P9-CLO-011

THE DREAM MERCHANT

The Dream Merchant

Isabel Hoving
translated by Hester Velmans

Candlewick Press
Cambridge, Massachusetts

First U.S. edition 2005

Library of Congress Cataloging-in-Publication Data is available.

Library of Congress Catalog Card Number 2005050182

ISBN 0-7636-2880-8

2 4 6 8 10 9 7 5 3 1

Printed in the United States of America

This book was typeset in MGaramond.

Candlewick Press
2067 Massachusetts Avenue
Cambridge, Massachusetts 02140

visit us at www.candlewick.com

For Jesse

Contents

PART IV – THE ROAD TO THE TEMBE

PART V – SATURA'S MAW

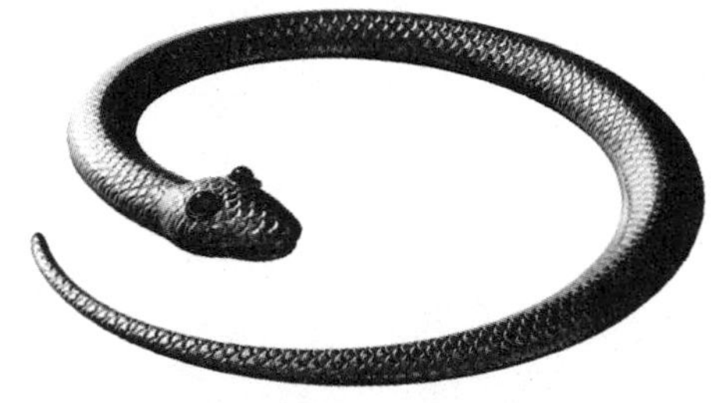

PART I
HE IS CALLED

1
Gadgets

Gadgets. It was all because he loved gadgets. When he looked back later on, Josh decided that was how it had started. Which wasn't far wrong: if he hadn't been so intrigued, Josh would have slammed the door in their faces right from the start, and then probably nothing would have happened. Why did they have to pick on him, of all people, to be the hero of their lousy adventures? He was just an ordinary boy – except for four things.

Four things. First, he was a collector, and quite a good one. He knew exactly how to organize all his stuff so he could find things easily, and so his parents didn't want to dump it all in the dustbin every few months. Mostly he collected useful things, like solar torches that also worked as a compass, whistle and penknife; but he also had shelves piled high with rusty bits of metal, skulls and skeletons, bunches of locks, picklocks and keys, computer games that no longer worked, and all sorts of tools and electrical devices. Second, he could fall asleep wherever and whenever he wanted. Third, he could always remember his dreams. Which could be a pain, especially when it was a nightmare, and then he'd go around all day with a sinking feeling there was something after him. And fourth: he was a thief.

A thief. No wonder he never showed his collection to anyone. Because it also contained jewellery: earrings, gold brooches and girls' rings. Why would a boy of twelve have things like that? He'd stolen them: half by accident, half on purpose. You might drop an earring when Josh was around, or put your ring on the edge of the washbasin when he was there and it would disappear while you were drying your hands. Or you might carelessly lose a bracelet, as a lady in a fur coat once did, when she let her gold snake bracelet (with genuine ruby eyes) slip off her wrist in a packed bus. If that bracelet accidentally got caught on the buttons of Josh's jacket, at the next stop you'd suddenly see him standing outside the bus, with something bright flashing in his hand, and you could say goodbye to your bracelet. But at least Josh never stole from his friends, and usually he'd only nick something if it was there for the taking.

Otherwise, he was an ordinary boy: lanky, pale, with tousled hair and shining eyes. There was nothing so special about him that would explain why he should have been called. With hindsight, perhaps his unusual birth may have had something to do with it. But that's hindsight, and every child's birth is different. There really was nothing special, then. But called he was. And not just called, but called to the phone.

The telephone rang in the middle of the night. Such a thing rarely happened, but when it did, his parents would normally leap out of bed to answer it. Their startled, hushed voices would wake Josh up, not the actual ringing. This time, though, Josh heard the noise shattering the silence. He groaned and struggled to the surface from the heavy depths of his sleep until he realized what the sound was. He sat up. What time was it? He listened to the shrill sound, his heart pounding. The ringing stopped for a second, then started again, making him jump. Why didn't Liz, his older stepsister, wake up? He lay down again, pulling the duvet over his head. Then he made up his mind, leapt out of bed and went down to the living room.

The room seemed larger than usual: empty, cold, full of shadows. Josh stared at the phone, his heart in his mouth. It must be something really awful; there was no other explanation. Death, or an accident, perhaps.

"Hello?"

"Am I speaking to Joshua Michael Cope, of 170 Pepys Avenue, Kentish Town, London?"

"What?" Who was this stuffy-sounding man, Josh wondered. "Who is it?"

"Gippart International here. My name is Marmeduke Fawcett. I'd very much like to ask you a few questions. Would that be convenient?"

"Well, OK, but—"

"Good, thank you *so* much. I have five short questions for you, for a youth market survey. First, may I ask you how old you are?"

"Twelve," Josh stammered. He was getting cold. "Mr…"

"Thank you. That is excellent. At present you reside with your parents?"

"Yes, I mean, with Mo, I mean my mother, and Edwin. My father lives down the street, and I go to—"

"Very good, thank you. Now for the third question. In what year did Christopher Columbus sail to America?"

"Huh? We haven't – oh, wait – 1492. I know it because of the rhyme about sailing the ocean blue." Josh began to think that this might be a competition and he might win something. A quad bike, he hoped.

"Yes, that is correct. Well done, I'm so pleased. I'll just jot it down. Now for the next question: what caused the dinosaurs to become extinct?"

Josh smiled. OK, it was a meteorite, *everyone* knew that; but he was getting cold and he wasn't old enough yet to ride a quad bike anyway, so he said, "They killed themselves laughing."

There was silence at the other end.

"Yeah," Josh explained, "because a meteorite landed on top of one of them, and the others killed themselves laughing. Something like that."

"I see." The man was quiet for a while. "Yes, of course. I understand. Just a moment…"

Josh hopped from one foot to the other. He heard whispering on the other end. He wanted to go back to bed. Sometimes they awarded a prize for the funniest answer. The one about the dinosaurs killing themselves laughing wasn't his joke, it was Baz's; he'd let Baz have a go on the bike too.

"Joshua?"

"Yes. Still here."

"Now, the final question – please think it over carefully, and answer as accurately as you can, will you?"

"OK."

"Think carefully before answering, now: how does one get into, or out of, a dream?"

"Pardon?"

"By what method, or methods, does one enter a dream? And, more importantly, how does one exit?"

"I don't understand. By going to sleep, of course. I mean—"

"Aha!" There was a deep sigh on the other end of the line, and Josh heard the man say to someone in a loud, excited voice: "Max was right!" Then: "Might I ask you to be just a little more explicit?"

Josh laughed. "I don't understand! You just go to sleep, that's all."

"Right," said the man eagerly, "but would you be able to demonstrate this, for instance?"

"Yes, of course, but—"

"Wonderful, thank you very much, that is very kind of you. Right then, we have come to the end of our interview. Location, time, history, technique. And your helpful co-operation. Shall we say two or three days from now? Thank you *so* much, and might I wish you a pleasant rest of the night! Goodbye for now."

Clutching the receiver, Josh listened to the dialling tone, nonplussed. Slowly he hung up the phone. He stretched. *What was that man really after?* Suddenly he started shivering in his green T-shirt and his pyjama bottoms that were too short for him. He padded back to bed and peered at his alarm clock. Half past two. He crawled under the lukewarm duvet, and replayed the conversation. How *did* you get into a dream? And out of it? Had the man been pulling his leg? Josh felt as if he'd told the man something important without understanding it himself, and that he should have just kept his mouth shut. After a while, he turned over on his side and fell asleep.

For the next few days, nothing important happened. Josh went to school, he did some more work with Baz and the others on the old shed they were rebuilding, he played games on the computer and at night he read in bed by torchlight. Edwin, his mother's boyfriend, came home drunk as usual, and Mo herself was irritable and short-tempered. Edwin's daughter, Liz, had an odd new boyfriend, all dressed up in a suit and tie.

"It's fine with me," said Mo, "but he can't stay to dinner just yet. I have to work overtime the next two weeks."

But he came to dinner anyway; Liz did the cooking, making pizzas with too many anchovies on them, and Josh and the new boyfriend ate them in silence. That may have been the first thing that was different, the odd-looking boyfriend. Liz's boyfriends never wore suits. But Josh hardly noticed; he was thinking about where he and Baz could find decent bits of wood for the shed. A week went by before he received another phone call.

Josh woke up a split second before the phone rang. He looked at the clock. Two fifteen. He breathed slowly and listened. The ringing came and went steadily. He sat up and calmly got out of bed. He padded along to his mother's bedroom, where Mo and Edwin were softly snoring. He stood in the doorway and said, as loudly as he dared, "Mum…" His mother always woke up when Josh called her, no matter how deeply asleep she was, no matter how quietly he spoke. Always. But this time she slept on. Strange. He braced himself, sucked in his upper lip and shuffled downstairs to the phone, which was still calmly ringing away. He picked up the receiver.

"Hello?"

"Yes, good evening, Joshua. Fawcett, of Gippart International, here. I should just like to verify something. Is this a good time? It's like this—"

"Wait," said Josh, "what is it you want from me, exactly? Did you want to talk to my mother?"

"No, no, no, that is quite unnecessary. If we had, we'd have set the telephone to the adult frequency. No, I just have one simple question for you: I was wondering, you see, when exactly you were thinking of visiting us. To tell you the truth, we've been expecting you for several days now."

"Visit you?" All the warnings about child molesters that Mo had drummed into him immediately flew into his head. So *that* was how they did it! "I'm not coming to visit you, no way. You must be joking!"

"Oh," said the man, hurt. "But … wait … I understood… Didn't you tell me you would, in so many words?"

"What? I didn't tell you anything, except about Christopher Columbus and the dinosaurs and all that. I'm not going anywhere."

"I see," said the man. "I *am* sorry, I'm afraid I have made a very stupid mistake. A minor misunderstanding. But it's of no consequence, don't worry. We'll arrange for someone to show you the way. In three days' time then? Would that suit you?"

"I'm not going anywhere!" Josh cried, alarmed. "Don't send anyone over here – I'm not coming!"

"But Joshua, truly I don't understand you. Surely it is an honour – it's every boy's dream! Gippart International is most popular with youngsters of your age! It's not as if there is any competition to speak of, certainly not at your level! Wait just a sec, could I be…" He was quiet a moment. "No, it's all here. Very good. I see that you are simply lacking information. That sometimes happens, of course. Our public relations department… Joshua, it will be a great pleasure for me to shake hands with you shortly. We shall make all the necessary arrangements as soon as possible."

He hung up again, and Josh was left staring stupidly at the humming receiver. Did this mean they were going to kidnap him? He wasn't going, whatever happened. Shaking his head, he returned to his bed and got back under the duvet. Half past two. He was starting to feel a bit warmer again, and sleepy. Before he knew it, he was out like a light.

The next days were filled with both ordinary and extraordinary happenings. One of his friends was given a PlayStation; another one fell and sprained his ankle. Together Baz and Josh valiantly sawed and hammered, but they didn't get very far. Baz, whose full name was Bhasvar Patel, was a fierce dark-skinned boy with straight black hair. He was quite strong, though he wasn't very tall. His heart wasn't really in this shed-fixing. He'd much rather be playing his drums. And Josh was pretty tall, but he got tired easily. He was pale to start with, and when he was tired he turned a transparent sort of white. The two of them bought some chips with Baz's pocket money, and they ate them in the shed while discussing how to make it watertight.

Liz's boyfriend came over again one night after dinner. He tried to start a conversation with Josh – asked to see his collection – but Josh decided he was a complete idiot. He didn't want to show him anything. He went to his room and flipped through some old comics for a while. He wished Baz lived next door. In the middle of reading his comics, he dozed off.

He was startled awake by the telephone, and his stomach

tightened. This time he really was going to make Mo wake up. He slid off the bed, stiff and cold because he had fallen asleep fully dressed, and crept cautiously to the main bedroom, with the ringing ripping the silence. He went up to his mother and shook her by the shoulder. "Mum!" Louder. "Mum!" No reaction. What was going *on*? Snoring, she turned over, muttering something (*"Wazzamatter?"*), and slept on. He said, as loudly as he dared, "Mum, wake up!" But she didn't hear a thing. Nothing for it then, but to try Edwin's side of the bed, even though he'd much rather see Edwin dormant than awake. But Edwin too was a lost cause, hopelessly fast asleep. Giving up, he made his way towards the jarring, insistent noise.

"Hello!"

"Joshua! Is that you? It's Max, Max Herbert, of Gippart. Well, my boy, didn't you understand what Marmeduke was asking you? Are you coming, or what?"

Josh felt dizzy. A "Max" now! Who on earth was he?

"Come where? And why? What are you talking about?"

"Oh. That's what I thought." The man on the other end clicked his tongue. "Look, it's a little hard to explain. Perhaps you should simply come and have a look. That way it'll all become clear. All I can tell you, Joshua, is that boys your age will do *anything* for the chance to visit Gippart. Do you know how to get here? Do you have the slightest idea of how to do it?"

The man sounded very insistent. When Josh didn't reply immediately, he went on earnestly, "I thought so. I suspected that was the problem. I can't really explain it to you, Joshua, you *have* to do it by yourself. But I know you can. Everything indicates that you are able to do it. Listen. I'll meet you at this end. You must go to your exit right away."

"You mean go to the front door?"

"No, your way out – to the gateway, Reception, you understand? No, just a minute. Listen carefully, Joshua.

You're to go back to your bedroom. Then you're to walk along the landing again, very carefully, down the stairs to the living room. From there you'll walk into the kitchen. From there, to the room beyond it. And on and on; you just keep going, understand? Make sure that you don't switch on any lights. We'll just see how it goes, and I'll help you. I'll be waiting for you. Oh yes, I almost forgot, your friend Baz is coming too. If it doesn't work, I'll call you again."

He hung up. Josh whistled through his teeth. The whole thing was mad. There wasn't another room beyond the kitchen. What was the man talking about? But it was odd: he was beginning to feel tingly all over. He didn't really care, he'd just like to find out what it was all about. So he decided he'd give it a try. And Baz was coming too! Whistling softly, he returned to his bedroom. The hairs on the back of his neck were standing on end; his whole body was humming with a lightly buzzing charge, as if he'd been plugged into an electric socket. He was very excited. Hastily he pulled on a warmer sweater, slipped his feet into his shoes (he realized there were advantages, sometimes, to falling asleep fully dressed) and strapped on his watch. Then he went back out on to the landing.

He felt all keyed up and a little scared – the landing seemed different, emptier and lonelier. He pulled his belt a notch tighter around his narrow hips. Down the stairs. The living room seemed larger too, and more deserted – a little sad, even. *Never mind, room, never mind; I'm coming back soon, don't be lonely.* He was so wound up he almost missed the door, the door he walked in and out of dozens of times every day without noticing – the door to the kitchen. It was as if the living room didn't want to let him go. The kitchen also looked darker, with strange white light radiating from the dials on the microwave and the oven and the face of the big clock on the wall. Everything looked so different at night. He walked over to the cage of his two lovebirds, Zizi and Dara – his little pet parrots.

When they felt his presence they began to stir, making soft noises. He pushed his finger through the bars of the cage door to tickle them. Zizi clamped on to his finger with her tiny claws. Josh grinned. It was a comforting feeling, those claws. Still smiling, he looked back at the kitchen – and his blood ran cold. He stared incredulously at the door that was supposed to lead out to the balcony. The balcony? Beyond the old glass kitchen door, he saw a large room that was the spitting image of the living room he had just left. Without thinking, he pulled back his finger, which got stuck, making the cage door fly open. Sucking his throbbing finger, he turned round, his heart beating wildly. That's right, there was the door to the living room, as always. And now, in front of him, was *another* living room. Which had never been there before.

He took a step forward. Max had told him: from the kitchen to the room beyond it. How on earth could *he* have known about this? Was Josh's house haunted or something? He tip-toed cautiously to the balcony door and opened it. He was standing on the threshold of a large room where everything was just a little bit different. Different, wider, longer – taller windows, and the curtains seemed redder and plusher. The light was different too. Not bluish-white, the way it had been in the kitchen. A warmer hue. A tawny gold. He took a deep breath, to compose himself. *I must keep going,* he told himself. *Baz is coming too.* But he couldn't move. Time seemed to have stood still. Then, quite unexpectedly, he felt something sharp digging into his shoulder. He spun his head round with a cry. "Ouch!" And his cheek grazed something feathery. Zizi had sneaked out of the birdcage and flown after him, silly old Zizi, with her sharp little claws. Josh laughed out loud with relief, and then a wing brushed his face, and cheeky Dara landed on his other shoulder.

Carefully he stepped into the new room, and walked through it slowly. He opened the door at the far end, and saw the kitchen – again. This one, too, was just the slightest bit different, like the living room. Josh glanced at the spot where the birdcage always stood, and laughed nervously: the cage was gone. There was a goldfish bowl in its place. He felt his birds against his cheeks and he was glad. "I'd much rather have you two with me on my journey than two goldfish," he whispered. He crossed the kitchen (it contained an enormous espresso machine and a round table instead of their own square one) and opened the balcony door. Again he stood on the threshold of the living room. This time it looked quite different. Early morning light was shining in. Before the open windows stood a large white table set with bright pink and red and orange crockery. On an enormous TV four men sang a discordant song.

He walked into the next kitchen. This time there was someone in there; a dark-haired woman was busy rolling out dough. She was singing along to the radio at the top of her voice. Two little boys were sitting at a table, playing a computer game. The woman glanced up briefly when Josh came in. "You'd better hurry," she said. "They're waiting for you."

Keep going, keep going! He walked into another room, then another kitchen, then another living room – it was just endless. Sometimes he encountered people, who urged him to hurry on. Most rooms were nice, except for a gloomy one containing a white bed on which lay a very old man, groaning. Shaken, Josh kept walking. Finally, on entering the umpteenth kitchen, he found himself in a small, square space, with a sort of check-in desk. A young woman was sitting behind the desk, typing. She glanced up at Josh.

"Ah," she said, "good morning. Just a moment, please. Cope, Joshua?" She was looking at her computer screen.

"Yeah," said Josh sheepishly.

She laughed when she saw his face. "Welcome," she said. "We're always delighted to have young visitors. Take a seat; they'll be along shortly."

She went on with her work. Josh lowered himself into one

of the red bucket seats. His little parrots scratched gently at his ears. *What if this is the dentist's?* he worried. *Oh, great. And to get home I'll have to walk back through all those stupid rooms again.* His spirits sank. He had the feeling he'd been walking for hours, though in truth he hadn't: it had taken him precisely twenty-two minutes and seven seconds, according to his watch.

"But then he must be in here – it's the only place left. Ah, indeed!" The door flew open and a man with dark eyes and a wild shock of grey hair walked in. When he saw Josh sitting there his face lit up in a wide grin.

"Well, well… Bravo! Bravo, Joshua! I knew you could do it! Congratulations, my boy!" Beaming, he grabbed Josh's hand and shook it vigorously. "And there was I, thinking you were coming from the opposite direction! But that doesn't make the slightest difference. The most important thing is that you made it. You've passed your first test with flying colours. Welcome, Joshua!"

Josh saw some other people crowded behind the man, all of them grinning at him just as idiotically. Some adults and some older kids, he thought – but they withdrew before he could have a good look at them. When the man let go of his hand, Josh stood up and looked at him uncertainly.

"Right then. I am Max Herbert, Joshua, and I am really extraordinarily pleased. You needed hardly any help from me at all. You only deviated off course by a negligible degree. Excellent! It's so gratifying to be proved right. I like the birds, by the way. Are they yours, or did they hitch a ride with you on the way?"

"But – where *are* we? Where's Baz?"

"At Gippart, of course. You're in Reception. Well now, shall we, then? They're waiting for you!" And he strode out of the room.

* * *

They came into a large central hall. Wide, gleaming corridors radiated out in all directions, with people hurrying everywhere, on foot or zooming along on little motorbikes. There was a soft buzzing and humming, a pleasantly busy sound. Josh hurried after Max Herbert through the hall while gazing about with interest. Everywhere he looked he saw people walking, sitting at computer terminals or talking on the phone. A door opened to his left and a tall man walked into the hall wearing nothing but a sort of short skirt made of animal pelts, with a bloody bandage around his arm. Behind him came a frowning girl, who looked at the man dubiously when he started shouting at a crowd of people walking up to them: "An order for three thousand pieces, would you believe it! It's an absolute record, you gutless book-keepers! And it's all thanks to Sita here!"

A little further on, four boys and girls aged around fifteen or sixteen, dressed in long turquoise gowns, slowly trudged down a corridor as if they were exhausted. A woman in uniform ran up to them, and suddenly they began laughing and talking to her all at once, and the uniformed woman exclaimed, "The imperial family? That's terrific! Six in one go!"

Josh and Max turned into a corridor and climbed a flight of stairs, walking on a blue carpet with a cat-face design. They arrived at another floor, and here Josh's heart almost did a somersault: he came face to face with a dazzling array of high-tech contraptions lying, hanging or hovering all around. Buzzing overhead were all sorts of model balloons and aeroplanes. Zipping along the floor were electronic cars, motorbikes and other vehicles that were difficult to define. Images swirled along the walls (flat-screen TVs? PCs? Recessed fish tanks?); and glass cases displayed clever items that made Josh's mouth water, even though he had no idea what they all were for: a drinking glass that had a light bulb in it, a little chair that slowly hobbled back and forth, a pen that seemed to be writing by itself. He even spotted a device he'd been dreaming about for as long as he could remember: a remote-control hand. It could move by itself, and was attached to a flexible, telescopic pole. Behind the glass it showed off what it could do: shoot out sideways, *bing!* turn off alarm clock, boomerang back, zip away again, flip light switch, pull open curtains; everything you've always wanted to be able to do from your bed but couldn't because your arm was about three metres too short.

"Come," said Max, "there's plenty of time for all that later. Now we have to hurry. They're waiting." He pushed Josh into a narrow hallway with a bank of lifts, and they zoomed to the upper regions of the building, which seemed to go on for ever.

They entered a room that was large and bright. Tall windows reached down to the floor, which had lights set into it. The walls were covered in a shiny design that showed a crowned cat. In the middle of the space stood a glass table that was lit from inside. Josh didn't dare look too closely at the people seated behind it. They had all stood up and were studying him very closely.

"Here he is," said Max with a note of pride in his voice, as if Josh were his very own creation. "It only took him twenty minutes. Hardly veered off course at all. A good sign, what?"

"Excellent, young man!" said a red-haired, slightly balding man standing beside the table. "Very good! Have a seat, do please sit down!" He pushed a tall stool forward, and Josh eased himself on to it carefully, so as not to upset his little birds. Max, smiling, joined the adults on the other side of the table.

"We are extremely glad you finally made it here, Joshua!" said the red-haired man. "It took some doing to get you to come! Welcome to Gippart International, the global conglomerate that stands head and shoulders above the rest, even if Katz says otherwise – but naturally you'd expect our largest competitor to say that, wouldn't you? Forgive me, we have already spoken but we have never met. My name is Fawcett, Marmeduke Fawcett, Secretary of Youth Affairs, and here in this room are some of the most important members of our Dispatch Board. You are already acquainted, of course, with Max Herbert, our Talent Scout and Director of Youth Affairs; and next to him you'll see Tal Sow Fall, our Chairman; then Miriane Comptesso, our Treasurer..."

Josh looked at the people without taking in their names, his mouth hanging open. "Close your mouth, darling, it makes you look so silly," Mo sometimes told him, smiling, and then she'd tousle his hair. But the Board members were returning Josh's gaze in exactly the same way, leaning forward, their mouths open.

"And, of course, the youngest family member on the Board, Garnet Gippart." The adults all heaved a sigh, then sat down.

"Joshua Michael Cope," said the woman named Garnet Gippart. She was a young woman with hair cut in a sleek bob and a rather determined expression on her face. "Welcome. I suppose you know we haven't asked you to come here just for fun. Actually technically you're too young to visit Gippart, especially on an individual basis. And this is no school outing, I assure you. Tal?"

To her left, a tall black man in an immaculately pressed dark suit and bright white shirt smiled and cleared his throat. "Well, young man," he said, "we'll come straight to the point. And the point is this: we need you. We need you very badly. We have invited you here to ask you to accept employment with us."

Before Josh could say anything, Tal held up his hand and went on: "That is to say, you could from time to time do us some small favour, for which you would be handsomely compensated. Gippart has a youth organization, the Junior Associates, for young people such as yourself, who do small jobs for us now and then. Such as taking part in simple sales campaigns, acting as couriers – all following our own unique techniques, of course. This work never interferes with any other obligations a young person may have—" A fat man sitting next to Tal coughed, and Tal corrected himself. "Actually, it can be combined with your school work quite easily. It involves, on average, just one or two afternoons a month. The laws of employment that apply to minors are sacrosanct to us. In short: we are offering you the opportunity to work for Gippart twice a month for one year."

A large lady with a swept-up hairdo leaned over towards Josh and whispered hoarsely, "The pay is excellent."

"Miriane, *s'il te plaît*," said Tal, and he went on, businesslike: "We'll be depositing five hundred pounds a month into an account to which you'll have access once you turn eighteen; moreover, once a month you may select one of our products, some of which you have already seen in our exhibit halls, up to and including the value of one hundred pounds. Questions?"

The adults again looked at him expectantly. On the far right a woman turned to the young man seated next to her. "It's positively unheard of… Are they quite sure?"

Josh coughed. "I don't really understand, exactly. Why *me*? And where's Baz?"

"Um, ah well," they all chorused, and, glancing at the laptop in front of her, Garnet Gippart said, almost impatiently, "According to our information, you possess a number of skills which may be of use to Gippart. The basic technique of how to get here, obviously, which is the very first condition. It also seems that you possess the knowledge of how to return – from, say, a dream. Next, you are able to fall asleep on command, and at Gippart that is worth its weight in gold. In addition, you have no trouble moving through the … shall we say the sectors. You run less of a risk, therefore, than anyone else. Even so, we are prepared to start you on a higher salary scale than the others. Will that do, for now?"

"Where's Baz?" Josh asked again. He didn't know what to make of it all. What he'd most like to do was get down off his stool and run: back to Reception, and then, if he must, he supposed, back through all those rooms with his birds, and then jump back safe and sound into his own cosy bed.

"Your friend has already been taken to meet the Junior Committee," said Tal, smiling. "We'll show you to their *nursery* in just a minute. Baz doesn't have the same qualities you possess; but Gippart has discovered that teamwork always turns out to be more profitable in the end. OK, that's it. Garnet?"

But the woman at the far right answered instead of her. "Tal, Garnet, with all due respect," she said vehemently, "I disagree. I don't accept that this boy, who looks rather frail, by the way" – she pointed a long arm at Josh, who was beginning to feel a bit insulted – "that this kid has the talents that Gippart... Well, you know what I'm getting at. I just don't agree. Before we sign him up, I'd first like to subject him to the usual Trial, if nothing else."

Max Herbert jumped to his feet. "Please, everyone, isn't it bad enough as it is? We have already agreed that we would handle this as carefully as possible. Gippart just can't afford another... I mean, children's lives are sacred to us, and not only because of the bad publicity – and I swear to you, if ever we were to endanger another child's life again, by God, Garnet, I'd go straight to the press."

There was an uneasy silence. Tal stood up, smooth and composed.

"You just heard it, Joshua," he said, with a condescending smile. "Your well-being is one hundred per cent guaranteed. And, besides, they do say most accidents happen in the home, don't they?" His smile faded and he turned to the silent group seated around him at the table. "Then I move to adjourn this meeting. I think we need a quick re-evaluation. Garnet, do you agree?"

Garnet Gippart nodded. She stood up, said, "Thank you, young man, we'll see you later," and walked out.

Marmeduke Fawcett bounded to his feet and offered to help Josh down off his stool. Then he trotted after the others without looking back.

2
The Associates

Before hurrying after the others with a rather long face, Max pointed Josh in the direction of the Junior Associates' quarters, which he called the JCR. "You can't go wrong. I'm sorry I can't go with you, dear boy. But don't worry, they are truly delighted that you are here. Really, everyone expects great things from you. Don't mind their misgivings; they'll get over it. See you later."

Josh didn't give a hoot about the Board's misgivings; he didn't have the foggiest idea why they should either trust or mistrust him. Uncertainly, he made his way to the lifts. Standing alone in the spacious, brightly lit lift, he was transported to Level –5: Junior Committee Room, Central Switchboard, Gym.

Following signs for the JCR, he thought about some of the high-tech gadgets he'd seen. Suppose he came and worked here. Not that he was going to, of course, but suppose he did. Would they let him pick something from that assortment? Then he thought about the five hundred pounds a month. That was six thousand a year, up to the time he turned eighteen – when it would add up to over thirty-five thousand pounds. Thirty-five thousand! He blew out his breath nervously. "They must be having me on," he said out loud to his parrots. He mustn't count on anything yet; he shouldn't expect anything. Sunk deep in thought, he turned into a corridor that seemed a little less harshly lit. Still, he *would* like to have another good look at those gadgets. As he was here, anyway. He thought he'd glimpsed a small laser pocket knife that would cut through wood or steel. He'd love to look at it properly. And just as he was beginning to wonder if he shouldn't give it a whirl, to work here on a trial basis for a month or so, two powerful arms grabbed him so suddenly from behind that the little parrots were knocked off his shoulders.

"Oooff!"

He kicked backwards with his feet and snapped his teeth at the arm wrapped around his neck, but he was caught fast in a stranglehold. "Easy, easy now, mate," a taunting voice hissed in his ear. "Where are we going then, in the middle of the night, all alone, here on *my* territory? What's a little guy like you up to in *my* neck of the woods?"

"Let me go!"

"Don't like it? Well, silly of you to come walking down *my* corridor!"

The grip didn't relax at all, but now a powerful hand tousled his hair, to annoy him. "Now then, you wimp. Why didn't you tell us you were coming, eh? You've got a nerve! Know what I do with little jerks like you who show the boss no respect?"

Josh was never that quick to get angry, but once he did, he was livid. A wave of fury took hold of him, and he started hitting and kicking madly, trying to wrestle his way out of the guy's clutches. When that didn't work, he yelled, "I don't know what you're on about. Leave me alone!"

His assailant suddenly hissed, "Hell, get off!" His grip relaxed for a second, just enough for Josh to twist his head round to get a good look at his tormentor, who was trying to ward off two green bolts of lightning viciously pecking at his hair, face and neck – Josh's fearless little parrots! But they were no match for this bruiser. He had pale skin, slicked-back, black wavy hair, little round gold-rimmed spectacles. He was wearing tons of gold chains and was heavily tattooed. But even though he was quite tall, he couldn't have been much older than seventeen. He'd already recovered his footing. Swatting the birds away with one hand, he kept a tight grip on Josh with the other. "It's not going to do you any good, sonny-boy. I'm waiting for an answer!"

Just then a boy raced up to them, shouting. "Moussa! What are you doing? That's the new kid, isn't it? Are you mad? Max just called about him. This is his new Associate – the special one. You know, the one they sent us that email about. Max just rang to tell us he was here. It's only his first day. We're supposed to make him feel welcome, and we need him all in one piece!"

"Yeah, right, I *am* making him feel welcome," said Moussa, "and as far as staying all in one piece, they never said a thing about that to me, the Chief Associate. None of us are going to stay all in one piece! If this kid had any brains, he'd turn and run as fast as his little legs could carry him. Such a baby. Such a pity, really. What's its *name*?"

Josh was speechless with rage. He scratched Zizi; she was perched on his shoulder again as if nothing had happened. The other boy spoke up for him. "You know as well as I do that this is Joshua Cope. Moussa, Chief, this is Max's star turn. Let go of him."

"I *hate* star turns!" Moussa pouted. "Besides, I like to be notified in advance exactly when to expect them, why, and how many of them there'll be. They're supposed to report to my office first! As Chief, I demand some respect around here. Otherwise I might get *really* upset. Besides, I'm going to go straight to the cops one day to file a complaint against that Max Herbert, you just watch me. Kidnapping minors!" But he did let go. Josh took a deep, seething breath.

The JCR, the place Tal had referred to so insultingly as the *nursery* a few doors down, was much nicer than Josh had been led to expect, after Moussa's rough welcome. It was a large, vaulted space, with all kinds of alcoves, balconies and a gallery. The floor was covered in thick carpet; and wide, low benches, also carpeted, lined the walls. Dozens of sparkling chandeliers and lanterns of multicoloured glass, silver and gold hung from the ceiling. In one corner was a widescreen TV, with at least a dozen boys and girls sprawled in front of it. On the benches and up in the gallery other kids were reading, sleeping, eating and chatting, or playing computer games. They were all a few years older than Josh, and they all looked very different. Some had fluorescent-green spiked hair, others wore hats; some looked studious and others looked like punks; some wore sparkly dresses and jewellery, others cut-off jeans. But they all seemed to be relaxed and in a good mood.

"Yeah, yeah," said Moussa moodily, and he clapped his hands. "Attention, ladies and gents. I bring you Gippart's latest star turn, and that's all I'm going to say about him. He fancies little birds. His name is … uh…"

He rolled his eyes and was silent. By then the entire room had turned towards Josh. Faces gazed at him from all around. Curious, friendly, giggly, mocking, bored faces. A girl in the TV corner cried, "Oh, this must be Joshua Cope, of course!"

"Well, you don't say," said Moussa. "Thank you, Teresa." He sighed. "Did anyone fetch his friend, Baz? Wasn't someone supposed to be bringing him? It was in that email, folks. Who's got Baz? Is he here?"

A small boy wearing pyjamas disentangled himself from the group of TV watchers, and Josh rushed over to him. "Baz!" Laughing, they punched each other on the arm and back, and a few tears rolled down Baz's cheek. "I want to go home, Josh. They just dragged me over here against my will!"

The girl named Teresa put her arm round him, but Baz shrugged her off. He rubbed his eyes.

"Did you get here by walking through loads of rooms, like I did?" asked Josh curiously.

Baz shook his head. "No, they came for me. At first I thought it was you, that you were calling me from outside my window, and then I opened the door and they grabbed me and pushed me into a car. And then they marched me all around this building till we got here." He rubbed his eyes angrily again. "I was scared stiff. I thought..." He bit his lip, frowning.

"Hey, calm down," said Moussa. "I want to know why Gippart has brought you here. Out with it. What's the deal with you two?"

"Yeah," cried a tall boy from the sofa. "Why are you walking around with those birds on your shoulders? Is *that* your secret?"

"Actually, it was an accident," Josh explained. "As I was walking through the kitchen—"

"Do you have Sense, is that it?" asked a black girl in a short white dress, who'd been reading a book. The red-haired girl beside her added, "*Great!* If so, you're the first kid with Sense that we've had here!"

"Sense?" echoed Josh. Whatever did they mean?

"Hey, hang on," said the girl called Teresa. "I don't think they know what on earth we're talking about. Tell me, do you know anything about Gippart? You don't look like you do, either of you."

Josh was glad there was finally someone who realized that they needed an explanation. Teresa was about fourteen or fifteen, with dark brown skin and a heavy ponytail consisting of dozens of black and silver braids, and cornrows with bright beads woven into them. She wore jeans and a short sweater with a large pink fur collar.

"Listen and I'll explain!" she said with the confident air of the practised storyteller. "Gippart, Gippart International I mean, the world-famous company we work for, is the largest trading corporation the world has ever seen. As an international marketing giant, there's nothing in the world like it!" She spread her arms wide and shouted, *"Ta-daaaaaa!"* Then she giggled and continued in her normal voice. "It was founded zillions of years ago; it's existed for ages and ages and ages."

"Founded in 1017," a boy whispered solemnly.

Someone pushed Josh and Baz down on one of the soft velvet sofas, and someone else brought drinks in tall glasses and placed a bowl of crisps in front of them, which the parrots immediately went for. Josh couldn't keep his eyes off a boy wearing a turquoise tunic and gold trousers, with a gold cap on his head. He looked like a Persian prince from a fairy tale. He sat up very straight, his handsome dark-rimmed eyes staring into space. All the kids were listening to Teresa's story, even though they must have heard it many times before.

"Gippart International specializes in selling the most inventive new products of its time," said Teresa. "They always manage to track down new ideas before they've even seen the light of day. They acquire the kind of stuff you only imagine in your wildest dreams, stuff you'd sell your soul to get your hands on. And then they turn round and sell them to their clients all over the world. They travel to the very corners of the earth, to as many different nations as possible, where they buy up whatever new things they've come across over there while selling our own products to them. And they've always been incredibly successful, because they've sold the stuff that you really, really needed but that your own country hasn't got round to inventing yet. How do you think the compass made it to Europe, or we ever started playing cards? How, I ask you? Gippart brought them all back over here, that's how! Windmills from Persia, wheelbarrows from China, chewing gum from the Mayan Indians via North America, and Arabic script to West Africa! It's made Gippart filthy rich."

"Really?" said Josh, and he took a sip of his drink.

"Arabic script to West Africa?" asked Baz doubtfully.

"It's true," said Teresa. "*I* should know. And that's how Gippart International has connected the whole wide world into one huge web."

"At the expense of the lives of quite a few travelling salesmen, adults as well as kids," a boy at a computer said loudly. A hush fell over the room. Josh and Baz looked at Teresa in alarm.

"Those were accidents!" she said. "As if Gippart would send its people to their deaths, or make use of child labour..."

"Well, don't they?" drawled Moussa.

"No, they don't! Because what we do isn't child labour, it's an adventure!"

"I'm glad *you* think so," said Moussa. "I hope Raphel saw it that way too, just before he—"

"Raphel was one of *my* best friends, and no particular pal of yours, Chief! And it was a terrible accident, a tragedy nobody could have prevented."

There was a deathly hush, and in the silence Teresa picked up where she'd left off, her voice steady. "Gippart sells only the very latest things, inventions ahead of their time, the hottest novelties. Always innovations! For example, right now they're working on a new sales drive for hypno-mail."

"Cool," said Baz.

"Not!" a girl standing next to him said gloomily.

Teresa nodded. "The trouble is, there are problems. Profits are down. You see, although Gippart's products are terrific – expensive as anything, but unbeatable – our competitors are better at marketing. Advertising, I mean. Much better."

"Katz," a few kids hissed in unison.

"That's right, Katz," said Teresa, wrinkling her nose. "Our arch-enemy. We hate Katz, and if you come to work here you have to swear you'll do anything to run the Katz company into the ground."

"Why?" asked Josh.

"Because they're always trying to do the same to us! Look, we just can't get rid of our stock any more. I mean, most of the world is too poor to buy Gippart's stuff, and the rest owns practically everything there is to own already. The point is, the rest of the world doesn't want any more *stuff*, it wants ... well, a *feeling*. Excitement, emotion, or simply the feeling that what you're experiencing is something absolutely unique. The trouble is, people don't necessarily get that feeling from Gippart's products any more. They used to, but not any more. I don't know why."

"I think it's because there are too many of those new high-tech gadgets around," a serious-looking boy added. "They just keep coming and coming, the most outlandish things you can think of. Next thing you know, they're already in the shops. Maybe they're just too much of a good thing. That's what *I* think."

"So anyway," Teresa continued, "people don't always get that special feeling from our stuff any more, but they *do* seem to be getting it from Katz, according to their ads. So Katz's profits keep going up, and ours keep going down."

"Then why don't you just come up with some brilliant ad campaign of your own?" asked Josh.

"Don't you think Gippart haven't been trying? But as soon as we've got someone who's really good at it, Katz snatches him or her from under our noses. Those Katz people have spies swarming everywhere."

"Can't you think of anything to stop them?" asked Baz.

"Of course we can. OK. Where do you go, once you've conquered the whole world with your products?" Teresa grinned. "It makes perfect sense, really. Where do you go next?"

"Time! Time!" shouted a girl from one of the alcoves.

Teresa made a sweeping gesture. "Yes, you travel in time, of course! If you could go back in time, if you could sell vitamin C tablets or paracetamol to folks in the Middle Ages, or the wheel to a caveman, or—"

"Or machine-guns and flame-throwers to the Vikings," sneered Moussa.

"The point is," said Teresa, glaring at the Chief, "that this has opened up a new market for Gippart. And we're the ones helping to develop it – us, our Committee."

"*Time*-travel, you mean?" asked Josh incredulously.

"Yes and no," said Teresa. "Gippart has been trying to travel back in real time, but hasn't had any luck so far, alas."

"Dream-time, though, is another story. We *do* know how to get there," said the Persian boy whose looks Josh so admired. "All you do is go to Reception, the same way you got here, Joshua, and then you just sort of alter the space, and then you leap and you glide, and – *wham!* – you're in dream-time."

Josh and Baz gaped at him open-mouthed. "Dream-time? Sleepwalking, you mean?"

"No, it isn't just your ordinary run-of-the-mill dream," he said. "It's called *umaya*, that's what we call it. *Umaya* is the collective dream-world of all mankind. Actually, it looks a lot like our own ordinary history, with the ancient Egyptian pyramids, the Incas and the Chinese Empire, and so on, yet it's different: it's made up of the collective dreams and memories of the entire human race."

To dream – how you get into, and out of, a dream. That very first phone call, in the living room, in the middle of the night...

"But it's still dreams," reasoned Josh. "You can't get into other people's dreams, can you?"

"Why not? You go to movies set in historical periods, don't you? You read books and magazines about the past and you see all those commercials and ads and cartoons, and they're nothing but other people's dreams about what history was like. Everyone is getting into other people's dreams all the time."

"That's how people share dreams," another boy added. "And because so many people share them, these dreams have become sort of real. Real enough to travel in, anyway."

"So that's *umaya*," Teresa concluded. "All those real dreams clustering together to make one huge dream-space. Now do you get it?"

"So, then you travel in time – but it isn't the real past you're travelling to, but a *dream* of the past?" Baz asked.

They nodded.

"But what for?"

"To sell things, of course," said the red-haired girl. "We're salespeople. And there are heaps of customers out there, and they pay good money for Gippart's products."

"Three cheers for the Associates!" Moussa suddenly jeered. "*We're* the ones risking our necks in that lethal stupid dream-time!"

"Well, some of the adults do too!" Teresa retorted.

"Yeah, but *we* don't have Sense, so we're the ones best suited to it," said the Persian boy.

"What *is* Sense?" asked Baz.

"Sense, *sense of time*, *Sinsi*, a sense of timing."

Baz chuckled. "Then you don't have one iota of Sense, Josh, because you're always late."

"That isn't the only thing," Teresa explained patiently. "If you have Sense, you can tell if anything's got mixed up, time-wise. For example, you'll know if you've carried something from *umaya*, from the dream-time, into the present time, or the other way round. Adults, of course, can always tell exactly what time it is, or which time-zone they're in, or where the time-barriers are. So if you have Sense, you can't dream-travel very efficiently, because you'll keep bumping up against those barriers, and you won't be able to cross them. It hurts, see? We, the Associates, can move easily from one time-zone to another, but people with Sense can't do that. Only adults have Sense, so that's why Gippart has assembled the Associates' Junior Committee, us kids, to be the time-travellers. We can explore that dream-time, get the lie of the land, and work out which time-zones are stable and which are a little rocky."

Josh still didn't get the whole picture. "That tall man, that Sow Fall, he only talked about selling stuff, he didn't say anything about time-travelling or dream-tripping or whatever you call it."

"No," said Teresa, "and that's because it isn't all that safe just now…"

Moussa stepped forward, his fingers hooked into his belt, his head tossed back arrogantly. "Let's just spell it out for you, shall we? First, dream-travelling is *extremely* dangerous. Last month, a kid died. And he was a tough, hard-as-nails customer, not some pathetic little wimp like you. There are, sadly, few adults who have the guts to go time-travelling. Second, you skipped the most important part, Teresa! Gippart is trying to push the kids *from* the dream-time world *into* the real past and future. That's what they're really after. Real time. That's where the big money's to be made! Hey, Switi, show them your leg."

The girl in the white dress stood up and limped towards Josh and Baz. One leg was bandaged. She stood before them, hands on her hips, holding her leg stiffly in front of her like a thick wooden pole.

"Next!" commanded Moussa, pointing to a tall boy with cropped blond hair. He stepped forward and showed them his hands: monstrously large, swaddled in bulging bandages.

"Teresa?" Moussa finally demanded, snapping his fingers. Hesitantly she pulled down the collar of her sweater: there was a vivid scar running down her chest. "Open-heart surgery," said Moussa nastily. "Her heart nearly burst. Time-tripping is far more dangerous than dream-travel, because your body can't take it. Gippart wants to see how far we can go forward in time, into the lousy future, before we explode. Well, we haven't been able to make it very far, that's obvious. And whenever the company tries sending us *back* in time, something invariably goes horribly wrong as well. So..."

"So they've put a stop to it," said Teresa softly.

Moussa, in a harsh and menacing voice, said, "So they're giving a reward of one million, plus a permanent job, to the one who does manage it. So there's always an idiot somewhere who'll be tempted to try it. So Raphel gets himself blown to bits. So they go and recruit some fresh blood, babies, like this kid here and his little crony."

The place was buzzing with short bursts of conversation:

"What? Is he here to be a time-tripper?" "How's he going to do it then?"

Josh's head, of its own accord, started shaking no, no, no. Baz looked at him questioningly. "No," said Josh, "that's not what I'm here for. I'm not an idiot – and I wouldn't even know how to go about it!"

"What *are* you good at?" asked Moussa.

"Collecting, and I'm good with my hands, machinery and electronics and stuff," said Josh. "Picking locks, and, uh, drawing, and..."

"Repairing sheds," Baz added helpfully.

"Swimming," Josh remembered.

"And dozing and sleeping and daydreaming." Baz giggled, his hand in the bowl of crisps.

True, the adults back there had mentioned that one too. "I fall asleep fairly easily, he's right about that."

"Oh yeah?" Moussa bounced on to the couch next to Josh like an uncoiled spring, startling the birds so that they flew off. He grabbed Josh's head in one hand and pushed him down with the other. "Go to sleep *now*!" he cried. "Sleep!"

Josh was lying uncomfortably flat on his back, his legs dangling over the side. Baz climbed over him and began pummelling Moussa's steely arms, shouting, "Let go of my mate," and Teresa was pushing from the other side, and all the kids ran up to see if Josh would manage to fall asleep just like that, right in the middle of a wrestling match.

"No," protested Josh, his face all red, "let me go. I've had enough, all right?"

Moussa let go, roaring with laughter. "Hey, that's the wisest thing that's come out of our little friend's mouth so far! Exactly! Take a walk, little man! Take a walk, get out of here before it's too late!"

"I wouldn't dream of it," said Josh firmly. He retrieved Zizi and Dara from the back of a couch, coaxing them on to his finger, set them back on his shoulders, and got to his feet.

"I'm going to look at those gadgets," he said, gazing down at Moussa, who was still laughing to himself on the couch, propped up on one elbow. "I'd like to have another look at all the stuff before I go."

Moussa shook his head. "Teresa, please take Cope and his loyal companion back to the game rooms and Reception area." He took off his gold-rimmed glasses. "And you'd better not come back," he hissed.

To the boys' delight, there were motorbikes. Just past the lifts, in a hallway on Level –2. On the wall above was a sign FOR PUBLIC USE. It was great; the electric bikes were easy to ride and extremely responsive – they read your mind if you wanted to slow down or speed up. Before the boys knew it, they found themselves in the corridor with the display cases. They left the bikes in a little hallway.

There was much more to look at than Josh had thought: rooms full of unheard-of inventions, all of which you were allowed to try out. There was a cavernous space with a soaring domed ceiling in which you could test flying objects, from mini-balloons with room for five, to compact individual hop-flight engines that strapped on to your back and with a big *whoosh!* shot you up to a height of about five metres, touched down smoothly at some twenty metres' distance, then let you bound back up in the air again. Teresa stood by proudly, as if all of it belonged to her.

"Great, isn't it? Gippart's absolutely wild about flying," she said. "They have the craziest things to get you up in the air." She gave them a quick pat on the shoulders. "I'm so glad that you're joining us. You're the youngest Associates we've ever had. You" – nodding at Baz – "remind me of my little brother. And you" – nodding at Josh – "look like someone I know. I forget who, but it'll come back to me." She laughed and gave them a little push into the room.

They tried out shoes that let you walk on water, and a very

small folding motorboat, to carry with you in your backpack when you were on the road. There was a smaller room with speaking, reading and writing pens. ("Handy for in the dark, in bed," said Baz. "You could get your pen to read to you.") There were fountain pens that automatically translated your writing into another language or a different alphabet. They also saw a pencil that drew lines that solidified in the air, ending up either flexible or stiff, depending on the thickness, so that you could use it to create proper chairs or ladders. There was a room crammed with books that adapted to your mood: if you were sad, they bombarded you with silly jokes; and if you were in a bad mood, the villains were shown no mercy, but got hacked to pieces in the most bloody and gruesome way imaginable.

Then there was what Teresa called the Gippart "family" room. It was a small, dark room with large oil paintings and a few display cases and bookshelves. Standing in the doorway, they glanced inside. "Gippart is actually only one branch of a huge mercantile family," Teresa explained, turning the light off again. "Besides Gippart, there were several brothers and sisters who all set up their own businesses. But they've all been taken over or gone out of business – except for Katz, that is. Katz Imagination. Our big rival. Books have been written about it, but nobody ever reads them." She hesitated, then whispered mysteriously, "There's a family curse, as well. It's something really nasty, supposedly, but nobody knows what it is, exactly – a fiend from hell, or some such thing, a monster they call Siparti. Nobody really knows. That's why you're not allowed on the top floor."

"What's on the top floor?"

"Didn't Max tell you? It's where the President hangs out. Stark raving mad, he is, and extremely dangerous."

She slammed the door shut.

There was a larger room with medical devices, such as a magnet that drew out the pain if you had a headache or hurt your knee, and a wheelchair that could climb stairs. There was even an ultra-sheer face mask that could completely alter your features. ("That's something for Liz; she's always whining about how boring her face is," said Josh.) Baz and Josh were also fascinated by the weapons room; they gazed wistfully at some blowpipes that could put a person to sleep in a matter of seconds. ("For the next time those kids down the road decide to come after me," said Baz.) They bent their heads over glue guns that would immobilize an opponent, and studied an electronic ankle-cuff that could whisk someone straight off to the nearest police station.

"Aren't these things for sale anywhere else? Except here?"

"They're nearly all prototypes. The Associates are the only ones allowed to buy them. That way, they can test them at the same time."

There was also a room with all sorts of ingenious bits and pieces, such as a portable hand-warmer for those endless waits on windy railway station platforms; taste-changers for when you had to go out to dinner, so the liver and artichokes tasted of strawberries and cream; and finally the softest, comfiest duvets imaginable, which hugged you ever so gently, and would even give you a back rub if you felt like one. Then they began to get tired. "I want to go home," said Baz. "Teresa?"

They turned back to the doorway where Teresa had been talking on her mobile phone. But she'd disappeared. They walked to the door and started looking for her down the corridors and inside the rooms.

"No point looking for her," came a voice. "I've sent her home." A man with a wild shock of grey hair walked up to them.

"Oh, hi," said Josh, relieved.

"Max Herbert, how d'you do," said the man, shaking Baz's hand. He looked them both over appraisingly, with an intense, mournful gaze. "Did the Associates help make you any the wiser? Did Moussa scare the living daylights out of you?"

"It seems Josh has been chosen to go dream-travelling," said Baz in his clear voice, "to sell things."

"Yes," said Max Herbert, nodding slowly, "and you're going with him. Moussa has probably told you that it isn't without its perils." He sighed. "And I *do* regret that. But you'll also get a lot out of it, I promise you."

"Five hundred pounds," said Josh dreamily, "and I can choose something every month. Does that include the weapons room?"

Max smiled. "Not all of the stuff on display in those rooms is there for the taking, no. But actually, I meant something else. I hope you will learn a lot from it. And all of the rest of us as well." He went on in a whisper, "We've never had any youngsters as young as the two of you. Fourteen's the preferred age, and even that is too young, if you ask me. But then again, sixteen's a little too old. Gippart is a business, a money-making venture, of course; no one will pretend it isn't. Still, dream-travelling is one of the most glorious things in the universe, and only Gippart can open up that dream-world – and explore its terrifying forests, and rid it of nightmares, and turn it into a paradise. And doing so will also make the real world flourish again. I truly believe in it, from the bottom of my heart."

They nodded and did their best to look as if they understood.

Max heaved a deep sigh and shrugged. "It's a dangerous little game, of course, and I do wish to impress upon you that, at all costs, you must avoid doing anything that might seem to you the slightest bit dangerous. Just trust your instincts, that should do it." He turned to Josh. "Joshua, it's quite possible that you'll be tempted to employ your talent. I would ask you not to do that yet. Not at this time. Not without some guidance." He continued to stare at him as if he was about to say something else. He lowered his eyes instead. "Oh well. The reason I came looking for you just now, boys, is this: sometime soon, I'd like to take you on a dream-walk, an *imayada*, to show you how it's done. I'll explain all about it later. I'll give you a call when the time comes, and then I'll be waiting for you at the usual entrance. Agreed?"

"Usual entrance?"

"Yes. Didn't they explain it to you?" Max pushed them in the direction of the escalators. "You see, each of you got here by a different route, didn't you? Well, there are two ways you can get to Gippart. Baz arrived here by car, via the usual entrance, but we made you go the other way, Joshua. That was your qualifying exam."

"And what about Baz?"

"Baz was invited because he's your friend, but *you* are the one we are really interested in, Joshua. If we find that Baz isn't able to follow us on the dream-walk, then we'll find you another friend."

"Huh, thanks a lot. That isn't very nice," spluttered Baz.

"I do hope and expect that you'll manage it, Baz," said Max, "and as Talent Scout, I can tell you that things look good, as far as you're concerned. I have an excellent nose for that sort of thing."

They had arrived in another large hall, with a gleaming reception desk and swishing glass exit doors. Max held open the door of a car waiting outside. "Don't say a thing about this at home, will you? Not a word! Teenagers can always be relied on not to confide in their parents, but in your case—"

"I never tell my parents anything," Josh lied.

"Me neither," said Baz quickly. "Well, most of the time."

Max Herbert shook his head. "We'll be sending them a letter, all in good time, but after a first visit such as this, you'd only be telling them some tall story they'd never believe. So keep it to yourselves for now. Just pretend you dreamt it."

"Fine," yawned Josh.

"See you soon," whispered Max. "See you very soon."

3
The Dawning of the World

It was impossible to pretend it had been a dream. Josh remembered everything down to the last detail, especially that Aladdin's cave of high-tech gadgets. In the days following their visit he was in dire need of the individual hop-flight engine (the time he was late for his judo lesson), or the solid-line pencil (when he needed a three-metre pole to get his badminton shuttlecock down from a tree). Sometimes he'd vividly remember the Board's probing eyes, or feel Moussa's stern grip on his neck again. Baz, oddly, remembered the music, to which Josh had paid hardly any attention. "In the corridor, remember? Where we found the motorbikes, didn't you hear it? *Ta-dada-dum, pum, pum, pum, ta-dada da-rum, parum-pum-pum.*" Baz had been playing drums, including Indian tablas, since he was five, and he could get a little carried away at times. But mainly they talked about what was going to happen next.

"I don't trust that Moussa," said Josh.

"But Max is all right, you can tell," Baz decided.

"Anyway, we'll go with Max just once."

"And then we'll see."

One evening, Mo said, "You're daydreaming again for a

change, sweetie." And Liz giggled. "He must be in love!" She was one to talk, with that creepy boyfriend of hers, whose name, it turned out, was Mervin Spratt. Spratt was trying so hard to please that he wouldn't stop pestering Josh with questions about school, his friends, his collection. Was it precious things he collected? Or unusual ones? Would Josh like to show him some, or swap? Josh just couldn't stand it, and looked forward to when he would spend the night at his father's.

Max's phone call came on Saturday afternoon, at five past two. Edwin, who'd been leafing through the newspaper and was just swallowing an aspirin with a mouthful of coffee, was the one who answered.

"Who? Scouts? Sorry, there's no Scouts here, and we'd prefer to keep it that way too."

He slammed down the receiver and shook his head. The phone started ringing again immediately. "What? You again? No, I'm *telling* you, aren't I, there's nobody here that goes to a Scout Group. What? An application form? Did she really? Today? Well I'll be... Wait a sec." He looked at Josh, who was scraping the chocolate spread off his bread with his teeth. "There's a Max Herbert, from the Scouts, or something, on the phone for you. Is it true Mo arranged for you to go there?"

Josh was so startled that he spilled his mug of tea on to his plate. "Oh yeah, right!" He nodded, grabbing the phone. "Hello?"

"I am sorry about calling you at this time," said Max, "but I do want our walk to be during the day, because it's best to be as alert and wide awake as possible the first time you do it. Do you think you could fix it at home so that they'll let you attend an introductory session for the Scout Group this afternoon?"

"OK," Josh stammered, "when, exactly?"

"Right now – if that is convenient, of course. Do you remember where Gippart is located?"

"Um..."

Max gave him the directions. "If you take the 134 bus, you can easily get here by three o'clock. Can you manage it? Right, now just say something into the phone that sounds enthusiastic, like 'Hey, cool' – isn't that what young people say these days? I really am not all that well up on our Associates' slang – and then you go, 'OK, see you soon.' Goodbye, my boy."

"Hey, cool. OK, see you soon!"

Edwin looked at him suspiciously. "What did that Scout leader want with you? Are you really thinking of joining that bunch of paramilitary boneheads? Has Mo gone completely off her rocker?"

Josh, blushing, bowed his head over his plate. "I dunno," he muttered.

Edwin folded the newspaper sloppily and tossed it down on the table. "I'll have to give her a piece of my mind tonight. What time's this shindig of yours supposed to start?"

"Soon. At three."

"At three?" Edwin glanced at his watch. "Well, actually, that's fine with me. For Mo's sake, go and see for yourself. Once bitten, twice shy, I always say. Where is it you have to get to, anyway?"

"Up on Hampstead Heath, near Kenwood. At least I think so. Somewhere around there."

"Then you'd better get going. Jump to it, move!"

Then the doorbell rang, and Baz was at the door. "It's *today*!"

A current of electric shivers coursed through Josh's body and the hairs on the back of his neck stood on end.

Edwin threw Josh his coat. "Hi, Baz," he said, burping. "'Scuse me. So you're off to learn all that dib-dib stuff as well, are you? Well, have a good time; see you later."

If Max hadn't been looking out for them, they could have been anxiously wandering back and forth past the gleaming office blocks and glass doors all afternoon looking for a sign that said

Gippart International. The nameplate was very inconspicuous: Gippart Int., in tiny letters, beneath a cat's-head logo.

"Gippart doesn't need brand recognition," said Max, leading the way into the building. "Let our subsidiaries sell our products under their own brand names, that's fine by us."

He took them to a very ordinary room on Level –3, the floor whose spacious central concourse had Reception areas all around the perimeter. He fiddled with a kettle and a hotplate in a corner. There was a worn carpet on the floor, and an old leather sofa near a gas fire. The walls were covered in photographs of children, teenagers and adults, as well as certificates, diplomas and medals. Max tossed some garments at them. "Here, put these on. Work clothes, for your first *imayada*."

"What language is that, anyway?" asked Baz, pulling a grey tunic over his head. "*Umaya, imayada, Sense.* Is it Arabic?"

"No, it's Tembe. Gippart's official language is the ancient tongue of the land of Gippart's ancestors – Tembe. We use Tembe words for untranslatable concepts, like *umaya*."

Max handed them two mugs. "Let's just go and take my favourite dream-walk. My *imayada*. Are you wearing your tunics? Here, drink this tea. It gives you a special sort of energy boost."

Josh felt a bit uncomfortable in his grey tunic. "Are there drugs in it?" he asked, staring into his mug suspiciously.

"Of course not. Drugs are not allowed here," said Max. "If you swallow a tablet, or a mushroom, or whatever's fashionable these days, it may very well send you off on your way, but you have absolutely no control over it, let alone the ability to move about freely or make any sales. Besides, you'll wreck your body that way. At Gippart, the point is to make yourself as strong as possible, body and soul, and that's all this tea will do for you. Inactive adults like myself, on the other hand, do have to take a pill to enter *umaya* for a dream-walk. If we didn't, we wouldn't be able to keep going for more than an hour. And even *with* the pills… But it's worth it."

They sipped the tea, which was sweet and slightly fizzy.

"Is it like finding your way through all those rooms?" asked Josh. "Do you learn to steer your way through?"

"You just roughly set a course in a certain direction," Max explained. "Each person's way into *umaya* has a special image or symbol. Mine, for example, is mist." He withdrew into an alcove to change his clothes. "So I have to make myself think of cotton wool, or whipped cream, or candyfloss, or snowstorms and then I'll get there. Except" – his voice was smothered by a piece of clothing being pulled over his head – "that with practice you learn there are barriers, so you've also got to think laterally, about a sort of detour. And initially you don't quite get to where you had in mind, either, but to a place that sort of points you in the right direction. So my own steps usually go: launderette, snowstorm, lift door with frosted-glass windows. OK, are we ready?"

He reappeared dressed in a tunic that reached down to his knees, and led them out into the hall, where the passers-by stared at them curiously.

"Everyone's staring at us."

"It's not because of the way you're dressed," said Max, "but because you're so young. You should feel honoured. They're wondering if you're as good as I've assured them you are." By this time he had opened another door, and they entered another of the many identical Reception areas. The receptionist behind the desk was a young man this time. He held up a hand in greeting.

"An *imayada* works basically the same way as your walk, Josh, through all those rooms to Reception," Max explained. And then he suddenly cried, "*Heavens*, am I looking forward to this! It's been months!" Soberly he went on, "It's practically the same kind of thing as walking to Gippart, except that the transition is more like a jump; it's a much more radical, much more intense experience. We're about to delve deep into the actual dream-world. I don't know what the effect will be on the two of you, but most Associates tell me that it's a funny feeling, as if you're on a roller coaster. Baz, just do as I say. Hang on tight to each other, whatever happens."

Josh gave Max one of his hands, and Baz's trembling hand firmly grabbed hold of his other one. Their hearts were pounding. Max pulled the door open a crack. Then the timbre of his voice changed, turning deep and hypnotic. "Think of a very wet, green frog, a lively creature, sitting on a water lily pad in the middle of a green river, at dusk, with silence slowly settling on the green, green forest..."

They thought they could feel themselves being lifted up. Their stomachs turned over and for an instant they couldn't tell if they were standing right side up or upside down. They gasped for air and then they heard Max say, "Well done! You can open your eyes now!"

"Wow!" said Baz, and Josh said, *"Jeez."* They were standing in a clearing in a sunny forest, beside a small pond.

"How was that?" Max smiled. "Pretty smooth going, as far as I could tell. Right? No one's hurt?"

They shook their heads and, laughing, looked around.

"Excellent, then on to the next. Think as hard as you can of a long, steep staircase going down. Not a ladder, though, a staircase. A solid staircase, straight down, down..."

They took a deep breath, squeezed their eyes shut, and had the sensation of slowly tumbling through the air, then abruptly landing on their feet again.

"Oh, *no*!" Max's voice sounded alarmed and yet at the same time amused, and once they opened their eyes, they understood why. They were standing at the top of a steep, wet, slippery waterslide, which ended below in the seething cauldron of a tropical swimming pool. A gaggle of dripping, screaming children crowded behind them, pushing to get on. "Oh well, here we go," shouted Max, and slid down the chute, clothes and all. Josh had no choice: a bossy girl shoved him from behind, and off he went, careering down, lurching wildly in the sudden turns; he came up spluttering, and swam as fast as he could to the edge. Baz surfaced behind him, just as a shrill whistle sounded. "Hey, you over there!" A lifeguard ran up to them. "What is the meaning of this? Off with those clothes, boys, and quick about it! Sir, are you mad? There *are* changing cubicles, you know!"

They ran, their shoes sopping and splashing, towards the MALE CHANGING ROOM sign. Max was hiccuping with laughter. "I can't wait to see what you make of the next one," he panted. "Please try to concentrate a little harder this time. Think of a lawn, an ordinary grass lawn, in a park. With no one around, OK? No footballers" – Josh immediately pictured a bunch of sweaty soccer players – "no dogs or anything…"

"Wait!" squealed Josh.

"Ready?"

They nodded.

"Go!"

After a short dizzy spell they found themselves in a quiet room. There was a round green rug on the floor and a great many clocks on the walls: tall grandfather clocks, cuckoo clocks, trick clocks with mirror-image faces or else illegible numbers, strident little tick-tock alarm clocks, railway station clocks.

"This is very odd," said Max. "I cannot explain it. Some of the adults, the Sensers, do sometimes experience this type of phenomenon. Oh my goodness, that would mean that one of you might be… But no, of course not. That's highly unlikely." He shook his head, annoyed. "Well, let's just get away from here. We seem to have veered somewhat off course, so as a corrective we're going to make a number of consecutive jumps. Hold on to me tightly. This time you really are going to go head over heels. It's absolutely crucial that you keep concentrating the whole time on a big, yellow moon on the horizon, filling up half the sky…" His voice sank again, insistent, hypnotic. They squeezed their eyes shut and thought about a moon, cheese – no, a moon. "A moon so big and smooth and round that you want to touch it; it rises slowly and majestically, and it's huge, it fills the sky, it swells and spreads until it's taken over the whole sky..."

His voice faded away and Josh promptly panicked. His stomach did a whole series of turns and, head and knees tucked in, arms flailing wildly, he lost hold of Max's hand. He heard Baz crying "Ouch!" in the distance, and blindly tried to find something to cling on to.

Suddenly he found something. He grabbed hold of something, something ice-cold and solid, and then it clamped itself viciously on to *him*. Something cold brushed his cheek, and he heard a shrill voice screech, as if from very far away, "I've caught you! Joshua *na* Jericho! *Gotcha!*" Josh felt a wave of icy fear. He froze, and then suddenly all about him there was the clamour of high-pitched children's voices and he felt cold little fingers gripping his ankles.

He screamed.

The next moment someone was hauling him up by the hair, and he was flying through the air. A voice from somewhere was shouting, *"Frog! Frog!"* Then he saw the frog. It was leaping and twisting and diving, and he tried to make the creature keep still by forcibly pushing it down on to its lily pad. The next thing he knew, it was pouring with rain, and the frog suddenly froze, as if turned to stone, staring at him glassy-eyed. "Are you OK, Josh?" he heard Baz say.

Josh groaned and swore. He was lying on his back in the wet grass, and heavy, lukewarm raindrops fell all around. Baz was kneeling beside him. Max crouched on his other side.

"OK, hush now," said Max. He offered him a bowl of something warm to drink.

"Is it tea?" Josh stammered anxiously.

"Well now, I can see you're already feeling a little better," said Max. "That didn't go quite the way we expected, did it!"

"What *was* all that?"

"When you go jumping, there's always the danger of running into a nightmare, to put it bluntly, somewhere along the line. I'm so sorry. It doesn't happen often, and I'll show you what you can do to prevent it."

Josh shuddered. "They were after me."

"That's what you think," said Max, "but it isn't the case. They can't really touch you, and they haven't got it in for you personally."

"For me, they have. They were as cold as ice, and they were calling my name."

"What? Your name?" Max rose to his feet abruptly. "Your name!" He turned to Baz. "And you, did they call your name too?"

"No. I told you, there was just that stabbing pain in my head and my chest."

Max stared straight ahead for a while, and then began pacing up and down, fidgeting with his hands.

"Were you the one pulling my hair?" asked Josh, getting to his feet.

"Yes," said Baz, "I'd lost you and I was really in pain too. I almost had a heart attack when I heard you scream. It's lucky I grabbed you as quickly as I did. And then we landed here, in the grass. Hey, Josh, do you really think we ought to be doing this?"

"I don't think so," he sighed. "But we can't just stop now, can we? Where *are* we, anyway?"

They looked around and saw, through a curtain of rain, the dim shapes of gigantic trees.

Max had stopped pacing and said, "The funny thing is that it's actually gone fantastically well. We've made it; we're in my favourite dream: the dawning of the world. Now that we're here, I might as well give you a tour. I don't know exactly what happened, Joshua, but I think it must have had something to do with your special talents. To my knowledge, such a thing has never happened before. But don't worry, we'll take a different route home, which is absolutely one hundred per cent safe."

Josh stood up. He had only just realized that he had, indeed, landed in a completely different world.

"Can you feel it?" asked Max. "Have you ever experienced anything like it? Can you smell that delicious young air, purer than crystal? As if it's never been breathed by anyone before?" He was right. Here they were inhaling not air, but a fizzy sort of energy. There was an undercurrent of contagious happiness everywhere that sent shivers up the spine. And above it, the air was light and supple, warm and playful; and also, for the moment, wet, wet, sopping wet.

Walking slowly through the glistening, dripping forest of ghostly giant trees, they saw animals flickering in and out of the currents of mist. Extraordinary animals. For besides ordinary rabbits, wild boar, birds, monkeys and deer, they also spotted long-haired porcupines, tapirs walking on large, ape-like hands, small white giraffes with downy feathers and little wings, and lizards the size of pigs, in scarlet and purple velvet. They were delighted when some creatures walked right up to them and licked their hands, or sniffed the backs of their knees, or nibbled softly at their hair. Baz stroked a young dark-furred panther with deep purple spots which was licking his right knee. "Aren't they dangerous?"

"In this world there is no fear, and no evil," said Max. "They're all very young and very curious, that's all."

No sooner were the words out of his mouth than one of the panther's sharp little teeth pierced the skin on Baz's knee, and a drop of blood welled up. The panther sniffed and squeaked, then licked away the blood. Baz patted it on the shoulder by way of goodbye.

"Now it's tasted blood," said Josh, worried. "Won't it—"

"No," said Max, "it won't eat you. It likes the taste of it, but that's mainly because it's something new and different." He was silent a moment. "Look, I'm not saying that the animals don't devour each other. But they're not driven by bloodthirstiness or the need to kill. It's as if these things happen by accident here, as if they just have to try everything, and are then either pleasantly or unpleasantly surprised by the taste."

"As if they're experiencing everything for the first time?" asked Baz, leaping nimbly over a huge pool of mud. Josh whistled in admiration.

"Yes, something of the sort, I think. Besides, if an animal puts up any sort of serious resistance, it won't get eaten. And the same goes for the two of you, remember. Look, the weather's clearing up; the sun will soon be out. Have you noticed, by the way, how little effort it takes to walk, run and jump?"

When the sun broke through, they stood rooted to the spot in awe. The mist slowly turned to gold. Next, there was just a soft, sweet haze over everything, and then the world about them was suddenly unveiled and crisply outlined. Everything glowed and glistened. It was as if the trees, the plants and the flowers were exploding with happiness.

"They're talking!" said Josh. From above his head and under his feet, from all around in fact, came the just-barely audible sound of laughter and whispering. He listened closely. "I can't understand it, Mr Herbert, what are they saying?"

"You won't be able to make it out, my boy. Everything's simply seething with life here, so that it sounds as if everything on earth is talking."

"Hush a minute." Baz lifted his hand. "Over there, in the distance – that isn't talking, it's music."

All three listened intently, and it was true. Under the chattering, they could hear snatches of music: a melody, a beat, drifting in and out.

Spellbound, they walked on through the music-laden air. The world was far more beautiful than they'd ever imagined. The trees grew smaller and then gave way to bright new sand dunes. Max's eyes shone as he looked around. He seemed to be pulsing with energy, and his messy grey hair was now a mass of springy waves. "The reason I love this world is not just because it's so young, and so full of life, but also because there really is nothing to sell here. Gippart's salespeople never come here. So peaceful."

"Do you live here then?" asked Josh.

Max laughed. "I like living out of town, though I wouldn't want to live *this* far! But I do have my own little retreat here. I'll show you my hideaway later. We'll be returning home from there. Come. Can you smell the sea? Can you hear the ocean?"

Josh heard a heavy, rolling drone behind the dunes, and Baz and he simultaneously broke into a run.

"Race you to the beach!"

"First one in the water wins!"

But they were in for a let-down. When they got to the top of a tall dune and looked down at the ochre beach, they saw that this wasn't the kind of sea that lent itself to swimming. It was heaving with creatures, living things that crawled out of the water and swarmed up on to the land.

"Ugh!" cried Baz, revolted.

"Don't say that – you mustn't!" Max cried, clambering up after them. "This is the primal stew, the primordial soup – look at it, look how absolutely marvellous…! Just *look* at it!"

Josh stuck out his tongue in disgust, but then looked at it anyway, and it was true, it was fantastic. It looked as though the ocean was emptying, as if everything that *could* was climbing up on land. There were crabs scrambling up, in an awkward sideways shuffle, but also great gobs of wriggly worms washing ashore, all helplessly thrashing about at first, and then, as if of one mind, starting their slow crawl inland. They saw how fish slithered on to the beach and then how they sprouted flat feet, which they used to move cautiously up on to the shore. They saw eels, once they reached dry land, metamorphosing into skinny lizards. They even saw a big old sea snake grow wings, shake itself dry and fly away. Birds were wheeling high above this wriggling multitude – bright red birds, or striped blue and yellow, all snapping their greedy beaks. They pecked and gulped and gorged themselves, and were beaten off from time to time, only to pounce once more, shrieking triumphantly.

"Is this really the way it all happened, aeons ago?" asked Josh, impressed.

"Of course not," replied Max nonchalantly. "Don't you remember? This is only a dream-world, or an *umaya* as we call it in Tembe. This is simply the way some humans have dreamt it could have happened, or maybe it's the way animals picture it – who knows? Or perhaps it's an amalgam of different dreams. Every time I come here it's a little different. But the power of it – that always remains the same."

At that moment three large catlike creatures leapt towards them out of the forest, agile and fast, dark as shadows. They were bigger than adult panthers, and Josh saw that their fur was black and deep purple. "Ha!" cried Max, and he called out something to the beasts in a language of clicking throat noises.

"This must be the family of the little panther that licked your blood, if I'm not mistaken," Josh told Baz, and Baz shuddered. "Let's hope they didn't get a taste for it."

Max patted the beasts, stroking their necks. "Here, climb on," he said. "When they come up to you on their own, you can ride them. Hold on tight. And watch your ankles and heels; they don't like being kicked in the flanks any more than horses do."

Josh decided later that, if he were ever sentenced to death and granted one last wish, this would be what he would wish for: to ride through the wind of the dawning of the world on the lithe, powerful back of a panther. It felt as if they were flying, propelled by blasts of pure force, their bare legs sinking deep into the warm fur. The wind whipped their hair, they squinted their eyes at the butter-yellow sun, they breathed in the wild air; they were heroic adventurers, and they didn't want it to end, ever.

At last the panthers slowed to a bumpy trot, then continued

at a more relaxed pace, tails swishing. Max, heaving a deep sigh, rode up alongside. "Look at the savannah," he said, pointing. "This is where humans originally came from."

They rode through the lofty grasslands, with here and there a stand of trees. There were apes in the trees, but they weren't proper apes: they had long white hair and hairless pink faces and blue eyes. As soon as the three of them drew near, the human apes began calling out shrilly, shrieking and swinging from branch to branch. Baz waved, smiling, but Josh couldn't help shuddering. "Is this the way it *really* used to be?"

"Oh, how do *we* know?" Max muttered. "Look, over there!"

In the next stand of trees they saw a group of darker anthropoids sitting on the ground, with long-haired white ape-children playing in their midst, as well as a smaller species of bluish-black monkey that seemed to be constantly busy with its hands – picking up twigs, knotting grass stalks. The anthropoid apes were climbing all over each other, jeering, and some of them were humming a weird tune, all in different keys. A little further they came to a towering rock formation with an assortment of anthropoids and other humanoids on it. Some were asleep, but others were busy working on rock drawings. On the top of the rock, a huge dark brown anthropoid was peering out into the distance. She was nursing a tiny ape with an intelligent face. Turning round, Josh saw something strange. "Mr Herbert, what's that? There, just beneath where that mother's sitting?"

Max looked back and his eyes lit up. "I call them wood-sprites, for want of a better word. What do you think? What would you call them? Nymphs? Elves?"

"No. They're so … so earthy. What do you think, Baz?"

"Wood-sprites," he said decisively.

The radiant creatures were hard to see, as if they consisted of nothing but mist or reflected light. But through the shimmering aura you could just about make out that they were greyish-green as lichen, silver as birch bark. "You'll probably get the chance to see them up close, later on," said Max. "Look, over there, there's another one, a night-spirit." They saw a very dark shape perched high up in a solitary giant tree. It seemed to be staring at them, frozen. Then, before their eyes, it vanished.

They rode to the edge of the savannah, and once there, the panthers turned their heads to look at them, growling. The three travellers quickly dismounted, and the panthers shot off and disappeared over the horizon.

"Is it that droning noise that's made them run off like that?" asked Baz. It was true: the earth was shaking, with a slow, heavy rumble. They felt the vibration in their legs and in their stomachs.

A thought suddenly popped into Josh's head. "They don't have dinosaurs here, do they?"

"Not usually," said Max, "at least, not in my personal *umaya*. Get down, quick."

They threw themselves to the ground, lying on their stomachs, shoulder to shoulder.

"Can you see them, over there?"

And then they saw it: close by, a parade of huge reddish-brown elephants, with long tusks and deep-set, sparkling eyes. Buoyantly they marched along, proud and uninhibited, as if they enjoyed stamping their feet as hard as possible. They were much bigger than ordinary elephants: masters and mistresses of the first savannah. When the parade had passed by and the dream-travellers were dusting themselves down, they suddenly heard chuckling and a tinkling sound: a big baby with a smiling elephant's face waddled behind the elephants on all fours. The baby caught sight of them, squealed, raised his little trunk and trumpeted. Then he scuttled on again after the elephants, with a baby rat following in his wake.

"Ganesh!" cried Baz. "That was the god Ganesh when he was a baby!"

"Of course," laughed Max. "Ganesh, Master of New Beginnings! Yes, he lives here. That's a good omen. Ganesh clears obstacles out of your way. Just what we need now."

They walked on through increasingly dense masses of green shrubs with bright yellow and orange flowers. They heard a rustling in the bushes, and a huge snake slithered out across Baz's path.

"So they *do* have bad things here, after all," muttered Baz, shaken.

Max placed a hand on his shoulder. "Quite the contrary. Didn't you know snakes mean life, fertility, the promise of life?" He walked over to the bushes and pushed them aside. "Hush now, and look – have you ever witnessed anything as lovely and magnificent as this?"

They saw an enormous coiled green snake, asleep; it was at least a metre in diameter, and perhaps twenty metres long. As they stared at it, it stirred, lifted its flat head and gazed at them pensively with its yellow eyes. Max stared back, and the snake slowly began moving its head around. Josh and Baz felt themselves growing sleepy. Then the snake shut its eyes, and Max took a step back.

"It was trying to hypnotize us!" Josh exclaimed.

"If you'd really been under hypnosis, you'd have been whisked back home. It was simply greeting us, giving us its full attention. Believe me, Joshua, snakes protect people, and they know the secrets of life. You need never be afraid of snakes. I know Associates who keep a snake as their guardian."

Josh, sunk deep in thought, remembered his snake bracelet at home as they walked on. The snake bracelet he'd stolen from the lady on the bus. "Do snakes protect you from nightmares as well?" he asked when they sat down to eat some yellow fruit.

"I think so," said Max. "If you treat it well, a snake brings life, and nightmares interfere with your life, so it's quite possible that it can."

So Josh decided that next time he'd wear his snake bracelet, as a good-luck charm. Who could tell? He had the feeling that it might be able to protect him from the terrifying nightmare he'd slid past while plunging.

They came to the slopes of a steep mountain, the first in a chain silhouetted against the purple sky. The air had grown even lighter and cooler.

"We're nearly at our destination," said Max. "My hideaway is up there, and we'll return home from there. It's a shame, really, but I must be out of here within an hour if I don't want to run into any problems. Are you boys still all right?"

They nodded. Baz was humming one of his rhythmic songs and Josh just kept gazing at everything around them, and at the huge clouds that were amiably drifting across the blue skies. Suddenly he saw a puff of black smoke against the white clouds. "Mr Herbert!" He pointed.

"Actually," said Max, "I forgot to tell you that my hideaway is inside a volcano. It's nice and warm in there, and in my *umaya* there's never been an eruption."

They climbed on, and soon they were standing at the top of a mountain pass, with a great panorama over most of the world. A huge wall of black clouds was gathering in the far distance. "Is that night coming on?" asked Baz.

"No, it isn't. Let's hope it stays exactly where it is. That is the end of time, boys. Chaos, the black void, I'm afraid. That's where my dream-world ends. Come, we'll go to my special place – it's more pleasant in there."

Max's hideaway was indeed safe and warm. It was a circular cave, reached by a short tunnel. There was an open fire in the middle, which flickered with little tongues of flame. The floor of the cave was covered in green moss, and the only other things in it, apart from some sleeping animals, were mugs and an earthenware jug containing a clear liquid. Max handed them each a mug of it to drink. They couldn't decide what it tasted of.

"What is it?" asked Josh.

"Water," laughed Max, "that's real water." He went and sat down on the moss between two sleeping foxes with green pelts and a long-haired deer. "Sit down, boys, so that we can think about getting started on our return journey."

They threw themselves on the ground, panting.

"I'm ready to drop," said Josh.

"That was the intention. Didn't you say so yourself, Joshua? Remember? You told us how one enters or exits a dream."

"Oh, yes," said Josh, who didn't really understand. "You do it by falling asleep."

"I'll explain it again, for Baz's sake. In order to enter an ordinary dream, all you have to do is fall asleep; but I believe you've already seen that it gets a little more complicated if you want to enter a live, conscious dream-world, or *umaya.* This is the collective dream of all mankind, where you can make conscious decisions as to what to do or not to do. That's why Gippart has developed the slide, or jumping method, by which you switch locations until you arrive at the dream-place of your choice, or else at Gippart's Reception, a transit area that's always within easy reach."

"Oh yes, really easy," Josh said sarcastically.

"All right then, easy for those with enough experience. But there's an infinite number of dream-worlds out there: not only the innumerable sturdy, solid *umayas* in which Gippart operates, but also all the flimsy dreams you dream in your bed at night. But there is only one single, hard-and-fast reality. So, it doesn't make any difference whether you're in a flimsy dream of your own making, or in *umaya*, the collective dream-world. Because once you wake up, you'll always find yourself back in the real world. So to get back there, all you have to do is to fall asleep. And *that* is something Joshua is particularly good at, and I don't think that after our trek, Baz, you'll have any trouble falling asleep either."

"I don't know," said Baz. "I feel quite wide awake, and this place is so strange." Then he gave an enormous yawn.

"But won't we have nightmares if we fall asleep here?" asked Josh, whose eyelids were beginning to grow heavy.

"No," said Max, "or at least not of the sort you experienced back there, anyway. Those are genuine nightmares, if I may put it that way. If you fall asleep now, you'll be dreaming your everyday, ephemeral dreams. And you'll probably wake up in Reception, at Gippart."

Baz curled up as close to Josh as he could. "Could you please not fall asleep until I'm asleep?"

"I don't know if I can."

"I'll stay awake until you two are off," said Max. "And I've a lullaby that works really well, Baz. Don't worry. We're in the bowels of the earth, you're sleeping in the bosom of the world – what could possibly go wrong?"

He stopped talking and then began to sing very softly in the same deep voice he'd used for the plunging – a reassuring and comforting sound. They couldn't understand the words. *Tembe*, thought Josh. Baz piped up in a small voice, "I'm not asleep yet!" Josh mumbled, "Me neither," and began to drop off, and felt himself grow wide and roomy.

It was true that it was easy returning to Reception: lying side by side on the ground, they were woken by a laughing young woman giving their hair a hard pull. But getting home from there was another matter. First, it took them ages to make their way along Gippart's many corridors to find Max's room and their clothes; and then, to top it all, they got on the wrong bus. It gave Josh such a shock to see how late it was that he slipped straight up to bed without saying a word. Which wasn't the cleverest move: late that same night, Mo, furious, grounded him for the next few days.

4
THE TRADERS' TRIAL

Mervin Spratt and Liz were getting to be a serious item. Spratt came over just about every night ("He doesn't have any family of his own, and the dump he's living in is cramped, nasty and draughty") after finishing work ("At the university, he's writing a very difficult book, it's *so* interesting," Liz gushed. "It's all about the concept of time!"), until not only was it driving Josh up the wall, but Mo and Edwin as well. To get rid of them, Mo presented the pair with tickets to the cinema, or she'd go down to the pub with Edwin, but Josh was stuck at home, helpless prey. At times it seemed as if Spratt deliberately had it in for him. "Hello, Joshie" – *Who said you could call me Joshie?* – "how about a game of draughts?" "Joshie, would you like some help with your homework?" "Joshie, are you interested in stamp collecting?" "Here, Joshie, would you like to go to the gemstones exhibition at the Science Museum?" "So, Joshie, why all the secrecy about that collection of yours?" Josh could really do without it. He was already a bit twitchy, ever since the adventure with Max Herbert, especially the clutching-hands nightmare, which he kept reliving over and over again.

That was why he wore the snake bracelet now. It really did seem to give him strength. He usually wore it around his ankle, under his sock, well hidden. He could just picture the reaction otherwise: "Ha ha, Josh is wearing a *bracelet*!" Or, worse still, a teacher, grabbing him by the wrist: "That thing's worth a fortune! Where *ever* did you get it, young man?"

One morning, a few days after his trip through Max's dream-world, he was reading the back of a box of cornflakes during an uncomfortable breakfast around the kitchen table. It was one of those silent mornings, with Mo in a touchy mood and Edwin grumpy with a headache; you could tell he'd go back to bed shortly. Liz was reading the newspaper and eating a tangerine very slowly; she kept dividing it into smaller and smaller segments. Only Spratt was unbearably cheerful and talkative. "There you are, Edwin. I always *knew* those shares were going to collapse! It's a lucky thing you don't dabble much in the stock market, isn't it! Delicious tea, Mrs Cope, could I trouble you for another drop? Liz, may I please have that section of the paper if you're done with it? Ah, look here, it says sunny weather tomorrow and rather cool; I'd really much prefer it that way than warm but rainy, don't you agree, Mrs Cope? And how about you, Joshie? If the weather's fine, you'll be able to go out – much better than moping indoors all day long. I should think you've had enough of *that*, what with being kept in and everything—"

"For God's sake, Mervin," Mo groaned. "Can't you just shut up for a minute, please!" She stood up and grabbed her coat and bag from the stool. "And it's been ages since I've used the name Mrs Cope, thank heavens. OK, I'm off, see you tonight, everyone. Joshie, don't forget your gym things." She put on her raincoat, a weird-looking one with a snakeskin pattern.

"I say," said Mervin, "what a perfectly splendid raincoat you have there. Rather viperous too, of course, genuine snakeskin – it takes guts to go around wearing such a devilish coat, but then you *are* such a plucky lady..."

"Oh, Mervin, spare me!" cried Mo, and she slammed the door shut behind her.

Josh had just about had enough – he went on the attack. “Snakes aren’t devilish at all. Max says they bring life and they protect you and –”

He could have bitten off his tongue. *Idiot, idiot!* He’d meant never, ever; to mention Gippart. He’d promised! He looked around, but Edwin and Liz were sitting there just as bored as ever; they hadn’t heard anything to arouse their curiosity. They couldn’t care less who Max might be – a friend, the guy at the Scouts. But then his eyes fell on Spratt, and his heart leapt into his mouth. Spratt sat frozen in his chair as if he’d been turned to stone. He was gulping so hard that his oversized Adam’s apple made a gobbling sound, and he was staring at Josh as if the latter had changed into a poisonous toad before his eyes. His face radiated toxic hate. The two of them measured each other up in a staring contest that went on and on.

At last Spratt stood up. With one last dirty look at Josh, and darting a glance at his ankle, he marched out of the kitchen without saying another word. The front door slammed with a loud bang. It was only then that Liz and Edwin were roused from their stupor. “Mervin?” called Liz, but then she shrugged and went on reading, picking at her tangerine.

Josh walked into the living room. One thing was certain: Spratt knew about Gippart, and Josh had given himself away. Spratt was the opposition. But how could he be? Why? He must phone Max and ask him what was going on.

He pulled the phone book from the bottom of a pile of old newspapers and feverishly tried looking up the number. But hadn’t Max told him that he lived out of town? As it happened, there were a few Gipparts in London. But which one was the right one? Or were you supposed to look it up under C, for Company, or I, for International? He didn’t feel like phoning lots of clueless people to ask them if Max happened to work there. When he’d combed through the Yellow Pages, he gave up. But he made up his mind then and there: from now on, he would sleep at his father’s, for as long as it took for Spratt to clear off. He stuffed the things he needed into a suitcase, and moved to his father's that very morning.

It was there that Baz reached him by phone, just as Josh's dad was busy in the kitchen preparing one of his elaborate meals for two.

"Josh, want to go over there together, for the Traders' Trial?"

"What?"

"You know, the Traders' Trial, the one Max told us about. Isn't it supposed to be tonight?"

"What are you talking about, the Traders' Trial!"

"Haven't you talked to Max?"

"No, I haven't. Baz, you remember Mervin Spratt, that boyfriend of Liz's? He knows something. I mentioned Gippart by accident and he went bananas. If there hadn't been other people around, he'd have attacked me. That's the reason I'm at my dad's."

"But what did you say? Why did he go bananas?"

"How should *I* know? I didn't say anything special, just that snakes are good. But you should have seen him – he just about hit the roof."

"Oh. Have you told Max?"

"No, I haven't talked to Max at all. Have you got his phone number?"

"No. But can I come to your place tonight? So that we can try and get there Max's way?"

"But what *is* a Traders' Trial, anyway? Actually, I'd rather go by bus, you know, because of those nightmares."

"The test for the Associates – the Traders' Trial. We're going to compete in a dream-travelling race, a salesmanship contest. Max explained it to me. To see if we're fast enough to be Associates."

Josh was quiet. He didn't much feel like finding out how fast he could leap his way through that unpredictable dream-world, with dozens of tough, critical Associates looking on. He was sure he'd get lost. And, worse: he could feel those icy hands around his ankles again. The thing he hadn't told Baz was that the creatures had used a most secret name. The name even Mo never mentioned. Joshua *na* Jericho. He shuddered.

"Getting a bus down there's fine with me. I'll come over at half past eleven then. Leave your window open, Josh, all right? I'll whistle for you. Stay awake, OK?"

"Of course I will," said Josh, and hung up.

He kept dithering all evening. Wouldn't it be better just to put an end to the adventure right now? Shouldn't he tell his father about it? Or Mo? No, he couldn't. It was already too late. Even if he did tell them now – if he told them what had really happened the afternoon of the "Scout orientation", and explained why Mo couldn't for the life of her remember signing him up for the Scout Group – Mervin Spratt would *still* be his enemy. He was clearly after something. Otherwise, why was he always whining about wanting to see Josh's collection? He'd probably still want to see it, no matter what. Spratt obviously wasn't going to go away just like that.

The telephone didn't stop ringing all evening. Mo, for Josh: "Hello, love, is everything all right over there? Are you coming home tomorrow? It's miserable here: Mervin Spratt's dumped Liz and now she won't stop crying. Will you try and cheer her up a bit? He was a pathetic creep anyway – can't you make her see that? Besides, I've got a bone to pick with you. Your room's a pigsty. It looks as if someone's dropped a bomb in there. Do come home soon, dear. Then we can all smile again, and we'll celebrate with a cake."

Baz, for Josh: "Didn't Max tell you what to wear, either? Wear gym clothes, or swimming trunks, under your ordinary clothes. And trainers. See you soon, no falling asleep, OK?"

And finally Max, for Josh: "Hello there, Joshua, is everything all right? Did Baz tell you about the Traders' Trial? Looking forward to it? Don't worry, will you? With your talent, you're sure to pass with flying colours."

"But Max..."

"I must hang up now, Joshua, I'm in *umaya.* I'll see you shortly. Goodbye, my boy."

Josh's father smiled. "You're pretty popular these days, Joshie. But now it really is your bedtime. Upstairs, please." The phone rang again. Josh's father picked it up. "Peter Cope speaking. Who? Oh, wait, weren't you Liz's friend? What can I do for you? Pardon? Just a moment. Joshie, come back in here, it's that Mervin fellow, for you."

Josh had been listening at the door with a sinking feeling in his stomach. "Oh, all right," he said nonchalantly. He took the receiver. "Hello?"

It was Mervin Spratt, but his voice now sounded unrecognizably cold and menacing. "Josh, let's just drop the pretence, shall we? You've been feigning ignorance long enough. I'm warning you, I've had enough of your infantile behaviour. This isn't child's play, it's a serious matter, and the stakes are high. I'm sorry it's come to this, but there is no other way. I'll be coming for you tonight, and together you and I are going straight to Gippart. And then you'll come clean with me, put all your cards on the table. Do you understand?" He hung up without waiting for a reply.

"What did that clown want with you?" asked Josh's dad, with a probing look at his son's white face. "Joshie?" He grabbed Josh by the upper arm. "Joshie, he isn't bothering you, is he?" He went all red in the face. "He isn't trying anything nasty with you, is he?"

"No," mumbled Josh in a choked voice. "It isn't that; he just wanted to ... see my collection." Now he was getting flushed: red, then white, then red again. "I think he's a creep too," he stuttered, "but ... all he wants is to see my collection."

The only one who could help him was Max. Tonight. He had to try to get to Max as soon as possible, before Spratt came for him. He hugged his suspicious father goodnight and ran up the stairs to his bedroom.

* * *

He hunted for his penknife, stuffed it in his pocket (with all the other junk – a broken computer game, a miniature pen, a battery, a small torch) and lay down on his bed waiting for the house to go quiet. He could hear his dad talking and laughing downstairs, involved in one of his endless phone conversations. It grew more and more hushed outside. Finally he heard his dad come upstairs, and the door to the main bedroom open. Wait, he was still walking around – bathroom, bedroom, toilet, bathroom, bedroom, down the stairs, kitchen, up the stairs, bathroom, bedroom. Finally it was quiet. The only sound was the TV rumbling softly in his father's room. Josh waited tensely for that to die away too – only then would the coast be clear for him to slip away, rush over to Baz's place, and both of them make their way to Gippart together. To find Max. He lay stiffly on his bed, worrying endlessly about what Spratt might be up to, and in the process of doing so, promptly fell asleep.

He was woken up by something rattling his window. Mervin Spratt! He leapt off his bed in alarm, groping for his knife, but then down below in the street, he caught sight of a head of familiar dark hair and then Baz's fuming face. He was gesticulating angrily with a fistful of pebbles. Thank goodness it was only Baz! Josh flew down the stairs making as little noise as possible, and out the front door.

"You lazy idiot, you promised to stay awake! And in the meantime I'm standing here looking like a complete fool! A man just walked past. He gave me such a filthy look, and he came back, as well, to give me the once-over! Maybe he's an undercover copper. Come on, we've got to rush for the bus – it's nearly ten to twelve!"

They managed to catch a late bus and then dashed through the peaceful midnight streets like two bats out of hell. At Gippart they found a uniformed girl waiting for them. She waved her arms impatiently. "Boys, you're really late! Come on, take the lift down. Run, boys, the Great Hall's already packed."

Indeed, Gippart's dusky subterranean hall, lit only by the emergency signs over the doors, was jam-packed with people. Josh and Baz elbowed their way through the crush of adults, who all obligingly helped push them forward. "Hurry up, boys, it's starting!" The Associates were standing on a podium, surrounded by ropes and barriers in the middle of the hall. Above the podium hung a large clock, and under it was a great big brass gong. Max was acting as a lookout at the edge of the stage, and when he spotted them he called out in relief, "Ha! There you are, you two! About time!" and helped hoist them up on to the podium.

They quickly went and joined the circle of Associates, who were all standing with their backs to the barriers. Josh looked around wide-eyed. The Associates wore hardly anything: their bright, extravagant clothes were draped over the barriers, and they were all standing around in their underwear, or in gym gear, or swimsuits.

"Why aren't you dressed?" Josh whispered to a boy standing beside him.

"Because it's so hot in here," said the boy sarcastically. He was covered in goose pimples, as the air was chilly. "We can hardly enter *umaya* wearing our ordinary clothes, can we! Come on, strip! It's starting."

Within a few seconds Josh, shivering in his underpants and T-shirt, had joined the line-up. Across from him he saw Teresa in a shiny purple leotard, chatting with a group of girls. She caught his glance, and waved. Then Moussa stepped inside the circle and made his way over to the gong with a heavy baton in his hands. Muscles rippling, he walloped the gong with an ear-deafening crash. The podium was suddenly bathed in light, and Moussa remained next to the gong, grinning widely. Max walked into the centre of the circle and climbed up on a red stool. He spoke into a microphone.

"Associates!" he cried, and all the young people raised their arms high in the air and roared in reply. "Associates!" Max shouted again, and again the kids roared, but now the adults were shouting too. "Associates, welcome!" cried Max, and now the whole hall was shouting and cheering and clapping with all its might. "It's finally here, and it's tonight, everybody: the Traders' Trial, as the Associates call it, or, as we say in Tembe, *imayada biris.* We have a wonderful team of Associates and candidates this year, led by the Chief of Associates, the incomparable Moussa!"

There was some applause from the hall, and a few Associates cheered, "Moussa!"

"The new team has only recently been completed. Our last two plucky participants first came to Gippart just two weeks ago, and they are very special agents, these two, on a special mission: Joshua Cope and Bhasvar Patel. They are the youngest candidate-Associates Gippart has ever invited to take part. Welcome!"

Again the hall exploded in applause. A shudder ran down Josh's spine. Special mission? It didn't sound all that pleasant. But Baz was beaming with pride at all the compliments.

"Everyone knows how the Traders' Trial works. We draw lots twice: once for the products to be sold, once to determine the destination. The Associates go in pairs, and they're awarded points for the time in which they manage to sell something and return to home base. The limit is, as always, one hour and forty-seven minutes. Whoever needs longer than that will not, unfortunately, make Associate-hood, and if it turns out he or she was an Associate already, they'll have to resign from the team. Jamie, the products! Associates, numbers, please, up to and including thirty!"

A boy with flushed cheeks carried a large box into the circle. Max started shouting out the Associates' names at breakneck speed. "Feng!"

"Fourteen!"

And Jamie threw an object from the box at him.

"Zak!"

"Twenty-six!"

"Erdogan!"

"Two!"

"Fatouli!"

"Ten!"

And in between, cries of dismay mingled with sighs of relief. "Great!" "Oh, piece of cake!" "Oh no, that's terrible!"

"Joshua!"

"Eleven!"

Josh caught a smooth little stick. "What on earth is it?"

Baz inspected it curiously. "What does it do? Is it part of something else?"

The boy next to him looked at it too. "Well, that's a stick," he said.

"Yes," Josh stuttered, "but how am I supposed to sell anyone an ordinary *stick*?"

"Working that out is what Associates have to do," the boy replied.

Baz's product was a fork. The girl beside him said with envy, "Oh, that's really easy. Want to swap?" She showed him a deflated little balloon.

"Contestants, listen carefully. The teams are made up as follows. Mikki and Sita, Fatouli and Amina" – cheers from the group around Teresa – "Erdogan and Zak…" Josh clenched his little piece of wood. What if he were to lose on purpose? If he did, it would all be over and done with. Yes, but what about that laser penknife then? And Mervin Spratt? "Joshua and Teresa!"

Teresa bounced over to him happily. "Cool!"

"Yeah," said Josh, not knowing if he would like to travel with a girl. Out of the corner of his eye he saw that Baz was paired off with the Persian prince, whose name turned out to be John.

Moussa clanged the gong loudly again and coloured light

suddenly shot up all around. "And now, finally, the destinations." Max passed around a blue bowl containing folded pieces of paper. The Associates opened them excitedly, loudly calling out their assignments to each other and the audience. Josh looked on tensely as Teresa opened the folded note.

LAMERIKA. Teresa wrinkled her nose. "Oh no. And you're new, as well – there's no way this is going to work. It'll be a fiasco."

Max, meanwhile, had climbed back up on the red stool and was shouting at the top of his voice, "Clear the way to the gates! Let them through, let them through, everybody. Fifteen seconds to go. Moussa, the starting signal, please. Associates, on your marks!"

A thunderous peal of the gong, and the kids leapt over the barriers, shouting and cheering, running as fast as they could to the doors. The clock had started the countdown.

Teresa was off like a shot in her purple leotard, striding on her long bare legs. Josh raced after her to one of the doors.

"What are we supposed to think of?" he panted. "Do you know?"

"A Cadillac," said Teresa, "I should think. Just make it black. Can't go wrong with black." She pushed the door open a crack and grabbed Josh's hand. "Off we go," she said.

Slowly the dizzy feeling took hold of them; they were lifted up, tossed head over heels, and they hit the ground stumbling.

"Hey, nice going, kid!" cried Teresa. They were standing in a garage filled with gleaming cars. "So what shall we do now? Lamerika: that must mean millionaires and film stars, and all that. What do you think?"

"Sports cars. Sunglasses?"

"Shades, terrific. Here we go!"

This tumble was higher and wilder. They must have flipped at least three times in the air, but they still managed to hang on tightly to each other. They even landed squarely on their feet.

"Wow!"

"Nailed it again!"

They found themselves by a large hotel swimming pool, with rows of sun loungers and parasols lined up the length of the terrace, which was completely deserted except for one smartly dressed waiter. The man was walking along the edge of the pool carrying a tray of glasses.

"Joshua, stay on course! Pink, do pink!"

The next leap was even higher and more spectacular. Josh recklessly kept his eyes open, and he saw a whirlwind of colours and lights, and heard a string of sounds chiming together.

"Yippee!"

Again they landed on their feet, and both burst out laughing. They were standing in a large cat basket lined in white satin, in which two Siamese cats were sleeping. The cats indignantly leapt from their basket and slunk off, miaowing.

"What's next, Teresa?"

"It's got to have a little more oomph, high tech and stuff. Hmm."

"What?"

"Rockets… Satellites. Satellite. Come on, hurry, let's go."

Did he forget to grab hold of Teresa's hand? Josh had no idea, but he did know something was wrong. The jump immediately veered off course. He flew through darkness and light, cold and warm currents of air brushed past him, and suddenly the thing he'd been dreading happened. The thing he'd been having nightmares about. Two ice-cold arms caught him, and squeezed the breath out of him. A frigid face pressed itself to his face. He felt two lips of icy snow against his cheek, and heard high-pitched laughter. Then that hideous little voice again – "Joshua *na* Jericho, gotcha!" – and cackling. Josh was drifting very slowly through the fog, in the grip of some invisible force. His nightmare. He thought he was screaming, and his one remaining clear thought was: *This is death.* "No, Joshua *na* Jericho, look at me! Look at me!" The voice sliced through his head like a piece of broken glass. Then, suddenly, a volley of sharp little arrows peppered his face and bare arms and legs, and cackling laughter was everywhere, and screeching, so high and shrill that it could have shattered glass. He felt sharp fingernails scratching him, teeth in his ankles, icy fingers poking in his ears. He was weeping, helpless, desperate. Then he was falling, he was falling and falling, endlessly.

When he finally landed, the world was warm again. He was lying on grass. And there was a warm hand on his forehead.

"Joshua! Can you hear me? Are you back?"

Josh opened his eyes and saw Teresa's worried face. "Oh God," he said, and burst out sobbing hysterically. "They caught me again, those weird ghosts. I'm not doing it any more; I refuse to go on!"

Teresa looked at him gravely. "But we're here now," she said softly.

Josh dried his eyes, sat up and looked around. "Did it work then?" he asked. "Is this Lamerika?"

His curiosity conquered his fear. It was a fresh, orderly world, dazzling, bathed in sunlight. They were sitting on a lawn next to a pavement that ran along a wide avenue, with open-topped limousines slowly cruising up and down. Men and women in tight-fitting clothes, all wearing dark sunglasses and flaunting shiny sculpted hairstyles, sauntered along the pavement. Diamonds flashed. Mobile phones rang. The men strutted like peacocks; the women, nearly all of them blondes, tripped along beside them, simpering and wiggling their hips. Nobody paid any attention to Teresa and Josh.

"I suppose so."

"I suppose so too," said Josh.

Then they looked at each other: instead of underwear, they were wearing unobtrusive navy blue clothes. Impeccable work attire, definitely.

"Shall we get down to business?" asked Teresa. "Would you like to have a go, Joshua?"

"I don't care." Josh shrugged. The fear of the nightmare still clung to him, and made him apathetic. "Why don't you go first?"

Teresa stepped resolutely on to the pavement, clutching the half-empty box of matches she was supposed to sell. Smiling brightly, she bounced up to a couple. "Ma'am, sir!" They didn't give her so much as a glance. "Madam!" She walked up to another couple with a winning smile. They continued their conversation, oblivious. "Sir, if you please!"

For ten minutes Teresa ran back and forth energetically. The most she got for her pains was a shove. "This way isn't going to work," she sighed. "I couldn't even sell these fatheads a laptop made of solid gold. They won't even have a look."

Josh had been thinking. "We've got to find a different sort of customer. You won't get through to those show-offs, swanning about in their designer clothes." He stood up and looked around. "Isn't that a filling station? Let's have a look over there."

"Petrol stations always have a shop too, Joshua. We won't be able to sell any matches there."

She was right: the shop was a large, brightly lit supermarket. Customers wearing dark sunglasses walked in and out of the swishing doors, flashing dazzling white smiles.

"But there must be pump attendants here, surely, and shop assistants?" Hesitantly they walked into the shop, but as they did, a loud alarm went off. Two little men in blue uniforms ran up to them and grabbed them by the arm. *"Out, out!"* they shouted, pushing them firmly out of the door.

"That's it. There's your other sort of customer," Teresa laughed.

"Hmm," Josh mused. "I think they only let rich people in there." He walked to the petrol pumps and looked around. "Yes, they're the sort of people we should be going for," he said.

There were quite a few of the blue men hovering around

the petrol pumps. They ran back and forth busily, filling someone's tank, washing someone's windscreen, inflating a tyre, being helpful and polite and attentive. But two of them were leaning against a pump, exhausted. "Those two," said Josh. He took the matches from Teresa and calmly went and stood next to them. "Hello," he said. "Busy day?"

The little men looked at him, but did not reply.

"I'd hate to have to work myself to the bone for those fatheads," said Josh. Again there was no reply. "They won't even let you into the shop, will they? So – were either of you wanting to buy any matches, by any chance?"

Now the blue men bestirred themselves. They straightened up and angrily pushed Josh away. *"Out, out, out!"*

Josh shrugged and walked back to Teresa. "Well, that didn't work either. Any other ideas?"

Teresa pointed a finger. "I think so. Hear that? Is that children I can hear?"

Behind the filling station was a messy patch of spare ground, with stacks of wooden crates and a group of children playing – the ones Teresa had heard. They were very small and dirty and dressed in navy rags. They stopped playing as the Associates walked up to them, and stared at them suspiciously.

"Hi," said Teresa.

"Hello," said one little girl, smiling at them. The other children glared at them.

"What game are you playing?"

The agreeable little girl showed them: they were playing marbles, using pebbles. Josh and Teresa crouched down beside them.

"Can we play?" They played for a while, losing on purpose, which pleased the children.

Then Josh took out the matches. "Want to buy?"

The little girl beamed at the sight of the matches and grabbed the box from Josh's hand.

"No, buy – swap, you've got to give me something in return!"

She shook her head no, and bent greedily over the box, the other kids crowding around her. Teresa grabbed the girl by the shoulder. "Come on, please – give us something. Anything."

Now it was Josh's turn. He'd noticed the little girl was wearing a rubber band as a bracelet, and he took her wrist. "You can keep the matchbox; we want the rubber band," he said sternly.

To his surprise, she nodded meekly and let him slip the band off her wrist.

"One down," he sighed.

Teresa smiled. "You're talented. That was a pretty good sales pitch, I'd say."

"But does it count?"

"Why not? These kids don't have any money. Hey!"

The children were striking the matches one by one, their faces beaming with delight.

"Wait," said Josh. "You want to light a fire? I've got some wood. Look!" He took his little stick out of his pocket. "Want to buy it?"

The girl nodded greedily.

Josh closed his hand around the stick. "You have to pay for it first. What've you got?"

They all looked around. Then the girl said, "Look," and she took a match out of the box and handed it to Josh.

"OK," he said, "it's a deal." He gave her the piece of wood and they stood up, relieved.

"Now let's get out of here, quickly," said Teresa.

Which wasn't such a bad idea, because a couple of the blue men, gesticulating wildly, had just come out to the spare ground with a tall man in sunglasses. They pointed angrily at Josh and Teresa. The children hastily gathered up their pebbles, matches and piece of wood, and scurried off behind a fence, out of sight. Teresa and Josh started to run too, across the waste ground, over a ditch and into a field. When they looked over their shoulders they saw the men had turned back, still talking angrily. The children were now hiding behind the petrol pumps.

They walked on until they were out of sight of the filling station, and lay down in the grass. Now that it was all over, Josh suddenly felt drained. He didn't even care whether or not he'd succeeded. He just wanted to have a talk with Max in private, that was all. Max would have to make sure that Mervin Spratt and those nightmares left him alone.

They lay quietly side by side for a while.

"I did have a good time with you," Teresa finally said drowsily. "It wasn't half as hard as I'd expected. You really did well. For a beginner, of course. Did you enjoy yourself, Joshua?"

Josh nodded sleepily. "Actually, my name's Josh."

"Josh," Teresa repeated. "You know, I'm sure I've seen you before somewhere, but I don't know where."

"Can you just fall asleep whenever you want?" he asked.

"Oh yes, I've done so much babysitting." Teresa laughed. "When the kids I was looking after finally dropped off, I'd be so shattered, I'd promptly keel over myself. I can fall asleep anywhere."

The timing was ripe for it as well: after all, for Teresa and Josh it was the middle of the night, even if in Lamerika the sun was shining. Their bodies, sensing sleep, succumbed immediately. At the very moment they were both nodding off, it happened. A huge explosion blew the petrol station sky-high. They awoke sprawled side by side on the floor of the Reception area, with the blast ringing in their ears.

"What the…?"

"My God!"

"Welcome home. Well done, Associates!" The boy at Reception ran out from behind his computer desk and pulled them to their feet. "Run, you've made excellent time. Run, quick!"

Still deafened by the blast, dizzy and sleepy, they sprinted through the hall, where the people stepped aside for them, laughing and clapping. Baz was already up on the podium, talking animatedly with some other Associates, all dressed in the bizarre clothes they'd acquired on their dream-walks. When Josh and Teresa climbed on to the podium, they all began clapping.

"Not bad!"

"Just look at the little squirt. Didn't you help him at all, Tess?"

"Sixty-seven minutes!"

Moussa walked up to them. "Did you sell anything?" he snapped at Josh.

"Uh … well, yes, I think so."

"Give it here!"

Josh, blushing deeply, handed over the rubber band and the matchstick. Moussa examined the little piece of elastic thoroughly. Then he scrutinized the match from every angle. He didn't jeer, didn't fling them into a corner. He gave Josh an inscrutable look and walked up to Max, who was giving them the thumbs-up sign, smiling.

"Well, that wasn't so bad," said Josh, and he sank to the floor, relieved. Baz, from out of nowhere, pounced on him. "Did you have a good time?"

"I suppose so. Did yours go all right?"

"It was underwater! Can you imagine? But it was a cinch. Except that I just couldn't fall asleep at the end. All those bubbles. Still, I got back before you did, didn't I!"

Leaning contentedly against the barriers, they sipped a fizzy drink, which was delicious, and swapped stories of incredible feats with the others, like athletes after a race.

"Lamerika? Wow! What did it look like? They say everyone there goes around wearing outrageous designer clothes!"

"It was pretty stupid," Josh concurred. "And there were all these little men in blue, as well."

The boy who'd been the first back had been to the top of a

mountain range. "I was one hundred per cent sure I wasn't going to manage to do it. The place was crawling with monks, and they never buy anything! They try to fob you off with their own things instead!"

"So how did you do it?" asked his listeners.

"Well, you have to understand your customers, don't you?" he bragged. "So if they're trying to get rid of their stuff, then you do the swap so that they're the ones left with a little less. So I exchanged my product for two of their spare begging bowls."

Josh tugged his sleeve. "What was your product?"

"A sock. Not a bad thing to have, up there in the cold."

They were all leaning on the barriers, watching the returning Associates. In the middle of all the excited chatter, Josh suddenly had a sinking feeling again. Turning his back to the Associates, he began observing the people in the hall as unobtrusively as he could. All of a sudden he was convinced that Mervin Spratt was out there somewhere. He probably would have gone to Josh's home and found him gone, so where else would he be? Maybe Spratt was waiting for a chance to drag him off without anyone noticing. Josh scanned the crowd. He recognized some faces – the Dispatch Board members: a flushed Marmeduke Fawcett; at a bar in a far corner, seated on a bar stool with glass in hand, a haughty Tal; and next to him, a frowning Garnet Gippart. He looked and looked … and then he jumped, because he'd finally spotted what he'd been looking for. Standing by the wall at the back of the hall, near the lifts, was Mervin Spratt. It was definitely Spratt. Their eyes met. Josh quickly turned his back, his heart pounding.

As more and more of the Associates came in, he sneaked over to Max's side. He was making entries in a big book next to the gong. "Hello, my boy," Max greeted him cheerfully. "Did Teresa let you do most of it by yourself? You really made record time."

"I don't want to do it any more," Josh began.

Max, eyebrows raised, waited for him to go on.

"That nightmare… And Mervin Spratt's after me. He's here."

"One thing at a time. That nightmare – you had it again?"

Josh nodded. "I can't take any more." To his great embarrassment, he began to shake.

"Aha." Max nodded thoughtfully. "I'm so sorry. I promised to give you something to counter those nightmares, and I completely forgot to do so, because of all that's been going on. Let me have a look at you." His eyes travelled probingly up and down Josh's skinny frame. When he caught sight of Josh's feet he whistled. He bent down and touched the snake bracelet. "For protection?"

Josh nodded.

"Then you'd better take that … *thing* off, for starters."

Josh had trouble slipping the bracelet off his ankle and foot.

"Listen, Joshua. This thing may indeed have the power to protect you and help you. On the other hand, I am not too fond of Associates relying on that sort of talisman. Superstition can increase your fear. I'd rather you wore our official protection. This." He tied a narrow leather band around Josh's wrist. Gippart's logo was stamped on it, and next to it J.M. COPE. "This is our proof of ownership. You belong to us. No one will be able to take you from us, certainly no ghosts and nightmares from the dream-world, you can be sure of that. All right, now get back into line. We haven't finished yet."

"But," said Josh as Moussa struck the gong again, "but – what about Mervin Spratt?"

"Mervin Spratt is a first-rate Senser in Gippart's service," said Max impatiently. "He's the very best at checking time-zones in *umaya*, and he's highly trustworthy. Now off with you; we'll speak later."

Josh ran back, tucked his bracelet into a special inner pocket of his jeans, which were hanging over the barrier, and quickly resumed his place. Moussa, standing on a stool, had begun boasting loudly: "One hour and forty-seven minutes! Practically all of my Associates made it back in time! We're the champions!"

The hall burst into loud cheers and laughter, while nearly all of the Associates raised their arms triumphantly in the air.

"Long live commerce!" cried Moussa. "Let the celebration begin! Scout Herbert is adding up the results for the prize ceremony. In the meantime – let's have a party!"

Right on cue, music suddenly started blasting out, and a wild light show lit up the hall. Waiters carried around trays with drinks and canapés, as if it wasn't the middle of the night at all. Josh chewed on some sort of potato fritter, anxiously peering into the chattering crowd. Aha, he thought so. There he was. Mervin Spratt was ploughing his way towards the podium.

"Baz, look!"

But Baz wasn't at his side any more; he was standing a little way off, in earnest conversation with Marmeduke Fawcett. Max, Moussa, Garnet Gippart and two other people were huddled in deep deliberation beneath the gong, gazing at Max's book and then at their hand-held computers, pointing at various Associates. Suddenly they all turned to look at him; Moussa seemed to be vehemently trying to talk Max into something. Josh turned his back on them, embarrassed. Spratt had got stuck behind a group of laughing red-uniformed receptionists. *I must get out of here. Surely I'm not just going to stand around waiting for him to catch me?*

He dived under the barrier and forced his way through the crowd, glancing back over his shoulder from time to time. Was Spratt on his tail yet? Wasn't that him, next to the podium? Grimly he wrestled his way to the closest Reception area. The little room was empty. He sank down on a chair. Just as he was beginning to wonder if it was such a good idea to hide in there, the hall door behind him was flung open.

"Moussa!"

"What are you up to?" Moussa glared at him suspiciously,

as if Josh were on the point of secretly setting in motion a devilish plot against Gippart.

"Nothing." And then he couldn't help saying it anyway, to his own dismay. "Spratt. Spratt's after me."

"Mervin Spratt? Well, of course he is. The whole lot of them, they're *all* after you, aren't they? Aren't you just lapping it up?"

"No, I'm not, not at all!"

"Well, then you can just relax, idiot, because I've come to help you. Isn't that nice of me? I'm going to help you fail the Trial. For your own good. Because we're not convinced, see? Sure, with Teresa at your side you made it look as if you could get the job done. But I don't believe for a minute you could have pulled it off on your own, in a real, tough *umaya*. I've asked for you to have to take the test again. Your first result is disqualified. This time it's for real. Here." He pressed something into Josh's hand: a bouncy rubber ball.

"Yes, but Moussa—"

"Quiet. Come with me." He opened the exterior door a crack and grabbed Josh's hand in a crushing grip.

"Ouch! Moussa, I don't want to—"

"Shut up. A rock. A big grey rock in the middle of the desert. The desert is red. Go." He flung open the door and gave Josh a shove. Josh tumbled head over heels, landing hard on his feet. "At least you got *that* one right," Moussa hissed. They were standing in a large hangar. "Next step. Red. Red and round. See it? Jump!" They jumped, and were drawn into a wildly spinning vortex. Everything turned red before Josh's eyes. Finally he crashed down on a rocky surface, scraping his knees and palms. But he immediately got to his feet without a whimper. Moussa was standing next to him, legs spread wide, wearing a brown leather tunic with a dangerous-looking dagger slung from it. "Good," he said with satisfaction. "We're here. At least you're not too stupid for this, dope. Though you're stupid enough to have returned to Gippart. Even after I'd warned you not to."

Josh looked around in silence. He too was wearing a leather tunic, and he had the same kind of knife as Moussa's. The wind was howling through the low, craggy hills. Here and there, trees contorted by the wind clung to the rock face. To his right he could see the sea through a gap in the rocks: seething, violent waves. On the beach there were fires burning.

"Where on earth are we now?"

"The year of the warrior," answered Moussa. "Hurry up. Sell your ball. This time it's the real thing. Hurry up, go and sell it."

"But I already did it once! And there's no one around!"

"Oh, stop your whining. You're the one who was so keen to be made an Associate. Just work it out for yourself. Or, even better, don't. Go!"

He gave Josh a push, and at the same moment they heard the beat of drums and the shrill blare of trumpets. A battalion of fierce, warlike horsemen thundered down the beach under streaming standards. Moussa's eyes glittered as they galloped past. "There must be an army encampment somewhere near by. Hurry up."

Josh walked down to the beach, his legs shaking. He had absolutely no stomach for trying to sell a ball to a soldier armed to the teeth. They wore helmets and carried long sabres, and some had knives clenched between their teeth. But the beach was completely empty again. Josh walked along the seashore for a while, heading into the wind, until he saw a path leading back up into the rocks, which he took. The wind here was a little less ferocious. He turned a corner – and jumped back in horror. There in front of him, in the middle of the path, two men were having a sword fight. They were uttering blood-curdling cries and dealing each other mortal blows. Blood spurted from their armour. Josh ran away as fast as his legs could carry him. "Fools, fools, fools," he muttered furiously. But he was in warrior-*umaya*, and he hadn't gone another five minutes before he heard the clashing of swords again.

How typical of Moussa, he thought to himself indignantly, to choose such a ridiculous destination. Did he hope that Josh would be scared out of his wits, so scared that he wouldn't want to have anything to do with being an Associate any more? Josh wasn't even sure he *wanted* to be one in the first place. But he wasn't going to fail this test on purpose and let Moussa win. Besides, there was no other way out for him. In order to get out of there, he'd have to sell something; and in order to sell something, he needed a customer.

Cautiously he crept towards the source of the noise. He soon arrived undetected at a few low huts surrounding a yard, in which a lesson in combat was being held. A bald old man wearing an orange robe was shouting at half a dozen children who were jabbing at each other violently with sharp curved swords. Josh spied on them from behind one of the huts. The children were evenly matched; no blood flowed. Finally they all cast their weapons to the ground at the same time, bowed to each other and their teacher, and went and sat down in an orderly row. The master began to speak. Josh noticed he could understand what the man was saying. He spoke about the different sorts of fighting weapons and held these up one by one, each more terrible than the last. Then he threw them on a pile and explained that weapons were useless without the right skills, or the right mental attitude; he spoke of courage, concentration, an alert, open mind. The children nodded and in chorus obediently repeated after him what he said. "Animals can teach us a thing or two," said the master. "Look at a dog's tenacity, a cat's nimbleness; they can show us how to shadow an enemy's movements – they are supple, resilient, indefatigable, always capable of bouncing back." And that gave Josh his idea.

Very cautiously he slipped out of his hiding place. Heart pounding, he walked through the little class. He knew the master had spotted him as soon as he came out of hiding, but the old man continued talking calmly. Only when Josh was standing right behind the students did he stop talking. Then he asked amiably, "Do you have a question, pupil?"

The children looked around, jumped up and assumed a fighting stance. Josh took a few steps back, hands raised like a kung-fu fighter.

"Sit down!" barked the master, and the pupils all promptly sat down again, Josh included. He put up his hand.

"Speak," said the master.

"I happened to be passing your school," said Josh very politely, "and I heard your wise lesson, and then it occurred to me that it always helps to have an example ready, if you're trying to explain something. And it just so happens that I have an example with me." He stood up and showed them the little ball. He walked over to a flat rock lying in front of one of the huts, and let the ball bounce from the stone against the wall. It wasn't a really bouncy ball, but luckily it bounced high enough. "Supple, resilient, and it always comes bouncing back. Just like a great fighter."

The children nodded attentively, and began clapping their hands. The master nodded slowly.

Josh held up the little ball. "Would you like to buy it?"

"What do you want for it?" asked the master, looking him in the eye without blinking.

"It doesn't matter, whatever you can spare," Josh stammered, suddenly feeling rather silly.

"Are you an apprentice salesman?" asked the master.

Josh nodded unhappily.

"Salespeople are indispensable to society," said the master. "But many salesmen are really nothing but thieves. And you, apprentice salesman, you have already stolen something from us."

"I beg your pardon?" Josh thought of the jewellery in his collection, which he hadn't come by honestly. "What have I stolen?"

"My lesson. You overheard at least five minutes of my lesson."

Josh opened his mouth, but could think of nothing to say.

"So you have already been paid." Calmly the master took the little ball from Josh's hand. "And that is the second lesson I will give you in payment: be careful with things that belong to others. You should never take anything without asking."

Josh blushed, and nodded.

"You may go now." The master fixed the boy with his stare. "But wait. You are not from around here, pupil. You are brave, but not yet brave enough. I will give you one other thing in payment. This lesson: stare whatever makes you afraid straight in the eye. Do you understand me? Stare the nightmare straight in the eye. Farewell! And thank you for the example," he said, tossing the ball from one hand to the other.

Josh got away as fast as he could. He was half expecting one of the pupils to attack him from behind, but that didn't happen. He ran until he was completely spent, and walked the rest of the way. He had no trouble finding the way back, but Moussa wasn't where he had left him. He combed the area, until finally he heard a heavy, smothered grunting. Moussa! There he was, and, naturally, he was embroiled in a fight. He was lying half on top of a fierce-looking warrior, whom he held pinned in a firm armlock. But they were riveted together; neither could let go of the other. They could hardly move at all. Josh ran up to them, and Moussa yelled, "There you are at last! Slit his throat, quick!"

"No chance!" shouted Josh.

"You brainless idiot, we're in *umaya*! Do as I say!"

"Not likely," Josh said, with trembling lips.

"You stupid louse, then bash his brains out! *Do* something!"

Josh let himself drop down next to the clawing, spitting warrior who, without warning, bit him on the shoulder. *"Ouch!"* Josh picked up a lump of rock, shut his eyes and dropped it on the man's head with a dull thud. He only dared open his eyes when he heard Moussa get to his feet.

"You wimp," the Chief Associate scolded him. "All you did was knock him out for a bit. Well, did you sell it?"

He was looking at him so intently that Josh hardly dared tell him. "Yes."

"Huh."

Moussa turned round and stalked off. Josh followed him at a trot. In a little valley Moussa leapt off the road and sat down behind a boulder. Josh followed hesitantly.

"Well," sighed Moussa. "That's all I can do for you. Now you're in for it, you little fool. No, be quiet, and listen. I'm going to give you a piece of advice. A warning. You're an idiot, but then you're also just a kid. You should never have come back. Now you're in deep trouble. They're going to make you an Associate. And then they're going to send you on a sales trip and it'll be the death of you. I know what's going on at Gippart. You're their guinea pig. They're going to push you into trying something that's absolute suicide. They know it'll be curtains for you. You're just a guinea pig."

"That's not true! Max would never allow it!"

"Max," said Moussa with utter contempt, "Max, that old *granny*. Max doesn't have a clue! Just listen to me, bonehead! They're experimenting with the boundary between dreams and time, don't you understand what I'm saying? Didn't you see Teresa's scar? Didn't you hear me tell you Raphel was blown to bits? You're their new pet project. You, Joshua Cope."

He pointed his finger at Josh. "There's something about you. They think you can do something special. That you have a unique talent that will allow you to travel in time. And you're *fluid* too. Fluid Associates are the kind they like best: they're the ones that travel the fastest. But listen to me, little man, in *umaya* they're the ones that disintegrate first as well. Raphel went splat, but a year before Raphel, Niri disappeared without a trace. First she split in two, then in four, then in eight – now there was a *really* fluid one. You're their next victim."

"So why should you care?" Josh shouted. He'd just about had enough of Moussa treating him like a complete moron.

"I *do* care," said Moussa, grabbing Josh by the collar of his tunic. "I care, because Moussa is the Chief of all the Associates, and because Moussa won't have Sow Fall, Garnet Gippart and that whole double-crossing gang messing with his Associates. Because the Associates are *mine* – my responsibility – and *I* demand some respect. Got it?"

Moussa was the last person on earth he'd ever confess his weaknesses to. And yet Josh suddenly found himself looking to Moussa for comfort. "But Moussa, I don't *want* to do it, actually, not really. Those nightmares…"

Moussa raised his hands in the air. "But if you don't *want* to do it, dope, why on earth did you enter the Traders' Trial? And here I was giving you another chance to save your skin – and you go and screw it up! Don't you understand?"

"I do… No, I don't… Well, I do sort of want to, I suppose, but I'm scared of the ghosts."

"*Umaya* is crawling with ghosts, that's just the way it is. I'm sorry to have to tell you this, but you're trapped. You passed the qualifying round of the Trial. You've even got yourself a Gippart band around your wrist already! All I can do is just give you one piece of advice: don't attempt anything out of the ordinary. Don't *ever* try to step over into time."

"I wouldn't know how, anyway."

"I believe it's done with sound," said Moussa. "Notes, trills. The others needed a Walkman for it. But I bet they'll have something new for you, take it from me. I forbid you to take part in their crazy goings-on. Do you hear? Your Chief absolutely forbids it."

"I promise."

"I'll give you one last piece of advice: in *umaya* there are danger zones. Unstable zones. We call these 'a chink in time'. It's where the different time-lines intersect. That's where they want you to go. Just don't fall for it."

"I promise."

"Good," said Moussa with a deep sigh. "Then let's go back." He suddenly looked at Josh curiously. "What did you get for that rubber ball?"

"Oh," stammered Josh, "a lesson. Three lessons, actually."

"What? A lesson? Are you mad? What good is a *lesson* to Gippart? God, what a bonehead you are." He leaned against a boulder, suddenly all smiles. "Hey, maybe you did fail after all! Let's hope so. Now, fall asleep, idiot, seeing as you're such an expert at it!" He tossed a pill into his mouth and swallowed it. "See you later."

In a couple of sickening convolutions Josh tumbled back to Reception. Moussa wasn't there. He walked gloomily back to the podium through the festive crowd. Spratt was nowhere to be seen. He didn't wave back at the jubilant Baz, but collapsed against the barrier like a sack of potatoes.

After a while Max wandered up to him. "Congratulations, Associate," he said. "Why so downcast? You made good time again, certainly better than your first test. Did my wristband help you on the retry? Besides, the second test was really just to please Moussa, you know. We didn't consider it necessary at all."

"Yes, but I've brought nothing back. I sold my product for nothing. I failed, Max."

"For nothing?"

"Well, for some lessons. Some wise lessons." He gave a scornful laugh.

Max took a notepad from his pocket and tore off a piece of paper. He handed it to Josh, with a pencil. "Write them down, Joshua. Chin up! Do you want to know one of Gippart's greatest success stories? In the year 1200, they bought a great new mathematical discovery, and then sold it to the rest of the world. That discovery changed the world. Do you know what it was?"

Josh shook his head.

"It was nought, nothing – the number zero. An idea, in other words, or a lesson, if you like. Write it down. Who knows, your lesson may also be worth millions."

Josh took the piece of paper and scribbled down the master's lessons. "But all I got for the box of matches was a rubber band," he whispered.

"Ah yes, the rubber band. Young man, that Lamerikan rubber band is worth at least three pounds here. Yes, just because it came from Lamerika! Not a bad return for a box of matches, eh? You certainly have good commercial instincts." He winked, folded the piece of paper, and walked back to the gong.

Josh sat down on the floor. He gradually began glowing inside. First, it was a gentle tickling; then he started feeling warmer and lighter; and by the time Baz came and sat down next to him, he was beaming.

"Was it *that* good?" asked Baz. "You went with Moussa, didn't you? What did he want?"

"To warn me off. But I'm doing it anyway, Baz. I'm going to be an Associate."

"Yeah, isn't it great?" Baz looked as pleased as punch.

Side by side they listened to speeches by Moussa and Max, interrupted by lots of cheering and applause. There was much praise for the candidate-Associates' speed and business sense, and then the names of the three fastest Associates were announced. They had to climb on the red stool and receive a medal and flowers and a gift. And luckily Spratt stayed away.

Then the podium began to revolve, and all the Associates held on to the barriers, laughing and shouting. Loud music filled the air, and some of the Associates started dancing in their stiff travelling clothes. Suddenly a rain of sweet champagne sprinkled down, and the waiters went around with platters heaped with chocolates and cakes. All of the Gippart employees were singing and dancing, nibbling and trying to catch the cascading champagne in their open mouths or glasses, howling with laughter. When everyone was thoroughly sweaty and wet and dizzy, the volume was turned down, and Max, shouting to be heard over the talking, laughing and singing, cried, "That was it, everybody: this year's Traders' Trial. The Associates are expected home now. It's time they were gone, before a new day breaks and the employment authorities slap another heavy fine on us. Remember, you must all abide by the employment laws. One last round of applause for our Associates, please. They're the hope for the future, both for Gippart and for the whole wide world. Children, get changed into your proper clothes, and watch for the postman. You'll be receiving a contract in the post within the week."

There were cheers and shouts as the Associates began changing their clothes. A pale light filled the hall. Josh noticed he was covered in cuts and bruises. His stiff jeans scraped his raw knees. Didn't he have a tissue somewhere? He fumbled in both his right and left pockets, and noticed they were empty. Only his bracelet was still there, safe inside the zipped-up inner pocket. What the…?

"Baz, did you take my computer game out of my pocket? And my knife? And my torch and my mini-pen and my battery? Where's everything gone?"

"Could they have fallen out?"

They hunted all around, but found nothing. Moussa said, "Hurry up, you two. What's up?"

"My stuff is missing."

A girl next to them said, "I saw someone going through your jeans. Just before you came back from your second Trial. But when he saw me looking, he ran off."

"Who was it?" asked Moussa sharply. "An Associate? A time-traveller?"

The girl shrugged. "I dunno. It all happened very quickly. He was a bit too big for an Associate, but it was quite dark."

Max joined them. "Problems? It's time you were out of here, boys."

"His things are missing," Moussa muttered. "Looks as if there may have been..."

"May have been...?"

"May have been a theft."

A few Associates who overheard him saying the words gasped. Max and Moussa looked at each other.

"Well, anyway," said Josh, "the most important thing's still in here. And there's so much stealing these days."

"You don't understand," said a boy gravely. "Theft..."

"Gippart is a commercial enterprise," Max explained. "Theft is quite beyond the pale. It simply cannot be tolerated. It is a capital offence."

Josh started feeling a little uncomfortable. "Well, but—"

"Anyone who steals from Gippart," said Moussa, "gets thrown into the deepest darkness."

"And you are now a part of Gippart, Joshua," added Max.

They stared at each other in the dim light. Finally Max spread his hands. "But you must go home, at the double. We'll get to the bottom of this, don't worry. Don't give it another thought. Congratulations, and goodnight. Goodbye, Associates!" He gave them a friendly push in the direction of the lifts.

Josh and Baz almost sleepwalked out of the building. They caught a night bus home and, smiling, wished each other goodnight.

"Shall I see you tomorrow?"

"I'll see you tomorrow."

"Associates."

"Yes." They smiled at each other. "Associates!"

PART II
THE EXPEDITION

5
The Assignment

It was lucky that the letter from Gippart arrived soon, because it was difficult to give a convincing explanation for his cuts and bruises, or his absence that night.

"You weren't in bed," said his dad stiffly, "not at four o'clock, nor at five. You can swear till you're blue in the face that you just went to the bathroom, but I'm absolutely certain you were gone for at least two hours."

Then, when he returned home after that unpleasant exchange with his father, he had to face Mo: "You must have been in lots of accidents, or someone's been beating you up round the clock. Don't try pulling the wool over my eyes, young man. How did you get all those cuts and bruises?"

He did look somewhat the worse for wear: his knees were black and blue and crusty from falling on the rocks of the warrior-*umaya*, his shoulder was blue and swollen where Moussa's enemy had bitten him, and below that were the yellowing bruises Moussa had given him the first time they met.

Liz laughed. "He's just turning into a real boy, Mo," she said as she tapped in her new boyfriend's number on her mobile phone. "You used to wish he'd go outside and play, and now that he is, you're still not happy!"

But Mo had another reason to be angry with him, and that was his room. Everything had been turned upside down, his entire collection had been ripped out of the boxes and cupboards it was kept in, and it was such a terrible mess that it brought tears to Josh's eyes. Mo didn't believe he hadn't done it. Three years earlier during one of his rare temper tantrums, he'd completely trashed his room – and Mo's room too, for good measure. Mo didn't believe it was burglars. And she didn't believe anything he said any more. The letter came as a reprieve.

"Ah, so that's what that Scout business was all about!" said Mo, carefully reading through all the paperwork. "I couldn't understand why you'd suddenly wanted to join. So you and Baz are going to lead a Cub Scout troop two Saturday afternoons a month! Let's see, it says under the supervision of the Head Scout Master, Max Herbert. And you're being paid a retainer for it too – my goodness! But I can't allow that: you're only twelve. Surely you don't need to be paid, at your age. I'll give those people a call."

Josh held his breath, but the phone number turned out to be correct, and after her conversation Mo didn't have a problem. "They give you a choice: you can either be paid in cash or you can choose a little something from the Scout shop. I'm OK with that. It's fine with me if you want to start a collection of Scout-thingamajigs." She ruffled his hair. Then she signed the contract and sent it back.

Josh and Baz met at every opportunity, to discuss what their special mission might be. As well as Gippart's shadier aspects.

"I think Moussa's just jealous," said Baz. "It's obvious why Gippart keeps trying to see how far they can get into the dream-world and into time, because they're explorers, sort of, aren't they? And it makes sense that they want to use us for it. We're much better at dream-travelling than the adults." Baz already felt himself to be an Associate through and through.

If there had been a uniform, he'd have worn it.

"I think Mervin Spratt pinched my things," said Josh. It still really bothered him that he'd lost them. "And he must have ransacked my room too."

"Or else it was Moussa, trying to scare you off."

They couldn't explain it, and they couldn't wait for Saturday September the twenty-third, their first official day at work.

They were actually summoned to appear before the Dispatch Board a few days before that date. They arrived at the building at exactly the same time, and were sent up to the sixth floor, to the offices of middle management. They had to walk along the imposing corridor again until they reached the door with the sign DISPATCH BOARD Z 6.39 C. To their surprise, Moussa was there, waiting for them. He nodded at them curtly, and moved aside to let them go in first. Then he followed them inside, and waited by the door. Only three Board members were sitting at the conference table, leafing through a stack of files. Tal Sow Fall wasn't there. Max rushed up to them with outstretched arms. "Sit down, Associates, have a drink!" Smiling, he poured them two tall glasses. "First of all, congratulations again on your achievements at the Trial. You both scored record times, if you take into account how young you are. Which means that we were right about your abilities. Let's see – Joshua, you shared seventh place with another contestant, in a field of thirty participants. Places one to four went to our veterans, the sixteen-year-olds. So that's splendid. And you, Baz, you were in fifth place! Well done. We're extremely gratified, particularly since we had no idea you would be just as talented as Joshua. So that is a most fortunate coincidence, is it not!"

"W-well, yeah," stammered Baz bashfully. "I also discovered something..."

Max nodded. "So it seems, and we are most pleased that you did. That is why we had you come here today, to give you your instructions, so that on Saturday you can start without delay. There's no time to lose. Garnet Gippart will tell you about the special assignment we have in mind for you. But of course you can always refuse."

"I'm not so sure about that," commented Garnet, looking up from her papers. "This assignment is of the utmost importance to Gippart, and these kids have been selected for it."

"Come, come," said the other man at the table, Marmeduke Fawcett, the Secretary of Youth Affairs. "Of course the young men don't have to do anything they don't want to do."

"The contract has been signed," replied Garnet icily. "Boys, your assignment is as follows: you are to embark on a chain-*imayada.*"

"Hmm," came Moussa's voice from the far end of the room. "Are you sure they're up to it?"

"Moussa!" cried Garnet, incensed. "Max, can't you be more vigilant? Top security, and you just let that big mouth stand there eavesdropping!"

"Oh come, you saw him sneak in too, didn't you?" Max muttered. "Sorry, Moussa, instructions meetings are closed. Just go out into the corridor will you, please?"

"*Really*, Max," said Garnet as Moussa retreated, annoyed. "Sometimes it seems as if you're trying to sabotage the entire project on purpose. Do you have a direct line to the press, then? Are you really so intent on shouting everything from the rooftops as soon as possible?"

Max turned bright red and he gaped at Garnet, speechless. Finally he said, "If you have even *one* good reason to doubt my total commitment to Gippart, if you can name just *one* instance when I behaved carelessly, or leaked anything—"

Garnet stabbed a finger in his direction. "The moment I have sufficient grounds for a legal action, sir, you'll be advised. Now, boys, again your instructions: you are to undertake a chain-*imayada* leading backwards through dream-time in leaps of approximately one hundred years."

"What's a chain-*imayada*?" asked Josh, who was beginning to wonder if he'd be able to carry out this assignment.

"A chain-*imayada*," Max hastily explained, "is a series of dream-walks, or *imayadas*, in which at each stage you keep going back further in time, in the same dream-world. In this case you'll be going back a hundred or a hundred and fifty years at a time."

"So we're going back in time?"

"That's right," said Max, "except that it isn't of course real time, but dream-time. It's very interesting to see how such a world has gradually evolved through the ages. I am very fond of chain-*imayadas* myself. That is how I originally reached the dawning of the world, by the way."

"But why? What do we have to sell?" asked Baz.

"It's not primarily about selling," said Garnet. "You'll be given a product to take along with you, but you'll have to be selective about selling it. Your task, you see, is to find the right customer. And since we don't exactly know where our customer is, you're going to have to work your way down that dream-world chain. Understood?"

"No," said Josh. "So we have to sell something to someone in particular? And you don't know where he is? Or in which time-period I can find him?"

"That's correct," said Garnet. "The point is that our customer isn't really a person, but a group of people – a tribe, a village, a company, or a sect. To be honest, we're not completely sure what name they go by."

"But then how will I know it's them?"

"The people you're looking for live on the border," Max tried to clarify. "You'll recognize the border by the darkness. Remember our dawning of the world *imayada*? Remember the darkness we saw, in the distance? Well, we think our client is located somewhere near one of those borders."

"But isn't that terribly dangerous?" asked Baz.

Max looked unhappy, and began humming and hawing.

"Oh, it's not too bad," said Garnet Gippart. "You'll be with an escort. And then you'll just have to follow your instincts, make your way to the border, and look for our clients once you get there. Since we don't know what time-period they live in, you'll probably have to give it a few tries before you find them."

Max added, "But you don't have to go back any further than the year 1000. We haven't come across any sign of their existence before that time."

"You can use their ancient name in your search," said Garnet, "even though we're not sure if they still use it themselves. But they'll certainly remember it, in any case."

"What name is that?"

"Tembe."

"Tembe?"

"You heard me. The Tembe. It's a legendary name here at Gippart. You should feel very honoured that you've been chosen to look for them."

Josh felt the hairs on his neck start to rise. "But *why* do we have to look for them? Who are these people? Why do they live on the border?"

Garnet pursed her lips. "If we knew the answers to those questions, boys, we wouldn't be sending you out to look for them. Your mission is to be the first to make contact with them." She hesitated. "I'm seeking authorization to give you a rough map to take with you. Long ago, someone in the family mapped out this *umaya*. The Royal *umaya*, we call it. If I succeed in obtaining permission, we'll include it in your travel kit." She stretched. "Well, I hope everything's clear. Of course, we expect a written report after every *imayada*, backed up with a verbal account to the full Board in this chamber."

It was beginning to sound more and more like piles of homework. Baz asked his question again. "What do we have to sell?"

"Don't laugh," said Max. "They're really your kind of thing,

Joshua. We'll be giving you a whole batch of them. Should you come across any customers keen on acquiring one, there might be a connection there with the Tembe."

"But what are they?"

"Wooden bird calls."

Max put a couple of wooden objects on the table. They consisted of two discs fitting together tightly, which made a high, squeaky sound when you twisted them. You could make all kinds of sounds with them, to replicate different bird calls.

Josh stared at them, disappointed. "Couldn't we sell something a bit more high-tech? Like one of those laser penknives or something?"

"I'm afraid that kind of product won't be suitable when you go back that far in time. They'd immediately cry 'witchcraft' and burn you at the stake for it. Besides, we have a hunch the Tembe are mad about birds. They wouldn't find anything else quite as enticing as these bird calls."

"So, are we finished then?" asked Garnet.

A mobile phone rang. The adults looked around, fumbling in their pockets, but it was Garnet who ended up taking her phone out of her handbag and talking into it. "No, we're just about done with those kids – OK then, see you." She snapped her phone shut and flashed the others a smooth smile. "Well, boys, the only other thing you should know is that throughout your assignment you'll be answering directly to me. It's my intention to accompany you as often as I can the first few times, for as long as the stress of the *umaya* doesn't get too much for me, anyway."

The boys looked at her open-mouthed, their hearts sinking even further. They'd hoped to experience their adventure by themselves, just the two of them; and now it looked as if they'd have to take orders from this smooth operator!

"Which reminds me," said Max, "that you'll have another travelling companion: Teresa Okwoma. We have analysed all of the Associates' results and their final Traders' Trial times, and our calculations show that the most efficient combination will be the three of you working together as a team. So what do you think?"

Neither of them knew what to say, after all these disappointments. Teresa was OK, but why couldn't they just go it alone? But they had no say in the matter; they were merely the two youngest recruits in an elaborate sales campaign.

"We'll be expecting you in Reception on Saturday afternoon at two o'clock on the dot. That's when you'll be given your kit. Marmeduke, didn't you have something else for them?"

Marmeduke Fawcett pressed a little square card into both their hands. "There you are," he said, nodding fervently. "It gives me the greatest pleasure to be able to present you with these at this point. With this special-purchaser card you may select your first item from Gippart's storerooms. The card has twelve punches, so it will last you exactly one year."

"Yes!" Josh's heart leapt. Finally! They quickly took their leave and rushed for the door with unseemly haste. But before they could get there and head for the display halls, the door flew open and Moussa came in again. "Hey! Excuse me, Board, but is it OK if I take these little runts with me now?"

Max hurried up to them. "Moussa, I'm warning you! No funny business with these boys! No tests, no excursions to forbidden *umayas* for a joke – you know perfectly well what I'm talking about. Or else you'll have to answer to me, my fine fellow."

Moussa was the same height as Max. For a moment they glared at each other, eye to eye. Then Moussa put his arms round the two boys' shoulders and turned them towards the door. Over his shoulder he cried, "I'm not the one endangering children's lives, Max Herbert!" and strode out, kicking the door behind him.

"What are the forbidden *umayas*?" asked Baz.

Two Associates passing them, apparently also coming to receive their instructions, heard his question and laughed. One of the boys turned to them. "The *umayas* for people over eighteen, kiddo! Naked women, that sort of thing. Or the extreme, hard-core scary stuff. Horror, sex and violence. At least three quarters of the dream-world is out of bounds to us! Sometimes we'll send new Associates like you in there, for a laugh."

Moussa exploded. "Shut up! That stuff is for men only. These kids don't need to know about it."

"Why not?" asked the boy, wide-eyed. "I was going to those movies when I was only twelve. And didn't you send me to that zone once, where—"

"Shut up!" shouted Moussa. "Do you hear me? Shut your trap!"

The boys, smirking, banged loudly on the door of the Dispatch Board room.

"Where are you taking us?" asked Josh defiantly. "I want to go and see the gadgets. We're allowed to choose one. I'm not going anywhere else."

"Who said you had to?" said Moussa. "I'm just keeping an eye on you. Daddy likes to look after you while you're here at big bad Gippart. And, Joshie, hold out your hand. Here's your stuff back." He deposited a handful of objects in Josh's hand: a broken computer game, battery, mini-pen, torch and penknife.

"Oh! Where'd you find these?"

"In the Associates' hang-out. I suppose the thief had no use for them. Or else he was scared. I'll track him down soon enough, and then he'll find out it isn't a good idea to steal from Moussa's boys."

They came to the corridor with all the display windows, and Moussa left them there. "The best of luck for Saturday," he said. "Come and see me afterwards. Remember what I told you, dozy. Don't fall for their tricks." And then he was gone.

At the entrance to the exhibition halls sat a receptionist. She gave them a friendly wink. "So, are you here to choose something? Take your pick! You can have anything that's marked with a white dot for one month's work. The ones marked with a yellow dot count for two months' work, the ones with an orange dot for three, and so on. You can save up for the things that have a black dot, but if I were you I'd take something now. If there's no dot, you can't have it."

It was awful. They saw so many things they really wanted that were too expensive, or too risky: the hop-flight engine had eight black dots, and the girl told them you needed to save for eight years to get it – which was exactly the total amount of time they would work for Gippart between them. To their great regret, the weapons were strictly out of bounds. Josh's laser penknife was worth two months' wages, and he dithered endlessly about it. In the end Baz chose the solidifying pencil that could draw concrete lines in the air, and Josh settled for a compass that kept pointing north with a pencil-thin beam of light until you switched it off. Just the thing for going on an expedition. They had their cards punched on the way out and went home satisfied, two proud Associates.

On Saturday Max was waiting for them in Reception, impeccably dressed in a dark grey suit with the Gippart logo emblazoned on the waistcoat pocket. Teresa bounded up to them in the corridor and shook their hands, smiling. "We're going to crack it. You'll see," she said enthusiastically. She nodded when she saw Zizi on Josh's shoulder – he'd secretly lured her along, his brave parrot, his little green guardian angel.

Along came Garnet Gippart in a grey short-skirted suit, also emblazoned with the Gippart logo. She was on the phone. "Back in three hours, definitely. No, just three kids. Yeah, ha ha. Uh-uhn, not exactly my favourite thing, no."

There were little groups of Associates gathered all over the hall, ready to start on their *imayadas*. Teresa waved at her girlfriends. Moussa bustled from one group to the other. "Here," Max told them, "here's your travel kit." He gave them each a black backpack. "A couple of co-ordinates, to start with – it's very precise, so pay attention. The town you're starting in is called Portilisi. Check everything: map, your supply of the merchandise. You know not to start selling too soon – rules and regulations. There's *umaya*-money in your backpack, and here, Baz, your Gippart wristband. Teresa and Joshua have theirs already. Next, important: your Gippart work clothes. They automatically turn into clothing appropriate to whatever *umaya* you're in. Joshua, let's just reiterate: you are the leader of this expedition. We have complete faith in your instincts as to where the Tembe might be. Just follow your nose. If it gets too frightening, stop and turn back. Baz, Teresa, you'll follow Joshua's instructions. Garnet Gippart has the final say, naturally, but Joshua is the one who sets the course. Everything perfectly clear?"

They nodded. Josh, worried, chewed his thumbnail. He hadn't a clue what he was supposed to do. But Max took his hand and whispered, visibly moved, "You're going to do a smashing job. But take care." He nodded at Zizi. "Good idea of yours, that, taking along your bird. It'll go just splendidly, you'll see." Then he darted off to the next team.

"Come on, kids, I don't have all day," said Garnet Gippart, walking towards one of the Reception areas. "I want to be back by five, not a minute later. Joshua?"

Josh followed with knocking knees. First, in silence, they hurriedly changed their clothes. Then Josh walked up to the door. He read what it said on the piece of paper Max had given him: "Locomotive." He turned to his companions. "Ready?"

Baz took hold of his hand firmly, and squeezed. Josh pushed the door open with a resolute shove, and leapt through it, pulling Baz with him. It was a lengthy fall, almost straight down, and when he landed, Baz, Teresa and Garnet fell on top of him. Teresa got the giggles and Garnet swore. They scrambled apart and found themselves sitting on the steps of a large, official-looking building with tall pillars and guards at the doors. Josh consulted his piece of paper.

"Next jump: conveyor belt."

They stood next to each other, hand in hand. Then Garnet Gippart said, "This is ridiculous. You can jump by yourselves, boys. I'll make my own way with Teresa here." She snatched the paper out of Josh's hands. "Balloon, Eiffel Tower, ape. OK. See you there." She grabbed Teresa's hand, who pulled a face, shut her eyes, and they were gone.

"Well, really!" said Baz. "Why don't we just go somewhere else, Josh?"

"No," said Josh, "we can't leave Teresa in the lurch. Come on, I want to get there before that *woman*."

They jumped hastily, dizzyingly. The next jumps all went well. Until the last one, which brought them up short in a blind dive. It took Josh completely by surprise.

Cold fingers deliberately prised his hand out of Baz's. An icy cheek pressed against his. Josh opened his eyes. He was looking at a whirl of blue-white hair, could see nothing else, felt a cold body entwining with his. Two arms of ice around his neck, a cheek against his face, then two lips like glass on his cheek.

"Finally I have you! I've got you!"

He took a quick, squeaky breath and hung there with his mouth open, petrified, felt the bracelet around his ankle searing his flesh, felt more than anything that bitterly cold mouth close to his. "Joshua *na* Jericho!" the voice keened in his ear, inside his head almost, very high-pitched and shrill, but with an undertone of despair.

"Say something!"

Josh gasped for air, his head buzzing and pounding. He shut his eyes, opened them again, saw only white, blue. Time stood still. He opened his mouth and spoke.

"Who *are* you?"

"Come on, *say* something!" the voice insisted, impatient now, furious almost.

Josh struck out with his legs as if he were swimming. With a few powerful strokes he broke out of the ice-cold embrace. He saw a white, strangely distorted face, first very close up, then far away. He saw a wide grin spread over the face. Then everything vanished in a blue mist, and he fell, eyes wide open.

He landed on his back. He heard himself mutter, "Now I've seen you. Now I've *seen* you!" He sneezed, shook his head, and sat up. He was sitting on a Persian rug, in a softly lit room. Zizi was still perched on his shoulder. Good old Zizi. A row of chairs was drawn up around him, with a hunched-up figure sitting on one of them. The only sound to be heard was the oily ticking of a clock. As he reached for his black backpack, a door was flung open behind him.

"Next patient?"

The form on the chair hunched itself into an even tighter ball. Josh looked around at a big, fat man with red sideburns, a red moustache and a bristling red beard. "Yes, you, young man. Do come in," said the man, nodding genially at Josh. He was wearing an old-fashioned suit of some kind of thick dark stuff, and his face was puffy and bloated above his stiff, high collar.

The room Josh walked into was opulently furnished: red velvet everywhere. There was a couch in a corner. The big man pointed at the couch. "Please lie down."

Josh hesitated. "I'm not really a patient," he apologized.

"Of course," said the man. "You are certainly not the first one to tell me that."

"But what I mean is, I got here by accident," said Josh. "I don't really belong here."

"Then please sit down a moment, to get your bearings," said the large man, and pointed at a chair by his desk. He went to sit behind the desk. "Has something happened to you? You seem tense, nervous."

Josh had no idea why he was bothering to answer the man. He was in some *umaya* or other, who knows where, so nothing that happened here was really important. But something horrible had happened in his nightmare, and a sympathetic person was asking him about it, and he couldn't help talking about it.

"I bumped into that ghost again... This time he was closer than ever. He hugged me and had his lips on my cheek and my mouth... And he was wrapped all around me. But actually, I wasn't as scared as I'd been the first times. I was dying of fright the other times. But this time I tried to look. And I saw him." He shuddered. "He's got a real face. An angry face. But he seemed sad too."

The man had been listening, nodding his head slowly, and taking notes. In a calm voice he urged Josh to go on. "Keep talking. Nothing surprises me. I've come across every nightmare there is." He wrote something, then put down his pen and asked pointedly, "Were words exchanged? Did you speak to each other? Words are important, you see."

"He said my name. My special name. The name no one else knows. And he said, 'Now you're mine,' or something like it, and he asked me to say something."

"Aha," said the man. "That's excellent. I don't think you have to worry. You are well on your way to being cured. Do you understand who this foe of yours is?"

"No," said Josh. "A ghost, it's just a ghost... Why, do *you* know who it is?"

"Never mind that. Doesn't the ghost remind you of anyone you know?"

Josh frowned. "No, it's just scary. Just vicious, evil and frightening. Besides, there's more of them."

"Naturally," said the man, "there are many fears and nightmares inside us. It is not uncommon for them to come out, and appear to the horrified patient in the form of ghostly apparitions. They are, ultimately, our own fears; we ourselves are they. The first important step towards a cure occurs when you are able to face your demons. It looks as if you may almost have reached that stage."

The door suddenly swung open and Garnet Gippart burst in, dressed in a rustling floor-length nurse's uniform, with a little white cap perched on top of her black hair. She was wearing round granny glasses.

"Please excuse me, Doctor," she said, "but this patient escaped from another ward. I'd like him to come with me."

"Certainly," said the big man, getting to his feet, "but are you sure he is receiving adequate mental help? Do please have the attending physician contact me about his case. I should like to see the boy again. One doesn't often get the opportunity to explore fear disorders in such a young person."

He bowed politely to Josh as Garnet Gippart dragged him outside.

"Well now," said Garnet as they walked down the stairs to the front door. "How did you end up being so late, and so far off course? What's wrong with you, can't you use your brains?"

"Now wait a minute!" cried Josh, pulling his hand out of Garnet's grip. "I'm the leader of this expedition! Where were you?"

"Your team has been waiting for you for half an hour at the appointed rendezvous! I'm starting to have serious doubts about Max's judgement. It's bad enough that I'm forced to endure these unhealthy *umayas*. Besides, I'm the one who's in charge here, you little squirt, and it's about time too. I've waited long enough."

"No," said Josh furiously. "I'm the leader. I decide what we're doing."

"Well, what are we doing next then?" She barged ahead of him, incensed.

They went out through a big door and on to a wide pavement. Josh's jaw dropped as he looked around. The pavements were swarming with people in clothes that swept the ground: rustling skirts, swirling cloaks. The road had four lanes, packed with all sorts of traffic: wagons, bicycles and cars he'd never seen before. He saw rockets on wheels zooming by, low to the ground, but he also saw lofty carriages pumping out foul-smelling exhaust fumes with an ear-splitting noise. Up above the traffic drifted ponderous blimps, and high above these, feather-light aeroplanes resembling crickets, and hot-air balloons suspended over baskets were everywhere. Josh hugged Zizi to his chest so she wouldn't fly away in alarm. *"Wow!"*

"Yes, just keep walking," ordered Garnet, marching on.

Josh ran after her, looking around open-mouthed. "Is this what people a hundred years ago used to dream about?"

"Yes, of course, and it's also the way we now envisage the people of a hundred or so years ago in our dreams – both those things," said Garnet, suddenly swerving into an alleyway that led to a small quay.

A flimsy boat with a canopy was moored to the jetty. Baz and Teresa, wearing fancy costumes, were sitting in the boat. Teresa wore a flattering, high-collared red velvet dress buttoned tightly at the neck and flowing voluminously down to her feet. Baz sported a dark green velvet suit with a big satin bow, and a beret. Josh laughed. "You both look silly."

"What about you?" Baz returned.

Josh looked down: he was wearing a simple suit of stiff black material, over a rough grey shirt. He even had a cap on his head. "You're poorer than us, I think," said Teresa. "Hop in, lowly knave." Josh jumped aboard, and Teresa started the engine. They cruised slowly along a canal of crystal-clear water, lined with stately white homes.

"Were you lost?" asked Baz. "I had the feeling someone was pulling our hands apart. Were they?"

Josh nodded.

"Was it your nightmare again? I felt this fierce blast of coldness, but I kept gliding, and next thing I knew I was here, on this boat. I've discovered a much easier way to jump, Josh. Shall I tell you how?"

Garnet was listening attentively. She lit a cigarette with angry, shaking hands, grimacing as if in pain.

"It was the same nightmare again. Max's wristband doesn't help at all. Baz, I ended up at this sort of doctor's, and he said something strange. He said it was all me – myself. My own fears, or something."

Teresa spoke up. "That's what they always tell you. But I know it isn't true. There *are* ghosts belonging to other people that come and bother you too. I can't tell you how often it's happened to me, Josh."

"I don't think it's just me, either. All of this, and all the *umayas* we've been in – those aren't just me, either, are they?"

Their conversation was interrupted by Garnet talking shrilly into her mobile phone. "Yes, just arrived. Splitting headache, of course. Yeah. It'll work in a minute. Oh, darling, you don't have to tell me. I'll try anything. We'll see. Ciao then, kisses." She put the phone away and flipped her cigarette into the water. "Very well. I've fetched Josh back so now we can continue. Where to, young man? You tell us."

Josh hesitated. "We've got to look for the border. For the darkness. Well, one thing's certain: it's really light here."

So it was: everything shone and glittered. The water was as clear as glass, the sky was bright blue, the houses were white and spotless. The Zeppelins glistened overhead.

"So?" Garnet's voice was extremely impatient.

"So, we've got to go and get the lie of the land. I'll have a look around with Baz. You can stay in the boat with Teresa. We'll be back in an hour."

Just a little while later Baz and Josh were walking side by side down Portilisi's busy thoroughfares, which were packed with people briskly going about their business. And yet, Josh noticed after a while, now and then he'd see – down an alley, behind a cellar window, or in a doorway – some crouching, huddled figure. "There are some pitiful people here too, you know," he said to Baz.

"It's the nineteenth century. Didn't they have terrible poverty and misery in those days?"

"But most of what you see here is positive, all about progress. Maybe this is an *umaya* that shows only the optimistic side of that period."

"Or else the bad things are hidden away somewhere."

"Hey, that's what that doctor said too. He said you have nightmares hidden deep inside you, and that they can suddenly come out."

They came to a tower, a lofty tower with acres of glass and steel, which it was possible to enter on paying 1.10. They didn't know how much 1.10 was, but, according to the cashier, the unfamiliar coins in their pockets would do. From the top of the tower they looked out over the whole city. Zeppelins dipped and bobbed before their eyes, with gentlemen in top hats puffing cigars in the baskets underneath. A silver aeroplane dived and looped the loop around the airships. Zizi, agitated, hopped up and down on Josh's shoulder. Far below them the strange traffic flowed. In the west, the sky was beginning to turn a light pink. And over in the east, far beyond the city limits, loomed heavy, black clouds.

"Darkness," Josh pointed out.

"That's just nightfall."

"But what time is it then? It isn't even three o'clock, is it?"

Baz checked his watch. "That's what it is at home, but in this *umaya* I'd say it's about six or seven. Look, everyone's leaving. They're closing."

They went down with the others. It was remarkable how quickly the traffic thinned out in the slowly falling twilight. Pedestrians scurried in all directions, and doors slammed shut, while lamplighters went around lighting the street lamps as fast as they could.

"Sir, excuse me, but what time is it?" Josh asked one of them. The man scarcely slowed his pace.

"Nearly too late! Hurry, you two, get inside, silly boys!"

Somewhere a sash window that was sticking was slammed shut, opened, slammed down again, and opened once more.

A woman in a white cap yelled at them through the crack, "Hurry home, boys! Are you mad? It's getting dark!"

There was no need for discussion. Automatically they broke into a run and raced back to the boat in alarm, as fast as their legs could carry them, under the flickering street lamps. A lamp burned in their boat too, a friendly little yellow light.

"Did you find out anything?" asked Teresa.

"I don't think we have to do anything – the darkness is coming to *us*. Because it's almost night-time, you see."

"Well, obviously!" Garnet sneered.

"But this is a different sort of darkness," said Josh. "I think it's the border between two worlds; between this bright world and something threatening and dark that lies beyond it."

As the city around them grew silent they began to hear other noises. Low, nearly inaudible sounds. Vibrations. Something that sounded like screams. Distant wailings.

Teresa shuddered. "If you ask me, Josh's right. There's something creepy going on."

They held their breath and listened. Underneath them the water began to seethe. "Maybe we'd better go ashore," said Teresa in a tight little voice.

Just moments ago the whole city had been buzzing with a current of excitement and optimism; now a different sort of tension crackled through the air. Pressed close together, they huddled in the narrow alleyway leading from the water to a broader avenue. The air felt oppressive and leaden.

"What do you feel now, Joshua Cope?" asked Garnet.

"Something scary," said Josh. "I see shadows. Ugh."

"Are we at a border?" she insisted.

Baz was the one who answered. "No," he said. "We're still in the same dream-time."

"How would you know that?" cried Garnet. "*You* don't have Sense, surely!"

Josh suddenly remembered landing in the room with all the clocks, on their jump with Max to the dawning of the world.

It was the sort of thing that sometimes happened to Sensers, Max had told them. One thing was certain: Josh wasn't a Senser himself. He looked at Baz with fresh eyes. "Maybe he does," he said softly. "Right, Baz?"

"That boy can't possibly have Sense," argued their peevish travelling companion, "or he'd be in terrible pain when he's plunging." She looked at Baz sternly. He kept quiet, his eyes set. "You'd be in pain!" she repeated.

Baz kept his mouth shut a little longer, but finally he couldn't contain himself and burst out, "So what? I never said it didn't hurt!" He lowered his voice, shaken. "Maybe I just don't whine about it, that's all. And I've already told you I've discovered something really important, something that makes it easier for me to bear."

Josh felt terribly guilty that he hadn't been aware of Baz's pain. Baz had mentioned it on their first *imayada* with Max, but after that Josh hadn't given it another thought. Teresa put her arm round Baz.

"Well, well, well," said Garnet softly. "You've got Sense. Isn't that convenient? So you can Sense there isn't a border here. Then perhaps we should get out of here, kids, because I'm afraid this *umaya* is in the process of changing into something extremely unpleasant."

She was right. The brilliant city had changed into a brewing menace of dark walls and bulging shadows. A wind had sprung up that made the shadows tremble and shudder. In the distance came a drawn-out, harrowing cry. "Ghosts," muttered Teresa. They huddled closer together.

"But how can we fall asleep like this!" said Josh.

"Well, you're the leader of the expedition, aren't you?" Garnet sneered. "Why don't you think of something?" She flipped her phone open again and turned her back on the others. "Yeah, it's me – things are getting a little out of hand here, but it's just occurred to me that it might not be such a bad thing. Yes, exactly. Right. I'll just try it. That way we'll know if it works or not. No, I've got enough tablets with me. No, are you kidding – Mervin, enough! Yes, yes, OK, definitely, bye." She turned round again, still holding her mobile.

Josh elbowed Baz. Had he heard her addressing the man as Mervin? Which Mervin might that be?

"Who is it you keep calling, anyway?" he asked suspiciously.

"Gippart's central help desk," said Garnet quickly. "Our behind-the-scenes assistance line. OK, here we go." She bent over her mobile phone and pressed some keys. Then something odd happened. Josh felt his heart involuntarily starting to beat faster. It wasn't because he was scared that his heart raced; it just started beating faster, rhythmically, of its own accord. His arms began to itch from the inside, and his eyes stung and burned. The snake bracelet felt as if it were sinking its teeth into his ankle.

"Ow!" Baz cried beside him, jumping up and down and scratching himself like mad.

Teresa looked at them in surprise. Then she looked at Garnet, who was clutching her phone and watching them intently. Teresa rushed at her. "What are you doing? Stop it!"

Garnet warded her off. "Stay where you are. What I'm doing, girl, is in Gippart's best interests. I'm just giving them a little push in the direction of this world's border. There's nothing wrong with that. Haven't you been to one of those borders yourself?"

Teresa clutched at her heart. "Yeah, and that's lethal, that is! Stop it, Garnet, these boys aren't up to it, and it was never agreed!"

Josh had the feeling that his head was swelling up, and that his whole body was about to burst. Wheezing, he hung on to the wall, staring into space, his eyes bulging.

"Oh yes, it *was* agreed," said Garnet, and again she pressed a key.

Josh gasped for breath. His heart started racing as if he was about to blow up. The world about him seemed to grow even darker. The shadows detached themselves from the earth and rose up into the air like clouds of terror that might at any moment come crashing down on them.

For one endless moment it felt as if everything was about to explode. Then Josh saw one of the shadows swoop down on Garnet and Teresa like a noiseless avalanche. He heard screaming, then a crash, and then everything before his eyes went black.

As he slowly came to again, he noticed he was lying on the ground, weak and spent. His twitching body gradually relaxed. His heartbeat was loud, but regular. He felt his chest and his arms and his legs: all in one piece. He sat up. Teresa was lying on the ground a little in front of him, her head cradled in her arms. Baz was stretched out beside him. His eyes were closed and he was as pale as a ghost, but he was breathing, shallowly and rapidly.

"Baz?" Cautiously Josh touched his arm. "Baz, are you asleep?"

Baz half opened his eyes. "If only," he groaned. "It was terrible. It hurt so much, Josh." He clutched his chest and his head, and tears rolled down his cheeks. "Oh, help! I'd give anything to be at the dentist's instead!" He laughed, and then he started to cry.

Josh sat there, helpless, looking worriedly over at Teresa. She gave a loud moan, and turned on to her back. "Oh God," she muttered. "Josh? Baz?" She sat up, casting around wild, fearful glances. "Has it gone?" She rushed over to Josh, hugged him, grabbed the crying Baz and held him tightly.

It was comforting to feel their warm bodies close to his. Josh gulped a few times and looked around. "Where's Garnet? And what the hell was she up to? *She* did it, didn't she?"

Teresa clicked her tongue. "That snake. I don't know how she did it, but she tried to force you out of this dreamworld. She wanted to get you to the border where real time begins, the real nineteenth century. They tried it with me as well. Just wait till I get my hands on her!"

"But then all those shadows suddenly came," said Josh.

"Maybe they came because of her," said Baz. "Because of all the trembling. And the pain."

"But where is she now?" They peered into the darkness.

"I couldn't care less," said Teresa. "Let those spectres around here just tear her to pieces, for all I care. If they can stomach her, that is."

"She arranged to do it," said Josh suddenly. "She told someone on the phone she was going to do it."

"The help desk," said Teresa.

"Mervin," said Josh, and then he and Baz exclaimed at the same time, "Mervin Spratt!"

"Spratt? What do you mean?" asked Teresa. "Isn't Spratt a Senser? Surely he's got nothing to do with the help desk?"

After they'd filled her in, she whistled. "So Mervin Spratt is after you for something, something you own or something you know, and Garnet is in league with him. But what can they possibly want from you?"

"I don't know," admitted Josh. "Everybody's been going on about my special talents, but the only thing I'm good at is falling asleep at the drop of a hat, and you're just as good at that as I am. I really don't understand any of it. There's something else. Something they wanted to steal from me, while the Trial was going on. Something for which they completely ransacked my bedroom."

"But *do* you own anything special?" asked Teresa.

"No! I can't think what!"

Then, near by, they heard a scream. They pressed closer together in alarm.

"I want to get out of here," said Josh in a strange, tight voice. "Would you two be able to fall asleep here?"

"I doubt it," said Teresa. "Look, I've got goose pimples all over, and my hair is standing on end. There's terror in the stones, can't you feel it?"

It was true. The entire city was pulsing with barely audible, weird music, a drawn-out spasm of dread.

Josh considered. "I know somewhere that might be safe. I know someone who isn't afraid. Who says he's already seen all the nightmares there are to see."

"Here?" asked Baz.

"Yes, that doctor, when I first arrived. Didn't you get here that way? Come with me. If we can make it to his waiting room, we'll be able to go to sleep."

Stealthily they crept out of the alley. The streets were weakly lit by the glow of flickering yellow street lamps. There were shadows skulking in all the corners, and sometimes a large shadow swept down from above. As they shuffled along with their backs pressed to the wall, to their horror a woman whose clothes were on fire ran past. Her streaming hair showered sparks, and she thrashed her arms about wildly. She uttered such heart-rending screams that the three of them threw themselves to the ground, clamping their hands to their ears. Zizi hid herself inside Josh's collar. In a little while the woman had disappeared.

To his relief, Josh found the way back without too much trouble, in the perplexingly flickering darkness. He had a keen eye for that sort of thing. There was that dull square building again. And next to it, he recognized the large door with the copper nameplate. He pulled hard at the doorbell. They waited, flattened against the door, out of breath.

"Listen," said Baz. High-pitched music was coming from the building. It was a comforting sound, compared to the monstrous noise of the street. As they were listening, the door opened just a crack.

"I'm one of the doctor's special patients," said Josh quickly, "and he was interested in examining me more closely."

The door opened a little wider and an old man in livery pulled him inside. In a calm, reassuring voice he told them to wait, and shuffled up the stairs. The music stopped. A little later a door opened and a voice called, "Come up here, young people."

They climbed the stairs, the butler held open the waiting room door for them, and there they saw the doctor, a striking figure with a violin in his hand.

"Good evening," he said in his deep voice. "I am delighted you have found your way back to me." Then he shook his head. "Nevertheless, I shall not be able to attend to you this evening. I am sorry. I am currently indisposed."

They saw that there were beads of sweat on his forehead, and that his hands were shaking slightly. "I play the violin at night, you see – and I take something. At night I descend into the depths of the soul. I explore the depths of the fears that we are only too eager to suppress, we people of the modern age, we world conquerors shaking in our boots, victims of our own bottomless greed." He turned round to go back to his office. "But if you will wait here, I can certainly give you a session in the morning. It will give me the greatest pleasure. Do please excuse me." He closed the door behind him.

"Doctors can't be on duty around the clock," said Baz charitably. He sat down on one of the chairs. There was a friendly night light in one corner of the room. Teresa settled herself with a sigh in another armchair. "This time-period is lousy, isn't it?"

"Lousy at night, but fun in the daytime," added Baz, arms crossed, chin resting on his chest.

The butler returned carrying hot chocolate on a tray and three large feather pillows. They snuggled down contentedly in their chairs. "But actually," said Josh, scratching Zizi's feathers to comfort her, "the nightmares here aren't *our* nightmares. Funny, isn't it? That you can be scared by the fears of others?"

They drank their sweet hot chocolate.

"Can you two go to sleep now?" asked Josh, remembering his responsibilities as expedition leader. Baz and Teresa nodded.

"We're never coming back here anyway," said Josh. "See you in Reception."

Sprawled languidly in their chairs, one by one they fell asleep.

Their instructions were as follows: *On completion of the* imayada, *check in immediately with the Chief of Associates; write your report (on form enclosed) within the fortnight, and present yourself before Dispatch Board C (Z 6.39 C) for an oral debriefing half an hour before your next* imayada.

Still a little weak-kneed from their frightening experience, the three of them obediently went, in silence, to find Moussa. Just as they approached the lifts, the clock struck five. Baz smiled. "We didn't do all that badly then."

They walked along a corridor lined with offices. From behind one of the doors came angry voices. They had already gone past when Baz suddenly stopped, his finger on his lips, gesturing.

"Oh stop it, Max. I'm just doing *my* job. Do I ever interfere with yours?"

It was Garnet's voice. Max's answer was inaudible.

She went on: "My instructions are perfectly clear! And those kids won't take the slightest initiative. If you'd only give one to me, no holds barred, you'd see some results. This way nothing's ever going to happen!"

Next came Max's angry voice. Then Garnet again. "What's the end game here, anyway? Is it about opening up new markets with zillions of new customers, or is our goal to coddle your thick little infants? Do you really want Gippart to restrict its sales operations to those ridiculous dream-worlds, none of which really deliver? Do you have any idea by what percentage our profits are shrinking? Have you seen last year's sales figures?"

Again they couldn't make out the answer.

"And do you know what Katz's profits were for the last two quarters?"

An angry mumbled protest.

"And I've had enough of it! Those Associates, as you call them, they're all little psychopaths, every one of them. Don't be such a hypocrite. You know they're only useful to you as long as they remain clueless about the difference between illusion and reality. And that boy Cope is the saddest case of all, if what Mervin Spratt has told me about him is true!"

A short grumble was the reply.

"OK, so it's true then. But you'll never find out this way, whether or not he manages to cross over into real time! If you ask me, the little idiot doesn't even know himself how he does it. Why don't you let me have him for a proper long, drawn-out *imayada*? If I were given free rein, I'd have no trouble sorting it out. A little push, I know just how to do it…"

There was a loud thump, and a yell from Garnet. "You sentimental old fool!"

They got out of there as quickly as they could, round the corner, before the door was flung open and Garnet came out, snorting with anger.

"How'd *she* get here so fast?" whispered Teresa.

Baz was spluttering, wounded in his new-found pride at having made Associate (fifth place). "Thick! Psychopaths! She says we're clueless!"

"Ha," laughed Teresa, "that's what they always call us. Don't let it get to you."

But Josh was frowning. So they thought he had solved the big secret! That he knew how to get from the dream-world into real history. But what made them think that? Lost in thought, he followed the others to the Associates' Junior Committee Room. Teresa immediately ran to a group of her friends, Baz bumped into John, who launched into an enthusiastic tale, but Josh just collapsed on one of the sofas, bewildered. What if they *did* just give him to someone to use as a guinea pig! If only he knew what it was, exactly, that he was supposed to be capable of; what it was that made them think that he was the only one in the world who knew how to travel through time!

Someone flopped down next to him, threw an arm round his shoulder and pushed a glass into his hand. "Nicely done, boyo, right on time. You're getting the hang of it. Well, I'm waiting for a report. Aren't you the expedition chief?"

Josh looked uncertainly at Moussa. "What am I supposed to tell you? It was horrible, and I think it's all supposed to be kept secret."

Josh felt Moussa's warm breath as he whispered in his ear, "Daddy knows everything. And what he don't know, he ought to know. Tell. Just tell me!"

Josh told. Not everything. Not about their mission to find the Tembe. But he did tell him about having to find the border. And about Garnet's mobile phone. About her disappearing act and reappearance at Gippart.

"They've got these little pills," said Moussa. "They're very bad for you, but without them you'd peg out in an hour, and instead they make you fall asleep in a flash, and get you back home. The adults never travel in *umaya* without their little pills."

"Nor do you," said Josh as it dawned on him.

"No, I don't," muttered Moussa. "Still, I'm not happy, Joshie. Garnet Gippart. Hell. They're messing with my Associates. Max—"

"Max and Garnet were having a row about it," Josh told him. "I don't think Max is in on it. Is Garnet Gippart Max's superior? I think she's working with Mervin Spratt."

"Spratt?" Moussa's eyes lit up. "He's Gippart's most accomplished Senser. He's good at it. If you so much as *think* about your grandmother when he's around, he'll react – that's how sensitive he is. He knows exactly where the borders between the dream-worlds are located. And where time begins."

"What does a Senser *do*, exactly?"

"All *you* need to know is that a Senser checks to make sure the dream-worlds aren't getting mixed up. And to ensure nothing gets carried over into real time out of *umaya* by mistake.

He's the bane of Associates with itchy fingers, that Spratt. Boy, if you ever nick something from *umaya* and take it with you, you're in big trouble – Spratt will sniff it out from miles away, and you'll hang for it."

"But why isn't it allowed?"

"Because of the environment, of course! Gippart has signed masses of contracts that say that they're not allowed to change a thing in nature, or in the sequence of time, or anything else. It's only on condition that they're very tidy and careful and change absolutely nothing that they're allowed to muck about with that dream-travelling business. Sometimes it can't be helped, if you're attacked, for example. But other than that, if its people so much as pick a flower in *umaya*, Gippart has to pay a hefty fine. Did you think the employment inspectors of the TTO, the Transgressive Trade Organizations, would stand for it otherwise? That lot keep a very close eye on what happens here. So at Gippart they try to do everything up front, by the book. That way, they think they can secretly get away with illegal activities somewhere else. Like using the kids for their time-experiments. The Associates." Moussa stood up and took Josh's glass from him. "What are you still doing here? Go home, sleepyhead. And remember, I'm your Chief. You're not to take part in Garnet Gippart's little games, or Spratt's. No time-travelling for you!"

6
The Teeth of the Inelesi

To Josh's annoyance, Baz wouldn't help him write his report. "You're the leader," he said, and he left Josh to it, with his forms – to be filled out in duplicate. *Number of items sold. Leftover stock. Sold/exchanged for ——, equivalent of ——pounds/euros/ dollars/yen.* Umaya *visited, code, department. Time-frame and duration of journey, hours/minutes Greenwich Mean Time/central European time/*umaya *time. Concise summary of sales strategies (in less than 500 words).*

Furious, Josh hurled his pen across the room. He stamped down the stairs.

"Bad mood?" asked Mo cheerfully.

Thanks for asking! Yes. With good reason: the nightmares about that ghost-city, Spratt and Garnet out for his blood, everyone constantly after him; at school he kept nodding off, and he was expedition leader of exactly nothing. But then he had an idea.

"Baz, we'll just get there an hour early next week!"

Baz was working up a sweat over his drums and he looked up, dazed. "Early where?"

"At Gippart!"

Baz beat one last drum roll, threw his drumsticks up in the air and caught them. "What for?"

"That way we can shake Garnet. She'll be up to her nasty tricks again. If we get there early, we'll give her the slip."

"Oh, right!" Baz laughed. "She'll be hopping mad."

"We'll just get there at one o'clock!"

"And what about Teresa?"

"As far as I'm concerned, she can come."

"But how?"

"When we were driven home last time, we dropped her off first at her house, didn't we? So we can just pick her up on our way, can't we?"

On Saturday October the seventh they got to Teresa's house at 12.30 p.m., a perky Zizi on Josh's shoulder. A lady wearing a suit opened the door. "Boys, we have visitors!" she called over her shoulder as she slipped past them.

"Mum, you forgot your bag!" Teresa came running into the hall, holding a handbag. "Oh, Baz and Josh!"

The lady took the handbag from Teresa and nodded at the boys. "These friends of yours from school, Teresa? I'll see you later tonight, honey. Don't forget to do your homework, all right now? Study hard."

Teresa waved Josh and Baz into the living room, where a couple of boys were sprawled on the sofa watching television. "I thought I'd be seeing you two in a while anyway, in Reception," she said. "Is something the matter?"

"We want to get there before Garnet, to give her the slip," said Josh. "We're going over there an hour early. Do you want to come?"

Teresa's face lit up. "Right!" she said, and ran out of the room. They heard shuffling, whispering, a protesting voice, and then a door slamming. "All set. Louisa will do the shopping."

"Which of your brothers is it I look like then?" asked Baz curiously as they walked to the bus stop.

"My little brother that died," answered Teresa. "Oh, how I'd love to see Garnet with egg all over her face!"

But when they got to Reception, the girl at the computer gave them a hard time. "Your appointment isn't for another forty-five minutes," she said firmly. "They can't debrief you before then. And there's absolutely no way you can leave earlier. Just go and hang around in the Junior Committee Room for now. Run along, shoo." She was adamant that she wouldn't let them go any further.

Fuming, they walked down the corridors to the JCR. But when they got there, Josh had made a decision. "We'll just go to a different gate. We'll fetch the backpacks and get changed, and then we'll choose a gate and jump before they can stop us."

They all nodded resolutely. "What are the co-ordinates?" asked Teresa as she pulled her grey tunic over her head.

Josh read from the piece of paper on which Max had written the instructions for the first few stages of the chain-*imayada*: "Skull. Wig. A Greek column."

They gave each other conspiratorial nods, then hoisted on their backpacks. They were in the central hall in five minutes.

"Ready? Let's go!"

They ran into one of the boarding areas. Josh slapped his report down under some young man's nose. "That's for Max!" He jerked the door open a crack and they grabbed one another's hands, shut their eyes and jumped, before the astonished young man could stop them. But just as they'd started their jump, they bumped into a couple of solid bodies. They were knocked down to the ground, completely disorientated, and heard a voice crying, "Grab them!" Josh scrambled to his feet and in a panic reached for Baz's hand, then Teresa's, and plunged again, shouting, "Skull!" And tumbled, and tumbled, and tumbled.

They landed on hard ground in a neat row. On their feet.

Baz scratched his head, dazed. "Damn!"

"I can't *believe* a group of Associates were coming in just as we were leaving." Teresa giggled, cupping her hand over her mouth. "We must have given them quite a shock."

"Have we been pushed off course now?" asked Baz.

"It's quite possible," said Josh. They were standing in a bare cellar with a low ceiling. It smelled mouldy and decayed.

"But then again, maybe not," said Teresa. "Shall we go on?"

"Wait a minute." Baz rubbed his head.

Josh suddenly remembered what Baz had told them. "Are you OK, Baz? Did it hurt again?"

"A little – but that's because I couldn't use my trick, because we bumped into those others. Want to hear about it now?"

"First let's make sure we aren't lost," said their leader. "Shall we do 'wig'?"

"Ready?"

"Go!"

They jumped, spun, glided, plummeted. Something must have gone wrong, or they wouldn't be careening sideways through space for such an endless stretch. A dreamy tumble. Everything sweet. A hazy mist, lukewarm. Baz singing, somewhere far off. He wasn't holding hands with anyone any more. With a smile on his face, Josh was sailing through an infinite void. He floated slowly down, hovered, swam, drifted. He was face down in the water. He stretched, lazy and contented. It was as if someone had caught his ankle in a warm-blooded grip. Everything felt quiet and good. Warm fingers caressed his face, tracing the lines of his jaw, his nose, his forehead. A delighted laugh. A finger stroked his eyelid. "Open your eyes, Joshua *na* Jericho. Look at me."

He wasn't even really afraid. It was so sweet. He opened his eyes. Close up he saw another face, so near to his that it was distorted: large nose pressed against his nose, two enormous eyes almost merging into a single eye. A face that mirrored his.

Swirling hair everywhere. Whispering. "Can you see me? Do you finally see me?"

"Just about," mumbled Josh. "Who *are* you?"

"Don't you recognize me?" The voice sounded a little hurt, a voice as familiar as his own heartbeat.

Another youthful voice piped up: "Of course he doesn't recognize you! He's never seen you before!"

"We lay side by side for nine months! He can't have forgotten me!"

Josh's body began to glow. He was beginning to understand something, and his body seemed to grasp it faster than his head. His ankle began to scorch and burn. He looked at the face in front of him, which seemed to be fading and melting away. The water started to flow.

"Let me go to him! The longer I'm with him, the more likely he'll remember!"

"Just wait for your next chance. He can't escape you now, after all."

Fainter and fainter, the voices. "You're right, I've got him now. He'll keep coming closer, he can't help it..."

Now he was flowing with the water, slowly but relentlessly. Flowing downstream. Faster. And then he was gliding over a smooth rock, and over another one. He switched direction, veered sideways, and then finally he was lying still. Head down, in the water. That was where he came to rest, his nose and mouth drinking water, breathing water.

"Josh?" They hauled him out of the pond, afraid it would be too late. The cold air in his lungs made him cough. Angrily he thumped his chest with his fists. He panted until he remembered who he was again. He opened his eyes. Green reeds. Baz and Teresa on their knees in front of him, looking relieved. Zizi was on the ground beside him, preening her feathers.

"We're all together again." Baz laughed. "Teresa was up in a tree, Josh. It took me *ages* to find her! And I landed in that thatched hut over there. I thought I was all alone. Are you OK? I really thought you were drowning."

"No," said Josh, wiping his face with his Gippart shirt. He didn't know what to say. He was beginning to understand something about his nightmare, but the thought frightened him so much that he immediately repressed it. This wasn't just any old ghost, the kind that just shows up and then moves on. It was something that was part of him, an ingrained piece of his life. Something he couldn't get rid of.

"You do look a bit pale," said Teresa.

"Do you want to go on?" asked Baz. "Did something happen? Ghosts?"

Josh shrugged. He shook his head and puffed out his cheeks, raised his hands in the air the way Max did, and then gave them a lopsided, unhappy smile. "I dunno. Let's go on."

He – no, it was a *she*, he knew it now – she had said, "*I've got him now. He'll keep coming closer.*" The Gippart wristband was no match for her, that was clear. And every time he plunged into an *umaya*, she had another chance to reach him.

Teresa observed him thoughtfully. "If you ask me, you shouldn't be jumping solo any more. Baz, that special trick of yours, do you think it might help Josh as well? Will you tell us about it?"

Baz beamed. "Yes, of course I will. I've wanted to share it with you for ages. Would you like to hear it too, Josh?"

Josh nodded. "Yes. Please."

"Good," said Baz. "It's like this. I just thought it through. When you jump, you move from one dream to another. Wait, let me try to explain it a bit better."

He looked around, found a long sturdy reed and a flimsier stick. "Listen. Pretend this is our ordinary world." He began hitting the reed with the stick in a quick, steady rhythm. "I can't tap it out the way it *really* goes, because that's much too complicated a beat. But let's just pretend. Next you have Gippart, Reception. That's a little slower. Like this." Now he was drumming a different, slightly more measured tempo. “Now. Then you move from Reception into *umaya. Umaya* can either be slower or faster, usually a little faster, but every *umaya* is different. One might go like this” – he tapped out a quick beat with a roll in between – “and the next one like this: *tad*adam, *tad*adam, *tad*adam. And then you get one of these: —x —x, or else: —= =———=-==, or this one: —xx/ —x/ —xx /—.” He drummed all kinds of different rhythms, each one slightly faster than the Gippart tempo. “See? Every dream-world has its own beat. And because I have Sense, I feel those rhythms in my bones. And then my heart starts beating along to the rhythm. When you leap from Reception into *umaya*, and from one *umaya* to another, those rhythms sort of interplay inside your body, in your heart, and that hurts. I mean, if you can feel it. If you have Sense.”

“I don’t have Sense, but I do love music,” said Teresa.

“All right, what do *I* know?” said Baz. “I only know that I can feel the rhythm in my heart and my belly. But listen, the thing I do when we jump, you know, is I try humming along to those rhythms. That way I turn it into music. And then I can make the different beats play together, and that makes it really easy to slide from one dream to another. It’s quick – only takes a couple of seconds. That’s my trick.”

“Oh,” said Josh, in disappointment. “But the only way to do it that way is to feel the rhythms! And I can’t feel a thing.”

“But I could sing them *for* you, or drum them,” said Baz. “Let’s try it together. Shall we?”

“Great – it’s a terrific idea,” said Teresa. “Now I suddenly understand why my heart nearly burst that time I tried stepping over into real time. Real time must just have a totally different beat!”

“I still don’t understand it completely,” said Baz. “But why don’t we try it?” He was itching to go.

Josh stood up. He was still ill at ease. But Baz had discovered something important, he could tell. “Why don’t you be our guide, then, Baz? If I’m the leader.”

Baz smiled with pleasure. "I've wanted to tell you about it for ages, but you wouldn't listen."

"And what am I then?" asked Teresa.

"What would you like to be?" asked Josh.

"Hmm. Champion long-distance runner, the only one here with the slightest bit of sense, the oldest and wisest, the master storyteller, the one who never gives up, and the clearest thinker. That isn't what I *want* to be, it's what I *am* already. Shall we get going?"

"You'll be the head," Josh decided. "I'll be the leader and Baz will be the guide. But I get to say where we're going, all right?"

"And I get to say how we get there," said Baz. "Right, on your feet. Now. Say with me: *ta*daka – *ta*daka – *ta*daka..."

"Is that the rhythm of this in-between world?"

"Yes, very straightforward. A real *umaya* is much more complicated. This is only a halfway stop. You'll hear it. What should we be thinking of, Josh?"

"A Greek column."

"It'll be hard to do it all right," said Teresa, "having to think of a Greek column at the same time as keeping the beat. *Ta*daka – *ta*daka..."

They jumped, spun through the air. Baz doggedly went on beating the rhythm. "*Ta*daka – *ta*daka – um – uh ... raha*ee*ni – raha*ee*ni – *ta*daka – denee – *ta*daka *dee* – *ta*daka denee..." He squeezed their hands, rhythmically, tentatively – and he was right: they landed in less than a minute, softly and surely.

"Fantastic, Baz!"

"Where are we?"

They were standing on the smooth cobblestones of a small town square, with a few starchily dressed people sauntering by. It was a fine day, though overcast, and the square was as neat as a pin. Some of the ladies and gentlemen were wearing impeccably powdered wigs. Josh quickly felt his head. Phew. It was still his own hair.

"We're in a town again. Oh, no!" Josh looked at the others in alarm. "We're in Portilisi again!"

"Naturally," said Teresa.

It was true. It was the same town, only it felt strange, and quite different from before. There was no trace of the crackling tension. This was a very stable place. The weather was calm, with the sky an even grey, and not a gust of wind. The buildings were uniform square blocks with evenly spaced windows, and the people were not agitated or desperate.

"It's a nice rhythm," said Baz, "calm and yet very strict, with interesting flourishes. Can you hear it too?"

"That's really odd," said Josh. "You hear a rhythm, but I'm more inclined to see colour – strange colours, which I think have something to do with this time. A sort of powder-grey-blue-purple. Can you see it too, Teresa?"

Teresa shook her head. "You know what springs to my mind? This town's stories. Not the wild kind of story that sends shivers up your spine, but the story of how they're always trying to keep a lid on everything here, to keep things in order. But there are other stories as well, which don't quite fit." She gazed at a little band of poor porters, at a beggar scurrying into an alleyway.

"Do you think they've got those nightmares here too?" asked Baz.

"Oh, probably," said Teresa.

They shivered, and Josh said, "Let's get away from here. I don't feel like being trapped by any nightmares at all."

They left the square in a hurry, Josh in the lead, in search of the outskirts. Fortunately they were in luck. Walking down the streets lined with tidy, symmetrical buildings, they came to a cattle market that was just finishing. All they had to do was follow the traders and farmers, who, having done their business, were leaving the town. Outside the town the paved streets gave way to a wide dirt road, lined with mansions set in elegant park-like estates. They walked on until there were no more houses to be seen, only farmland. The road meandered to a friendly forest. It was early autumn, and the sun finally broke through the clouds, shining gold. The first red leaves twirled through the air. They sat down at the side of the road to decide what to do.

"Why don't you get the map out, Josh?"

They pored over it intently. "Baz, can you sense a time-border anywhere?"

Baz cocked his head to listen, and Josh and Teresa scanned the horizon for signs of oncoming darkness. "Nothing."

"How on earth are we going to find those Tembe, then?"

"Maybe," said Josh, tapping the map, "maybe we have to make our way to the coast. That's the only kind of border I can see here. And we'll just have to ask people on the way."

He took out his Gippart compass and twisted it until a pencil-thin beam shot out of it, pointing miles into the distance. Proudly Josh turned it off.

"That isn't a good idea." Teresa frowned. "If they spot you here with that thing, you're in big trouble."

"All right, but it seems so quiet here," sighed Josh, "for a change. Shall we go? This road leads straight to the coast."

It did seem to be a very calm *umaya.* Perhaps because it was lacking the buzz of last time, they didn't feel the paralysing terror of the nightmares, either. It seemed to be a very ordinary world. But there was no doubt they were in *umaya.* The air was rich in oxygen. It made them a little light-headed as they strolled along the road, chatting and singing. Their clothes were comfortable; Teresa's dress was long and flowing. It felt good to be playing truant from the house of Gippart. Zizi fluttered along above their heads, happy as a lark. They joked about everything they saw: fat people in wigs and stiff costumes on horseback, large families crammed into carriages, a herd of huge red and white cows crossing the road, pedlars, students in long cloaks, soldiers. Everyone nodded hello to them, and sometimes they'd exchange a few words – "Where are you from?" to which the Associates would answer, "Persia!" – and then they'd each go their way again. No one had heard of the Tembe.

"It's such an ordinary world, I don't really understand," said Baz.

"There are quite ordinary *umayas*," said Teresa. "I was once in an *umaya* that looked exactly like my own normal world. I even had to go to school. Boring. It turned out it was a sixteenth-century peasant girl's dream of the future."

"She must have been psychic then," Josh decided.

After they'd been walking for half an hour he began to worry. "We'll never get back in time this way. Shouldn't we hop on a stagecoach or something?"

"We have plenty of time," said Baz. "Here, time passes faster than at home. Three hours here may be the same as only two hours at home. Or even less. And we're making good progress."

He was right: the landscape was beginning to look different. The pastures and wheat fields were giving way to waterlogged farmland – rice, according to Teresa. In some places the land along the road was nothing but a swamp, and the further they went, the more muddy the road became. From time to time a proud white mansion complete with veranda would appear in the distance, sheltered by towering trees. But something in the sky had changed as well. Something was brewing up there. They couldn't put a finger on it, but all three of them felt it.

"I haven't seen anybody for ages," remarked Teresa.

Josh opened the map while walking. "There aren't any more villages or towns until we reach the port, Damara, on the coast. Hopefully they'll have heard of the Tembe there."

"Well, someone's coming," said Baz with a nervous little laugh. "You can ask them."

It was two big men riding in an open horse-drawn cart. As the cart slowly rocked closer, all three fell silent, frozen in a strange state of apprehension. The men were alarmingly large, they noticed, when the cart drew closer. They were both over six feet tall, and at least three feet wide. But they didn't notice the worst thing about them until it was too late.

"Ugh!" cried Teresa, and she turned and ran.

One of the men jumped down from the cart and lurched after her, surprisingly fast on his feet, waving a long whip in his hand. The other fellow grabbed a gun and pointed it at Baz and Josh. "Into the cart, and quick about it!" he growled. "Or I'll blow your bleeding heads off, scum!"

They immediately raised their hands in the air. It was the first time anyone had ever pointed a real weapon at them, and automatically they did what they'd learnt from television. The man glared at them menacingly until they'd climbed in the cart. Then he thrust the gun aside, flung a dirty old blanket over their heads and tied it fast. As he was doing so, in the dark they could hear someone else being thrown into the cart; and from the cursing and swearing, they could tell it was Teresa. The cart lurched into motion.

"What kind of people are they?" Baz asked Josh anxiously in the stuffy darkness. "Why did they take us prisoner?"

"Did you see their skin?" Josh whispered. "Are they ill?"

Teresa, who was close, hissed, "I know who they are. They're called the people without skin. In my dad's family there are stories about them. They're the mad, sadistic slave traders! Oh, damn, how did we manage to fall into their clutches!" She sounded more furious than frightened.

The ride took so long that Josh thought he'd suffocate. The stinking blanket irritated his nose, and Baz and he were bound tightly together. Baz's backpack poked into Josh's stomach irritatingly. Baz was panting quietly. They didn't dare talk.

Finally the cart drew to a halt. Josh and Baz were picked up like a sack of potatoes, carried some distance, and then flung down on to a stone floor. They felt another body land beside them.

"I caught three," drawled a phlegmy voice. "Just walking along the road in broad daylight. Stolen fancy clothes too. Lock them up in the cellar; we'll decide what to do with them tomorrow."

"We can have some fun with them," gurgled a second voice. The brutes belched and laughed. There was the sound of rattling keys and the creaking of a door, and then someone kicked Josh in the back, hard. They rolled down some steps, jolting and bumping, until they came to rest on a hard floor.

"Ouch, ouch, get off me," squeaked Baz.

"I can't," panted Josh. "I can't breathe; I can't move."

They writhed and squirmed, snorting and groaning, but in vain.

"Wait, wait!" came a familiar voice. They felt a firm hand pulling at the ropes, fumbling with the knots. At last they were able to pull the foul cloth off their heads. They found themselves sitting in a pitch-black cellar. They could hardly see a thing.

"Right," said Teresa, always the practical one. "What do we do now?"

"We've got to escape," said Baz, rubbing his arms. "What do those fat pigs want with us?"

"Oh well," said Teresa, "that's obvious: they want to sell us, or get us to work as slaves on their land, or maybe murder us as gruesomely as possible, for sport, if they decide we aren't worth anything. Something along those lines."

"They look so disgusting," said Josh. "Did you see their flabby transparent skin? They're like human jellyfish. You can see their veins and bones right through their skin – *yuck*!"

"It's only an *umaya*," said Baz nervously. "It's only an *umaya*."

Teresa was relentless. "You wouldn't be the first to snuff it in *umaya*. Didn't you hear what happened to Raphel? *Umaya* is *umaya*, yes, but they're real dreams and real nightmares – you should have worked that out by now." She changed her tone. "But we'll get out of here, don't worry. This is the slave trade and plantation nightmare, the nightmare about the people who used to work on the plantations as slaves. I've heard so much about it from my grandma that I know all about it."

"Was she a slave?" asked Baz, shocked. "Your grandma?"

Teresa clucked impatiently. "Think, boy! Britain banned that slave business in 1808! She wasn't even born then. Can you two see anything yet?"

Josh could. His eyes were becoming accustomed to the dark, and he peered around. "I'm going to have a look at that keyhole. Baz, can you hear anything?"

Baz crept after Josh up the short flight of stairs, and pressed his ear against the cellar door. "I can't hear a thing. I think they're outside, on the veranda."

"Boozing," sneered Teresa.

Josh started poking at the lock. "Simple mechanism," he muttered. Locks were his hobby, especially old rusty ones like this one. He fumbled around in his pockets. But no, in *umaya* his pockets were empty.

"What are you looking for?"

"A stiff piece of wire or something. Do you have anything on you?"

Teresa pulled a long pin from her dress. With great concentration Josh started fiddling with it in the keyhole. "There – yes. And there – right – *yes*!"

The lock clicked, and slowly the door swung open. Butter-yellow light streamed inside. Josh stood up, dusted off his knees, hoisted on his backpack and motioned to the others. "Come on, let's go!"

"Don't even *think* about it," came a deep, slurred voice.

At the far end of the kitchen stood a blubbery mountain of a man. His skin had the appearance of soft, see-through plastic, with gobs of yellow fat and red muscles underneath. Blue veins throbbed deep inside his neck. He stared at Josh with beady eyes. "Come over here, squirt," he said menacingly, waving his jelly hands.

Josh looked around in panic. There was no way out. The giant went on staring at him intently. Then he turned his head round and called over his shoulder, "Bill! Tom! Come and see what you caught!"

Two other monsters clumped inside. The first one's pale mouth fell open. "Hadn't you noticed, Tom? Is that ... or isn't it?"

Tom shook his head. "Can't you see for yourself, man? It is, it's one of ours." The three giants rolled up to Josh, drooling.

"Don't touch me!" Josh yelled shrilly.

"Now, now," clucked the monsters, patting his shoulder with their flabby hands. "It was just a misunderstanding. We didn't notice. But how come you were walking along the road with two of those blacks? Were you being kidnapped? Come on, little man, everything's turned out all right. Come and have a drink with us. What's your name?"

They went on making comforting noises, prodding him out on to the veranda, where they pushed him down into a rocking chair. Bill went back into the kitchen and locked the cellar door again.

Their rancid, quivering presence made Josh feel sick. He didn't understand why they were being so friendly, and he didn't trust them for a minute. The giants pulled up chairs close to him, belching and farting, and they wanted to know everything about him: his name, whose son he was, what had happened to him. And they made him drink a strange, sour drink, and offered him sausages dripping with fat, and slices of wet liver. He was feeling more and more nauseated. "He's from the north," they finally decided, after he'd convinced them he had set out with his two friends of his own free will. "Those people just don't understand. But those two there" – they stabbed their podgy fingers at the cellar – "will realize that they have broken the first law. Befriending one of ours! The scum."

"I need some fresh air," Josh begged. All he could think of was that he wanted to get away from the fetid stench of his gelatinous hosts. "Would you mind if I went for a walk?"

They stood up, nodding. "You can walk over to the next estate," said Bill, "as far as the Smidders'. But watch out. You have to be back by the time it gets dark, or the brutes will get you again. Those savages come out when it gets dark! And they'll gobble you up, son, mark my words. Joe and I will visit the other estates, to discuss what to do."

They hitched up their beige breeches and tightened their belts, from which hung guns, knives and whips.

Josh stepped down from the porch, breathing a sigh of relief. Now that he was alone he was able to think again. He decided he'd walk a little way – he could see the next mansion in the distance – and then creep back to the house to set Baz and Teresa free. A good, simple plan, he thought. And as if she agreed with him, Zizi appeared out of nowhere and settled on his shoulder.

He walked along the quiet paths, over lawns dotted with large golden trees. Their leaves glowed in the slowly falling dusk. As he strolled through the fragrant gardens, the contours of the bushes and trees became indistinct. It struck him as strange that the landscape here was so beautiful. At any moment he expected to see ladies in ample rustling gowns coming out of the mansions. How could such lovely surroundings harbour such disgusting, evil beings? He imagined he could still smell them, all around. He could hear their voices everywhere: in the distance, behind him, but also near by. From the bushes right and left came snatches of whispered conversation. More distinct voices rose from the home of the Smidders ahead him. They were carrying oil lamps out on to the veranda, and he wandered on in the direction of the yellow light. It looked warm and welcoming in the rapidly cooling autumn nightfall.

"Damn mosquitoes!"

"What did you expect, Garnet? We're in the middle of a swamp here!"

Josh dived behind a bush. Impossible! Had they followed him, then, after all? And were his eyes deceiving him, or was it really Mervin Spratt sitting on the veranda up there, next to an overdressed Garnet? But Sensers weren't supposed to be able to dream-travel – or were they? Josh peered until his eyes hurt. It really was Garnet Gippart and Spratt, but from what he could see in the dancing light of the oil lamps, they looked pale and ill.

"We're all right here. It's far from being a picnic, but as long as I have my pills and my brandy, I can live with it." Spratt was rabbiting on again. Suddenly he slammed his glass down on the table. The cloying tone was gone from his voice. "Garnet. He's here."

"What do you mean? Who? That Cope boy?"

Spratt stood up abruptly. "I can feel it. He's very near."

"Where, in which direction?"

Josh stole backwards. So it was true. Mervin Spratt was an extremely good Senser! But how did he do it? Were Sensers able to Sense dream-travellers? He turned and ran.

"There! Over there, I can see him!"

He heard footsteps behind him. Hurried footsteps, closing in fast. He was desperate, but he just couldn't go any faster. He wasn't swift enough. Any moment now he'd be grabbed by the shoulders. He was tackled from behind, and the next instant Mervin Spratt was sitting on top of him.

"Now I've got you, little twerp." His hands searched him all over, looking for something. "And you're going to explain it to me, down to the very last detail. You damn little pest. But I've got you now – I have it! *Ow-ouch!*"

As Spratt's hands closed around Josh's ankle, the ankle with his snake bracelet, he gave a wavering scream. He shot up in the air, fell flat on his face, and lay still, lifeless.

"Mervin?" Garnet's voice was very close. "Have you got him? What's wrong?"

Whispering. Suddenly Josh found himself surrounded by

dim figures looming up out of the darkness. Strong hands lifted him and carried him off. Garnet's voice sliced forlornly through the night. "Mervin?"

They carried him to a stand of trees, lifted a trapdoor in the ground and lowered him in. Crawling, he followed them into a circular underground chamber. They lit some small oil lamps, and finally he could see who they were. And they, in turn, could have a good look at him. They were a small band of normal-looking, well-built people with healthy, normal skin. Wonderfully ordinary people with real, black skin that wasn't at all transparent. The only thing that worried him a little was that they were backing away from him, staring at him in dismay.

"Have we gone and rescued one of the Inelesi?"

There was grumbling and feet-shuffling. Then a woman leaned over and touched his cheek. She grinned. "My people," she said in a firm voice, "these things happen in the world. He is of the Inelesi, but also of us. Maybe the father is Inelesi, the mother one of us. These things happen. He was being chased by the Inelesi, and that says it all. These things happen."

"Who are you, white-face?" asked an old man. "And why were they after you?"

Josh stammered his name. "The man chasing me is my enemy. His name is Mervin Spratt. He's with Gippart, you know, the trading company." He wasn't sure they understood a word of what he was saying. But they were nodding attentively. "I don't know why he collapsed like that, all of a sudden. He's been after me for a long time."

The people began to laugh and prod each other with their elbows. "He doesn't know why he collapsed!"

"We walloped him on the head, Joshua," the woman explained. "Where are you from?"

"I come from up north," said Josh.

The friendly woman patted him on the back. "Just sit here for a moment." She gave him a beaker of water and left him.

All around him the other people began chattering again, or started cooking, or picked up their books. The Inelesi seemed very far away, in this subterranean refuge. But when suddenly at the far end of the chamber a fierce rustling was heard, everyone jumped, brandishing a stick, a wooden spoon, or a knife. Then they all relaxed again, relieved, smiling. And Josh smiled too when he saw his faithful little parrot winging towards him. Twittering away, Zizi clamped herself to Josh's shoulder with her sharp claws.

"Ai!" laughed the woman, from the kitchen corner. "Do you have a bird for a friend, white-face? That is good, very good. Where are you travelling to, anyway, all the way from the north?"

"To the Tembe," said Josh. "People that live on the border of the darkness, or something. But nobody seems to be able to tell me who they are."

The woman walked up to him and smiled, dumping a large basket of apples on the ground. A few others came and sat down beside her, paring knives in hand. They all began peeling and slicing apples together, convivially seated in a circle. Someone pressed a knife into Josh's hand. Obligingly he joined in. But he almost cut his thumb when the woman continued, "In the north they may not know who the Tembe are, and there's no point asking the Inelesi, of course, but it would be very odd if *we* didn't know who they were."

She chuckled on seeing his expression. "Does that surprise you?"

"But nobody knows – not even the people at Gippart!"

The whole circle laughed. They found his bewilderment quite amusing. "Not everyone knows the same things about life," said the woman gravely. "And I can tell you that we've paid dearly for what we know. For our knowledge of the Tembe and their tragic history, which isn't so very different from our own."

Josh became so excited his mouth went dry. "So you really know them?"

"Of course! Every self-respecting, decent person knows about the Tembe. Maybe there are less decent people than I'd thought, up north."

"But … could you please tell me where they are? Please?"

The woman pursed her lips and went on peeling her apple in silence.

"Oh, come on, sister." A woman with a green headscarf nudged her. "The child is trying to find them. Doesn't that say something about him? Go on, tell him."

"Tell him, do!" the others buzzed.

"Oh, please," implored Josh, as politely as he could. "Please!"

The woman still wouldn't answer. After a while she finally sighed. "As long as you're peeling apples." She nodded. "And seeing as you love birds. All right then." She cleared her throat and spoke a few words in a foreign language. The people beside her murmured something in reply. Then she began to sing, and the others softly joined in. She stopped for a moment to explain. "The stories of the Tembe and of Temberi himself have been handed down by the master storytellers of the desert, the Mabeh of Ixilis; they are also recorded in the Six Books of the Cat. I was taught that ancient song by one of the Mabeh, a nomad. The meaning of the song is: Temberi, the eldest brother, has met his fate; his rapacious younger brother has caused his downfall. That's what the story is about."

As she was talking, Josh had the strangest feeling that this truly was of vital importance to him, this story he was listening to in the bowels of the earth. He listened with the utmost concentration, staring at the woman's grave black face and completely forgetting about peeling his apple.

"Many years ago, two brothers lived at the edge of time, in paradise. Awè, which means 'the first', was named Temberi. His younger brother Kide, which means 'the second', was known as Kide the Cat, and also by another terrible name: Siparti. Temberi loved the birds; he conversed with them all day long, fed them from his store of planting-seed, and built nests for them in the forest where they lived together in harmony. His brother Siparti was a lover of cats. He lived among the hot desert rocks which the felines make their home, slept with them during the burning-hot days and went stalking their prey with them at night. With his companions the cats, he hunted for treasure, diamonds and precious stones, because cats, as you know, are grasping, greedy animals."

The people in the circle murmured their agreement. Josh knitted his brow.

"One day, paradise succumbed to a famine. So the brothers decided to go out into the wide world, and become merchants. Kide, whose name is also Siparti, set out to sell his diamonds, and Temberi sold his songs and moulted feathers. They became rich, saved their people from starvation, and each built a large palace in their own favourite surroundings, where they settled with their extended families."

She stopped a moment, and all the listeners nodded and sighed. When she continued, she first sang again the two verses of the ancient song. Josh was all ears. He was hoping he'd finally understand what the story had to do with him.

"But Kide the Cat, whom they referred to in whispers as Siparti, was not satisfied. He decided he'd make more money if his brother didn't sell his treasures at the same markets, because people were eager to buy from Temberi, who made their hearts glad, rather than from himself. Then Siparti suggested to his brother that they divide the wide world into two. The crafty Siparti told his good-hearted, dreamy brother, 'The world consists of two things, space and time. So let us divide the world along those lines. One of us can claim space as his sales territory, and the other one will have all of history as well as all of the future in which to operate.' Temberi, the singer, the dreamer, walked into the trap with his eyes wide open: he agreed to the plan. Siparti chose space; Temberi chose time."

"What a stupid fool!" Josh blurted out, and the other listeners nodded in agreement.

"Thereafter, Temberi couldn't sell a thing any more. He wandered dreamily through the mountain forests among his birds, dreaming of walking through time, into the future and into the past, but naturally he couldn't sell anything. That scoundrel Siparti returned home from his travels on a few more occasions, each time wealthier, each time more extravagantly dressed, each time with more big cats with diamond collars, earrings and gold-painted tails in his train. But he started returning home more and more infrequently, sharing less and less of his wealth with his brother, who grew poor, and with his clan suffered great hunger, living in a palace that was crumbling bit by bit.

"And still Temberi tried travelling in time. And because of his attempt to do so, the palace eventually slipped right out of the world and time, and that's where the ruins hang now, between heaven and earth, at the end of time. The place from which nobody ever can return. Not even the traitor, that crook Kide the Cat, whom they call, with a shudder, Siparti.

"When Siparti visited Temberi for the last time, he told him, 'Dear brother, I see that you're having difficulties gathering wealth on your travels through time. I cannot help you, since my territory is the world itself – the earth, space and everything contained therein – and so you see I already have my hands full. But my heart bleeds to see you suffer. That is why I want to make you a promise. If on my travels *I* should ever manage to solve the riddle of travel in time, then I'll send you my six clever children, or else my youngest son and daughter – Gip and Kat, the children of my youngest wife – on the others' behalf. They are the ones dearest to me. They will help you escape from your misery.'

"When he had spoken, he turned and left. Temberi never saw him again, neither him nor his children."

She stopped, and again sang the refrain. The circle of listeners hummed along softly.

"Kide, whom they gave the terrible name Siparti, went out into the world and with his six children built an immense trading empire, driving many unfortunate people to their ruin. And that is how the wickedness of greed came into the world. But Awè, the first brother – the saintly Temberi, the sweet, the gentle – has been disappearing from living memory bit by bit. They say that his descendants, the Tembe, are still bitterly waiting for the children of the brother-killer Siparti to arrive. And should Siparti's offspring ever dare come near, riding to the end of time on the back of a winged cat, they'll have to pay dearly for their father's misdeed."

The story was finished, and Josh hastily finished peeling his second apple. He threw the slices into the bowl. This was it then. This was the information they had been seeking. The Tembe did indeed exist!

"There now," said the storyteller. "That's enough, I should think. Thank you, white-face. Did the story make you happy?"

"It did. Thank you very much," said Josh. "But do you have any idea when all that happened, or where they are now?"

She shrugged and picked up the bowl of peeled apple slices. "They're at the end of time. Perhaps the Mabeh of Ixilis will know more. In these parts, unfortunately, we are more familiar with Kide the Cat, with Siparti, than with the saintly Temberi."

"What do you mean?" He followed her to the kitchen corner.

She smiled grimly. "That brother-murderer must have been the ancestor of the Inelesi, those brutes. Beasts, they are, not human. One of Siparti's most notorious sons was called Beast, or Beez. The Inelesi must definitely be descended from him."

Josh suddenly became agitated. Oh heavens, the Inelesi! He'd nearly forgotten all about them, down here. What had they done to Baz and Teresa while he'd been gone? "Madam," he said hastily, "thank you so much for your story, but I must go now – there were three of us, you see, and my friends are still held prisoner! Could you help me free them, please?"

Friendly as she had been at first, she now turned standoffish. Silently she busied herself with pots and pans, pursing her lips.

"Why should *we* set *your* friends free?" she finally asked coldly. "We only saved you because you almost ran into us. Our life is hard enough as it is, and it's very dangerous for us to go anywhere near the Inelesi. What's it to us, anyway, little northerner? None of our business."

Well, that was true. Josh understood all too well. He shrugged. "Then I'll go by myself. I have to rescue them."

"Very well. Where are they being held?"

"In that big house. Not the Smidders', the other one."

"The estate of the Jonoos. We'll show you our tunnel leading to that house. If you are successful in setting them free, you can make your escape by using our tunnel again."

At a signal from the old woman, a younger woman walked up to Josh. She nodded at him and said gravely, "I'll be waiting at the exit."

Josh took heart. "Thank you," he said and bade farewell to the whole assembly. "Thank you for saving me."

They waved and wished him luck as he followed the young woman into a wide tunnel.

The tunnel was brown and warm, with a pleasant earthy smell. The corridor was faintly lit by sparse lamps. Josh mused about the tale he had just heard. "There's an entire underground city of tunnels dug by us," the young woman told him after they had gone some way, "to keep us safe from the Inelesi if we wish to visit friends or family, or our forest, or the beach."

"Is there a tunnel leading all the way to the beach?" asked Josh.

"Yes, so that we can fetch fresh fish. It isn't all that far. And the Inelesi never go there." She glanced at him, wrinkling her nose. "Don't come too close, please. You look a bit strange to me, white-face. And I don't like the way you smell."

Insulted, Josh followed her at a distance until she stopped short. "There, we're at the end of the tunnel. You're in the Inelesi's grounds here. This is as far as I'll go, because it's more dangerous for me here than it is for you. I don't think they'd kill a white-face like you."

Josh climbed up the wooden steps at the far end of the tunnel. Night had fallen, and a balmy breeze ruffled his hair. Overhead amazingly bright stars shimmered in a velvety black sky. He crept over the lawn, past a bush with late-blooming roses that suddenly overwhelmed his senses with their heady scent. But then something else caught his attention: out of the corner of his eye he noticed something move. He strained his eyes in the dark, and listened closely. Then he was sure: he could hear voices. Lots of voices, rapidly coming nearer. The thundering sound of a loud report, as if from a shotgun, made him jump. He dropped to the ground and lay frozen on his stomach in the wet grass. He heard shouts, roaring. Shadows were approaching, wavering in the torchlight. The mob was close to the house now. Lights were already entering the garden. He was shaking so much, he could hardly make himself move. He crawled in the direction of the house, not even sure if he was moving away from the mob or towards it. But he completely lost his bearings when suddenly he saw figures rear up right in front of him. With a cry he leapt to his feet. Whoever they were jumped back. One of them tripped and fell, and the other one cried, "Let's get out of here, come on!"

It was only then that Josh realized who it was. "Baz! Bazzer! Teresa!"

"Josh! What are *you* doing here!"

"Quiet!"

They froze, pricking up their ears, their hearts in their mouths.

"Did any of you *hear* that?" asked a voice rising from the mob behind them.

The three children grabbed each other's hands and began stealing away as quietly as they could from the ominous hum of voices.

"I'm telling you he's around here somewhere," a voice whined over the noise.

Josh would have known that voice anywhere. His relentless enemy. He gave Baz's and Teresa's hands a squeeze, dragging them along even faster, back in the direction of the rose bush.

"We can't see a thing, Merv," gurgled one of the Inelesi. "Why on earth would he try to return to the house?"

A general muttering seconded the question.

"How many times do I have to tell you! To free his little friends and set fire to your house! Don't you know what that scum from up north are like?"

Josh tried to gauge the distance to the rose bush. The tunnel entrance was just behind it. Only a short sprint, and they'd be safe. "Follow me," he whispered to the others.

He raced ahead of his companions to the rose bush. Loud shouts. He'd been spotted! Never mind, just two more strides – they were at the entrance to the tunnel. But then his relief changed to incredulity … and panic. The tunnel was shut. They couldn't get in. He dithered for a moment like a horror-stricken rabbit. Then he did the only thing that was left to do: bolt. They were off like a shot, Teresa and Baz right behind him. They ran as fast as they could. They leapt, they flew. Behind them the night exploded in yelling, thudding feet and lights. The Inelesi roared bloody murder. It seemed as if from all sides more of them came running to join in the fray, and the world thundered and blazed at their backs. The Associates jumped through the undergrowth, sloshed through a sopping wet field and waded laboriously through flooded terrain, tripping over tangled roots.

"They've reached the swamp!"

The brutes were closing in. Somehow the creatures seemed able to move more easily in the shallow water than they could. Josh's heart hammered in his ribcage. Breathlessly they stumbled among tall trees anchored in the water by their gnarled aerial roots, the monsters splashing behind them. But they were no longer drawing closer. The splashing and squelching sounds grew faint. Were they staying back? They heard their pursuers jeering in the distance. One of them shouted, "So long, filthy northerners! Here come the alligators! Have a good time!"

They could hear Mervin's shouts of protest, with only repulsive laughter and belches in reply.

They stood still, panting, knee-deep in the oily water.

"Are there alligators here?" asked Baz.

"Very probably," said Teresa, glancing around fitfully. "But they haven't got us yet. Josh, where do we go now? Have you any suggestions?"

"Well, there were these people that helped me, but then they left me high and dry – they barred the tunnel. It was our only hope of escape."

He took out his compass and twisted it so that its light beam flashed on for no more than half a second, and then he switched it off again. "But they told me the seashore is near by. The Inelesi never go there. Come on, we're going south."

Meanwhile, Baz had tugged free three long, stout branches. He quickly sharpened them to a point with his penknife, and handed one each to Josh and Teresa. "Spears," he said.

Armed with their spears, they splashed on, clambering with difficulty over the aerial roots of the mangroves, tripping over vines, slipping in the mud. For a while they made good progress. Until…

"Shhh," said Baz, "I can hear something."

They stood still in the water. It was true: behind them, very stealthily, came a soft splashing.

"Alligators," breathed Teresa. "Get ready!"

They stood shoulder to shoulder, spears pointing. The water surged and swelled. An indistinct form suddenly loomed before them. They caught their breath. There were two of them, approaching slowly: enormous, shapeless things surfacing out of the water.

"Hippopotamuses," hissed Baz.

But their gaping mouths revealed rows of razor-sharp alligator teeth. Josh, staring petrified at the teeth, had no idea if what he was looking at were hippos, alligators, or some other kind of water-fiend. All he knew was that these unwieldy beasts were just as jelly-like and transparent as the Inelesi; and that they were hungry. He felt Teresa stiffen beside him.

"It *is* them, the Inelesi," she mouthed. "They've turned themselves into alligators."

"Beasts," Josh whispered hoarsely. "They're animals, not humans."

And then it happened: the brutes went on the attack. They knocked down Josh and Teresa, who tried helplessly to level their spears at them. Baz danced around them, screaming and jabbing his spear into the wobbly blobs. Josh, half submerged, half buried under a suffocating weight, fought for air, trying desperately to push the great toothed mouth away from him, thrusting his spear blindly into the air, into the water. Then he felt razor-sharp teeth fastening themselves on his left arm. He screamed. He struggled blindly to escape, but he was pinioned. He was swallowing alternately mouthfuls of water and mouthfuls of air. Then he saw red. A raging fury overtook him. Firmly he grasped the spear he was holding in his free right hand. Clenching his teeth, he aimed and, with a yell, thrust the spear with all the power of his rage. The spear slithered easily through the spongy flesh, but when it finally met resistance deep within, the beast suddenly gave a deafening roar. Bellowing, it reared up on its hind legs, its mouth yawning wide open.

Josh's arm was freed. He scrambled backwards in the water as fast as he could, slipping and sliding in the mud, *quickly, quickly*! The beast collapsed into the muck, thrashing about helplessly. Josh felt a tree root behind him and pulled himself up on it. He clung there for a while, panting. His left arm was throbbing with pain, but he couldn't see to that now, because right in front of him a ferocious water fight was still in full flow. In the gloom it was hard for him to make out what was happening, but suddenly there was another roar, and a triumphant victory cry. The huge pale bulk of the monster crashed into the water, bellowing, setting free two figures that splashed towards Josh.

"Good for Teresa, good for Teresa!" Baz cheered deliriously. "She really walloped him! We got him, we got him!" He bounded up to Josh. "Did you get yours too?"

Josh nodded, unable to speak.

"Wow!" Baz shouted. "I'd never have thought it of you! Terrific, Josh, good going!"

"Quick!" cried Teresa. "Let's get away from here, before more of them arrive. Josh, are you OK?"

"Yes," he replied in a shaky voice that didn't sound at all OK.

As they stumbled forward Josh's arm began to throb more and more. It felt as if it had swollen to ten times its size. He sloshed blindly after Baz and Teresa. From time to time he tried to listen for noises behind him. Was that an ominous splash, or was it just the wind? Was he hearing the ordinary sounds you'd expect to hear in a swamp, or should they make a run for it? But the woman in the tunnel had been right: the beach wasn't far away. They only had to make their way through the shallows a bit further, then they were clambering up solid banks. They forged ahead through low shrubs and tall grasses in the direction of a new noise: the relentless pounding of the waves. They discovered a narrow sandy path that led up to hilly scrubland. In silence they plodded on, Teresa in front, then Baz and, bringing up the rear, Josh. He was exhausted, and the pain in his arm made him feel sick. "To the sea," he kept muttering to himself, "keep going, to the sea – we're very close – to the sea, to the sea..."

They climbed the last slope, and suddenly there they were. Panting, they stood and stared. Before them stretched the endless, shimmering sea. There was nothing but a strip of grass and a narrow band of sand between them and the water. White gulls skimmed along the water's edge. Zizi flew off Josh's shoulder, darting towards the other birds. They walked slowly towards the remains of a bonfire on the beach. Josh dragged himself there behind the others, then sank to the sand, spent.

"Are you all right?" asked Teresa.

"My arm." Josh pointed at it, grimacing. He hardly dared look at it.

Teresa frowned and examined his arm with a look of concern. "There are lots of deep puncture wounds," she said worriedly, "on either side of your arm. You're bleeding a lot. But I don't think it's broken. Just bruised, I think."

By some miracle, all three of them still had their Gippart backpacks with them. And fortunately, Teresa's contained a first-aid kit. She dabbed Josh's wounds with stinging antiseptic, and then wrapped several metres of bandage around his arm, to dress it. While she did this, she told him how Baz and she had managed to escape. It had been easy. "They're disgusting brutes, those Inelesi, but as thick as planks," she said. "One of them came back to have another look at us – at least that's what the scumbag said – and then some visitors arrived and they forgot to lock the door again!"

The burning pain in Josh's arm eased slightly, and he began to feel a little better. Now it was his turn to tell them about how he had been saved, and about the tunnel people.

"Well, actually I do understand why they closed their tunnel to us," Teresa mused. "If we had run in there with the

Inelesi hot on our heels, we'd have betrayed their secret, wouldn't we?"

"Right," said Josh, ashamed that he hadn't thought of it. But he did have something to be proud of: he had unearthed vital information about the Tembe. He reported as accurately as he could what the woman had told him about Temberi and his greedy brother, Kide the Cat, whom they called Siparti. Teresa and Baz grew excited on hearing his story. They showered him with compliments and bombarded him with questions.

"Siparti," said Baz. "Hmm, I've heard that name before. What was it again? Something nasty."

"The curse," said Teresa quietly. "The Gippart clan is jinxed by the curse of Siparti."

"But how? It was the Tembe who were jinxed by the curse of Siparti, weren't they? Because Kide the Cat – in other words Siparti – ousted *them*. But what's it got to do with Gippart?"

"I haven't the foggiest idea, Josh," said Teresa. "Maybe we'll learn more on our next dream-walk. But it doesn't look good. The Tembe out for revenge! The end of time!"

Baz glanced at his watch. "That's more or less where we are now, actually, the end of time. I don't know exactly what the time is, but we've been in this *umaya* for hours and hours, and I'll bet we're terribly late."

"We're really in trouble now," Teresa grumbled. "We've broken heaps of rules. They'll put the curse of Gippart on us, just you wait and see. They'll be out for revenge!"

"But let's not forget all the things we found out," pointed out Josh. "We didn't do too badly, did we?"

"Hmm," said Teresa.

They curled up on the sand, and closed their burning eyes.

Alas, Josh's expectations were much too rosy. Their welcome at Gippart wasn't exactly positive. As they staggered into a Reception area, worn out and filthy, their three bosses were in the hall waiting for them, seething with fury – Max, Moussa and Garnet. Moussa was punching his knuckles into his fist as if he had to keep himself from beating them to a pulp right then and there.

"I'll kill you!" Moussa fumed. "I swear, I'm going to kill you! What the hell were you thinking of! I'm going to beat the living daylights out of you!" He was so incensed, he couldn't go on.

Garnet Gippart put her oar in. "If it were up to me, we'd lock you up right now in the top-security unit. You have saddled Gippart with incredible problems. The employment inspectors have already phoned twice."

Moussa couldn't contain himself. He barked, "Never has any one of my Associates—"

But Max came between them. Even he was white with rage. "You are two hours late. Two hours! And what's even more reprehensible, you left an hour early, without authorization! Without your team-mate and leader, Garnet Gippart! And I don't know how you did it, but you even managed to injure the search party sent out to rescue you so severely that, as we speak, Mervin Spratt is lying in hospital with concussion! On top of that, you exposed three other Associates to harm by jumping through their gate as they were coming in. One of them slipped back into *umaya* and couldn't get home for hours." He raged on. "You have been absolutely irresponsible. This is dangerous work. We entrusted you with a special mission, and you go and behave like a bunch of total idiots! I wouldn't even trust you to go to the grocer's by yourselves!" He was ranting the way Mo sometimes did when Josh came home late. It suddenly occurred to Josh that Max had been beside himself with worry.

Garnet started again. She rushed at Josh and viciously pinched his ear. "And if you think that you can go on playing your little games with us, you pea-brained truant, if you continue refusing to co-operate…"

Max pulled Garnet back, but Josh had had enough. "You

can all go to hell with your poxy *umayas* and your stupid old time!" he yelled. "That's it. I've had enough, you idiots!" He hurled his backpack at Garnet's feet and ran down the hall. Blinded by hot tears, he stumbled his way through the building until he reached the deserted Committee Room, where he swiftly changed his clothes before rushing out again, all the while seething to himself. *"That's it! That's it!"*

His reception at home was, by comparison, tolerable. Mo was hopping mad about his coming home from his Scout meeting over two hours late, but was so shocked at the state of him that she immediately fussed over him and was full of sympathy. She put him under the shower, dried him with her own two hands and then drove him to the hospital, just to be sure.

"I'm not going back to the Scouts," Josh told her in the waiting room, and Mo nodded.

"If this is the state you're going to be in when you come home, I think it's best if you stopped going too."

The doctor on duty didn't believe his story about a Rottweiler mauling him; his wounds were nevertheless thoroughly cleaned, stitched up and dressed.

That Sunday night he awoke from a long-drawn-out, haunting dream. He stared for a while at the street light shining into his room, and then he got out of bed. He went downstairs. There was still a light on in the living room. Mo was lying on the sofa, reading two books at the same time and chewing a pen.

"Mo?"

"Hello, sweetheart. Aren't you asleep yet? It's past eleven thirty, dear."

He sat down next to her. She put the books on the floor, took off her reading glasses and gave him her cup of tea. She gazed at him a while without saying anything, until he started to talk.

"Mum, when I was born, you know…"

"Hmm." She didn't look surprised, didn't move.

"There was another baby as well, wasn't there?"

She nodded. "Your twin sister."

He fumbled for words. "Was she already dead when I was born? Which of us was born first? And was she alive when she was born?"

Mo rubbed her face. "Oh, my dear boy. You were born first, and I think she must have been still alive at that point. But she never took a breath. She never lived on her own. She only lived until the time when you swam into the world."

Josh stared into the lamp. "Didn't you have a special name for her?"

"Oh yes, we did," sighed Mo, "and I still feel bad about it. It was so silly. When you two were in my belly we made up a silly name for her; she never had a proper name. Well, she did, a rushed name. But it wasn't the right name for her. Jenny."

"But what did you call her then – the silly name?"

He already knew the answer. Mo had told him a long time ago. They hadn't spoken about it for seven years, but he still remembered.

"Your name was Joshua, that we already knew long before you were born. And when we heard we were having twins, we came up with the other name. Jericho. Joshua and Jericho, we told each other. Because in the Bible, Joshua overthrew the town of Jericho. We thought the two names sounded good together. But it wasn't a very nice name for a baby."

It had never occurred to Josh that it wasn't a nice name. The name of a city that was destroyed.

"Joshua's people blew on their trumpets," he said, *"and the seventh time, the walls of Jericho came tumbling down."*

"That's right," said Mo. "And Jericho never lived."

Josh began scratching his head. "Did you bury her?"

"She was cremated. For a while we celebrated her birthday, which was also the anniversary of her death, but then we stopped."

"Why? That was mean of you!"

"Because it was also your birthday, sweetheart. Don't you see?"

He nodded.

"You know," said Mo, "one in twelve of us starts out as a twin. It's quite common in fact. But when only one of the twins survives, it's so terribly sad. Oh, my poor Joshie."

Josh gulped. "I dreamt about her."

Mo looked up, smiling. "Really? Oh, that makes me happy. What did she look like?"

"I don't really know. She had long hair."

"Was she … happy? Was she…"

"I don't know. I don't think I could really tell."

"But she wasn't… Did she make you feel frightened?"

Josh shook his head slowly. "No. Not really. Maybe she was a little angry, but … she had friends. She sounded, well … normal."

He stood up awkwardly. Mo got to her feet as well, and held him gently by the shoulders. Then she gave him a wet, salty kiss. They remained like that for a few seconds, not saying anything. Then Josh shyly disentangled himself, and made his way back to his room.

Only when he woke up the next morning with a sinking feeling in his stomach did he work out what else was wrong. His brave little Zizi hadn't come home with him. She had stayed behind, in *umaya.*

7
A Chink in Time

The first one to come and see him was Teresa. Josh was going to the door to open it, but when he saw Teresa through the window he turned round and went back into the living room. He sat down on the sofa, turned on the TV and began flicking through the channels.

"Josh, open the door! Are you deaf? Someone's ringing the bell!" Edwin, annoyed, steamed past him into the hall, holding a tea towel. Teresa walked in. Edwin, slipping behind her to the kitchen, gave Josh a funny look. Josh kept his eyes sullenly on the TV.

"Hi," said Teresa. Today she was wearing a green hat. She kept her hands in the pockets of her green leather jacket and stood there wobbling on ridiculously high platform-soled gold trainers.

"Hi," said Josh. They both watched *Looney Tunes* for a while without exchanging a word.

"Aren't you going to Gippart any more then?" asked Teresa, staring at Daffy Duck. Josh shook his head.

"That's just silly."

"Let's go to my room," Josh sighed.

Once there, he flopped down on his bed.

Teresa squatted on the floor. "If you're not going any more, I'll have to leave too."

Josh bit his lower lip.

"I need the money," said Teresa. "I want to work there another two years, till I'm sixteen. Then I'll have earned enough to pay for college for my sister Louisa and me."

Josh took his broken Game Boy from the chest next to his bed and started fiddling with it.

Teresa waited. Then she said, "Between the three of us, we can keep Garnet and Spratt in their place. And now that we've got Baz's rhythm-trick, we can zoom through *umaya* so fast, your ghosts won't be able to catch you ever again."

Josh remained silent.

Teresa stood up. Shrugged. "Right then. Bye," she said and marched out of the room. The front door slammed with a loud bang.

The second one to come and speak to him was Baz. Josh had been avoiding him, which wasn't easy because they were in the same class at school. But Baz had kept his distance too. Until Thursday afternoon, when Josh was walking home in the rain and Baz came and walked by his side.

"Aren't you going?" asked Baz quietly.

Josh shook his head silently.

"Then I can't go any more either," said Baz. He sighed. "I was really hoping to try and see how quickly we could time-hop, using my rhythm-trick."

Josh shrugged. "I'm not going, and that's that."

"Max said Garnet was carpeted by the top brass. She's been warned not to try any funny business with us any more."

"So what?" said Josh, stamping his foot in a puddle.

Baz jumped from puddle to puddle beside him, humming under his breath. "I thought it was terrific," he said suddenly. "Remember that baby panther that licked my blood? And those big panthers that let us ride on their backs?"

Josh smiled. "And that hop-flight engine."

"Or the way we taught those alligators a lesson – *yes*!"

"I'm not going," Josh repeated.

They walked on in the pouring rain.

"If you ask me, those *umayas* are all chock-full of nightmares and terror," said Baz.

Josh nodded, and then said something he'd been mulling over in his mind for some time. "You know, the funny thing is, in a way, I myself belonged on the side of the nightmares in that last *umaya*. At first those people in the tunnel thought that I was one of those horrid brutes."

Baz licked the rain off his lips. "As long as you *know* it's only a nightmare, it isn't so bad."

"Well, you seemed pretty terrified."

"So did you."

"I'm still not going," said Josh.

The phone rang incessantly all night long, and Josh had to bury his head under his pillow. When he was on the bus he'd jump every time a mobile phone rang. He kept expecting someone to hand him a phone: "Max Herbert. For you."

In the street he kept thinking he saw Mervin Spratt, and he'd have to duck into a doorway. Mo stroked his head. "Did that Rottweiler business give you nasty dreams, love?"

But the third one to ask him to go back was his parrot, Dara. He sat hunched forlornly in his cage. Josh went and sat down beside him, tickling him through the bars of the cage. "Are you *that* lonely?"

Dara glared at him.

"Yes, but it isn't my fault, old boy. Zizi chose to stay there. It was *her* choice."

Dara turned his back on him.

"She's with the other birds, by the sea, and she's very happy. She's free; she can fly wherever she likes."

Dara drooped, hunching his wings. Tears filled Josh's eyes. He sat by the cage a long time, his stomach churning and his head pounding, all the while stroking Dara, who maintained a reproachful posture. Finally he made up his mind and went to the telephone.

"Hello, Baz?"

"Josh?"

"When's the next *imayada*? Is it this Saturday, or next week?"

"Huh?"

"I'm going in again, to fetch Zizi. Is it this week?"

Baz squealed and cheered and whooped with joy. They made a date to present themselves at Gippart at the appointed time, with Teresa. Mo frowned when she heard about it, but Josh assured her that this was the very last time he was going to Scouts, that they were only going canoeing on the lake, and that he had to go because it was a farewell party for him. He could lie through his teeth when he had to.

They presented themselves on Saturday October the twenty-first at 1.30 p.m. at the door of the Dispatch Board room, and were ushered in, only to come face to face with the full Board. They received an official reprimand and a fine (to be deducted from their next month's pay). Garnet Gippart took great pleasure in slowly and distinctly reading out the judgement. But once that was done, everyone relaxed again. Garnet shook hands with them. "From now on we'll have a perfectly agreeable working relationship," she told them, poker-faced.

Relieved, they walked to the Junior Committee Room. But that was tougher. Moussa didn't behave very professionally. Sprawled on a bench, engrossed in a game of chess with another Associate, he drawled nastily, "Well, well, look what the cat's dragged in!" Then he sent the chessboard flying and pounced on them.

"First, I won't accept any violation of the rules. I demand absolute obedience and complete respect. Second, I need a full report from you about your idiotic shenanigans on the last trip. And I mean now."

"We have to be at the gate in fifteen minutes," said Teresa.

"Now!" yelled Moussa. He waved them over to the bench and sat down next to them. He seemed to be simmering down slightly. "Listen to me, kids. I don't think you have the faintest idea how much trouble you're in. The only way I can save you is for you to do just as I say. What went on, exactly, on that last utter balls-up of a trip?" He was staring at Josh.

Josh had to think quickly. His plan was to leave *umaya* and go home as soon as he'd found Zizi. Maybe Moussa could help.

"Mervin Spratt," he said. "Garnet and Spratt were in the *umaya* of the Inelesi."

"Whoa, hang on, idiot! Who or what are the Inelesi? Oh, never mind that. Just go on."

"They seemed to be in league with them," said Josh. "They tried to hunt us down."

"Go on."

"Well, Spratt caught me, and now I finally know what he wants from me."

The other three gasped. "You know?" Moussa grabbed him by the collar. "Out with it then!"

"Well, I know *what* he wants, but I don't know *why* he wants it."

"Birdbrain! Tell us what it is!" shouted Moussa, shaking him.

"Let me go!" cried Josh. He pulled up the leg of his jeans. "This is what he wants. My snake bracelet."

They gazed at the shiny gold bracelet on his ankle. Baz whistled. Moussa narrowed his eyes. "Where d'you get that?"

"Um, well…"

Moussa closed his eyes and sighed. "Hell. Now on top of everything I've got an Associate who's a thief." He opened his eyes and stared at Josh. "Did you steal it here, at Gippart? Or when you were in *umaya*, is that it?"

"No!" cried Josh. "I'm not a thief, I don't really rob people – just this..."

"Just this, just this," growled Moussa. "All right, but then tell us what it's all about. What's so special about that thing!"

"I don't know. But Spratt was after it. I think he went through my pockets during the Traders' Trial, but he didn't find it that time. So he pinched my other things."

"I know what it's about," said Baz.

They all turned and stared at him in surprise.

"I have Sense," Baz explained to Moussa, blushing. "Some Sense, I mean. I can tell that that snake bracelet doesn't belong in our time."

"What do you mean?" asked Teresa. "Does it belong in *umaya*?"

"That's the funny thing. It doesn't belong in *umaya* either." He tried to explain. "Everything that's from a certain time-period has a similar rhythm. But this bracelet has a rhythm of time past. It isn't any *umaya* rhythm, as far as I can tell. I'm beginning to get the rhythms of *umaya*, and I know what real time sounds like too. I think that this bracelet is from the past – it's three hundred, maybe three hundred and fifty, years old."

"You mean," Moussa pressed him, "that this bracelet just somehow made its way – *wham!* – from the actual past into the present time?"

Baz nodded. "It's as if Josh had zipped back three hundred years, and brought this bracelet back with him."

"But I didn't!"

"Aha," said Moussa. "Good work, Baz. Now I get it, stupid. Now I see why all of Gippart is after you."

"But I didn't," Josh said again.

"That's your problem," sighed Moussa. "It turns out you're able to time-travel, but you don't know how you did it. If only you could show them how you did it, Gippart would stop bothering you. Now they'd cut you up into little pieces before they'd leave you alone. Huh! Star turn!"

In the distance a gong sounded. Teresa jumped to her feet. "It's two o'clock, we've *got* to go to the gate!"

Moussa held them back. "Leave that snake bracelet here, Joshie. Give it to Moussa."

Josh refused. He didn't know why exactly, but he wouldn't have left the bracelet behind for all the gold in the world. He raced off, calling airily, "I'll leave it at the gate!"

He didn't think Moussa would believe him, but Moussa didn't come after him. They dashed to the gates, first on foot, then on motorbikes. Most of the Associates had already left. Max was waiting impatiently for them. Garnet was leaning against one of the gates, bored.

"It's just too bad that you young people have no concept of time," Max grumbled. "Please try to consult your watches more often."

"My watch tells the wrong time in *umaya*," said Baz as they hastily changed their clothes.

"Of course it does," said Max. "But you can still tell if you've been gone one hour or three hours." He looked on, shaking his head, as they prepared themselves for the journey. Josh pulled a fistful of keys, metal hooks and picklocks out of his pocket and dropped them into his backpack. Ever since being locked up by the Inelesi, he'd been determined to be better prepared the next time. Baz frowned at his watch, hesitating for a moment, then put it inside his backpack.

"Do please try and follow the rules today," Max was saying earnestly. "And listen to Garnet Gippart. You are still so young. It won't kill you to take orders from an adult for once, now will it?"

They nodded meekly.

"Joshua, what with all the confusion, we haven't had a report from you on your last sortie yet. We'll expect two from you next time. Well, boys and girls, all the best of luck then. Don't do anything foolish. And come back on time. Or with time to spare, if you prefer. Good luck!" He patted them on the back and pushed them through to the gate.

As Josh read out the co-ordinates, Garnet kept a watchful eye on him. Taking Teresa's hand, she positioned herself behind the two boys.

"We're going to do it to the rhythm," Baz hissed in Josh's ear. "I'll whisper it in your ear, OK?"

Josh nodded. He pushed the door open a crack.

They jumped swiftly and without any problem. On their final, perfect somersault, like a three hundred and sixty degree loop on a roller coaster, Josh heard excited voices in the distance saying: "There he is! Grab him! There he goes!"

But no one caught him. They landed with a thud in the sand, shoulder to shoulder, and to their surprise found themselves on exactly the same beach where they had gone to sleep two weeks earlier. It was almost exactly the same place – they recognized it from the remains of a bonfire scattered around.

"Everything OK?" asked Baz.

"Yes. You?"

They sniffed the air, tasted the salt on their lips, glanced at the sun, and looked around the beach. A cloud of gulls swarmed over a sandbank. To Josh's disappointment, no green bird detached itself from the flock to flap eagerly towards him.

"Everything's the same," said Baz. "Only the tempo is a little faster. It's quite upbeat, actually. Sort of higher, with a tremolo."

"I think the sun looks a bit more orange," Josh observed.

And their clothes were different too – a definite improvement on what they were wearing before. They inspected themselves: loose, long black trousers; white shirts tied with a floppy dark red bow; woollen winter jackets with shiny buttons, elegantly trimmed in red fur; and striking wide-brimmed black hats. As they took their time looking around, they discovered for the first time what it looked like when someone appeared in *umaya*. There was a flash, a mirage-like shimmer, and then suddenly two solid bodies landed out of nowhere.

"Wow!"

It was Garnet and Teresa. Teresa quickly scrambled to her feet. "Hello, boys, where are we? What's it like here?"

Garnet stayed put in the sand where she'd landed, rubbing her head and looking peevish. She didn't deign to look at them. The young dream-travellers, standing at the water's edge, scanned the horizon. Josh took out one of the bird calls and made all kinds of quacking and tweeting sounds with it, but with no luck. No Zizi.

"I just want to find Zizi," Josh told the others softly. "And then we're going back."

"But she doesn't seem to be here," said Teresa.

"Then we'll have to go and look for her a bit further on," said Josh reluctantly.

"I suppose we'll have to," agreed Baz.

"We might as well start off in the direction of the Tembe," Teresa suggested. "They're supposed to be fond of birds, aren't they?"

At that point Josh decided to open his map.

"The people in the desert must know where the Tembe are. The Mabeh."

"Then let's go to the desert," said Teresa. "It's on the other side of those mountains, along the coast. We'll have to follow the coast south until we reach the mountains, and then we'll have to cross them."

"But that, over there, is a swamp," Baz pointed out. "If we keep to the coast we'll have to wade through a swamp for at least – uh – sixty miles. And I'm not doing that, I'm telling you now."

"We'll have to cross a couple of very wide rivers as well," added Teresa. "Is there no other way we can go?"

"We could go inland, but we'll still have those rivers to deal with," said Josh.

They pored over the map. Garnet had come up behind them.

"Ah," said Josh. "But if we went to this island, here, just off the mainland – Trellis – we'll only have to go a short way. We can cut off that whole triangle with that short cut."

All three smiled. Cracked it!

"But where will we get a boat?" asked Teresa.

"Well, there's a port over here, called Damara," said Josh. "There must be a ferry, or a boat we can hire. It can't be more than a mile or so to the island."

He studied the map again. "The island is part of an archipelago, the Skirides – the bird islands. That's what it says." He squinted as he read the name of a small slip of land near the largest of the islands.

"Then that might be where Zizi is," Baz suggested.

"Yes."

They took off their soft leather shoes and walked eastwards in the lukewarm water. Garnet, puffing a cigarette, trailed behind with a face like a sour lemon. Teresa bent down to pick up seashells. "Look at this one," she said, showing them a beautiful gleaming pink coiled snail-shell, and, a little later, a black and gold striped scallop. "I think this is a pretty good *umaya*."

Her clothes, too, were comfortable; although she had to wear a long skirt with a tunic over it, it was easy to run in, and was not cumbersome. Garnet was wearing a much heavier brown dress, with a flurry of white pleats at her throat.

It was a sunny world, cheerful and vibrant. They could tell by the orange and blue birds doing somersaults in the sky, and from the billowing bright white and red sails of the ships sailing past, their colourful flags fluttering in the wind. They could tell by the fishermen who greeted them enthusiastically as they hauled their shiny painted boats up on to the beach. They could tell by the fluttery feeling in their stomachs.

They hadn't been able to pinpoint their exact position on the coast, but after less than an hour's walk they arrived at the port of Damara. There they suddenly found themselves in the midst of frenetic, bustling activity. Fish merchants were selling delicious fried fish, a woman on the beach served raw oysters to richly dressed passers-by, and children were roasting potatoes in the embers of a bonfire. They walked on, their mouths watering, put on their shoes again and climbed the steps to the quayside, where they followed a gravel path to the harbour. The sights were dazzling, the sounds deafening: gulls screeching raucously, ropes and flags flapping and fluttering everywhere. Carts rattled over the cobblestones, porters staggered beneath enormous loads, muscular fellows pushing wheelbarrows shouted at them to move out of their way. The stench of rotting fish, urine and sea water mingled with the smells of tobacco, roasted chestnuts, beer, tar, paint and wood smoke. They slipped on wet rubbish and tripped over ropes and crates. There was colour everywhere: this was definitely a colourful dream. All the boats had been painted dazzling hues, often in a combination of three colours or more. Dozens of these were moored gunwale to gunwale in the harbour, their tall masts proudly pointing to the sky.

This must be a typical seventeenth-century dream, thought Josh, the age of exploration, of greed for gold and sea salt, the age of scurvy and colonization. He thought he could make out ships from all parts of the world. *Those long, open ships must be from the south, and so are those tubby boats of woven reeds. And those big fat ones come from the north.* Whether or not he was right, he saw mariners from all corners of the world swaggering by. Half-naked sailors marched, saluting, past sea captains in gold-embroidered purple uniforms, and an old seaman with an anchor tattoo sat tippling in the company of a female in jacket and hose, who was armed to the teeth. An enormous three-master was moored at the mouth of the harbour. It was being loaded by bare-chested sailors, who were rolling barrels aboard. They were telling jokes, shouting to be heard over the din. A black cat streaked up the ship's gangplank, dodging the barrels. The Associates looked on, captivated.

"Come on," Josh sighed finally. "Let's find ourselves a boat!"

They turned round and walked along the jetties of the inner harbour. "Do you know anyone who could take us to the island?" Josh asked a sailor.

The man looked up from the rudder he was repairing. "To Firin?"

"No, we need to get to Trellis. The big island."

"Have you lost your mind? Never!"

Taken aback, they walked on.

A little further on, three sailors were eating fish. "Trellis? You've already had enough of life then, even at your age?"

"But what's wrong with it?" asked Josh.

The sailors snorted and spat into the water. "Most dangerous place on earth, and the kid asks us what's wrong with it! How about if I told you there are volcanoes? Don't you remember the earthquakes last month?"

"But we've got to go there, no matter what," said Josh. "Is there anyone who sails there?"

The oldest sailor growled "Well, none of my business, I s'pose. Brand goes to Firin, on occasion. Once you get to Firin, you might even find some crazy fool prepared to make the crossing to Trellis. Brand is the skipper of the *Conchita.* It's the last tub on this jetty."

Captain Brand was leaning against the mast of his small yellow fishing boat, sawing away at a fiddle. On his shoulder sat a blue parrot – the sight of it pierced Josh to the heart. They hailed him and asked politely if he would take them across to Firin. He was willing, no problem. "Ten coppers a head," he said, putting away his fiddle. "Do you know how to sail a boat?"

They shook their heads; only Teresa's eyes lit up. "I've done it before. You know, the foresail and jib."

"Well, well," laughed the skipper, scratching his head of carroty curls. "And your mother? Does she want to come too?"

Suppressing giggles, they turned to Garnet, who was fuming.

"I'm not their mother," she said. "Thank God. How long is this little jaunt going to take?"

"Oh, missus," said Brand, looking her over from head to toe, "motherhood is the most beautiful thing there is, ain't it! And I wouldn't mind going seafaring for a week or two with you."

"Oh, don't talk rot," snapped Garnet. "How long?"

"About two or three hours, me darlin'," said Brand, bestirring himself to get his boat ready.

"That's too long," Garnet said shrilly. "Come on, kids!"

"No," said Josh, who was really looking forward to the trip. "We *have* to go there. Besides, time goes more quickly here, doesn't it, Baz?"

"Oh, just let them come with me, me darlin'. They want to so badly," said Brand. "Give me a hand there, boys, and you, little fo's'lmiss, help me hoist that sail."

As Garnet whispered into her mobile phone with her back turned to them, they helped to ready the boat.

"Ahoy, Twinkle-eyes, cast off the bowline there!" Brand finally shouted at Josh, who cast the rope off the mooring ring on the jetty.

"My name's Joshua!"

"Who cares?" Brand roared. "For heaven's sake, help your auntie on board, quick!"

In the very nick of time, Garnet managed to jump aboard the boat that was already bobbing away, and they were off – first by rowing and punting, until they were out of the harbour. They felt the boat shiver when the mainsail suddenly caught the wind, and then off she went, sailing before the wind.

"Keep it taut, keep it taut, fo's'lmiss!" Brand yelled at Teresa from behind the tiller. "Hit the deck, Twinkle-eyes! Head down, Jumping-bean!" This last warning was to Baz.

It was a rough trip: the waves were enormous, and the spray splashed around their ears. Garnet sat hunched up near the skipper, who kept up his non-stop chatter as if she hadn't turned her back on him. "Isn't this delightful, me darlin'? To go boating with the handsomest man in all Damara and your nephews and niece. What a lovely outing on your day off, ain't it!"

A big wave broke right over their heads, and Garnet didn't look as if it was at all delightful. The three Associates, on the other hand, were in heaven. They would have liked to sail to the end of the world, with the wind at their backs, in this proud, shuddering, bucking vessel. Brand distributed ship's biscuits and rum. The rum burned their throats and made them choke, but they valiantly took big gulps from the jug and after that, they couldn't stop laughing. Finally they joined Brand in belting out some off-key sea shanties.

"Firin, ladies and gents, the port of Firin!" Brand cried at last.

They saw a small rocky island with just a scattering of houses and millions of screeching birds. Brand barked out his seafaring orders at Teresa, and they swept elegantly into the harbour.

"All right, everybody out," cried Brand. "Quick, because I'd rather not hang around here too long. I want to be off."

Josh chewed his lower lip. "But there are no other boats here."

Teresa, who had already jumped ashore, looked around and, crestfallen, agreed.

"Aye," said the skipper, "that doesn't surprise me. All right, out you go now!"

Josh remained seated, and Teresa climbed back into the boat.

"We'll give you eight coppers more," she said, businesslike, "if you'll take us over to Trellis."

Brand chewed hard on something in his mouth. He squinted at the sun, tugged angrily at the rudder and cursed. "Trellis? No bloody way. Out! There'll surely be—"

"Sixteen coppers apiece more," said Garnet unexpectedly.

"God help me," mumbled Brand.

"Twenty," said Baz, grinning.

"Stop!" yelled Brand. "For God's sake, you haggling twisters! It's not about the money; it'll be the death of us – and it's strictly against the law. Out, I said!"

"Thirty," said Garnet.

Brand chewed and chewed. Then he took a big gulp from his jug. "I'll do it for five pounds. Oh, it's a bad job."

With an angry shove, he pushed off. Excited, they settled in the bottom of the hull again. Teresa nudged Josh with her elbow. "Garnet's looking cheerful, isn't she? That doesn't bode well for us."

"Let her stew," Josh hissed back at her. "She won't have the nerve to try anything, anyway."

The boat turned out of the harbour and was caught by the wind again. Brand heeled out over the side of the boat to prevent it from capsizing, while Teresa hung on to the small sail's sheet with all her strength. They skimmed over the water, listing at a precipitous angle. They had to cling on tightly in order not to slide down the other side. Their wet hair slapped in their faces; they were completely drenched. They gasped for air. The initial crossing had been rough enough, but this time the going was truly tempestuous.

Brand adjusted his steering so that the boat heeled at an even steeper angle, going even faster, and they streaked over the water at breakneck speed. Then, out of the blue, Brand shouted a loud command; Teresa understood what it meant. Little by little they fell away. The boat slowed down, and ended up bobbing across the waves.

"Now here comes the best bit, hard alee!" shouted Brand, who seemed to be enjoying himself; and off they went again, almost directly into the wind this time, scrambling up towering waves and then dropping with a sickening thud into a trough. Their stomachs were lurching.

"Choppy, ain't it!" cried Brand. "You asked for it! Here comes another one!"

And again they pitched and slammed down hard on the water.

"This is nothing," said Baz. "When you jump into *umaya* you get hammered around much worse than this."

They pitched and rolled for a while, but when they reached a rock sticking out of the water in the middle of the sea, Brand made the boat come about again, to race with the wind for another nautical mile before turning the boat into the wind once more. At last they drew near to the green island they'd spied from a distance. From the boat they could see hills thick with vegetation, with here and there a sandy beach at their base. Above the greenery flew a multitude of birds: large white ones, small coloured ones, all screeching, piping and whistling in a cacophony of sound. Josh peered at them intently.

They sailed up to the entrance of a small bay.

"This is it," said Brand stormily. "I'm not going any further, not for all the gold in the kingdom. Scram, on the double!"

They stared at the beach hesitantly. It did seem temptingly close.

"Must we?" asked Teresa.

But Josh laughed. "Course!" he cried, kicking off his shoes. "Come on, we're already soaked, aren't we, and it isn't far!"

"But in this long skirt…" Teresa complained.

"Take it off and roll it up. You can carry it on top of your head. Simple. I've swum that far millions of times!" Easy for Josh to say – dolphin-boy Josh, with his seven swimming diplomas.

"Five pounds," said Brand, looking around nervously.

Josh fumbled in his pockets and his Gippart backpack, where he found a purse with coins. He gave Brand a fistful of strange dark brown and silver coins.

"That's too much, sailor," said Brand. "Ye're a bunch of crooks and blackmailers, but I can't accept all this." He gave a few coins back to Josh, and then shoved him roughly towards the rail. "Right, get out!" he growled as the boat started drifting backwards out of the bay.

Josh pushed his hat, coat and shoes into his backpack, and was overboard before the others could stop him. "The water isn't even cold," he called cheerfully. "Come on!"

Baz and Teresa plunged in after him, without looking to see what Garnet would do. Without too much effort they swam the short distance to the beach. It wasn't until they'd reached it that they noticed Garnet hadn't joined them. She was still standing in the boat, quarrelling with the captain.

"Oh, that's Garnet Gippart for you," sighed Josh. "Always making trouble. Are we supposed to fetch her back?"

"Max said we should listen to her," said Baz.

"Yes, but what if she doesn't come with us?" Teresa cried.

"Let's just wait and see." Josh started wringing out his clothes.

"The most important thing is that we're here," said Teresa. "And let's just hope that there's nothing really wrong with this island. Sailors are awfully superstitious, aren't they?"

She managed to make a washing line using rope that had washed ashore, which she tied between two trees. She made the boys strip off to their underwear, hung their clothes in the wind, along with their jackets from their backpacks, and then shooed them away. "Why don't you go for a swim or something. You're not seeing *me* in the nude. Or try and get a fire going."

Shivering, covered in goose pimples, they crossed the windy beach.

"You're still wearing that snake bracelet around your ankle," commented Baz.

"Oh dear. I was supposed to leave it at the gate, wasn't I?"

"I don't think it's very clever to be wearing it," said Baz. "There's something wrong with that thing. And Mervin Spratt can Sense it."

"Spratt isn't around."

"You never know. He certainly seems to want that bracelet very badly, and he's already come after you once in *umaya.*"

Chilled to the bone, they sat down on the stiff seagrass, in the shelter of a stand of trees.

"Where'd you get that bracelet, anyway?"

"By accident. It slipped off someone's wrist on the bus. I found it."

"And you didn't give it back?"

"I got off, by accident," said Josh, blushing.

"Then you really did nick it. Wow." Baz whistled. "Can I touch it again?"

Josh stuck out his ankle and Baz carefully ran his fingers over it. "That's odd," he muttered. "It's different now. It's got the rhythm of real time, but it's very similar to the rhythm of this *umaya.*"

"What do you mean?"

"I think we're in the dream-time equivalent of the real time this snake bracelet came from. The year 1660 or 1670."

"That's quite possible. We've been going back a hundred years each time. So we must be in a dream of about three hundred years ago."

"So you never went back in time, did you? You don't really know how to time-travel, do you?"

"Exactly. I don't really understand it either. That bracelet must have jumped out of the past on its own. Or else somebody else went and brought it here."

"Well, you can tell the bracelet is from the time-period we're in now. It certainly looks brand new. Look at how shiny it is! But it's strange, Josh" – Baz shook his head and glanced around uncertainly – "on this island, the *umaya* we're in has an awfully shaky sound. There's something not quite right about it."

"No nightmares, I hope…"

"No, it's more as if it might explode at any moment. Can't you hear it?"

"I can see that the air seems to be shivering, but that's probably because *I'm* so cold. Let's run!"

They raced each other, and Baz won. Josh shouted, "You useless Jumping-bean!" and Baz shouted back, "You nitwit, Twinkle-eyes!" and they wrestled in the sand until they were warm again. Then, from a safe distance, they asked Teresa for their backpacks, as Josh had had an idea. The beam of the compass could be adjusted so that it focused tightly into a ray of white-hot light. They experimented with it until they got a fire going. Triumphantly they called for Teresa to come and see, but her clothes weren't dry yet and she stayed where she was. The fire made them think of roasted potatoes and toasted marshmallows, until they couldn't stand it any more. They took their trousers down off the line and pulled them on, wet though they were, to go exploring and looking for food. Teresa could wait there for Garnet.

They walked under the trees up the gently sloping hillside. It was covered in strange and weird trees: ancient conifers with star-shaped needles, a few palm trees and deciduous trees with leathery fronds. It felt very quiet after the whooshing of the sea and wind, and the screeching of the birds. From time to time they'd hear an animal crashing through the undergrowth. Once, they saw a couple of goats bounding away in the distance. They came to a rushing stream of fresh spring water, and drank greedily. There wasn't much to eat; all they could find were some dried-up blue berries, which they didn't dare try. They climbed on in silence. Every now and then a beam of golden sunlight would break through the canopy of leaves, only to slip away again almost at once, leaving behind a dim, greyish light.

"Quiet, isn't it?" whispered Baz.

"At least there're no earthquakes or volcanic eruptions."

"I have a strange feeling, though."

Josh nodded thoughtfully. "Sometimes it's as if it's suddenly hard to see. Everything sort of flickers, have you noticed?"

"Something's happening. Let's get out of here as quick as we can. Please? Do you really think Zizi is around here somewhere?"

Josh took the bird call out of his pocket and made it whistle. In response a complete silence fell on the forest. A breathtaking silence.

Suddenly gripped by a cold fear, they spun on their heels and started walking back. Now they could hear a louder kind of rustling behind them. They walked faster. The rustling became a crackling sound. They broke into a run. Then a shadow sheared right over their heads. There was a thud, and something blocked their path. Before them stood a tall, red-skinned man, dressed in a sleeveless jerkin of rabbit fur and a crude pair of trousers. His shiny blue-black hair was knotted into a ponytail on the top of his head. He was holding a rusty gun and a spear, both of which were aimed at the two boys.

"Halt!"

They stood rooted to the ground.

"Who are you!" demanded the man. "Answer! What are you doing here?"

"I am Joshua Cope. We were on our way back to the mainland."

"Lost?" The man poked them aggressively with the barrel of his shotgun.

"No. We were just taking a short cut."

He noticed that the man looked jittery. He seemed distracted, only partially paying attention to them, as if he had one ear listening for sounds behind his back.

"How many of you are there?" he barked.

"Us two and Teresa, that makes three of us."

"There are more," muttered the man, glancing over his shoulder.

"Garnet, maybe," said Josh helpfully. "But aren't people allowed to come here then?"

The man turned his full attention on them again. "Not allowed? Where the deuce are you from, that you didn't know that? Who brought you here?"

"A captain from Damara. But he didn't really want to—"

"I should have known," the man bristled. "Those miserable Damarans. I'll have to load the cannon again – it's the only thing that keeps them away."

"We'd like to leave again as soon as possible," said Baz. "Couldn't you help us get away from here?"

"I'd be more than happy to help you by kicking your behinds back into the sea. But it's probably too late now. Your arrival has made the vibrations start again, although I fear the other intruders may be doing even more harm. There's nothing I can do now to prevent the disaster."

"But what have we done?"

"You've disturbed the equilibrium! This island, as everyone knows, is right on top of the fault line! At even the slightest provocation, some part of it will cave in, or a volcano will erupt, or autumn will turn into spring, or the butterflies will turn back into caterpillars! I spend my whole life trying to keep everything under control, but intruders from the outside are constantly upsetting the balance just when I've got the place more stabilized!"

"Oh, sorry," said Josh. "We didn't know."

The man lowered his weapons. "Anyway, they shouldn't allow children like you to travel unaccompanied," he sighed. "It's irresponsible scamps like yourselves, in search of adventure, that in their foolish ignorance always set the cat among the pigeons."

"May we go then?" asked Baz.

"How were you thinking of leaving here?" asked the man, looking over his shoulder again. "Do you have your own ship?"

They shook their heads. "Is there anyone here who could ferry us across?"

"Here on Trellis? Of course not. I'm the only one that lives here. Except for those shipwrecked scoundrels that keep washing ashore – supposedly by accident." He suddenly whipped around. "Show yourself, you bastard!" he roared into the undergrowth. "Come out or I'll shoot!"

To their bafflement, the response was a chuckle.

"Oh, Uju!" sighed the man. "Stop playing the fool, will you? Come here."

A tall boy emerged from the bushes, laughing. He was wearing the same kind of clothing as the man, only he wore his long black hair loose, cascading down to his shoulders. He looked at Josh and Baz with a glint in his eye.

"Don't let my old dad frighten you! Me, I love it when everything starts to shake around here. You never can tell what's going to happen next."

"Uju," said the man, "you're supposed to take my place as the next Guardian some day. It is high time you started acting a little more responsibly. You're sixteen years old!"

"Oh, that'll sort itself out all in good time," said Uju. He stared at the boys, fascinated. "Have you come from the north coast? Do they still have the fastest horses on earth, over there in Damara? Who won, in this summer's races?"

"Hold your tongue, Uju! We have other things to worry about at present."

The earth beneath their feet rumbled long and deep.

"We have to find those other intruders. Uju, I think it would be best if you showed these boys the way to East Beach. When it's all over, perhaps you could paddle them across to the mainland in the big canoe. I'm going to look for the other intruders before it's too late."

"But Teresa," said Josh. "First we have to fetch Teresa."

"And I'm hungry," added Baz.

"Very well," said Uju, "In that case we'll collect this Teresa of yours first, and we'll pick up some supplies on the way."

They followed Uju, who, with a hasty farewell to the

Guardian, leapt like a hare down the hillside. Uju jumped so effortlessly over fallen logs and streams that they soon lost sight of him. Then he came sprinting back, elated and teasing. "Come on, little piggies, can't you move a bit faster? We must reach shelter before the storm."

The rumbling and shaking was certainly getting stronger. Now and then Josh felt as if he might faint, because everything seemed to be spinning around him so wildly. Everything was shifting at different angles. Still, he knew that it wasn't just him. The world itself was shaking and wobbling. They rushed uneasily after Uju.

"Wait here," Uju shouted when they reached a crevice in the hillside.

He disappeared into a dark hole and came out again a few seconds later with a wicker basket slung over his arm. "Let's be off," he cried. "Let's find your Teresa. Is she pretty, this Teresa?"

They covered the last yards to the beach leaping down a nearly perpendicular slope. Josh slipped, landing heavily on his arm, but ignored the pain. They started calling Teresa's name before they reached the beach. Fortunately, there she was, dressed, sitting by their dying bonfire in the middle of the beach. She was alone. Garnet was nowhere to be seen. Uju ran up to her, gesturing wildly. "Come, lovely Teresa, princess of the desert, we have to get to East Beach straight away! Can you run?"

Teresa didn't have to be asked twice. She knew it was serious. She gathered the rest of the boys' clothes, threw them at Baz and Josh, slung the backpacks over her arm and ran after Uju. Baz and Josh hurried after them. They scrambled up a hill, puffing and panting. Thunder boomed overhead. A strange kind of rain started falling: red-hot ashes rained down on their heads. Uju waited for them to catch up with him. "I don't know if we will be in time," he said. "We need to get to the middle shelf. That one's usually quite stable. We can eat up there."

Josh wasn't hungry any more. He was feeling dizzy and sick, and he wished everything would stop rippling before his eyes. It was giving him a headache. Besides, he was out of breath, and had a stitch in his side.

Fortunately, Uju's shelf wasn't too far away, and by the time the first bolts of lightning flashed in the sky, they were safely installed on the flat ledge, halfway up the hill. They gazed across the sea, where in the distance the skies were calm and sunny.

Uju sighed. "Don't be afraid. It may just blow over. And if not, it'll be amusing. Maybe we'll turn into goats this time. Would you like to be a goat, Teresa, my night princess?"

Teresa chuckled. "What are you talking about? What's happening?"

"We're on top of a fault line," Josh explained.

"Ah," said Teresa. She slapped her hand to her mouth. "If I'm not mistaken, this is what at Gippart they call a chink in time! Uh-oh. That's bad news, that is."

"We should have stayed away," said Josh.

"Yes, and it's because of us coming here that it's started to go all wobbly," said Baz. "What a pain!"

"Oh, I don't know," protested Uju. "My old dad tends to exaggerate. It can't possibly be just your fault."

He jumped up to spread out the contents of the basket on the ground. "Here you are, that should take care of your hunger. Have something to eat, and then get a little rest. This is a fairly safe place. My sisters like to come here during the storms. And they're sensible girls, my sisters. I'm going to see if my father needs any help. I'll be back." And he was gone.

Teresa laughed. "He's a live wire, that one. But just look at all this!"

There was a mound of food on the grass: bananas, mangoes, berries, oranges and fruits they didn't recognize, hunks of black bread, some white roots and green stringy vegetables.

For just a moment they forgot all about being in a chink in time. Teresa took a cautious nibble at a fruit she'd never eaten before. "Yum, juicy. I was very thirsty. Must have been the rum, I think. What about you two?"

Eagerly they bit into the strange fruits and roots, sucking on the sweet stems. Josh was starting to feel a lot better, in spite of the fact that the entire island was shaking and the skies were blazing with lightning. Baz began to hum again – one of his wordless, rhythmic songs.

"*Bon appétit*, young people," said a voice behind them.

A voice like a whip. Their hearts leapt into their mouths. Teresa spat out some mango at the shock.

"Garnet!"

"Garnet Gippart, yes, the one who is in charge here. That's right."

She stepped on to the shelf. She was no longer the morose, sulking woman they had set out with. She seemed to know exactly what she wanted. Shining with malicious determination, she stood unmoving, feet planted firmly, mobile phone in hand.

"Good," she said. "The conditions are perfect. A line of fracture, and right at the crucial climactic moment too. In that case, we'd better not waste any time. Mervin?"

In dazed astonishment they saw Mervin Spratt climb up on to the ledge after her. He looked terrible. His face was green, and his whole body was shaking. He immediately sank to the ground, as if he were about to pass out.

"Are you all right?" asked Garnet, without looking back.

Spratt hawked, spat and groaned. "The pills will start to work in a minute." He stared at Josh with bloodshot eyes. Josh stared back at him. Slowly Spratt lowered his eyes to Josh's ankle. Josh expected him to jump up and hurl himself at him. But Spratt stayed put, panting, unable to tear his gaze away.

"Good," said Garnet. "Get out your measuring equipment. I'm starting."

"What do you mean?" cried Teresa, who had finally found her voice. "You're not doing anything, Garnet! No funny business! You were told not to!"

"You shut your trap!" shouted Garnet. "Do you think I even care? I can easily cough up ten thousand pounds for the fine! I'll be overjoyed to pay it. Are you ready, Mervin?"

Mervin was twiddling the knobs of a small square box. Lightning was flashing all around them.

"What are you doing?" cried Josh.

"Scientific research!" Mervin gasped. "Garnet, I … I think it would be better if you immobilized them."

"Right," She said, taking a step towards them, and before they realized what was happening, before they could believe it was happening, she'd knocked Teresa and Josh to the ground with two well-aimed blows. Baz ducked and ran, but in one smooth lasso move, Garnet caught him, using the same strong cord she'd just looped around the other two, and hauled him back. The electronic cord automatically snapped shut and anchored itself firmly in the ground. The whole thing took less than a minute. Flabbergasted, they found themselves chained fast to the earth.

The realization hit them that they were nothing but guinea pigs for Garnet and Spratt. Troublesome guinea pigs. Ready for the experiment.

"But you're going to kill us!" cried Josh. "Uju! Help!"

Garnet seized him by the throat and addressed him in a deliberate, icy voice. "Listen to me carefully, Joshua Cope. The dream-time we're in has split open. We're going to push you out of this *umaya*. Your only chance of survival is to flee into the real past. So that's what you're going to do. Travel in time. Understood?" She let go.

"But I don't know how to travel in time!" cried Josh in a choking voice.

"Oh stop it! It's not as if we don't know perfectly well what that idiotic bracelet of yours means – and if I had succeeded in lifting the thing out of your pocket during the Traders' Trial, or if Mervin had found it in your room, then we'd have been able to prove it scientifically too! Well, enough of the chatter. Ready, Mervin?"

"Ready. Zero point two-five."

"Perfect," said Garnet, and she took out her phone and aimed it at them.

The last time she had pointed her mobile at them, they had felt its effects: their hearts had started beating faster until they'd nearly burst. This time it was the world that quite simply exploded. One moment Josh lay there thrashing and yelling, the next there was nothing but a brutal whirlwind of pandemonium and pain. He heard screams, then an ear-splitting explosion whose shock waves shook his body, the world, the universe. He became a thread of high-pitched shrieking, ever more shrill, ever more piercing. Until the thread snapped. And then there was nothing.

Nothing.

Silence.

8
JERICHO

Josh knew it was nothing because that was what he was drifting in. In nothing – the void. *I'm dead,* he thought to himself in amazement. He couldn't see, because he no longer had any eyes. He didn't feel anything either, neither joy nor sadness. He was as wide as anything. As weightless as nothing.

This lasted a long, long time. Several years, several centuries. Then he began to fall. It was hardly noticeable at first. It wasn't all that pleasant. Then he began to fall a little faster. He tried to put the brakes on. Beat his tail to swim against the current. Flapped his wings helplessly. But he couldn't stem his fall. There he went, plummeting into a sea of clouds. He opened his eyes and felt the thick mist caressing his cheeks. Now he was adrift, bobbing around in the void, half blind. He stretched out his arms and legs, felt other bodies near by. Heard voices.

"Who is it?"

He pricked up his ears and peered around. Eyes, lighting up, glided past. He saw hair, hands, a smile coasting by.

"Is he here?"

The sun broke through. He began to fall again.

"Quick, quick!"

Feverish voices all around him. Then a familiar voice,

triumphant: "It worked! Hooray, I've got him!"

He was hurtling down at terrific speed through lifting, soft golden mist. Then he felt solid ground beneath him. For a brief moment he stood there on his own two feet, suddenly blasted by an overwhelming, burning joy.

The next moment a heavy weight landed right on top of him. An opponent had attacked him from above, and lost no time wrestling him into a tight armlock. He put up a fierce struggle.

"Let go!"

"Not likely!" cried a young, devil-may-care voice.

He kicked and bit and thrust. He nearly managed to work himself loose, but then two muscular legs pinned him in a tight hold again. They rolled over the ground, kicking and lashing out at each other. Finally Josh ended up flat on his back, with his opponent seated on top of him, sharp knees pressed into his ribs, hands pushing his hands into the ground. He looked his attacker in the face for the first time.

It was a girl.

A pale girl with light, almost colourless, flashing eyes. A girl with long, tousled, bluish-white hair. A girl with a mocking, beaming face. Josh stiffened. A face he knew all too well. He couldn't quite place it, but the blood was pounding in his ears. He couldn't think.

The girl sat there gazing at him for a long time, smiling, enjoying her victory. Then she leapt off him. Josh sat up and looked at her open-mouthed. She bent over his leg and with some difficulty prised the bracelet off his ankle.

"There," she said, "I'm taking it back. It belongs to me."

Afterwards Josh couldn't tell when it had finally dawned on him.

"You're such an idiot," said Jericho. "You only realized after I told you who I was."

"That's not true," he said, offended. "I even knew it, you

know, that time you pressed your face against mine. As a matter of fact, I knew it the very first time you called my name."

"You don't have to lie about it," Jericho teased him. "You see, *I'm* the one with brains, and you're a fool and a liar."

It was true that it had taken a while for Josh to work out why Jericho's face was so familiar. It was his own face. Only bluish-white.

"That will all sort itself out," said Jericho, "once I've been here a while." She looked around with an air of satisfaction, with that funny grin of hers that revealed her sharp little canines.

They had landed back on the same ledge on Trellis – the one Josh had been blasted off. Only, Josh couldn't really remember what had happened. His head was light and empty. He sat in the grass in a daze, as the flashes of lightning slowly faded towards the horizon. This strange, new Jericho couldn't keep her hands off him. She ruffled his hair, she prodded him in the neck and licked his nose as, laughing, he struggled to get free. She poked a finger in his ears and tasted some of his earwax.

"Stop it! Stop it!" cried Josh.

"Well, I have to find out who you are again, don't I?"

"You don't have to eat me; that's disgusting!"

She jumped up, caught hold of a tree branch and hung there, swinging back and forth. She did a handstand and then roared as loudly as she could, savagely beating her chest. Finally she dropped down next to Josh and put one hand on his heart, the other on her own.

"Yes," she said contentedly. "Together, at the same time. Can you feel it? Isn't it wonderful, our heartbeat?" Then, eyeing him up and down: "You hair is either too long or too short."

"I hate barbers. Mo sometimes gives it a trim."

"Then it should be longer. A bit more like mine."

Little by little, she quietened down. She chewed on a blade

of grass, feasting her eyes on everything: Josh, the trees, the sky, the sea, the grass, and then back to Josh again.

"It's so lovely to be here again," she sighed. "They all thought that I'd make you come to us, but I felt like doing it the other way round. I decided I'd rather come to you. They'll be livid, probably. Especially Lucide. Are you angry with me?"

"Angry?"

Josh laughed, bewildered. He didn't understand any of it. He had exploded and died, and now he was alive again. Next to him sat his dead twin sister, as real and concrete as could be. Only a little bluish-white. He tore his gaze away from her and looked up, at the mist from which he had fallen to earth. He saw clouds, motionless, ranging from dark grey to light grey. The lightning storm had withdrawn to the very edges of the sky.

"Let's do something, shall we?" Jericho suggested. "What were you doing when I arrived? I mean, before you were blasted over to our side?"

He frowned. "I don't remember anything," he muttered. "Isn't that strange?" He stared at his hands, his feet, the earth around him. "I was here, I think. And then there was that big bang. And then you came. But what was I doing here?"

"How should I know! Anyway, it was something you needed hardly any clothes for." She giggled.

"But I wasn't alone. There were other children as well. I think they murdered all of us. Why can't I remember any more?"

"Who cares?" Jericho decided. "*I'm* here, aren't I! Finally! So, what shall we do?"

Josh shook his head. "It was something important. I *must* remember."

"Very well, you decide. I'm ready for anything." She got up and wandered over to the edge of the shelf. "Look, those children you were talking about, was one of them a tall girl in a dress? A Moorish girl, perhaps?"

Josh bounced up. "Yes! Teresa!" He suddenly remembered. He ran over to Jericho's side and saw Teresa. She was sitting on a rock a fair way back from the edge of the shelf, hugging her knees.

"Teresa!" he yelled, running down to her, with Jericho at his heels. He knelt down next to her.

Teresa turned her tear-stained face towards them. "What...?" She began crying and laughing all at the same time, throwing her arms around him. "Josh! Oh, Josh, you're alive! Oh, you're alive, great God, you're alive!" She almost squeezed him flat until he disentangled himself, suffocating. She dried her tears with the hem of her skirt. "Oh boy, how wonderful that you're still alive. What happened to you? Where were you?" At that moment she caught sight of Jericho. It gave her a shock. "What's *that*?"

"Oh," stammered Josh, who was becoming confused again, "this is Jericho."

Jericho grinned at Teresa. She said nothing, smiled, flashing her sharp teeth, and ran her pointy tongue over her lips.

"Josh," whispered Teresa, "this isn't right. She looks exactly like you! Where'd she come from? This isn't a normal kid."

"No. She is, ah … oh, well. I mean, I was dead too. It isn't *that* strange."

"You're talking rubbish," said Teresa sharply. "Where's she from?"

"From the mist. This is my ghost, actually." He laughed nervously. There was no rational way to put it. "She's my twin sister. She was dead. And now she's back."

Jericho added, "I caught him. With my bracelet." She raised her arm and showed Teresa the snake bracelet around her wrist.

"I don't get it," said Teresa. "But it isn't right. You're from the other side, and you have no business being here."

Jericho threw Teresa a fierce look. "Oh no? Haven't I had to put up with being born here, over and over again, even if I never asked for it?"

"Then you're … you're a comebackchild," Teresa stammered. She slapped her hand over her mouth and, speechless, looked from Jericho to Josh, and from Josh back to Jericho. "Oh, *now* I see."

"A failed comebackchild," said Jericho. "My bad luck started a thousand years ago and has been going on ever since. I get born, and then a few months later it all goes wrong. I'm born again; three years later it goes wrong again. I'm born once more, and guess what, it's finished in just two days. Ad nauseam. It makes you sick; it makes your head spin, it does, all that coming and going, coming and going."

Teresa stared at her with pursed lips, appalled. "Then why don't you stay there for good!"

"You didn't stay back there, did you? So why should I?"

Teresa stood up. "Josh, it was that time-quake that caused all this. It ripped a hole in this dream-time, and that made everything get all jumbled up. We've got to get away from here."

Josh sat shivering on the forest floor. He was still wearing nothing but his trousers, and it was chilly. "But what *happened*?" he demanded. "I know there was an explosion. But why? And haven't we any warm clothes to put on?"

"Don't you remember?" asked Teresa, looking worried. "You did make an incredible bang." She pulled him to his feet. "Come on, let's look for our clothes. And then we'll go to East Beach. I don't know what else to do. I've looked everywhere, but I can't find him."

"Find who?"

"You really don't remember?"

"There were others," said Josh, straining to think.

"Baz."

Josh felt a tremendous shock. "God, Baz!" He froze in his tracks. "Teresa, where's Baz?"

"I couldn't find him. I don't know either."

"He can't be dead, because I'm not dead. I fell back to earth. And he's so much cleverer than me. He isn't dead."

Teresa said nothing.

"What happened, Teresa?" asked Josh. "Tell me, please!"

As she gathered up their clothes, which were scattered all over the place, Teresa told him everything, starting with their departure from the gate, and it all came back to him as she spoke. He hadn't been missing from time all *that* long then. Finally she got to the part he didn't remember. Lowering her voice, she shuddered. "And then Garnet turned on her mobile phone. You and Baz started screaming and having convulsions. Then, suddenly, you were blown backwards down the hill like a shot out of hell. And Baz – he simply blasted off into space. He flew high up in the air, landing with a thud behind the bushes, and then I heard him tumble down the hill." She shrugged, trembling. "Garnet was laughing. But Spratt had to throw up."

"But what about *you*?" asked Josh.

"Yeah, I can't understand it. I didn't feel a thing. Garnet approached me and then I think she turned up the juice even more. But I still didn't feel a thing. My heart just beat a little faster, that was all. Then Garnet wanted to follow you and Baz, but just then, all hell broke loose overhead. You've never in your life seen anything like it! Non-stop lightning, but in all the colours of the rainbow, and then the oddest things started appearing in the sky: winged horses, Josh, and gigantic exploding balls of fire, and all these tiny coloured lights changing into butterflies, and the longest snake you ever saw swimming very slowly along the horizon. And it was raining ashes and the earth was shaking and I could hear this horrendous roaring and howling. And the trees around us turned into pillars and then into bare red trunks, and then into trees again. And the soil changed colour and suddenly thousands of fireflies came crawling up out of the earth. Then a big chasm opened and down at the bottom of the abyss I could see a roaring subterranean river in flames." She sighed. "It was the end of the world."

Josh listened open-mouthed.

"Garnet and Spratt were lying on the ground with their hands over their ears. I tried to see where you'd gone. Then, finally, everything went quiet. But once it was quiet, the strangest thing happened. It felt as if the island was turning around, like a giant rolling over in his sleep. It tilted, and then it righted itself again. Since I was tied down, I didn't slip, but Garnet and Spratt slid right off the ledge." She gave a bitter laugh. "I never saw them again. I hope they fell into that river of fire."

"And then?"

"Well, I waited, but everything stayed calm. The birds began to sing again. And some rabbits came hopping along. Then I just wriggled free and began to look for you and Baz. I searched for hours. I thought you were dead, and that I was the only one left alive. Even Uju is nowhere to be found. I've shouted myself hoarse."

Josh looked over at Jericho. "But Jericho came."

"She isn't the strangest thing that's slipped through that hole in time. I spotted a giraffe, and, if my eyes didn't deceive me, a silver racing car. And a band of little white men with beards, like gnomes."

Josh laughed doubtfully.

"I don't care if you don't believe me. Everything got all mixed up, I'm telling you, and your Jericho is just part of the mess that fell in through the hole. It's all got to go back to where it came from, though. If not, there'll be total mayhem in *umaya*."

"Oh well," said Josh, confused. Little by little, he was starting to remember what had happened, but he didn't quite know what to make of it. Jericho, Jericho – suddenly he had a sister, a twin sister who was the spitting image of himself. That wasn't something to turn your nose up at. It was amazing.

Teresa pulled him close. "Josh," she whispered, "do you remember I said I'd seen your face before, but I didn't know where? It's come back to me now." She glanced over her shoulder and went on. "I was wrong. It wasn't you I'd seen before. It was Jericho I'd seen. In my dreams about my dead brother. He came back to me in my dreams, in the company of other dead souls. Jericho was among them. She's a ghost, Josh, a comebackchild. And they're bad news, they are, according to my grandmother on my dad's side. She has no business being here."

Teresa found their backpacks on the ledge. She didn't have to look very hard. "The Gippart backpack is very practical," she explained to Josh. "It comes with a guarantee that you'll never lose it, and that's true." Josh, shivering, pulled on his creased shirt and his woollen coat. He also jammed the wide-brimmed hat back on his head. Finally, after tying the leather shoes on his bare feet, he felt a little warmer.

Jericho laughed at him. "Now you do look smart. Can I have a hat like that too?"

Teresa shook her head. "We only have the one that belongs to Baz, and you can't have it."

"You can have my velvet bow," offered Josh.

Jericho tied the red velvet ribbon around her neck; it made her look slightly less pale.

They followed a narrow trail that meandered from Uju's shelf in an easterly direction. Behind them the sky was turning a dazzling pink, shot through with purple stripes. The noise of the seagulls carried clearly in the silent evening.

"Teresa," said Josh, "maybe Baz fell asleep. Perhaps he's back in the real world."

"I wondered about that too," admitted Teresa. "But we can't be sure."

Silently they walked through the twilight. Suddenly a small black shadow flitted across their path. It disappeared into the underbrush on their left. Startled, they stood still. Then the beast poked its head out of the bushes again. They found themselves staring into a pair of yellow eyes.

"It's a panther or something," muttered Josh.

The animal slunk very cautiously towards them.

"It's a large cat, black, with purple spots."

"It's too large for a cat," said Josh anxiously.

The little panther crouched as Josh spoke, then leapt back over to the right side of the path.

"I've seen that panther before," he said. He scratched his head under his hat. "I know! In the dawning of the world. It licked Baz's blood."

Teresa didn't know what he was talking about, but pointed. "Look, it's slipping into that gap. There must be a cave, I think." Josh hesitantly followed it. Could it really be the same panther? He stuck his head through the gap. There was a small cavern. In the dusky light from outside he could make out a dim shape lying on the ground.

Even in the dark Josh immediately knew who it was. He was lying on his stomach, the top half of his body bare, spreadeagled as if he'd fallen from a great height. "Baz!"

They rushed over to him, felt his pulse, his neck, listened to his breathing, and laughed, relieved. Teresa rubbed his back and said over and over, "He's only sleeping, he's only asleep!"

Josh poked him. "Baz, wake up. Hey, wake up!"

Groaning, Baz turned on to his back. He opened his eyes, blinked a few times, and asked in bewilderment, "Josh? Teresa? Where am I?"

They were so ecstatic that for a brief moment they forgot that something was wrong. So did Baz. He sat up, rubbing his head. "Oh, my head. What happened? That bang!"

"Garnet and Spratt were fiddling about with that phone thing. Then the whole world blew up, more or less, and you fell. How do you feel?"

"Awful. But I'm glad to see you. What a nightmare. I thought I was getting blown to bits. I was hurled into the air, I think. Was that what happened?"

"Yes," said Teresa. "At least two metres."

"It felt more like a hundred. Oh, I felt all broken up inside. Everything was going haywire. Did you feel the same thing?"

"No," said Josh, "but what exactly happened to you?"

"Nothing, my heart was just out of sync, I couldn't think or breathe, and nothing was the way it should be. The only thing I could think of was that I had to try and get hold of a good rhythm from somewhere. I thought I could hear something coming from deep down in the earth itself. So then I crawled into this cave, to try and hear the beat properly, and I must have fallen asleep listening. But it did help, I think. My heart seems to be beating normally again."

"Well, we're on our way to East Beach," said Teresa. "Then we'll cross over to the mainland so that we can begin our next dream-walk from there. We must make sure we don't get stuck on this island again next time."

"Oh no," cried Josh. "Never again. I'm never coming back to *umaya* again. Are you out of your mind? After all that's happened? We're never coming back. Let them find the Tembe themselves!"

"But didn't you want to find Zizi?" asked Teresa. "If so, you'll just have to return another time, won't you?"

"Well, then I'm not leaving here before I've found Zizi. Once I've found her, I'm never coming back!"

They glared at each other.

"Please, let's not fight," said Baz, "let's just go and find that East Beach. Where are my clothes? I'm freezing."

As he was getting dressed he caught sight of the little panther sitting in a corner of the cave, its yellow eyes gleaming in the dark.

"Hello!" He walked over to it, hand outstretched. "Hello, little panther."

The creature licked his hand carefully.

"Josh," said Baz in an unsteady voice. "Josh, this is the little panther, you know, from the dawning of the world."

"You're right, it is," said Josh. "Several things that belong in some other time seem to have landed here."

"That panther isn't the worst of it," muttered Teresa.

"What else then?" asked Baz, stroking his panther's thick fur.

"Me," said Jericho, stepping forward. "I'm the worst of it."

Baz's mouth fell open. "Who are you?"

"Have a good look," said Josh, smiling. "Jericho, stand outside. Baz, come over here and guess who she is."

Outside, in the evening light, Baz stared at Jericho, baffled. "You look just like Josh. Are you his mirror image come to life? What sort of thing are you?"

"Polite, aren't you?" Jericho commented. "I'm a *someone*, not a something."

"She's my twin sister," announced Josh proudly. "She was dead and then she followed me here."

Baz didn't know what to say.

"That little panther followed you," Josh explained, "and she followed me."

"Did you know you had a twin sister? Is she real?"

"She died when we were born," Josh explained, and Jericho added, "And all that time I've been working out how to come back. Are we going to that beach now? I'd really like to see more of the world."

Baz darted Teresa a puzzled look. She shrugged and pulled a face. "Let's just go," she sighed.

They hoisted their backpacks over their shoulders and walked in single file down the dusky path, into the night. Teresa was in the lead, then Baz, then Josh and, right behind them, the little black and purple panther, with Jericho bringing up the rear. She skipped back and forth, taking in everything with her luminous eyes, touching everything, sniffing everything. Josh kept waiting for her. Then they'd walk side by side for a little while, and he'd ask her a question – Where had she come from? How had she managed to catch him? What did her bracelet have to do with it? But she'd only flash him a crooked smile, pinch his cheek and ask what his favourite food was. And then she'd stop short to study a column of ants on the move, hailing them with, "Hello, my friends, here I am again," and would seem to forget all about Josh. So then he'd just walk on ahead of her.

Every so often he'd whistle up into the sky, but to no avail – yet he was still hoping that Zizi would hear him. But even if Zizi were here, he told himself, the huge blast would have made her lose her bearings. He didn't dare hope that he would find her. There was perhaps one last chance: on the map of Trellis, he'd spotted, like a mysterious omen, a tiny island just off the coast of East Beach.

After a long walk along the shadowy trail they finally rounded a hill and saw, far below, a glistening white beach. They scrambled cautiously down the rocks. There was a large, round boulder in the middle of the beach. They walked over to it, shrugged off their backpacks and sat down on the sand. Only Jericho, in her flimsy white dress, remained standing. "It's beautiful," she sighed. "It's so beautiful."

"More beautiful than where you're from?" asked Josh.

"Different," said Jericho. "This is beautiful because it isn't permanent. Everything around here comes to an end, and so it's incredibly beautiful, in the saddest sort of way."

The three Associates, leaning back against the rock, shut their eyes.

"But how are we going to get back to the mainland?" Teresa cried suddenly. "We mustn't fall asleep yet! Can any of you see Uju's canoe?"

They rubbed their eyes and looked around.

"No," said Josh, who had the keenest eyesight. "Wait, I'll just climb up on top of the rock. Maybe I'll be able to see better." With a leg-up from Baz he managed to hoist himself up to the top. There he stood, high above the beach and the sea, the evening breeze lifting his hair.

"Baz?" he called down after a while. "Could you just hand me my bird whistle?"

Baz threw the bird call up to him, and Josh caught it on the third try. There, in the distance, near a few rocks close to shore, flew a huge swarm of birds. It was at the very tip of Trellis, and his very last chance. But he had reason to be hopeful. After all, he'd read it on the map. He made the bird call squeak and screech, then shouted at the top of his voice, "Zizi! Zizi!"

And the miracle happened: out of the multitude of birds preparing to roost for the night, one detached itself and flew straight for the boy on the rock. For a moment she hovered overhead, to make sure it was him, then gave a triumphant squawk and shot straight up in the air, before letting herself waft down slowly on to Josh's right shoulder. Josh cautiously spread his arms wide, and with a heart bursting with joy yelled, *"Yes!"*

He climbed down carefully until he was standing proudly on the sand, with his bird on his shoulder. Lovingly he scratched the downy feathers of her throat, and she snuggled her little head gently against his ear.

"You really are the Pied Piper of Hamelin," said Teresa in a tone of both admiration and disapproval. "You just seem to attract everything to yourself – Mervin Spratt and parrots and dead girls. And a load of trouble."

"Josh is the best," Jericho declared contentedly.

"Now we can go back," said Josh. "Is that all right with you, Teresa? Shall we go to sleep now?" Now that he had his parrot back safe and sound he'd suddenly become aware of how much the day had shaken him. He was more than exhausted, and he was still confused. He could think of nothing better than to be home again, safe.

"I can't come up with any other solution either," admitted Teresa. "We'll just have to work out how to get away from here next time. That will be another hundred years before this

– there'll probably be people around again."

"There isn't going to be a next time," argued Josh irritably.

"Not for you there isn't, maybe, but there will be for me," said Teresa, who wanted to have the last word.

They lay down on the beach, the little panther curled up against Baz's back. Only Jericho was still on her feet, looking up at the stars.

Josh suddenly sat up. "Jericho!" he exclaimed. "We've got to tell her!"

"What?" asked Jericho.

"That we're going. We're going to fall asleep, which means we'll be leaving this dream-world. We're going back to our own world."

Jericho looked at him blankly. "Aren't you in your own world now? You aren't dying, are you?"

Josh didn't know how to explain it to her. He walked up to her. "You won't be able to come with us, I'm afraid. I'm *really* sorry. But this is only a dream; it's *umaya*."

Jericho stared at him with a cryptic smile. "Just go to sleep, Josh," she said. "You can't get rid of me. I caught you, didn't I, remember?"

"You don't understand."

"No, I don't. But it doesn't matter. You really can't get rid of me any more. Sweet dreams."

Josh gave up. He lay down again, letting Zizi climb on to his head. He took one last look at Jericho, who was gazing at him with her brilliant eyes.

"Farewell, Jericho," murmured Josh sadly. He was already drifting off, into the deep sleep of warriors and dream-travellers.

Early the next morning he was woken by the sun shining in his eyes. "Switch the light off," he groaned, turning over onto his other side. He inhaled a noseful of sand and sneezed. "Yuck!" Annoyed, he wiped the sand from his nose. Sand, sand everywhere. Cold sand too. He was freezing. Why was it so cold, and why all the sand? He tried to fall asleep again, but couldn't. Something felt terribly wrong. He opened his eyes. He was lying on the beach, and next to him were Teresa and Baz, in a deep slumber. The little panther had draped itself over Baz. Josh sat up and shook the sand out of his hair. Then he caught sight of Jericho, who was sitting a few metres away. She looked at him with triumph in her eyes.

"Good morning, little brother. Did you sleep well?"

He jumped to his feet. "Jericho!"

"I told you, didn't I? You can't get rid of me."

He looked around in bewilderment. No Reception gate, no Gippart. They were still in *umaya*. They'd fallen asleep, but they were still stuck in *umaya*.

He ran over to Baz and Teresa in panic, shouting, "Wake up! Wake up!"

Reluctantly they opened their eyes, but were immediately wide awake, shouting at the same time, "How did this happen?" "Where are we?"

Teresa stood up and said, trembling, "This isn't possible! No one has ever fallen asleep in *umaya* without returning to the real world!"

They looked at each other in alarm.

"But – oh dear," said Baz. "Yesterday. Didn't I fall asleep yesterday?"

"Oh no!" said Teresa. "Oh no! This is the very first time this has ever happened. Do you know what this means, boys? Yesterday the doors between the times must have swung open for a bit, and then they must all have slammed shut. Every one of them. We can't go back. We're trapped in *umaya*!"

Jericho was watching them from a little distance. She had her hands on her hips, and her mouth was drawn in an odd, almost malevolent smile.

PART III
DRUMMERS AND THIEVES

9
Waves, Wraiths, Wolves

There she stood, early on a Sunday morning, October the twenty-second, on a beach on Trellis island: a girl playing truant from eternity. Just standing there whistling to herself. She was already looking a little less blue than yesterday. Her hair was now a wild mane of cobweb-fine creamy brown, though her skin was still a translucent white.

And before her stood three stranded dream-travellers, staring at her with distrust.

"Can I help you?" she asked mockingly.

"I think you know more about this," Teresa snapped at Jericho.

Jericho fixed her with her pale eyes, and whistled a little tune without answering.

Baz grabbed her by the arm. "Have you taken us prisoner? Are you the one who closed off time?"

Jericho slapped his hand away. "Don't touch me! And don't ask such stupid questions. I've got nothing to do with *you*, drummer-boy!"

Josh touched her shoulder. "Jericho, did time slam shut on us because you caught me?"

"It was about time, wasn't it, that I caught you?" Jericho

rubbed the snake bracelet on her wrist. "But the other two are none of my business. As far as I'm concerned, they can go and take a running jump."

"So it isn't your fault, then?"

Baz interrupted him. "What's all this about the bracelet, anyway?"

Jericho gave him an icy look. "It's nothing to do with you. That's between my brother and me." She turned her back on them, pulling Josh along with her.

They climbed up to the forest and walked a little while beneath the fragrant, rustling pine trees. Jericho seemed to be in a good mood again: gazing around in curiosity, she licked the rough bark of a spruce tree and took a delicate bite out of a blue pine cone. Josh said, "Come on, Jericho, why won't you explain?"

She sighed, tossing the pine cone away. "There's nothing much to explain. I don't know anything about time, and if you ask me, you're all talking nonsense as far as that goes. But if you're talking about the way I caught you, it was with my bracelet. It was my favourite bracelet. Don't you see? My most precious possession. So that's what did it."

"I just don't understand. Aren't you Jericho, my twin sister? How could you have owned a bracelet?"

"Oh, that's perfectly possible," she said patiently. "Because I'm a comebackchild, you see. I've been here before, many times. The last time I decided to come back, it was as your Jericho. But I'd been here before as well. Three hundred and fifty years ago."

Josh tried to understand. "And that time you were alive, like an ordinary child?"

"Just like you. Do you want to know what my name used to be? Elisabeth Cope. Betty Cope."

"Cope? The same name as mine?"

"Yes. I was your great-great-great-great-great-great-uncle's daughter, something like that. I was an only child, which was awful, and I was always sickly: that was bad too. When I was twelve I'd had enough. It was 1665, you know, so it was easy to get out. That's why I left my bracelet in your time. So I could be born again. As a daughter of the Cope family. It's easier to get reborn into your own family."

"But you didn't get reborn properly in my time."

"No. Something went wrong, and I was furious with you because you just went on by yourself. The ironic thing was that that bracelet was lying there waiting for me. It was pulling me, but I couldn't get to it, and then you started feeling its pull a little as well. Then I had this idea: I'd try and get hold of you. If you found that bracelet and picked it up, then it would forge a way for me to you. Because that bracelet is always pulling at me, I'm sort of part of it. That way I could reach you, or you could come to me. That would make up for everything." She laughed, and kicked a seashell. "But you wouldn't pick it up!"

"But where was it, then?"

"It was in the garden of the house of our birth at first, behind the potting shed. Back when I was Betty Cope, a group of us had crept around behind time to put it there. It was all very exciting. Except that tiresome old Lucide saw us do it. He was livid. I still think I wasn't born that time because he wanted to punish me."

"Oh? What a lousy thing to do to you."

Jericho shrugged. "Well, I managed to get to you anyway, didn't I? We kept sneaking into your time to make you find that bracelet. Twelve years we were after you. And you didn't take the bait!"

Josh's head was reeling. "I had no idea."

Jericho ruffled his hair. "Oh, you're so hopeless." Then, out of the blue, she tugged viciously at one of the longer locks of his hair. "You abandoned me. It was awful, so don't think I've forgotten. I'm just going to have to teach you a lesson or two!"

"Jericho, I was just a baby, I couldn't help it!"

"A baby! Babies know everything! We stayed around you for

months, and all you did was blithely chuckle at us, and pull faces at us! Babies know everything, didn't you know that? They forget it all later."

"OK, OK," said Josh, laughing. "Come on, let's see if we can find something to eat. Aren't you hungry?"

"I probably am, I think. Isn't it that funny feeling in your stomach? I've forgotten."

They walked on. Jericho skipped ahead of Josh, but then came running back, gaily asking, "Don't you think it's wonderful, this bracelet? It's the most beautiful thing I own." Both of them bent their heads over Jericho's wrist, and the salty sea wind tousled their hair.

"It's really great," agreed Josh with some regret. "Terrific."

"Real gold," said Jericho, polishing the snake's back with her fingertips. "And can you see how beautifully it's fashioned, the little head?"

"And those rubies. They are real, aren't they?"

"My mother gave it to me, for my tenth birthday."

"It was the most beautiful thing *I* owned too," said Josh. He stared at the golden snake.

"You can borrow it sometimes, if you like. But it's mine."

They walked on through rustling woods where little boar grubbed in the bushes, and they came upon rocky slopes scored with interesting crevices and caves. They saw birds everywhere: brightly coloured, raucous seabirds, fluttering forest birds and, circling over the crater of a tall volcano they spied from a hilltop, stately highland birds. They didn't see any people. From time to time they did hear some sort of creature scampering away. But when they called out, no one answered. The place was littered, however, with strange things that obviously didn't belong on Trellis: a child's pink bicycle, a shattered green light bulb, a large shiny illustrated book, *The Art of Glass-blowing*, and, hanging high in a tree, a fluorescent orange garden hose. But the best thing was waiting for them in the middle of the path: a bulging orange plastic carrier bag from the supermarket. Josh ran over to it, thrilled. It was chock-full of groceries. He rummaged through it, amazed. "Jericho, look: crisps and salami and scones! Just look at all this!"

"That's handy," said Jericho. "Food from your world! Terrific!" Together they carried the heavy bag back to the beach.

Baz and Teresa had lit a fire with the help of Josh's compass, and they were just putting in some apples to bake.

Baz looked up anxiously. "Have you sorted it out now, Josh? Can she open up time for us again?"

"I don't think so," said Josh, and he explained how Jericho had caught him by using the bracelet.

"You mean that she left that bracelet in our time three hundred and fifty years ago? That she paid our time a quick visit three hundred and fifty years ago?"

Josh nodded and gingerly picked a hot apple out of the fire.

"So then she really does know how to time-travel," said Baz. "Then it was all *her* doing, Josh! *She* knows the secret of time-travelling! Oh, if only they knew that at Gippart! So she's the one who knows how, not you!"

Josh nodded again.

"But," Baz continued, "if she could only teach us, we'd be saved!"

Jericho was hissing under her breath with rage. Josh prodded her gently. "Could you do that? Will you help us get back to our own time, Jericho, please?"

Jericho spat on the ground. "I really don't have the faintest idea what you are talking about – your own time this and your own time that. There's only one time – the one we're in. And people who are alive can't travel in time. And you, Josh, you're here and you're staying here. And that's that."

They all stared despondently into the fire in silence. So Jericho didn't know how to do it. Even if it really was all her doing, she had no idea how she'd accomplished it. Or how to undo the damage. Now, at last, the gravity of the situation really hit them. Taking careful bites of their steaming apples, they talked it over. And suddenly thought of home.

"My dad's going to kill me, I know, if I simply don't turn up!"

"They're going to think I've had an accident," said Josh. "Or that I've been kidnapped, or murdered."

"My sister is getting married on Wednesday," grumbled Baz. "That's in three days' time!" He angrily tossed the core of his third apple into the water. "And I'm still as hungry as a horse." He nodded his head at the supermarket bag. "What did you find, by the way? Is there any food in there?"

Josh unpacked the bag. "Just look at this: crisps, scones, and look, a carton of milk, a tin of Whiskas, a bag of salt – well, that's not much use to us, is it!" Uncooked spaghetti, tea, a big bag of toffees, bananas, a washing-up brush, passion-flower shower gel, sliced salami, a box of matches, muesli, a bag of mixed salad, two bottles of lager and a pot of banana-flavoured yogurt. It felt like Christmas. They sat around the fire eating scones with salami, taking turns to sip from the pot of yogurt and drink the milk in big gulps, and that soon made them heartened and warm and happy again. They opened the tin of cat food and let the little panther lick it clean.

"If Jericho can't help," Josh muttered, delving for leftover raisins in the empty plastic bag, "then there's only one solution left, if you ask me."

"What solution is that?" They looked at him expectantly.

"We've got to find the Tembe. If they live at the edge of time, then there must be a way out of this *umaya* where they are, surely? Our only hope of escape from here is to find them!"

"The Tembe." Baz frowned. "The embittered Tembe, intent on vengeance. I wonder if that's such a good idea?"

"Anyway, Gippart wants us to find them," said Josh.

"But what for?" Baz licked the yogurt lid clean. "Why do they want us to find them so badly?"

"Because the Tembe know something about time-travel," Teresa explained. "According to the story Josh heard from the tunnel people in the Inelesi *umaya*, anyway."

"According to that story, actually, the Tembe *don't* possess the knowledge of time-travelling at all," said Josh, but Teresa shook her head.

"That was ages ago. They may very well have discovered how to time-travel in the meantime, and I think that's exactly what they're counting on at Gippart, if you ask me."

"But for us the point is that they live at the furthest edge of *umaya*," said Josh. "Where the exit is. They're really our last remaining hope of getting home, even if they're demented flesh-eating zombies."

He'd meant that as a joke, but nobody laughed. All stared sombrely into the fire. Until Teresa jumped to her feet. "You're right, Josh. And if we can find the Tembe, it'll be killing two birds with one stone. We'll have carried out our mission for Gippart, and we'll have our chance to escape from *umaya*! Let's do it, and let's hurry up about it!" She looked around, frowning. "But first we have to get off this island. Everything's changed. There are no people, and those trees look different too." It was true: this time there were more blue spruces than before, whispering in the westerly breeze. And next to them brand-new deciduous trees fluttered their bright yellow leaves. It was lovely, but disturbingly different from the way it had been before the explosion.

"We'll have to build a raft," said Josh. "I know how. First we have to gather lots of branches. Straight, dry branches."

They split into twos and went back into the forest to gather the wood. Josh and Jericho went together, with Zizi flying cheerfully overhead. Jericho took pleasure in the task. She kept darting ahead of her brother, searching for branches and fallen logs. Sometimes she'd pick up something unfamiliar to her and taste it, and once she put something in the pocket of her white dress, to take with her. They hauled slender tree limbs, gnarled roots and rotten pieces of bark. Then, to their delight, they found an old porous tree trunk that had fallen years ago. It was just light enough for them to drag it away. Josh pushed and Jericho pulled. They slipped and fell, scrambled back to their feet, laughing, and finally managed to push it bit by bit down the hill to the beach, where Baz and Teresa had already made a pile of strong branches.

"You'll never make a raft out of *that*," said Jericho, giggling. She twirled round to skip back up to the forest, but then she suddenly froze. "Oh no!" she said, slapping her hands over her mouth in horror.

Josh looked over his shoulder in alarm. "Spratt? Garnet?" He never stopped worrying that he'd bump into those two.

"No," said Jericho. "Lucide!"

He was sitting high on a branch at the edge of the forest. Huddled like that in the shadows, Josh could hardly make him out. But when he finally spotted him, he recognized him: Lucide looked just like the night-spirit Josh had seen in the dawning of the world. From his dark form only his eyes could be seen, glinting in the gloom.

"Has he spotted me?" Jericho moaned.

"He's looking this way," Josh whispered. "Is this the same Lucide who's so angry with you all the time?"

"He's come to take me back. Please help me, Josh! I don't want to go back yet!"

"He isn't moving."

The night-spirit was seated upright, hugging his knees, as if he'd been sitting there for centuries and wasn't intending to move for the next few centuries either. As Josh stared at the forest, Baz and Teresa returned with more armloads of strong branches. They deposited them carefully on the sand and came and stood beside Josh.

"What are you looking at?" wondered Baz.

"Have you spotted someone?" asked Teresa.

Josh pointed. "A kind of night-spirit, or wood-sprite. See him? Up there, on a branch of that yellow tree."

Baz gasped. "A wood-sprite!"

Glancing at Jericho, Teresa said, "Not a particular friend of our own ghost, by the looks of it."

"That spirit is like the law for them, I think – their policeman," Josh explained.

"That's good," said Teresa. "Then he can put things straight around here."

But the night-spirit didn't look as if he wanted to get involved. They stared at him a little longer, but when he just continued sitting motionless up there in his tree, they went back to work. They sorted the branches into piles and eventually managed to lash them together into a rickety, two-layered raft. Baz improvised some ropes out of flotsam and reeds, which he and Teresa used to tie the branches together with professional-looking sailors' knots. Josh walked along the beach gathering useful bits and pieces that had washed ashore: an empty wicker demijohn, a headless plastic doll, big chunks of cork; also their empty milk carton and the plastic yogurt pot. He tied all of these underneath the raft. Then they pushed the messy stack of wood and flotation devices into the water. There the contraption floated, bobbing around on the surface.

"It's not bad," said Teresa.

Josh peered at the mainland on the other side. "We might just make it. It isn't all that far."

"Do you think the current's very strong here?" asked Baz.

"It floats," said Josh, "that's the main thing. We're going to get wet no matter what. Let's give it a try."

Teresa looked at him dubiously, and Baz pulled a face, but then Teresa shrugged. She waded into the water and climbed carefully on to the wobbly raft. It stayed afloat. "It's all right," she said. "Come on, Baz!"

Josh tied the backpacks on to the raft and then went back for two more long pieces of wood. "Oars," he muttered.

"Do we have everything? Jericho, come on!"

Jericho anxiously got to her feet and, with a worried glance over her shoulder at Lucide, waded to the raft and obediently settled down right in the middle of it. Josh whistled for Zizi, who had been hovering around all this time. With his parrot on his shoulder, Josh felt competent and strong. He pushed the raft off into the sea until he was standing waist-deep in water. He looked back once more. The night-spirit was still sitting motionless up in the tree. But at the water's edge, swishing its tail, stood Baz's little panther.

"Come!" Baz called to it, but it couldn't summon up the nerve. Baz whistled shrilly. The panther nervously ran along the shore, then suddenly plunged into the water, paddling desperately, its ears flat against its head, and scrambled up on to the raft, where it shook itself vigorously. It stood stiff-legged, pressing itself up against Baz.

"Yes!" shouted Josh. On the water he was in his element. Gippart Associates at sea! He swung himself up on to the raft, picked up an oar, and had Teresa grab the other one. And then they paddled slowly out of the bay.

If they had been using this rickety raft to cross the Serpentine in Hyde Park, on a sunny day in London, everything would have been fine. But this was the Gulf of Trellis, on an autumn afternoon, with a gale-force wind. Their raft was no match for this turbulent channel. Nobody ever crossed the rough sea between Trellis and the mainland unless they were in a very sturdy, seaworthy vessel – not even Captain Brand. The current was ferociously strong here, and the waves around Trellis were pitiless. Josh realized this as soon as the first towering wave picked them up and hurled them down again. This was a really bad idea.

They had to cling on with all their might, or be flung off the raft. Even worse, with every crash the raft came to lie lower in the water. The Associates gasped for air, blindly flailing around for something to hang on to, and braced themselves for the great quantities of water crashing down on them. But the moment came when the raft was so violently submerged that there was no way to hold on any more. The sea was playing a vicious and lethal game with them. It yanked the raft out from under them, and then let it shoot back up to the surface, sometimes just next to them, sometimes some way off, so that they had to swim desperately to grab hold of it again. Within ten minutes they were exhausted – even Josh, who was by far the best swimmer of them all.

Josh saw Teresa's anguished face, saw how she was trying to keep Baz and him in sight and how she grabbed for Baz's hand when he was sucked under. He saw how time and again Baz fought like a madman to stay with the raft. He saw how the little panther kept clawing its way back to the raft as fast as it could. He saw the grey-green waves towering all around them, the grey foam that was flying about their ears, and from time to time he'd catch a glimpse of a distant sun, or of Zizi, a calm little dot in the sky high above. He was surprised to see how Jericho would let herself be swept away by the furious waves, and then gracefully slip back on to the raft as if it were the easiest thing in the world. She was even smiling, and seemed to be singing to herself. It was the strangest thing. Here the living children were losing the battle before his very eyes, himself included. But the girl from outside the realm of time seemed to be enjoying just drifting around their hopeless thrashings.

Gasping for breath, he shouted over the din, "Help, Jericho!"

She stared at him in surprise, and was at his side in one stroke. "What's the matter?"

He was doused by a wave, and it took him a few seconds before he could regain his breath to speak. "Help us! We're drowning!"

She frowned. She swam back with him to the raft, where Teresa and Baz were desperately trying to hang on. Jericho took it all in: the choking, ashen-faced seafarers with their screwed-up eyes; Josh starting to panic. She lifted her face to the sky and began uttering strange sounds. Over the din of the sea Josh couldn't quite make out what she was doing. But he did notice that something was happening. The colours changed. The sounds changed. All around him he heard faint snatches of high-pitched voices calling. Faintly colourful shadows flashed in and out of the crashing waves and foam. The sea was too wild to see exactly what these shadows looked like. But Josh wasn't surprised to recognize the shrill tinkling sound. These were Jericho's friends. The Still-Dead-Children had come to their aid.

As another torrent of water gushed over him, Josh felt himself being lifted by countless prickly hands. He felt a cheek being pressed to his, and he thought he heard his name being whispered by giggling children's voices. They held him, keeping his head above water, lifted him right over the next wave, and tossed him easily back on to the raft. The raft was now proudly afloat in the water. It didn't list or sink any more when it landed in a trough. Dozens of children's hands were supporting it and keeping it afloat. Jericho's friends were everywhere, a flurry of hands, eyes and voices. There were lots and lots of them. Josh sat up on the raft, feverishly scanning the horizon. "Baz!" he yelled. "Teresa!" *Ah, there they are.* They shot up out of the water like dolphins, landing with a hard smack on the raft. Moments later, the little panther joined them.

"Ugh!" cried Baz, spitting out green water. He struggled to a sitting position and started hitting out at the ghosts.

"Don't!" cried Josh, as Jericho flipped herself up on the raft, screeching with laughter. "Moron, they're trying to help you!" But Baz wouldn't listen. Now that he was on firm ground again, he fought like a tiger, lashing out at the ghosts like a madman. That made his adversaries go on the offensive. They pinched his nose and ears, they poked him in the ribs and slapped him in the face, they pulled his hair, and finally tossed him overboard with an enormous heave. He didn't even scream, but fought desperately to keep his head above water. Josh stuck out his hand to pull him back on to the raft, but before he could do so a trail of mist wrapped itself around Baz and pushed him under. There was the sharp cackling of many voices, spiteful and jeering. Jericho was roaring with laughter too, holding her sides, but then she became serious.

"Stop!" she cried in a commanding voice. "Pull him up!" There were piercing sounds of protest in reply.

"Get him out!" Jericho bellowed. "He's going to be the best drummer in the world some day!"

The voices ceased. Suddenly Baz was floating on the surface again, and was hauled up on to the raft. He lay there on his side, spitting out water and clinging to the logs for dear life.

"Just calm down!" Jericho called. "They'll leave you alone now!" She sat up straight and proud, riding the raft as easily as a rider on horseback, her hair swirling in the wind. Teresa was prostrate. She glowered at Jericho, but didn't say anything.

They made the rest of the crossing in silence, cruising from the crest of one wave to the next as if on a roller coaster. In less than an hour they reached the breakers and were propelled across spray and sandbanks into calmer waters. The raft grated over the bottom, coming to rest on a dry strip of gravel. The colourful, luminous shadows started rising from the water.

Josh felt his hair stand on end. He braced himself for the sight of something not meant for his eyes. The shapes were growing more distinct. He was so sure he wasn't supposed to see this that he averted his gaze. And that was why he didn't see what happened next. He didn't see it – but he heard it.

A gigantic osprey smacked down on the water. Completely out of the blue. With a crash as if it had plunged from a height of a couple of miles. At least, that was what it sounded like to Josh. Jerking his head round, he couldn't understand what was going on in front of his eyes. There were high-pitched shrieks and blinding flashes of light all around, and for just an instant it sounded to Josh like the protests of a class of schoolchildren who were being punished. The shouting swelled to an unbearable, ear-splitting screeching, and then it was over. The noise died away as if a switch had been turned off, and the shadows dissolved in the air.

Knees trembling, Josh climbed off the raft. Jericho had collapsed backwards into the water, and there she sat now, nervously running her fingers through her hair.

"Are you all right? What happened?"

"They've gone," said Jericho shakily. "Chased away. Didn't you see it? Was it him? It was, wasn't it?"

"What do you mean? Who?"

But she shook her head, struggling to her feet with some difficulty. Side by side they waded to the beach. Suddenly she looked tired and dishevelled. Her flimsy white dress was soaked, torn and dirty.

"Well," said Josh, "they did save our lives, anyway. Thank you."

Baz and Teresa sat down next to them on the pebbly beach. "Yeah, thanks," echoed Teresa. "I'm not thrilled about your presence here, but I suppose it was useful this time."

"Absolutely," sighed Baz, who seemed to have come to his senses again.

Jericho nodded. "Fine," she said. She stared wide-eyed at the sea. "Shall we go?"

But they weren't ready to go on yet. They lay stretched out on the pebbles, out of breath, listening to their own wildly beating hearts. The earth seemed to be bucking wildly beneath them. In a corner of the beach the little panther sat grooming itself.

Little by little, they started to unwind. The monotonous pounding of the waves began to sound peaceful and relaxing after a while. The ferocity of the murderous sea already seemed far away. The sun shone sweetly and kindly on them, and the beach stopped rocking and came to rest.

"That wasn't the best of rafts," Teresa said, after a while.

"Oh, it wouldn't have mattered," said Josh. "Even on a good raft, we'd have been in trouble."

They lay on their backs looking up at the clouds.

"Your knots were terrific, though," he added.

But Teresa muttered, "Stupid raft."

"Idiotic raft," Baz agreed.

"Idiotic plan." Josh chuckled.

"Whose plan was it, anyway?" asked Teresa severely.

"Mine, of course!" Josh laughed.

Teresa laughed too. "Those stupid oars of yours!"

"Ridiculous," said Josh. And he had to laugh again.

"And me thinking those ghosts were trying to make me drown," said Baz. "I must have been nuts, laying into a bunch of ghosts."

"Whew – when they tossed you overboard, Baz!" said Teresa. "That was an amazing belly flop."

Baz snapped to a sitting position and poked her in the ribs. "What about you? You came shooting up out of that water like a rocket!"

"Look who's talking, Bazzer," said Josh, tickling him under the armpits.

"All your fault, you fool of a leader!" cried Teresa, who was now starting to pull Josh's hair.

"Oh, what now? *Who* thought it was such a cool plan? *Who* built the stupid raft in the first place? Teresa! Stop it!"

They rolled over the ground, tickling and poking and pinching each other until they were helpless with laughter. It wasn't until the panther began licking and nibbling their faces that they stopped and came to their senses, nicely warmed up.

"Have you noticed? It's much warmer here than on the island," said Baz. "We'll soon dry off."

Teresa smiled. “See? We’re in the south. Every cloud has a silver lining.”

Eating bananas, they took in their surroundings. Before long the narrow beach turned into a rough grassy hillside. Beyond it were meadows dotted with wild flowers, and a purple mountain range rose up on the horizon. Out of the distance came faint noises: a horse whinnying, bells chiming, snatches of conversation. It was a mild autumn afternoon in a southern clime.

“What do you reckon, Baz?” asked Teresa. “Are we safe here?”

“I think so. It’s just about the same kind of rhythm as yesterday’s. That upbeat excitement. But—”

“The colours are much the same too,” Josh added.

“But … something’s a bit odd.” Baz tilted his head to the side. “Can’t you hear it? There’s something I can’t quite get.”

“*You* don’t get the *rhythm*?” asked Josh.

“Well yes, of course I get it. It goes like this.” He tapped out two different beats on his knees simultaneously. “The first rhythm is a bit faster than yesterday’s – a fraction faster – and that means that we must have gone back in time again last night. Not all that far, though. I think we only went back thirty years, more or less – to around 1630. But on top of that, there’s this other rhythm that seems to be slowing the other one down, and chopping it up. And I don’t know what that means. Except…”

“What?”

“Except perhaps it means that time is running backwards right this very minute. That would explain the double rhythm. Don’t you see? The rhythm of the time we’re in and the rhythm of time running back.”

They looked around uneasily, but there was nothing to make them think time was running back, like a movie spooling backwards. “I can’t see anything unusual,” said Josh.

“I told you I didn’t really understand it.”

“But we’re definitely in an earlier era than we were yesterday,” said Teresa. "Wow, a spontaneous chain-*imayada*! Do you think we'll automatically end up in the time of the Tembe?"

"Let's hope so," said Josh. "Maybe Gippart's behind all this. Perhaps they're steering our *umaya* in the Tembe's direction!" The thought cheered him up.

Teresa sucked in her cheeks. "The seventeenth century," she said. "That's when global trade began. As well as the slave trade, of course. That got going around the same time. Trade and plunder! We have to be super careful. We're still in the same *umaya* – that of the Portilisi-nightmares and the Inelesi, only a couple of centuries earlier. I bet it's crawling with monsters here too."

"But Baz isn't Sensing anything," said Josh.

"Well, I didn't feel it in Portilisi either," said Baz.

"The seventeenth century," Jericho said suddenly, "was the best time. My grandma used to tell me. She was born around then, just after the Gunpowder Plot. There were lots of exciting new people in the city – architects, painters, writers, actors. There was Shakespeare, and the Globe Theatre, and all sorts of lovely political intrigues. That's when they built Covent Garden too. Don't you remember, Josh?"

They looked at her, startled. But Jericho's attention was fixed on a small dark object in her lap that she was flipping over and over, shaking it as if to guess what was in it. Josh leaned over to see it and had the shock of his life. He recognized it immediately.

"Garnet's mobile phone! But how…? Jericho, watch out! It could go off!"

Teresa bounded over to Jericho's side. "Don't touch the buttons! Where did you get it?" She snatched it out of Jericho's hands.

"Give it back!" Jericho tried to grab it, to no avail. "I just found it, over on the island!"

"Oh!" Teresa was bouncing up and down with excitement. "Can't you see how incredible this is? We can call Gippart for help! If it still works; let's just hope it still works!" She pushed some buttons and her face fell. "Oh dear. Address book almost empty. There's just a number for Mervin on 1, and some overseas number on 2."

"I know my own telephone number by heart, and my dad's, and Baz's. And 999," said Josh.

"Hmm," Teresa grunted.

Baz asked, "Do *you* know a more useful one, then?"

Teresa nodded, smiling mysteriously.

"Really?" Josh insisted. "Whose?"

"Moussa's," said Teresa. "Moussa's mobile number."

"What? Do you know that one by heart?"

At that Teresa lifted her chin and glared at them haughtily from beneath half-lowered lids. "*Every* girl at Gippart knows Moussa's number by heart," she drawled. Then she giggled and quickly punched in the number. Josh and Baz leaned close to her, their ears as near to the phone as they could get.

It was hard to believe, but someone answered. Moussa!

"Moussa?" she cried. "It's Teresa! We can't come home!"

There was a short bark from the other end.

"We're stuck! Spratt and Garnet messed about with the time, and now we're stuck!"

Moussa was responding in a loud and urgent voice, and Josh heard "terrible problems here" and "Max Herbert blowing his top" and "absolutely top secret". Then he asked something Josh couldn't hear. Teresa answered, "Yeah, but we want to come back! Can't you fix it?" She listened intently and nodded. "We'll try." Then she gave the phone to Josh. "He wants to speak to you."

Josh gingerly put the phone to his ear. "Hello?"

"Josh? Josh, everything OK?"

"Yes," said Josh, "only—"

"Shut up, little brother, and listen. No time to lose. One, you're stuck. We don't know why, and we can't help you right now. We're doing everything we can, I promise you, but all gateways into *umaya* are frozen. Two, try everything you can to get back. That Baz of yours is a fund of ideas. And Teresa's on the ball too. Listen to her. And you yourself are capable of much more than you think. Your best bet is to get to the frontier, if you can find it. Three, call your parents and invent some excuse. Tell them you've gone camping in Wales with a mate or something. It's half-term, so it works out well. Make sure they don't get worried."

"Moussa," cried Josh, "can't *you* find out where the Tembe are? Can't *you* come out here?"

"No, I can't, stupid. The connection between Gippart and *umaya* has been cut! And I don't know a thing about the Tembe. You'd better get off now, in case your battery goes dead or you run out of minutes. I'll call you. Tomorrow morning at nine. Make sure you're by yourselves. We'll know more by then. Joshie, chin up, eh, you can do it! Ciao!" And he was gone.

Josh folded the phone shut, crestfallen. But Teresa was positively beaming. "Right, let's call home," she said. Which they did, one by one. Teresa spoke to Louisa, Baz to his furious dad.

"Phew," said Baz, passing the phone to Josh, "it's only half past eight at night over there. *Last* night! And he's already livid."

Josh, to his relief, got Edwin. He was slurring his words and must have been at the whisky again. Which suited Josh fine, for once. Now Mo would think that Edwin had simply failed to get the message straight.

Having been in touch with home made all three of them feel better. They crouched down and studied the map, which Josh had taken out of his trusty backpack. By some miracle, the map was still dry.

"Where to now?"

"Over there is a road into the desert," Josh pointed out. "Just outside that town over there. Tsumir. Look, the road goes over those mountains – past those villages – straight to Ixilis, in the desert. That's where the Mabeh live."

"And the Mabeh know where the Tembe hide out."

They took their black hats out of their backpacks and put them on. Zizi perched contentedly on top of Josh's hat. Hoisting on the backpacks, they then clambered up the grassy embankment to the road.

Josh turned to Jericho, who was still standing barefoot in the water, staring out at the sea. "Aren't you coming?" he called.

She shook her tangled hair as if she was dissatisfied about something. Frowning, she kept looking back over her shoulder as she climbed up the hill after him.

"What is it now? Are you upset because Teresa took that phone from you? But it's no use to you anyway," said Josh.

But she shook her head and didn't answer.

A narrow footpath led through overgrown fields to the small town on the coast. It was pleasantly warm, the warmth tinged by a brisk sea breeze. Steep mountains rose to their left, and there were even snow-covered peaks glistening on the horizon. On their right was the turbulent sea, which from a safe distance looked playful and sunny. Just ahead of them they could see the walls of a modest fortified town. They had to make their way among goats, scrawny brown sheep and small herds of piebald horses. Baz firmly held on to his softly growling panther by the scruff of the neck. But when, just outside the town of Tsumir, they came to a wharf bustling with noisy people, the panther tugged free and ran off into the fields.

They stood and watched the scene from a little way off. People were unloading large bundles and baskets from the ships moored to the quay, and setting out their contents on carpets and tables. There were glistening fish, crabs and seashells, as well as linens and fabrics, pottery, herbs and jewellery. Townspeople were strolling up from the town, many of them carrying things to sell. Others had set up stalls for their wares. Baz trotted off towards the milling crowd, curious to see what it was all about.

Josh felt Jericho's hand sliding up his arm. Grabbing his upper arm, she pulled him close, resting her chin on his shoulder, her lips touching his ear. Her voice was wheedling and as soft as the buzzing of a bee. "Won't you buy me some new clothes, Josh? Nothing too fancy – that would attract too much attention. But something pretty. My favourite colour is dark red."

"Clothes?"

He sounded so amazed that it made Teresa look up.

"Clothes – Teresa, Jericho needs something to wear," Josh stammered. "Maybe we should—"

"We spent much too much of our money on Brand already," Teresa said bluntly. "We can't buy anything that isn't absolutely necessary."

"But Teresa," Josh insisted, "Jericho saved our lives! And she's the one who found the phone too!"

"The answer is no."

"All right, but look at me, you bitch!" said Jericho, suddenly livid. She plucked at her wet, torn dress that was no longer white. "You can see right through the holes! They'll arrest me for vagrancy looking like this!"

"She's right, Teresa," said Josh. "Look at her."

Teresa turned away. "Oh, all right. If you're going to start taking that ghost's side, Josh, then suit yourself!" She hopped on to the road and marched off towards the town centre.

"Well, fine," said Jericho. "We *will* just suit ourselves in that case, whether Madam Teresa likes it or not. You can just steal some, can't you? That way the money's not a problem."

Josh went red, and started shaking his head.

"Oh, please, for *me*? I always *did* adore pretty clothes. And besides, you're a liar and a thief, so you might as well behave like one too." She gave him a shove towards the market stalls. "In the meantime, I'll start walking up the road into the mountains. See you later, then! And remember, I prefer dark red."

* * *

Dumbfounded, Josh walked on to the wharf, where the market was now in full swing. The ships' merchants were touting their wares at the top of their voices to the townsfolk, and pedlars from the town offered their merchandise to the seafarers with equal enthusiasm. Josh was nervous, but determined. Jericho was right about her clothes, of course. She couldn't possibly keep walking around in those rags. Besides, one good turn deserved another. She had made it over here from the great void with the utmost difficulty, and if it hadn't been for her they'd be dead by now. He was going to nick something really special for her. After all, wasn't he her big brother? And he had a lot to make up for.

He threaded his way slowly through the stalls towards Baz.

"Toilet water! Coconut oil! Goat's milk to soften the skin!"

"Dates, the very best! Figs! Pitted dates!"

"Blue cottons! Silks in every colour of the rainbow! Every colour, every design! From far across the ocean and from the distant deserts!"

"Hey, merchant, you, with the kettles… Do you by any chance have any coffee pots from Ixilis? Those silver ones inlaid with turquoise stones?"

"Ho, man, *I'm* not Siparti! Coffee pots from Ixilis, he wants, no less! I have kettles from Wartsigir-on-Sea, perfectly respectable, decent, ordinary wares!"

Had he heard right? Josh blinked. "*I'm* not Siparti!" Siparti? He glanced at Baz out of the corner of his eye, but he was busy talking to a woman selling musical instruments and appeared to have heard nothing out of the ordinary. Josh shrugged and went reconnoitring. Food, brassware, salves and oils, glassware, birds. Zizi, still perched on top of his hat, started chirping excitedly. Ink, perfume, leather bags and shoes, necklaces. Then at last, over there: clothes! A little group of men and women was seated on the ground, sewing. A customer was waiting for them to finish, with a happy smile on her face. Ready-to-wear outfits hung from the gunwale of the boat behind them. Long robes, scarves, shirts – everything you could think of. Blue, white, or with yellow flowers. Josh looked at everything as discreetly as he could. Those over there were too small. Trousers? Would she like a pair of red trousers? Then he suddenly spotted them: a couple of dark red dresses hanging at the end of a row of dresses in all colours of the rainbow. They were hanging near the prow, and were just the right size.

He leaned nonchalantly against one of the mooring posts. What should he do? Rip the dress off the hook and make a run for it? No, that wouldn't be very clever. Raise a fire alarm? Too conspicuous. *Come on, Josh, master thief: how do you usually go about it then? Well, usually I only steal when the opportunity arises.* He sauntered back and forth in front of the tailors until he had the unpleasant sensation that he was being watched. Glancing over his shoulder, he found himself looking straight into the eyes of a girl. He looked away, but it was too late.

"Hey, you, boy!" She was wearing a simple black dress and a little black cap, and she had a very penetrating gaze. She was carrying a pile of slim red pamphlets in her arms. Reluctantly he turned to face her. "What's your name, boy?"

"Joshua Cope," he said sullenly. "But—"

"Joshua Cope, nothing escapes notice." She brought her face close to his. "Do not succumb to the sin of greed, boy! Theft is a deadly sin." She snared his shoulder in a pincer-like grip. He tried to shake off her hand, but with no luck.

"Oh, leave the poor lad alone," grumbled a passing sailor.

Now, to Josh's relief, she turned to the sailor. "And who, then, will champion virtue, if not I? Yea, thyself would do better to reflect on how best to conduct business in a virtuous manner, most especially over the seas, where there is no one like me to be on the lookout for rampant greed! For he who desires to obtain gold over the seas must bring the light in return, sailor!"

This seemed to Josh like a good time to make his escape, but at the last minute she stopped him, pushing one of the red pamphlets into his hands. "Read this," she commanded. "For the sake of your eternal soul!" Josh let it drop to the ground, uninterested, but she picked it up again and pushed it firmly into his backpack.

Two women had been looking on, shaking their heads. "Nobody wants those boring Kauri pamphlets, sister. Stop bothering us all the time!"

"It is a great shame that you do not support me in my work, madam," said the girl. "Greed sets out from here to sail all the oceans of the world. Is this not the last chance we have to curb rapacity, and to remind our sailors of their moral duty?"

"For all I know, sister, the moral duty your sect preaches chiefly consists of making as much profit as possible," replied the woman sarcastically, which made the sister gasp and take a deep breath to embark on a lengthy rebuttal. But Josh didn't stay around to listen to a debate about trade and morals. He made himself scarce, leaving the sermonizer to her new victims, and went back to casing the joint, sizing up the tailors, trying to decide how to go about it. He thought of and rejected all kinds of plans. Finally he ran his fingers gloomily through his hair. He'd just have to wait until thieves' luck was with him.

And just the way these things sometimes happen, on a day when the sun is shining and the sea breeze is blowing, good luck did come his way. Suddenly, unexpectedly, he had his chance. There! A small black shadow streaked up the quay from the right. He saw at once what it was: Baz's panther! One of the tailors sprang to his feet, shouting at the other merchants, and they all jumped up, waving their arms and yelling, "Liparti! Liparti!" A crowd formed around the panther, which had frozen in its tracks. No one was watching the merchandise. That was the moment in which Josh pounced. With trembling fingers he pulled two, three dresses off their hooks, then took to his heels, everything a blur before his eyes, his heart pounding in his mouth.

A great shout went up from the quay. He didn't know if it was because he'd been spotted, or because they were yelling at the panther. It didn't matter; it had worked; he'd got away with it! He ran into the town, dashed blindly along the streets and alleys, pushed people out of his way, jumped over a sleeping dog, hid in a doorway, inspected his booty, tossed the dresses that were a lighter red in through an open window and finally strolled out of town again, as cool as a cucumber, Zizi winging along above his head. He took the main road east, the dark red dress rolled up inside his backpack.

He could have jumped for joy. He'd done it! *Need to have a job done? You can count on Josh, master thief, no problem.* Oh, the world lay at his feet. He would be rich and have anything he wanted! He'd wear dark clothes, so that he'd melt into the darkness at night. He could lead a double life. During the daytime, Josh Cope, a bit of a dreamer. And at night, the avenging wolf, the master thief.

He was walking on air during that first part of the journey into the mountains. The noonday sun smiled down on him, and the sea breeze caressed his hair admiringly. Bright horses whinnied as if greeting a friend. *Umaya* was fantastic. He leapt off the road when he saw Jericho sitting in the shade of a large rock. She sprang to her feet on seeing him.

"Have you got it?"

Slowly and triumphantly he took the dress out of his pack.

Jericho whistled in approval. "Good going, brother!" She patted the dress and looked it over appraisingly. "Nice material, a little on the heavy side perhaps. The sleeves are a bit funny." She held the dress up against her body to see how long it was, then quickly took off her white dress and put on the new one. It looked amazing on her. She was transformed from a drowned cat into a lady. Yes, she looked more than presentable now.

"Well, *I* like the sleeves," said Josh. "You really look good like that."

She glanced at him with her sly, crooked smile. But her face fell abruptly as she caught sight of something over his shoulder. That voice – it came like a slap in the face to Josh.

"That bloody dress could cost us our lives, you bonehead!" Teresa came up behind them in a fury. She marched over to Josh and grabbed him by the arm. "Have you lost your marbles! What the hell is wrong with you!"

Josh jerked free and wanted to shout in her face that she should mind her own business, when Baz ran up, breathless. "Josh, they're looking for you! They're asking everyone in town if they've seen Joshua Cope!"

"What?"

"You stupid oaf," cried Teresa. "They even know your name!"

Josh was dumbstruck. All his high spirits seeped out of him and a gnawing feeling of shame and fear took hold of him instead. But he was also seething. He'd just about had enough of everybody constantly getting at him.

"So what? We're not going back there anyway, are we?"

"And what if they come after us, smarty-pants?"

He'd already started walking, heading for the mountains. He heard the others scrambling to follow him.

"Stupid thief," panted Teresa. "Don't you understand? We're in *umaya.* Who knows what might happen here if you steal their stuff! Do you really want to have man-eating monsters nipping at your heels?"

Josh stepped up his pace, and didn't answer.

"They might even have werewolves here," Teresa went on, her voice suddenly a little shaky. "Or we'll be tortured and beheaded, or they'll burn us at the stake!"

"They haven't caught us yet," said Baz, and Josh was grateful to him for that.

He started walking even faster, even though his heart felt fit to burst. He did his utmost to stay ahead of the others. The grumbling noises behind him were dying down. *Good for you,* he thought, *you bunch of pessimists.* He was sure it wasn't as dire as all that. And anyway, it wasn't as if he'd had any choice, had he? Hadn't Jericho needed new clothes, yes or no? Hadn't she saved their lives, yes or no?

Josh trudged on, a good distance ahead of the others. The road began to climb up windswept rocky inclines. His indignation evaporated. At the top of a short steep bit he stopped, out of breath. They were up so high that he could see the town of Tsumir lying far below, a glistening dot on the shore of a turquoise sea, in the middle of which rose the proud island of Trellis. He could even see the market quay, and the ships moored there. Jericho quietly came and stood next to him, and grabbed his hand.

When Baz and Teresa got to the top, they sat down on the ground without a word, massaging their calves. The panther stretched out beside them. Teresa unpacked her backpack. She'd been carrying another bundle, which she now untied. With the money that remained she had bought provisions in Tsumir for their journey: food, towels, a pile of strange long underwear and knee socks, water, and four blankets. Then they each packed the supplies into their own backpacks. Jericho rolled up her extra underwear in her blanket, tying it in such a way that she could carry it on her back. Satisfied, she tried out her backpack. But she didn't say anything, didn't say thank you.

Despite the rush, Teresa had even managed to swap a few bird calls and the bag of salt for some extra cash. "You're either an Associate or you aren't," she said.

As they drank some water from a leather gourd, munching on honeybread, goat's cheese and almonds, Josh looked back at the road they had just climbed. There were dots down there. Well, why shouldn't there be? But there were an awful lot of them: dots marching in their direction at a rapid pace.

Jericho crouched beside him. Following his gaze, she nodded. "It was to be expected," she said. "But you'll think of something, won't you?"

"What?" asked Baz.

Teresa clicked her tongue angrily. "They're after us!" Hastily she started putting away the food. "Get off the road," she snapped. "Hurry up. We're going north-east. Follow me."

They dived after Teresa into the underbrush, through thorny bushes, over rocky alpine meadows full of frisky sheep that bleated much too loudly, and across mountain streams. They left the road far behind, and when they tried to find it again it wasn't where it should have been. After an angry hour of bickering, during which each blamed the other for getting lost and Josh's compass had led them to a number of wrong mountain trails, they finally found the road again. Better still, their pursuers were nowhere to be seen.

"Well, I'd rather be chased than lost," said Baz. They all fervently agreed. Henceforth they stuck to the stony road, nervously glancing over their shoulders.

When evening began to fall, they breathed a sigh of relief. They felt that the pitch-black shadows of the trees and rocks, far from being creepy, would protect them. Finally they felt invisible. So invisible that they made straight for the dilapidated hut that they had spied in the middle of a rocky sheep meadow. It was a shepherd's hut. Inside they found sacks, stores of salt for the sheep licks, and a crude bed. Mutely Josh sank down on a pile of sacks. Mutely Teresa distributed dates and bread. Mutely Baz, Teresa and Jericho stretched out on the bed, the panther between them. They rolled themselves up in their blankets, and then there was complete silence.

* * *

Silence? After a little while there was the sound of bare feet padding over the stone floor. Jericho sneaked over to Josh's bed of sacks and crept quietly in beside him under his blanket.

"I'm joining you," she said softly. "Is that all right?"

Josh nodded in the dark.

"Thank you for the dress," she whispered in his ear. "I think you're the best, really I do."

Josh shrugged. But a warm glow coursed through his insides and made him smile.

Jericho sniffed and grumbled something inaudible. After a little while she sighed contentedly. "Snug as two bugs in a rug. The way we used to be. Two little wolves."

"You do remember all that then, do you?"

"No," yawned Jericho. She pushed her head into Josh's shoulder and snuggled against him.

"Tell me," Josh insisted. "Tell me how you caught me. Before you forget."

"Hmm. Shall I tell you something? I always wanted to have a sister."

"Yeah. I always wanted a brother."

"So that didn't work out too well."

"But you know, I don't mind having a sister. I think you're great. Honestly."

"Honestly?"

Josh nodded.

"Good," said Jericho. "How do you say it? Cool?"

"Cool."

Jericho grinned. "Before, you wouldn't have known that you thought I was cool. It took so long before you let me catch you! We'd been dangling that bracelet right in front of your nose for years and years. It took twelve years for you to take the bait. I swear, we tried everything we could to get you to take it. Once I even left it in a locker at your school. Turns out it was someone else's locker, so I had to snatch it back from the girl who had it. My, did she scream, when I came to her in the night to get the bracelet back!"

"Oh," said Josh. "Who was it?"

"I think her name was Diana. Could it have been?"

Josh had to think. "Diana Masters? Perfect! So were you after me all those years?"

"Yes. And there you were, thinking you were the great master thief – pfff, rubbish! You didn't even catch on when I shoved it right in your face."

"But in the end I did," said Josh. "I took it from that lady in the fur coat, on the bus."

"Huh, dirty thief, she was! She'd pinched the bracelet from a stall in the flea market. You were the one who was supposed to find it. We made her get on and off buses until you finally came along and stood next to her. We went to a lot of trouble to make it happen."

They lay side by side in silence. "This is the way it should be from now on." Jericho laughed softly. "Josh, you and I – we can do whatever we want. Between the two of us we can beat anyone. Shall we? How about being wolves again?"

Josh listened motionless, heart pounding.

"We can steal anything we need, and I'll teach you how to float, both in the water and in the air, so that nobody will ever be able to catch us. And I'll teach you how to sneak around the back of time." She laughed again, wickedly. "We can become highwaymen, time's terrorists, Josh, and they'll be scared to death of us. The two terrible wolves of Cope, they'll say, Josh and Jericho. And then they'll have a fit."

Josh saw himself streaking through the dark starry night, a masked figure with a black cape fluttering behind him. He saw himself hauling Edwin out of bed, the eternally drunken loser with the lame jokes. He saw himself slinging the wretch around in the air. Edwin screamed in terror and begged for mercy, until Josh flung him right over the horizon, where he crashed splat on the hard ground. He took a deep breath.

"Well?" Jericho insisted.

Josh thought of Baz and Teresa. And the expedition. "I can't desert Baz," he said. "Nor Teresa."

"Teresa!" Jericho snorted. "She'd like nothing better than to give me a kick in the backside and send me flying back to where I came from."

"But Baz..." Josh suddenly remembered something she'd said. "Is he really going to be the best drummer in the world?"

"Oh yes," said Jericho. "Of course. Bhasvar Patel. Baz, right? The best drummer in the land, anyway. But how about it? Baz doesn't need you, really he doesn't. That Teresa will look after him."

Josh shook his head. "Baz can look after himself. But that's not it. I can't leave them in the lurch now. Baz is my best friend. When we get back we'll do it, Jericho. OK?"

Jericho was speechless. Then she growled, "Back *where*? And when?"

"Back in our own time."

"Oh, stop that silly nonsense, will you! I just want to know where and when. That way we'll have a definite date."

"We *have* a date," said Josh. "You don't have to go on about it."

Jericho turned her back on him.

"Anyway, I'm the oldest," said Josh firmly.

Then, a little later: "I promised, didn't I?"

But Jericho didn't say another word.

10
Royal Blue

"I can't go on," said Josh, halfway up a barren gradient of scree.

A few hours ago they had all been startled awake at the same time, as if a cannon had been fired. They'd rushed outside into the grey dawn, and it had been quite a while before they'd realized there was nobody on their heels. They kept walking, chewing crusts of bread, occasionally stopping for a quick pee behind a rock or to gulp some water from a stream. They climbed higher and higher as the sun came up: past the treeline, into the raw world of naked rocks and stiff bare grass. And halfway up that sun-baked slope, Josh's legs suddenly refused to go on. He stood there swaying dangerously for a while, as if paralysed. Then he collapsed backwards, in slow motion. On top of his backpack. He didn't move, but stayed just where he fell.

"Time for a rest," declared Teresa.

They sat in silence, peering down at the road they had climbed yesterday. Only the panther, greedily guzzling the dates Baz was feeding him, seemed content. And Zizi, of course. She was pulling a date apart, chirping softly to herself.

"They must have given up," said Baz.

Teresa shrugged, cutting a slice of bread into quarters. Then she looked up, concerned. "Hey, wait a minute, wait a minute! Hasn't time gone backwards again, Baz? Didn't it run back automatically? If so, we should be safe."

Baz shook his head. "That's the odd thing. I don't understand either. We're still in the same rhythm as we were yesterday, around 1630. But something doesn't feel right. It's as if it wants to slow down, but can't. As if someone were trying to hold back time." He shrugged. "I simply don't have a good enough grasp of this time-rhythm thing. I ought to ask a professional Senser about it some day."

"Don't tell me you mean Mervin Spratt," said Teresa.

"Actually, I wouldn't mind having a word with Spratt about it."

"With that *murderer*?"

Baz shook his head. "He's a real Senser. The best. I'd just like to discuss it with someone who really knows his stuff. A real professional."

"Know what *I* think is odd?" asked Teresa. "I think it's odd that Moussa hasn't called us yet."

"Do you think there's something the matter at Gippart?" asked Baz, as Teresa checked to see if the mobile phone battery was still full. "It's past nine o'clock!"

"It seems to me we're the ones in trouble, not Gippart," muttered Josh, shakily getting to his feet. "I bet Garnet and Spratt are after us. I don't trust those two one bit." He took off his jacket. Despite a hefty west wind, the climbing had made him sweat. And he started feeling even warmer when Jericho hissed, "You'd better watch out for those people following us, Josh. You can't rest here too long."

"So they're still back there?"

She nodded gravely.

"Well then, you'll just have to chase them away, you and your ghost friends, won't you?" said Baz with a laugh.

"Why don't you just try and solve your own problems

today!" she snapped. "I've enough to worry about."

"What do you have to worry about?" asked Josh.

She sighed. Today her hair was nearly as brown as his. But her eyes were still strange – unnaturally colourless. Whispering so softly that only Josh could hear, she breathed, "He was here again last night. He was on the roof. And he was playing that wretched violin."

"Spratt?" he asked.

"No, no," said Jericho. "Lucide!"

They were by no means rested, but didn't dare take a longer break. Sighing and groaning, they got to their feet and hoisted their heavy packs on to their exhausted backs again.

Josh, leaning against a rock to get his breath back, stared at the mountains up ahead. He saw how the road kept zigzagging up and up across bare rocky expanses, before disappearing beyond yet another ridge, behind which lay even higher peaks. It made him think of their summer holiday in the Pyrenees last year. There had been thunderstorms every night of the three-day hike; all night long they had lain quaking with fear in their little tent above the treeline, caught in a bombardment of lightning and thunder for hours on end. Edwin had slid down an expanse of scree, they'd had to cross a dangerous glacier after getting lost, Josh had fallen into a mountain stream and hadn't stopped complaining about all the walking, and on the return journey Mo had sighed, "Never again!"

It was nearly noon, and they ate some crisps, cheese and bread. The west wind at their backs pushed them along. From time to time they thought they could hear voices behind them, and they'd step up the pace a bit. When the light began to fade, the trail brought them to a narrow sheltered pasture hemmed in by two sheer cliffs. Further on, the trail led precipitously up to their first real mountain pass: a narrow corridor between two peaks. It was marked by an oddly shaped black rock positioned in the middle of it. They climbed up to it slowly, panting and perspiring. The little panther was the first to the top, followed by Baz, who called down, "Come have a look – it's amazing!"

The others followed him, scrabbling with hands and feet, and then they were all standing pressed close together on the windswept, narrow pass between two sheer rock faces. A grey, magnificent mountain landscape stretched out before them. On the other side of the pass was a small green valley with a stream running through it, but beyond that the real peaks began: enormous, sharp-toothed mountains – the Takras – reaching high into the sky. It was as if the entire world consisted of inaccessible, threatening mountains, above which loomed an ominous evening sky.

They had a tough job ahead of them if they were going to cross the Takras. Josh's heart sank. He was in an ice-cold sweat, shivering, his feet were burning, and his legs trembled with exhaustion.

Teresa whistled through her teeth. "Awesome. It's the beginning of the world!"

"The end of the world, if you ask me," said Josh, sinking to the ground. "Those mountains are impassable!"

"Of course they're not," said Teresa. "All we have to do is follow the trail. It doesn't look that far on the map."

"Anyway, we have to cross them," said Baz, looking around breathlessly. "We have to be home by Wednesday. Listen to those birds! Way up there in the sky. Enormous birds of prey. Can you see them?"

Josh glanced back nervously at the road they had just climbed. He couldn't see anyone in pursuit. To his concern, he couldn't see Zizi either.

Baz flung his backpack on the ground and crouched down next to him. He ran his hands over the black rock in the middle of the pass with great interest. "I think this is some sort of monument," he said. "What do you think it's supposed to represent?"

"A bird of prey," guessed Teresa. "With a nasty beak."

"There's an inscription in the rock over here," said Josh. "If only I had that translating-pencil!"

Teresa rubbed her finger over the cursive, strangely slanted characters. "I bet it says KILROY WAS HERE. Or I LOVE BERNIE."

"Or PASS ON PERIL OF DEATH," said Josh.

"Oh, will you stop it?" grumbled Teresa. "Who'd like a toffee? We'll look for a sheltered spot down in the valley below, and we'll have something to eat and then go to sleep. There's water to drink down there, and we have our blankets. We can make a fire too, with your compass, Josh."

"No fire," he said. "That would attract our pursuers."

"I almost forgot, we've got *that* to worry about as well! All your fault, you stupid thief!"

"Excellent thief!" cried Jericho. "If it had been up to you, I'd still be walking around in those disgusting rags! Josh is a master thief! He fooled them all!" She'd shouted it out at the top of her voice, and suddenly it came echoing back from all directions. They all jumped, except Jericho, who was glaring at the others, her eyes glittering with anger, and she hadn't finished yet. But then a pebble rolled down the hill. It came to rest at their feet. They stiffened. A few more pebbles clattered down. They stared at the little stones, and then all four looked up at the same time.

It wasn't Jericho's voice that had made the stones come loose. Halfway up the slope leading to the summit to the left of the pass, a man was looking down at them. He was dressed in blue with a belt around his waist, into which were stuck two long, slender swords, studded with precious gems. He tilted his head back and greeted them solemnly.

"Welcome to Braxassallar-Takras," he said. "Master thief, cat, and friends. Customs Inspector A. Marchrizar welcomes you. Your identification papers, please."

Customs Inspector Marchrizar, the border guard, didn't seem dissatisfied with the identity cards they dug out of their backpacks. As Gippart Associates, they had been given all kinds of impressive passports, visas, residency and travel permits. Only Jericho had nothing to show him.

"If you don't have a passport, you'll have to find someone who is prepared to vouch for you," said the border guard. His piercing eyes rested briefly on Jericho's bracelet, on Teresa's gold necklace, and on the shiny buttons and red fur collars of the boys' jackets. Then rubbing his prominent nose he looked Josh over from head to foot. "Master thief. I assume you are the leader?"

Josh nodded, taken aback.

"Then would you please sign here?" The man took a document out of his blue tunic. He handed Josh a sharpened pencil, and Josh signed his name to something.

"Not to stand on ceremony," said the border guard, smiling at last, "we are delighted to receive a party such as yours. There aren't many of our kin that come this way – certainly no young people."

Then he did something odd. He bent over the little panther and, laughing, rubbed his fist against its sharp fangs. The animal snapped at his hand, but the man spoke to it cheerfully and intimately, *"Chraskir, haksamtra dikri,"* or something to that effect, and gave the animal a friendly shove. Then he climbed back up the incline. Clambering nimbly up to a lookout platform, he peered towards Tsumir, then slid back down in a few long strides. "Follow me, if you please. You may spend the night with me in the border patrol hut. Tomorrow you may resume your journey into Braxassallar. The cost of your night's stay will be sixteen trikli."

They hurried after him, down into the valley.

"Great, isn't it, that we can sleep in a hut!"

"Did you hear that? He said we were kin!"

Josh looked at the border guard with admiration. His blue tunic hung nearly to the ground at the front and back, but it was left open at the sides, so that the long panels flapped impressively around his legs as he walked. His sleeves, too, were long and wide. His clothes glittered with gemstones and jewels sewn on here and there, and around his waist he wore a feather-trimmed sash, into which were stuck two rapiers. Josh thought he looked magnificent.

They had to run to keep up with him, taking care not to trip in the rapidly darkening night. At last he leapt up a small incline on the other side of the valley and, hopping up over the brow, turned left. And there, hidden behind a boulder, stood a small hut, half built into the rock. He led them inside and lit an oil lamp. It was a brown hut with wooden bunk beds, and in the middle there was a big table surrounded by a few chairs. Pinned to the wall was a large map. The place names had been written in the same slanted script they had noticed on the rock, up at the top of the pass.

"Sit down, visitors," he said. He took bread, meats, jars of honey and other sweet things from a cupboard, and placed everything on the table in front of them. Then he poked the fire in a cast-iron stove in a corner, and began to stir the pot of soup that was on it. They kicked off their shoes and contentedly sniffed the smell that soon wafted from the pot.

Meanwhile, Josh counted out a few coins on the table. He didn't have all that much left, after Captain Brand. "Is this enough?"

The border guard leaned over the coins, fascinated. He handled them and inspected them carefully. "Ah, coins from the north! Here, some coppers from Damara! But they seem to be of a new sort. These ones here I don't recognize – oh, of course, this one must be from Portilisi, but it's rather unusual. What form of government do they have in Portilisi now, guests?" They had no idea. The guard shook his head as he walked back to the pot. "You ought to know these things. Knowledge is power. I'm not sure of the exact value of these different coins, but if you pay me eight coppers plus five of those Portilisi coins, that should suffice."

He took the soup pan off the stove, placed it on the table and tossed them four spoons. Then he walked to the door, opened it and stared out into the night. "Master thief, I understand that someone is after you, am I right?"

They had started on the hot soup. Josh choked on his.

"Not to worry. Your pursuers have not yet scaled the pass, and they are unlikely to do so tonight. Besides, this hut is well concealed. The west wind blows the smoke and sounds away from the pass, in the opposite direction. But come tomorrow morning you will have to be on your guard. I am prepared to help, naturally. Kinsfolk must always look after one another." He patted the panther on the head.

When they were getting ready for the night, after finishing their meal, Josh dug his bird call out of his backpack. He went outside and climbed to the top of the boulder in front of the hut. Standing with his feet apart, he started making bird sounds, then listened intently. There, now! But then he'd never had a moment's doubt, although he had no idea where she'd been all day. Here she came – Zizi, streaking back to him like a flaming arrow, landing with a triumphant squawk on top of his head. It wasn't until he was about to climb down, pleased as Punch, that he noticed the customs inspector watching him from the roof of the hut. He was squatting up there motionless, his keen eyes glittering in the cold darkness. Josh quickly slid off the boulder, scurried into the hut and dived into one of the lower bunks, Zizi still clinging to his head. Although shivering with fright, he fell into a deep slumber almost as soon as his head hit the pillow.

Something wasn't right. Josh woke up reluctantly. Voices, light. An argument! Dazed, he sat up. Edwin? No. In the light of the oil lamp he saw Baz, in his underwear, standing in the middle of the hut shouting at the border guard. Marchrizar was perched on top of the table, surrounded by the contents of the Gippart backpacks.

"What the…?" muttered Josh.

Baz swung round to face him. "So you're awake, finally! Look! The man's a thief! He's emptied all our backpacks!"

Teresa's voice came from the top bunk. "Give Mr Marchrizar a chance to explain, Baz. How's he supposed to explain if you keep shouting at him?"

Baz, spluttering, turned back to the guard, who was watching him with glittering eyes while still running his hands over their things. Then the man fixed his gaze on Josh.

"There seems to be a most peculiar misunderstanding," he said. "You know, surely, that guests are sacrosanct? No one would ever dream of stealing from a guest, nor would a guest ever rob his hosts and hostesses. You must have come from a long way off not to know this."

"But why are you going through our things?"

"Why, wouldn't you do the same, in my place? A guest, surely, allows his host to satisfy his curiosity and hunger for knowledge? What is a guest's duty if not to supply new knowledge?"

Teresa laughed. "Baz, I think they have different customs here from at home."

"He's just making an excuse, if you ask me," said Baz angrily.

The border guard was at his side in one big, fluttering leap. "My dearest guest," he said with suppressed vehemence, "you come from very far, and for that reason there is much I will forgive you. But I cannot allow you to accuse me of stealing from or lying to guests and kinsfolk. If you will not behave as a guest and kinsman, I'm afraid I shall be obliged to escort you back across the border and hand you over to the Tsumir police. And you know what that means."

"No, I don't," said Baz.

"No?" The customs inspector raised his eyebrows. "You don't know what they do with thieves in Tsumir?"

"No, we don't," said Josh apprehensively.

"They eat them, of course," said Marchrizar. "The reason we guard the border so carefully is that we don't want our best thieves to end up in the stomachs of the Tsumirans."

He jumped back on top of the table. "Might I ask you a question? This object" – he held up Josh's compass – "does it really serve as a lighting implement? And how does it work?"

But Josh was too shaken to answer him.

The next morning the hut was shrouded in a thick white mist. Shivering, they ate the breakfast Marchrizar had prepared for them: warm porridge, sweet tea, bacon and peppered sausages. Zizi was on the table, tucking into the porridge and making a big mess.

The guard was extremely kind and friendly today. "Your pursuers haven't yet crossed the pass," he informed them. "I will lead you up to the highest corridor, the Pass of Srixoch. It will not be difficult for you to make your own way from there down to our settlement. There you will be safe. Please do not worry." He patted them on the back and shoulders, poured them another cup of tea, stroked their seventeenth-century Damaran clothes and then sighed, "Royal, truly royal."

Josh took advantage of the opportunity to touch the inspector's clothes in turn: the jewels sewn on his long tunic, the feathery sash around his hips, the flashes of little mirrors embroidered on his sleeves and trouser legs. With his wide, flapping sleeves he looked like a large, gleaming, human bird of prey.

Outside, all sound was hushed and muffled. They followed Marchrizar in a straight line over a narrow trail marked with black stones. The white mist made it difficult to see anything. From time to time Baz would halt and listen. From the left, the right, in front and behind came snatches of human voices, faint sounds. It was impossible to determine exactly where these came from. Baz tugged Josh's sleeve. "There are people behind us," he whispered hoarsely. "I'm sure of it now."

"Close?"

"Not very," said Baz, but, contradicting himself, added, "I have no idea, in this fog."

Teresa had heard him. "Baz, what time are we in?" she asked. "I don't suppose time has run backwards again?"

Baz shook his head. "Can't you see for yourself? Marchrizar is still here. It's still the same rhythm, around 1630. With the same strange kind of tension. Someone really is holding back time, I'm sure of it."

"Damn," said Josh. He felt terrible. He'd had nightmares last night, for a change. And now the fog was making him claustrophobic. He felt like a rat caught in a trap. Who was holding back time? And why?

"Maybe it's Gippart," said Teresa. "To help us get back home."

"Then why haven't they called us?" said Josh.

"I turned off the phone," said Teresa. "The battery is half empty. As soon as Marchrizar leaves us at the pass, we'll call them ourselves."

In the endless hours of that morning they toiled up endless steep inclines. Marchrizar bounded ahead of them, and he kept urging them to go faster.

"I thought you were supposed to take it slowly in the mountains," Josh complained.

"Not if there are cannibals after you," said Baz laconically.

After hours of climbing at a steady pace through the mist and faint voices, Marchrizar finally gave them permission to take a breather. They had landed on a ridge, where, beside a shallow rushing brook, they came upon a black statue. It was very much like the bird statue at the border, but this bird of prey was larger, and its wings were spread as if it was about to fly away.

"My guests may rest for half an hour," said Marchrizar, putting out bread and salami. "Drink and eat. I have to take care of some customs formalities."

He vanished into the whispering, shuffling mist. Josh just caught sight of him drawing one of his rapiers before he disappeared.

"Can you still hear our pursuers?" Teresa asked Baz, chewing a piece of bread and salami.

Jericho smiled. "Can't you smell it? Marchrizar is taking care of things."

"What can you smell, then?" asked Josh.

Jericho sniffed deeply, her eyes closed. "Fear," she whispered. "Fear, and blood."

They went on eating, ears cocked for any sound. Suddenly Baz nodded, muttering to himself.

"What?" Teresa demanded.

Baz nodded again, tense. "Fear," he said quietly. "A fight."

Exactly half an hour later Marchrizar was back, still with sword in hand. He was chewing something. Wiping his sword, he stuck it back into the wide sash at his waist. "Not to worry," he said. "Follow me. We'll soon be out of this fog."

Silently they stood up and followed him, not daring to ask any questions. They had gone only a few paces uphill when a strange thing happened. The fog seemed to lift briefly, revealing a magnificent, sun-drenched mountain landscape. The next moment they were trudging through the blinding whiteness again. Then the fog parted once more. They stepped into clear sunlight and looked around, blinking. All around them lay the Takras mountain range in its full glory. There were no trees up here, only naked, rough, glittering blue rocks. The peaks were covered in snow. Here and there great greenish rivers of ice blanketed the slopes. They inhaled deeply. Ice-cold air, sharp as knives, rushed into their lungs, and they felt recharged with a new vitality. Their feet hurt and they'd been scared stiff, but all that was now forgotten. They looked in awe at the great birds soaring over the mountain tops. Zizi let go of Josh's shoulder, and flew higher and higher until she was just a little dot against the blue sky. Josh looked behind him. He was startled to see that they had just come up from a mountain valley that was filled to the rim with a thick white mist. Wisps of fog still lapped at their feet.

"We are now leaving the world of the lowlands behind," announced Marchrizar. "Follow me, visitors. We have another hour or two to go before we reach the Pass of Srixoch."

They walked on more slowly, and the guard pointed out the earth underfoot: the grass glittered with dewdrops that refracted the sunlight as if it had rained diamonds. The radiance was eye-dazzling, and Josh imagined himself collecting handfuls of those crystalline diamonds, taking heaps of them home with him, saw himself sleeping and swimming in diamonds. But he was perfectly well aware that they were really just drops of water. Drops of water in the sunshine.

Marchrizar pointed to the highest peaks and told them their names, proudly telling them tales about glaciers, waterfalls and birds of prey. He told them about his people's high-mountain fort, about their raids on Tsumir, about the centuries-old strife with the coastal settlers. He said that they, the mountain people, were in the habit of eating their own dead (a question of hygiene, he stressed) and explained that it had sometimes come to pass that they had disposed of the Tsumirans' corpses in the same way. In retaliation, the Tsumirans had decided, hundreds of years ago, to eat Braxassallar-Takrian thieves, in the hope of solving the riddle of their unbridled greed and rapacity. He laughed. "But what's so puzzling about greed? You, my kinsfolk, surely you must agree that greed is a most natural urge of all young people?"

They didn't quite know how to respond to that (although Josh did find his comment reassuring). But Teresa ended up posing the question that had been bothering her for a while. "Why do you keep saying we're related?"

Marchrizar glanced at her quickly. "Why, do you think we're not?"

"I don't know."

The customs inspector shook his head. "Travellers accompanied by a royal cat! Could these be anything other than relatives of ourselves, the Braxans – the Eagles of the sign of the Cat? Cat tamers and bird catchers, you are. It is hardly possible that you are not related to the Braxans, descended, via the noble daughter Brax, from Siparti *na* Temberi."

"Siparti *na* Temberi?!" they echoed in chorus.

"Surely that is your lineage?" asked Marchrizar.

They looked at each other in excitement. "Do you mean, you mean that you are descended from Temberi?"

"Not from Temberi, from Siparti. From Siparti *na* Temberi," said Marchrizar patiently. "Aren't you?"

"Of course we are," said Josh quickly; he thought it safer to be as closely related to these dangerous people as possible.

"That's the reason for our journey," said Teresa. "We are seeking the Tembe. The Tembe of Temberi. Do you know where we might find them, by any chance?"

"Knowledge is power," said the man, "but that, alas, is not within our knowledge. We know where Siparti's distant offspring are – that is to say, our own tribe and the five other tribes in the wide, wide world that wear the crown of Siparti *na* Temberi. But as for the Tembe, those extremely wise, extremely ancient, ill-fated bird catchers, the most star-crossed of them all, I am sorry, we haven't a clue. That knowledge was lost when our forefathers broke their vow that they would visit them and seek a reconciliation. A most terrible mistake, I must say. May I ask why you wish to pay a visit to the Tembe?"

"On account of their knowledge," said Teresa cryptically.

The border guard nodded. "Their knowledge must be extraordinary. After having lived for so very long in the most calamitous adversity. But are you not too young for that type of knowledge?"

"Knowledge is power," said Teresa.

"That is very true," agreed Marchrizar, "but this would be a lethal sort of knowledge, the *ultimate* knowledge – for even if you were to survive the harrowing voyage, you would surely find them so full of wrath at the way we have betrayed them that you'd be executed on the spot. And quite right too!" He sighed. "You must have received unprecedented permission to undertake such a fateful journey. Ah – so young! So young to die! Oh, well. While we are on the subject, I need a few particulars from you." He took a small notepad out of his tunic and turned to Josh. "Which lair do you belong in, if I may be so bold?"

"Uh… I don't belong to any lair."

"Magpie, Falcon, Buzzard? I am a Goshawk, as are all of us border guards, but you already knew that."

"Where we're from they don't have any of … those," Josh said apologetically.

The man frowned. "But you must, if you are to stay in our settlement. How old are you, thirteen, fourteen? From four to seven it's Sparrows, from eight to eleven or twelve, Jackdaws. After that you are allowed to choose between Magpies, Falcons, Kites, and, for the most talented youngsters, Buzzards. You, master thief, bird catcher, you'd certainly be justified in calling yourself Buzzard. What a pity that in your country this custom has been lost!"

"I'm a junior," said Josh, "and in the Scouts we've got the Beavers, the Cubs and then the Scouts, and finally the Explorers."

The customs inspector seemed interested, so Josh explained all about the school system and the names given to the different houses, about the different categories of Scouts and about ranks in the army.

"Knowledge is power," Marchrizar finally said with satisfaction. "Thank you. So, then, while you are staying with us you will introduce yourself as a member of the Buzzard lair, and you are to present yourself to Ych Kraslichar, who will sign you in to the Buzzard House."

* * *

The trail to the Pass of Srixoch was relatively easy. They made their way slowly up a wide trail that afforded them a spectacular view of the mountains. Before they knew it, they were on top of the pass, where a new panorama unfolded before them. "There is our fort, our Eagles' nest: Braxassallar-Takras!" cried the guard. Tossing his head back, he uttered a few raucous cries.

They peered into the distance. Yes, over there, at the foot of a waterfall lay a few black dots grouped against the mountain side: houses, barns. A clearly marked trail led down to the settlement.

"This is where I leave you. You will report to Kraslichar, of the Buzzard House. I hope that you will study our native customs, and that you will similarly share yours with us. Kinsfolk must share both knowledge and power." He took Josh's hand in his, bowed low over it and rubbed his pointy nose on the back of Josh's hand. Then he gave the fur collar of his jacket one last longing caress, muttering, "Royal, truly royal." He sighed deeply, shook the others by the hand as well, and then he was gone.

They began to descend the trail on the far side of the pass. Suddenly Teresa stopped and sat down on a rock. "Let's call Gippart now," she said. "This is just too crazy." She dug the phone out of her backpack and resolutely tapped in the number. The others crowded around her apprehensively. Except for Jericho, who lay down in the coarse grass, which was shimmering with blue star-shaped flowers, and played with Zizi, unconcerned. It took ages for someone to answer. Then came Moussa's voice, hoarse and fierce: "Yeah?"

"Moussa!"

It was wonderful to be in touch with reality. Josh and Baz bent their heads as close as possible to the phone, to hear what Moussa had to say.

"What! God Almighty, what time is it?" His voice sounded groggy. "Five in the morning. Teresa? Teresa!" He was suddenly wide awake. "What's the matter? Everything all right?"

"Yes, yes, we're fine. We're hanging in there, but why haven't you called us? Is everything OK at Gippart?"

"I was going to call you at nine, sugar. It's only five o'clock. I didn't get to sleep until three, damn it. We've been working round the clock here, all Sensers have been called back from leave, every technician's at his post in the control room. It's a twenty-four-hour operation." He yawned. "Just a minute, Teresa. I'll call you right back."

A click. They stared at the phone, perplexed.

"It's only five o'clock over there," said Baz. "Monday morning, and here it's already Tuesday! Wow, then we're really running fast. Well, yes, I suppose that's about right too." He snapped his fingers.

"They're working round the clock," said Josh. "All just so they can bring us back."

"Then I'm sure it'll work," said Teresa.

They waited impatiently for the phone to ring again. A few seconds later it did. "Tess, girl, here's Max. He'll give you further instructions. Keep your chin up, OK? We're working like mad here; it's going to be all right, kid."

Max's voice sounded agitated. "Teresa? How marvellous to hear your voice. How are you? Are the boys holding their own?"

Teresa nodded, muttered something, and Max continued. "To be perfectly frank, we haven't made much headway as yet. We're pulling out all the stops, but our top expert is missing. Listen carefully now to what I'm telling you. Our only chance, and I repeat, our only chance, lies in getting in touch with Mervin Spratt. He is the only one in the whole world who can help us solve this technical nightmare. We know he's still in your *umaya.* I am sure that he is looking for you. For God's sake, Teresa, see that you find him and get him to call us."

"But we have no idea where he is – and he's trying to kill us, Max!" Teresa cried. Josh nodded vehemently.

There was a deep sigh at the other end of the line. "Listen, Teresa, I know that Mervin's been in a terrible muddle recently.

He was stressed, under great strain – and, to be honest, Garnet Gippart was pushing him in a direction I did not approve of. He should never have been in *umaya* at all. But Garnet is back here now, and Mervin is on his own in your *umaya*; surely he has come to his senses by now."

"But then – Garnet has returned to Gippart?" cried Teresa. Josh's jaw dropped.

"How the hell can that be?" asked Baz.

"Well," said Max, "Gippart must have mounted some sort of lightning emergency raid to rescue a stranded family member. Garnet was back at Gippart less than a minute after the *umaya* borders had slammed shut. You see, Gippart can use its special influence and resort to specific techniques, and it's possible – but that may have been just gossip – it might even have had a little help from our arch-rival, Katz..."

They gasped. Garnet had been rescued. Garnet, not them. They *could* have been rescued. It slowly dawned on them what a dirty trick Gippart had played on them.

"And they just *ditched* us?" roared Teresa, who was the first to find her voice again. "They could have rescued us all and they just rescued that cow? And we can go to hell, for all they care? And you – you just let it happen, didn't you!"

They'd never seen Teresa really lose her temper. It was a sight to see, the way her fury boiled over, starting at her toes and welling all the way up to her head. She was furious. She ranted and raved and yelled into the phone. Then she hurled the thing to the ground and stalked off, seething.

Josh picked up the phone. "Max?"

"Joshua? Oh, my boy, my dear boy..." Max couldn't go on. Josh swallowed, and waited. "Yes, Joshua, this is a disaster, and I'm so sorry. I warned you that Gippart can be ruthless. But that's beside the point. We have got to get you out of there. Did you understand what I said about Mervin Spratt?"

"Yes, but Max, I won't do it, really I won't. You haven't seen him. He honestly wants to see us dead." He shuddered.

"Nonsense!" cried Max angrily. "This is not the time to be stubborn, Joshua. Your lives depend on it. It's your only chance! Find Spratt and tell him to call us! You have the phone!"

"But he's still on that island and I'm not going back there, do you hear?"

"If you could get off that island then he can do the same. You must find him. You must!"

Josh was silent. Max begged and pleaded. Finally Josh said coolly, "Listen, Max. You've said it yourself: Spratt is after us. So we don't have to go looking for him, 'cause he's looking for us, and if I have my way, he'll never catch us. We're going to the Tembe!"

Max interrupted him, shouting, "Please, my boy, please just try to be realistic! It won't do you any good to reach the Tembe by yourself! All of our research attests to that. Without special expertise and special safeguards you won't get through an exit point like theirs alive! You need Spratt in order to get past the Tembe. Now do you see?"

"No," snapped Josh savagely, tears springing to his eyes. "The only thing I see is that you could bloody well have brought us back, and you didn't, that you want us to throw ourselves into a murderer's arms of our own free will, and that you're sending us to an exit point we can't get through alive. Well, thanks a million, Max."

He broke the connection and flung the phone down on the grass. "They just abandoned us! The *bastards*, they..." He buried his face in his hands. Cursing, Teresa went over to him and put her arms around him. Baz sat next to him on the ground, biting his nails.

They sat like that for a while. Then Jericho – pale, savage, cheerful Jericho – came skipping up. "Come on, chin up," she said, smiling. "Isn't it lovely here?"

They glared at her. But Josh shook his head and wiped his nose. "She's right," he said. "It isn't as if we have much choice. Chins up."

"Chins up," Baz agreed. He jumped to his feet. "Right, come on, we aren't going to let idiotic old Gippart get us down, are we? Max hasn't got a clue. He hasn't ever visited the Tembe himself, has he? Who knows, it's probably not as bad as all that."

Nobody could stay depressed for very long on the high trails of Takras. The sun shone exceedingly brightly, the air was bracing and as clear as glass, and they found themselves walking on the top of the world. The entire world lay at their feet, and it felt as if, with every swing of their arms, they'd rise to even greater heights. Josh heard Baz and Teresa behind him chatting, singing and laughing. They were animatedly discussing groups and songs Josh had never even heard of, and then they'd rap a few lines, or belt out something in two-part harmony, before collapsing with laughter. Jericho ran past Josh, hid behind a rock and then leapt out to startle him. "Boo!"

She took his arm and matched her steps to his. "Let's stay here, Josh, and do what we said we'd do. Oh, let's!"

"Jericho, I've already *told* you we first have to get out of here alive. After that, maybe."

Jericho smiled her crooked smile. "I understand. But isn't it so much nicer here? Here you're a master thief, and they think you're really somebody. And it's so lovely here! I could teach you how to fly in no time, in this place." She looked at him expectantly.

Josh shook his head. "No, no! No means no! I've told you a thousand times!"

Jericho pulled a face. "You're mad, you. At home it's always your school, school, school, and then on top of that homework, homework, homework, and you're just a nobody there who's always being teased and bullied, while here you could so easily be a king or a chieftain, I bet."

Josh glared at her. "How do you know what it's like for me at home?"

"Idiot, didn't I tell you I've been sneaking around the back of time? I saw you, didn't I! Maths and biology and English and Lord knows what else. Don't you go thinking I know nothing about anything, just because I was twelve years old three hundred and fifty years ago."

"Whatever. We're still going home first." Josh walked on, deep in thought. "But Jericho," he said, more friendly all of a sudden, "are you *sure* you don't know any way to get us home? You can teach me how to sneak around behind time, can't you?"

"Course. But I've told you a hundred times there's only *one* time, and that you really can't jump out of it. Anyway, I don't feel like teaching you how to sneak around time just now. And besides, you'd have to change a little before you could do it."

"Change?"

"A little bit."

An unpleasant thought struck him. "You mean I'd have to be dead, like you, first?"

Jericho shrugged her shoulders. "Who can tell?"

"You really are no help at all!" Josh said angrily.

Jericho tapped him on the nose and darted away.

An hour later they were standing on top of a second, lower, pass with a good view of Braxassallar-Takras, which lay across from them, close enough so that they could distinguish the settlement's inhabitants. People clad in blue were sitting on top of the roofs of tall huts, while down below both adults and children, also dressed in blue, were milling around the huts. A waterfall cascaded down from a great height above the village, and at the foot of it a few people were bending down, doing something in the foaming water.

Teresa muttered something to herself. She stood stock-still, staring at the village with eerie concentration.

"What is it?" asked Josh.

She didn't seem to hear him. Then she exhaled, and laughed. "Nothing."

Josh suddenly felt faint. The world was spinning around in a sickening way. Shapes and colours were whirling before his eyes. Then everything went back to normal again. Baz clapped a hand to his mouth and cried out. Teresa turned back to them in alarm. "What's the matter with you two?"

Josh felt around for a rock to lean on. "It's over. I'm just tired, I think."

Baz didn't answer, but drummed a rhythm on his fingers, muttering to himself. He shook his head. "Let's go," he said.

It took them an hour to cover the last stretch of road to the settlement. First downhill, then back up. Finally, in order to reach the village they had to scale a sheer, high wall. They pulled themselves up by a sturdy rope that was fastened to the rock with iron spikes. But when they arrived at the top, a thin iron sword stopped them from heaving themselves up and over the edge. A stern face leaned out over the side.

"Halt! Your names, please!"

"Oh *come* on," yelled Teresa, who was clinging to the rope with shaking muscles, her feet planted against the rock wall. "Can't I come up first?"

"Your names!" came the voice again.

"Gippart expedition composed of Teresa Okwoma, Joshua Cope, Bhasvar Patel and Jericho, plus royal cat and bird, destination Tembe. Permission to pass from Customs Inspector Marchrizar and on our way to Ych Kraslichar. Now may I continue?"

"Thank you," said the border guard. "We have been expecting your arrival. Welcome to Fort Braxassallar. Your lair is Buzzard?"

"Yes!" squeaked Teresa. "Can I please come up now? I can't hold on much longer!"

The man took a step back and Teresa flopped over the edge on to the plateau, under an iron rail. After getting her breath back she helped Josh and Baz up over the last hump. The panther clawed its own way up the rock face and leapt nimbly on to the plateau beside them. They found themselves on an expansive piece of flat terrain abutting the rail that fenced off the cliff they had just scaled. Across from where they stood, a road led into the village proper, most of which was built up against the mountain side. There was a busy hustle and bustle: people in flowing blue robes coming and going; children scurrying in and out among the adults, shrieking and shouting in high voices. The border guard was a short man with a stern face and was dressed similarly to his colleague Marchrizar. He shook hands with them, then he took down their names in his notebook.

"Welcome," he said again, "dear kinsfolk. The Buzzard House is expecting you. However, first I must read you the rules."

He took a blue booklet from his breast pocket and started reading at top speed. They didn't understand much of it. It was about rights of larceny, rights of possession and dispossession, about age groups and death rights, categories of kin and categories of guests. After about ten minutes of this, the guard snapped the book shut and put it away. "You are expected to know the law, and abide by it," he said with a solemn nod of the head. "Ych Kraslichar awaits you. Take this trail, then the third trail on your left, which will lead up the mountain to the Buzzard House. I wish you a pleasant stay." He shook their hands again and went back to standing sentry at the gap in the railing.

They went the way he had shown them. The inhabitants dressed in blue stared at them with great interest and greeted them heartily: "Welcome, kinsfolk. Good afternoon, welcome!"

From time to time someone would reach out and touch them. The little panther, especially, came in for quite a bit of cautious, reverential patting. Annoyed, it hissed, and eventually leapt up the mountain side, swishing its tail, in order to get away from all the fuss. But for the Associates, it was the children that were the most annoying. A mob of little kids toddled after them, snatching at their clothes and then running off again, giggling. Halfway up the hillside, things got a bit out of hand. Suddenly little children were hurling themselves at them from all directions. They jumped on their backs, pulled at their packs, scratched their hands, bit the buttons off their jackets, tugged at their necklaces and bracelets, and started ripping their clothes to shreds.

"Have you gone mad?" cried Teresa, and Baz shouted, "Stop it, you little pests!" They started hitting and kicking at the children to get them off, taking care not to hurt them at first, then lashing out with more force. But, shrieking with laughter, the children kept coming back at them for more, with their probing little fingers and sharp teeth, as if they didn't feel any pain. Suddenly a figure in flowing blue robes ran up, brandishing a long stick. "Sparrows, stop it! Guest Rights! Guest Rights! Stop it at once, I say! Guest Rights!"

The children halted. The little girl who had clamped herself to Josh's back clung on as if frozen in place. "Guest Rights! Really?" she asked, disappointed.

"It's mess duty tonight, for all of you," said the woman, pulling the little girl off Josh's back and carefully prying open the jaws of a boy of about five who had his teeth fastened around Baz's ankle. "Anyone who walks about freely is a guest. Repeat after me!"

"Anyone who walks about freely is a guest," the children echoed in chorus.

"Is that clear? Run along then. And all of you, mess duty tonight in the Sparrow House. You too, Gix, I saw you." The children ran off, jeering and laughing.

"My sincere apologies," said the woman. "My name is Kraslichar, Ych. Those Sparrows get more stupid by the year. Do please excuse them." She shook hands with each of them, smiling. "It's as if they just can't manage to get even the very first rules into their little heads. One does not steal from guests. I knew that rule even in my sleep when I was just three years old. Please accept my apologies."

She walked on ahead of them, a striking woman in blue, her garments shimmering with white jewels. She halted at a large wooden house erected next to a statue of a bird. "Welcome to our Buzzard House," she said solemnly.

She strode up the three steps to the bare wooden door and motioned them inside. As they squeezed past her into the house, she ran her hands over their clothes. "Royal, indeed," she sighed.

The Buzzard House was a bit like the border hut: very plain and brown. It consisted of a large room that had a number of bunk beds filled with straw, and walls covered in bookshelves, and another large room with tables and narrow benches. A tall boy crouched motionless on top of one of the tables, watching them through half-closed lids. On the ground floor, three steps down from where they stood, they saw a large kitchen with an open brick hearth and two cast-iron cauldrons. Next to that was a scullery with a sink carved into the rock, and a simple pump. Behind a brick partition there were a couple of toilets consisting of a cubicle over a hole in the ground. Ych Kraslichar showed them around with great pride. The most unusual thing in the Buzzard House was the open cupboard hanging on one wall of the great room. It was bulging with precious objects. Gemstones, both polished and uncut, silver daggers, shiny gold, silver and bronze bracelets, a necklace and rings set with lapis lazuli, piles of gleaming coins, and a piece of gold brocade. Josh stared at the cupboard's contents.

"The Buzzards' treasures," said Ych Kraslichar. "Woe betide the Magpie that even thinks of touching it. We are always on our guard."

She showed them to their beds, where they deposited their backpacks.

"You are free to explore the settlement at your leisure," she said. "When night falls we assemble for the evening meal. We hope to welcome you into our midst at that time, and to hear about your experiences." She bowed. "We are honoured to give you shelter. Your experiences will enrich us. We also hope to have the opportunity to share our knowledge with you."

"Thank you very much," they replied, and went back outside.

"Well!" said Baz when they were alone again. "I'll be glad to ditch this bunch of thieves. It's lucky that we're their guests and kinsfolk. If we weren't, they'd rob us blind and then cut our throats, that's for sure."

"Well, I think they're fantastic," said Josh. "Did you see those jewels? *Wowee!*"

"Yeah, but you're a pickpocket yourself," said Teresa. "Baz is right, this is a dangerous place. Do you have any idea where we are? Do you?"

"Course I do," said Josh defensively.

"These people are Siparti's descendants! Don't you see how dangerous that is? Siparti had six offspring, and one of those six children was called Brax, remember, and the Braxans are descended from that daughter, who was obviously as much of a criminal as her father was before her! We have no business being here, and tomorrow we're getting out of here. I'll be glad when we get to the Mabeh."

Jericho shook her head. "*I* love it here. If Josh says yes, we're staying here, he and I."

"No way," said Teresa. "That's not even an option."

They were just passing an elderly, scantily dressed man. He was strolling along with a gentle smile on his face, in nothing but a worn blue loincloth, and with a string around his neck from which hung a light blue gemstone. He greeted them quietly and cheerfully. Just as they were returning his greeting, a young man strode resolutely up to the old fellow. "Good afternoon, sir. What's this, then, around your neck?" To their dismay, the young man whipped out a knife and cut through the piece of string. Pulling the stone off the string, he examined it appraisingly. "If this isn't the Blue of Garris! Thanks a million, old man. I've been itching to get my hand on a Garris stone for a whole month!"

The old man did not put up a struggle; he didn't shout, but just smiled and muttered something softly to himself. The young man ran off, clutching the stone in his fist, and the Associates were left standing there, bewildered, facing the old man.

"What should we do?" asked Teresa. "Do you want us to go for the police? Was the thief someone you know?"

The man gazed at them amiably. "Dear guests," he said in his gentle voice, "I am an Eagle, can't you see that? I do thank you for your concern. But I am, quite simply, an Eagle. And a pleasant afternoon to you." He went on his way, as if nothing had happened.

"What was all that about?" Baz asked.

"It must be something to do with those rules," mused Teresa. "If you ask me, they have very complicated laws here."

"If you ask me," Josh laughed, "stealing is permitted here."

"But not from guests," said Teresa.

"No, not from guests, or hosts and hostesses. But old men are fair game, it seems."

That afternoon they learnt quite a bit about the way things were run in Braxassallar. Some people sat indoors or on the roofs of their huts, scribbling on sheets of paper, or immersed in books, mouthing the words to themselves. Others prowled about, chatting with each other, until suddenly they'd pounce on some victim – always an elderly man or woman – who'd then almost always placidly allow himself or herself to be robbed. Only once or twice did one of these burst into tears. When that happened the thief would give the victim a severe talking-to before making off with the booty. Other inhabitants busied themselves with more normal occupations: men and women washed clothes in the waterfall, sold foods door to door, or taught groups of children in cramped sheds. The Associates stood listening in on one class of eight-year-olds: a lesson in the rules. The teacher, a bare-chested shabby old man, was testing them on their homework.

"Rule 13A. Chrikkig?"

A skinny boy jumped to his feet and slapped his hand to his forehead. He stuttered, blushing, "Every person by the name of Eagle shall have the right to be dispossessed, also Owl, uh, and Hawk..."

The class exploded in laughter.

"Hawk!" cried the teacher. "Young man, isn't your mother a Hawk? Well, does she have the right to be dispossessed?"

The poor boy blushed even deeper. "No, I mean ... I mean... Griffon Vulture?"

"No, not Griffon Vulture," said the teacher dryly. "Griffon Vulture falls under Rule 16, Nomads' Rights of Possession. Chrikkig, you will copy out Rules 1 to 13, thirteen times for me by tomorrow morning. You ought to be ashamed of yourself. You're a Jackdaw now, yet you still don't know what every Sparrow ought to know! Shoo! Out of my sight!"

Chrikkig turned round and trudged unhappily out of the shed as the other children eagerly waved their hands in the air. The Associates just caught the correct answer (Bearded Vulture) before they had to stand back to let the student through.

Teresa went up to him. "Hello, Chrikkig!"

The boy, startled, raised his head. "Oh, yes, you're those guests, aren't you? Family, right?" His eyes ran over their clothes and jewellery. "Guest Rights," he said regretfully. "Rule 4. I know that one."

"May I ask you something?" said Teresa.

The boy pouted. "I have to go and do my homework. I'm being punished. What do you want to know?"

"Could you explain to us when exactly you're allowed and when you're not allowed to rob somebody?"

"Don't ask me. I haven't sorted it out yet."

"But is anyone allowed to steal from us?"

"No, of course not. That's Rule 4. Guest Rights. Uncontested right of ownership is due to all guests, et cetera, and a guest is anyone whose arrival is announced and whose name is written in the guest book. Here's how you remember it: anyone who walks about freely is a guest. Anyone who's detained is prey." Then he took off.

"So, now we know," said Teresa. "We're safe."

A howl went up from the classroom. They were just in time to see a girl prising a ring off the teacher's finger. The teacher let her have her way, smiling. The whole class was shouting, "Rule 27! Rule 27!"

The Associates walked over to the waterfall. It was late in the afternoon and no one was doing laundry now. There was just one tough-looking woman standing sentry. She wore the same outfit as the other border guards, and she was brandishing a drawn sword.

"Greetings," she said gruffly.

"Greetings," they said.

"Please return to your lair, guests," said the sentry. "The mountains are not safe."

"Are you expecting an invasion?" Teresa asked.

"Guests always bring strife. The guest rules specify that we must defend our guests. You may arm yourselves, if you like. Buzzard, right?"

They nodded yes.

"All you have to do is request a weapons-ban exemption from Kraslichar. Then present yourselves to Station Number 3."

Baffled, they found their way back to the Buzzard House.

"Do you think she meant we're still being followed?" Josh asked. "Do you think those people from Tsumir might still be after us? Or Spratt, after all?"

"I thought Marchrizar had settled their score," said Baz.

"Maybe he didn't," said Teresa. "But this kind of thieves' nest is probably constantly under attack. They must be forced to fend off other gangs, or the police, if they even have such a thing here."

They were warmly received in the Buzzard House. The great

room was filled with young, blue-clad Braxans with their hair bristling with buzzard feathers. When the Associates entered they all stood up, applauding enthusiastically. A few cried, "Siparti! Siparti Xarxal!"

Shyly they waited for the applause to die down. Ych Kraslichar showed them to their seats, at the head of the centre table. She turned to face the gang of Buzzards, and, smiling, introduced the travellers. Patting Josh's shoulder, she announced, "Knowledge is power, brave ones. Let's hear the honourable master thief and his travelling companions describe for us over dinner the different laws governing our various Siparti tribes, all interconnected through the crowned cat."

Then she let out a blood-curdling yell. All of the Buzzards followed suit, and promptly big platters of food were carried in. The menu consisted of a sort of millet with a red, spicy meat sauce that made Josh's eyes water; it was delicious, but so hot that you could only eat it in little bites. He had to drink gallons of water. Meanwhile, more and more children came crowding around him, or perched in front of him on the table.

"Hey, master thief, what kind of laws do you have in your country?"

"What kind of birds do you catch?"

"Where's that cat of yours?"

"Do they cut off thieves' hands where you're from?"

They just kept peppering him with questions, until Jericho, bored, took her plate and sat down on the floor underneath the table. They had to listen to endless stories about the laws of the royal Braxans, Siparti's offspring via his noble eldest daughter Brax. Thus they learnt that the right of dispossession applied to everyone aged forty or older; and that anyone who had passed his Falcon or Buzzard exam could freely rob these Elders (the Eagles, the Owls and, on the top rung of wisdom, the Bearded Vultures) of all that they possessed.

"The Elders have wisdom," said one of the girls with awe, "and knowledge is power. They are the most powerful among us. *They* are the greatest minds of the mountains. Possessions weigh you down."

"But in that case, why do you all steal everything in sight?" demanded Teresa. "Don't you weigh yourselves down that way?"

"Of course we do," said the Buzzards. "But young people suffer from greediness. Therefore you have to find a way to satisfy that hunger, and do it thoroughly, before you can rise to the highest level. How do *you* deal with greed, then, if you're not allowed to steal?"

"Well," said Teresa, "you just have to control yourself! If you really want something, you have to earn the money to buy it."

And then they wanted to know exactly how that worked, earning money.

"Knowledge is power," said Ych Kraslichar contentedly.

But her pupils shook their heads, protesting, "We really can't see what good this knowledge is to us."

"The Tsumirans think along similar lines," Kraslichar explained.

The Buzzards giggled. "The Tsumirans! Those feeble beach-combers!"

"But you're descendants of Siparti too, aren't you?" asked a girl who had kept quiet until now. "Then how is it that you disapprove of stealing?"

Teresa chewed her lower lip and blurted out, "We Gippart travellers are merchants, not thieves."

"I don't understand," said the girl earnestly. "Hasn't the noble Brax Siparti told us that *commerce* is thievery? Book V, Verse 29; and Book VI, Verses 3 to 8."

"Well put!" cried Ych Kraslichar.

"Could I have a look at those books?" asked Teresa. She went with the girl, leaving Josh and Baz to the inquisitive Buzzards.

Josh yawned. Their hostess immediately put her arm round his shoulder. "Do please retreat to your lair," she said. "We can continue this conversation tomorrow."

"Tomorrow," said Josh sleepily, "we have to be on our way."

"No, no," said Kraslichar, "tomorrow you will share your knowledge with the Hawks, the day after that with the Wise Ones, and over the following couple of days it will be the younger ones' turn. Your day of departure is set for October the thirtieth. It is recorded in the guest book."

"That isn't possible," said Baz. "We have to continue our journey!"

"Of course," said Kraslichar. "And we shall be very sorry to see you go. Monday October the thirtieth we'll see you off. That is six days from now – not a moment sooner. Goodnight."

11
Deception, Betrayal and Apple Pie

The battle was already in full swing before Josh had any idea anything was the matter. He awoke to find himself all alone in the dormitory. Outside he heard shouting and the clash of steel against steel. The red glow of flames flickered in through gaps in the wall.

He sat up. He felt the warmth of a little bundle of feathers against his cheek. "Oh, Zizi," he groaned. "I hate fighting."

But there was nothing else for it. He got dressed, sighing, put on his hat, paid a visit to the deserted latrine, and then walked reluctantly to the front door. All he could see through the crack was the darkness of night. The din came from the village green by the cliff wall. Zizi flew off his shoulder and flapped back to the dormitory.

Josh sidled through the dark, icy streets, keeping his back to the huts. He turned the last corner and came to a halt. It made him think, oddly enough, of the alarming, exciting commotion of Bonfire Night on Primrose Hill in London: the bonfire, shrieks of fireworks, people screaming and shouting, children bubbling with excitement and trepidation, plunging into the crowd. Only now there was also the only too real, painfully cruel, ringing of steel against steel.

It sounded as if the heaviest fighting was taking place right on the edge of the cliff. He wondered where the others might be. Was Jericho in the thick of the fray, grinning at the sight of spilt blood? Was Baz slugging it out in there? He stared indecisively at the rowdy brawl. What could he do? Wouldn't it be best perhaps if he just turned back and crept out of there quietly? As he stood there, dithering, the mountains suddenly shook with a violent explosion. A huge burst of flame shot out from the centre of the plateau and people ran in every direction, screaming. Then a strange hush fell over the scene. Josh pricked up his ears. At the far end, by the cliff fence, somebody was talking. The silence deepened. In order to hear what was being said, Josh had to leave the safety of the houses. The crowd, too, listened intently to the speaker at the precipice, as the flames from the explosion in the middle of the green died down, flickering. Josh walked right up to the flames. There he halted, because he could now make out what was being said. Worse yet, he recognized the voice. From where he stood, the words sounded muffled and muted.

"It isn't necessary, surely, for Tsumirans and Braxans to continue to spill one another's blood? You know perfectly well what it is we want: we request that you surrender the outlaws to us. As soon as you comply with our rightful demand, we will withdraw immediately. And then we can start negotiating a lasting peace settlement."

Josh had heard Mervin Spratt speak too often not to know that it was he. Only Spratt was capable of droning on and on so sanctimoniously, in such a blatantly slimy and hypocritical whine. Except that his voice sounded hoarser than normal. As if he had a bad cold. Josh fervently hoped he'd caught a nasty ear infection or something.

Then he heard the response: firm, businesslike. "In joining battle with you, we are but obeying the guest laws, esteemed envoy from Tsumir. We would never surrender guests, certainly not kinsfolk of ours." It was the border guard who had welcomed the Associates when they arrived.

"Ah, my very dear Goshawk! I'm afraid you have been misled. Your sticky-fingered guests are no kinsfolk of yours. They pulled the wool over your eyes, in order to obtain your protection. Can't you see through their tricks? Have you tested them on their knowledge of your *Book of the Cat*? I can assure you that they haven't got a clue."

The border guard's answer was swift, cool and deliberate. "We cannot grant your request, envoy Spratt. There is no question of our turning them over to you. Shall we take up arms again then, most esteemed foe?"

The other side deliberated. Josh told himself he ought to get out of there, but he couldn't seem to move.

"I am so sorry, Goshawk," drawled Spratt menacingly. "I'm afraid we must have Cope. We will lay waste to your entire lair if we have to. We must have him."

There was a ringing of steel, and a sigh went up from the multitude. They all braced themselves for the next onslaught. But suddenly a very different sound was heard. A reedy voice. An acerbic laugh. Josh's heart missed a beat. "But dearest enemy, you are making an incredibly silly mistake!"

There was murmuring around the cliff wall. Josh craned his neck, but he couldn't see her.

"You say you're looking for the Cope boy, but there's nobody here by that name! I think my presence must have confused you. My name is Jericho Crope. I am on my way, in the company of some relatives, to a wedding up in the mountains, and I assure you that I haven't stolen anything. You may search my luggage, if you like. Can it be that you mistook my name for his?"

Spratt gave a shout of disbelief. "But you *are* Cope!"

"I'm sorry," giggled Jericho, from somewhere in the crowd. "You really must be very confused. Can't you see I'm a girl? How can I be the master thief you are looking for?" Her voice hardened. "And you'd better hurry up and retreat, before the

Braxans get hopping mad about your vile, unprovoked attack, and before we decide to raze Tsumir to the ground."

There were catcalls and loud shouting. Spratt's voice was lost in the belligerent cries of the Braxans. Josh came to his senses. He jammed his hat down over his eyes, turned round and ran as fast as his legs could carry him back to the Buzzard House, where he collapsed on the front steps. The little panther jumped up at him, nuzzling its snout in his armpit. Josh hugged it tightly, shaking all over. He felt Zizi's light little feet landing on his head.

"Panther, what am I supposed to do?" He buried his face in the big cat's thick pelt. "Do you think I'm a coward? Should I have joined in the fighting? God, they're all going to make fun of me when they get back." He sighed. "It's all my fault, isn't it? Spratt with an entire army at his back – I'm sure they won't fall for the fib that I'm not here. And what if we lose?"

"We're not going to lose," said Jericho. She had crept up, all cheerful and unconcerned. "What did you think of my little ruse? Quick thinking on my part, wasn't it?" She sat down next to him, drew a handful of toffees out of her pocket and gave him two. "Spratt didn't fall for it. But it certainly took him by surprise, and his friends the Tsumirans now think he's mad. Really! Half of them have already turned back. Isn't that fantastic?"

Josh looked at her, shaking his head. "You had a nerve!"

"Well, I'm not scared of that Spratt. He can't hurt me. But what *is* it about him – why does he scare you? And why does he want to get his hands on you so badly?"

There were some things Jericho knew without having to be told – like what Baz would be when he grew up, or Josh's life at school – but the most important things going on right then seemed largely to have escaped her. Josh tried to spell it out for her. He told her about the Gippart trading company, about Garnet and Spratt, about time-travel and the Tembe.

Jericho wouldn't sit still to listen. "The stuff about time-travel is nonsense, of course. That's impossible. No wonder Gippart hasn't discovered how to do it, because there's no one alive that can actually travel through time. What a bunch of fools they are." She was silent for a moment, picking and tearing at her toffee. "But where are we now, then? That's what I don't understand."

"In *umaya*," said Josh for the umpteenth time. "In dream-time. That's the problem, you see."

Jericho drew a deep breath and angrily threw the pieces of toffee to the ground. "You're real," she said crossly, "you're no dream. Nor am I. And those people here aren't, either. You can't make me believe this isn't earth. The real, living earth."

Josh opened his mouth and closed it again. She simply didn't want to know. He picked up a piece of toffee, brushed the dirt off it and stuck it in his mouth. The noise in the distance had abated, and it looked as if the sky in the east was beginning to grow lighter.

"It was a terrific battle," Jericho mused. "You know what? That stupid Teresa, she fights like a Viking. You should have seen her when that swine crept up on me from the side. She knocked the sword right out of his hands. I owe her a thank you, I think."

"Teresa?" Josh was flabbergasted. "And Baz? Did he take part as well?"

But Jericho was looking the other way, towards the green. "Listen, the fighters are returning!"

Indeed, there they came: the Buzzards, swords in hand. They were all talking at once, banging their swords on a rock from time to time, and uttering warlike yells. Josh wasn't particularly looking forward to the heroes' return. They had fought his battle for him, while he'd almost slept right through the whole thing – would you believe it! He braced himself – they were going to make fun of him, and then give him a talking-to about cowardice and duty.

But that wasn't what happened. When they saw Josh they

ran up to him, threw down their swords enthusiastically and slapped him on the back, congratulating him, all smiles. "What Teresa said is true," cried a young man with a bloody arm. "You people are masters of self-control! Master thief Cope, it must have taken a lot of will-power to hold yourself aloof from the fray the way you did!"

"I'd never have been able to," said a girl admiringly, pulling a steel cuirass off over her head.

"You are certainly endowed with great intelligence and self-discipline," gushed another girl. "It's only because you kept out of the way that your sister's ruse worked!"

Josh, who didn't see how he deserved all this admiration, grabbed a handful of toffees from Jericho's bag and distributed them among the Buzzards. They chewed them, curious to see what they tasted like, while disarming themselves and inspecting their wounds.

Two more exhausted warriors hobbled up. Josh jumped to his feet when he saw them and ran over to them. "Did you fight? Hey, did you really fight?"

Baz's face was bleeding, he was limping, and he let his sword drag behind him over the rocky ground; he was completely worn out. Yet he was smiling proudly. "Josh, you really missed something! Teresa and I must have sent at least seven Tsumirans flying over the cliff!"

Teresa was holding him up, her own sword slung through her belt. "No need to crow about it, Baz," she scolded him, but she too had a smile on her face. "It turned out all right in the end, anyway. No one's dead, and we'll have some peace and quiet for a while. Whew, what a bunch of hooligans!" She helped Baz sit down and then flung herself down on the hard ground. "My arms really ache!" She stretched. "It's lucky you didn't show yourself, Josh! Spratt was there. He must have found a way to get off Trellis as well. He's the one who whipped up the Tsumirans and made them come after us, I'm sure. But Jericho managed to throw him off. It was a clever move. She undermined the morale of the troops, as they say."

"So I heard," said Josh, helping them out of their metal breastplates, and tending their wounds with the help of Gippart's first-aid kit.

Baz tentatively touched his cheek. "That was the only blow that really hit home," he said. "I was terrified he'd put my eye out."

"You have a huge gash down your cheek," said Josh.

"Do you think there'll be a scar?" asked Baz hopefully.

"Oh, definitely." Teresa nodded.

"Terrific," said Baz happily.

Teresa had a few nasty scrapes on her arms, but that was all. "I've had five years of fencing, first at home and then at Gippart," she explained. "I'm not an easy target."

Josh was glad to have something to do. When he was finished dressing Baz's and Teresa's wounds, he started administering first aid to the Buzzards. He dabbed antiseptic on their cuts and scrapes, which made them howl, then dressed them with miles of bandages and stuck on plasters till he was blue in the face. By the time everyone was taken care of, it was morning.

The Buzzards sat outside their house, finishing the toffees while bragging about their exploits. Just then, Ych Kraslichar returned. She was wearing an imposing helmet topped with a rigid blue crest of feathers. When she reached them she halted, raising her sword. "Honours to the Buzzard division!" she shouted. "Glory to all the young warriors! Tirchax and Mazakirig, heroes of the hour, to you go the top honours. Today I am going to propose you for the rank of Goshawk, before the Braxas-Xal. My congratulations."

All the Buzzards cheered and applauded, slapping a grinning young man and young woman heartily on the back. Then Kraslichar turned to the Associates. "Congratulations to you too, our guests, for your cunning, your courage and your self-control. I have learnt much this night. Thank you." She took off her helmet and sniffed the morning air. "The time of bloodletting is past. It is time for rest. Skerprix and Slich, will you please get breakfast ready? After breakfast, there will be a four-hour nap in the lairs. Does anyone still need any medical attention?"

While she examined the Buzzards' wounds, the clatter of the table being set came from inside. There was a smell of bacon and, strangely, freshly brewed coffee. "Breknax!" Kraslichar called through the open door. "Would you go and check on the Jackdaws? They are supposed to be clearing the battlefield."

A girl came out, but Josh cried, "I'll go!" He wanted to do something to repay them.

"You can come with me," said the girl. "I don't think the Jackdaws will listen to you if you go by yourself."

They walked in silence through the sharp morning chill. Here and there, exhausted warriors sat in front of their homes, raising their hands in greeting, smiling. The green, now quiet, was a mess. It was covered in wrecked weapons, feathers, sticks, pieces of blackened steel, garments, and tons more loose stones than there had been the previous afternoon. The fire was still smouldering in the middle of the green.

"What exactly was that explosion?" asked Josh.

"A little memento from Tsumir," hissed the girl. "They always bring explosives. The yellow-bellied cowards."

Children armed with baskets and wheelbarrows were sifting through the rubble. Some of them hauled stones off to the side. The girl walked over to the edge of the precipice, where the border guard was coolly standing sentry. "Congratulations," she said. "Your daughter's getting nominated for the title of Goshawk, isn't she?"

The guard smiled proudly, but said nothing. They peered over the edge. Down below other Jackdaws were collecting the weapons the Tsumirans had dropped in their flight.

"Just the weapons!" the girl called to them down below.

A little boy called back loudly, "*We* know, Buzzard!"

She shook her head. "These kids get cheekier by the day. Come, let's go and see how they're doing here on the top."

Josh picked up an empty basket with carrying straps, and started tossing weapons, pieces of rusty metal and scraps of clothing into it.

"Take only the useful stuff, master thief," said the girl. "The Sparrows will come and get the useless junk later. Look, this sword is still intact, it's just lost a few gemstones." She threw it into the basket.

Josh looked at it greedily. The hilt was adorned with glittering blue and green stones; it was a fine weapon and looked razor-sharp. He scanned the green feverishly for more of such finery. Whoever would drop a weapon in the heat of battle? Seemingly, countless Braxans had: he found a dozen daggers and swords that were hardly damaged at all. When his basket was brimming with swords and daggers, metal gloves, dented helmets, unmatched shoes and a few feathers, he hoisted it on to his back with a groan. "Where does this basket go?" he called to the girl.

"Take it up to the Buzzard House. We'll take the stuff to the smithy this afternoon. I'll be back shortly – you go on ahead."

Josh walked back, staggering under the weight. He'd already made up his mind, even though he didn't know yet how he was going to go about it: four of these swords were theirs. They'd need weapons for the journey ahead, wouldn't they? He felt the familiar, tingling sensation of excitement and determination that always preceded stealing. Anyway, stealing was allowed here. And besides, they had no other choice. They needed to be able to defend themselves, with Spratt and the Tsumirans hard on their heels.

As he made his slow way to the Buzzard House, his back ached and sweat stung his eyes. He had to stop and lean against a rock, to take the weight of the basket off his back for a moment. He rubbed his eyes, and then he saw him. Like an omen. Sitting on top of the Buzzard House roof. Josh knew that this one was following Jericho, not him; still, he felt his heart pounding, and he was one hundred per cent sure that those piercing eyes were now fixed deliberately on *him* – stern, commanding. Lucide! The dark shape on the roof did not stir, but the eyes were wide open, eerily luminous. Josh returned his gaze, anxious, then watchful, and then defiant. He hoisted the leaden basket on his back again, and staggered forward until he dumped it in front of the house. He took a step back to have another look. Lucide was still staring at him, an imposing figure. Josh had wanted to say something nasty, something like "What do *you* want?" but, seeing him up close like this, he was suddenly awestruck. The majestic black form scintillated and gleamed as if radiating light from within. But more than that, he seemed to be carrying inside him a profound, very ancient silence, a silence that surrounded him like a halo. *Magnificent,* thought Josh. *Splendid, royal.* He stared at Lucide open-mouthed, drinking in the amazingly brilliant, incandescent colour. Lucide's skin was so dark that it seemed to reflect the light, and the long flowing tunic he wore was of a warm black material that glowed a deep rusty brown. His angular face did not smile. His long, graceful neck was slightly inclined as he looked down. His black hair lay close to his skull. Josh couldn't stop staring, powerless to break the spell. It was lucky Kraslichar came out just then to call him inside for breakfast. Josh shuddered and tore his eyes away. He followed Kraslichar into the dining hall.

The Buzzards had almost finished their victory breakfast of coffee and bacon. They carried their plates and cups to the kitchen and then hung around the scullery and latrines, chatting softly. A few had already gone to bed. Josh sat down next to Jericho on one of the benches. He sipped cautiously at a cup of steaming sweet coffee, which he didn't like very much.

Teresa pushed a bacon sandwich over to him. "We have to talk," she whispered into his ear. Josh nodded. "After the meal, outside," she whispered again, with a glance at Kraslichar.

A little while later they were perched on a rock out of earshot of the houses. The sun had risen above the mountain peaks in the east. There was a strong westerly wind. Josh glanced at the Buzzard House roof, but Lucide had vanished. He felt both relief and disappointment.

Baz had something to tell them. Something important. The bright red scar on his left cheek made him look strange. "Time, Josh!" he began excitedly. "Time has started running backwards again! I *thought* there was something funny going on yesterday afternoon, when the rhythm suddenly skipped. Remember, when we saw the village in the distance, and we all had a brief dizzy spell, and felt sick? But it wasn't until very early this morning, since the battle ended, in fact, that time started running backwards properly. Do you understand what this means, Josh? Soon the Braxans won't even remember we were ever here! We'll have skipped back in time!"

"Oh," said Josh. "But I don't get it, Baz. I don't feel a thing. Time isn't really running backwards, is it?"

"I think it goes in fits and starts," Baz explained, making circles in the air with his finger. "It does run back, but only at night, or when everyone's asleep, and then it'll skip thirty or forty years. That's when you notice it."

"And the Braxans are all about to go to sleep," Teresa added, "so in just a little while from now, time's going to be rolled back. If we make for the hills now, we'll be safe."

It took a moment for this to sink in. Then Josh nodded. "OK. Let's go! Let's pack our bags and get away from here!"

"Great," said Teresa. "I was shown that book yesterday – you know, the *Book of the Cat* that they keep going on about? I wasn't allowed to leaf through it myself, more's the pity, or I might finally have been able to sort out the story about Siparti and Temberi. What I did see was that the laws here are incredibly strict. It was all about 'their throats will be slashed', bloody vengeance and so on. We really have to get out of here."

Josh did some quick thinking. "I'll have to go back inside," he said, "to collect the backpacks. I'll hand them out to you through the scullery window, all right? And then get going. I'll follow you."

"It would be best if I went," Jericho insisted. "They don't pay as much attention to me as they do to you, Josh." And before he could argue with her, she'd run into the Buzzard House.

But Josh had another idea. Once Baz and Teresa had hoisted their packs on to their backs, he told them to go on ahead, as he'd forgotten something; and in a few strides he reached the front door of the Buzzard House. He shrugged off his jacket, grabbed four short swords from the basket of battlefield debris, wrapped them up in his jacket, stuffed the bundle into his backpack, grabbed Jericho, who'd just come outside, by the hand and dragged her up the hill. "Hurry, run!" Josh cried. He was expecting to hear hoarse shouts behind them at any moment.

They sprinted down the trail along a narrow mountain ridge, with the young panther and Zizi following close behind. Not paying any attention to the mountainous landscape around them, they sped to the far side of the ridge, leapt with great, slithering bounds down the scree, then clambered up another short incline, across a plateau with a dark mountain lake, then down again, this time a long, sloping hillside covered with patches of snow. Baz crouched on one of the snowy stretches, sliding down on the soles of his shoes. It worked well. They coasted, they ran, and then slid down again. An hour later they came to a lovely valley basking in the sun, with soft green grass and blue flowers. Large guinea pigs cavorting among the rocks started whistling as they came near. The Associates flung themselves down in the grass, laughing. They'd escaped!

* * *

They were alone again at last. They took turns drinking from the leather gourd Teresa had filled with water at the Buzzard House. Once their sweat dried off and they got their breath back, they looked to see what food was left in their backpacks. Enough for the day ahead, anyway. They stretched out on their backs to rest, relieved. Chewing muesli, they gazed at the clouds speeding by above.

Baz pointed at a curiously shaped wisp of cloud. "Look! It looks just like an eagle, with its wings spread. See it?"

"That one? It looks more like a lizard..."

"Well, yeah, now it does. It's losing its shape."

They stared up at the sky and listened to the howling of the mountain wind.

"Trust us to run into Siparti's descendants, of all people," sighed Josh. "Do you think there really are six tribes of thieves? If so, then we've just experienced the Braxans. And then there are the two youngest ones, Daddy's favourites, Gip and Kat. And then that really nasty gang – what did that woman call them again, the one who sheltered me from the Inelesi? And the Inelesi themselves, they were probably Siparti descendants too. Maybe they were the offspring of the son called Beast, or Beez, or something."

Teresa sighed. "Nice *umaya* we're in, isn't it? With all those Siparti crooks."

"But they aren't *all* bad," reasoned Baz. "Those people in Damara and Trellis and Tsumir weren't Siparti. You don't have to lose any sleep over it, Teresa."

"I shall lose a lot more than sleep if you eat all the muesli. We were going to save half for tomorrow morning! Stop it, Baz, it's got loads of calories – you only need a handful."

Reluctantly they got up. They stretched, packed the backpacks again, and pored over the map. They looked for landmarks, decided what was north, what was east. After much measuring and calculating, they decided that it was probably about two days' journey to the nearest village on the east side of the mountains: Mur.

"Two days' march!" Josh exclaimed.

"It's already Wednesday," Baz said. "Then we won't get there until Thursday night. And my sister's getting married today. Damn it."

"But time runs differently here, Baz, doesn't it?" Teresa reminded him. "It may still be Monday in the real world."

Baz shrugged. "But before we're home it will be long past Wednesday. You'll see." He pointed to the map. "From Mur to the Mabeh – *if* they are really somewhere around Ixilis, that is – is at least another four days' journey. OK, and even then we're nowhere near the Tembe. How do we know where they are hiding? Over there, all the way in the east perhaps? Or on the far side of Portilisi? Or at the South Pole?"

They all stared at the map, which would not divulge the secrets of this *umaya*.

"When's your birthday, Teresa?" Jericho suddenly asked in a friendly voice. "Isn't it soon?"

"No, why? My birthday is May the seventh."

"Oh, what a pity," said Jericho. "All right, let's go, shall we? Or do you want to hang around here and wait for Spratt to come along?"

They jumped to their feet and followed Jericho, taking an easterly course, keeping the beam of Josh's compass to their left.

"Why did you want to know if it was Teresa's birthday?" Josh asked his sister curiously.

"I've got a present for her."

"A present? Are you two friends then, all of a sudden?"

"No. But she saved my life. In the battle."

Josh smiled, pleased. Then he said hesitantly, "I saw Lucide."

Jericho didn't say anything.

"Did you see him too?"

She nodded.

"Does he really want to make you go back with him?"

She shrugged, and kept silent.

They trudged on slowly, up and down the trail meandering through the rough terrain of Takras. It was very quiet here in the mountains. High above them circled great birds of prey. Baz and Teresa told of their exploits in the battle against the Tsumirans. They had fought side by side surrounded by the Buzzards, who had occasionally come to their aid when necessary. They were honest about that.

"But it was amazing, Josh! As soon as a head came up over the edge, we'd smash him – *kapow!* – back down."

"Remember," said Teresa, "that huge fellow in the checked suit?"

"Oh, him. Josh, you must hear this. This man crawls up over the edge with a sword in his hand, Teresa after him and me right behind. Know what we did?"

"We rapped!" Teresa exclaimed.

"Rapped?"

"Yeah, we just rapped in his face – all kinds of nonsense but a very tight beat, you know – and then we brought in a counter-measure! Great, wasn't it, Teresa? I was just pummelling him to this drumbeat, *ta-dam, ta-dam*. When you do that, they can't offer any resistance. You have to picture your opponent moving to a certain beat, and then you have to confuse him, break his rhythm. It really does the trick!"

They walked all day through the central mountains, growing more tired and quiet as the afternoon wore on. Sometimes they'd have to push through undergrowth, but more often they would cross rocky ledges, until, late in the afternoon, they reached a sheltered meadow with a stream running through it. From here the trail led up steeply to another mountain pass.

"Let's make camp down here for the night," Teresa suggested.

In the soft red sunlight they shrugged off their backpacks and took out their food and blankets. Teresa had even brought along a little red copper pan, and they made a fire with the twigs and branches they'd gathered on the way. They succeeded, with difficulty, in bringing some water to the boil, for spaghetti. They ate greedily out of the pan, scalding their fingers: plain spaghetti, with salami and bread.

By the time the food was all gone, it had grown cold and dark. Shivering, they wrapped themselves in their blankets and huddled close together around the fire, taking turns to sip tea from the cooling pan.

"Do you think there are wolves here?" asked Josh, leaning against Baz.

"It's Spratt you ought to be worried about. He's the one snapping at our heels." Baz poked the dying embers with a stick.

"We'll keep watch tonight," said Teresa. "I'll go first. Then I'll wake you in two hours' time, Josh, then Jericho, and then Baz."

"Wait." Josh pulled his pack towards him and took out the wrapped-up swords. "Here, take one. We should be prepared." He threw a sword at each of them and put on his jacket.

"Joshua Cope!" Teresa exclaimed. "You didn't steal these, did you?"

Josh tossed his head back, so that his hat fell off. "Come on, they were leftovers, rejects! Look, they're not perfect, and besides, stealing's allowed in Braxassallar, and we're not in their time any more, anyway!"

"Oh, you thieving idiot! You never learn, do you! You never steal from your hosts and hostesses! Haven't your sticky fingers brought us enough trouble already? Can't you just stop it for once?"

"Yes," said Baz, feeling the edge of his sword, "but you've got to admit, these *will* come in handy just now, Teresa. Hey, come and get me, Spratt!" He slashed his sword savagely at the empty air.

Teresa stood up, muttering, but she was nevertheless gripping the sword, testing its weight. Then she flung her blanket around herself like a cape. "Well, get yourselves some shut-eye. I'll wake you up in a couple of hours, Josh. Baz, could I borrow your watch?"

"It isn't working properly," Baz reminded her, handing it over.

They huddled together in a tight pack, the panther curled up on top of them, and closed their eyes. Teresa began slowly pacing back and forth, singing softly to herself. As he dozed off Josh heard her swish her sword through the air.

When she woke him it felt as if he hadn't been asleep more than five minutes. He spent much of his watch hunched on top of a rock. Then, to get warm and to stay awake, he started walking in circles. Above him stretched a terrifyingly immense expanse of night sky, with stars so dazzlingly bright that he didn't dare look directly at them. He was sure the temperature was below zero. The cold penetrated his clothes and seeped into his bones. He didn't hear any suspicious sounds, but from time to time the blood would pound so loud in his ears that it made him think an entire cavalry was thundering towards them, led by Spratt. Then he'd squint around anxiously, only to be greeted by a deep, inky silence. He was all alone in the sleeping mountains. Zizi had taken off again. Was she up there with the eagles?

After two hours of this, he felt like a pathetic little kid who wanted nothing more than to climb into bed beside his mother. But he shook Jericho awake, who scrambled to her feet without a murmur. She blew out a puff of white breath.

"Is it freezing?" she asked.

She climbed up on a rock, her blanket draped around her head and upper body. Josh gratefully snuggled up against the clump of bodies around the fire and fell asleep shivering. He slept, a block of ice, and woke up frozen.

Jericho was sprawled on top of him, and Baz had squeezed

his legs in between them. Lying on top of the numb cluster was the panther, with Zizi nestled in its neck fur. They all looked ashen from the cold, especially Teresa, whose lips were blue when she woke them up. Teeth chattering, they rubbed their own and one another's arms and legs, hopping up and down, but nothing helped.

"Never again," said Teresa, taking the food out of her pack with shaking fingers. "And we don't even have any wood for a fire!"

But Josh had an idea. He aimed the beam of his compass at the pan, which Teresa had just filled with cold water at the mountain stream. He twisted something, adjusted the distance, then zapped the pan from all sides with the light beam. And, unbelievably, the water started to boil! It felt wonderful to sip hot tea. As the warmth spread into their stomachs, they stopped shivering. They finished the last of the bread from Tsumir and the final crumbs of muesli.

"Now all we've got left is tea, nuts and dates," said Teresa. "We *have* to get to Mur by tonight."

For the first hour they walked huddled in their blankets. When the sun broke through and their muscles had thawed out, they packed away first the blankets, then their jackets. They plodded on staunchly across mountain plains, skirting steep ridges, and sliding down endless slopes of scree. In the afternoon they walked through a stark mountainous landscape, stepping up the pace in spite of their sore feet, pushed along by a fierce mountain wind. They entered a rustling pine forest, and suddenly found themselves in a twilit gloom reeking strongly of resin. They zigzagged down woody trails, and when they finally emerged from the forest they saw they'd arrived at the foot of the mountain range.

Before them, a friendly rolling landscape, ochre and green, interspersed with dark patches of trees, stretched out in the dusk. A brilliant white star twinkled in the dark blue sky. They took out their blankets and slung them around their shoulders again.

"I'm hungry," grumbled Baz.

"Mur *must* be very close," said Teresa.

"We're in a new part of the world," said Josh. "It smells good here."

They walked on slowly, tired but vigilant.

"Look! Lights, over there!" Josh pointed out, after less than an hour's walk. To the left of the road some yellow lights flickered in the dark.

"I can hear voices," said Baz. "This must be Mur!"

Hesitantly they stepped on to a path leading to the first of the village's low, round houses. Two wide steps led up to a porch that encircled the house. The front door stood half open, and a beam of yellow light fell on to the grass. When a homely smell of cooked food came wafting outside, their mouths started to water, and suddenly they all felt terribly homesick. They were still standing there dithering when a stout figure stepped outside carrying a bucket, talking and laughing to someone inside while calling out, "Tockie! Silly pig, where are you! Dinner time!"

She dumped the contents of the bucket into a feeding trough on the grass below the porch. When she straightened up, she caught sight of the four travellers. "What the –" Putting down the empty bucket, she clapped her hands. "Oh, my dear heavens. *Dear* children! What are you doing there, in the middle of the night?" She went up to them and grabbed them firmly by the arm. "Oh, please, come inside, quick," and she led them inside her warm round house.

The woman seemed to have at least four hands, the way she bustled around. She pushed them down on to a sofa with soft pillows, pulled off their shoes, dusted off their clothes, and patted their cheeks. She tickled Zizi and patted the panther. She was big and strong and dark-skinned, and she smelled of soap and pie. More than anything, she gave the impression of red flowers: she was wearing an enormous red-flowered dress that made her look impressively huge. A man and woman similarly attired in red sat at the kitchen table, the man with short red hair, the other woman olive-skinned and wearing a red headscarf; both looked at them with the same friendly, solicitous expression. The man got up to put the kettle on the enormous black stove, and the other woman stoked the fire in the oven.

It felt wonderul to be mothered and fussed over, and they surrendered to it without any protest. The first woman didn't ask them any questions. She poured hot tea for them and gave each a big biscuit. She rubbed their feet until they glowed and then swaddled them in thick woollen socks. "Oh, my darlings," she said, "you have terrible blisters. That's what you get from all that traipsing across the rocks. First, you'll eat, and then you can have a bath – what do you think of that? And just look at those clothes, my duckies. You can't travel in those, can you!" She tousled Baz's hair, and said, tut-tutting, "And has a doctor had a look at that cut on your cheek, my boy? I'll see what I can do about it, after your bath."

The other woman gave them a plate of chicken and rice to eat on their laps, and they eagerly wolfed it down, slurping, using their hands and making a mess, while the adults looked on approvingly.

"It's been a while since we had children here in our house," the first woman told them, "and I do miss it, you know, when you children don't visit." She pinched Jericho's cheek gently. "I'm so happy you came."

"Are you a cannibal?" Jericho suddenly asked, in her clear, cheeky voice. The others choked on their food.

"Cannibal? Whatever gave you *that* idea?" The woman stared at her wide-eyed. "Cannibals don't exist, dear child, that's just silly make-believe."

"Oh," said Jericho, gnawing on her chicken leg.

"Don't you worry, now, my little angels. In Mur you certainly don't have to be afraid of anything. Everyone knows that! It's just that we love to have visitors, children *too*, because they're such a pleasure to take care of."

"But we have to be on our way again first thing in the morning," said Josh. "We really can't stay."

"No, of course not. Children always leave the nest, and that's the way it ought to be. Do you want more chicken? We killed them yesterday – there's plenty. What about you, dear, are you still hungry?" She directed her question at Teresa, who was thoughtfully cleaning her plate with her fingers.

Teresa shook her head and asked, "Are you descendants of the Tembe, by any chance?"

"The Tembe? The Tembe of Temberi?" Not answering the question, the woman stacked their plates and waddled to the sink.

The warm kitchen suddenly smelled mouth-wateringly sweet. The other woman had just taken a pie from the oven; she sliced it and divided it among seven plates. "You're lucky," she said. "Lopper here, he turned forty-five yesterday, and this pie is the last leftover from the party."

All four were given a big crusty piece of apple pie, which they fell upon, puffing to cool it, as if they hadn't yet had a thing to eat.

"Ah, well, those ancestor stories don't really interest me that much," said the first woman finally, her arms crossed over her chest. "Come on, if you're all done, it's time for your bath. There's nothing better after a long day's walk than a nice hot bath, is there!"

They were reluctant to get up from the comfortable sofa.

"I can't move," Josh whined, but the woman pulled him to his feet, smiling.

"You can sleep as much as you want in a little while," she said, "but you'll see, my little lad, there's nothing that refreshes like a nice hot bath."

She led them into a scullery with two large metal bathtubs filled with foamy water. A red-hot little wood stove sizzled between the two tubs. Lopper poured one last kettle of hot water into the baths. "Boys in this one, girls in that one," the woman pointed, taking their clothes and throwing them into a large wooden washtub – except for Jericho's dress, which she draped over a washing line. (And which Jericho grabbed again as soon as she could, because she didn't want to let it out of her sight, she was so fond of it.)

The woman was right: it was wonderful. The last remaining chill and stiffness dissolved in the warm suds, and they leaned back blissfully.

"Do you think we can trust them?" asked Baz once the adults had gone back into the kitchen.

"Oh, I just *want* to trust them," Teresa sighed, from the bottom of her heart. "And I can't sense any nightmares. It's just lovely here, that's all."

"Yes," said Baz. "I can't hear anything creepy either. What about you, Josh?"

Josh was lounging back, his eyes closed. Baz splashed water in his face. "Yoo-hoo, master thief, we asked you a question! Do you feel there's anything fishy here!"

Josh sat up, splashing water all over the place. "Stop it, Baz!"

Baz giggled. "It's just like being at home here. Or just like at my grandma's. 'Would you like another biscuit? Would you like another drink, sweetheart?'"

"Lovely, isn't it?" sighed Teresa.

"Yes," said Jericho, who was blowing flecks of foam into the air.

The first woman came to wash their hair and let them brush their teeth in the bath. Then she disappeared to take care of the panther and Zizi. The man, meanwhile, was busy with their laundry, singing to himself. The woman brought them enormous rough towels and thick flannel nightgowns, showed them the lavatory, and then took them to a small bedroom with two beds next to the kitchen. "Girls here, boys there." Red as lobsters, they snuggled obediently between the fresh, soft sheets. The woman spread a green smelly salve on Baz's cut, gave Josh's old Inelesi-bite a smear of it as well, and tended to Teresa's scratched legs. Then she rumpled their hair, turned down the oil lamp and wished them goodnight.

"This is heaven," groaned Baz, curling up beside Josh.

"This is *home*," muttered Josh, slinging his arms around the feather pillow and snuggling as deep down into the blankets as he could.

Josh was woken by somebody's elbow poking into his eye. "Don't, Liz," he grumbled, pushing the arm away. He opened his eyes. Oh, no, of course. *Umaya.* The village of Mur. Blissfully he closed his eyes once more. Then opened them again. He had the feeling something wasn't quite right, and propped himself up. It wasn't Baz lying next to him. A little boy of around seven years old lay there snoring, his arm slung across Josh's torso. Next to the little boy was a larger, gangly boy with short red hair, and next to him was Baz, fast asleep.

The door opened and a woman entered carrying a tray and humming softly to herself. "Good morning, my precious darlings. Wake up, my little luvvies!" she cried, then froze in her tracks. She glanced from Josh to the other bed and back. She put the tray down on a little side table, clapped her hands together and hooted with laughter. "Well I never! I put three to bed and next thing I know there are seven of them to wake up!" She pulled the curtains aside and patted Josh on the head. "Well, my little stranger, did you just wander in here and decide to crawl into bed with my little ones in the middle of the night?" She pinched Baz's cheek. "And you, my little friend, did you sleep well?" She kissed the two boys in the middle and went over to the girls' bed. "Two more girls as well, what an amazing morning! Manne, what did you do, did you decide to smuggle two of your friends into your bed last night?"

A girl with two long braids gazed shyly at her bed-mates.

"I've never seen them before either," she murmured, and then she started giggling.

The woman went out of the room to fetch four more steaming beakers of tea, and a whole loaf of raisin bread. She cut seven thick slices. "Here, have some breakfast first." She started laughing again. "Jonas, come and have a look," she called to the kitchen.

A fat old man came in. He too started to laugh when he saw the beds crammed with children. "Mansura," he said, "I knew you were fertile, but this really takes the biscuit."

"What're your names?" asked the little boy.

Josh told him. "What're yours?"

"I'm Mup, he's Lopper, her name's Manne," the boy said. "Are you staying?"

"Actually, we have to continue our journey," said Teresa from the other bed.

When the adults had left the bedroom, Baz said, "What idiots we are. Of course, time must have run back again last night."

"We're lucky," said Teresa. "This house might not even have existed. We'd better watch out next time."

"But I did sleep really well," said Josh, pulling the blankets back up to his chin.

The little boy crawled on top of him. "Where are you off to, then?" he asked. "Can I come?"

"We're going to the Mabeh," said Josh, "and you're much too young for that kind of trip." He gave the little boy a ride on his knee.

"The Mabeh live in Ixilis, in the desert," the little boy piped up, "and I've already been there, with Mallum. He goes there every Saturday and comes home every Tuesday. Are you going to go with Mallum?"

"No," said Josh, "we're going by ourselves."

"Do you have any zebras?" asked the other boy, who seemed to be about ten years old. "Or camels?"

"No. We're just on foot."

"Are you meaning to go to Ixilis on foot?" asked the girl, getting out of bed and putting on a long knitted jersey. "You must be mad. On foot, through the desert?"

"Can't it be done?" asked Teresa.

"It can be done, I suppose, but it'd be silly to try," said the girl. "Considering the bandits and the soldiers, the quicksand and the sandstorms, and the lack of water, and the jackals, and everything."

"We came on foot all the way from Portilisi," said Josh, "through the swamps and via the island and over the mountains. All on foot. We did."

There was no response from the children. They got up and carried the empty beakers to the kitchen.

"Well, now," said Teresa. "Did you hear that?" She took one last bite of the bread and licked her fingers.

"Maybe we should go with that Mallum instead," said Baz. "Tomorrow is Saturday."

"And hang around a whole day for Spratt to find us? Spratt is in the same time as us, remember! He's right on our heels!"

"Let him come," said Baz. "I wouldn't mind a little chat with him."

"But we can't, anyway," agreed Teresa. "We can't go with Mallum."

"Why not. Don't you trust him?"

She laughed grimly. "Think. By the time it's Saturday, another night will have passed, and time will have jumped back again. We'll have gone back in time another good number of years, and Mallum won't even exist yet."

"Oh, of course. Damn."

That backward shift in time did create all sorts of problems for them.

"As long as the Mabeh still exist when we finally get there," said Josh.

"They're very ancient," said Teresa, "so that shouldn't be a problem. But you're right. We've got to move on. If time really is running backwards as rapidly as it seems to be, then we risk flying right past the Tembe and missing the exit. We'll end up lost somewhere in prehistoric time."

"I'm not much in the mood for dinosaurs," said Baz.

"Baz, how much time have we been losing every night, exactly?" asked Teresa.

Josh answered without hesitating, "Thirty-five years."

"How do you know?" asked Baz.

"Do you remember the man with the red hair, last night? Hadn't he just turned forty-five? His name was Lopper."

"Oh," said Teresa, "you're right. The boy's name is Lopper! Wow! He's the same person, only when he was young!" Frowning, she started doing the calculations. "Max said we shouldn't go back any further than the year 1000. We're in about 1535 now, so we've got just over two weeks to reach the Tembe. And that isn't a lot – it's taken us almost a week to get here!"

Baz started calculating too. "If we stayed here, we'd be going back about thirteen thousand years in time every ordinary year. In that case, if we were fifty-two, we'd be living in the year 520,000 BC. What kind of time was that?"

"Humans didn't exist then," said Teresa. "They only got here around a hundred thousand years ago. The intelligent species of Homo sapiens, I mean, real humans."

"But it wouldn't be the age of the dinosaurs either," said Josh. "They became extinct sixty-five million years ago. There's no way we'd ever get there."

"I know one thing for certain," said Teresa, "and that is that we have no time to lose. We have to keep going, boys!"

But Josh too had done some calculating. "You know," he said dreamily, "I'm supposed to be paid five hundred pounds for six hours' work a month. We've been here six days or so, that's twenty-four times more – that means I've already earned twelve thousand pounds!"

"Ha!" sneered Teresa. "Don't count on it, my boy. Gippart would never reckon it up that way." But then she raised her eyebrows. "You're getting five hundred pounds for two afternoons? Hey, those cheapskates! I'm only getting six hundred for four afternoons!"

Then they heard their names being called and went in search of their hostess.

The other children were already sitting round the kitchen table, and Mansura was pouring beakers of milk, slicing bread and spreading it thickly with yellow butter and dark red jam.

"Well, well, visitors," she said. "Tell me, where are you off to, then? To see the Mabeh of Ixilis, is that right?"

They nodded, taking greedy bites of the gritty bread. As if they'd gone hungry for days.

"How are you getting there? Do you have transport?"

They shook their heads.

"Oh dear," said the woman. "Then you'd best wait until tomorrow, and beg a ride with Mallum. He'll get you there in a day."

"We've got to go today," said Teresa.

"Are you in such a hurry, darling? But the road to Ixilis isn't safe now. You know, with the border skirmishes, all those patrols – they kill every stranger on sight."

That was bad news, and the more they asked Mansura about the situation, the more obvious it became that their plan of going to Ixilis on foot was quite impossible. The danger posed by Spratt was nothing compared to this. They ate the rest of their breakfast in silence, until they couldn't swallow another bite. After breakfast they went looking for their clothes, but in vain. The house was recognizable enough, but they found no clothes in the scullery, or hanging outside on the line to dry. Only Jericho's red dress still existed: she had taken it to bed with her for safekeeping. And, of course, their three trusty backpacks lay on the floor of the bedroom, with their hats, of all things, stuffed inside.

They told Mansura of their problem, explaining that they'd lost their clothes, they had no idea how it could have happened, and could she help them?

The strange thing was that Mansura didn't ask them how they had ended up in her house. She helped them look for their clothes without success and then shrugged her shoulders, stuck her head in the huge kitchen cupboard and took out some clothing: navy blue and purple wide-legged trousers tapering to the ankle, and long tight-sleeved shirts in similar colours. They were comfortable, and quite different from the sturdy Damaran clothes. She inspected them critically. "Now you look just like children from Mur. Are you sure you want to wear trousers, my dear?"

"Oh, yes," said Teresa. "Thank you very much. How much do we owe you?"

Mansura shook her head. "Oh, no, darling, I would never. Can't I be allowed to take care of children? Whatever next! I'd be ashamed to accept money from you."

Teresa hesitated. "But you're just helping us out of the goodness of your heart – yet you have no idea who we are! Don't you want to know where we're from? Do you always allow any strangers to stay with you? Without asking any questions?"

Mansura turned round, opened another storage cupboard, and set vegetables, sausages, bacon and bottles of oil on the table. Then she put an enormous black pan on the stove. "But, my darlings, it's not as if armed robbers and murderers come knocking at the door every day now, is it!" She started chopping onions with a big carving knife, and threw them into the sizzling pan. Then she turned to Teresa again. "I think it's very polite of you to offer to tell me about your past, but it really isn't necessary. It doesn't matter, don't you see? It doesn't matter where you're from." She turned back to the pan on the stove. "What matters is where you're going, *that's* what matters."

And then she shooed them outside, because they were getting in the way of her housework.

They strolled about the village. Children came crowding around them. It was an airy village of low, round houses with porches. Goats, chickens and pigs grubbed around among the white and yellow whitewashed houses. Round, motherly women lugged baskets back and forth, gossiping with men carrying washtubs on their heads, or children on their shoulders. Everywhere they went they were hailed or patted on the head, and some man or woman would cry, "How lovely to meet you! Where are you going? You *will* come and visit me, won't you, the house with roses?" or something like that. They'd never been patted on the head as much as they were today; never had they experienced adults who were so delighted with them, and so interested in everything they said or did. It was heartwarming. Josh found that he could go on and on ad nauseam describing the problems he'd had trying to reprogram his old PC to a man with a beard, even though the man had certainly never even laid eyes on a typewriter. Then a blacksmith let him try out his entire collection of locks, until Teresa came and hauled him away, grumbling. They had to talk! They had to get going. But how?

They sat in Mansura's yard kicking at pebbles and staring into space. Even Zizi was glum, hunched up on Josh's shoulder. Teresa kept clearing her throat as if wanting to say something, but then changing her mind. Josh finally noticed that Baz was busily muttering to himself. "What's up, Baz?" he asked.

"I'm trying to decide if it's possible," said Baz, "but I don't know if it would work."

They all waited for him to finish.

"I don't know if it's possible. But it does do the trick when we jump into *umaya*." He shrugged and looked at Josh uncertainly. "I don't know if it's possible," he said again.

"*What* isn't possible?"

"To hold back time."

"What? Can you do that?"

"I don't know. And if I can't, we've had it. Because in that case we'll have missed hitching a ride with Mallum through the desert."

"But how?" asked Teresa.

"Tonight, the moment when the rhythm changes. That's when I'll have to try to hold back the beat!"

"Can you do that?" asked Josh.

"But you'd have to be up all night!" cried Teresa.

"No, I think the changeover happens only once." He added hastily, "But I'm not sure if it'll work."

Teresa whistled. "Baz, we've got to try it! Just think what it means, if it works! If you can really figure out how to influence the rhythm of time, then that would be a way for us to get out of *umaya*!" She slapped him an enthusiastic high-five, which somehow got mixed up with his hair. "Wow, this is fantastic!"

They told Mansura that they'd like to stay for another night, and she looked genuinely delighted. Then they sought out Mallum, to ask him for a lift. Mallum lived at the other end of the village, in a large round house next to a pasture filled with zebras and bizarrely spotted ponies. In the midst of the milling ponies circled two ragged, evil-tempered camels. It was fine with Mallum if they wanted to come with him. He looked a little tougher than his neighbours, but seemed just as amiable. Only, he was willing to accept payment. Four Tsumiran ducats, that would be more than enough.

"Tomorrow morning at dawn, young visitors," he said as they left. "Ask Mansura to wake you up, all right?"

They had to wait till the other children were fast asleep before they finally had a chance to discuss it.

"I'll just stay awake until I feel the rhythm switching over," said Baz, with a drawn, pale face. He had taken a wooden stick and a bowl to bed with him, on which to tap out his back-beats.

"In that case I'll stay up too," said Teresa.

"Me too," offered Josh.

"No," said Teresa, "you've got to get some sleep, Josh. One of us has to be alert tomorrow. We've got to be on the lookout for Spratt."

All of a sudden Jericho leapt from the bed, clutching her red dress. She extracted a square package from its folds. "If you're going to stay awake, Teresa, then here's something for you to read." She pressed the package into Teresa's hands with a big grin and then got back under the covers beside her again. "Because you saved my life. It's for you, my thank-you gift. It's what you wanted, isn't it?"

Teresa was sitting up rigid as a board. She stared in horror at the book and let it fall from her trembling fingers. "But this is … this is… Oh, you shouldn't have, Jericho!"

"But you wanted it so badly, didn't you?" Jericho, nodding at her encouragingly, pressed the book into Teresa's hands again.

"But Jericho," panted Teresa, "this is a forbidden book. You can't!"

"Why not? I just took it, for you. It was no trouble, really. Look, it's got pictures too."

Josh and Baz eagerly craned their necks to see the book. It was bound in blue leather, and the paper was old, yellowing and fly-specked. "What is it?" asked Josh.

"The Braxans' *Book of the Cat*," said Teresa softly.

"What?"

"That's right," said Jericho, "Teresa had said she'd like to have another look at it, and so I just took it. Those Braxans know the whole thing by heart anyway. And it could be of use to us. Didn't I do the right thing?"

"But this is their holy book," said Baz, rubbing a finger over the leather cover.

"We've got to take it back," Teresa decided.

"We can't," said Baz, "because Jericho stole it in the future. If you follow what I mean."

The thought made them dizzy. "Are there now two books, then, one with the Braxans, and one here with us?" asked Josh. "Why didn't the book disappear when time ran back?"

"It was tucked inside my dress," said Jericho, "and I carried it in my arms."

"I just don't understand," said Baz.

Teresa leafed through the book. "Everything's written in here. Everything – about stealing and trade, about Siparti … about Temberi … oh my Lord. Maybe it'll tell us where the border is. What kind of exit it is. And how we should act when we meet the angry Tembe." She flipped through the pages, read a bit, skipped from chapter to chapter.

"You see?" said Jericho. "Isn't it a really good present? Isn't it exactly what you wanted? Thanks very much, Jericho."

Teresa looked up. Her eyes suddenly filled with tears, and she smiled. "Silly girl. You funny ghost, come over here." She pulled Jericho close and gave her a big bear hug. "Thanks, sis. But you mustn't steal any more, OK? Promise?"

"No," laughed Jericho. She pulled the blankets over her head, grumbling softly, "Funny ghost." And didn't say another word.

Teresa read. Baz listened, counted and hummed under his breath, and Josh tried to fight off sleep. He'd be aware of nodding off every so often. And then he'd be convinced he was wide awake, only to wake up with a start. A few hours went by. Teresa was still reading by the faint light of the oil lamp. From time to time she'd read something aloud to Baz. Then, around one o'clock, Baz suddenly caught his breath. Teresa sat up, startled.

He started tapping on the bowl, an easy beat, listening open-mouthed. He whispered, nodding at Teresa, "You take it over. The rhythm of the bowl."

Teresa started copying the first beat, tapping her fingers on her book. Baz was now drumming a different beat on the bowl and started making staccato sounds at the same time. Together they wove a fast, complicated beat, and they kept it going endlessly. Baz stepped up the pace, nodding to Teresa that she should follow suit. It went on so long that Teresa's hand started aching and she began to feel dizzy. Baz seemed almost in a trance. He just kept drumming and chanting with the same stresses, only a little louder from time to time. All of a sudden he shot Teresa an urgent glance. "Now!" he cried.

She saw he was pouring with sweat, and did her utmost to follow along. The children started stirring restlessly in their sleep, and she prayed they wouldn't wake up and ruin everything. Baz drummed faster and faster, harder and harder, keeping up an impossibly rapid, steady tempo; and then suddenly it was over.

"Yes!" He gave the bowl a boisterous drum roll. "*Tatekketatit*, we *did* it!" He tossed the stick in the air, and looked at Teresa with a big grin on his face. "Piece of cake!"

"Is it OK for me to stop then?" she asked painfully. Baz nodded.

"Piece of cake!" she cried. "Ouch, my hand is dead!" She looked around. Mansura's children still lay motionless beside Josh and Jericho, fast asleep. "Did it really work?"

"It worked." Baz leaned back against the pillow, ecstatic. "Can't you feel the change, how easy the rhythm is now?"

"Not exactly." She tried hearing it. "But – so it really worked? Oh, Baz, that was great!"

"Thank you. It really was a cinch." He yawned, then smiled euphorically. "Hey, *I* know how to stop time. Crazy, isn't it?"

"It's very important, that's what I think it is. For getting out of *umaya*. Maybe we'll be able to use it for that."

"I'll have to think about that one." This time Baz yawned so widely that the corners of his mouth nearly split open. "Shall we get some sleep now? I'm really tired."

Teresa tucked her book under her pillow. "You're terrific. Did you know that?" she asked.

"Yes," said Baz contentedly. "I'm a pretty good drummer," he chortled. "That's true. I'm a great drummer."

At dawn they said goodbye to Mansura and the others. Packed up and all set to go, with heaps of hearty sandwiches for the journey, bottles of tea and loads of cake and pie and fruit, they climbed up into one of the carts of Mallum's caravan. Wrapped in blankets, they made themselves comfortable on the cushions at the back of the wagon, with Zizi and the little panther tucked between them. Mansura and the children waved goodbye until they were out of sight. So began the final leg of their journey to the Mabeh. As long as they were safe inside that wagon, flanked by strapping, armed horsemen, they didn't have to worry about running into any bandits – or Spratt.

12
The Thief Who Used His Eyes

The white covered wagon jolted on relentlessly, and the four travellers slept until the heat of the sun had turned the cart into an oven. When they awoke they were bathed in sweat. Through the opening at the front they could see an endless yellow plain. The zebras hitched to the wagon trotted on grimly; Mallum was seated up front, chatting with his mate.

Josh nudged Baz. "I sort of had this idea I'd dreamt it all, last night. But you did it, didn't you?"

"Easy," said Baz. "And it's even simpler when there're two of you."

"Great," said Josh, gazing at his friend with thoughtful admiration. "You really are some drummer, aren't you!"

"Yes," said Baz, smiling to himself.

"And what about that book?" Josh asked. "Does it say where the way out is?"

Teresa shook her head. "Not exactly. But I did find out some very important things. Want to hear them?"

They looked at her expectantly.

"If I've understood properly," she began, "Gippart isn't all it seems. Haven't you worked it out yet? You know, about Temberi and Siparti and the rest, and what business Gippart has with the

Tembe?" She paused a moment. "Listen carefully. Kide the Cat, whom they called Siparti. His son, Gip Siparti. Gippart."

"Oh," said Josh. "*Now* I get it. Damn!"

"You can say that again," said Teresa. "Damn! Gippart is Gip Siparti! Siparti's favourite son. The favourite son of the greedy monster who brought ruin on his own brother so that he might have the whole world for himself."

They were dumbstruck. "So then we're working for a louse," Josh spluttered.

"*Now* I understand why they ditched us," said Baz.

"And why they wanted to kill us by pushing us into real time. They're a bunch of crooks, that's all there is to it!"

"And to think we've been scared of Siparti all this time," said Baz, "while all along we've been in Siparti's team ourselves!"

"On the other hand," said Teresa, "Gippart is sending us to the Tembe. So it's possible he's sorry for what he did! Remember? Siparti promised Temberi he'd send his favourite children to his brother. To share with him the secret of time-travel."

"But he never did," Baz objected.

"But he did, Baz, he did! His favourite son Gip *did* go to Temberi. Or, rather, he's on his way there now. Right this minute. Don't you see? Not in person, but he is sending children there on his behalf."

"Children?" The enormity of what Teresa was saying slowly dawned on Josh. "You mean … you mean … it's *us*?"

Baz echoed incredulously, "Us? Siparti's favourite children?"

"We're from Gippart," Josh muttered. "We belong to Gip."

"So we are. You've got it," Teresa said softly.

They looked at each other, speechless.

"Well then, that's just too bad, isn't it?" Josh finally said with a nervous giggle. "Too bad for the Tembe. Because we haven't got the faintest idea how it's done, time-travelling. Have we?"

* * *

Teresa started telling them what she'd read. "The whole story begins in a prehistoric land called Zaam. Temberi is still supposed to be somewhere near there, but if I remember correctly the word *zaam* just means the past, or olden times, or paradise, or something. God, how I wish I had my Tembe dictionary with me now! Anyway, Book I tells much the same thing you learnt from the people who rescued you from the Inelesi, Josh. Temberi and Siparti went out into the world to sell their goods, and that was the beginning of the end. Because before that time there was no personal property, and there was no greed. And also, before that time, people could fly."

"You're kidding!"

"That's what it says in Book I, one of the first verses. The *Book of the Cat* tells how people learnt to covet things and how they gradually forgot how to fly, and how they got heavier, and greedy and bloodthirsty. The Braxans believe that they have to work through their greediness in order to become possession-free and weightless, and that once they reach that goal they'll be able to fly again. And if you can fly, then you can return to Zaam. But that's probably just a myth."

Baz and Josh frowned. "So do we have to go to Zaam?"

"I don't know that it really exists. It says that Temberi fled with his clan to the lands next to Zaam, where the wind is all-powerful. And then they fell prey to the deadly storm of time, and were swept away by a great whirlwind, which tragically ran them aground at time's outer boundary. And there they remain to this day, in rage and despair, that's what it says."

"Where they've been waiting for the children of Siparti to come along, so they can wreak horrible revenge." Baz shuddered.

"But doesn't it say where?" asked Josh.

"No," said Teresa, "but wait, I've not finished. It says something else, something very important. I'll read it to you." She took the book out of her backpack and leafed through until she found the right passage on the page she'd marked by folding over a corner. "Book IV, Verse 15: 'And when a hundred years had passed, Siparti knew his time had come, and he wept and he shuddered, because he was overcome with remorse about the great injustice he had done to his brother, and he greatly feared death.'"

"His own bloody fault," said Baz.

"Shut up and listen. 'He gathered his six sons and daughters around him, and he kissed them all, and spoke to them. And he made each one of them swear to seek out his unhappy brother Temberi, and strive to lead him out of his adversity, so that they might travel through time together.' See, he wanted his children to make up with his brother. But here comes the important part." She raised her index finger. "'He embraced his youngest son Gip to his bosom, the apple of his eye, and to him divulged the last of the roads leading to Temberi. Then he embraced his second son Beez to his bosom, the deadly one, and to him he revealed the fifth road to Temberi. Then he embraced his eldest son, the generous-hearted Mono, to his bosom, and to him he revealed the fourth road to Temberi.' Then it was his daughters' turn – his favourite, sweet Kat, and Kauri the globetrotter, and the noble Brax – and to each of them, too, he revealed a different section of the route. Do you see now? He gave each of his children a little piece of the puzzle of how to get to Temberi. It says here that his last wish was for them to kiss and make up, to stop feuding and make their way to Temberi as a group. But they never did."

"That rat must have had something else up his sleeve; I can't believe he had good intentions," said Josh. "He was probably hoping Temberi had already discovered the secret, and thought his children would worm it out of him."

"No wonder the Tembe are so vindictive," said Baz. "They don't trust those Siparti con men one bit."

"You may be right," said Teresa. "But don't you get it now? This is the Braxans' *Book of the Cat* and they're descended from

Brax. Brax Siparti. Now for the good news: the first section of the route to Temberi is described in this book. Get your map, Josh, because I've been dying to look it up."

They pored excitedly over the map as Teresa slowly read to them from Book IV, Verse 30. "'These were Siparti's last words to his noble daughter Brax: "The dead river leads to the hills, where the town of Nan lies buried beneath the sand. From this grave the road leads down to the cattle herds that graze Myndinak's fertile fields. Go now, lead thy brothers and sisters to Temberi, and share with my brother the secret of time."' Can you see those names anywhere on the map – Nan, or Myndinak?"

"Which direction are we supposed to be looking in?"

"Oh, I forgot to tell you, Siparti died at Ixilis. That's why Ixilis is marked in bold on the map. The tomb of Gippart's patriarch. It makes sense, doesn't it?"

"Near Ixilis… Look, here it is! That must be it, Myndinak! Look, Teresa! Look, Baz!"

"That road on the map, what is it?" Teresa wondered excitedly. "Is it a dry river bed? It's leading into the hills! To this little dot here… Nan! So that's it!"

"Yes, that's it." Josh clicked his tongue. "We've got it! We're going to the Tembe!" He slapped Baz and Teresa on the back. They laughed elatedly, hardly able to believe their luck.

"Pretty good, that book, isn't it?" came Jericho's sleepy voice at their backs. She'd finished the leftover apple pie all by herself, and now lay sprawled on the cushions, stuffed.

"Yes, it is," said Teresa. "Except that it's just the first part of the way to the Tembe."

"We'll have to seek out the other tribes," said Baz. "Each of the six knows a different part of the route."

"Oh yes, as if they're dying to share their secret with us," said Josh.

"Maybe they all have a sacred text," said Teresa, stroking the cover. "Maybe the Mabeh know. The Mabeh know everything."

"Maybe they have a library," Baz suggested.

"A library, in this century?" asked Josh sarcastically. "Oh yeah, we'll just look it up on the Internet."

"Doesn't it say anything in that book about the other tribes?" asked Baz.

"Oh, there's lots more in this book. The other brothers and sisters aren't all straight either, you know. Some of them are just plain traders, but there are some that are real crooks. Siparti's other little darling, Kat, was brilliant at sales talk and publicity. Mono was also all right, a dealer in fine art, but Kauri was, like, a trader – one of those really dreary missionaries."

"What about Gip?"

"And Gip, well, Gip, see Book II, Verse 13: 'And Gip took up his staff and spoke: "I shall go forth and seek out wonders in all corners of the world, and sell in the east what has been invented in the west, and sell in the north what has been discovered in the south, and many will be the hands in my employment, and I will reward them handsomely. For I will be my father's pride and joy and my domain will stretch from horizon to horizon, and from the beginning of time to the end of time."' That's our Gippart! Great, huh?"

"It isn't exactly against the law," reassured Baz.

"No, the *real* scoundrel, that's Beez. Book II, Verse 14: 'But Beez, the cruel and violent one, took up a spear and said: "But I will live in the shadows of the earth, and the anguish of the sick, the maddened and the starving will be my gain. From blood and groans shall I spin gold. I shall sell numbness and delirium, and in payment they will give me their lives and their gold, and those will be my spoils."'"

"Sounds shady to me."

"But exciting too," said Jericho softly behind them.

Teresa closed the book. "So we're on our way to the Mabeh at Ixilis, and from there we'll go on to those Myndinak pastures. And while we're among the Mabeh we'll try to find out where those other tribes live. Or where their holy books are."

Josh said, "I've heard that name Kauri before. Something about a book of Kauri. Can either of you remember?"

They shook their heads.

"Still, we're really risking our necks looking for the Tembe," said Baz. "Once they hear we've been sent by Gip Siparti … well … they'll…"

"Execute us," finished Josh. "They'll execute us. Just as the border guard said."

"But the Tembe are the good ones," said Teresa encouragingly. "Nothing like that's going to happen all that fast."

"I certainly hope you're right," said Josh.

When they stopped around noon by a thicket of thorn bushes, Mallum seemed nervous. The escorts also appeared tense and on their guard. They didn't have to explain, for the children could see it for themselves: a dust cloud on the road behind them. They ate in a hurry, and then went on their way. Once a small group of riders on horseback swerved towards them from the south, but withdrew without attacking. The dust cloud behind them, however, remained. Josh kept an eye on it through an opening in the canvas all afternoon.

It was late in the evening when they finally entered Ixilis through the eastern gate. Mallum manoeuvred his small caravan into the courtyard of a hostelry. People came running up to tend to the zebras and the horses, rub them down and tether them in a paddock. Mallum greeted them warmly. So these were the Mabeh, the children thought, inspecting them with curiosity. The wisest people on the planet. They couldn't detect anything particularly unusual about them for now. Just jovial black people wearing long coats. After a little while Mallum introduced them to a couple of the Mabeh, and they shook hands and had to reply to a lot of questions that Teresa seemed quite familiar with: "How do you do?" "How are your parents?" "Where are you from?" "How are the people you left behind?" "Is everything all right?"

At last they were shown into a large dining hall, where they sat down on thick mats and ate communally from large platters: couscous with a spicy vegetable sauce. Then they were offered plenty of sweetmeats and mint tea. They sat talking for a long time with Mallum, the Ixilians and other travellers staying at the inn, chatting about the border war, about the places they'd come from and the places they were going, and it was all very convivial.

Finally it was time for bed. They said a long-drawn-out goodbye to Mallum. "Please give Mansura our greetings," said Teresa, "and tell her that we had a wonderful time in Mur, and that we wish her the very best, and that we'll always be thinking of her and the others."

"Hey, my darling," Mallum laughed, "you haven't left yet, have you? I'll see you at breakfast, you know. But I'll certainly tell her, sweetheart." He kissed all four of them goodnight.

"I'll be curious to see what the world looks like in the morning," Baz whispered when they were lying side by side in bed under the heavy blankets.

"We should have asked," Teresa suddenly said. "Whether, for example, thirty-odd years ago, they were at war too. We should remember to ask next time."

"It's Spratt we should be worrying about," sighed Josh. "Don't you think that dust cloud was—"

An annoyed *"Shhh!"* came from one of the other beds. They curled up obediently, shut their eyes and plunged into the eighth night of their journey through *umaya.*

They had the impression it was violin music that woke them up. But as soon as they opened their eyes and sat up, all was quiet. They looked around eagerly. Yes, it was the same dormitory. But it seemed barer, emptier, whiter. There were red carpets on the floor and the other beds had not been slept in. When they got up they noticed it was already very hot: a heavy, dry heat lapping at their ankles. They pulled their wide-legged Mur trousers on over their undershirts and went outside to visit the latrines and the bathhouse. The courtyard was quieter than yesterday. Two camels were snapping at each other in the paddock, and in another corner a beautiful black horse hung its head motionless over a watering trough. A man dressed in a loincloth was pumping water. Another man and woman stood next to him, waiting their turn. They hailed the children in surprise. "Good morning, visitors," the shorter man cried. "Here I was thinking the guest quarters were empty! But you are most welcome." And he greeted them with the same string of questions that Baz and Josh were beginning to become familiar with too.

"What, you wish to journey to the Tembe?" the woman finally asked them, and she shook her head. "It's none of my business, but you mustn't think of attempting it. A journey to the Tembe, that's a journey into death. Oh, children, do not imagine you are immune to death."

Jericho smiled. Teresa decided to take the bull by the horns. "But *why* is it a journey into death? Are the Tembe really that dangerous?"

The woman shook her head. "I can't tell you any more than what I've just told you." She made them follow her to the bathhouse. "There are some here who know more than I do about it. But everyone will tell you the same thing I just told you: *don't go.* All the stories state that the road to the Tembe is the road to death. It's written in all the books, and all our storytellers will tell you the same thing."

"It's written in the books?"

"So it is," said the woman. She poured water into four buckets and handed each a bucket, a bowl, a cake of soap and a length of cotton cloth. "The shower stalls are over there. Breakfast is almost served."

They showered by dipping the bowls in their buckets and pouring water over themselves. It was wonderful: they hadn't noticed how dusty and sticky they were. Refreshed, they walked to the breakfast room wearing nothing but the cotton cloth tied around their hips, or pulled across their chests and knotted under their arms. Teresa had wrapped her purple Mur shirt around her head like a turban. "My hair's a disaster," she grumbed.

At breakfast they made their plans. It was simple. First, they'd try to find out where the books were kept. They had to get their hands on them at all costs. After that, they'd make a quick getaway. "As we did at the Traders' Trial," said Teresa. "Go, Associates! Zip in, zip out, fast, furious and unstoppable!"

They paid the bill and left. But when they stepped outside, they looked around in wonder. They weren't in the city at all. The inn was within the outer ramparts, but a considerable way from the city proper. With a strong west wind at their backs, they walked up a gentle incline. Zizi sat on Josh's hat and the panther loped along behind. Suddenly, as if they were coming up from below ground, the city walls of Ixilis loomed up before them, huge, majestic, impressive.

"Wow!" Teresa gasped. Baz whistled. Josh and Jericho stared, open-mouthed. Cautiously they drew nearer. The tall mud walls stretched right and left as far as the eye could see. Before them was a gigantic arched gate, flanked on both sides by huge round towers ending in a sharp, gold-clad steeple. The towers and the walls had been painted in red and orange designs, and they gleamed and twinkled in the morning sun. The reason, they saw when they came closer, was that the walls were inlaid with gold and precious gemstones. Groups of people were strolling about on top of the walls; some were leaning out over the parapet, peering into the distance; one or two of them waved.

"This is a huge city," said Josh. "Bigger than London! We'll never find our way around!"

"We'll see about that," said Teresa.

They presented themselves at the main gate, and requested politely if they might enter. But the little panther had another idea. It found itself a cool resting place in the shade cast by the wall and Zizi flew up to find a niche for herself.

The sentries greeted them cordially and sprinkled scented water on their hands. As they stood there, two men galloped through the gate on their fiery steeds. Both were dressed in leather combat gear, with an intricately decorated shield slung over the left arm and a long spear with streaming ribbons held proudly in the right hand.

The city was dizzyingly large. The centre, situated on higher ground, consisted of neatly clustered streets radiating from a tidy circle, with elegant buildings and white stairs leading up to six palaces. But down below and beyond snaked a maze of narrow streets and courtyards. Here lived the storytellers, magicians, stargazers, fire-dancers, thieves, counterfeiters, minstrels, boxers and sages. Josh had the feeling that even if he were to spend his whole life in Ixilis, he'd still come upon something totally unexpected in these lower reaches at least once a day. All agog, the Associates wandered down streets that kept forking into more alleyways.

Baz's eyes sparkled. "Hear those drummers, over by that dead tree? I've never heard anything like it! Don't you love it? They're amazing. Hear it?"

But Teresa sternly dragged him off. "The books first. There may be time for that later." She went up to a passer-by, a tall man wearing a woollen hat and a red sarong. "Excuse me, sir, but we're looking for the library. Could you tell us where we might find it?"

"If it's books you want, you'll find them up there, in the city on top of the hill. Are you well?"

"Very well, thank you. And yourself?"

"Excellent, thank you. Well then, I wish you good day, young lady. Good day, young people."

Slowly they climbed up to the city on the hill. They passed people sitting out in front of eating-houses, cradling bowls of tea or coffee in their hands. Most of them were dark-skinned:

some of them blue-black; many were brown-black like Lucide, or deep brown like Teresa. Several were light brown like Baz, and just a few pale like Josh. The people of Ixilis exchanged elaborate greetings before loudly sharing the latest gossip. In among them roamed goats, stately porcupines that looked as if they might shoot off their sharp quills at any moment, and the occasional scurrying monkey. Brilliant birds twittered high up in the rustling trees. Birds also nestled under the roofs or soared through the air with raucous, boisterous cries. And then there were the pungent odours: the earthy smell of cooking fires, the aroma of coffee, of stewing millet porridge, of manure and flowers, the invigorating scent of the coconut oil the people used on their skin, and the smell of fruit and spices offered for sale along the streets. It made them hungry, so they bought a bag of warm roasted peanuts and a couple of bananas.

When they got to the top of the endless white steps, they enquired left and right where they might find the books, and finally someone directed them to a low, round building next to a college. When they got to the steps they hung back. Every now and then someone would go in through the open door, after first having a word with a woman dressed in dazzling blue and wearing an impressive headdress. Then they would disappear into the building.

"Come on," Teresa said, "let's just ask. The Gippart Associate's first course of action: just ask. You never know, it's always worth a try."

She stepped inside, the others close behind. The woman in blue looked at them sternly.

"Good morning," said Teresa. "How are you today?"

"Quite well, thank you, and yourselves?" replied the woman, unsmiling.

"Very well indeed, thank you. And your family?"

The woman nodded. "Excellent, and yours?"

Now Teresa was free to ask her question. "Do you by any

chance have any books about Temberi or Siparti?"

If the woman had been wearing glasses, she would now be peering at the Associates over them. "My dear readers, have you been initiated? Where are your insignia?"

They stared at her, mystified.

"Only those people who have passed certain tests, and who have attained a certain level of maturity, are allowed to look at the books dealing with Temberi and Siparti. Besides, you have to be fluent in Tembe, and by the looks of it you won't have passed that exam yet either." She flashed a smile at Baz. "Although you, boy, do indeed have the sign of the first test on you. But it is for the drummer's test, not the reader's." She touched the scar on his left cheek.

"Oh," he said, baffled.

"But we're foreigners," Teresa tried again, "and it so happens we do know some Tembe, and we've passed all sorts of exams and tests."

"Tili sinarulo aa ene-o?" the woman barked at her. Teresa blanched, and floundered for the right words. *"Ee,"* she began, "*a ili anam* … *anam*… Oh, damn, I don't remember."

"Just so," said the woman. "You've got the beginning right. However, I think you'll have to wait a couple more years before they call you up for the initiation rites. Trust me, you really can't do much with this information until you are good and ready for it. One cannot rush these things. But I'll tell you what. Go and seek out the storytellers in the lower city. They can tell you about Temberi. And they also know plenty of other stories, more appropriate for children your age."

They went outside again, disappointed. "If I'd remembered more Tembe, she'd have let us through!" said Teresa regretfully. "I should have said, *'A ilu amane ita sirule-o.'* Oh well, let's just go and find those storytellers. Oh damn, what a drag."

They were already walking away, but suddenly Teresa jerked her head up. "Wait! I've got an idea! Of course!" She spun round and walked back. The librarian glared at her disapprovingly, but before she could say anything Teresa had whipped the *Book of the Cat* of the Braxans out of her backpack. "If you'll let us have a look at the other Books of the Cat, madam, then we'll be happy to give you this valuable one in return – do you see now that we are mature enough for such knowledge?"

But the woman in the blue headdress stiffened. Slowly she stuck out her hand for the book, then snatched it out of Teresa's hands.

"So is that a deal?" asked Teresa.

The librarian stared at the children standing before her in consternation. "But this book," she said, "is unique. There is only one copy of it in the whole world. It is the most carefully guarded book on earth." She clutched it to her bosom. "I had not heard that this book was stolen. It can't have been stolen, and it hasn't been! My most esteemed colleague saw it just last week, during a visit to the Braxans of the Takras. Is this a forgery? How did you obtain it? What *is* this?" She stared at them, her eyes popping out of her head.

Teresa bit her lower lip and turned round. The others trooped anxiously outside after her. Before reaching the corner, before the librarian could come after them, they broke into a run. It wasn't until they'd left a whole succession of streets and squares behind them that they dared to slow down. "I messed that up," said Teresa. "We'd better forget about the library. Come on, let's go down to the lower city."

"Don't you think she'll come after us?"

"Why should she? She's got the book now, hasn't she?" Teresa shook her head sadly. "I'm sure she's going to take her time examining it, with that highly esteemed colleague of hers. Nothing we can do about it now."

They passed palaces and courtyards where goats with gold collars capered about. Then they came to a strangely hushed square, where all was still. Even Ixilis's ubiquitous twitter of birds was muffled. There were no goats here. In the middle of the plaza stood a square mausoleum.

"Look," whispered Josh.

On top of the tomb was a cat – a marble statue of a cat with eyes of red rubies. They tiptoed closer. There were Tembe words chiselled into the stone. The name of the person buried here didn't come as much of a surprise to them. SIPARTI NA TEMBERI it said above the text, in big round letters. 950–1050. Solemnly they stood still in front of it. Josh touched the cold stone.

"So then he really *does* exist," he muttered.

They walked down the steps to the lower city, where there was less wind. It was also hotter, and teeming with life. They criss-crossed the dusty streets, where everybody said hello to them, and exchanged polite pleasantries as they strolled on in search of the storytellers. They came upon two speakers battling it out, cheered on by a crowd of onlookers. Baz and Josh stayed to listen, smiling. But Teresa wandered off towards a group of women who were braiding one another's hair on the wide front steps of a dwelling. Out of the corner of his eye Josh saw them looking up warmly at Teresa. They exchanged a few words, and then Teresa sat down on the ground, leaning against one of the girls' knees.

Josh went over to her, worried. "Teresa, how long is *that* going to take?"

The young woman had already started undoing Teresa's messy, fuzzy cornrows. "Hmm, I've a wonderful idea for your hair," she murmured. "It'll take four or five hours."

"What?" Josh exclaimed.

Teresa let her head loll back, her eyes shut. "All right, Josh," she said with a wave of her hand, "just go and find something else to do. I'd really like to have this done."

Josh turned to find Baz, but couldn't see him any more. The two speakers had disappeared and the street was empty. Only Jericho remained. "Come on," she said, gesturing with her head, "let's go pilfering."

"What?"

"The Books of the Cat. From the library. Come with me."

Josh, puffing out his cheeks, followed her reluctantly.

They climbed the white steps to the upper city again, the sweat pouring in rivulets down their faces and backs. Cautiously they drew near to the library. The wide avenue in front was now deserted. It was almost noon and at this hour nobody went out into the sun. The city fell silent in the heat. Only the voices of students could be heard coming from the windows of the college next door. The two thieves hid in the doorway of the college, from where they could survey the library.

"How are we going to do it?" asked Jericho.

Josh stared at the round building. "Up there!" He gestured towards a small round window with no panes, a little over two metres off the ground. They could get in that way. "Come," he hissed, flattening himself against the college wall. They sidled along until they were facing the round window. He pointed. "Up there."

Jericho nodded. They shot across the narrow alleyway. Jericho, planting her feet, interlaced her fingers to give Josh a leg-up. Josh stepped into her cupped hands and hoisted himself up. He could tell he'd been in *umaya* for a while; he was definitely stronger than before. He stuck his head through the window and saw that he'd be landing in an empty chamber no bigger than a walk-in cupboard. He wormed his way inside, scraping his elbows, and briefly got stuck; but then he was through, and toppled to the floor with a thud. It wasn't until he was on his feet again that he realized that Jericho wouldn't be able to follow him. There was no way for him to climb back up to the lofty window to pull her up. Hesitating, he looked around. He heard Jericho's voice outside. "Josh! Josh *na* Jericho! Can I come too now?"

He tried calling to her as softly as he could, but she couldn't hear him. After a brief silence, he heard her walking away. What was she going to do? Would she be back? He waited a long time, but nothing happened. Then he put his ear to the door, listening intently for any sound inside. Nothing. It was as if the whole world had dozed off, and the building were softly breathing. He opened the door very cautiously and inched his way forward along the corridor. When he had gone halfway down, he heard whispering. He froze, but the whispering died away. He crept on, a small shadow in a big, slumbering building. He passed chambers and halls filled with books, where people lay sleeping on mats and tables among the bookcases as if this was the most normal thing in the world. *So they must be in the habit of taking siestas here,* Josh decided. Readers and academics would naturally prefer to sleep among their precious books. But where was he going to find the Siparti books? There were no computer terminals, of course, on which to type in a book search, but shouldn't there be a card catalogue or something, or just a simple list of subjects? He stopped at the door of a round chamber that seemed deserted, and slipped inside. There were shelves along the walls, as well as cases filled with scrolls. He ran his fingers along some of the spines. *AYAYLIREM PANI LUYMALINI!* it said brightly on one of the spines, and, ominously, *DAV* on another. Some of the titles were written in a weird kind of alphabet. It was an uphill task to find Siparti's sacred legacy among all these folios and scriptures. He pressed his cheek against a pillar in the centre of the room and whispered, defeated, "I just don't know!"

A shudder went through the pillar. From deep inside came a voice, barely audible: "What is it you just don't know? May I ask what you are looking for?"

Josh jumped back in alarm. Was the heat getting to him? Was he starting to hear voices now? He took a deep breath and looked around. There was no one in sight. He whispered, his heart pounding, "I am looking for the books of Siparti."

There was a rustling sound, then a flat little laugh, and the voice again: "And who are *you*, reader, that you should want to read the books of the terrible Siparti?"

"I am Joshua *na* Jericho, sent by Gippart."

"Ah, an envoy from Gip Siparti," the voice whispered. "The son beyond compare of an awe-inspiring father and a remarkable mother! Come closer, child of Gip Siparti."

Josh took a couple of hesitant steps towards the pillar.

"You will find them in the small red room in the rear hall, past the atlases and the forbidden bookcases. Bookcase B, second shelf. You'll find only Kauri and Kat, as well as our own Mono, Mono of Ixilis... Actually, no, Mono and Kauri were taken out, to be returned by November the eleventh, and ... oh, curse it, by October the twenty-sixth, and it's not back yet! Ah well, you can find the Book of Kauri on any street corner; there are hundreds of them. But Kat – I have no doubt that that one would be your favourite? Gip and Kat Siparti, cut from the same cloth. Go, reader, I'll pass on your name to the book warden, so that you may read without being disturbed."

The voice died away before Josh could cry, "Wait! Don't!"

He had no clue what was going on, but one thing was certain: the book warden would be alerted very shortly, so there was no time to waste, or he'd lose his chance. He dashed out of the room and ran to what he thought was the back of the building. The place was still dead to the world, mumbling in its sleep. The readers were happily snoring on their mats and their tables. But the building might wake up and turn against him any moment now.

He rushed through a few rooms, but then found himself totally disorientated. In desperation he put his mouth close up to a wall and whispered, "Could you tell me please, where is the small red chamber?"

A sleepy voice mumbled back, "Two rooms down, dear reader."

He rushed on, past bookshelves full of whispering books, past people grinding their teeth in their sleep. And then – he could hardly believe it! – he stumbled on the little red room at the end of a dead-end corridor. The heat hung stagnant among the bookcases. He wiped the sweat out of his eyes.

"Kat Siparti!" he said out loud and walked confidently up to the second bookcase.

"Gip Siparti!" came a loud answer. A small red book hurled itself off the second shelf.

Josh bent down and picked it up, and it was as if the book gave a shudder before relaxing in his hands. He darted out of the room again, looking for a back door. But the corridor had no exit, and he pressed his mouth against the wall once more, pleading, "The back door, please?"

The voice that answered him sounded confused. "The title of the book? Title, please?"

The building started to tremble. The whispering became louder and suddenly seemed to come from every direction. There was a shout from somewhere, and a door slammed. So this was it. The chase was on. And he was the one they were after, for a change. But it was odd: he wasn't paralysed by fear; he felt instead the prickling of excitement. He laughed out loud. Joshua *na* Jericho, master thief of time! Kat's *Book of the Cat* seemed to be throbbing in his hand, to inspire him with courage. He hurried down the corridor, opening doors left and right, startling readers who were waking up. He raced through a hall where readers looked up in alarm from the books they had just opened again, darted into a study carrel where a very old woman was chanting in a croaky voice from a songbook, discovered a flight of steps, leapt over the gate barring the way, and ran upstairs. He found himself in a large attic space under a domed roof filled with archives. But here at least there were some small windows. His salvation. Sticking his head out of one of them, he didn't linger. From downstairs came the sound of a gong. "Come on," he told himself firmly. "Siparti!"

He squeezed himself through the window, legs first, and dropped on to the stone ledge encircling the entire building. A useful ledge. He sat down on it, took a deep breath and jumped to the ground below. His ankles almost gave way, but that didn't slow him down. He glanced over his shoulder. Some people with scowling faces were walking towards him. He shouted, and took to his heels. And suddenly he felt someone grab him by the hand, and he found himself running with increased speed and ease. It was Jericho sprinting at his side, smirking little devil that she was! They ran as hard as they could, but the Mabeh had started running too. It sounded as though there was a whole mob gathering behind them. "This way!" Jericho urged him on, and suddenly they found themselves in the hushed square that housed Siparti's tomb. Josh slowed his pace, wiping the sweat off his brow. Jericho pulled him over to the tomb. The stone cat stared at them, frozen, with flickering red eyes.

"*What*, Jericho?"

"Over here!"

To Josh's astonishment a dark opening appeared at the side of the marble tomb. Like a door into the deepest night.

Jericho stepped through without hesitating. "Come on!" she insisted, and was gone in the blink of an eye.

Josh looked back. A large, noisy crowd came swarming into the square; some of the gang were brandishing sticks. When they caught sight of him they pointed and started shouting. He gulped, clutched the book tightly, stepped over the stone threshold and slammed the thick stone door shut behind him.

It was pitch dark. "Jericho?"

Echoing sounds. It was stifling. He didn't dare budge for fear of disturbing some partly decayed corpse. Jericho and her bright ideas! Here they were, blind as bats, entombed in a smelly, boiling-hot grave!

"Jericho!"

Her voice came from the other side of the darkness. "Over here, Josh."

He felt around him in the dark. Suddenly he was convinced

he couldn't possibly move another foot.

"What's taking you so long?" shouted Jericho. "Come on, you aren't scared of some silly old bones, are you?"

Something hard hit his nose, then clattered to the ground. Josh screamed and kicked it away from him in panic, arms flailing. "Stop it!"

She giggled. "Don't be such a baby. Come here."

She came shuffling towards him, through piles of bones by the sound of it. Her hand found his. Josh put Kat's *Book of the Cat* in his pocket and let Jericho pull him along across the tomb's littered floor.

"Want one of Siparti's bones as a souvenir?" she teased him.

"Stop it," said Josh again. The deathly air in this nightmarish crypt was making him feel sick.

They shuffled forward cautiously, until Jericho suddenly seemed to disappear, dropping down a little way. "Trapdoor, careful," she whispered, helping to guide Josh's legs through the hatch and on to the rung of a ladder. Carefully they lowered themselves down the ladder, landing in a still darker small space. "There's another ladder going even further down," said Jericho. "It's just like that thief said. A good escape route, isn't it? Can you see, or do you need me to help you?"

Josh came to a standstill, his hand on the ladder.

"What's the matter?"

"It's not right," he muttered.

"What isn't?"

"Those bones, belonging to Siparti. It isn't right, is it?"

"What are you talking about?" asked Jericho. "Did you want to take them with you?"

"No, of course not," said Josh, who suddenly knew what he had to do. "Wait for me here, I'll be back in a jiffy."

He felt for the rungs of the ladder and climbed back up to the stifling crypt. Once up there the smothering heat again overwhelmed him. He had to stop a while before he could begin what he'd come to do. His heart pounding, heaving from time to time with disgust, he started fumbling around for the bones and collecting them. After much hunting around he found the skull in a corner. The thing felt a little clammy, as if it was sweating. It would be days before Josh would eat with the hand that had touched that skull. While he was working he tried to do as little thinking as possible. Oddly enough, Lego sets kept flashing before his eyes, as if he were putting together a complicated assembly of tricky, living Lego pieces.

"Come on, what are you doing?"

"I'm just trying to tidy up these bones," said Josh hoarsely. "Can you see a coffin or anything anywhere?"

He heard Jericho scrambling up the ladder. "That stone sarcophagus over there, it's toppled over on its side," she said. "Do you want to turn it right-side up?"

"Let's," said Josh. "Oh wait, I'm such an idiot." He fumbled in his backpack for his compass, and switched it on.

The dim blue light made Siparti's scattered bones glow in the dark. Brilliant jewels flashed among the white ribs and hip bones. Jericho went to pick one up, but Josh gave her a warning slap on the wrist. "Leave it!" he barked. "This is a *burial vault*!"

"So?" But when she saw his solemn face she complied.

They turned over the sarcophagus, which weighed a ton. Next, they carefully arranged the bones in their proper places, measuring and puzzling over where each one was supposed to go, until the skeleton was complete. It was a complicated job, and took ages to finish. At last the only thing left was to slot the skull into place at the top, and to scatter the jewels all around. As they slipped the last stray toe bone into place, Jericho said, "I still don't see why you needed to do this so badly, but it's done. Can we go now?"

Josh stared thoughtfully at the inert skeleton. "He isn't all that tall, is he? I thought he'd have been taller."

"Dearest Josh," said Jericho. "It took us hours to assemble Siparti, and I've helped you without complaining, but now we're getting away from here, all right? Or are you going to hang around here another few hours praying or something?"

"Isn't it strange, though, that we're actually looking at Siparti himself?"

"In his own grave? What's strange about that? It would have been strange if you'd met Dick Whittington in here or something. Come on, slowcoach, hurry!"

They clambered down the ladder, and then another one, their way dimly lit by the compass, and then they were standing at the top of a set of wooden steps, which they took two at a time, landing in a circular space.

"Where to now?"

"Here, to the left. This is how all the thieves make their getaway. That little pickpocket I met told me about it."

As they rushed through the passageway, Jericho told him about the helpful thief who had struck up a conversation with her outside the library, and told her about the thieves' secret escape route via Siparti's tomb. In listening to him, she'd stumbled upon yet another of Ixilis's secrets: that nothing here remained private if it was anybody's business. The blacksmiths always found out almost at once whatever it was that concerned blacksmiths (and there was a lot funnier stuff going on there than anyone might think), while the latest burglary was immediately known to all the burglars. And not just to the burglars, either.

At last they emerged into a dusky, roofed-over alley, creeping past mud walls from behind which came voices and domestic sounds. The alley led into a wide avenue, sunlit and busy. Yet even here they weren't safe. Josh noticed people looking at him suspiciously. Someone shouted, "Stop!" Someone else asked him loudly where he thought he was going, and he felt a hand grab his shoulder. Another held him in a tight grip. He struggled helplessly, but an instant later was saved by an armed ruffian's fiercely galloping horse nearly running them down, whipping sand up in their faces. As the fellow who'd grabbed him jumped back to avoid the horse's hooves, Josh tugged himself loose and darted up a steep alley across the way. He turned into a side street, and then another one, and had just begun wondering how he'd ever find Jericho again when she dashed up to him from the opposite direction.

"Quick," she cried, "hurry!" and pulled him into yet another alley. "They're after us!"

And it was true. They heard voices near by as well as further away. People were no longer just staring at them, they were calling out at them sharply, or grabbing for their arms. There was a mob of children running after them. This was the real problem about Ixilis, they realized: everybody immediately knew everything that was going on. And everything that was going on was everybody's business. People came streaming out of their houses to help catch the thieves they'd heard were on the loose. Josh and Jericho were still managing to give their pursuers the slip, but they knew the noose was tightening and there was nothing they could do about it. The whole city was after them.

"Over here!" Jericho suddenly yelled. She leapt through the door of a small flat-roofed mud hut, slammed the door shut behind them and barred it. Josh didn't know how she'd been able to tell from the outside that the house was empty, but it was, and for the time being they were safe. Gasping for breath, they sat down on a low bench. Meanwhile, a raucous crowd was gathering outside, and started hammering on the door and the walls. The little house shook to its core.

"We're trapped!" panted Josh, wiping his drenched hair out of his eyes.

"I think you're right."

It was a hut with no windows. There was no trapdoor to a secret cellar, no emergency exit.

"What are we going to do?" moaned Josh.

From outside came angry voices: "Come out, thief!" "We're going to get you!"

Someone had climbed on to the roof and was now banging on it hard. The plaster came raining down on their heads. Glancing up worriedly, Josh pulled the book out of his pocket. "I'll just read here what it says about the route. And after that, well…"

"By the time you're done they'll have smashed this house to bits," said Jericho. "And us as well."

With trembling fingers Josh leafed through the little red book. He read a few words, leafed on and read some more. Slowly he let his hands drop to his sides and gazed at his sister. "We're done for. This is no use to us."

"What?"

"It's in some foreign language." He hurled the book to the floor in frustration.

"Ha," said Jericho. She didn't appear to care much one way or another.

Josh picked up the book again and stared at it in despair. "Kat Siparti," he moaned. "Blasted Kat Siparti! Damn, damn, damn –"

The book trembled. At first he thought it was caused by the whole hut shivering and quaking under the blows of the furious crowd outside. But that wasn't it. The book itself was vibrating. Faintly, but agitatedly. And then he heard it whispering something, very softly. He pressed his ear to the cover and found he could understand what it was saying. His stomach lurched.

"Gip Siparti, you feather-brain…"

"What?"

The voice was asking, "Can't you read Tembe any more, dimwit?"

"No," he stammered. "But who—"

"What is it you want to know, little brother?"

"I…" Josh gulped. "The way to the Tembe," he muttered.

The book tittered, nearly inaudibly. "Really? Even now, after all these years? You are a silly billy, Gip Siparti." It hesitated.

"May I ask if you yourself are Gip, or are you his child's child?"

Josh had to swallow again. "His child's child, I suppose, more or less," he whispered.

"Ah," breathed the book, "I thought so. Just as I am Kat's handbook, not her actual self… My dear, for our incomparable blood brother's sake, I'll tell you. But do you truly wish to visit Temberi, our kind-hearted uncle, who has been dead these many years? All by yourself? Don't you think it is a little late to correct the great wrong done by our heartless father? Why do you wish to go there?"

"Because…"

The book, nestled in his clammy hand, sighed. "Well, it's none of my business, is it? Gip always likes to keep us in the dark about what he is up to. Well now, since you have returned I am obliged to reveal to you our section of the road."

Josh glued his ear to the warm cover to catch the book's words, which were growing fainter and fainter. The phrase it recited made little sense: "'From lake through mud to a waterfall; to guidance, to punishment; the road to Maam Sagal.'"

Although it didn't mean a thing to him, he repeated the words carefully several times. "Right, dearest," said the voice, getting even fainter, "and now you'll take me back to the library, won't you?" The book went still, and lay inert in his hands.

Josh looked around at his sister, dazed. His improbable conversation with the book had lasted no longer than a minute or two. In that time the commotion outside had grown louder, and dangerous cracks had appeared in the wall. It was getting so bad that here and there whole chunks of plaster were breaking off and crashing to the floor. It felt as if a horde of aliens were laying siege to them, hostile beings from an enemy planet.

Jericho was moaning softly to herself, a strange sound at the back of her throat. It took a while before he understood she wasn't whimpering or crying. She spread her arms and gazed up, radiant. She looked intensely happy. Josh followed her gaze upwards. Suddenly he felt the air around him throbbing. But it wasn't coming from up there. They were swarming in from all sides, all around, charged with static. They had piercing, laughing voices. Their amorphous shapes swirled through the air like a mirage. He braced himself. Was he about to see them clearly at last? Were they going to grab him and carry him off? Were they going to set themselves on the Ixilians, and chase them away, and sweep the whole town clean of its inhabitants? He quite forgot to breathe. When the crash came, it gave him such a shock that he felt faint. Blinded, he collapsed in a heap on the ground.

He lay against the wall of the hut until he could get his breath back. His heart was pounding. Had they all come crashing down at once, those spectral friends of Jericho's? Opening his eyes took too much effort. But when he heard Jericho swearing furiously, he looked up. She was ranting and raving in a wild-haired frenzy, screaming at the top of her voice at an unruffled figure standing opposite her. The Still-Dead-Children were nowhere in sight. The electric charge had been banished from the air as if by magic. The figure facing Jericho wasn't smiling, but drilling her with his piercing stare. He had an aura of stillness about him. He was holding her by the wrist and didn't move.

"You just *had* to go and spoil everything, didn't you! You just want to ruin everything! When are you going to leave us alone? Why can't I call on my own friends to come and help us? You won't be satisfied, will you, until my *living* brother is dead as well! In your book does everything have to die, then? You mean, meddling bastard, always sticking your nose in!"

Lucide did not open his mouth, but held her tightly, and gazed. From where he was seated up against the wall, Josh could feel Lucide's calmness, felt him giving off serenity like a glowing ember, and it did make him feel a lot calmer himself. It had the same effect on Jericho. She kept up her ranting and raving a little while longer, then burst into furious tears. Lucide slowly let go of her wrist. He stayed still, impassive.

Impulsively, Josh stood up and took a step in the direction of Lucide, who suddenly turned his gaze on him. As if bewitched, Josh froze. Then he spun round towards the front door, and, without knowing what he was doing, unbarred it and stepped over the threshold, out into the bright sunlight and the raging crowd.

For just a moment there was silence. Then the cries and jeers started up even louder than before. "The thief!" "There's the piece of scum!"

Many hands grabbed him. He was lifted into the air and then hurled to the ground. People were pushing and kicking him. Somebody hit him in the back with a cudgel. A hand tugged his hair viciously. He cringed, not uttering a sound, still clutching the book to his chest. He heard people rushing into the hut behind his back, and heard Jericho's angry shouts; and he felt Lucide's presence, faint, but somehow comforting. A little space opened up around him, the beatings stopped, and he peered round cautiously through narrowed eyes. A couple of people stood facing him; the rest had formed a circle around him. Josh wiped his face. He noticed he'd bitten his lip, and it was bleeding. It didn't matter. He took a deep breath, stood up straight and handed the book to the person in the middle. He had no trouble recognizing her. It was the librarian, regally arrayed in blue.

"Well, well," she said, taking the book from him. She inspected it from all angles, then, to Josh's astonishment, burst out laughing. The crowd surged forward, curious to see what was so funny. "Kat Siparti!" the woman laughed. "What else would Gip Siparti's incomparable kinsfolk steal but Kat Siparti's book! Gip and Kat, Kat and Gip, they're inseparable, those two – if they're not at each other's throats, that is!"

A ripple of laughter and murmuring went through the

crowd. But then the woman continued, stretching herself to her full height. "Thief!" she said loudly, and the mob echoed in agreement, *"Thief! Thief!"* "You have robbed, you have stolen from the library! You have shamed and betrayed your entire clan – because the fearsome Sipartis of the House of Gip do not tolerate theft!"

Josh stared at his feet. He wished it was over. Were they going to flog him, hang him, banish him for all time?

"We shall now mete out the penalty you deserve, and after that you had better get out of here, you and your accomplice. You may very well be related to our own Sipartis, the Sipartis of the House of Mono, but we certainly never want to see your faces here again."

Well, at least they weren't going to kill him. It hadn't all quite sunk in yet, but what he did understand was that his wretched predicament would soon be over. He braced himself to hear what his punishment would be.

"Come here," said the woman. She was holding a long knife. She looked him in the eye and then gazed past him. "Hmm. I see the two of you have a guardian."

Josh glanced over his shoulder. There stood Lucide, quiet and dignified next to Jericho. Jericho's eyes were fixed on the knife, but Lucide's gaze was on the distant horizon. It had grown very quiet and very hot. Everyone waited with bated breath.

"Give me your right hand," said the woman. "I, Nilim Memue of Ixilis, guardian of the books, am authorized to punish the thief who steals my books. So I now raise my knife to shed the blood of Gip Siparti's offspring, who this day, Sunday October the twenty-ninth, in the year 1490, unlawfully took Kat Siparti's *Book of the Cat*."

She raised her knife, nearly crushing Josh's hand in hers, and turned it over, palm side up. "This hand has plundered, and this hand will pay for that deed," she said in a loud voice, and brought the knife down.

The blood drained from Josh's face and he broke into a sweat. He tried with all his strength to pull his hand away, but she held him fast. He shut his eyes in panic. A cry went up from the crowd and then he himself screamed, at the sudden sharp pain in his wrist. Two harsh, burning slashes; and then it was over.

She let go, and he clutched his wrist. The blood was welling up from two cuts just beside the artery. "Ouch!" he cried. Tears streamed down his cheeks. *"Ouch!"*

The woman carefully licked off the knife and nodded at him gravely. "The sign of the thief. A V-notch on the right wrist."

Then she did something unexpected. She threw the knife down on the ground and offered him her hand. He stared at it nonplussed, sucking at his bleeding wrist. "Come on, hit me," she said. "Hit the hand that dealt you the wound. Go on, do it, then it will be done."

He didn't understand why, but using his left hand he did slap her, hard, with all the strength and fury that suddenly surged in him.

She gasped, and then she nodded. "Thank you, Gip Siparti. Come, I will accompany you and your companion to the North Gate."

The crowd dispersed, chatting and laughing. All the tension had suddenly evaporated. Jericho rushed over to Josh. "Did it hurt a lot?" she squeaked. She patted his forearm, which was still dripping blood, though more slowly now.

He rubbed his eyes. "A little," he whispered in a shaky voice.

"Come," ordered the librarian.

Jericho tugged at her sleeve. "Won't you do the same thing to me? Please?" she pleaded.

"Certainly not. It is the thief who is punished, not his associate. The mark you would receive would be quite different. A notch by your nose or something."

It was a long way to the North Gate. As they walked

through the streets in the sweltering afternoon, they were hailed and greeted everywhere again. The voices had no venom in them any more. The people of Ixilis gazed at them pleasantly and wished them well. "Good afternoon, librarian and thief; good afternoon, Gip Siparti," they said cheerfully, and asked them where they were from, where they were going, and how they were; but Josh didn't answer them. He was sucking his sore wrist.

The woman left them outside the city under a palm tree, out of sight of the city walls. She turned and hurried back towards Ixilis without saying goodbye.

"*Now* what do we do?" said Jericho. "It's all been a waste of time, hasn't it? You've lost Kat's *Book of the Cat.* And Teresa lost the Braxans' *Book of the Cat.* That's the last time I'm giving her a present." She pulled up a withered grass stem and began chewing it.

"But I do know the way," said Josh, who was watching Lucide settling himself down on the sandy ground on the other side of the road. Lucide crossed his legs, rested his hands in his lap and then gazed straight ahead, immobile, in their direction. It made Josh a little nervous.

"How, then?" asked Jericho.

"Didn't you hear? The book told me."

"What? You mean that book spoke to you?"

"Yes it did," said Josh. He had to admit it sounded a little far-fetched, even to himself. "You know, that whole library could talk. There was a voice that told me where to find the books. And Kat's book just jumped off the shelf when I called it."

"Amazing. So you know the way to go?"

"Yes." He took the crumpled map out of his backpack and spread it out in front of him. "Kat's route is the third leg of the journey." He remembered the words exactly: lake, mud, waterfall, Maam Sagal. Guidance and punishment. But it suddenly dawned on him, too, why he wouldn't find it on the map.

"Look," he explained to Jericho, "obviously it's only after completing the second leg of our trip that we'll be able to find this third name. If not, you'd need only the instructions for the last stage in order to find your way there. Who knows if Maam Sagal is somebody's name, or a place, in the language they speak there." He folded up the map, suddenly very tired. They still had so far to go. And at the end of their journey, a totally terrifying final stage awaited them. Impossible to get out alive, Max had said. "What do we do if Baz and Teresa can't find us? Do you think they're looking for us in the city?"

But Jericho did not reply. She was lying on her back, staring up at the sky, humming under her breath. Then she sighed. "I wish Lucide would just get lost." She turned to Josh. "You know, you're very brave, really."

"I am? Why's that?" asked Josh languidly, flat on his back now too, slowly licking his throbbing wrist.

"Well, staying all alone in that library for one thing, and having the guts to put Siparti's bones back in place, even though I still don't understand why you did it. And having the courage to walk out of that hut."

Josh thought it over. Had he been brave? "But I'm no good at anything," he finally said, voicing what he'd been brooding about the entire expedition. "I can't play the drums and hold back time like Baz, and I don't have Teresa's way with words, and she always just seems to know what to do. I'm not much good at anything, actually. Stealing and getting caught. That's all I'm good for."

"Nonsense. Know what you're good at? Looking."

"Oh, big deal," Josh scoffed.

"No, I mean: you look, and then things change."

"What do you mean?"

"Take those bones – Siparti's bones, I mean – for instance. You were really scared of them at first. And then you started seeing them as just ordinary building bricks. Right or wrong?"

"Lego," Josh said, surprised. "I was seeing Lego pieces."

"And inside that hut. It felt as if we were being attacked by a horde of terrifying monsters, didn't it? And then you thought to yourself, *If I can see them, it won't feel so bad.* And then you went outside and it really wasn't all that bad."

"I wasn't thinking anything. I don't know why I went outside."

"You were thinking: *I have to see the thing that's making me afraid with my own two eyes,*" Jericho continued.

"So you think you can read my thoughts now?"

"I can sometimes," said Jericho. "Why not?"

"But that wasn't what I was thinking then. It's what the combat master told me, in the *umaya* of the warrior: 'Stare the nightmare straight in the eye.'"

"It was in your head, anyway. And then things changed. At first they were a mad, bloodthirsty crowd, and then suddenly they were just normal people."

"The Mabeh," Josh muttered, "they're supposed to be the wisest people on earth. They can't have been mad, I suppose. Hey, wouldn't *they* know where Temberi lives? We should have asked them straight out."

"I just wish Lucide would get lost," said Jericho.

Far away, in the lower city, Baz ended his solo. He'd been playing on three unfamiliar drums simultaneously, delighting in their sound: the heavy, booming timbre of the first, the elastic, nimble pitch of the second, and the hollow, spicy tone of the third. He'd worked himself into a sweat showing his new friends what he was capable of. They were standing in a circle around him, three master drummers, three of Ixilis's most dazzling players. When just a few minutes ago they had made his ears ring and his heart race with their playing, he'd been practically hopping up and down with excitement. And disbelief. To think you could make that kind of sound with your hands and feet and a couple of drums! Then they said, "Your turn, little drummer," and he couldn't very well refuse. He was in his element. He played his own riffs and tried to copy what they'd been playing, and when that didn't work, never mind, he'd mess about and play around with it. And after finishing he jumped to his feet as his friends clapped and cheered. "Bravo," they cried, but in the Mabeh language, using a word reserved only for drummers.

First they earnestly discussed what he'd done and where he could improve or do something differently. Then they let him join them as a fourth drummer, which almost drove him wild because he had such a hard time following them, tripping over their far too complicated beats. But they steered him back on track, showing him how to play in a foursome. They taught him that during a solo you were allowed to really show what you could do, but they also showed him how to play discreetly, as back-up, so that the listeners heard only the singer, letting him or her shine.

As they were standing around chatting, the drummer called Swap suddenly pulled out a knife, and caught Baz in a tight hold. Baz the gutsy drum-maniac immediately managed to kick himself free, but the others cried, "Calm down," and Swap explained, "You already wear the mark of the drummer, but that one's just the initiation-stage sign. I want to give you the mark of the second drumming exam. I have the right to give it to you." Baz squeezed his eyes shut and – *"Ouch!"* – felt a second cut just underneath the first scar, ending right next to his ear.

Swap took a pungent leaf from his pocket and pressed it on the bleeding cut. "Congratulations!"

The other two started drumming a lively beat. "That's the second exam's special beat," they told him. Then they switched over to a really odd, very annoying rhythm.

"Hear that?" asked Swap. "You can make people really mad with that one. And listen to this one. This one will make some-one burst into tears."

Baz picked up his drumsticks again and tried to copy them. For several hours he forgot all about the expedition. He forgot he was in *umaya*, he forgot about their assignment, and he forgot that Josh and Teresa might need his help.

A few streets away, in front of a mud hut, in the shadow of a pergola smothered in passion flowers, a group of girls were busy braiding one another's hair in intricate patterns using hair extensions and beads, telling one another endless stories. Teresa listened open-mouthed as her matted hair was untangled with infinite patience, then brushed, washed, oiled and braided once more.

They told horror stories so scary, they made your nose bleed. Ancient tales about the beautiful, one-legged girl who flew up to the sun on her flying camel to find gold. About the weeping palm tree whose tears turned into grains of sand which filled up the entire desert. About the wicked witches tricked by the clever young girl with the goat. About a crafty one-eyed zebra that was addicted to tobacco. Stories about rogues, sailors and merchants. Stories about Lamerika, about the haunted forest, about the South Pole and the aromatic Far East. The Mabeh were great travellers, Teresa learnt, and they knew the globe like the backs of their hands.

When all these stories had been told, everyone suddenly looked at Teresa. "And you, stranger? Do you know any stories?"

Teresa smiled. She sat up straight as the girl went on carefully braiding her hair. "I will tell you about a great trading company of legendary renown," Teresa began in the low, mysterious voice she always used to capture an audience's attention. "It goes by the name of Gippart International, and it has outstandingly courageous traders. But the bravest of all are the youngest traders, who dare to go where adults fear to tread: the fearless Associates. I will tell you about the terrible adventures of three young Associates who were sent on a lethal mission by Gippart, and who were then falsely betrayed and left to their own devices..."

As she told her story, the others listened with bated breath.

The girl doing Teresa's hair forgot her work and let her hands drop into her lap. Teresa didn't notice. She went on with her glowing tale, fibbing a little here, embroidering there, concocting heroes and fabricating monsters. But suddenly she found she had come to the story about how Baz stopped time in Mur. It occurred to her it would be best to end it there.

Townsfolk kept strolling past, chatting, smiling and greeting each other, but the small circle around Teresa didn't budge, listening transfixed.

"Ai," said the girl Liam at last with a deep sigh. She jumped to her feet and went up to Teresa, hands outstretched. "Teresa, Teresa, I name you Daughter of Zim, acrobat of storytellers!" She turned back to the others, waving her hand at Teresa. "Look, my bosom friends and Mabeh cousins, storytellers, second-class, have you ever listened to a teller of tales such as this? To such a young, unmarked girl in dusty travelling clothes and wild hair? And doesn't she speak just like one of us Mabeh?"

They clapped their hands and shouted their agreement. The girl who was supposed to be braiding Teresa's hair pulled her close again. "I'm going to give you a different style," she said, and started undoing the part she had finished braiding. "I was going to give you the hair of the stranger with the keen ears, but now I'm going to weave your hair in the style of storyteller, second-class, Mabeh's pearl, tongue of gold."

Teresa buried her blushing face in her hands in order not to burst out laughing. But that wasn't the end of it, for Liam went to fetch someone: a short, swarthy woman in a towering, gold-embroidered headdress. All the girls quickly got to their feet, but the woman made straight for Teresa. This was master storyteller Zim, the girls whispered. She who had once chased off a hungry lion with her sharp tongue; she who with sweet words could coax rain from the drought-stricken sky.

Zim took Teresa's face in her strong hands and gazed long and deep into her eyes. Then she smiled. "I see your cheeky head brimming with stories, young lady from the north, ward of Mother Earth," she said softly. "How I should like to be your teacher. You know" – she lowered her voice – "I can teach you to change the world around you with just your words; I can teach you how to make men fall in love with you and how to change timid females into fierce warriors." Her eyes roved over Teresa's face and she laughed. "Aha, you saucy thing, but perhaps you already know how to do that – am I right?" She went on staring at her intently. "I read you, young lady. You do not wish to stay. But I shall give you a gift, whether you want it or not." She plucked a small, sharp knife out of the folds of her skirt. Teresa jumped back, but Liam grabbed and held her. Zim stroked Teresa's chin. "We storytellers wear our mark with pride, for it reminds us always that we have made people laugh and we have made them cry, and that our power has stood us in good stead and will do so again, yea, even in the hour of our greatest need. Because the earth itself is our protector. Come, my pride and joy. Come, storyteller of mine."

And before she knew it, Teresa had a vertical cut just beneath her lower lip, stinging, sharp. It startled her, but she did not scream. The blood dripped slowly down her chin. Zim carefully pressed a dressing of spiders' webs over it. "Long live Teresa Okwoma, storyteller, second-class!" they all cried.

Then, while her hair was being braided with gold beads and a red feather in the distinctive style of a storyteller, second-class, they presented her with several secret tales reserved only for the ears of the initiated. To Teresa's delight, one story they told her was that of the two favourite offspring of Siparti the terrible, Siparti the almighty: Gip and Kat Siparti, the two youngest siblings of Ixilis's noble ancestor, Mono Siparti. Gip and Kat, the two richest merchant-traders in the world; twins who loved each other passionately, but who also quarrelled incessantly because neither wanted to be outdone by the other in power or wealth. Zim related that both were sly and crafty;

and with their smooth tongues they could sell you just about anything, for just about any price. Kat was the more persuasive of the two, but Gip had the advantage of being more skilled at sniffing out the most tempting baubles to sell. Teresa heard how one would trick the other to come out on top, and how the other one would then settle the score in their never-ending rivalry. And she heard that they were jinxed with the terrible curse that clung to all of Siparti's kin: the curse that goaded them on, and that fuelled their hate and envy. "But Gip and Kat, Kat and Gip Siparti," Zim concluded her story, "they actually can't bear to be apart, those two. Some day they will go side by side into eternity."

And last of all, tersely and with loathing, she told Teresa about the hideous Beez Siparti, the black sheep of the family and his siblings' nastiest foe. Beez had made earth a living hell until his kingdom was razed to the ground. "All that remains of the place Beez and his henchmen used to live is scorched earth," Zim whispered, "but from beneath the ashes you can still hear the groans of their victims. The earth is still hot there, and even if the soles of your feet could stand the heat, your heart would break from the fear and despair that linger."

All this Teresa heard in Ixilis on that extraordinary afternoon in the shade, and she remembered all of it, every word.

A thin sickle moon was just sinking into the westerly horizon when Teresa and Baz reached the palm tree that evening. The faint moonlight slipped over the sleeping forms of Josh and Jericho before disappearing. Teresa and Baz took the blankets out of the backpacks and tucked in first their companions, and then themselves. The little panther came slinking along, and nestled down beside them. They didn't notice Lucide, sitting there like a statue. Under the reassuring rustling of the palm tree's leaves, they promptly fell asleep.

PART IV
THE ROAD TO THE TEMBE

13
THE DOVE OF LIGHT

In the stillness of the dawn a bird came flying out of the south, the morning sun glinting on her pale green wings. Silently she glided down, and Josh was asleep when she landed on his head, and he was still asleep when she rubbed her beak against his ear. He was asleep until she began impatiently pulling at his hair.

"Zizi!" He tickled her warm neck and let her hop down on to his hand. "Zizi, you've missed all the excitement. Wherever were you? I've had such a mad time." With his lips pressed to her feathers, he began telling her the whole story. She listened attentively, cooing softly when he'd finished. "Yeah, and now I'm a real, honest-to-goodness thief. But Jericho says what I'm good at is seeing things. So, what do you think, Zizi?"

"It's a great story, anyway," a voice piped up from Teresa's blanket-cocoon. "Did they really give your wrist the mark of the thief?" Poking her head out, she stared at his hands.

Shyly Josh stuck out his right hand.

Teresa whistled. "Good-looking scar. What do you think of mine?" She pointed to her lower lip.

"Did they catch you stealing too?"

"No, it's the mark of the storyteller, second-class!" Teresa shook off the blanket and stood up proudly. "And what do you all think of my hair?"

She looked very impressive, a proud black girl with towering hair of intricately woven cornrows, sparkling with gold and crowned with a scarlet feather.

"You look very different," said Josh, awestruck. "Much older, I dunno..."

With the help of the compass they brewed some tea and ate the last of the bread from Mur, and the fruit and bread Teresa had brought from Ixilis. Baz told them about his session with the drummers. Josh listened enviously. *How fantastic, to be given a scar for something you're really good at!* he thought. He leaned his back against the trunk of the palm tree and stared straight ahead at the windy plain. Lucide was still sitting across from them, in the shade of a hill. Josh made a decision. He stood up, poured himself a mug of tea, grabbed a hunk of bread and one of the passion fruits, and carried them across the road. Lucide's eyes were shut, but when Josh approached him he opened them slowly. That clear, attentive gaze again! Josh stopped short, uncertain, lulled by the shimmer of calm surrounding Lucide. "I've brought you something to eat," he whispered.

Now he could smell Lucide too: a light, spicy scent, pithy and rich in oxygen. A smell that reminded him of the dawning of the world. Josh blinked, then placed the tea and the food at Lucide's feet. Lucide inclined his head and smiled faintly. Then he said softly, almost inaudibly, "Thank you."

The voice was just a breath, gently brushing Josh's cheek. But it made Josh grin and he felt elated as he returned to the others.

"Are you feeding that swine?" asked Jericho. "He doesn't need food, you know."

"But he's eating," said Josh. "See for yourself. And he can talk too."

"As if I didn't know," said Jericho, studying the seeds of her passion fruit. In a nasal voice she whined, "*Jericho*, this really is the last time. *Jericho*, mortals are not permitted to cross the border. *Jericho*, if it happens again, I'll have to take you back. Of course he can talk!"

"Who *is* Lucide really, anyway, Jericho?" asked Teresa.

"A lousy creep."

"He prevented Jericho's friends from helping us," Josh explained. "When we were trapped in that hut in Ixilis. And he's ... he's..."

"He is from the dawning of the world," Baz said suddenly. "Isn't he, Josh?"

"He's a watchdog," Jericho snapped. "He doesn't want us crossing any borders. He'd go to any lengths before he'd allow any of us, in an extreme emergency, to hop over to the other side now and then."

Teresa stared at her, shocked. "But Jericho..." She turned to the others. "If what Jericho says is true... It's suddenly occurred to me that it may not have been Gippart's fault that time was slammed shut. And it wasn't some natural disaster, either. Maybe it was Jericho – maybe she had something to do with it!"

"Jericho had nothing to do with it," said Josh.

"No," said Teresa, "but I was thinking... Lucide."

"What do you mean?"

"Well," said Teresa, "Lucide doesn't want anyone crossing the border between life and death. And that border was opened when Garnet and Spratt were messing around with the mobile phone and that other piece of equipment. That's when Lucide must have just slammed all the borders shut. Maybe he was being just a little overzealous."

"That makes sense, I suppose," said Josh. "Whenever Jericho tries calling her friends, he always intervenes. When we were on the raft, too, he chased them off in the end, I'm fairly sure. And ever since yesterday, which was the last time she tried calling them, he hasn't let her out of his sight for a minute!"

Jericho puffed out her cheeks in annoyance. "Mean, interfering bastard," she muttered.

They all turned towards Lucide, who was calmly seated across the road from them. His eyes gleamed softly.

"Can't we just explain it to him?" Teresa suggested.

"You can't explain things to Lucide," Jericho snorted.

They fell into an uneasy silence.

"Myndinak first, and then we'll go on from there," said Teresa, strapping her blanket to her backpack. "It'll be Kat's route next after that, won't it, Josh? How did it go again?"

"Maam Sagal," said Josh. "Oh, but Teresa..."

"What?"

"Kat's route is the third leg of the journey. There's supposed to be another one in between. A second one, between Myndinak and Maam Sagal."

"Get the map out," Teresa ordered, businesslike.

Josh took the map out of his backpack, and a lot of other stuff came tumbling out with it: dirty socks, the *Gippart Associates' Instruction Manual*, sticky dried dates, some wire and his compass. They pored over the map, reading all the small print, but Maam Sagal was nowhere to be found.

"Damn, damn, damn," swore Teresa. "So which leg of the trip are we missing? Kauri's?"

Jericho was playing with the compass. "It's north you're supposed to be going, isn't it?" she said, turning it on. The beam shot straight at the northerly horizon.

"How should I know!" snapped Josh. "We don't know, do we! We're supposed to look it up in the Book of Kauri, but wherever will we find it? Where is that wretched Kauri?"

"I've stolen one book for you," said Jericho. "You can find the next one yourself. You'll only lose the ones I get for you." She shook the compass. "Josh, your compass is going wrong, you know."

"What are you doing!" Josh angrily snatched it from her

hands. She was right, though. The beam was no longer pointing due north. It was pointing down, at the ground; at the things that had fallen out of his backpack, to be precise. "*Now* what! The compass is broken."

He shook it and twisted it. Then he saw Teresa's face. She was staring at the compass, frozen, her mouth hanging open. "Josh," she said in a strangled voice. "What was it you just said?"

"The compass is broken. Why?"

"No," said Teresa. She rose slowly to her feet and took the compass from him. "You said, 'Where is that wretched Kauri?'"

They all saw how the beam of the compass was flashing at Josh's things. Josh's mouth fell open. "It listens!"

"Multifunctional," said Teresa. "If only we'd known."

"But it doesn't make sense," said Josh. "Kauri isn't in my backpack, surely!"

Without answering, Teresa began sifting through the stuff scattered on the mossy ground. The beam fell on a tattered little red book. "What's this?"

Josh shook his head. "No idea. How did *that* get into my backpack?"

Teresa opened it. "Josh, you really are unbelievable."

"What is it?" demanded Baz. "Is it Kauri?"

"Yes. Josh is unbelievable. This is the Book of Kauri."

"What? How on earth…?"

Josh slumped backwards and groaned. "What an unbelievable moron I am! That preachy pest, in Tsumir, that missionary girl, shoved it into my backpack – a Kauri pamphlet, the people called it! I've been carrying it around with me all this time!"

"That's right, wasn't Kauri supposed to be a missionary?" Teresa laughed. She started leafing through the booklet. "It's a very short book. The laws, and that, and Kauri Siparti's ten commandments. Oh, wait a sec." Muttering to herself, she turned the pages. "Right, it's here. Out of the city gate, over the meadows northwards as far as the lake, the Long Sors. Simple!"

It was great to have done something so unbelievably brilliant purely by accident. Gleefully Josh snapped his compass beam on and off. "Where's Jericho?" he asked it, and *flash!* the beam shone at Jericho's face.

"Stop!" cried Jericho, covering her face with her hands.

"Where is Ixilis?" asked Josh, and *zap!* the beam spun round and pointed south.

"Where are the Tembe?" The beam hesitated a moment, flickered, and died.

"Broken," said Jericho.

"It doesn't know," said Baz.

"How about north then?" asked Josh. And, sure enough, the compass obediently swung north again.

"It isn't a compass at all," said Teresa. "It's a searchlight. Of course! I know someone else who has one: Zak. He always said it was really useful."

"Wow, Gippart's gadgets are amazing," marvelled Josh.

"Give it to me," said Baz. He gripped the compass tightly and said, "Spratt. Where is Mervin Spratt?" The beam pointed towards Ixilis. "We'll get that Spratt," he swore. "If he tries to come after us."

"If," said Teresa. "He's most probably long given up, after the battle with the Braxans."

Josh held his tongue.

That Monday was boring. They hauled themselves, sweating, up over the mountains before heading down again, sighing, towards Myndinak. Every so often they checked to see if they were being followed, but except for the leisurely figure of Lucide, they couldn't see any distant specks on the road. They weren't that bothered, anyway, today. Baz couldn't stop talking excitedly about the drummers of Ixilis, and he kept halting in his tracks to play them another example of the Mabeh's drumming skills. He often made a mess of it, though, and then he'd hang back, muttering and counting to himself.

Even Teresa had had enough after a while. She couldn't wait to tell them all the stories she'd heard. Josh listened willingly to the one about Gip and Kat; he was quiet and attentive for that one. But he didn't have the patience for all her other tales. He needed some peace and quiet, to think. They left him alone in the end, and, bringing up the rear, he walked by himself over the windy terrain with Zizi perched on his hat, his head bent down like an old mule. But he wasn't really thinking properly. It was as if the thoughts were chasing each other round and round his head without ever managing to catch up with each other. He wished one of those elusive thoughts would finally snare another one, so that he might come to a decision. *I'm turning into a thief,* he thought. *I could become really good at it, and that'd be pretty cool. Except that stealing means trouble, and I don't like getting into trouble. So, what if I wanted to be something different? But I'm no good at anything else! Jericho says I'm good at using my eyes, and that it makes it possible for me to change things, but I haven't the faintest idea what use that might be. And besides, I'm already a thief, aren't I? Only, I don't really want to be a thief...* And so the thoughts went on; thoughts that nagged at him like a toothache.

As they followed the path downhill it soon started growing colder. The vegetation was changing with practically each step. Fragrant blue bushes grew, followed by low, silver-green olive and citrus trees rustling in the west wind. Suddenly they were surrounded by clouds of pale yellow butterflies fluttering up from the ground into the bright sky. Little by little this Mediterranean-looking terrain gave way to a more lush and humid landscape, with trees that were turning yellow and gold, relinquishing their leaves one by one to a stiff autumn wind. It was pleasant to walk in the cool shade on the north side of the hills, under the dripping autumn trees, with the chirping of small blue birds and the rustling of forest animals in their ears. The trail changed into a shady forest path winding through a deciduous wood and leading into a windswept clearing, where the path forked. At that point there was a wooden signpost. They halted, elated. CITY OF DINAK, 3 HRS, read the arrow pointing north; and TANZEL, 8½ HRS, it said on the other.

"Dinak," said Teresa. "Myndinak must mean the city of Dinak, it *has* to. Three hours! Associates, we're doing great!"

"It is a pretty exciting world, this," said Baz.

"Has the rhythm changed again, then?" asked Josh.

"It changes a bit every day. Can you see anything unusual?"

As they walked on through the forest, Josh tried to look right through everything. How did one look at things in that special way Jericho was talking about? He tried taking in every tree individually, and saw each one sharply drawn with gracefully symmetrical branches, and on the floor of the forest he saw lovely plants with dark green leaves growing side by side. It was as if someone had drawn the trees and the plants for him one by one with the finest of brush strokes, as if it were a set design for some play. He tried to explain it to the others, and Teresa nodded. "Something's about to happen," she muttered to herself.

They all felt it: a landscape made for adventure. But what kind of adventure?

They didn't have long to wonder. Suddenly, with thundering force, a heavily armour-plated rhinoceros thing crashed out of the bushes. It pounded across the path and disappeared into the undergrowth. Before the dust had settled, a second one followed. But this one advanced more slowly, so that it was visible in all its glory: it was a strong, armour-plated horse, and on top of it rode something that looked like a squarish robot. But instead of flickering red lights, the steel helmet was crowned with a stiff comb of yellow feathers. The rider carried a square shield on one arm and with his other metallic hand he brandished a gigantic, heavy axe. He appeared to be shouting something, but his voice could barely be heard over the deafening pounding of hooves. The war machine soon vanished from sight. The little panther scrambled away, its tail between its legs.

"Knights!" exclaimed Baz. "Oh, of course. We're in 1455, nearly the end of the Middle Ages. There were still knights then – just!"

"I thought they'd be much lighter and swifter," said Josh.

"*Umaya*, Josh, we're in *umaya*," Teresa said. "Let's hope they don't give us a hard time."

"It *is* a bit over the top, isn't it?" Baz asked Teresa with a touch of mockery in his voice.

"Yes, just a little overdone, don't you think?" she replied with a smirk.

To Josh, it sounded as if they were talking in code.

"Let's have some fun, shall we?" suggested Baz.

"Yeah, let's relax them a bit!" Teresa giggled.

They walked on in silence.

"Aha!" said Baz, and pointed to something in the distance.

Through a cloud of dust, another one of those metal bruisers was coming towards them – at a calm pace initially. Suddenly he halted. He shifted his shield and spear and tilted forward in the saddle. Then he spurred on his steed. There was a thundering din of hooves – and here it came, making straight for them: a massive mountain of steel, and a viciously sharp spear pointing at them. Josh stared open-mouthed at the colossus lunging towards them. Jericho jumped up on a rock by the side of the road. But Baz, holding two sticks in his hands, had started drumming. Laughing and talking, he slipped easily into an intricate, strangely accented beat, with weird little shifts and backbeats. Teresa was standing at the side of the road, her lips moving rapidly. Josh couldn't hear what she was saying, but it was clear she was addressing the knight in a taunting voice. She didn't seem to be the least bit worried.

And then the most incredible thing happened. The knight appeared to stagger and nearly fall. Or maybe his horse stumbled, or it tripped over something. Anyway, it slowed him down, and suddenly the horse was trotting sideways, like a giant crab, as if executing a smart dressage step, only in slow motion. The knight ended up stuck in the undergrowth at the side of the road, slashing at the branches in fury. Baz and Teresa were doubled over laughing, though Josh couldn't see what was so funny. Their steel-plated enemy was wheeling his mount back on to the road menacingly and lowering his spear at them. Baz simply picked up his sticks again. This time it was a very rapid rhythm he hammered out; and the odd thing was, the horse seemed to be responding to it. It started cantering very fast, with tiny prancing steps, so that the rider was thoroughly shaken and jerked around. He lost his balance and, thrashing his spear helplessly about in the void, was swept past them, looking extremely silly.

Teresa howled with laughter. "Good going, Baz!" But then her face became serious. "Right, now let's get down to business," she said, and began to declaim. Although Josh was able to hear what she was saying, he still didn't understand a word of it. "Tea rose," she said, and, "from beyond the mountains, glistening."

He listened so intensely that it made him dizzy. The world seemed to be pitching and shifting. Just for a moment he couldn't see anything clearly, as if the picture had gone all wavy. He clutched the rock Jericho was sitting on, and then it was over. Teresa had stopped talking. She walked into the middle of the road, hands on her hips. Baz went and stood next to her. Cautiously Josh joined them. All three stared in the direction in which the knight had disappeared.

Something slowly started to dawn on Josh.

"I know," he whispered in Teresa's ear. "Teresa, you changed it! You've changed *umaya*! Just the way you did when we were in Braxassallar-Takras. I can tell, it's exactly the same feeling!"

"Hush," murmured Teresa.

They stared along the road, past Lucide, who was leaning

comfortably against a tree. And then they saw the knight coming their way again, but his appearance had been changed. "Terrific!" said Teresa.

The knight was now somewhat lighter accoutred: he wore a bright white cloak and carried a shield with a white dove on it. His black steed wore no armour and the knight had raised his visor. He carried his spear vertically, like a standard. But he didn't look very happy. He rode right up to them and looked down on them haughtily. "What did you mean by that?" he asked sternly.

Teresa looked at him with a twinkle in her eye. "What, my lord?" she asked, most politely.

"Causing my horse to shy and panic. I *must* say – as a courtesy I ride past you as carefully as I can, and then you cause my horse to bolt! Do you *know* who I am?"

Teresa smiled at him sweetly. *Any moment now and she'll start batting her eyelashes at him,* Josh thought, embarrassed. Although he had to admit that this was a handsome knight.

"Please excuse me, my lord," said Baz. "I am a drummer, and your horse must have shied at my drumming. I do beg your pardon."

The knight growled. "I have to get back in time for the Dove. I am not permitted to spill blood today. Although surely the Dove would not look askance on my chasing off the likes of you – drummers, jesters and salesmen." He trotted off without a farewell.

"Ai-ai," said Baz.

Teresa looked at him with a twinkle in her eye. "Feel like relaxing him some more? Him and his Dove!"

Baz shook his head. "We're right up against a time-border here. It's likely to flip over completely if we push it any more, and then we'll be even further away from home."

Josh couldn't keep it in any longer. "What are you two up to! What are you messing with?"

They turned to him calmly, and explained the whole thing:

they had worked out how to twist reality slightly in *umaya* by telling the story a little differently. Or by adding a different beat. "You were right, Josh," said Teresa. "I did do it in Braxassallar-Takras as well. I decided to cheat a bit. As we drew nearer, I could see those tough warriors in the distance, and that village high up on the cliff, and then I thought I spotted a washerwoman up by the waterfall. And I thought to myself, *No, there's no way I'm going to let you boys play the war-hero with those guys, and get stuck peeling carrots in the kitchen myself.* That's the kind of thing you often get, you know, that kind of ridiculous macho *umaya*, and I just wasn't having it. So I tried concentrating really hard, and kept reminding myself about the Amazons, you know, and all the other heroines my mother used to tell me stories about; and I think that's why the Braxan women turned out to be warriors too. You both felt it, didn't you?"

Josh nodded. "I saw it. It kind of shimmered, like a mirage."

"And I heard it," said Baz. "The rhythm was suddenly different."

"Yeah," said Teresa. "I didn't know what came over me. I had no idea I could change *umaya* around."

Josh laughed with relief. "But then that means we never have to be afraid again, in *umaya*! We can change everything around!" He suddenly went red in the face. "Hey, we can get out of here!"

Teresa and Baz both shook their heads. "You can only tweak it a little bit," said Baz. "It won't actually let you break out of this *umaya*. You can never turn this into the dawning of the world, for instance, or that Lamerika of yours. You can fiddle with it a little, but that's all." He snapped his fingers and grinned.

"But wait, someone else is coming," said Jericho. "Is that what you expected? It isn't a knight."

Indeed, someone was trotting towards them, coming from the direction of Dinak. It was a young woman, they saw, when she came close. She flung down her bag on the ground, breathless. There was a clash of rattling metal. "Is he a long way ahead of me?"

"Only a few minutes," said Teresa. "Are you his squire?"

"I am, and may God have mercy on my soul," the woman sighed, casually scratching her head of short flaxen hair. A rough girl, she was, muscular and gruff. "A pox on all this hauling and carrying! And what for, I ask you? Just so that this marvellous new era can begin? Not that it isn't high time, mind you, after the hundred years' misery we've had. Oh, all the starvation, and the wars, and the pestilence – we've had *more* than our fill, isn't *that* the truth!" She looked at them with a gleam of hope in her eyes. "You wouldn't happen to have anything to eat, would you? Aren't you from Ixilis, with nice bargains? Haven't you got any bargains?"

They didn't mind giving her some bread, but as for bargains, they were sorry, but they didn't have any.

"But you *are* pedlars, aren't you? Come on, confess, are you from Ixilis, or aren't you?"

"No," said Teresa, "we aren't. Actually, we're from Gippart. I mean from Gip Siparti."

"Gip Siparti? You don't say! And you're on your way to Dinak? On the Day of the Dove, of all days!" She threw her head back and guffawed. "But that's a laugh! You children certainly have guts, don't you!" Shaking her head, she took a big bite of bread. "But now don't you go telling me you don't have any delicacies on you, or any of those Gip wonders and marvels! Never mind, I don't have money anyway. But watch yourselves in Dinak!"

"Why?" asked Teresa.

"Do you have to ask? Surely you know that in the new age there'll be no room for pedlars, least of all for the Siparti scoundrels! The new era's supposed to be all calm order and purity. Just like in the olden days, when people used to walk the streets dressed in white robes, spouting philosophy. That's what they've been telling us anyway, our noble knights."

"But why shouldn't there be room for merchants?" asked Teresa. "In our world, the knights disappear for good just about this time. And the merchants and commoners rule."

"Fat chance, but I'll keep my fingers crossed," said the squire. "My Lord Asichem dreams of nothing but finding the Dove, wiping out both greed and trade, and reinstating the ancient virtue of purity!" She sighed wistfully. "But do you want to know what I dream of, myself? I dream of having enough to eat for once. Of the market, with all the good things to eat, and tasty boys. But what do I do? Do I follow my dream?"

"No." Teresa smiled.

"No," said the squire, hoisting the bag back over her shoulder, "I trot after Lord Asichem, in the unlikely hope he'll soon find his Dove, and the even more unlikely hope that he's right about that paradise that's around the corner. If God grants my wish, I'll be lucky for once in my life, and it'll be revelry and merrymaking for evermore. But what's the betting that, at the end of all this misery, you'll see me stumbling around in *his* version of paradise instead? Stuck in the middle of all these haloed holy boys that you're not even supposed to look at, let alone touch! Well, hail and farewell, fellow travellers."

The first thing that came into view was the castle, on top of a hill. It was a white-plastered edifice, with a lofty tower topped by a flag fluttering proudly in the rough wind. A little later they could see that both large and small houses had been built up against the castle. In 1455 the city of Dinak had not quite recovered from the disasters that had befallen its inhabitants a century earlier. The population was slowly increasing again, and recovering from the worst of the despair and abject poverty, but life was far from normal yet. A new wind was blowing in the land; that was something the Associates didn't need to be told.

The closer they got to the city, the more congested the road became. Farmers dressed in brown, driving their small herds to pasture, hawkers pushing their carts, monks rushing past. A band of religious brothers briefly gathered around Lucide. They spoke a few words to him, greatly moved, but Lucide kept his solemn silence. Then they bowed deeply, and kissed his hand. One of them started sobbing as they left him. Meanwhile couriers clad in hose rushed past them, and knights in shiny armour came clanking along, some of them bearing a falcon on their gloved hands. There were also solitary knights, their faces hidden behind their visors, their metallic bodies wrapped in a white cloak. All of these carried a shield with the emblem of a white dove.

"There goes Partrak, the Arrow of Mindouminin!" a girl in a black and orange dress walking next to them cried excitedly. She gazed after the knight in awe. "Isn't he wonderful? He's in fifth place now, isn't he, behind Lord Asichem! Of course, Angor d'Ivernes is impossible to beat. But Partrak is the youngest of them all, and I think that in a few years' time he'll be able to joust Angor right out of the saddle. Who are you behind?"

"We're strangers here," said Josh, who was walking closest to her.

"But how about at home, then? Who's your champion?"

"Spurs," said Baz. "Spurs!" sneered Teresa. "They're rubbish. It's been *years* since they were any good! Spoilt brats with far too much money, that's Spurs for you!"

The girl grinned. "That's what they say about our knights as well. That's why I like Partrak! He's an orphan, like me, and he has taken the vow of poverty."

"And he carries the shield of the Dove?" asked Teresa. "Same as those other knights?"

"Oh," said the girl, "you really are strangers, aren't you? Don't you even know what the shield of the Dove means?" When they shook their heads she looked perplexed. "Heavens!" she said. "So you don't know what day this is?

Everyone's going to Dinak to wish the seven unblemished knights Godspeed on their quest for the Dove of Light! But who *are* you then? What are you doing here, if you don't even know that much?"

"We're from Gip Siparti," said Jericho provocatively.

The girl's eyes widened, she pursed her lips and slipped away into the crowd without a word of goodbye. Jericho giggled.

"The Dove of Light," echoed Teresa. "Sounds sort of Christian."

"There are no spoilt brats in Spurs," said Baz, offended. "They train incredibly hard."

"Too bad they never score," said Teresa. "Well, everybody, let's be super careful in Dinak. We really need to earn some money, and we need to find the Book of Mono and the other books as well. But make sure you don't attract any attention, and pay for everything you need. No stealing. Agreed?"

Dinak was a very clean city. Not that it smelled good: there was a fine medieval aroma everywhere, the stench of manure and urine. But everywhere people were busy scrubbing the streets and whitewashing the houses, as if it was time for the annual spring-cleaning. The Associates looked around eagerly as they strolled past the freshly scrubbed half-timbered houses and workrooms, passing whitewashed cloisters as well as some sad burnt-out ruins. It was festive, and busy. The medieval burghers of Dinak, sturdy, pale or tanned, were walking around in their Sunday finery. Here and there a sheet with a picture of the Dove was draped from a window. Josh began hanging back a bit again, deep in thought, musing about the new era, and about what Baz and Teresa had discovered. Was there really no way to use their trick to break out of *umaya*? It would be so much simpler and easier than the laborious business of trying to find the remaining Books of the Cat, which entailed making enquiries – enquiries that only seemed to arouse suspicion – and then the danger of breaking in and stealing. Especially now that this new era was around the corner – the era of purity and cleanliness. He kicked at a pebble, and it bounced off a door against which a man with a tankard of beer in his hand was leaning. *"Hey!"* Josh was going to apologize, but the man motioned him closer, smiling. "Are you by any chance a pedlar, stranger?"

Josh nodded.

"Are you by any chance with Gip Siparti? They're saying he's in town. What are you selling?"

"Bird calls."

The man raised his eyebrows. "Really? That's odd. No red wool from Damara? No Skudish silk? Dyed Bizellian lace? I need cloth, you see. I'm getting married."

"Can't you buy any cloth here? In the market, or something?"

The man sniffed. "Now that I'm getting married, I'd better not show my face in the marketplace. With all that fuss the nobles are making over the Dove of Light, and the Duke's spies snooping everywhere, I'd just as soon not be caught trying to buy anything. Besides, what you can get in our market is nothing compared with Gip's wares. Here's to you, young man, to your excellent profession!"

As Josh walked on, bewildered, he realized that he'd lost the others. He trailed through alleyways, up steps, across tucked-away courtyards, and tiptoed over a rickety bridge spanning a smelly canal, until he was hopelessly lost and finally slowed to a halt, annoyed.

"Psst! Hey, over here!" A woman in a grimy orange smock and a nightcap stepped from a side street. She dragged Josh by the sleeve into a dark corner. "Have you got any goodies?" She winked at him cross-eyed.

"What kind of goodies?"

"Oh, come on, no one'll see it. Got anything good?"

Josh tugged himself free. "Sorry, I've got nothing good."

He got away as fast as his legs could carry him, out into the street, dodging left and right, until he stopped, panting, at the far end of a dead-end alley. He hadn't recovered his breath yet when a shutter opened right beside his head, and a man in a woollen hat hissed at him, "Hey, my boy…"

As he turned away from the man, Josh heard someone land next to him on the ground. He froze, but a hearty voice said, "Gip Siparti, aren't you?"

This time it was a chubby fellow with a bright red face. "I saw you running! I won't ever let a bargain from Gip slip past me! What've you got for me?"

To Josh's bewilderment, a chorus of excited voices piped up behind him. "Hey, Barry, you old greedy-guts, did you think you were going to buy up all of Gip Siparti's wares all by yourself? What's he got to offer?"

They thronged around Josh. "What new things have you brought us?" "Do you have those eyeglasses? Those new ones you had the last time, the ones even a blind man can see far into the distance with, as far as you like?" There were greedy hands and flushed faces everywhere. "Those new clocks, Gip, the ones with the special spring in them! You can take them with you anywhere you go; it's true, he's got them, I heard it!"

"No, the last time he had one of those mirrors, the kind in which you can see yourself just as clearly as if you're looking at someone else. They're made of glass. It's the very latest thing, I swear!"

"The little green bird you have there, how much are those?"

"No, what I need is weapons, armour – haven't you anything with gunpowder, some new-fashioned blunderbuss, or anything?"

They pressed around him, they pinched his arms, they snatched at his backpack. He choked helplessly, "No, please go away – no, I'm sorry, I don't have anything. Please!"

They didn't give him an inch of breathing space. Pleading didn't seem to be having any effect, so he started shouting for help, louder and louder, until his voice rose about the greedy clamour … and was finally heard. Dinak was Dinak, after all, where law and order ruled.

"What the deuce!" an angry voice rang out behind them. The greedy horde fell silent. One buyer took to his heels and disappeared into a neighbouring courtyard in a flash. The others looked over their shoulders guiltily.

"What's this, then?" the voice repeated sternly.

Two men marched up to the crowd. They looked intimidating and powerful as they stood there, the arm of justice. One of them wore a helmet and a tabard with the sign of the Dove over his leather sentry's jerkin. "By God, it's the Holy Day of the Dove! And I find you people attacking a defenceless pilgrim? What's going on?"

"This isn't a pilgrim," said an old woman, grinning. "It's Siparti! Gip and his marvellous rarities! Praise the Dove!"

"Gip Siparti?" the sentry's voice boomed out, surprised and indignant. "That's *this* close to blasphemy, that is! Wallowing in greed, are you, today of all days? In the name of the Duke, this calls for punishment!"

The customers weren't waiting around to hear any more. With one last regretful glance at Josh, cursing under their breath, they scattered – diving into an alley, over a wall, in through a window. The helmeted guard, furious, thundered in pursuit of the dispersing crowd. Doors slammed shut, footsteps died away. A plaintive voice could still be heard in the distance whining, "If only I had a pair of those eyeglasses, I tell you I'd…" And then all was quiet.

"Thank you," said Josh, relieved. He turned to his rescuer, the one who had stayed. He was a tall, skinny, hunched fellow in a long green coat. His hat was pulled down low over his eyes. "Thank you. I had lost my way. It really wasn't my intention to sell anything. Or to show any disrespect."

"I know," the man replied. His voice was almost inaudible – wheezy, ill.

Josh raised his eyebrows. A shudder ran up his spine. A vague apprehension seized him. "Well, thank you, then, I must run along," he said nervously, and started walking away.

A hot, bony hand shot out to pin his wrist in a vice-like grip. "Wait," the man snapped. He pulled Josh close and dragged him along with him, down the street, into another one around the next corner.

"No," Josh pleaded, as his terrible foreboding grew stronger and stronger. "Please, I truly am sorry… I couldn't help it, believe me! Please let me go… I won't do it ever again, please!"

Of course it didn't do him any good. He was pushed roughly into a dead-end alley. Behind him, a blank wall. In front of him, that faceless green coat.

"Well now," said the hoarse voice. "Finally. Joshua Cope!"

The hairs on Josh's neck stood on end. How could he have let himself be tricked so easily by his arch-enemy? He should have been more vigilant since leaving Ixilis. His mind had been so preoccupied with stealing and the art of seeing that he'd forgotten about the only truly nightmarish threat – this one, deadly foe.

"Mervin Spratt," Josh said in a choking voice.

"A pleasure. On second thoughts, not such a pleasure." Spratt was wheezing, bent over. He was giving off a strange, sour smell, and he was shivering as if he had a fever.

"What do you want with me?" asked Josh, looking over Spratt's shoulder. Could he give him the slip, if he made a run for it?

"You stay right where you are, young man," panted Spratt. He stuck out a claw-like hand and brushed Josh's cheek. "Such an unmarked, dreamy little face. Nothing to show for it, eh, no trace of the days you've spent in *umaya*, while I—"

"What do you want with me, you dirty murderer!" Josh screamed at him.

"Ho, ho! *You're* the murderer. You."

"What? You must be mad!"

"No, no, Mervin Spratt isn't mad." He wiped the sweat from his brow. "Who's the one who sent a bloodthirsty Braxan border guard, armed to the teeth, after me? Huh? It's a wonder I got off with just a stab wound in my shoulder. And who is deliberately sending me to my death – and not just me, but your two little friends as well? Who's the one who knows how to time-travel and how to cross the borders separating *umaya* from time, and yet *refuses* to share that knowledge with anyone else?"

"Oh, stop it," said Josh. "I have no idea how to time-travel. You're all mad. It was Jericho and her bracelet that gave you all the wrong idea. *You're* the one who almost murdered us with that vile instrument of yours – you and Garnet!"

Spratt peered at him from beneath his hat through bloodshot eyes. "Jericho," he muttered. "Jericho. The little piece of work I came up against in Braxassallar-Takras, eh? How'd you do it, Copey? Are you schizophrenic or something? What kind of mirror-image trick was that? Or did you split into two, the way children do who turn soft?"

Josh shrugged. "I won't tell you, because you wouldn't listen anyway. Let me go!"

"Not likely! You are my only hope of ever getting out of *umaya*, now that Garnet's left me in the lurch." He sniffed. "I could kill you, of course. There's a good chance that it's your fantasy world we're stuck in, and your death could even cause it to disintegrate – but I'm a decent chap, and I could be wrong. I'd rather have you break out of here alive and well. So that I can follow you. We're going to do a little experimenting, you and I. I've got my instruments with me..."

"Hell, Spratt, I don't know how to get out of here! Or I'd have gone long ago!"

"You just don't *know* that you know. I'd like us to work together on this, Copey. I mean Josh. Let's make it pleasant, shall we? And snappy and quick, all right? We'll just find ourselves a nice quiet spot."

He fumbled in his pockets. Josh made a wild lunge to get past him, but Spratt was on his guard. He pulled Josh back roughly. "Stay!" he barked. Then he hunched over, coughing his lungs out. He leaned against the wall, and slowly, breathlessly, recovered.

"You've got to co-operate," he groaned, almost begging. "Please understand... Joshua Cope, my dear boy, just look at me, please."

Very slowly, he pushed his hat back. The lower part of his face was covered with a piece of cloth, which he slowly pulled down. Josh clapped his hand to his mouth.

"Not a pretty sight, is it?" whispered Mervin Spratt.

It was vile. He didn't look human any more. His face was sunken, a disgusting grey-green, like a death mask. His skin was wet and flaky, and his hair hung greasily over his gleaming bony skull. His nose seemed half melted away. Bloodshot eyes stared hollowly at Josh from gaping eye sockets. Then Spratt covered up his face again. He gave a ghastly laugh.

"I used to be good-looking – wasn't I, even if I say so myself? Your sister Liz..." He stopped. Then: "A Senser isn't supposed to travel in *umaya*. I'm getting sicker by the day. Do you really want to have my death on your conscience?"

Josh's head was throbbing. He was feeling sick. "You've got those pills, haven't you?" he managed.

"Joshie, Joshie. What good are pills, if the way out of *umaya* is blocked? If I have to ration them?" He clawed at Josh's wrist. "Are you coming? Are you going to co-operate or not?"

Josh looked around. If he remained a minute longer in Spratt's sour company, he'd throw up. He broke into a cold sweat. He was at his wits' end.

It was as if the three of them had been waiting for Spratt's question. Of course they had missed Josh, had gone looking for him, and had found him. So it was with indescribable relief that he heard a familiar voice break in.

"Don't even think about it! He'll never co-operate with you, not on your life!"

Spratt's head jerked up. "What?"

Josh turned round with a gasp. There they were, all three of them. And the little panther, swishing its tail, next to Baz. And behind them, detached, gazing into space, their silent escort. The best thing of all was that all three had their swords drawn. And they were pointed at Spratt.

"Hello, Joshie! Everything OK?"

Spratt leaned against the wall, breath rattling. His eyes flitted from one to the other. Teresa cautiously stepped forward, and then took a wide-legged stance at a safe distance from him. The Braxan sword glinted in her hand.

"Well, well," she said. "Mervin Spratt."

With a sigh of relief, Josh detached himself from Spratt's side and made his way over to Jericho, who was in the rear. She put an arm round him contentedly.

Baz moved forward, looking the Senser up and down with glittering eyes. He was balancing his sword loosely in his hand. "*I* don't mind co-operating," he said.

Spratt looked at him contemptuously. "*You* can't time-travel," he said. "It's Joshua Cope I need."

"You're wrong," replied Baz. "He doesn't know how to time-travel either. But I'd be happy to discuss it with you."

"Nonsense." Spratt was obviously very ill at ease to be in the company of the three Associates, and Lucide waiting at the end of the alley in silence.

"But you've got to help us," said Baz. "That's what Max said. Without you we'll never make it out of here."

Spratt made a chortling sound. "Of course you won't! You don't even know where the weak spots are! You don't know a thing about safety measures, about navigating – about Sensing."

Baz went and sat down on a wooden barrel, prepared for a good chat. He laid his sword across his knees. "But that's just the thing, you see," he said pleasantly. "I'm a Senser too. Same as you."

Spratt spun round to face him as if he'd been stung by a bee. "You, a Senser? *You?*"

Baz nodded proudly.

"Impossible. In that case you'd be in a bad way too, same as me. You can't possibly be a Senser." Spratt lowered himself to the ground.

"Listen," said Baz. He started tapping a finger into the palm of his hand, and clicked his tongue to indicate a different rhythm from the first. "Isn't that right?"

Spratt listened. "Rhythm..." he muttered. "Rhythm. Yes, it is possible, of course." He was seized with another coughing fit.

"Can you hear it?" Baz asked, when Spratt had recovered.

"It isn't very accurate, but I do see what you mean. I've never done it that way myself."

"How do you Sense, then?"

"With dual sensitivity. Intuition, especially as it relates to smell and sound. It involves my entire organism these days. Accurate only with technical support."

"Smell," muttered Baz. "That's strange. Sound, I understand. But you see, for me, *that* isn't a very accurate method either."

"Why aren't *you* sick?" asked Spratt.

"It hurts, at times. Especially during the changeovers. And then I'll drum until those changeover rhythms match mine, or the other way round. Do you see?"

"On an intuitive, artistic level, yes, I do, but scientifically speaking, no, I don't. Oh, my God." He coughed again and stared at Baz helplessly. "And ... how about time? How do you see time, my boy?"

Baz laughed shyly. "I'm not really sure, of course. I've never studied it or anything. But I see time as rhythm, quite simply. Every being and every landscape has its own rhythm, and that's what you call time. If there's no life, there's no time either. Am I right about that?"

Spratt groaned and banged his fist on the ground angrily. "I should have known! Leibnizian nonsense! We might as well be talking anthropology here! I'm a scientist, idiot!"

Baz, startled, clammed up. But Teresa was indignant. "Just you be a bit more polite, will you, Spratt! Baz is better at Sensing than you are! Besides, he's right. You and your silly nonsense about time. You can't travel through time! Time is within your own being. Right, Jericho?"

Jericho took a few steps forward, which had a strange effect on Spratt. He doubled over and promptly threw up. "Ugh!" said Jericho. She pinched her nose shut and said in a nasal voice, "Living beings can't travel through time. All right?"

But Mervin Spratt had fallen into a dead faint.

The others hadn't succeeded in tracking down the Books of Mono, Beez and Gip, even though they'd asked around for them everywhere. But Teresa told them that she had sold the shower gel and the dishwashing brush from her grocery bag for a hefty sum. She'd sold them to people who had come flocking around her like flies around honey, begging for a bargain from Gip Siparti, something new, something amazing. She had used the money to buy rolls, which she now handed out, as well as some apples, carrots and strips of salted beef jerky, which were extremely tough to chew. But the rolls were delicious, plump and soft.

Out in the main street people were rushing back and forth, which reminded them that there were big happenings in the town. "I saw a knight from Ixilis," Teresa told them. "Milin the Thunderer. A really cool black guy. I'm sure he must be the champion."

"Aren't you from Africa originally?" asked Baz.

"I thought you were from Surinam," said Josh, surprised.

"My dad is Igbo, from Nigeria," Teresa explained, "and my mother is from Surinam. But my parents met each other in London, and I've lived just about everywhere in the world – Lagos, London, Paramaribo. Why?"

"No reason, really," said Baz. "It's just that you seem to have this knowledge about Ixilis."

"You understand the rhythms far better than I do," she replied, "and it isn't because that's where you come from, is it?"

"Of course not!" Baz laughed. He scratched the panther, which lay stretched out beside him on its belly.

"As they say in Mur," said Josh sagely, "it isn't about where you've come from, it's about where you're going."

Teresa raised an eyebrow at him, but Jericho said, "That's right, and where are we going, then?"

"Out of this city," said Teresa. "We'd better get a head start, before the entire crew of knights depart. They aren't too fond of pedlars and traders, Siparti's lot least of all. But shouldn't we try to get hold of those Books of the Cat first? What should we do? Keep asking around?"

Josh had walked to the corner of the street, to see where the happy commotion, which was getting louder and louder, was coming from. Several people ran past him, excitedly shouting, "They're coming, they're coming, the quest is about to start!" The entire city seemed to be heading towards Cloister Square, to witness the glorious departure of the Knights of the Dove: the champion Angor d'Ivernes, Asichem van Ousamaye, Milin the Thunderer from Ixilis, and the other braves, led by the pious Duke. It was strange – and perhaps it was because the lovely golden evening light cast such a painterly glow over the medieval houses – but Josh was overcome with a kind of joy. With shining eyes he gazed at the people passing by. He was suddenly seized with a desire to go with them, to see the knights, to welcome in the new age. Just as he stepped into the road, someone bumped into him. On purpose. The man hurriedly dragged Josh back into the alley.

"Sorry," he said, out of breath, "I'm a little late. I had a bit of trouble getting it. But I've got it. So can I please have one of those glass mirrors, that wonder of wonders? I'd also be interested in one of those clocks too."

He pressed a parcel into Josh's hand. Josh looked at it, bewildered. "But I'm afraid I could only get you Mono's," the man continued anxiously. "Is that a problem? I know it isn't worth a lot. But it's in quite good condition."

Josh ripped open the package and, indeed, he found what he'd thought he would find: Mono's *Book of the Cat.* The cover was decorated with designs of all sorts: he recognized animals, plants and people, all intertwined. The letters were so stylized that he had a hard time deciphering them. But it was there: *Mono.* He also recognized a golden cat with a crown on its head, looking rather smugly at the creatures swarming around it. The man watched anxiously as Josh turned the pages one at a time.

"All the maps are still intact, see? That's the most important thing, in Mono, the maps and the pictures." He babbled on. "Look, it's only hand-done, of course. You people of Gip Siparti, you're probably already selling those newfangled printing-press books, but here we're not that advanced in our science. Your books are probably much finer than this one. Still, you had to have Mono, is what they told me. Isn't that right?"

Leafing through the book, Josh came upon an austerely plain, cryptic map. On the left he saw a dot with the letters M. SAGAL next to it. The square map was dissected on the diagonal by a wavy line that read ROM. In the top right-hand corner there was a square with a W under it. And next to it, a square with the caption BZ. Around these were playful squiggles and drawings he couldn't make head nor tail of.

"Strange map, that one, isn't it?" said the man. "It's typical of Mono, though – a riddle, or it's in code, or something."

He was hopping up and down. "What will you give me in exchange? I'm in a hurry – I should be at the knights' departure by now. My patron insists that we all attend. I am sorry I don't have the other ones to offer you. But I was told, 'Gip Siparti is looking for the Books of the Cat,' and this is the only one I could lay my hands on. That miraculous mirror, that will be of the most vital use to me, actually."

Josh coughed and scratched his head, at the same time trying to memorize the map. He felt really bad that he had to disappoint the man, or, worse, make him angry. But he didn't have a mirror, and he couldn't very well give away Baz's watch or the compass, and he couldn't think of anything else that would make the man happy. What did he have to give him – his dirty socks? He just stood there with the book in his hands, giving it another quick look, this time from back to front. He stood there dithering so long that the man started getting impatient. "Is something wrong? Please hurry! I went to a lot of trouble to get it!"

Josh seized the chance. "It isn't the right one," he said, blushing, and handed back the book. "Please forgive me. I've got to have the other ones. I cannot make the trade." His face grew redder and redder. The man stared at him, incensed.

"You pedlars aren't to be trusted, are you! First I hear that you have to have Mono at all costs, and when I risk my hide to get it for you, you weasel out of the deal!" He snatched the book angrily out of Josh's hands. "I'll never fall for a promise from any Siparti again! You Sipartis are all bastards, and if you ask me, they're right when they say the whole nightmare is all your fault!"

"Nightmare?"

"Wasn't it? Oh, maybe you Siparti people don't consider the Black Death a nightmare; maybe you see it as more of a joke!" He was in a towering rage now. "But surely you must know all about the plague, seeing that it was a gift from one of your own Sipartis! From Beez Siparti. May his bones burn in hell!"

"What?"

But the man had already stormed off into the dusk, leaving Josh behind, stunned.

Quietly he walked back to the others waiting for him in the dark alleyway. They hadn't overheard his encounter with the man. He was glad that he could bowl them over by revealing his unexpected discovery of Mono's route. They hung over his shoulders as he carefully drew the map from memory on the back of one of his merchandise forms, by the light of the compass. But his elation had passed. He was sorry he'd had to cheat the man, and even sorrier about what he'd heard about Beez Siparti and the Black Death. When he told the others about it, they were all shocked. Baz said slowly, "If we go back in time now, we'll be landing right in the middle of the plague!"

"We'll just have to make sure that we don't end up anywhere near that Beez," Teresa declared resolutely. She gave the panther the toughest strips of meat to eat and packed up the rest of the food. Josh studied Mono's map. "I'm not really sure, of course," he muttered softly to himself, "but I think BZ could very well mean Beez."

They had no choice. They had to leave behind Spratt, delirious with fever, in the alleyway. He was a danger to them, and much too heavy to carry. They knew that Spratt should phone Gippart, but they could hardly be expected to sit around and wait for him to regain consciousness; it could take hours. And Teresa refused to call Gippart on his behalf. Scouting for a way out, they crept along the dark streets of Dinak, away from the noisy throng in the square. It took them a while, but then Josh found an opening in the north city wall. They were able to slip out unnoticed; and finally they were out in the countryside again. They were standing on a vast grassy plain, under a starry, ink-black sky filled with scudding clouds. They found a path, not much more than a track, that seemed to lead in the right direction.

"I wish that wind would die down," said Josh. "It seems to be getting stronger every day. It's making me fidgety."

Zizi too was restless. She kept hopping from his shoulder to the top of his head and back again, until finally he tucked her inside his turned-up collar. It was now growing really cold, and you couldn't see a hand in front of your eyes. They saw a warm light shining in the far distance. They all peered at it intently.

"A farm, maybe," guessed Teresa. The light winked at them, lured them, and slowly they drew near.

"Strange light," said Josh.

"Would that be a normal kind of light, in your world?" asked Jericho.

"What do you mean, Jerrie?"

Jericho shook her head. "That isn't any light from here."

The world around them was dark and windy, but it was beginning to shimmer at the edges. They heard snatches of sound. Out of the corner of his eye Josh saw other points of light appearing. "There are people coming this way," he said to Jericho. He called out to Baz and Teresa, who were walking ahead, "Watch out! People coming!"

The lights were approaching from seven different directions, flickering in the wind, and it seemed as if they were all heading for that one, strange radiance.

"Let's go and investigate that funny light," said Josh.

"Hmm," said Teresa. "Maybe it's another chink, a weak spot, like the one on Trellis. Don't you think? We're right on the threshold of the new age, and it's quite possible that there'd be a hole in *umaya* here."

The wind made it hard to hear what was going on. Voices seemed to be coming from all directions. Sometimes snatches of music caught their ears; other times they had the feeling the sky was splitting open behind them, but when they turned around it was as dark as ever.

"Lucide is nervous," Jericho whispered in Josh's ear.

He glanced over his shoulder. It was true. Lucide was no longer walking at his usual calm, measured pace. He seemed tense, and a red light seemed to glow in his eyes.

Gradually they were able to make out a few of the sounds. Suddenly Baz pulled them to one side. *"Watch out!"* Very close by, a dark shape on horseback was coming down the track. He carried a flickering lantern, and for an instant it lit up his shield: the shield of the Dove. His visor was open, and they caught a glimpse of his weather-beaten, ardent face. He passed them without noticing them.

"Angor d'Ivernes," said Josh, awed. "Did you see the initials on his horse's mantle? *AdI.* It was him! The champion!"

The walked on cautiously towards the light ahead of them, whose form they were now able to see. It was streaming out of the open door and windows of a small, chapel-like building on the crest of a low hill. They could also now hear the chiming of melodious bells and, underneath, a different kind of music, faint, almost inaudible.

Seven lights, from seven different directions, had now arrived at the foot of the hill. By the faint light of the lanterns, the Associates recognized the seven Knights of the Dove of Light. The knights tentatively drew near; they rode up the hill in unison, almost as if in a dance.

"I'd like to have a look at it close up," said Josh. "What if it really is a hole in *umaya*? It could be, couldn't it? Or Lucide wouldn't be so nervous."

"I'm coming with you," said Baz, hugging the little panther close.

"You go," whispered Teresa. "I'll follow at a distance. That's safer."

Doubled over, the two boys crept up to the chapel through the tall grasses, at the midpoint between two of the swaying lanterns. Every so often they'd catch a whiff of the horses to their left or to their right, or heard their earthy, reassuring snorting. Slowly they were caught up in the light, and in the web of dulcet sounds: a wondrous kind of music, which Josh couldn't quite get a fix on. They smelled the blessed scent of roses, of honey, of lovelorn blossoms and spicy wood. It made them hungry and very happy, but at the same time sad, with such an intense longing for something, for something... They wriggled forward on their stomachs the last few metres, wide-eyed and open-mouthed, oblivious of the knights around them. The knights paid no attention to them either.

They all arrived at the clearing around the chapel at the same time. The knights dismounted, and their horses came to a standstill. They formed a circle around the chapel, those mesmerized, yearning people, and the one little panther.

A knight came forward out of the circle and walked slowly to the chapel's radiant door. At the threshold he sank to his knees, remaining in that position for a long time. The light dimmed, but the music continued to quiver and hum. Then the knight abruptly stirred. It seemed as if a voice rang out; the knight leapt to his feet and took a stride forward, but the door slammed shut in his face. A shudder went round the circle. The spell was broken. The other knights stood up and walked over to their comrade. The knight who had just had the door slammed shut in his face turned to the others with great indignation.

"Impure of heart! Me, I am not truly pure! That's what the voice said!"

"You're no virgin, anyway, my liege!" There was a burst of laughter, but then they were silent again and knelt down. One of the knights began praying aloud.

The Associates crept around to the far side of the little chapel. There they lay on their stomachs on the cold earth, hidden from curious eyes in the tangle of wilted autumn vegetation. They saw the door to the chapel opening again; and they heard the music beginning once more, the scents blending with the light.

"It's a holy chapel or something," Josh whispered to Baz.

"It isn't a hole in *umaya*."

Baz bit his lower lip, and looked avidly at the chapel.

"What do you think, Baz? Can you Sense anything?"

Baz shook his head.

Josh felt Baz's body quivering next to his. He was wound as tight as a spring. "What's got into you?"

There was a commotion in front of the chapel again. Another knight had been refused entry. Now the others, too, tried to step through the doorway. One by one they were prevented from going in. Several knights walked away in silence, mounted their steeds and trotted down the hill, without looking back. Three knights stayed behind, kneeling in the clearing in front of the chapel. Josh recognized Angor d'Ivernes, Milin the Thunderer and Asichem. Nothing much was happening. Angor sank forward, his hands pressed to his face as if he was weeping. But none of them made any attempt to climb the steps to the chapel. There the little building stood, radiating light in the very heart of the darkest night.

Baz stirred. A shudder went through him. Then he stood up, gave a deep sigh and, head held high, started walking towards the chapel.

"Baz, what are you doing!" cried Josh as loudly as he dared. He scrambled after him, aghast, remaining in the shadow. He heard Jericho rustling along behind him. *Oh, what the hell, why don't we* all *go,* he thought to himself, desperate. *We're so inconspicuous anyway, inconspicuous as hell, the five of us, why don't we just get hold of a megaphone, for good measure?*

But Baz was oblivious. Without a moment's hesitation, he climbed the chapel steps and stopped in front of the brilliant doorway. Josh ran after him, but on reaching the steps he had a strong feeling that he shouldn't be there. *"Baz!"* he hissed.

But Baz wasn't paying any attention to him. He was talking to something, or someone, inside the chapel. His grave face was lit by the other-worldly light coming from inside. Josh now saw that the chapel's whole interior appeared to be ablaze; and the smells, the colours and the music were infinitely richer than he'd been able to tell from a distance. A lump rose in his throat. Suddenly he too wanted to go inside. He wanted to more than anything, more than anything in his whole life. He heard Baz's clear voice saying, "I don't know, but I would just so much like to… Please may I?"

And from inside came a soft laugh, or could it just have been the sound of a smile? To his consternation, Josh saw Baz take a step inside. "Baz!" he roared. He rushed forward and tackled him, caught hold of his leg. Dazed, Baz looked round. It was as if he had forgotten all about Josh's existence.

"Oh, Josh," he stammered, "I'm just going to… That rhythm… Even that drummer Swap couldn't… Wait…" A look of intense concentration came to his face, and he turned round and stepped over the threshold.

Then everything seemed to happen all at once. The door slammed shut with a thundering crash, the little panther threw itself, whimpering, against the unyielding door, and then Josh felt something explode, right in his hands. He fell backwards, down the steps. Two familiar arms caught him, a face pressed itself against his, and someone was whispering in his ear, giggling nervously, "Look, Josh, look!"

He looked – poor boy – he looked and he saw, outlined against the door, impotent and raging, Lucide, aflame. His eyes were spewing fire, and flames seemed to be shooting from his glowing form. He leapt upwards, and for a moment was silhouetted against the sky, arms spread wide, as a fearsome, towering inferno. Then the fire abruptly went out. Lucide jumped down the steps and walked past Josh and Jericho halfway down the hill. There he halted. Vigilant as ever.

"Too late, too late! He didn't realize!" Jericho giggled. "He was too busy watching me; he hadn't the least idea that Baz could do it too. What a laugh! He can't even curse! Poor Lucide! The bird has flown!"

Josh, bewildered, stood up. In front of him was a plain, dark chapel. There was no longer any light inside. The three knights had jumped to their feet and were conferring, gesticulating wildly. There was no trace of Baz.

"Jericho, where's Baz?"

"He's crossed the border."

"Which border?"

"Don't ask me. He's gone, can't you see that?"

Josh walked up to the chapel; he walked all around it and peered through the keyhole. A little of that amazing fragrance still hung in the air.

As he pushed against the door, he suddenly felt an iron hand on his shoulder. It was Angor d'Ivernes, gazing at him despondently. A silent Lord Asichem stood immediately behind him. Josh saw that he'd been right. The big man had indeed been crying. "Boy," barked the hero in a broken voice.

Josh looked at him, disconcerted. "My lord."

"Who are you? Who was it that just went inside – who was worthy enough to go up in the Dove of Light?"

"Baz."

"Baz? Is he a knight? Surely he's much too young to be a knight! A squire, perhaps? But even so!"

"He's a drummer," Josh explained. "A good drummer. I think he's gone after the music."

Angor d'Ivernes looked at him, speechless.

"I am sorry, my lord," said Josh, who suddenly felt completely drained. "I don't understand it either. He was just allowed to go inside. I wasn't."

"Nor I," whispered the Lord of Ivernes. "Not one of us was deemed worthy." He lifted Josh's chin, and looked at him searchingly. "Where are you from? Not from around here, that much is evident."

"No," said Josh.

"They're from Siparti," Asichem whispered very softly. "My squire told me."

"Siparti? And not one of our own was deemed worthy?"

the champion repeated. He turned round and walked heavily over to the third knight, with Asichem close behind.

"Friends," Josh heard him say, "Milin, Asichem, excellent knights, none of us has been deemed worthy! Our time has passed, blood brothers! A commoner, a mere boy, in the employ of Siparti's merchants! It is a sign of the times, and a bitter message from the Dove of Light! Not one of us has been found worthy!" He flung his sword down with a crash.

Jericho wrapped her arms around Josh from behind. "Let's get back to Teresa. Coming?"

Josh, exhausted, walked down the hill with her. The little panther padded along behind them, nuzzling Josh's hand, whimpering softly. Behind them came the sound of Lucide's footsteps.

The wind was chasing its own tail across the fields, in jerky fits and starts, the way it had been doing since time began.

14
Three Pigs in a Rich Lather

Baz's disappearance was the beginning of the end. The weather changed as if the earth had decided it might as well drown itself now. It rained and it poured in torrents and in buckets, as if the world would never be dry again. In silence, sad and frightened, they traipsed one behind another through the endlessly falling rain. The paths turned into muddy puddles, then into shallow streams. Halfway through the morning of the next day, there wasn't a dry stitch on them.

Jericho was the only one who didn't seem to care. She danced ahead of them through the puddles, laughing. It was the first time Josh really held it against her, her indifference to other people's pain. "But *he* was the one who wanted to go, wasn't he?" she asked, startled, when Josh shouted at her.

Baz's sudden disappearance had deeply shaken Josh. He hadn't been this conscious of being frightened of *umaya*'s dangers since that fateful morning on Trellis. Which was even more reason to miss his friend. He missed his sturdy presence, his worried expression, his maddening passion for drumming, his jokes. All right, maybe he had been paying a bit less attention to Baz ever since Jericho had arrived on the scene. But now that he was gone, Josh knew that he couldn't function without him. His very best friend in the world, without question. His comrade-in-arms in the treacherous worlds of dreams.

They hadn't let him go just like that. Teresa and he had searched the small chapel's exterior brick by brick; they had even broken down the door and run their hands over every inch of the dark interior. Cold, dead stone was all they found. And when they'd finally fallen asleep, exhausted, woke up again the next morning, shivering in the drizzling rain, they discovered that the chapel had vanished into thin air. Even then, they'd hung around for a while, quite beside themselves, despite the fact that the compass only flickered uselessly when they said Baz's name. They decided to leave only when the little panther gave up, and wretchedly started down the hill. There was nothing left of Baz except his backpack, and inside it his blanket, a set of rhythm sticks, and some dirty underwear.

And now they went slipping and sliding like pitiful drenched cats past shuttered rural villages and sodden farmland. They were on their way to Long Sors, the lake mentioned in Kauri's book. Josh's trousers slapped at his legs like a cold, wet mop at every step he took. The clothes from Mur felt as heavy as lead with all the rain they had absorbed. Josh was grateful for his hat; at least it managed to keep the rain out of his eyes. Zizi sat on his shoulder, wet and bedraggled, as close to his head as possible. The rain bubbled up and broke through the surface of the earth. It obliterated the trees and it turned the landscape into one grey, steamy body of water. When they reached the lake and stood on its banks, it felt as if they were standing on the bottom of a grey sea. A misty nebulousness enveloped them, so that they could no longer tell what was up and what was down.

Teresa wrung out the scarf she had wrapped around her head. "Where to now, Josh? Maam Sagal?"

Josh nodded. He sneezed.

"Do you have any idea where that might be?"

"No idea. That verse in the Book of Kat makes no sense: '*From lake through mud to a waterfall; to guidance, to punishment; the road to Maam Sagal.*' We'll just have to ask someone."

They looked around. But there was no one to ask. There was just the noise of the driving rain clattering down. Josh suggested, for the fourth time, "Shouldn't we just phone Gippart, Teresa?"

But for the fourth time Teresa shook her head. "Not now that we've made a mess of everything. I really don't feel like getting shouted at and being told what idiots we are to have left Spratt without letting him make a phone call, and losing Baz. Let's just call them sometime later on." She pulled the scarf back over her head. "Maybe we'll find someone to give us directions once we've crossed this lake." They peered at the other shore. It wasn't all that far. The lake was no wider across than the Thames.

Jericho came running after them out of the sheeting rain, startling them by leaping on to Teresa's back, so that she almost toppled over. "Jericho! Watch it!"

"Want me to show you how you can zoom through the rain?" Jericho asked them brightly. With hair dripping in her eyes she confronted them, beaming, carrying Baz's backpack. The rain streamed down her face in rivulets, and her red dress flapped in the wind like a wet sail. Smiling, she stuck her tongue out to catch the raindrops running down her cheeks.

"No!" cried Teresa. "Jericho, you've really got to stop trying to get us to do the things ghosts do. We want to stay alive."

"Oh, all right," said Jericho. "But stop whining then. And stop looking so down in the dumps too." She waded into the lake and started splashing the water high up into the air with her hands.

Josh crouched down by the water's edge. He pushed his hat off his face and looked around. Was it really impossible to see anything? He peered so intensely into the distance that the mist seemed to start to move. He saw dark wavering forms taking shape, then dissolving, rippling into nothing. That made him look more closely. And suddenly he saw, to his left, thick tree trunks in the mist. And once he'd seen those, seeing seemed to get easier. Very slowly he used his eyes to tease shapes out of the murkiness. On the opposite shore of the lake: there, a little house. A boat bobbing on the water. Above, to the left, the sky was clearing almost imperceptibly, as if the sun was hiding behind it. He smiled and honed his vision. Ducks on the lake. No, swans, two brown ones and one white. Well, why not? Reeds, tall reeds along the shore. And, on the far shore, a series of hills. He thought there might be a few houses on them, and indeed, there they were: he could see them more clearly now. A horse on the road, walking down to the lake's edge. A horse with no rider? No, no: there was a person sitting on it. The boat was now heading straight for the horse and rider, leaving behind a wake in the water.

Josh stood up. "Look," he said.

Teresa was staring at him. "Josh, what were you doing just then?"

"I was looking," he replied. The rain had noticeably lessened, and the world around them seemed a bit wider and brighter.

Teresa half closed her eyes. "That wasn't just looking."

Josh smiled. "I don't know. But look! At least we can see something again now. Can you see that boat coming towards us, the one that picked up that horse and rider? Maybe he'll ferry us across as well."

The boat gently nudged the shore on their side, and the horse made an impressive leap jumping out. It scrambled to find its footing in the slippery mud. "Good morning, fellow travellers," the rider greeted them cheerfully. "May God grant you a drier afternoon!"

They returned the greeting politely. The rider was a sturdily built girl with long black hair, dressed in combat gear of leather and iron plates. She carried a shield with a red and green emblem, and wore a short sword at her side. She spurred on the horse and it galloped off in the direction of the city of Dinak, sending up sprays of mud.

Josh walked up to the boat. "Would you please take us across?" he asked the ferryman, who was leaning on his pole, chewing.

He sized Josh up from beneath his brown cap. "What will you pay me?"

"What do you charge?"

"Four people, four coppers," said the ferryman, placidly continuing to chew.

"Fine," agreed Josh, and he waded a few steps to the boat.

When they were all seated, the ferryman spat in the water and pushed off. "Bail 'er out," he ordered.

Obediently they started scooping water out of the bottom of the boat. Josh sneezed ten times in a row.

"God bless you," said the dour skipper.

"Thank you," said Josh. "Excuse me, but do you know where we could find Maam Sagal?"

"Maam Sagal?" The ferryman punted on, his attention focused on the currents of the choppy lake. "Never heard of it."

"'From lake through mud to a waterfall,'" muttered Josh. "Are there any waterfalls around here?"

"Plenty of mud, anyway. In the forest. A few nasty waterfalls too."

"Where is the forest?" asked Teresa.

"Up the hill, near Muk. Ask them."

On the jetty they spent some time comparing and trading coins before the ferryman was satisfied. Then they walked up past the ferry house, where a frenzied dog barked at them. They followed the trail into a vast forest that spread across the hills. The naked tree trunks gleamed in the wind, and yellow leaves blew into their faces. It smelled of earth and mushrooms in there.

Slipping on the muddy paths, they reached a huddle of

straw huts in a valley that was speckled with little pools. Muk. The ground was so sodden that at every step they sank ankle-deep into the mud. A woman was in front of one of the huts, chopping mossy branches.

"Good morning," said Teresa.

"Mornin'," answered the woman, who dourly went on chopping.

"We are looking for Maam Sagal," Teresa tried.

"Go with God," said the woman curtly.

"Could you tell us where we might find Maam Sagal, please? It's supposed to be somewhere near a waterfall."

"Go with God!" the woman cried, hacking a slippery green branch in two with all her might.

"Well, a good morning to you too then," said Teresa by way of goodbye.

But the woman called after her, "Ask the acorn man. He's in the forest with the pigs, foreigners!"

"Thank you!" Teresa shouted.

They plodded laboriously back up the hill behind the huts. "Friendly place, Muk," said Teresa sarcastically.

"Those people are as poor as church mice," Josh excused them.

"Right, we're in the age of catastrophe now, aren't we?" Teresa realized. "Famine, wars, the Black Death."

"And it's all thanks to Siparti," said Josh. "We shouldn't tell people we're with Siparti any more, Teresa."

They walked through a groaning, dripping world of ancient wood and smelly fungi. Even Jericho was silent now. Behind her strode Lucide, a dark wraith. Since Baz had vanished he had retreated deep within himself. He burned no brighter than a dying ember. At his side, pitifully listless, plodded the little panther.

"Teresa," whispered Josh, "do you think Baz has just gone back home?"

"I don't know," said Teresa unhappily. "Maybe he's landed

in one of those wonderful *umayas* that the knights are dreaming of. I just don't know."

They followed the trail blindly, and would have missed the pigs if Jericho hadn't called them back. "Weren't we supposed to find a man with pigs?" she asked indignantly. "You haven't been paying attention!"

To the left of the trail some shadowy forms were grubbing about in the bushes. Five dingy brown hogs, covered in bristles. They were rooting around in the earth with their noses and forelegs, making snuffling, smacking sounds. There were no people in sight. Sighing, Teresa walked on. But Josh hesitated. He stopped and pulled his hat down low over his eyes. Very quietly he sidled up closer, crouching down not far from the bushes and peering at the indistinct shapes among the ferns and twigs. Was there really nobody with them? Could he swear to that?

He stared until his eyes started watering, and then he saw what he had been hoping to see. There very definitely were people there. At least two of the animals were wearing clothes: two stooped, weathered humans, in torn rags the colour of the pigs' hides. Just like the pigs, they were digging something up and shoving whatever it was inside their dirty rags. They were making the same kind of grunting and smacking sounds as the hogs. He didn't dare call out to them, but scurried on hands and knees after the others, signalling to them to come back.

Teresa's mouth fell open when she saw the hog people. She nodded and took a step in their direction. *"Pssst!"*

The hog creatures nearly collapsed from the shock and instantly scuttled back into the undergrowth.

"Don't be afraid! We come bearing gifts!" Josh shouted.

There was a moment's silence. Then shrill voices rang out. "Who are you from?"

"We've got to get to Maam Sagal, if you please," said Teresa.

"Maam Sagal?" They heard some grumbling, and then one of them edged closer. He was a drab brownish colour from head to toe. His matted brown hair, moustache and beard were the same colour as his clothes. There were acorns caught in his hair. His entire body was covered in a greenish mould, and he reeked of smoke and decay.

"Do you have any news? Any grub?"

Teresa shook her head. "Please could you tell us how to get to Maam Sagal?"

The acorn man started chewing furiously on his moustache. He fixed her with a withering stare. "Liar. You're not from Maam Sagal."

"No, I know," said Teresa. "We want to *go* there. Can you show us the way?"

"You said gifts," the man said shrilly. "Where are they, then?"

With some difficulty, Josh managed to wrench his wet backpack down off his shoulders. "Two bottles of ale," he said, "and a box of matches."

The acorn man blinked nervously. He touched the glass of the bottles. Then he sniffed at the matchbox. He looked up, glowering. "Sorcerers," he said, "pedlars. Devils. Is this from Maam Sagal?"

"If you'll take us to Maam Sagal, then it's for you," said Teresa.

"To Maam Sagal," the acorn man repeated. "Why?"

"We are on our way to the people of Temberi," Jericho piped up suddenly. "And the way there is past Maam Sagal, that's why."

The man looked from one to the other, and started shaking his head. "Saint Temberi," he said. "You're lying. It wasn't Saint Temberi. It was the other one." He snatched up the two bottles of ale and clutched them to his chest.

Josh and Teresa exchanged a quick glance. Teresa took a deep breath and said, "We have been sent by Siparti's offspring to go to the Tembe. Our road takes us past Maam Sagal."

The acorn man stiffened. "Siparti," he whispered hoarsely. "*That's* the name." He was silent for so long that they were afraid that his mind had wandered. But then he opened his eyes wide. "She did say it!" he announced loudly. "She said, 'Bring her to me,' that's what she said. 'My hogs, mud-grubbers, bring me Kat Siparti.' That's what *she* said!" Suddenly he was hiccuping with laughter. "You are entitled to know the secret! All the hogs know that. Entitled to your punishment, the Siparti punishment!" He looked up at them with gleaming eyes. "That's how the story goes! After centuries of being racked by guilt, Siparti comes crawling back, back to Maam Sagal, the washerwoman in charge of meting out the punishments, and she sends him on to the saintly Temberi! *We* know!"

He stared at them, chewing ferociously, then abruptly turned his back on them and started limping ahead, surprisingly fast, straight into the forest. "Well? Are you coming or not?" he snapped at them. "I haven't got all day!"

It wasn't easy following him; they had to duck under thorny branches, wade through wet hollows and across fields of dying ferns plastered together with spiders' webs. Ahead of them, the acorn man barged his way through the undergrowth. The Associates kept at a safe distance. But they didn't have a chance to talk until they reached an easier trail, where they could walk upright.

"Nice, isn't it, to be working for such a popular company?" Teresa grumbled. "He seems really delighted to be leading Siparti to his terrible punishment, doesn't he!"

Josh was staring into space.

"And I can't get over the fact you spotted that acorn man, Josh. He wasn't there at first, definitely. That was lucky!"

He looked up, tense. "I did it again," he said.

"What do you mean?"

"I looked. I used my eyes, and it changed things."

Jericho laughed. "Didn't I tell you? That's the thing you're good at."

"What do you mean, Josh?" asked Teresa again.

"Well, I was looking at those pigs, and then suddenly there was a person there as well. But I made it happen."

"Seriously?" Teresa looked at their guide, frowning. "The same way you did when we got to the lake?"

"And the same way he did it in Ixilis," said Jericho. "Josh knows how to look around. I mean look out. Look through. Alter-look. Well, something like that. He can change things by using his eyes."

"Great!" Teresa cried in a startlingly loud voice. "But Josh, that's fantastic! Now *we* can team up, the same way I used to do with Baz! I'll talk and you'll use your eyes! Now we're getting somewhere!" She turned to him and flung her wet arms around him. "Now we'll make it! I know it! God, how happy I am! I already knew there was something special about you, back when we were doing the Traders' Trial together. But I'm glad that what turns out to be special is this talent with your eyes, and not that sleepy head and those sticky fingers of yours!"

The acorn man glanced over his shoulder with a suspicious look and hissed angrily, "Quiet! Follow me, Sipartis! Hurry!"

Josh felt very happy all of a sudden. Drenched and chilled to the bone, anxious – and yet very happy. They hurried on behind their bad-tempered guide, along muddy paths in a northerly direction.

"Do you think that Kat Siparti was meant to be punished too?" Josh asked softly. "Since these people seem to be under orders to deliver her to this washerwoman who doles out punishments."

"Kat was his favourite, wasn't she?" said Teresa. "Maybe the punishment won't be that bad. It might be more like a kind of test. Don't you think?"

"I hope it isn't something horrible."

"I'd like to find out a bit more about that Kat. She was very clever, they say, cleverer than Gip. She could persuade anyone of anything with that sharp tongue of hers."

"The problem is, we don't belong to Kat, we belong to Gip," said Josh.

But Teresa grinned. "Gip and Kat are cut from the same cloth. We'll find a way to talk our way out of that one."

It was surprising how stubborn October rains could be. That afternoon the heavens opened with renewed vigour and poured another deluge on top of them, as if until then not a drop had fallen out of that leaden sky. Their wet clothing chafed their skin until it was raw. They were shivering and their teeth chattered. But there was nothing to be done about it. There wasn't a house or an inn in sight. There wasn't a single sheltering haystack along the trail to tempt them. Nothing but miles and miles of dark, dripping woods stretching in all directions, coldly inhospitable. Rings of bright orange fungi gleamed wickedly among the tree trunks. There was no end to the rain, and there was no end to the forest. The indefatigable acorn man tramped on ahead of them as if the rain didn't touch him. Josh felt his throat swelling up, sore and hot. He sniffed angrily. A cold, the flu, snot. Oh well, couldn't be helped.

Suddenly the trees ended and they found themselves standing on a rock ledge. The acorn man halted, panting heavily. A steep drop yawned below their feet. On the other side of the ravine a waterfall cascaded down. On a lovely summer day it must have presented a gorgeous sight. Now it was just another downpour in the unending deluge.

Josh blew his nose into a fallen leaf. "Which way now?"

"Down!" the acorn man panted hoarsely. "This is your last stop, Sipartis! That's where Maam Sagal is! Down, down, and then up, up! She's waiting! Down you go, to take your punishment!"

Without warning he gave all three a shove in the back. Startled, they tripped, tumbled, slid down the steep incline.

They tried desperately to grab on to something, but the ferns came away in their hands and the brambles tore at their fingers. Josh heard his trousers rip as he careened down the slope. High above them, they could hear the acorn man laughing.

Filthy and battered, they came to rest on the bank of a seething river. It was wider than Lake Long Sors, so there was nothing for it but to follow the river down towards the waterfall. Josh noticed that his right trouser leg was ripped from the ankle to the knee.

They were surprised to find a stone washing platform by the water, not far from the spot where the waterfall came crashing down, with a neat stone path leading up to it. They followed the path with pounding hearts. This must be Maam Sagal's path, the washerwoman they had heard such disturbing things about. The path turned into a slippery stone staircase that climbed up next to the waterfall. Panting for breath, they reached the top. The path now led away from the thundering roar of the waterfall, through a pine forest groaning and rustling in the westerly wind. Eventually they could hear each other speak again.

"I want some dry clothes and some food," Josh grumbled.

"I want to go home and sleep for hours and hours and have lots and lots of hot food to eat. I don't care what it is, as long as it's nice and hot," said Teresa.

"Chips," said Josh. "Mountains of fish and chips."

"Just chicken, spicy chicken in a red-hot sauce, with fried rice," said Teresa.

"Those tiny spring rolls. You know the kind I mean – really delicious. Much tastier than the big kind."

"Chicken chop suey. With lots of prawn crackers."

"One of those crispy pizzas, with pepperoni and olives."

"With anchovies, you know, to give your mouth a nice salty kick."

"And loads of melted cheese."

"Or toffees," said Teresa. "A bag of toffees. Chocolate éclairs and sherbet lemons."

"Crisps," said Josh. "And Coke. As much as you want. A big bag of salt and vinegar crisps."

Sighing, they climbed over a fallen tree obstructing the way. And then they saw it. It was drifting around in a lazy circle and then it popped. A soap bubble. They turned round, because the bubble came from somewhere behind them. Jericho was already playing with another bubble. The bubbles were spilling out of a dark opening in the rocks behind her. Every so often a whole cloud of bubbles would gush forth, wobbling along sluggishly at first, then suddenly, without warning, darting forward, pushed by the wind. Sometimes it was just a single big fat bubble, blue and purple and red. Teresa giggled.

"Washerwoman," she said.

Josh imagined a sort of headmistress in uniform, with mean spectacles and thin lips. And a whip. "Do we *have* to?"

"She's the one who knows the way to the Tembe," said Teresa.

Grimly they walked in, through the gap.

It was a rough, dark corridor filled with drifting soap bubbles, reeking strongly of soap and smoke. They carried on, fumbling in the dark, until they reached a door that was half open, as if they were expected. Hesitantly they edged across the threshold. Before them was another corridor, as dark as the first. This one, too, ended at a door that was ajar. From inside came a loud cacophony of popping, spluttering and splashing sounds, and an awesome bellowing. They peered inside cautiously.

"Good grief," said Teresa softly. For a few seconds they couldn't believe their eyes. A confetti storm? A blizzard of wild colours? They rubbed their eyes in disbelief. Whirlwinds of foam and bubbles whizzed through the air – red, green, gold, purple, blue, all shades of the rainbow – and the bubbles kept popping in spectacular cascades of colour. But that wasn't all. The large room was covered in thousands of dizzying tiles in crazy patterns, dancing in the glow of fires lit here and there around the room. On these fires, huge kettles and copper tubs were boiling away, and only now did they see that that was where the floods of foam and lather were coming from. And behind the cauldron in the middle of the room was a big strapping woman, her arms plunged in the suds up to her armpits. She was singing at the top of her voice, over the sloshing and gurgling and the roar of the wood fires.

"The washerwoman," whispered Teresa.

The woman was belting it out as she lifted a large flowered curtain, or whatever it was, out of the soapy water, wrung it out and flung it, dripping wet, over a clothes line behind her. Then she dried her hands on her apron and called, "Come on in, intruders, I see you!"

They didn't have a choice. Zizi and the little panther stayed behind in the corridor, but the Associates reluctantly stepped forward, into the hurricane of soapsuds. Maam Sagal stood waiting, hands on her hips. She inspected them minutely from head to toe.

"Well, well," she said. "Mudbugs, eh! Look what the cat dragged in! What's this supposed to mean? Who might *you* be?"

"Teresa Okwoma, and Josh and Jericho Cope, on a mission to seek the Tembe, on orders of Gippart," said Teresa in a clear voice.

Maam Sagal rubbed her chin thoughtfully. "And how about that one over there?" She nodded at Lucide.

"That's Lucide, a guardian," Teresa explained.

The washerwoman hum-hummed suspiciously. Then she fixed her attention on the Associates again. "Who did you say sent you? Gippart? What kind of person is that?"

"Gip Siparti," Teresa and Josh chorused.

"Well, well," said Maam Sagal. "Well now!" She abruptly turned her back on them and plunged her arms in the soapy water again. She began kneading, scrubbing and lathering furiously, so that billowing suds flew all around. Swathed in clouds of bubbles, Maam Sagal bellowed, "And I should be jumping for joy, I suppose! News from the Sipartis! And I'm expected to be ready to help, I suppose!"

"You don't *have* to do anything." Teresa cautiously made her way over to her, across the slippery floor. "We're just following orders, and we have to reach the Tembe. Can you help us? Or would you like us to leave?"

The washerwoman snorted. "Not so fast, you cheeky piglet! Give me some time to think here. You're a bit late, don't you think? Wouldn't you say?" She kept on scrubbing energetically.

"We were only sent a few days ago," said Teresa. "We didn't know the way at first."

"Over *three hundred and fifty years*!" Maam Sagal sloshed towards them menacingly with dripping arms. "Over three hundred and fifty years I've been waiting for one of those annoying, quarrelsome, greedy Siparti brats to come along! Don't you think that's just a *little* too long for you to come marching in here, the picture of innocence, with your muddy feet?"

She was seething with anger. But Jericho shoved Josh aside and said tartly, "Well, I'd been waiting for Josh here, for the last three hundred and fifty years too. And you don't see *me* whining about it."

Maam Sagal looked at her flabbergasted. Then she laughed. "Well now!" she cried, tapping Jericho on the cheek with her fat, wet hand. "Cheeky shrimp, aren't you! So is this what's become of the Sipartis? A bunch of insolent brats?"

Jericho reddened with indignation. "You *could* try to be a little more polite yourself, you know! Do you know who we are? *She's* the best storyteller in the world – she can talk anyone into anything! And that's my brother, who is a master thief and an alterer-seer, and if you're not careful they'll blow *you* right off the surface of the earth. And you're lucky Baz isn't with us too!"

Maam Sagal crossed her arms over her chest. "And what about you?" she asked darkly. "What might you be?"

"Me, I'm Jericho!" She stretched herself to her full height: a muddy, barefooted girl with hair like an old broom, with twigs and leaves sticking out all over; a pale little waif in a sopping-wet, torn and crumpled dress. "I am Jericho the time-traveller, I am master of life and death, I am my parents' nightmare and my brother's keeper! I can fly, and I can spy, and I can wallop old witches to kingdom come, do you hear me?"

Maam Sagal didn't move. She glared at the drenched little band, her stern eyes roving from one to the other. Josh found himself tugging at the rip in his trouser leg to hide it. The washerwoman stuck out her bottom lip. "It sounds just like Gip and Kat Siparti," she muttered to herself. "Conceited braggarts. But it doesn't *look* anything like them."

"But—" Teresa began.

Maam Sagal raised her hand. "Kat Siparti would *never* appear before me in this state. Never! And I wish to speak to Kat Siparti. I have a message for Kat Siparti."

"We're from Gip Siparti," said Teresa.

Maam Sagal nodded. "The wrong one. It's Kat I have a bone to pick with."

"But Gip and Kat are twins," Teresa objected.

But the washerwoman plunged back into her suds and cried out angrily, "Tell me something I don't know! Just try to make me change my mind, you glib-mouthed little swine, if you've got the nerve. If what that little smart alec there just said about you is true, that is. Go ahead, try and persuade me Kat and Gip are one and the same!"

Teresa stiffened. She was feverishly trying to think of something. Jericho was looking at her expectantly. Josh was trying to stuff his trouser leg into his sock.

"Josh," cried Teresa, "Jericho, come on!" She dragged them to a corner of the foamy laundry, where they were hidden in a blizzard of suds. "Listen, we're going to do it together. Josh, listen to me. Do you think you can do what I'm about to ask?" And she told them the plan she'd thought up.

"I'll never manage it," stammered Josh.

"If you can turn a pig into a human, Josh, then you can do this just as easily! All we have to do is persuade the woman that twins are interchangeable!"

"But they aren't," said Josh.

"No, but that doesn't matter. We just have to persuade *her* they are. Ready?"

They went back through the clouds of lather and bubbles to Maam Sagal, who was just hanging up some socks on the line.

"Mrs Sagal," said Teresa politely. "I'd like to explain something."

Teresa drew herself up to her full height, her hands spread. She motioned Jericho to come forward and grabbed her by the hand. "Here's a girl, one half of a pair of twins. This is the bad one, the ruthless one, the heartbreaker and the witch." Then she gestured at Josh to come forward. "Here's a boy, the other half of this pair of twins. This is the sleepyhead, the collector, the daydreamer and the thief."

She gripped their hands, and squeezed. Josh took a deep breath and stared hard at Jericho. Jericho returned his gaze intently. Meanwhile Teresa went on in a smooth and rhythmic patter. "Kat is the chatterer, the ruthless, the heartbreaker, the witch. Gip is the traveller, the collector, the novelty-seeker, the boss."

She stole a sidelong glance at Josh and Jericho. They were gazing deeply into each other's eyes. Teresa saw that Josh was beginning to sweat. His lips moved, and his breath was coming very fast.

"He is her mirror image, and she his," Teresa continued. "She is his opposite, and he hers." She threw another quick glance at Josh and Jericho. Nothing yet. "Gip is water, Kat is fire. Josh is water, Jericho—"

"Air!" said Maam Sagal suddenly, who, while continuing with her scrubbing, hadn't been missing a thing.

"But he is her mirror image, and she his!" cried Teresa, full of conviction. "Can't you see? She is his bad side, his vicious side! But they are the same, only the vicious side never came to the surface in Josh's case, because he was such a sleepyhead – I mean, until Jericho came and turned him into a thief – but it *was* in him, it was always there. They are one and the same, just like Kat and Gip. Do you see it now?"

Maam Sagal was staring at Josh and Jericho with such astonishment that Teresa spun round to look at them herself. It had worked! Jericho was still standing in the same place, but her face had turned into Josh's face. And Josh's skinny frame was now crowned with Jericho's head. Teresa clapped her hands to her face and started laughing hysterically.

Maam Sagal also began to laugh. She put her hands on her hips and threw her flushed head back. "Mirror image! They are the same! They can switch heads! Oh, those incorrigible Sipartis. Tricky devils, they are!"

"Josh," cried Josh's head from Jericho's body, "please make me go back to normal, will you? I want my own head back!"

Jericho's face on Josh's body frowned. "Wait a minute," she muttered. "It isn't that easy..."

Teresa and Maam Sagal looked on breathlessly, as Jericho's eyes fixed on Josh's face, trying to get it to change, frowning and blinking rapidly. "Come on," begged Josh's head impatiently.

Maam Sagal roared with laughter. "That's my Sipartis, *now* I recognize them! Always hoisted with their own petard! All those grand schemes of theirs for ever ending up in the soup!"

"Quiet!" cried Teresa, and *wham*! Jericho suddenly regained her long, wild locks and Josh got his own dreamy and yet rather bad-tempered face back. And Jericho's pale eyes glinted with their usual wicked mockery once more. Head on body to which it belonged, right body for right head.

Teresa was jumping up and down, laughing wildly. She slapped them both on the back, and kissed them excitedly. "Josh, Josh, you're fantastic! You're the greatest!"

"And me too," said Jericho. "Didn't I do a good job cooperating, Josh?"

Maam Sagal just laughed and laughed and laughed. She couldn't stop laughing. Finally she wiped the tears from her eyes, panting, "Children, you win! You have me completely convinced! If only that old coot Siparti could have seen you! Gip and Kat are definitely *not* one and the same, you filthy little piggies, and besides, Gip is earth and not water – but your tricks are Kat's kind of tricks, and you've earned your answer from me fair and square. Come here."

They were fully expecting a quiet explanation now, at long last, something good to eat perhaps, a little praise and a short rest; they had more than deserved it, after their clever sleight of hand. But that wasn't what was in store for them at all. Maam Sagal grabbed all three of them at the same time, and with a great splash dropped them, clothes and all, into her bubbling cauldron.

"There, there," she grunted contentedly, "three mudbugs, three tummies full of dung, three dirty heads filled with snot and nasty thoughts, into my suds, my suds, my suds."

They tried to scramble out of the hot cauldron, but it was impossible. The water hissed and bubbled, they were buffeted from side to side, the lather blinded them, and they needed all their wits about them to keep their heads above water and gulp some air. Maam Sagal ducked them under a couple more times, and then started soaping and scrubbing them.

"Ash and fat," she sang, "ash and fat! A nice soapy bath for your little head, head, head! Fat and ash, fat and ash, all those grubby grimy dreams come out in the wash, wash, wash!"

"Ouch!" cried Jericho when the washerwoman started on her hair, and Teresa squeaked, "Not my hair! Not my hair!" But Maam Sagal went on singing, deaf to their pleas: "Lather it well, mix it up well, the greasy gloop! All shades, all grades go into my soup, soup, soup!" She pulled Josh's jerkin over his head and flung it into a corner, then started scouring his back so roughly that his shirt ripped. "Know what?" she yelled loudly over all the noise. "Those Sipartis are right in one respect! Everything has to be thoroughly mixed up! That makes for the best, most fertile mix. The reason my fatty suds are so nice and rich is that I mix everything into them – every thought, every memory and every desire! And that's why my suds produce the very best ideas in the world! My soap bubbles are the best!"

Now she grabbed Teresa, poured several ladles of hot water over her head and began scrubbing her long legs as if she really meant business.

"A smidgeon of Ixilis and a pinch of Damara, a dash of Dinak and splash of Mur! And then? Keep it rich, boil it, stir it, and there you have it: soapsuds crammed with ideas and plans, and colours and tastes never known to man."

Now she grabbed Jericho. "Air, air! Come here, little girlie of air! Ha, three I've got: boy of water, girl of earth, wraith of air… But where's fire? Where did fire get to?" She tapped Jericho on the head with her ladle. "Did you chase fire away, missy? Where is he, where's my fourth? Ah well, not to worry, I'm sure he'll be back. He'll certainly be back."

She stoked the fire hotter. They were sweating more and their hearts felt about to burst. Maam Sagal danced wildly around them, singing and washing, pounding and kneading. "Come on, let go! Give up your tastes, your smells, your dreams, your colours! Come on, make my suds nice and rich! It's all got to get mixed in, so give it up, let go, let go!"

And then, seizing them in her gigantic fist, she lifted them out of the water and dropped them on the warm floor tiles. They lay there panting, as red as lobsters. Maam Sagal didn't even give them another look. She bent over the seething water in her cauldron.

"Ah," she cackled, "nice and fat, lovely, lovely. What have we here? Hunger, hunger, greed for gold, gluttony, we know it well: ah, flying machines, flying engines, airships! Hunger for flight, for flying, for voyaging! Wheels? Machines? Engines? Electra, energy, white lightning? Wait, ha! What lovely goodies you've brought me. I had no idea, oh what lovely fat!"

The Associates dizzily got to their feet.

"The woman is mad," Josh spluttered.

"She's just a witch," said Teresa. "She's taken something from us. Gosh, I'm hot."

"It's better than being outside, anyway," laughed Jericho. She took off her dripping-wet, tattered dress. "But my dress has had it, I'm afraid."

"My clothes too," said Josh.

"And my hair," added Teresa. "How *ever* will I fix my hair again?"

"Oh, I'll draw you a picture of it," said Josh. "I had a good look at it before. Actually, some of it's still in there; it's not completely ruined, but the feather's gone."

The washerwoman turned back to them. "Well now, silly things," she cried heartily. "My soup's ready! And what are you doing, standing there half naked? Shame on you! Come on, into the drying room you go. We've got some business to take care of there!"

They went into a side room. The rafters held a maze of criss-crossing washing lines on which laundry was hung to dry, and the walls were lined with ironing tables. A tiled stove was blazing in the middle of the room; a cat lay curled up in front of it, asleep.

"Gift from Siparti, that stove." Maam Sagal nodded. "I suppose I do owe my former master a favour. But having to wait three hundred and fifty years to do it, that really is a little too much. Here, take this, take this, take this."

She threw a handful of clothes at each of them, in a medley of colours and patterns. It felt wonderful to put on dry clothes again. The icy torrential rains had been steamed out of them, and they felt as clean as little piglets.

Maam Sagal leaned against one of the ironing boards, stroking the cat, as the Associates got dressed. Teresa put on a pair of trousers in blue, black and purple stripes, topped with a crimson blouse and tawny yellow jacket. Jericho, naturally, had chosen dark red: a dress with a long skirt. Josh's trousers were black and his shirt was navy blue, with little gold and purple stars.

"If there's one thing I hate," said Maam Sagal, flipping open a little shutter in the stove and taking out a pot, "it's purity and drabness. Here you are, some buttermilk porridge and syrup. Go on then, stuff yourselves till you're nice and full again, skinny bunnikins."

It wasn't chop suey or pizza, and at home they'd have turned their noses up at it, but here they fell on the porridge as if it were their favourite treat. At around the twentieth mouthful, Teresa spoke. "But aren't you a laundress? So isn't cleanliness what you like best?"

"Ha!" Maam Sagal snorted and sampled the porridge herself. "Do you know what soap is made of, Kat-kins? Fat and ashes. The only reason I do washing is to make nice rich suds. And then I mix the whole world into it. It's only a rich, fat lather that will ever produce anything new, just as you need a rich, fertile soil, which is made up of all sorts of dirt, to grow new crops. Didn't you hear what I was singing?"

"I did," said Teresa, "but what is it, then, that you took from us?"

"The thoughts inside your head," said Maam Sagal, smacking her lips, "and everything you know and everything your body feels. I now know about everything in your world, thanks to the memories you brought me. And all that is now in my melting pot; and from it come the bubbles, bubbles with new ideas we may be able to use. Perhaps, perhaps…"

Dazed, for a moment they couldn't think of anything to say.

"I still have all my memories," said Josh uncertainly.

"Well of course, you still keep what I take from you," said Maam Sagal. "Not like it is at Siparti. Whatever *that* one takes from you, you never get back. Oh well, Siparti does help me stir the whole world together, I do have to give him that. That's the positive aspect of trade, I suppose. The world gets stirred up together. That's about as much as I have to say for it."

Teresa cautiously ventured, "You knew Siparti, didn't you? Was he really such a monster?"

Maam Sagal gave her a strange look. "Siparti a monster? Oh, my dear…" Absent-mindedly she took a couple more mouthfuls of porridge. "*That* you'll have to decide for yourself. The whole Temberi business was a dirty trick, anyway. It's been the cause of much evil in the world. Temberi should have tempered Siparti's greed with his own lightness of being, you see. That was the way it was supposed to happen. And now the whole world is gripped by Siparti's kind of greed, that rage to conquer, that ruthless craving for profit…" She shook her head, smiling. "But I myself always got along very well with Siparti. Although one did always have to watch one's back with that charmer. Oh my Lord, Siparti!"

"But what about that curse?" asked Josh.

"So you children *are* connected to Kat after all, are you?" muttered Maam Sagal. "The old trickster wanted me to have a serious word with his daughter Kat, a nice little heart-to-heart about the evils of trade, and its positive aspects as well. You're dying to know too, aren't you, piggies? Kat was always keen to know exactly how things stood – Gip didn't care so much."

"But what about the curse?" Josh insisted.

"How should *I* know! I'm Maam Sagal, I'll have you know, not Siparti's mother-confessor! Yes, of course he was cursed after that whole Temberi business, cursed tenfold, and some of that curse was visited on his children. But what it was exactly… I know he used to complain to me he had only six children, instead of the hundreds he'd always wanted. Lord knows he did his best to try and sire thousands! He thought it was because of that curse that he'd had only six. But don't ask me what it was really about, the curse that hung over his children's heads."

"What about the evils of trade, then?" enquired Teresa.

"That's something I should have discussed with Kat in person," said Maam Sagal. "You're only in their service, and you're much too young for that kind of discussion."

She sounded so firm on that point that they didn't insist.

"In that case, please could you tell us how to get to the Tembe now?" asked Teresa.

"No," said Maam Sagal. "That wasn't part of the deal either." Teresa wanted to say something else, but the washerwoman went on. "Besides, I don't know. Siparti wouldn't tell me, the dirty double-crosser. And anyway," and suddenly she turned vague and hesitant, "I don't know if it's such a good idea to go there. If it were Kat, that would have been another story – but you, foolhardy children… And who knows what they'll do to you, if you arrive there with greetings from Siparti?" She sighed. "Ah well, suit yourselves. I've done what the rogue asked me to do. All that's left is for me to give you my parting gift." Then she had a thought. "Tell me. Is Kat dead? Is that it? Did Gip finally bash her brains in?"

"No," said Teresa. "She can't have been killed, because she built up her business into a great company. As far as I can tell, except for the House of Gip, the House of Kat is the only one of all the Sipartis that's left."

"In *our* time, you mean," said Josh. "In the twenty-first century."

"Aha," said Maam Sagal, "Aha!'

Josh blanched. He had betrayed what should have been left a secret.

"Doesn't matter, anyway," said Maam Sagal. "I always knew

there was something strange about you youngsters. You are from so far away! So, then Gip Siparti has discovered how to time-travel, has he? Well, if that's the case, the Sipartis are cleverer than I'd given them credit for. In which case, you may just stand a chance with the Tembe; who knows."

They finished their porridge in silence. Maam Sagal kept staring at them, muttering to herself. The cat was nestled on her lap. After a while she asked, "Tell me, in your time, has the world really become a nice rich, fat stew? And what's it like?"

"It really *is* a melting pot," Teresa laughed, "London especially. You can find the whole world in London. It's been that way for quite a while. That's the way it should be, isn't it?"

Jericho nodded. "In the days when I was Betty, it was the same. Even more than in your time; much of the city housed new immigrants. There were people in huge fur hats, you know, and others wearing turbans, and Irish, and Germans, and Huguenots, and Moors, and people like that. I had a friend who was from Persia."

Teresa was thoughtfully playing with her spoon. "It still isn't integrated enough, yet. People still live very separate lives – and of course there are always those complete morons who tell you to go back to where you came from. You know, that kind of stupid nonsense."

Maam Sagal shook her head. "People are fools. Come on, piglets, get finished. I must get back to my suds."

Josh, wandering around the drying room, soon found himself back in the laundry proper. He started sniffing around the bubbling cauldrons. Something funny was going on inside the large tub they'd been bathed in. He bent over the fiercely gurgling and sputtering lather. Strange things were going on in there. The water kept turning different colours. It turned viscous, then fizzed back into a watery liquid. As he looked, it started boiling so wildly that an absurdly large bubble welled up and grew larger and larger, until it boiled over and landed on the floor, where it went splat at his feet in a riot of smaller bubbles. These swirled about Josh's head. He gazed at them, captivated.

Inside the smooth, lustrous bubbles, pictures swam into view. But it wasn't his surroundings that were reflected in them. In the squall of shifting images glinting and shattering before his eyes, he could see, to his utter astonishment, Gippart itself: the Great Hall, with a crowd of travellers and Dispatch Board members milling about. He saw Tal pacing up and down, deep in agitated discussion with Garnet Gippart, just as the image popped. He saw Moussa asleep, his head on a computer keyboard, while next to him a red-eyed Max was peering at the screen. He saw Zeppelins being struck by lightning. He saw a herd of Inelesi alligators retreating in panic as they were being attacked by a herd of horned zebras. And he saw Spratt with a hat pulled low over his eyes, collapsed in a chair, bargaining with a man dressed in a khaki military uniform. Then, to his delight, he saw Baz. He had a worried expression, and was running, muttering to himself and – true to form – tapping a stick on the tree trunks as he went by. Next he saw himself, eyes open wide, and he saw his likeness in the bubble gazing at Jericho, and was stunned to see for the first time how very much alike they looked – except, of course, that Jericho looked so much more mischievous and wicked. But then her face changed. It was pitch black all around her. Her hair, oddly enough, had been hacked off in a messy cut, and to his distress he saw that she was starting to cry. He blinked, and the image dissolved. The bubbles ballooned, spun around in the air, and burst.

Now he heard a deafening bubbling and sputtering coming from somewhere behind his back. Curious, he turned and walked over to a little cooking pot in a corner. Here too something was happening. A foaming volcanic eruption. Cautiously he drew near the riot of soap bubbles spewing out of the pot. A puff of bubbles revealed a trading caravan approaching. The lead wagon was ably driven by a little girl – she couldn't have been more than six years old. A great cavalcade followed: camels, wagons, war horses festooned with bright tassels and trimmings, tinkling bells, flashing gold. Over there, on a tall, magnificent show camel, sat an arrogant-looking fellow in a Tartar hat. He inspected the convoy with searching eyes. Nothing escaped him, this proud, keen-eyed merchant king. Josh saw him come into closer view. His eyes scanned the string of bubbles to get a good look at the man's face.

Josh had never seen a face like it. Dark, aquiline, animated. A face twinkling with passion and determination. A predator's face, yet at the same time too sensitive, too ironic and mocking to fit that description. The eyes took in everything, estimated the value of everything in an instant, and could immediately tell if something was worth having or not. That was when the fellow would make his move. Josh was so engrossed that he jumped when he felt a hand on his shoulder.

"Hey, young nosy-parker," the laundress was hissing into his ear. "Are you happy now? That there's Siparti!"

The picture suddenly changed before their eyes. Panic had set in at the front of the caravan. The caravan had drawn up sharply at the edge of a precipice, scattering in all directions. The man on the show camel bellowed at his mount to move, and the animal set itself heavily into motion. And now here came a little black boy speeding along on another camel, outrunning the leader himself. A racing camel!

"Ha, and there's Mono," laughed Maam Sagal. "Good-looking Mono of Ixilis! He must be nine here, swift as an arrow, the apple of his papa's eye."

Mono stormed towards the first wagon, where the little girl, screaming, was pulling at the reins with all her might.

"She's six years old there, little Brax," whispered the washerwoman. "Six, but already as proud as an eaglet, and as fierce as a hawk. Siparti was just crazy about his eldest daughter. Mountain-girl Brax with the robber's blood."

Mono was already beside her and caught the bolting horses

by the reins, leaping down off his own camel. With sheer might he dragged the horses back from the precipice. Brax was screaming something at him, incensed. Now the wagons reordered themselves, Brax in the lead, glaring, with Mono beside her.

Josh could breathe freely again. His entire body began to tingle from head to toe. All of a sudden he found himself fervently wishing he were Mono, who was treated as a grown-up; or Brax, a girl so trusted by her parents that, at the age of six, she was allowed to lead a caravan of riches; and he wanted to be Siparti himself, a man who collected treasures and then resold them, who was rolling in gold and precious jewels, and whom nobody could resist.

As he went on staring hungrily, flushed and open-mouthed, a new image appeared. A sunny urban scene, but in what age, or what far-off country, he could not tell. There they went, Gip and Kat, proud and straight, strolling with long, lithe strides, both of equal height, both fleet of foot, evenly matched. Seeing them laughing, boasting about profits and grandiose trading plans, they took your breath away. They were both extravagantly dressed, this black-haired, black-eyed pair, in outlandish hats and flowing cloaks. Having inherited Siparti's weakness for flash and glitter, they were dripping with jewellery – necklaces, brooches, bracelets and rings. Josh's heart started beating fast, and his body began tingling again. That was what he wanted to be like, as magnificent and indomitable as those two! He wanted to be like Gip Siparti and Kat Siparti, as they were when they were first starting on their illustrious careers, heading for their successful young companies.

His eyes devoured the wonderful scenes that came next: a youthful Gip with a big smile on his face, racing to tell his sister what he'd found among a seafaring people from the east, a discovery that would change the world and make him rich, namely, the compass! Then Kat with a wicked grin on her face, writing Gip a note to inform him that she'd made a huge profit and when was he going to catch up? But he also had a quick glimpse of Gip and Kat, aged fifteen, circling each other with drawn swords, their black-rimmed eyes spitting hate. Gip's dense black hair was standing on end. He was deadly serious. This flare-up of hatred was almost immediately erased by a flood of cheerful images of storehouses filling with gold, voyages of discovery, eager buyers awaiting the market's opening.

And as he watched, the picture changed again. There was Siparti's face. But this time it was blank, rigid with grief.

"Ah," sighed the laundress. Josh had nearly forgotten her. "He has finally realized it. Too late, Siparti, your brother is dead. Gone, gone, gone for good, and it's all your fault. You're the assassin..."

The hot, humid laundry suddenly seemed to turn to ice. Josh shivered. Oh, the pained despair on Siparti's face! He couldn't make himself look away as the next terrible scenes flashed before his eyes. Dark, dirty, deafening factories; rubbish dumps; bare, scorched earth; a line of prisoners shackled together trudging down a forest path; gangsters shooting a man in the back; drug dealers in a blind alley. He didn't want to see any of this. He gulped, squeezed his eyes shut and turned away.

The washerwoman followed him to the drying room, cackling unkindly. "Looking is painful, isn't it? Well, it's your own stupid fault! Those sorts of things aren't meant for your eyes, my piglet."

She tweaked his nose. He rubbed his eyes and then quietly slipped back to his seat by the stove.

Maam Sagal raised her finger in the air. "Oh, that reminds me of something. Siparti! Yes, I was supposed to give you your parting gift. If only I could remember where I'd left it..." She bustled through the drying room, disappeared into the laundry, then returned, grumbling. She shooed away the cat that was slinking around her, butting its head against her legs. "Three hundred and fifty years," she muttered, "plenty of time to lose something. For goodness' sake, cat, buzz off."

She dug around in a huge pile of laundry waiting to be ironed, then turned back again, and grabbed the cat by the scruff of the neck. She paused. "Aha! Oh, do please excuse me, most excellent puss," she breathed, taking something off the cat's neck. "Got it!"

The cat streaked away, and Maam Sagal was left holding a round, glittering piece of jewellery. The three of them stared at it. Teresa stood up to have a better look. "But that's –" She looked back at the others. "Isn't this the one that belongs to Jericho and you, Josh?"

Josh jumped to her side and took the gold snake bracelet, knitting his brow. "How can that be? No, this one's different. Mine doesn't have its tail in its mouth."

"Do you know it?" asked Maam Sagal. "Do you know what this is?"

They nodded, and compared the two bracelets. Jericho's bracelet, which she stubbornly insisted on wearing on her wrist, was indeed different. The end of Jericho's bracelet was open: the snake's mouth was closed, and the tail ended in an elegant swirl next to the head, not in the mouth. But the heads were uncannily alike, and both had eyes made of red rubies.

"I don't know the whys and wherefores," said Maam Sagal, "but this is the gift I was supposed to give Kat. And now you'd better pay careful attention and listen, because there was a message that went with it, and it wasn't a short one, either." She closed her eyes and began speaking slowly and with earnest concentration. "Listen: 'The earth is round.' Siparti states: 'So, too, the end of time is nothing but the beginning of time.'"

"A riddle?" asked Teresa.

"Heed," said Maam Sagal, "Siparti's second bidding: 'Tell your uncle that I love him. And that I did him a great wrong. I miss him terribly. Tell him that.'"

"Yes," said Teresa, "but—"

Maam Sagal interrupted her again. "Quiet! Thus spake Idadde, Kat's mother: 'Everything is interconnected: brother and sister, parent and child, family and friends, friend and foe. The curse on Siparti's head is borne by his children, and Siparti's promise must be fulfilled by his children. Should they fail to do so, they shall have to live with that curse for all eternity.'" Maam Sagal opened her eyes. "Well, that's it, I've now done more than enough to honour the memory of that awkward old scoundrel. Did you get it all? Can you repeat it to me, word for word?"

Teresa was able to repeat almost verbatim what Maam Sagal had just told them, and the latter nodded with pursed lips, satisfied. She straightened her back and placed the bracelet in Teresa's hands. "The end of time is the beginning of time. Everything is interconnected. That's it."

Teresa clutched the bracelet. "Are we supposed to give this to the Tembe? Do you mean—"

But the laundress clapped her hands decisively. "This visit is now over. I have nothing else to tell you. I've got to get back to work, to my suds, and I don't need you children getting in my way. Just – wait." She walked back into the laundry, and came back a few moments later with three lengths of some shiny stuff and three pairs of boots. "Mud is good," she said, and grinned, "but if you have to travel far, you'd better protect yourselves from the rain. Come on, wrap yourselves up, wrap yourselves up. Tomorrow is November the first!"

Teresa wavered. "Wouldn't it be better if we spent the night here?" she asked politely.

But Maam Sagal firmly shook her head. "I've done my duty, and now it's up to you again," she said, pushing them out into the corridor.

"I thought you were supposed to punish us," said Josh, draping the oilcloth around him like a cape and pulling the roomy material over his head. Little Zizi, who was dry and fluffy once more, eagerly hid herself by his neck, snug inside the waterproof hood.

Maam Sagal puffed out her cheeks. "Who am I, to punish the Sipartis? Did you think I was a saint or something? No, it was old Siparti himself who spread that rumour, to make sure that even those who can't stand the Sipartis – and there are plenty of those, believe you me – would still lead you to me. I'm glad it worked, and that my swine finally brought you here." She smiled. "Well, off you go, you wicked little cheats. Go and make a lovely dirty mess for me!"

When evening fell, the weather changed yet again. It turned colder. From time to time the cloud cover would break, and a bright shaft of yellow light would suddenly beam down through the wispy clouds, only to be snuffed out just as abruptly again, and then the rain would merrily start pouring down once more, with an occasional hailstone thrown in for good measure. It didn't bother them. The moors might not provide any shelter, but they were huddled deep inside the washerwoman's stiff oilcloth capes, as if each had their own private tent. Only Lucide, bringing up the rear with the little panther at his heels, was getting a thorough soaking, exposed as he was to the elements in his short tunic.

They walked in single file at first, then huddled together in order to solve the new puzzle.

"But how come they are so much alike?" asked Josh, who couldn't stop thinking about that bracelet.

"Why not?" said Jericho. "It was my birthday present; my mother simply decided to buy me something very beautiful and old. She bought it from the very best merchant, from Katz's. She did, she bought it from Katz's."

"Katz's?" asked Josh and Teresa at the same time.

"I *think* that was the name of the merchant," said Jericho. "Everything there was ridiculously expensive. When she gave it to me, she said, 'Betty, this came from Katz's.'"

"Katz," said Teresa. "Kat Siparti. You've got a bracelet that came from Kat Siparti's trading company! Isn't that a coincidence!"

"It's no coincidence," said Jericho, "it's the best of the best."

"But this one's a little different, and that must mean something. Do you think it might have special powers?"

"Perhaps the Tembe can tell us," mused Josh.

"Hmm," said Teresa. She turned the bracelet round and round. "I'll keep it somewhere safe. We'll see."

She started walking faster, towards the dark forest in the east. In silence they hurried after her, with Lucide's slow, steady footfall following behind.

But as the long hours of walking multiplied, dejection set in again. There was no sight of warm or dry shelter for the night. There was nothing at all in sight. Dark, ominously creaking, dripping forests alternated with windswept moors, and not a single light flickered for miles around. Standing, they had each chewed an apple and a carrot from Dinak, and gulped down a hasty drink of water, and as they walked on, they finished their last crust of bread. Their stomachs were growling. But what could they do about it? If what they had witnessed in Dinak had indeed been the final days of a century-long nightmare, then all they could expect from now on was abject poverty, even more mud and even more calamity. They were now truly in the Dark Ages – the age of the Black Death. They thought nostalgically of the apple pie they'd had in Mur. The only thing they had going for them was that they knew where to go on this next stage of their journey. Mono's map was easy to read; from Maam Sagal they had to go in an easterly direction, cross a river, then continue east on a main road that led to two points on the map, W and BZ. So they trudged on down that dark road, silent and moody.

"If there's a ferryman's hut at the river, let's sleep in there," Josh suggested.

"I wouldn't count on it."

"What are *you* hoping for, then?"

"Dense tree cover," Teresa grunted.

Jericho hissed angrily. She'd been in a foul mood for hours. It wasn't really like her. But Teresa didn't react, and grimly pressed on.

Drained and exhausted, they trudged through the inhospitable autumn night, their stiff capes flapping and creaking like old sailing boats. They forgot about Baz's disappearance, Maam Sagal, and the difficult road ahead. They just stumbled on, as stiff-legged as robots, their brains nothing but grey static. Familiar scenes from home unreeled before Josh's eyes. The school cafeteria. The kitchen breakfast table at home. His room, and his collections. Dara and Zizi. Mo. He was so tired he didn't even feel homesick or depressed any more. He wasn't even waiting for a sign from Teresa that they could finally flop down and go to sleep. Never slackening her pace, she marched on ahead of them, into the woods, out of the woods, across a soggy field that was a sea of puddles, across another bleak plain where it started raining again, and into another wood. Josh was convinced they were going over and over and over the same terrain. He was beginning to wonder how soon he'd reach the stage when he'd just fall down senseless, like a block of wood. He felt himself drifting off, and he didn't really care.

It happened just at the point when he started to fall asleep on his feet. A totally unexpected sound. Straight ahead of him. A high-pitched noise urgently drilling through the sound of the rain. Fresh, other-worldly. He froze in his tracks, bewildered. The sound hurt his ears and his nerves.

"Telephone!" cried Teresa, who was walking a couple of paces in front of him. She fumbled under her oilcloth cape for her backpack; the phone slipped from her frozen fingers and fell on the ground. Josh picked it up and raised it clumsily to his ear. With his hood flung back, rain pelting in his face, he panted, "Max, is that you?"

With a shock, he realized he didn't recognize the voice at the other end.

"May I speak to Teresa Okwoma, please?"

It was a woman's voice. She had a curious foreign accent.

Mystified, Josh gave the phone to Teresa, who was standing beside him, her mouth open in disbelief. She turned up the volume, and the voice echoed through the night. "Hello? Is that Teresa Okwoma?"

"Yes?" said Teresa. "Who is it?"

"Ah, it truly is Teresa! Finally! This is a great moment. Teresa, my rose, how are you faring?"

"Fine," said Teresa, frowning. "Who *is* it?"

"Teresa, my rose, may I call you by your first name? Is this a convenient time to speak to you? You don't object?"

"Yes," said Teresa. "What's the problem? Who are you?"

There was a gentle laugh. "Ah, Teresa, there is a problem here, in my office. Teresa, all day long my people speak of Teresa. They tell me: this Teresa, she speaks so well, she makes the words sing and dance – and everyone who hears her falls under her spell, and does her bidding. Teresa, they say, Teresa can make the seas part, and make the trees bow low to her, and make the sun break through the clouds. When I hear my people talk, my rose, I think they are all in love with Teresa. That is my problem."

"Who are you?"

A brief silence followed. "That is why, my treasure, I am asking you directly: please come and work for me. I think my people cannot live another day without Teresa. I need her, and I think that she needs me too."

Teresa heard her out in silence, her heart beating fast.

"Haven't you already guessed who is speaking to you?" the voice came again, teasing. "I will be honest. We are but a small concern, unlike Gippart International, the mighty, glorious Gippart of the whole wide world, with its thousands of courageous traders and its thousands of magnificent subsidiaries. We are very small. But this year, Teresa, our little business has made a far greater profit than giant Gippart has. We do not hide from taxes and inspections; we do not take refuge in *umaya*'s borderlands, going underground to avoid being caught. We are as clear as crystal; we are unbeatable, quick and clever…"

Josh saw that Teresa was listening intently, wide-eyed.

"Tell me, Teresa, my gorgeous girl, is my brother treating you well? Is he paying you a fair wage? Is he looking after your welfare? Does he guard and protect you? Is he there for you when you're in danger, to save and rescue you?"

"Kat Siparti," whispered Teresa. "You are Kat."

She laughed softly. "My treasure," she said in a low, slow voice, "we are the word-merchants. We entice people with words until they swoon with love. We instil hunger and passion in people, and then we show them what will satisfy the hunger, what will temper the passion and convert it into a sated contentment. And then, thrilled to the core, they will buy. Our jewellery, our exquisite accessories, our lovely designs. She who works for us is an artist, a virtuoso, a magician and a reader of souls. Teresa, please come and work for us."

"You're the ones with the best ads, aren't you? Katz Imagination is famous for its advertising campaigns."

"But you are the storytelling artist, you are the sweet magician of words, my rose. You are much too seductive for Gippart. Tell me, Teresa, are you happy working for my brother? If you are happy there, then good, Kat embraces you and kisses you farewell. If you are not, then it is very simple. Phone me and I'll come and get you. My number is preprogrammed, just dial 2."

"Get me? Out of *umaya*?" Teresa gasped.

"But yes. Kat never lies. I need you, just as you need me. It won't be easy, but we will find a way, we two. For you alone will I do this, for you are worth gold to me, and more. Only one person will I rescue, and that person is you.

"Finally – please forgive me – I must confess something to you. I have been eavesdropping on you in secret. By means of your invaluable mobile phone; practical, isn't it, to have spies at your competitor's? I have overheard you, and this is my invitation. My incomparable Teresa, I long for your phone call. Don't wait too long, my morning star."

She was gone.

"Kat," said Josh, flabbergasted.

"Kat," whispered Teresa, turning towards him.

Both stared into space. The wet wind slapped in their faces.

"She can get you out of here," said Josh.

"That's what she claims. I don't believe a word of it."

Josh was silent.

Teresa kept quiet.

"You've got to risk it," said Josh. He was wide awake once more. His dull gloom had lifted completely. He felt on edge, and, in some weird way, afraid. Very afraid.

"She's lying through her teeth. Huh! Kat Siparti, on the phone. Do you think she was calling from *umaya* or from the real world?"

"You can call back and ask her."

"She can't be the real Kat. The real Kat was born a thousand years ago, just like Gip. She's a descendant, of course. She must be the head of that advertising firm. But do you think *they* travel around *umaya* as well? I thought that was just Gippart's thing. They're always telling us Gippart's the only one that knows how to travel around *umaya*. Or did she manage to steal that ability from Gippart as well, through espionage? Oh, Josh, what should I do?"

Josh put his arms around her and pulled her wet face close to his. "You have to risk it, Teresa! Even if it's just one chance in a thousand, you've got to try and get out of here!"

He saw the tears rolling down her drenched cheeks. "I

won't leave you here alone, Josh. How could I leave you behind?"

He was crying too, without really knowing why. "You *have* to go; we're all given just one chance! Baz grabbed his, and you've got to take yours, and as for me, I…"

Teresa hugged him tightly. The wind tugged wildly at their wet capes. "I'm not going," she whispered in his ear. "Either we go together, or we don't go at all. I'm staying with you."

"You're completely out of your mind. I'm the leader here, remember? And I'm ordering you. Go!"

"I'm the head, and I'm telling you I'm staying." She wiped the tears from her face. "Come on, let's keep going."

"To the Beez?" cried Josh. "To the most terrible place on earth? You *must* be out of your mind!"

"Oh, it'll probably be even worse when we get to the Tembe," said Teresa, smiling grimly. "Come on, we're going home. Just two more stops. The third stop is the end of the line, and then home."

As he walked on, Josh wept. He wept because of the burning pain in his chest, because of a scorching sore throat, and because of an overwhelming feeling of loneliness. He didn't really know why he was crying, and he didn't know why he couldn't stop. When he finally calmed down, he felt strangely at peace and cleansed. Not strong. And yet indomitable, in some slight, weak kind of way.

And in the night, when they had retreated into a thicket of dense thorns to get some rest, he didn't go to sleep. He stayed awake until Teresa had dropped off into a fitful slumber. Then he woke Jericho, and dragged her drowsy, unwilling body into the wet, windy night. Lucide soundlessly rose too, and followed them. The panther stole along behind him.

"Wazzamatter?" asked Jericho sleepily, rubbing her eyes.

"We must leave," whispered Josh. "That way Teresa can phone Kat and go home."

Jericho yawned. "But why does that mean I can't get any sleep?" She finally opened her eyes and glared at him with unmistakable venom. But he paid no attention.

"She doesn't want to leave us in the lurch here, and that's why *we* have to leave *her*."

"Oh," said Jericho sullenly, sleepwalking.

They stumbled on until they collapsed in the shelter of some tall pine trees, where they fell into a shivery, restless sleep.

15
Josh Alone

The day looked quite different when you were alone. Alone except for your dead sister and her silent guardian. The day seemed more impersonal, somewhat malignant, acrimonious and threatening. But then again, it was yours alone. Your enemy, your friend. Yours to tame.

When Josh woke, he lay there uncomfortably stretched out for a while longer. He noticed his mind was strangely clear. He felt a gnawing hunger. He was stiff, cold and tired – but also determined and resolute. "It's the right thing to do, isn't it?" he muttered, sitting up.

It certainly was the right thing to do. It wasn't something that happened all that often, but this morning he was truly proud of himself. He had saved Teresa by sacrificing himself. He stretched, hopped up and down a bit, rolled up his blanket and blessed the morning, which was dry and windy and white. The clouds were still scudding across the sky against a bright white backdrop. The sun was probably brushing her hair somewhere. *Soon,* thought Josh, humming to himself, *the sun will come out. And if it refuses to come out on its own, I'll* make *it come out, using my eyes. Enough's enough.*

He made a list of his supplies. Four nasty, icy carrots, two wrinkly apples and a handful of almonds among his dirty underwear. His trusty little sword – that gave him a good, warm feeling. Money: a purse with about thirty coins. He had no idea what they were worth. A little pile of well-thumbed forms, three of which he had filled in neatly. *Gippart Associates' Instruction Manual*, a bit damp, strangely enough. His supply of picklocks and metal hooks. Kauri's book. Five toffees somewhat gritty, which he wolfed down then and there – or, rather, three for himself and two for Jericho. A handful of bird whistles. It was hard to remain optimistic.

"We've got to find ourselves some food, Jerrie," he said to Jericho's right eye, the only one peering out of her blanket-cocoon. She sucked noisily on her toffee.

"Bacon!" she said. "Eggs and bacon. And beer. I feel like a beer."

"Beer?"

She sat up. "Josh," she said, "this has got to stop. I don't want to sleep out in the open any more. And I want to have proper food. It can't go on like this."

Her eyes were paler and fiercer than yesterday. He noticed worriedly that her hair seemed to be a lighter colour as well. There was that prickly feeling again, the one that he sometimes got when he looked at her. That faint flesh-creeping feeling in his stomach, at the back of his neck.

Annoyed, she combed her fingers through her hair. "Insects! Leaves! Dirt! That isn't what I came back for!"

It occurred to Josh that she'd been sulking since yesterday afternoon. "When we reach the Tembe things will be a lot better, I expect," he said to reassure her. "And back home is definitely a *lot* better. If you come home with me, Jerrie, you'll have the best food you've ever tasted. Pizza, and fish and chips, and ice cream. And you'll sleep under a feather duvet, and you can watch TV, and play video games. You won't believe your eyes. You've never had anything like that, have you?"

"Hmm," said Jericho. She stood up and shook out her

blanket, rolled it up and shoved it in Baz's backpack. Shivering, she wrapped herself in her oilcloth cape. He could tell she was cold. Maam Sagal's clothes were flimsier than the dress he'd stolen for her in Tsumir.

"I don't want to come with you," she suddenly burst out. "I want *you* to stay *here*." Before he knew it, she had drawn her sword, lunged and thrust the point against his chest.

"What are you doing? Put it away!"

"Only if you'll say we're staying here." Spitefully, she pressed the point of her sword in a little deeper.

"Ouch!" shouted Josh, losing his temper. "Have you gone mad? Stop it!"

Jericho said nothing, pressed deeper.

Josh felt the sword prick his skin. Something warm and wet soaked the inside of his shirt. "I'm bleeding, idiot! Stop it!"

"Say it!"

"Ouch!" yelled Josh.

Abruptly she pulled her sword back and hurled it into the leaves behind her. "I've had enough!" she cried, and leapt on top of Josh, knocking over his backpack and spilling all its contents. She grabbed him by the collar. "I've really, *really* had enough! For days and days I've been obediently going along with whatever Teresa's decided, and what you and Baz decided, and now everything's ruined and you and I are the only ones left, and now it's my turn! You've had your chance, and now I want to have mine! It's November already, and *I'm* going to be in charge for the next eleven days. What I say goes, and what I say is this: we're going to rob and steal and have a good time!"

Her eyes drilled into his, her nose was squashed against his and her sour breath steamed up his dirty face. Her eyes glittered maliciously. He pushed her off him hard, one hand pressed to his chest, where it stung. "Nothing's ruined yet! We're on our way to the Tembe and we're getting very close. Jerrie, I promised you..."

"You promised," she said, icily calm, "that you'd do whatever I wanted once Baz and Teresa were safe. Don't you remember? You didn't want to leave them in the lurch."

"I said 'home first', and then I'll do what you want."

"Home!" she cried. "You don't understand at all, do you! *What* is that, home!"

Josh stared straight ahead. It did seem doubtful. Was it still possible to go home? He tried to find the words. "Jericho … we've got to try. My mother … Mo." He suddenly realized what it was that was so important. "Jericho! I want you to come and meet Mo, because, you know, she's *your* mother too!"

The fierce light in Jericho's eyes dimmed immediately. She sat down on the forest floor, deflated. "Yes." She looked at him earnestly. "How is she, anyway? Does she ever get upset? I mean…"

"She's OK." What could he tell her? "She's often really tied up with her work. She can really blow her top, but she's funny too, sometimes. She's a little forgetful." None of this was what he really wanted to say. "But she's really stupid when it comes to men. They're divorced, you know, and now she's got that total idiot Edwin. He drinks like a fish and acts as if he's really somebody, but the worst thing is that he's *constantly* on my back. He thinks I'm a bit slow, sort of, and he wants me to be different, but whatever I do, it's never good enough for him, and then he starts making idiotic jokes and I get so mad!"

"So he isn't our dad? Actually, you *can* be a bit slow, sometimes."

"Our dad's name is Pete. He lives down the road, and I stay with him quite often, and that's great. We'll do something together – go to a late movie, rent a video, or recently, for instance, we went fishing. We left at the crack of dawn." He thought it over. "But I don't know if you'd like him that much. He's my dad in one sense, but in another sense he isn't. And

I'm not allowed near that other side of him. If I call in for no reason, he'll just tell me to go away. He won't have it."

Jericho was listening open-mouthed. "Are you rich?"

Josh laughed. "Oh, no." He corrected himself. "In your eyes, I suppose you'd say we are. We have a lot of stuff they didn't have in your time. And loads of things to eat. But for our time, we aren't rich. We aren't poor either. Just ordinary."

"How big is your house? And where is it?"

"On Pepys Avenue," said Josh, and Jericho started giggling.

"What's so funny?"

"Samuel Pepys. Did they really name a street after him? He used to live in a grand house near us. A street named after him! He would have liked that. Is it a fancy street?"

"Well, no," he admitted. "Not at all, in fact. Oh, come on, come with me!" Josh pressed her. "You'd be living with a real family. Isn't that what you've always wanted? With you it will be much more fun. You can sleep in my room. We'll sneak out and watch TV in the night. And go to school together," he went on excitedly. *Ha, wouldn't that make them sit up! Hey, meet my twin sister; yes, we only just found her.* "And Mo asked me about you just the other day – she really wanted to know how you were!"

"Really?"

"You *must* come! I'll show you the local swimming pool, and you can come with me to judo, oh, and the Imax Cinema – you won't believe your eyes!"

Jericho was sunk deep in thought. And Josh just kept babbling on about the fun to be had at birthday parties and Christmas; he got quite carried away about video games, DVDs, sailing weekends, about paintballing and laser tag and finally – hesitantly to start with, then more and more enthusiastically and shamelessly – about stealing things. And then he told her about school and about staying at home, reading sci-fi comics on the sofa, with a bag of crisps and a glass of Coke.

She was all ears. He was sure he'd already won. All of *umaya* had vanished in his torrent of words, the lovely descriptions of home, home, home. His excellent, very own home. Jericho had a faraway look in her eyes, swept up in his dreams.

But then, slowly, she shook her head. "It wouldn't work. I'm bad. Can you really see me going off to school, and doing my homework, like a good girl?"

"But we'd have adventures together, and when we're a little older we can go hang-gliding, and travel around the world, and visit the North Pole!"

But Jericho shook her head again. "I'm telling you, I'm bad. I'd probably set the train on fire, and rob the captain, and push someone out of the hot-air balloon."

"But you haven't done any of that so far, here, have you?"

"I've been trying to be on my best behaviour up until now, little brother! And my best behaviour has finally run out. That's what I'm trying to tell you. Now that it's just the two of us, I want to do what *I'd* like. It's only fair."

Josh was so disappointed that he lost his temper. "Right, but I'm telling you we're going to the Tembe no matter what you say, Jericho! And after that, we're going home! And if you don't want to come, so what, I'll go by myself, and you can just go to hell!"

"You idiot!" Her face had gone bright red. "Three hundred and fifty years I've done everything in my power to reach the stupid fool, and now he's telling me I can just go to hell! Spoilt brat! Spineless jellyfish!"

"Did I ask you to haunt me, stupid? As if it's *my* fault that you never got born! Stop pretending you're the boss."

All the colour drained from Jericho's face. She seemed to freeze for an instant. Then she flew at his throat, a raging fury. Zizi fluttered off in alarm, disappearing high up in a tree. They slammed to the ground, her hands round his throat. Josh punched at her face blindly, thrusting his knee into her stomach, while she for her part spat in his face and, screaming at the top of her voice, jabbed him with her knees whenever she had the chance. The little panther ran around them in a frenzy, yelping and nipping at them. They rolled back and forth in the wet leaves, seething with anger. Oddly enough, it came as a relief to Josh finally to be able to lay into his sister. As he pounded and kicked, the fear he had of her, deep down, evaporated. Under his fists she was no longer a ghost, but an ordinary warm, skinny body – nothing creepy or supernatural about her. From that day on, he would never again have that hair-raising feeling when he looked at her; in the course of this fight she really became his sister for the first time. Not exactly of the sweetness and light variety, of course. She was a pig-headed, hard-hearted pain in the neck.

The fight raged on in deadly seriousness until their arm muscles started trembling and they were aching all over. They panted heavily in each other's faces, slack-jawed, as they gradually came to their senses. And they began to feel that they were acting like idiots. And that they were being watched.

Which was, indeed, the case. An unfamiliar, cold male voice reached their ears. "Well, well. A little tiff, children?"

Jericho gave Josh one last kick in the ribs before turning round.

A smartly dressed gentleman was standing behind them. He was dressed in a flowing brown cloak and a brown bejewelled hat. Below his cloak he wore white stockings. Josh was still flat on his back, trying to catch his breath. Jericho was speechless too, for once.

"Brother and sister, are you? Come, come, young man, surely it is most ungentlemanly to treat your sister in this fashion! Please get up, dust yourselves down and introduce yourselves to me properly." He ran his left little finger over his neat black moustache.

Josh stood up, dazed, and brushed off his clothes. "Joshua and Jericho Cope," he muttered, bowing, "at your service."

The gentleman grinned. "Good manners, that's what I like

to see. Count Beraz Imendoni of Siparti, at your service likewise." He sat down on a tree trunk and crossed his knees elegantly. "Are you just passing through, dear children?"

"Siparti? Is your name Siparti?"

"But of course. This is Siparti country. The Sipartis of the House of Beez, in case our most august name means anything to you."

Josh and Jericho exchanged a warning glance. *Don't give anything away.*

"Well now!" said the gentleman cheerfully, taking a small flask from under his cloak. "And where is your journey taking you, if I may be so bold? A little sip for you, young man?"

"No, thank you," said Josh. "We are travelling east. Nowhere in particular, actually."

"Travelling students? Orphans?"

"No," said Josh, but Jericho broke in. "We were part of a trading expedition, but we lost the others."

"Aha," said the Count. "So I take it you are all by yourselves?" Before they could answer him he got to his feet. "But in that case I should very much like to invite you to come with us. Children alone on the road, that can be very perilous in these times!"

"Oh, we're armed," said Jericho.

The Count smiled. "Come, come. Not so bold. Accompanying me may very well be in your best interest. Do forgive me for being so impertinent, but I just overheard this young lady declaring that she is bad. I do not exactly know what she meant by that, but we too are … bad. And we have found it to be quite profitable. Perhaps you will consider helping us in our work for a while? I assure you, you will be generously recompensed."

"What kind of work?" asked Josh, who was trying, with some effort, to remain polite.

"Trade," said the Count. "We deal in healing, in hope, in life. A most sought-after product, in these pestilential times."

"How is it that you are bad, then?" asked Jericho.

"Well, how are *you* bad?" asked the Count.

"Well, I just like being bad. I like doing wicked things – causing accidents and stealing, things like that."

"Just so," said the Count. "And we, in turn, gravitate to those places where the most bad things happen. Disease, war, catastrophes – that is where our trade flourishes. Come, why don't you just come along and have a look for yourself at what we do, anyway?" He gestured invitingly to somewhere down the hill.

"Where would we be going?" asked Josh.

"To the capital of the House of Beez's domain. Ancient Bat Zavinam, currently, alas, in the throes of a great disaster. Won't you follow me? My servants are waiting."

"We're *not* going with him," Josh whispered in Jericho's ear. "Come on, let's get our things and run in the opposite direction."

Jericho shook her head. "I'm going to do what *I* decide. It's my turn, remember? And I wouldn't mind having a look at that disaster of his. I'm still angry with you, you know." She pinched his ear nastily.

"But don't you see? He's one of the lethal Beez! He's trying to get us to come with him to that filthy city of his!"

"But we have to go that way anyway, Josh, don't we? Bat Zavinam, BZ, aren't those the initials on Mono's map? W, BZ!"

He was taken aback by her words. It was true, it had clean escaped him. Jericho was already skipping off down the hill, tauntingly humming to herself. Suddenly the bushes behind them came to life. It was Lucide, getting to his feet to follow Jericho, as usual. Looking neither right nor left, he walked straight past the Count, on the heels of his ward. The little panther trotted along behind him.

The Count looked at Josh in alarm. "Who is *that*?"

"That's Lucide" Josh grinned. "Our guardian."

"I was not aware that you had an adult servant with you."

"He isn't our servant. He's our guardian. He never leaves our side."

The Count nervously watched Lucide's tall form stride off. "Well, in that case…" he muttered, hurrying downhill to his servants.

"Fine," Josh said out loud to himself, "but *I'm* not going."

He heard shouting down below. Orders were given. He heard the crack of a whip, a horse neighing and the clatter of hooves. A little later all was quiet. Had they really gone, then? Were Jericho and Lucide really mad enough to go with that man? Josh packed his things into his backpack, Jericho's sword too; his own sword he strapped around his waist. When he got to the foot of the hill he found the road deserted. There were fresh hoof prints. Freshly disturbed sand.

For a while he stood wavering on the quiet road. Then he put on his oilcloth cape again. He pulled the hood down low over his face and turned right, walking east. He really had no choice. To reach the Tembe, he would have to pass through the city of the Beez, whether he liked it or not – to find Beez's *Book of the Cat*, if for no other reason.

He trudged down the road deep in thought, head down, the rugged wind at his back. Strange, how quickly it had all happened. The day before yesterday – Baz. Yesterday – Teresa. Today – Jericho. And here he was, suddenly, traversing the treacherous dream-world all by himself. He was all too aware of the danger of travelling in *umaya* as a single, unaccompanied boy. Even more so in this particularly foreboding *umaya* of the Black Death. But he wasn't scared; it was as if this was the way it was meant to be; as if he had seen it coming. Last night, before they'd left Teresa, he had cried so much that he didn't have any tears or any fear left. It wasn't recklessness; far from it, his heart quaked at the thought of the Beez, and of the terrors that lay ahead on the road to the Tembe. But he was ready to go where he had to go. He felt clearer about that than ever.

As he tramped on in Maam Sagal's leather boots, he decided

he would try to find Jericho again. She could be nasty and aggressive, and a horrible pain in the neck, but she *was* his sister. He was, above all, responsible for her. Wending his solitary way, thinking it over, it finally dawned on him. Baz and Teresa were both capable of finding their way home from *umaya* by themselves, but Jericho wasn't. She was the only one who couldn't get away. And – he suddenly saw it clearly – it wasn't because she was bad; that wasn't it at all. It was Lucide. As long as she had Lucide guarding her, there simply was no way for her to cross from *umaya* into real time. As far as Lucide was concerned, it was bad enough that Jericho had managed to cross from death into *umaya*. There was no way he'd let her cross another border, into real time.

He could have kicked himself for having gone on and on so ecstatically about home. Praising all the things she'd never have! Josh sighed, and a wave of pity swept over him. Did she know? She wasn't stupid. Surely she must have realized by now that she hadn't actually broken through into the real world? Was *that* why she kept whining about staying here? But was that what she really wanted, haunting the *umaya* world for good, flitting from one terrifying dream-time to the next, always looking for excitement, constantly plunging deeper into the forbidden worlds of violence and terror? With Lucide always on her heels?

What else was there for her? Well, the world of her companions, for a start, still beckoned. The Still-Dead-Children – her comrades. The sinister world of icy hands, shrill voices, glowing eyes. "Jericho!" he said out loud, miserably. *If I were in her shoes,* he thought, *I would go back, and then give getting born again another try. But what if it never worked?* he asked himself earnestly. *What if you finally had to admit to yourself that you'd never lead a normal human life, with loving parents, brothers and sisters, and, later on, children of your own?*

Another thought occurred to him as he walked on, an ice-cold thought that pressed on him like a stone. Would Jericho try to keep him in *umaya* by force, against his will? When they finally reached the exit, would she, if it came down to it, would she try to hold him back and rob him of his only chance of returning home? So wouldn't it be sensible to stay out of her way? But at that point his mind went blank – he couldn't bear the thought of it. *Maybe,* he thought, grinning in spite of himself, *maybe something went wrong when I changed us around, you into me and myself into you. Or maybe when Maam Sagal stirred us up in her melting pot. Maybe a bit of you remained inside me, and the other way around. That's why I can't even conceive of abandoning you. Didn't Siparti say that we're bonded to one another? OK, I'm going to look for you.*

First, hunger. Reluctantly he chewed on an apple and a carrot. It didn't help much. It was cold, hard food that scarcely filled him up. Next, the creeps. Not the quite understandable fear of what-on-earth-am-I-doing-here-all-alone? But a more profound dread, a dawning that something definitely wasn't right. A scorched tree: well, there could be an explanation for that. A mound of earth with a rough wooden cross on top? Fine. But what about row upon row of messy graves lining the road? And great swathes of burnt forest, with just one or two charred trunks sticking up gloomily here and there? And what about back there, away from the road, a thing he wished he hadn't seen: a mess of rags hanging from a rope, flapping in the wind. Rags? He quickly turned away, before he could catch sight of a rotting skull, claw-like hands. No, there was something sinister going on, on the road to Bat Zavinam.

Yet he kept walking. He was glad to have Zizi perched on his shoulder again. Crossing a wooden bridge over a broad river, he refused to look down, so that he wouldn't catch sight of any swollen corpses in the water. And when he passed a village that had been reduced to ashes, he hurriedly walked on, keeping his eyes fixed on his boots, muttering, "Ah, that must be W. I'm getting close." He daydreamed about diving into a swimming pool full of crisps, blotting out the empty ache in his stomach and the dismal surroundings.

And then, all of a sudden, he was there. He was standing on top of a hill, somewhat dizzy and nauseous, looking down on Bat Zavinam. It wasn't a very large city. He sized up the dark settlement at a glance. Smoke curled from some of the sagging, semi-demolished houses. From here it looked as though the city had just been bombed. Fire, clouds of black smoke; everything was blackened and in ruins. What in God's name had happened here? "The Beez," he answered himself with a sigh, surveying his surroundings: the barren moors, the smoking middens, the mass graves.

He scanned the horizon. Could he see the edge of *umaya* from here? Darkness? Over there, behind the mountain range far to the east, he thought he detected clouds. A thunderstorm approaching, no doubt. How appropriate.

Down by the city walls he spotted something moving: a small band of people dressed in grey rags, led by an armed man in a khaki uniform, was dejectedly making for a field of crosses in the distance. He saw they were carrying a stretcher with something wrapped in sheets on it. Now he also noticed the sentries posted at the gate. They were all dressed in the same uniform: khaki tunic, wide belt, khaki trousers and boots. He wondered how he could continue without being spotted. He wished he could do this like in the Traders' Trial, when he could have just nipped in there, found Jericho, stolen Beez's *Book of the Cat* and slipped away again unnoticed, all preferably in less than an hour. He watched the funeral procession stop at the burial ground, and then start wending its way back to the city again. Josh didn't wait any longer. He dashed across the crackling black heath. Making a wide circle, he ended up on the road some way behind the funeral procession. Alternately sprinting and walking, he soon caught up with it; and, without the guard having noticed him, he joined the mourners. Nobody took any notice of him. He pulled his hood even lower over his face and trudged along at the same sad pace, head bowed, hands folded. He pushed Zizi gently into her usual spot under the hood, by his neck. And so he entered the city of Beez unnoticed. Bat Zavinam. The most horrible place on earth.

As the procession shuffled its way up foul-smelling streets, Josh darted into a side alley. He turned a few corners, and was alone. He was standing in front of a dilapidated shed with closed shutters. In front of the door, which was swinging and banging in the wind, a little boy of about five was sitting drawing pictures in the sand. Josh knelt down next to him.

"What's your name?"

The child did not look up. "Sbran," he mumbled, or something like that.

"Tell me," asked Josh, "do you know where I could find a library around here?"

The little boy now peered up at him, his head cocked to one side. "Libba-what?"

"I'm looking for a book. Do you know anyone here that has any books?"

"Oh, books," said the boy, going on with his drawing, "they don't really want books, they want blood. Are you looking for blood?"

"No, a book. Beez's *Book of the Cat.*"

"Beez," the boy echoed. "To buy blood, you have to go to the House of Beez, on Blood Square. Have you come down with it yet? I haven't. My mother bought blood for me."

"Do they have books," Josh insisted, "in the House of Beez?"

But then the door was flung open, and a dishevelled woman stepped outside. She swept the little boy up in her arms, whisked back inside and barred the door with a loud thud.

Josh walked on, looking around for someone who might be more helpful. There weren't many people out in the street. He couldn't blame them for staying indoors. From alleyways and cellar holes all around came the sound of moaning and weeping. There were piles of smouldering rubbish everywhere, and the smoke mingled with other smells into a strange, disgusting stench that pervaded the entire city. He pulled his shirt collar over his nose, gagging. Even though he needed information desperately, he couldn't bring himself to question a group of weeping people pushing a wagon loaded with a number of bodies wrapped in sheets. He also wisely kept his distance from a greyish form lying huddled on the ground groaning. Bat Zavinam reminded him of one those awful computer games in which you find yourself walking through a bombed-out, radioactive American city, a ghetto of high blank walls pocked with bullet holes, being spied on by bloodthirsty aliens and horribly deformed mutants. The only thing missing was the graffiti. When they got back, he would tell Max to add this *umaya* to his out-of-bounds list. This was no place for children.

As he cautiously sneaked past a pile of burning rags, someone grabbed him. Josh found himself staring into the grimacing face of a man in khaki uniform, who, oddly, was wearing a loop of rough rope around his neck, like some poor excuse for a tie. "Hey, young bullock! Need any blood? Any *good* stuff?"

"I don't need anything," Josh shuddered, trying to pull himself free. But the man tightened his grip, and waved at a body lying motionless among the rubbish in the street. "Do you want to end up like him, then? How much do you need? I'm much cheaper than the folks in Blood Square."

"Books," Josh blurted out, turning his face away from the man's alcoholic breath. "I'm looking for a book!"

"Books," sneered the man. "Are you a student? A stranger? Tell me, are you by yourself?"

"No," said Josh. "I live here, actually. My father is waiting over there." He waved his hand behind him.

The man pulled him a little closer. Josh stared reluctantly

into his strange red eyes. Even his irises seemed dark red. "Rich folks, eh? So then go and fetch me your father, all right?"

"No," stammered Josh, "thank you. I have to go."

But the man did not release him. "You're not from around here, are you? Come along with me – there's a feast. I'll give you some good stuff, to make you forget all the misery. We'll have a drink! I'll get you an emerald too, to protect you from the pestilence! Come on!" He dragged Josh with him, down the street.

"No, thank you," Josh protested. He tried to wriggle free, but the man had a fist of iron.

"Don't be such a misery," he growled "We adore unaccompanied children here!" Revealing his strong, pointy yellow teeth, he began to laugh: a rough, spitting laugh that turned into a coughing fit, right in Josh's face. Josh wiped the disgusting spit off his chin, nauseated. He didn't know what to do. He simply didn't have the strength to pull himself free. But suddenly he remembered something he had learnt from Teresa. *Create a distraction. Sow confusion. Sidetrack your opponent with words.* "Why," he quickly asked, "why are you wearing that piece of rope around your neck?"

"Piece of rope?" The man felt at his neck. "Aha, that piece of rope! The necktie! But my boy, every self-respecting man of work wears a necktie! Don't you know that?" And he threw his head back and guffawed uproariously. It was lucky the fellow was drunk, because that was about the limit of Josh's diversionary talents; but it was just enough to tug himself free and make himself scarce. Hoping for the best he darted into one alley and out of another, down reeking passageways, across a square where a great bonfire was raging, and then he ducked into a quiet street. There he finally stopped to catch his breath. He was panting painfully, trying to breathe in as little of the greasy, filthy air as possible. How to evade those lurking men in uniform, who seemed to be so fond of unaccompanied children?

He backed into a space between two wooden houses and felt around in his backpack for the compass. It was heartening to feel its smooth shape in his hand. He brought it up to his lips and whispered, "Jericho." The beam brightly shot sideways, to the right, and then went out. Josh smiled, satisfied. Cautiously he continued in that direction, taking care never to cross one of the uniformed men's path. At the end of one of the smoke-filled streets a crumbly set of steps led upwards. He started hauling himself up them, but suddenly felt so faint and sick that he had to sit down. Was it the nasty smell? Fear? *I'm hungry,* he suddenly thought; *I'm famished.* And once he realized that that was what it was, he almost started crying. He'd hardly eaten a thing since Maam Sagal's porridge yesterday afternoon, and in this whole rotten *umaya* there was never anything good to eat, and he was so terribly hungry! He shrugged off his hood and let Zizi fly away. "Go and look for something for yourself," he whispered.

The little bird flew off, higher and higher, grateful for the fresh air high above the pestilential smog of Bat Zavinam. Alone and abandoned, Josh leaned against the sooty wall and closed his eyes. Oh, it was all very well to be noble and brave, but it didn't do you a blind bit of good if you ended up dying of hunger. He began to drift into sleep.

But after only a few moments, he felt sharp little claws digging into his knee. Groggily he opened his eyes. "Ah, Zizi." His eyes drooped shut again. But – what was it? Zizi hadn't just returned for nothing; she had something in her beak: a grubby piece of bread.

"Zizi!"

He took it carefully from her beak, and she let go of it without protest. He nibbled at it cautiously. It had a faintly sweet taste, and was as dry and crunchy as a mouthful of sawdust, but it was food. He tickled his little parrot under her chin. Who ever heard of a bird feeding its master? "Good girl," he said. "Zizi, you're the best."

She fluttered away and soon returned with another piece of bread. He ate it, chuckling, and she left again to fetch another mouthful. But on her fourth foray she ate it herself, perched on his knee. Then Josh got up and hauled himself stiffly up the steps, and when he reached the top he surveyed the scene again. Where had Zizi found the bread? It must be near by. She fluttered ahead of him, staying low to the ground, and he followed her, a bright spot of colour in all the bleakness. When they came to a square, he hung back. Zizi flew across the square, making directly for two ragged figures in an alleyway across from him, sitting with their backs to a drab building of heavy grey stone. They had a large basket in between them. Josh followed Zizi as unobtrusively as he could, staying close to the houses. He didn't feel like walking openly across the square, for all to see. There were too many people about. Some of these, laden with crocks and bottles, were lined up by a door beside the arched entry of the forbidding building. Men in uniform strolled about, alone or in groups. Luckily he managed to sneak to the alley without being seen. The two old people looked up, startled, but then waved him over, hissing, "Young gentleman! Rich young master! Here's what you're looking for!"

In the basket Josh saw a quantity of grey buns, including two that had obviously already been nibbled at considerably. The rolls didn't look very tasty, but it was food. Real food. He took one out of the basket, blew the dust off it and cautiously took a bite.

"It's good," whispered the man. "Healthy, normal food, none of that Beez blood! Rich young master, eat!"

It was as dry as dirt and it tasted of ashes, but it was sweet enough, and when you got to the middle you bit into something sticky and good. He handed the man a coin and ate two more.

"Eat, eat," said the man, happily playing with the coin Josh had given him.

Josh sat down in the shade of the alleyway with his rolls, and from there he assessed the situation. Another customer came up: a skinny, hollow-eyed man clutching a jug under his arm. "Three, please," he whispered.

"May God bless you," murmured the old ones, handing him his rolls and accepting his coin. "God bless you, wealthy Zubad! But it is shocking to see even you, Zubad, knocking at the Blood Palace's door for blood – shame on you!"

"What do you want?" answered the man. "Must I lose my only remaining two children to the plague as well, after it has already taken my wife and my youngest ones? Do I have any choice, old man? We have been delivered body and soul to the blasphemous Beez, and the laws of God don't mean anything any more!"

As he finished his last roll, Josh stared after the man. Now he understood what it was, this ominous building against which he was sitting. And he also understood what that queue of slumped people was waiting for. Zizi had led him to the evil heart of this city. The House of Beez: the Palace of Blood.

Just as he was uneasily wondering if that was where he should go looking for the Book of Beez, inside this creepy bastion, he heard a sound on the other side of the wall. A desolate sound that made his flesh crawl. He listened, stunned. Turning round, he saw a grate low down in the wall. He tried to peer inside. There was a bright light burning in there.

"Don't, little master," the bread vendor beside him hissed. "Don't look! Don't look at the virgins! In God's name!"

Josh jumped back as if he'd been stung. "What's in there? Who is that crying?"

But the old ones shook their heads and refused to answer. Another customer came shuffling up, and another one, and only after they were done with those did the old men turn their wrinkled faces towards him. "You must be a stranger here, wealthy young master. How did you manage to get so lost as to end up in our doomed city of Bat Zavinam? Don't you know that the black plague and the Beez have us in thrall?"

"I came looking for my sister. We were on a trade mission. I lost her."

"Trade mission? Here, in Bat Zavinam?" They shook their heads and stared at him incredulously. Through the thick wall at their backs came the sound of weeping again.

"Special assignment," said Josh. The stifling air here robbed him of the will to mislead or tell lies, and he decided he might as well put all his cards on the table. "To the Tembe. The road to the Tembe passes through here."

The bread vendors were quiet for a moment, and then suddenly started conferring with each other as if Josh's news had shocked them deeply. They asked more questions. He'd lost his sister? Here, in Bat Zavinam? And he was all alone, unaccompanied? On his way to the Tembe? They pulled him closer and started whispering to his face. Josh heard more than he wished to hear. About how nobody who entered the city was ever allowed to leave. That he had fallen into a trap, since the Beez were always on the lookout for virgins like him, and that after hunting them down they locked them up in the Palace of Blood. That he was in grave danger, he as well as that sister of his that he'd lost, and who must already have been caught. But they also told him about the resistance, the partisans who made the occasional foray to free the virgins; and that – but this was a secret, mind – even this very day perhaps there might be an assault on the Palace of Blood. And if he was armed, then he, scion of a noble line, fierce crusader in the name of the Holy Tembe, he would be more than welcome to join their party.

Flustered, Josh crumbled a piece of bread between his fingers. The old ones gazed at him expectantly. They touched his sleeve with their gnarled hands, and lowered their voices even more. "But beware of the Beez, little master – a virgin such as yourself. Take care that they don't catch you! Keep an eye out for their traps! And above all, avoid Desastre!"

He nodded, baffled. Desastre? "Well, thank you very much," he said. He realized that they had just given him valuable information. The problem was that, with all their gloomy advice and dire warnings, they had also managed to quash the last scrap of courage remaining to him. As he staggered to his feet, the city's stench took his breath away again. "Don't you have anything, an antidote, for that foul smell?" he complained, pulling his collar back up over his nose.

The vendors' grey faces fell. "No," they growled, "there is nothing, except for God's mercy. And if anyone tells you to open up your flesh to let the bad blood out, and that you should drink some fresh blood and eat some warm organ meat, don't you believe them, master! Do not trust the Beez!"

Without another word Josh slunk off down the alley. No, thank you very much, he'd never get that stuff down his throat. He'd always found that sort of food disgusting anyway: liver, kidneys, black pudding. A horrible image flashed before his eyes, of screaming pigs hung up on meat hooks, being bled to death for the sake of some pricey quack remedy for the plague.

By the time he sat down in a sheltered spot a little further on to think it over, he had in fact already reached a decision. He scratched Zizi beneath her beak. Getting out of here wasn't an option any more. He was constantly inhaling the contagious plague stench, and there was nothing to protect him from it. The Beez – who, he decided, must be blind drunk if they weren't completely mad – were out in force, intent on hunting children like him. He didn't stand a chance. But, oddly enough, it didn't really make any difference. He'd simply have to do whatever there was to do. Like a pre-programmed robot. He had to find Jericho, and find the book. Whether he was scared or not, whether he knew it was hopeless or not – it didn't matter. He wondered vaguely if it was because he was on his own now that he seemed to be so calm and determined. He felt himself to be quite a different boy from the one who'd left Damara twelve days ago. He played around a bit with Zizi, fiddled with his compass, and kept an ear cocked for the noises surrounding him. He didn't have to wait very long.

As the bells rang for four o'clock a group of men and women began gathering near the back door of the Palace of Blood, in an unobtrusive spot. There were about twenty of them; all were masked and armed. Josh thought he recognized one of the bread vendors, but wasn't sure. Cautiously he crept nearer. They were fiddling with the locks. It took them ages, but they managed it in the end: one by one, they slipped inside.

Josh was the last one in.

He followed them at a respectful distance, his sword at his side. Zizi, her feet planted firmly on his shoulder, seemed considerably more ready to do battle than he was. Halfway down the first passageway he stubbed his toe on something solid. He only just managed to stifle a cry, and quickly stepped over it without looking at it too closely. He knew, of course, that it was a dead body, a dead Beez sentry probably, and he didn't have the least desire to know what he looked like. Gratefully he let the stealthy group ahead of him lead the way. They crept along the passageway, then down some stairs to the right, ending up in another passageway, lit this time. Suddenly there was a shout from the front of the group. In a flash they all had their backs pressed up against the wall. Josh dived into an alcove. He too heard it now: footsteps approaching.

It was the jailer. A heavy-set, unsuspecting man waddling down the passageway, whistling through his teeth. He was jiggling an enormous key ring hanging from his belt. Josh recognized the red eyes, the rope around his neck, and the khaki uniform of the Beez. A couple of partisans at the front moved out as if by pre-arrangement, and Josh saw it all happening in front of his eyes: the men plunging their daggers at the same time into the jailer's soft flesh. There was a gargling sound, the body gave a few strange jerks, and the face twisted into a sallow grimace. Josh turned his head away, revolted. He remembered. He didn't like fighting.

The body of the Beez was dragged off and hidden in a dark corner. Something green came rolling out of the flabby mouth, and one of the partisans jumped forward in a flash to pick it up and pop it into his own mouth. *"Ugh!"* cried Josh. But then it dawned on him that it must have been an emerald, and hadn't he heard that if you held an emerald in your mouth, the plague wouldn't touch you?

The gang conferred briefly. Josh heard them drawing their swords. He glanced at his own weapon. Apparently the resistance fighters were expecting a battle. Perhaps he'd better start thinking along those lines himself. Could he do it? When he was much younger, he had often played at fighting with his friends, and Baz had given him a few demonstrations when he'd started taking martial arts classes – but how would he do here, in a real sword fight? *An ambush, that's the way,* he thought. *You lie low and then you leap out without warning, and next thing you know* – pow! – *the enemy is eliminated.* He sighed and pressed his lips together. He just couldn't see himself doing it.

Ahead of him the group split up. One band went left, a smaller group turned right. Josh hesitated for a moment. But when he heard the pitiful wails coming from the passageways to his right, he padded quietly after the smaller group. A little further on they turned into a wide passageway, brightly lit with flares and oil lamps, and lined on either side with metal doors. The partisans in the lead began trying to fit keys in the lock of the first door with much noise and ado. Josh held his breath. But it seemed to take an agonizingly long time before the lock clicked and the iron door swung open. It stayed strangely quiet inside the liberated cell. It wasn't until the partisans went inside that there were exclamations of relief and joy, and Josh heard someone bursting into tears. Then they came shuffling out, hand in hand: four teenagers of about fourteen or fifteen. Jericho wasn't among them. They started talking to their rescuers in low voices, and he heard them refer to someone named Desastre. They were led away by a couple of friendly partisans, back along the passageway, out of the dungeon. The rest started silently on the next locked door.

Josh sighed impatiently. It was all too obvious that the conspirators weren't very experienced at picking locks. They also seemed to be too relaxed, these fighters. A group of them were standing near him, chattering away as if they were at home, the fools. He was only listening to them with half an ear, more concerned with how the work on the locks was progressing.

"But there have never been as many as there were today," said one. "They're flocking to Desastre like flies to honey! Thank God we got here in time."

"I saw her myself," said another one eagerly. "She walked through the streets like a noblewoman, so beautiful and radiant! Some of the children believe she is a special guardian angel, and search high and low to find her. Desastre!"

"Perhaps she really is an angel," a third one remarked. "Isn't it possible that God might be calling his children gently to him, through her? Couldn't he be sending us a new sign, in the blackest days of our despair? And was her coming today not foretold by the appearance of the comet? Comets usually announce the coming of salvation, do they not?"

"Well, *I* think she's just another of the Beez's tricks," said the first one, upon which the third said softly, "Not everything is the Beez's fault. Do not assign blame too hastily, friend! Who *hasn't* been unjustly accused of this pestilence, this chastisement from God? We have heard rumours that southerners were responsible, or people of a different faith, or else that it was the nobles, or the poor. But I believe that it is God's hand we see at work here – it is nothing if not God punishing us for our greed!"

"But then how do you explain that it's the poor and the

children who are most at risk, sister?" the first one objected, but at that moment the next lock finally gave way, and a second group of children streamed out, blinking in the light. But no Jericho. Josh took a deep breath. Then he put his backpack down on the ground, took out his own hooks and picklocks from home, walked over to the door nearest to him and began jamming his sturdiest hook into it. There was a sudden complete silence; he felt everyone's eyes on him. But he doggedly went on with his work, picking the lock; and then, hey presto – *click* – open! He grinned broadly. He *knew* his picklocks would come in handy some day. *Expedition leader, eh?* Looking neither left nor right he pushed the door open a crack, then immediately went on to the next lock. He noticed that he was now flanked on either side by two of the partisans.

"Who are you, helper? How did you get here? Speak!"

"Look! Didn't I tell you? It's the young nobleman on a pilgrimage to the Tembe!"

Josh glanced at him. It was one of the old bread vendors. He seemed much sprightlier than this morning, and Josh smiled at him, then bent over the job at hand once more. The two resistance fighters stayed at his side without saying another word. He picked open four locks, one after another, and it wasn't until he was done that he looked back over his shoulder: there were, all told, about twelve children back there now, standing uncertainly in the corridor. But no sign of Jericho yet. Conscientiously he bent down again to begin on the next lock, on a large door in the far wall of the corridor, but one of his companions stayed his hand.

"Young nobleman! Leave that door shut! That is the Satan cell!"

"Satan cell?"

"That's where they keep the Black Box, with all their devilish books of spells and poisons, evil charms and torture instruments! The Satan cell, home of the dead and dying!"

Josh froze. "Is their *Book of the Cat* in there too, by any chance?" he asked, breathless. "Do you know? Beez's *Book of the Cat*?"

The man crossed himself and nodded. "Their Satan's bible, I suppose you mean! Aye, master, but the Black Box harbours the plague, and everything inside it likewise." When Josh stubbornly started working on the lock anyway, the man cried angrily, "Leave that door shut! To open that dungeon is certain death!"

"All right," sighed Josh. He followed the man over to the other side of the corridor, and quickly picked the last few locks. The freed virgins milled about for a minute or so, pale and fearful, before rushing off as fast as their legs would carry them.

"My sister isn't here," Josh said.

The man laid his hand on Josh's head. "Oh, how awful. May God rest her soul."

Josh looked at him annoyed. "So she must be somewhere else. Where else are they kept?"

"No other place. The butchering takes place down here, in the butchery next to the cells. Come along now, in God's holy name, before the alarm is sounded!"

Josh refused to budge. The book was there, right behind him, but unattainable – and Jericho, where could she be, for crying out loud? The horrible word "butchery" evoked a gruesome image he quickly tried to blot out: Jericho as a bloody corpse, chopped into little pieces. His knees started to buckle when it finally dawned on him whose blood it was that the Beez sold as medicine to ward off the plague.

He might have stood there all night frozen in horror, but his escort shook him out of his petrifying thoughts, and they followed the small band of comrades back up the torch-lit passageways. A few paces past the dead prison guard's corpse, they stopped in their tracks. Josh, still numb from his terrifying discovery, hadn't been paying attention. But ahead of them, a menacing phalanx of the Beez was barring the passageway. They were drunk; but that only made them even more bloodthirsty.

They had red eyes, the rope tie pulled aggressively tight around the necks. And all five of them brandished really wicked-looking swords. It was true that Josh had tried to prepare himself for such an eventuality by analysing his own will to fight – but it had never occurred to him that it wasn't *his* sword that was the problem. The problem was the *other* men's swords.

With a pounding heart Josh pulled the sword out from under his cloak. It gleamed in the light of the passageway. The Beez across from them, having recovered from the shock, had arranged themselves in fighting formation. "Thieves!" the first Beez shouted loudly. "If there's anything men of business absolutely loathe, it's thieves, isn't that right, partners?"

The other Beez jeered and crowded closer, their swords raised.

"Since you seem to be so keen on having the Beez's merchandise, thieves, you're going to have to pay for it!" And with that, their leader lunged at them.

His attack was met by the two foremost comrades. Josh did a quick count. Five Beez against eight of their own. Seven and a half, if you counted him as a half. Next to him one of the partisans gave a harsh shout. It was the old bread vendor, Josh saw, but almost unrecognizable now, ferociously aggressive. One of the Beez managed to wound one of the partisans. The man collapsed, his hand clutching his side. The bread vendor leapt forward fiercely, and for a moment Josh thought he was going to throw himself straight on to the Beez's sword. But the old man slashed at it with such force that it flew out of the Beez's hand; the Beez hadn't expected such resistance from somewhere in the rear. *"Ye-esss!"* cheered Josh.

His foolish shout attracted the attention of another Beez, one who'd remained out of the fray until now. *"Virgin!"* he roared. "Blood!" and lunged at Josh.

Josh was so horrified, he forgot to parry. He just stared at his attacker, stupefied, with his arm down at his side. It wasn't until the Beez grabbed him by the hair that he suddenly remembered his sword. He slashed it awkwardly at the Beez's arm and by sheer beginner's luck – bull's-eye! His keen little sword found its mark, and he immediately pulled it back again, ready to deal another blow. The Beez hadn't counted on this pipsqueak being armed. Roaring bloody murder, he let go of Josh's hair, and, after a horrified glance at the blood pouring from his arm, switched his sword to his other hand. Josh saw him raise it high, and his instinct took over; quick as a flash, he ducked behind the broad frame of a fighter beside him, and the sword landed with a dull clang on the stone floor, just missing his foot. Josh zigzagged through the battling throng, dodging the hacking, slashing swords and cudgels, and just managed to slip by unharmed every time. Then, suddenly, he found himself face to face with a heavily panting Beez wielding a broken sword. When he noticed Josh, his face contorted and he rushed at him, hacking his jagged blade at him wildly. But Josh jumped backwards and then delivered it such a thwack that it flew laughably wide of the mark. With a growl, the Beez came at him again. There was no room for Josh to slip past him. He couldn't go backwards either: that way was blocked by a pair of fiercely duelling warriors. He started to sweat. He held out his sword in front of him, vaguely remembering something about needing to protect your upper body. The Beez was whirling his half-sword around like a madman, getting closer by the second. He looked like a crazed windmill on the rampage, ready to slice Josh into neat little slivers. Josh feinted with his sword, waving it around in front of him, but that hardly seemed to deter the snarling Beez.

As he stared in horror at those red eyes closing in on him, Josh suddenly saw a flash of green. The broken sword clanged to the ground, and the Beez clutched at his burning face with two hands; a little green bird with a hard, razor-sharp beak seemed to have selected his eyes for target practice. The Beez gave an agonized roar. Josh snatched up the broken sword and ran past him, crying with relief. *"Zizi!"* She must have been waiting for her chance, the brilliant creature! He raced down the passageway until it turned a corner; there he glanced back. Floundering in the middle of the passage, the Beez was attempting to ward off his vicious little attacker. He was the only thing still standing there. A few bodies were sprawled on the floor around him. The distant sound of clashing swords came echoing down the corridor. The battle, which seemed to be fizzling out, was taking place somewhere else, out of sight. Suddenly, abruptly, Josh was alone again.

In a dark corner of the Palace of Blood's beer cellar, hiding behind some large kegs, he examined his wounds. He discovered he had a few nasty cuts. He had no idea how he had got them. He bandaged his upper arm as best he could with a clean sock from his backpack.

"It wasn't that bad," Josh told himself, to give himself courage, "for my first time, anyway."

He sank backwards, sucking his throbbing hand.

He had learnt one important thing: he wasn't a fighter. He wondered if it was something to be ashamed of. But why should it be? He had proved himself a more than valuable asset tonight, when he'd opened all those dungeon doors in record time. "You probably need all sorts in times of war," he muttered to himself. The ferocious warriors that stand their ground, and the nimble specialists. The brawn and the brains; the compassionate and keen-eyed beside the merciless. He wished he could discuss this with Baz. Baz was an honest-to-goodness fighter, no two ways about it. But Josh was different, and he thought he'd like to keep it that way. Being a thief and an observer wasn't such a bad combination either.

He waited until he thought everything had completely quietened down again, and then he waited a little longer still. And then, sweet as a butterfly, Zizi came fluttering back to him.

"Oh Zizi, you hero!" cried Josh. "You saved my life *again*!"

He petted her a long time, and, cooing with delight, she let herself be tickled and fondled. Then he took out his compass, and asked it to show him where Jericho was. It pointed straight up! Did that mean she was still around here? He hauled on his backpack again, keeping his sword in his hand.

"Come on, Zizi, let's investigate! Are you coming? Let's go and look for Jericho!"

He crept along the passageways like a practised thief. His tensed body knew exactly what to do. Duck down low, scurry back instinctively at every sound, sneak up a flight of stairs, noiselessly push a door open and slip through on tiptoe. His agile limbs obeyed him like a dream. When he got home, would he become awkward and clumsy again?

The Palace of Blood appeared to be deserted. Apart from a few oil lamps flickering here and there, there was no light. Most of the halls he walked through were empty and dirty. It wasn't until he entered a deserted scullery that finally, to his relief, he heard somewhere far above his head the faint sound of music. Ah, so they did live here then, the Beez. Were they having a feast? Were they drinking blood from golden goblets, or did they just drink it straight from the throats of their victims? Would he find Jericho up there tied and bound, lifeless, sucked dry?

Higher and higher he climbed, until he came to a hall lit by many torches and lamps. Yes, this must be it. He heard voices and shrill music to his right. A door flew open, and two inebriated Beez tumbled out. They scrambled to their feet and tottered past Josh, singing out of tune. From within came an unearthly racket. Cautiously, very, very cautiously, Josh sidled up to the door and put his right eye to the crack. Just as he thought – a drunken orgy. Clusters of drinking, dancing and drooling Beez. But no children.

Taking a deep breath, he crossed the hallway. More closed doors. And sounds coming from inside. His heart pounding, he pushed open the door slightly.

He could hardly believe his eyes. This room glittered and smelled as if the plague and the Palace of Blood did not exist. There was a blazing fire in the hearth, and golden dishes on the table, and platters of roast chicken, crusty breads and lemons. He saw savoury pies, a dish of honeycomb, and blue glass bottles filled with what looked like delicious drinks. Seated around the table were several elegantly dressed ladies and gentlemen deep in conversation. Josh felt just like the Little Match Girl peering in from the cold. Had he accidentally landed in a different *umaya*?

No. Because there she was. It was unbelievable. His ears began to burn. *What the…?* She was sitting at the far end of the table with a goblet in her hand. She was wearing a gown of dark red velvet and brocade. It had such wide sleeves that they trailed over the table and down to the ground. When she moved, the pearls sewn on her gown shimmered. She seemed twice as tall as she'd been that morning. That was partly because of her ornately styled hair, piled on top of her head and studded with pearls and rubies. He barely recognized her. She seemed several years older, as if in the past few hours she had blossomed into a young lady. She seemed flushed with a kind of malicious overconfidence, drinking noisily from her goblet as a richly dressed young man on her left leaned over to her, smiling. And on her right sat the Count himself. The treacherous Count Beraz Imendoni of Siparti. He patted her bejewelled hand and asked her genially, "Wouldn't you be willing to fetch some more, my dear?"

Jericho tossed her head back and said snootily, "Some more of that pie, first. With lots of honey, Zomiran." The young man nodded and went to do her bidding.

Jericho the queen of the hive! Promoted in half a day from stray waif to lady-in-chief! And he'd imagined her imprisoned or, worse, fallen into the clutches of child-murderers and butchers!

Jericho drained her goblet and then rudely banged it down on the table. And she spotted Josh.

"Ho!" she said loudly. Then turned her icy gaze away again.

For a moment Josh thought she was going to pretend she hadn't seen him. But as he crouched there paralysed, peeping round the door, Jericho got up, a rustling whirlwind of velvet and fur, her jewels glittering.

"Now then, my lord. I think I shall stretch my legs. I'll have that piece of pie later."

The Count got to his feet, but she waved at him to sit down. "I'll be back in an hour or so."

Josh scurried away from the door, down the hall, into the darkness of the stairwell, and down the steps, until he found himself on a faintly lit landing. There he waited for her. And there she came, gliding along like a queen. A delicious flowery smell preceded her. Without seeming to be in any hurry, she made straight for the stairwell. Humming, rustling and fragrant, she descended the steps towards him. On the landing she stood still. Again she coldly looked him up and down. No hello, no sign of recognition or surprise. Absent-mindedly she stroked the blood-coral necklace circling her white, powdered neck, and stared into the light of the oil lamp. Then she turned her pale eyes on him.

"Well?" she said coolly. "So you're here too?"

"Jericho!" exclaimed Josh, bewildered. He didn't understand. "Have you lost your mind? I thought you'd been murdered! Don't you know that these people here drink children's blood?"

She grinned at him, baring her sharp little canines. But she didn't reply.

"Well, are you coming or not? Let's get out of here."

She sighed, and played with the pearls on her gown. "And sleep outside again? And go hungry?"

"Do you really want to stay here, then, with those butchers? It wouldn't surprise me at all if they had brought the plague here deliberately, so they could make a killing with their filthy blood potions!"

"And they haven't done badly either. I've never eaten so well in my life."

Josh pursed his lips. "Why didn't they kill you, anyway?"

"Well, because they need me, naturally," said Jericho icily. "I lure the children here for them. They call me Desastre. The bad-luck star."

"You… It's *you*?" he gasped.

She stared at him without blinking. God, how pale and transparent her eyes were!

"*You're* Desastre? Jericho, do you know what they do to those children? Jericho! What have you done?"

"Of course I know. They slaughter them, and then they sell off their blood and their organs."

"And you're collaborating in this? You're a part of it!"

It was over. His skin blistered with disgust. She was no sister of his. He wanted nothing to do with her. As he recoiled from her, she held out her hand.

"Josh…"

But he turned his back on her and raced down the stairs, as if there was a ghost after him.

16
The Deep Valleys of the Night

At first he just wandered blindly through the Palace of Blood. He trudged down some stairs, landed in a hall cupboard and collapsed on the floor in there. When he started feeling chilly, he ventured out into the corridor again. He trailed his sword along the walls. It cut a deep groove in the plaster, until it occurred to him that he was leaving an all too obvious trail. In a storeroom he found sausages hanging from the rafters, and racks laden with pastries and pies, but all he stole was some bread and a piece of hard cheese. This made him thirsty, so he peered into all the jugs until he found one he was sure didn't contain anything gruesome. He left the empty jug in the middle of the floor. Then he carved the words *Gip Siparti was here* into the wall in big letters. *There, let them wonder about that a while,* he thought to himself. *I am the ghost of the Palace of Blood. I am the shadow that plunders your cupboards. Catch me if you can.*

Almost unconsciously he found himself back down in the dungeon. He shuddered, but he knew exactly what he was going to do. He was going to break into the Satan cell and steal the Black Box without touching it. And then make his escape. Without Jericho.

His resolve made him both cold and alert. So much the better. It was much more dangerous down here than upstairs. At one point he had to hide from a Beez guard patrol stamping past him, deep in conversation. Another time he had to run to avoid lighter footsteps. He huddled in the dust beneath a low stone vault with his heart pounding – as if he was more terrified of those soft footsteps than of the marching boots.

Then he started to recognize where he was. With his back pressed against the wall, sword at the ready, he slipped down familiar steps. Yes. He found himself in the brightly lit passageway again near the back door, where the fight with the Beez had taken place. A broken sword hilt still lay on the ground, abandoned after the battle. He could hardly believe that he had been right there, in the midst of the fray. Now it was as quiet as the grave. Cautiously he retraced his steps of a few hours earlier, when, blinking in the flickering light of the oil lamps, he had shadowed the partisans down corridors. A little later he recognized the wide, brightly lit corridor with the prison cells. There, at the far end, was his objective. He took a deep breath, touched Zizi's claws, and walked into the corridor, making straight for the Satan cell.

He had covered only half the distance when he heard the stomping boots of the patrol approaching. Of course. He should have expected it. He clicked his tongue and looked around, annoyed. What should he do? There wasn't time to go back. There were no side passages. As the footsteps grew louder and louder, he took the only option left to him: he darted into the closest empty cell, pulling the door to behind him, leaving it slightly ajar. Just in the nick of time. The Beez thundered into the corridor. The ground trembled under their thumping feet, and his limbs were shaken along with it.

Unintelligible orders were shouted. Then someone barked, "About-*turn*!" And off they went again, marching in step.

Josh breathed a quiet sigh of relief. Would they stay away long enough for him to pick the lock of the Satan cell? He stuck his head very cautiously round the door. And withdrew it just as swiftly. There now was a Beez guard posted in front of the Satan cell, his hand resting heavily on the hilt of his sword.

Quiet as a mouse, Josh retreated to the back of the cell and sank down on a pile of straw. As long as he didn't make any noise, he'd be safe. He sighed. There was nothing for it but to wait. To wait, mute and motionless. Like a rabbit in its hole.

So he resigned himself to the inevitable. If he must wait, he might as well make himself as comfortable as possible. As he tried to take his blanket noiselessly out of his backpack, he felt dear little claws digging into his shoulder. A tickly head butted his ear. He pressed his lips to Zizi's little body. "Well, old girl. We're in the soup again."

Zizi's company was more than welcome. He was tired and stiff, and what was worse, he was starting to feel hungry again. For a long time he sat staring into the deepening gloom. Wondering if he would ever get out of there, he fell asleep.

His sleep was shallow and restless, and plagued by frightening dreams. Dreams full of grumbling, quarrelsome voices. "Well, *you* left *me* in the lurch too, you know. You always have." "Now it's *my* turn. Fair is fair." "You *promised*!" "Did you really think you could hide from me?" He was startled out of his sleep by shuffling and whispering outside his cell, but then heard nothing more, and fell asleep again.

The night passed this way, between waking and dreaming, until he finally woke up properly. For one dizzy moment he didn't know where he was. Then it hit him all at once: the pale light of dawn shining in through a grid; his sore throat, headache, and thirst.

With a sigh he closed his eyes again. Anxiously, he tried to identify the sounds around him. He heard rustling, creaking noises he couldn't quite place. Smelled new smells. Manure? What time had he landed in now? *Please let it be a happy time,* he prayed, *a safe time*; but then he changed his mind. If it was before the Beez had arrived in Bat Zavinam, then he was lost. Because then Beez's *Book of the Cat* wouldn't be here yet either. He rubbed his forehead and wondered if he would make it through the day. He felt full of flu. Seriously full of flu.

He nearly succumbed to self-pity. All alone, scared, in grave danger, and now sick as well – it wasn't fair, to be laid low by the flu as well, on top of all his other troubles! But before he could start really wallowing in despair, Zizi began tugging at his hair. Startled, he opened his eyes wide and shook himself. Sick or healthy, he had to get moving. *Remember, Siparti,* he told himself firmly. *Nothing's lost yet! Come on, Siparti!* He clenched his teeth and stood up.

The initial signs were good. Today his cell looked more like a storeroom than a dungeon. All around him there were piles of goods: chests, baskets, some spears, shields marked with the initials BS. He coughed into his fist and cautiously peered round the door. Other cells were wide open as well. Stranger still, out in the corridor, rummaging about in untidy piles of straw and hay, were several goats. Yet not everything was different. To his right, in the wall at the end of the corridor, was the same heavy metal door as there had been yesterday. The door to the Satan cell. And this time there was no sentry.

Josh listened keenly for the early-morning stirrings of the palace. He was fairly sure now that the Beez must already have taken it over. But he could hear nothing particularly alarming. No marching boots. No sound of other captives. Not even the sound of a girl coming to ask her brother for forgiveness. Where might she be today, anyway? Was she still sleeping snugly in a warm, soft bed, that child-killer? He shrugged his shoulders. It didn't matter to him where she was. He had decided yesterday on a course of action, and he was determined to stick to his plan today, no matter how ill and lonely he might feel. Rubbing his sore throat, he got out his picklocks and hooks. He slung the backpack over his shoulder, picked up his sword, put on his cape and stole out of the chamber, making for the Satan cell.

Once he stood in front of it, he noticed that his hands were shaking. He glanced anxiously back over his shoulder, saw nothing but the innocent goats, and then stared at the door in front of him again. It looked menacing, somehow. It was as if there, on the other side of the door, something terrible must be lurking, something that knew he was standing here: that was waiting for him. Could that be true? He thought he could smell something – the stench of decay – from behind the door. Yet something was also telling him in no uncertain terms that he had to go inside.

That message came through so clearly that without further ado he stuck a prong into the lock and began poking and twisting. *I wish I had an emerald,* he thought to himself glumly, but then the lock clicked, and the heavy door swung slowly inwards.

He stepped over the threshold, kicked the door shut behind him, and then leaned against it, breathing heavily. As his eyes became used to the darkness, they began to make out some shapes: racks against the walls and, in the middle of the floor, a square chest. He didn't notice any corpses, although it did smell very bad. And there certainly weren't any living, breathing soldiers in there. Burying his nose in his sleeve, he crept cautiously towards the chest.

It was black, and an insignia was painted on it: a noose, and inside it a red eye. This was clearly it. The plague-infested Black Box. Shuddering, he crouched down in front of it and stuck his best picklock into the lock, prodding and twisting. Suddenly he froze. He'd heard something. For one terrifying moment he thought the sound was coming from the box. But then he realized that there was something alive in that room somewhere – something, or someone, very gingerly moving towards him. He stood up and peered with watering eyes into the shifting shadows. Of course there must be something there. Something guarding the box. A poisonous snake, perhaps? Tarantulas? Or a victim of the Black Death, in a state of advanced decay?

He took a few steps backwards and bumped into the door. Confusing lights danced before his eyes. The pounding of his heart made seeing and hearing nearly impossible. He was about to give up, to turn round and run from this horrible darkness, when something latched itself firmly on to his ankle.

He tugged his foot loose and jumped aside. It was coming at him again, relentless – the sound of something dragging over the floor. He heard himself groan, as if he couldn't stop himself. He raised his hand to his gaping mouth, bumped into one of the racks, and something crashed to the ground. That seemed to make the thing crawling towards him pause. Josh shrank a bit more, and suddenly he had a better view of the thing on the floor.

And instantly such a shudder of relief ran through him that his legs failed him and he sat down on the ground. *"Jericho!"*

He saw her ghostly pale face light up. "Hey! How could you tell?"

She sounded irritated, not at all amused. He was too upset to respond. He was shaking so badly that he had to hug himself with his arms. He gasped for air, forced himself to take long deep breaths. It wasn't until he'd finally managed to calm himself down a bit that Jericho snapped, "I don't feel the least bit sorry for you. I felt lousy too, when I was on my own. Oh well, just take that book out of the box and let's get away from here. I've been waiting here for you for ages." She stood up, pale in the shadowy light, almost luminescent.

Josh was still trembling. "You almost gave me a heart attack! What are you doing here?"

"Waiting for you, of course. Weren't you listening?"

"For me?"

"Yes, for who else? I didn't know where you'd gone, but I did know that you'd have to come here eventually, of course. And didn't you just hear me say that I feel lousy without you?"

"Huh! So then you go and scare the living daylights out of me!"

"You deserved it. Because you never go along with what *I* want, not even when it's my turn. So now we're even. Shall we go?"

Josh coughed painfully, then got up and walked over to the chest. His indignation flared up again. "Jericho, you don't *see*, do you? You make me sick! What you did, that just wasn't right. I'll never, *ever* forgive you for helping those children get killed."

"But they weren't killed, were they? You set them free."

Josh shook his head gloomily, making scratches in the side of the black chest with his metal spike.

"Listen," said Jericho. "I know what it is to be dead, and it really wouldn't have been such a bad thing for those children. But look, time has run backwards again. I'm here with you now. So you can just stop your whining. Besides, without me you'll never get out of here alive. I know my way around this palace now, and I've stolen the key to the front door for you. Either we go together, or we don't go at all. Come on, hurry up, get that chest open!"

He didn't know what to do. He desperately wanted to get it into her thick head that it was truly over between the two of them, that she could go to hell for all he cared. On the other hand, her presence did comfort him. It was almost good to have someone to squabble with, here, in the very heart of the nightmare.

"Yeah, easy for you to say," he said. "That rotten chest is full of germs too. I don't much feel like getting infected with the plague."

She scratched her neck thoughtfully and then looked him straight in the eye. "Let me open it then. I don't care about that." As if needing to atone for something, she knelt down beside the chest.

"That's really stupid. It's just swarming with the plague in here!"

"Pooh, that doesn't worry me. Remember, I've seen 1665."

Josh forgot he didn't really want to talk to her any more. "So, what was 1665 then?"

"Don't you people remember anything any more? In 1665 just about the whole of London snuffed it. It's true! It was a terrible catastrophe, because it was so crowded at the time, with workers swarming to the city from everywhere. It was bursting at the seams with people from all over the world, and there was so much to do and to see – the most exciting playhouses, and paintings and intrigues – and then the plague came! And I was so furious to be missing all the fun because of being ill all the time. In the end I was so fed up, I just upped and left. Whoosh! Within an hour I was dead."

"Oh – did you die of the plague?" Josh asked, somewhat doubtfully. She did have a waxen pallor about her, and her face was drawn. Still, she didn't look anything like someone who'd died of the plague.

"Well, you have to die of *something*. It wasn't that bad; it was pretty quick. But of course I co-operated. One-two-three-out!"

"Yesterday we were around 1385," said Josh, who was beginning to forget about his anger. "So it must be thirty-five years before that now, around 1350. Do you know anything about that time?"

"That surgeon, he told me something about how the plague started. I wanted to know all about it, so that I could die as quickly as possible. So I kept asking him about it – nearly drove him mad. Come to think of it, he did tell me it was in about 1348 that the Black Death first appeared in Europe. That time, I think, it killed off about a third of the population."

Uncertainly, Josh handed her his tools. "So if you've already had the plague once – can you get it again?"

"Well," said Jericho, starting to poke one of the picklocks into the lock any old way, "I'm not really sure. But it doesn't matter."

"It *does* matter," retorted Josh, grabbing her hand. "Besides, you don't know what you're doing. Here, let me do it. I'm breathing those germs anyway." He pulled his collar over his nose and bent over the lock. "But what *does* help to protect against it then? Do you know?"

"Nothing really helps. It spreads so quickly. Well, making sure the air is nice and fresh, that might help a little. You purify the air by burning camphor and sulphur, and you have to make sure to burn all your rubbish straight away. But that's no good to us – it stinks to high heaven in here."

"But what do the Beez do to protect themselves?"

Jericho snorted. "Their 'stuff', and drink the blood of virgins, of course. And other than that, they take the same precautions as everyone else. Not eating fruits and greasy food, and no cream, and not taking a bath, and vinegar for your nose, and enjoying drinking lots of white wine, and having fun. But surely they've discovered a cure for it in your time?"

"I don't think it exists any more, in our time. But I don't really know anything about it. Why should I?"

"Well, it would have been useful to know what medicine they used in your time. In our time there was nothing that worked. And the Beez are fools as far as that goes too. The only thing that will save us is to get out of here."

The lock clicked open. Josh lifted up the heavy lid. An unpleasant stench wafted out of the chest; he buried his nose deeper in his collar. He peered inside, his heart pounding. Was that all? No skulls, no deadly scorpions. Only some stinking earthenware jugs, bottles, baskets, dried herbs, and a pile of shredded documents. He hastily looked through it all. Everything was dirty and sticky. At the very bottom he found the front and back covers of a book, with just a couple of pages left inside. But to his great delight the stained front cover had the gold symbol of a cat wearing a crown. He quickly leafed through the few ragged pieces of paper remaining. They were mainly pages of strange anatomical illustrations and illegible texts, but among them he finally stumbled on – thank goodness! – a little card: a sketched map of a river, a tunnel through a mountain, and an inn. And, underneath:

"Downhill at Ferry, and seven miles through the darkness; in the sun to Hiuja, and there drink to me."

He let the lid bang shut, wiped his sticky fingers on his clothes and picked up his backpack and sword. Without paying any attention to Jericho, he stalked out of the Satan cell, letting Zizi perch on his head. But when, halfway down the corridor, he looked back over his shoulder, he saw that she was just behind him, her eyes darting around nervously.

"Why, you're scared, aren't you!" He said it scornfully, but she came right out and admitted it.

"Of course I am. You know what the Beez do to children. Here, in this time, I'm no longer Desastre, I'm just a nice juicy virgin full of fresh blood."

He grinned wickedly. "Didn't you just say it wouldn't be that bad, for those children?"

"Being dead, I meant. The rest is pretty nasty, of course."

Josh saw a familiar dark shadow waiting for them at the corner. Next to him sat the little panther. "You're forgetting Lucide. We don't have to worry, with him at our side."

"I wouldn't count on it."

"But, I mean, he's our protector and guardian! He'd never allow us to … to cross over to the other world, would he? Isn't that why he's constantly watching you?"

"You're wrong. He couldn't care less if we die or not. The only thing he's concerned about is that it should happen the right way. Don't you see? Whether someone beheads us or drowns us, or strangles us or chops us into pieces, that's all right with him, because we'll have died an ordinary death. But woe betide us if we try and get across the border and back again on our own. Woe betide me if I try and get my friends to come over sometime! *That's* when Lucide steps in, and only too eagerly, the meddling fool."

Josh couldn't believe his ears. "Do you think he'd really just stand by coldly and watch if the Beez came and carved us up?"

"Certainly. He might come fluttering over with a serene

smile on his face, and maybe he'll even lovingly hold your hand. Reassuring, isn't it!"

"We'll just have to be extra careful. Break out of here. Simple enough."

It isn't easy to stay cool and vigilant when you're feeling so ill. Especially if you find out that the danger you're in is far greater than you'd feared. After sneaking around stealthily for what seemed like ages, they eavesdropped on a conversation between two servants in the Palace of Blood scullery, and discovered what year they were now in:

"I'm getting out of here as soon as I get the chance!"

"Hey, careful, the chief might hear you. Just think of all the gold we're going to earn instead, you coward."

"Gold! What good is gold to me if I'm dead?"

"Have you forgotten we have a remedy that's foolproof? A medicine that will make us rich as kings, richer than all the Siparti houses combined? Have you no trading sense at all? You must grab the opportunity by the horns! Now is the moment for it!"

The other servant lowered his voice. "That medicine – if what I've heard is true – I wouldn't touch it with a bargepole. I swear."

"Oh, don't make such a fuss. So the occasional scrofulous waif dies. So we ease him out of his suffering. And what of it? One death produces enough medicine to save hundreds of lives."

"Liar. In the time since the Beez arrived here, on All Souls' Day, 1347, exactly one year ago to this day, nine children have already met their fate. It was supposed to be just one, a beggar child, a single one! Next you'll be hunting children like animals!"

"Whose side are you on anyway, you whiner? Do you want me to report you? Shut your big mouth, and help me carry these serving trays inside."

The children hastily retreated into another passageway.

Josh sighed, disheartened. The year was 1348. They had landed right in the middle, in the worst year of the Black Death. Trying to suppress his coughing, he trudged on behind Jericho.

She tripped along lightly once more, wearing the simple red dress Maam Sagal had given her, as if she had never known Desastre's extravagant gowns. Josh wasn't really angry with her any more, even though he still considered what she had done unforgivable. But he felt too ill to get all worked up about it. He was above all incredibly glad that she was here to lead the way, with Lucide and the little panther behind them; glad that they were with him in this hellish den of the Beez, now that he wasn't sure how long he would be able to keep going.

Josh was no longer the leader of the expedition. He tried his hardest, but he was having trouble enough now just keeping his eyes open. When they worked out that the front door key Jericho had stolen yesterday didn't fit the door today, it took him much too long to pick the lock. The sentries marching up and down the hall spotted them almost at once.

"Trespassers!" they barked, and came thundering towards them.

Perhaps they could have talked their way out of it. They might have saved their skins with a fib: that they had just been hired as servants; that they were pages, couriers. But Josh felt too ill to think of something, and Jericho didn't think at all. Instinctively she dived into Baz's backpack, and then in Josh's, for their swords. In a matter of seconds she was brandishing her sword at the Beez, thrusting Josh's sword into his hand, then she lunged at the nearest noose. She stabbed the Beez right in the stomach. He screamed, made a rattling sound in his throat, and sank to his knees. Shaken out of his stupor, Josh now started waving his sword around, and felt it strike home. Hoarsely he yelled, *"Siparti!"* and jabbed the weapon upwards. He felt faint. He coughed, his head was pounding, but he stood his ground.

His battle cry made the Beez pause. "Siparti?"

"Hey, poxy virgin you – you a fan of Siparti's, then?"

Josh took a deep breath and yelled, "Gip Siparti! Gip Siparti! A pox on the Beez!" And he hurled himself at them.

Coarse hands pinned his wrists; loud, snarling voices threatened them. "Gip! It's one of Gip's, by God!" "We've got to tell the boss. Dirty tricks! Gip has made his way in!" "Crush them! Hack them to pieces! What stinking bloody cheek!" "Let's cut off their heads and send them back to Gip!"

If Josh had hoped that the name of Gip Siparti would confuse the Beez, he now realized he'd guessed wrong: Gip's name was adding fuel to the flames. He started kicking and thrashing wildly, until he received such a terrific blow to the head that he tumbled to the ground. Everything went red before his eyes. Suddenly his sword was gone; one moment he'd still been hacking at the air with it, the next it was no longer in his hand. Someone dragged him to his feet and then slammed him back to the ground. He tried to crawl away, but was pulled back by the leg. He heard laughter behind him.

"Take them away," said a cold voice.

"Where to – the dungeon? Or the questioning room?" A clamour of voices broke out.

The commanding voice cut through the din. "To the butchery. Go and fetch the surgeon and his assistants. These brats aren't locals; they won't be missed! The little rats will bleed, and Gip along with them!"

They all pounced on Josh at the same time – at least, that was what it felt like. He was almost torn limb from limb, so eager were they to get their claws into him. Along lengthy passageways, down steps – he knew exactly where they were going. He squeezed his eyes shut against the light of the dungeon. The last door on the right screeched open. He was kicked inside by several Beez boots. Jericho tumbled in after him. The door crashed shut. They were trapped.

Outside, the Beez were laughing and kicking at the bolted door. One of them jeered, "I'm gonna use that pretty little sword of yours to cut out your liver, you little worm! We'll be back soon!" And then all was quiet.

The butchery wasn't a very pleasant place to await the return of the murderers. It was a dingy whitewashed space lit by many oil lamps, with a channel in the floor to drain excess blood. Iron meat hooks hung from the rafters and buckets were lined up underneath. It was very cold in there.

Josh sat for a while with his head between his knees. His courage had deserted him. All his bones ached, a fierce headache and sore throat took his breath away, and he felt completely drained. Their luck had turned – they were now prisoners of the Beez. Prisoners? Lambs to the slaughter, more like, and soon they'd be mincemeat. He just couldn't fathom it, get it through his befuddled, painful head. Jericho, meanwhile, was a bundle of energy. She had jumped to her feet and started examining all the walls, nooks and crannies, running her hands over another metal door. She rattled all the grilles and gratings, but there wasn't a single opening large enough for even a squirrel to get through. Or Zizi for that matter, who had luckily flown off in the nick of time. Eventually Josh joined Jericho in her search. Lucide sat serenely in a corner, as usual, the panther snuggled against him: the only spot around emitting any warmth. But it was a warmth that really couldn't help them now.

When the door was flung open, they froze in alarm. Instinctively they flew into each other's arms. A man wearing a white apron and a kerchief over his mouth and nose cast a quick, businesslike glance inside. Then he came into the room and opened a metal box screwed to a narrow table in the centre. He took out a couple of knives, as well as some other instruments Josh couldn't identify. Seeing the man going about his preparations in such a clinical way made his throat tighten. The man tested the knives with his finger to see if the blades were sharp enough, glanced down at a piece of paper and muttered, "Liver, heart, kidneys – twice – keep the heads separate."

He put the knives back in the box, locking it again conscientiously. "I'll just go for the assistants, and then we can begin," he said cheerfully. "Wait a moment," and he hurried out of the room.

Josh's heart sank when he realized there was no escaping their fate any longer. In less than a minute they would feel the sharp metal cutting into their skin. His knees shook, his stomach contracted and a tremor passed through his entire body. He had held the Beez at bay for one whole day. But that day was now behind him. He was finished!

On an impulse he turned round and sidled over to Lucide, as if Lucide were his mother, and he her terrified little child. He sat down on his lap and buried his face in Lucide's warm chest. Lucide folded his arms around him as if his arms were wings. He whispered into Josh's ear, almost inaudibly, "I cannot help you, my boy. I am so sorry. I cannot do anything for you."

Oh well, it wasn't as if he didn't know that. But it didn't matter. He wasn't at all angry with Lucide about it. He was so deliciously warm and fragrant. Josh closed his eyes and inhaled, deep, comforting breaths. He heard singing – Lucide humming a lullaby. Then he heard Lucide talking softly to him again. "You do know, my boy, don't you…" He seemed to be searching for the right words. "If the very worst should happen, then I will come to you. Then I will stand by you. Do you understand?"

Josh nodded drowsily. He wasn't sure if he really understood. Lucide gently stroked his hair, humming a wordless tune. Everything faded away. The soreness in his head and throat, the exhaustion, the fear. Lucide's power of consolation was so strong that right there, at the most terrifying moment of his life, he'd have dropped off to sleep if Jericho hadn't started tugging his leg.

"Josh, are you mad? We must do something! You're not falling asleep, are you?" There was panic in her voice.

"No…" said Josh. But it would have been such an easy way

out: to fall asleep right now and go to another time, or maybe never wake up again. And it was beginning to look as if he had reached the final chapter – that of never waking up again. Why not just allow himself to slip away gently, rather than having to endure the most terrible agony first? Still, he disengaged himself from Lucide's warm arms, went over to his sister and put his arms around her. She was trembling too, the same as he.

"We have to put up a fight," she said. "We can't just let them slaughter us! Oh, God!"

She screamed because at that moment the door flew open again. The surgeon marched in, followed by two assistants, both dressed in khaki. All three wore a neat rope tie around their necks.

"The boy first," said the surgeon.

"No!" cried Jericho, but before she could throw herself at the surgeon, an assistant had grabbed her.

"What about that fellow?" The other assistant, who was dragging Josh to the table, nodded at Lucide.

"Oh, he's just some kind of deaf and dumb monk," said the surgeon. "He won't interfere. The guards said all he did was look on when they were fighting. Come on now, I haven't got all day."

As the assistant bound Josh to the table, the surgeon, humming to himself, took out his instruments again. "Did you hear Maziva Gorna singing and playing the harp at last night's feast?" he asked his assistant genially over Josh's head. "She was magnificent, didn't you think?"

"Oh, I don't really care for that sort of singing myself," the assistant said, buckling Josh's kicking ankle to the table. "Give *me* the sort of tune you hear in the whorehouse, ha!"

The surgeon chuckled. He cut open the front of Josh's shirt and ran his hand over Josh's skin, pressing the spots where his heart and liver lay, and nodded approvingly. "You're just a horny lecher, you pig!" he said to the assistant. "Let's listen to this boy soprano. Just a squeak, mind, and then you'll shut him up."

I can't feel any pain yet, thought Josh. *I can't feel anything yet. And I'm not going to either. Because this just can't be happening.* Petrified he was – his head drained of all fear. Time stood still. Tense and breathless, he waited for the searing pain that would finish him off.

And then Jericho yelled something. And he heard it, and understood in a flash. He snapped out of his trance.

"Use your eyes!"

It felt like a slap in the face. *Of course!* He stared up at the surgeon, who was looking around at Jericho in surprise, and then Josh really *saw* him – saw his bloodshot blue eyes above the kerchief, saw the wrinkled brow, the bushy eyebrows, the pimple over his nose; and in the interminable second it took him to concentrate on the man with all his might, it suddenly dawned on him that he looked like someone he knew. He looked like the hospital doctor who had once stitched a cut over Josh's eye. What an ordeal that had been: first an injection of anaesthetic deep into the wound, and then a few stitches. The whole time Josh was being worked on, he had stared intently into the doctor's face, and now he recognized that same look of concentration on this man's face. *You're a good man,* he mentally told the surgeon, *you're a good man.* And he saw … a spark of kindness in those bloodshot blue eyes; and he heard the surgeon say in a businesslike voice, "Let's just begin with the alcohol to kill the pain, shall we?"

Josh heard Jericho giggling nervously. The assistants looked at each other nonplussed. *"To kill the pain?"*

"Well, it's going be a nasty cut. Come on, hand me the alcohol. And hurry up about it!"

"But we don't have any of that," said one assistant. "What's the matter with you? Don't you want to have a laugh?"

"A laugh?" The surgeon slapped his forehead. "A laugh? What do you mean? I don't understand… I… What?"

"Keep going," cried Jericho. "Keep it up, Josh!"

Josh gazed at the surgeon, who seemed to be coming to his

senses again. He pulled out his instructions from his apron pocket and stared at the paper in confusion. "First the organs," he read out slowly. "Then the bloodletting. Yes, of course..."

"Well then, why don't you start?" said the assistant standing by Josh's head. "You really fancied it only a moment ago!"

The surgeon frowned. He steeled himself, and raised the knife in the air.

"Right," he said. Josh balled his fists, fought off his headache, and caught his gaze. Ha! He saw that the surgeon trembled slightly, that he was a little confused. As the knife slowly started its descent, he began trembling more and more violently. The surgeon's hand and arm shook and jerked so badly that they missed their mark. The knife came down next to Josh's chest and stuck fast in the table. Jericho cheered. The surgeon looked at the knife, flabbergasted.

"What now?"

"Shame on you!" cried the assistant who was holding Josh. "Did you have too much to drink? You don't deserve this job!"

"No, that isn't it!" cried the surgeon. "This is sorcery!"

"What an excuse," said the assistant. "Shall I take over? Are you feeling sorry for them now?"

"No, of course not," said the surgeon crossly. "Come on!" He pulled the knife angrily out of the wood and held it poised right over Josh's ribcage. "The heart first," he muttered.

Josh saw drops of sweat welling up on the man's nose. Now that he was focusing his entire will on manipulating that butcher, he no longer felt the slightest bit afraid. *I can do it,* he thought to himself, and as he fixed the wavering surgeon with his stare again, he felt a wave of joy. *I can do this!* Again he caused the surgeon's hand to tremble, shake, and then jerk back and forth uncontrollably. The knife flew out of his hand in an unfortunate trajectory, just grazing Josh's temple next to his left eye, before clattering to the ground.

Josh felt the blood oozing from the shallow wound. That knife really was razor-sharp.

The nearest assistant picked it up, cursing. "Let *me* do it!"

Josh gasped in alarm. He couldn't see the assistant, who was standing behind him. Maybe he'd stab him from behind! *I can't use my eyes on both the surgeon and his assistants at the same time,* he thought. *I can't change all three of them. Especially not if they're standing behind me.* His head was pounding dreadfully, and he was having trouble breathing. Painfully he twisted his head to the side and caught a glimpse of the assistant, who seemed a little nervous. He was poised with the knife above Josh's ribcage, but didn't seem to know exactly where to cut.

"Shall I just stick it in there?"

"Certainly not," said the surgeon. "Give it to me, that's a surgeon's job! What on earth do you think you're doing!"

To Josh's relief, the surgeon snatched the knife out of his assistant's hands. But he didn't do anything with it. He just stood there playing with it clumsily. *Come on,* Josh was taunting him mentally, *come over here, and I'll make you trip and fall on to your own knife. Come here, you dirty killer.* But the man didn't budge.

He was badly shaken. "A different plan," he said. "Untie him."

Obediently the assistant loosened Josh's bonds and he sat up, trembling. Breathing deeply, he felt the cut next to his eye with his fingers.

"Hang him up on a meat hook," said the surgeon. "And put a bucket underneath. We'll drain all the blood out first, then work on the organs. I'm not taking any more risks."

"No," said Josh, when the assistant tried to grab hold of him. *"No!"* He thrashed his arms and kicked his legs wildly. The assistant couldn't get a hold on him anywhere.

"Stop kicking, you little brat!" he cried angrily. "What a mess, this morning! Master, come on, help me, I—"

To their alarm the door was flung open and a group of spectators walked in, about to witness their embarrassing bungling. What was supposed to have been an interesting surgical demonstration had degenerated into a wrestling match, in which the victim was making complete fools of his assailants. The captain who entered took it all in at a glance. "What's this, Buzim?" he roared. "Are you letting the boy get the better of you?"

Five other people entered. Three military guards, smartly dressed in the uniform and rope tie, and two others: a hooded lady in a red cloak, and, behind her, a tall figure in a cloak and hat, his face hidden behind a cloth pulled up over his nose, as if to protect himself from the plague.

"Is this what you call efficiency?" said one of the guards. "What time did it start? *Pah!*"

"You must realize that this means disciplinary action, Buzim," said the captain. "They should have been hanging from those meat hooks, cleaned and bled by now!"

Since no one was paying any attention to him, Josh slipped off the table and went to stand next to Jericho. He grabbed her hand. She touched the bloody cut by his eye. He swayed, staying upright with difficulty. But he had to: he had to be on his toes, because it still didn't look too good for them. How would they even begin to defend themselves against this mob? How could he use his eyes on nine hostile, bloodthirsty adults all at the same time?

"Can't you help me?" he whispered in Jericho's ear.

"I can't do what you can do," she hissed. "We'll have to fight. Grab the knife!"

Josh saw that the surgeon had indeed left the knife on the table. The man was standing near it, but not touching it. Perhaps if he inched closer very carefully... But he had missed his chance. The captain turned and made straight for Josh and Jericho. He dragged them over to the visitors.

"Just look at this," he said in an oily voice. "Have you ever seen anything like it? Two identical virgins. What extraordinary potency a pair like this must have, would you not agree?"

"Yes," the surgeon stammered, "that ... that must be it! They aren't normal!"

The captain gave him a withering look and turned to his

audience again, smiling. "We can count ourselves fortunate that the surgical procedure has run into some delay, so that you may now observe for yourselves the unique properties this magnificent purchase offers. I would venture to guess that a potion made from their entrails will surely provide a year's worth of protection, at the very least. Drinking the mixed blood of twins will boost your own life force eightfold. But of course there is also the option of having a little fun with them before proceeding with the slaughter, because a set of virgins of this calibre is most suitable for all kinds of, shall we say, activities – especially since we have both sexes here, to suit any taste! Yours was the highest bid, sir, I believe?"

He turned to the man standing at the end of the row. But the lady was nervously licking her lips. "I'll double my bid," she said in a hoarse voice.

The man at the far end raised a finger in the air.

"You too?" asked the captain. "Then the price now stands at sixteen thousand."

The lady was panting. "Eighteen thousand," she said loudly.

"Your original offer was for the processed carcasses," the captain hastened to clarify. "Now that, happily, they still appear to be intact – so that you are, as it were, purchasing the enjoyment of the slaughter on top of other … pleasures – the price has gone up, naturally. I would say twenty thousand would have to be the very least."

The man at the far end held his finger up again.

Josh's brain was spinning. To be sold – it gave them a chance. But they had to remain alert, on their toes. Even if he was feeling so terribly ill.

The lady held up her hand, and walked up to them. Her chilly, bloodshot eyes glittered from her hood as she looked them over closely, stroking their cheeks with her clammy hand and pinching their arms and legs. Jericho pulled a face and crossed her eyes, as if she were a bit simple, and let some foaming spit drool out of her mouth in the most revolting way.

"Twenty-five," the lady panted.

"Thirty," the man snapped.

The lady wrung her hands, glanced at her rival – and then, with an exclamation of disgust, stormed out of the room, cursing under her breath.

"My congratulations," said the captain. "Well now, Buzim, it seems you have been saved by the skin of your teeth. But I shall still have to report you. Most esteemed patron, do you wish to take them with you as they are? Or would you prefer to have us prepare them for you after all? It will be no trouble, either way!"

But the esteemed patron shook his head. "Will take them the way they are," he said very quietly.

The captain was at his most helpful. "Are you going to take them now?"

The man pulled a heavy purse from beneath his cloak, and counted out almost its entire contents into the captain's hand. "There. Thirty. Please bind their hands. Did they have any possessions with them? That was included in the sale."

"Just a minor misunderstanding, I believe," said the captain. "I'm afraid it wasn't. Standard charge, five hundred more."

The customer flew into a flaming rage. He grabbed the captain by his necktie, pulled him close and snorted into his face. "You foul Beez, you disgust me! Have their belongings sent for, or I'll strangle you with your own tie!" He started pulling the noose tight so that the captain grew purple in the face. He squeaked at one of the assistants, "Their things, quickly!"

The man pushed him away. He leaned heavily against the wall, appraising his acquisition with a sidelong glance.

They looked back at him. "What do you think he's after?" Jericho asked softly. "I won't let him touch me, just you wait."

Josh didn't answer. He stared with increasing anxiety at their buyer. There was something familiar about the man. If he hadn't been feeling so groggy and sick he'd have worked it out by now. But who could he possibly know, here in Bat

Zavinam, in the year 1348, a year he'd never been in before?

Just then, the man briefly turned his face towards him. It lasted just a second, and then he turned his red eyes away again. But it was enough. It hit Josh like a sledgehammer. Of course. It was Spratt.

He whispered his discovery in Jericho's ear. She gasped.

That Spratt! To have followed them all the way to the city of the Beez, the most terrible place on earth – and buy them from the Beez! But to what end? *Ha! The murderer decides to buy us back from other murderers. Is it because he wants the pleasure of the kill for himself? Is that what he is risking his life for?* Well, whatever the case, there it was: Spratt was alone, and unwell, and they'd already beaten him at his game once; their luck had suddenly turned!

When the assistant returned with their backpacks, the captain took it upon himself to tie Josh and Jericho firmly together, and then offered the end of the rope to Spratt with a formal bow. Spratt grunted and stepped outside, dragging the pair along after him. Behind them they heard Lucide getting to his feet to follow them. Their dear, useless shadow.

Spratt led them into a back alley near the east wall, and pushed open a narrow green door. They found themselves standing in the parlour of a small house, where he untied them. Mutely he motioned them to a low bench against a wall, close to the hearth. They sank down on it, and Spratt lowered himself on to a large settle opposite. Josh was more than exhausted. He leaned his back against the wall, eyes shut. Now that the nail-biting tension was over, he felt like weeping. His head, throat and chest ached. He coughed again, a raw, painfully hacking rasp from deep inside. When he wiped his mouth, he noticed his hand had blood on it. No, he hadn't recovered from the terror of the past few days yet.

But Spratt hadn't bought their freedom for nothing. After they had sat there a while opposite each other, coughing and sighing, he opened his red eyes and nodded at them.

"Well now, young Cope."

"Well now, Spratt," replied Jericho. "What do you want with us?"

"Not even a word of thanks," said Spratt bitterly. "Sad, really."

"Thanks a lot," said Jericho. "How much is thirty thousand anyway? Must be quite a lot. How did you get all that money?"

"God!" groaned Spratt, pressing a skeletal hand to his brow. "Shut up, little minx. Joshua Cope, listen to me. As I have told you before, we have to work together. *Umaya* will end up being the death of you too. If it weren't for me, you'd be dead already."

"Nonsense," retorted Jericho. "Josh managed to beat those butchers all by himself, Spratt. We're perfectly able to save ourselves!"

"He looks rather ill to me, though."

"I'm fine now," said Josh, and made himself sit up, coughing. His chest was feeling tighter and tighter, and he was chilled to the bone too, or burning hot, he didn't quite know which. It was as if it wasn't his body any more. Everything felt wrong.

"That's good," whispered Spratt, in all sincerity. "You and I need each other, young man. It's our last chance."

"Don't you want to kill us any more then?" asked Josh.

Instead of answering, Spratt got to his feet and shuffled out of sight. A little later he returned with a tray laden with steaming bowls of soup, bread and beakers of ale. Jericho fell ravenously on the food, and since Josh only wanted to sip the ale in his beaker, she wolfed down his portion as well. Zizi had to fight her for the crumbs. When Jericho was done, she belched rather disgustingly, mouth open wide, and leaned back. "What *do* you want then, Mr thanks-a-lot-Spratt?"

"The same thing you yourselves want. To get out of here. The sooner the better. Get Josh to force open an exit. Using my instruments."

Josh was already beginning to shake his head, but Spratt held up his hand. "Listen, Cope, you have my word: I promise I won't zap you with the highest dose this time. I've already seen that *that* doesn't work. Besides –" He started chortling behind the cloth covering his face, which led to a coughing fit. Haltingly he continued. "Besides, I wouldn't want to risk your splitting in two another time, so that I'd be lumbered with *four* Copes." He took his time recovering from his coughing spell. "The mobile phone. That's the first thing. Have you got it?"

"No," said Josh. "Teresa's got it. And I don't know where she is. She's gone."

"But I have to contact Gippart! They must have come up with some new data by now – absolutely crucial data – for us! You're not lying to me, are you, sonny?"

Josh was too sick and groggy to answer him. Spratt muttered to himself, pressed his hands to his eyes and then gave a deep sigh. "Then I'll just have to do it without their help. That really is too bad. Boy, you listen to me. I am going to have to ask you to work the instrument yourself."

"What? Me?"

Spratt pushed a square electronic box towards him. "I'll give you some numbers. You'll set the dials to those co-ordinates. Then you must use your own judgement to increase the intensity, and tell me what you're feeling as you're doing it. You have to find a certain equilibrium, which is when you suddenly reach a point when you feel yourself detaching from this *umaya* – when you start Sensing the chink in time."

"You mean a gap? Like the one on Trellis? Can you make that happen with this thing?"

Spratt shrugged. "To a certain extent. There does happen to be a weak spot here in Bat Zavinam. You're the one who can crack it open, and thus carve a viable exit. My God, with the nightmare of the Black Death and all its evils, it really does seem as if the gates of hell have been flung open." He wiped his forehead, breathing laboriously for a while. "I am very ill,

Josh. My pills are almost gone. I won't last another two days."

"I want to get out of here too," whispered Josh. "I just feel awful."

"*Umaya* is terribly dangerous," agreed Spratt. "You do look a bit green. We've got to hurry."

"And what about Jerrie?"

Spratt waved at the instrument. "Red dial: six-three-two."

"What about Jericho?" Josh repeated hoarsely. "Will she feel it too?"

"I have no idea what will happen to Jericho. We'll see."

"No," said Josh. "If it puts her in any danger—"

"Listen, kid," said Spratt, "it is quite possible that it's all thanks to you that *umaya* got stuck shut. No, let me finish. It's only a theory. A conjecture by Gippart's head shrink. *Umaya* is, after all, a hallucination. Shut up! It may very well have been your fault! You *owe* it to me to co-operate here!"

Josh could barely follow what he was saying. It was hard enough staying upright, and out of pure wretchedness he gave in. "All right. So what next?"

"The little black dial, on medium. That one, on the left. No, no, the other one… Yes, that one. B."

Listlessly Josh followed a whole series of instructions. Jericho looked on tensely.

"Very good. Now switch on the power. Point that side at your heart. Yes, very good."

Josh's heart began beating a little faster. "That doesn't feel good," he said uneasily.

"Fine, then leave it exactly where it is. Green dial on five-eight-zero. How do you feel now?"

"Sick," groaned Josh. "I can't breathe. Ringing in my ears."

"No unusual kind of pain? Then turn on that green switch, down there."

"I'm feeling very … light. You both look funny to me. You're slowing down. *Ouch!*"

Spratt stared at him. Drops of sweat appeared on his grey

forehead. "Are you OK? Can you keep going?"

Josh panted desperately. "Can't I turn it down? Ouch! Can't I turn that green switch off?"

"No! We're nearly there. Keep going!"

"Ooo-ouch!" came Jericho's voice from far away. "I'm getting so heavy. Josh, turn it off!"

Painfully Josh turned his enormous, foggy head towards her. His burning eyes detected Jericho in the remote distance, as if she were at the far end of a tunnel. He could see right through her. "Jerrie!"

"Turn it off!" She seemed to be stretching out an arm a mile long towards him. Someone grabbed at the instrument. There were cries and a loud scream, and he tumbled off the bench, helpless. He slipped smoothly into a dark, warm lake, happy to be allowed to leave the painful world behind.

Later something warm and wet trickled into his mouth. Most annoying. He weakly tried to push the cup away.

"No, come on, drink," someone insisted.

He opened his eyes. Jericho had her arm round him and was trying to make him drink some tea from a large cup. She was back to her old self again. He saw that even her eyes had lost their unearthly pallor. He leaned back and obediently took a sip. Ouch! His chest felt painfully congested. Everything hurt. It was hard to breathe. "Where's Spratt?"

Jericho giggled maliciously. "He flew away," she said. "I grabbed the instrument, and then I think I aimed it at Spratt by accident. He's so sensitive, isn't he, that one! A scream, and then he just flew off. Whoosh!"

Josh was too ill to give it much thought. "Just like Baz. A chink in time. But why can't we do the same?"

Jericho jerked her head to the right, indicating the corner by the hearth. "Lucide, of course, sticking his nose in as usual. I'm sure he'd have held me back if I had tried slipping away."

Josh felt Lucide sitting there, glowing.

"Well anyway," said Jericho. "At least we're rid of that awful Spratt! And now it's time we really got out of this pest-ridden city. Once we've done that you can rest as much as you like. You really are poorly, aren't you! Well, same here, let me tell you. I could sleep for days. But first we've got to get going. Here, here's a handkerchief – you've got blood on your mouth."

Dabbing the cloth to his lips, Josh tried to stand up. But he couldn't. His whole body started shaking and shivering. His head, throat and chest hurt like mad. Collapsing back on the bench, he was seized by a coughing fit. But even once the hacking had subsided, he still felt he was suffocating. He tried to spit out the disgusting slime that kept bubbling up from his throat and tightening chest, but it was no good. He just wasn't getting enough air. In panic he crumpled up the soiled, blood-stained handkerchief in his fist, and he began to cry, gasping and convulsing.

"Don't!" Jericho had briskly picked up their backpacks and capes. "Come on, you can bawl as much as you like later, once we're out of here. We've got to get you some fresh air. Don't think of the Beez. I'm not thinking about them either. Come on!"

Josh wiped his eyes and smudged mouth, panting heavily. There was nothing else for it, they really had to go. Making a superhuman effort, he tried to make himself stand up. But it was no good – until Jericho briskly pulled him up off the bench. Leaning on her shoulder, he wobbled outside, into the deadly city.

For the first twenty metres or so the open air made Josh feel a little bit better. But after that, every step became harder. His body hurt all over, and he was seized with agonizing pains. He was simply not getting enough oxygen. Everything inside him fought for air. He was breathing rapidly, madly fighting off the phlegm bubbling up from his insides. Stars, lightning bolts, pain, screaming pain. A rattling cry came from his throat.

Jericho turned round, excited and impatient. "Just keep walking!" She bent down to peer under the hood into his face. "What's the *matter* with you? You were feeling better, weren't you? We must get out of here!"

Josh gasped for air, waving his arms around blindly, looking for support; and then the world around him just dropped away, as if the earth had melted, in one simple, dizzying twist. Next he found himself lying on the ground, wildly trying to ward off the thing that was suffocating him. He seemed to be wrestling with a strange, cruel demon that came from somewhere deep inside himself, and that was trying to strangle him and drown him from within.

Next to him stood Jericho, thunderstruck. She tried to pull his convulsing body up on its feet, but in vain. He no longer responded to her.

A few concerned passers-by wandered up to them, but when they saw the boy lying there stretched out on the ground, rattling and choking, they shrank back in fear. They conferred in whispers, never taking their fearful eyes off him.

And as they huddled together in the dusky square, dithering over what to do, a dark figure made his way, slow and dignified, through the crowd. Silently they stepped aside to let him pass. With measured step he walked up to Josh. When the people saw that, they crossed themselves, and then took to their heels. In the middle of the deserted square Lucide knelt by Josh's side. He picked up the boy tenderly and hugged him, lovingly, to his chest. Solemn, almost smiling, he carried him off, carefully picking his way over the broken cobblestones.

No one knew better than Jericho what it meant when Lucide took a dying soul into his arms and carried him off, away from the living. "Lucide!" she cried. "What are you doing? Let go of him, Lucide! Let him go!"

But Lucide looked neither right nor left. He kept walking.

Jericho ran after him in fury. "God help me, Lucide, can't you see he's just worn out; he's been through one ordeal after another! He hasn't had enough to eat, and that stench is really bothering him! Don't you touch him, do you hear me? Lucide, I'll get you for this!"

But he would not look at her.

Jericho tugged at his tunic. "He isn't dying!" she bellowed. "He doesn't even have the lesions! You bastard, mind your own business, damn you! *Lucide!*"

He strode past citizens, who fearfully shrank out of his way, and advanced imperturbably to the city gate. The two sentries crossed themselves and stepped aside, averting their faces. They didn't look at the little green bird or the big cat that followed Lucide, and didn't even glance at Jericho, who was running behind him, sobbing and cursing. Ah, it was something they had seen so often, the frantic reactions of mourners – the distraught, going into frenzied rages, or the unseeing, numb with grief, or the weepers, crying their eyes out, their throats raw, their cheeks etched with salt. The sentries of Bat Zavinam had seen it all before.

Lucide carried Josh a long way out of the city. He was going east, the wind at his back. He finally halted when they came to a small wood. There he sat down carefully, keeping Josh in his lap, his warm arms protectively wrapped around the convulsing body.

Jericho danced around him in despair. "Lucide, *do* something! You can't just take him, *do* something! I won't have it, I won't have it!"

Lucide looked down at Josh mutely and stroked his fevered head. As if to soothe the terrible breathlessness.

Jericho knelt by her brother's side. "Josh," she pleaded, "Josh, you're not going to leave me *again*, are you? What a useless brother you are! I hate you, you fool, you stupid idiot. Josh, please listen to me! *Josh!*"

To her immense relief, his eyes fluttered open. He stared at her as if from a great distance, cross-eyed, intensely. And suddenly she had a terrific idea. "Josh, listen, can you hear me?"

He nodded, but then clawed at Lucide's tunic again in panic.

"Keep looking at me! Josh, you can save yourself! Don't you remember you turned me into you, and yourself into me? You've got to do it again; you have to use your eyes! Turn yourself into me, before it's too late! Josh, hurry, hurry up!"

He forced himself to open his bloodshot, burning eyes. He breathed shallowly and painfully. But he did manage to get a few words out. "You'll get sick… I don't want to…"

"I don't care! I've been sick and dead so often already! I don't care! You *have* to do it now, quickly, please, I can't…"

He stared at her. "You're – spinning. I can't…"

"Now! Do it now," she screamed, "or it'll be too late!" She pressed her forehead against his. "It's our only chance! Come on, do it, my brother, Josh, come on, my darling, do it…"

Coaxing, sobbing, swearing and pleading, she tried to make him stay conscious. But his eyes rolled into the back of his head, and his legs started kicking again, and blood started to foam around his lips once more.

"Josh!" she screamed. Jumping up, she unsheathed her sword and pressed the cold steel to his face. Like an animal fighting for his life, he stared at her.

"Look, look, I'm going to help you," she implored him, standing before him. Using the sharp blade of her sword, she began hacking at her long hair. "Look, I've got short hair now like you, we're nearly there. Josh?"

She stood before him, her head messily cut off, and it was true: she looked more like him than ever. But Josh wasn't able to answer her any longer. He had fallen back, unconscious.

She let her sword drop from her hands. Shaking, she sank to the ground. Lucide, with his charge on his lap, began to hum very, very softly.

They sat there for hours. At first she could still hear Josh tossing and turning every so often, while Lucide apparently whispered soft nothings in his ear; but then it grew quieter and quieter. Jericho didn't dare look up. She was shivering with cold, but was so paralysed with dread that she couldn't make herself get up to fetch a blanket.

In the middle of the night, just at the moment when all was at its quietest – in the dead valley of the night, when nothing stirred – Jericho suddenly heard something moving behind her. Lucide was very calmly lifting Josh in his arms. Carefully he laid him down on the ground and gently wrapped him in a blanket. And then he got to his feet. He glided past Jericho, out of the wood. At the edge of the wood he stood still, his handsome face raised to the stars.

Jericho noticed she was holding her breath, and that she had clapped a hand to her mouth. Very deep inside, a burning pain rent her heart. She didn't dare move a muscle. *This,* she thought, horrified, *this is what my parents went through, with me. I never realized.*

In the silence of that terrible night she couldn't help herself. Like a wounded animal she crawled towards Lucide. He was the only thing for miles around that was breathing and warm. They were alone, he and she; both of them had strayed over to this side by accident. And now there was no longer any reason for them to stay. They were two useless wraiths in an empty world.

She was surprised to see him holding his violin. Just as she was close enough to touch his calf, he began to play. A lovely melody. She listened, spellbound. No shrill squeaking. No melancholic, heart-rending dirge, this. Just a cheerful, gentle and even rather catchy little tune.

"Why did you play that?" she asked softly when he stopped. She could hardly breathe, and it took her much effort to get the words out.

He smiled mysteriously.

"Shouldn't you be playing a funeral march?"

He looked at her mutely. His eyes twinkled strangely. As if he was amused by something.

"*Why* did you take him, Lucide?" Jericho asked miserably. "Was it to punish me? To let me really feel what it's like, for once?"

Lucide shook his head. He laughed low. "If there's anyone who ought to be punished, it is I, I'm afraid."

"But it's your job, isn't it? To lead the living to … to hold their hand when they…"

"Oh, Jericho, have you felt now how serious, how real, the border is separating life and death? Do you see now that that border must be guarded? Do you understand how much pain is unleashed when the border is breached? Do you understand now how it will break your heart?"

Jericho realized she was crying. Strange: they were tears of a sort she had seldom shed. Warm, human tears, tears that came from the pain of a terrible loss.

"You are a brave soul," Lucide whispered in her ear, "but jumping across the border is no child's game." He pulled her close to console her. And she let him, willingly. "But today, I must confess to you, I have committed the very same sin as you have. Forgive me." He let go of her and said, "Go, watch over him, tonight! Go, hurry!"

"I don't want to," said Jericho, her bottom lip trembling. "I'm scared!"

Lucide picked up his violin. "Now you feel it! You do have a heart! Go, it is the lot of the living. Watch over him!"

He had started playing his violin again, a soft and very sweet sound, an eerie song for the stars.

Sobbing and shaking, Jericho went back to the wood. Once she was surrounded by trees again, she noticed that the wind had started to pick up. The west wind had returned, and with it the noise, the creaking, the swaying and the groaning.

Groping her way in the dark, she found the place where she had left Josh. The first thing she found was his backpack. Then his inert body, stretched out on the ground. His dear, pale face gleamed in the dark, and the wind was playing softly with his hair. Through her tears she saw that the little panther had curled up against him, and that Zizi was sitting on his chest.

That's the way I looked too, she thought. *Three hundred and fifty years ago. White and completely still.* She realized that in the end she wasn't really scared. *Is it because I've been dead myself so often that I'm not afraid?* she asked herself. She had seen enough corpses, back in her harsh seventeenth century, to know what death looked like: that complete blankness. But here, she suddenly realized to her surprise, it wasn't blankness.

He was still here.

He wasn't dead.

She crept towards him, her heart beating fast. Touched his throat. It was throbbing, slow and regular. Warm. Not hot. She swallowed. He was asleep! The idiot, what a complete cheat. One minute at death's door, dying of the plague in Lucide's arms, and the next minute just happily sleeping, with a cat by his side, even! She was so elated, she didn't know what to do. Dance, yell, kick the tree trunks! Make him wake him up by stepping on him!

"*Yes yes yes!*" she cried, hopping up and down, crying and sneezing. "Lucide! Lucide!" She ran towards him, but he and his violin were already high up in a tree again. She jumped up and down underneath him, delirious. "You knew! You didn't let him die! He's alive! He's alive! Lucide, you saved him, didn't you?"

Suddenly she understood everything. She fell to her knees and then jumped up again, hardly able to take it all in. "*You* love him too!"

And then, as if *he'd* lost his mind, Lucide blurted out with reckless abandon, "Just as I love *you*!"

The next thing she knew, he was scraping away at his violin once again, and the high, soaring notes were swept up in the howling wind.

Jericho ran back to Josh. She wrapped herself in her own blanket and cuddled up against him. She had never been so happy.

17
Higher, Higher, Higher

And what did that silly Josh say when he woke up the next morning?

"What the hell happened to your hair, Jerrie?"

Jericho, who'd been contentedly chewing a carrot next to him, looked at him, insulted. "Well, I cut it, can't you see?" Then she smiled, baring her canines. Her face was dappled with flecks of sunlight. "Are you feeling better?"

"I'm feeling great." Josh sat up, yawning, and stretched himself luxuriously. "I think I must have had some kind of asthma attack yesterday, mustn't I? Because of the stench. I had no idea it was that bad. It was a scary feeling. It feels as if you're drowning." He shuddered.

Jericho gave her brother a sardonic look. "Yes, it does, doesn't it! Do you want anything to eat?"

"A carrot, I suppose."

"I had brought some cake from Bat Zavinam, but I threw it away. I refuse to eat anything from that plague-ridden city."

"It's lucky we didn't catch it," said Josh. "How long does it take before you notice you've got it? I was starting to get a little worried yesterday…"

"Well, we haven't got it," said Jericho cheerfully, "I'm sure of that. Where are we going? What did it say in that Beez book?"

Josh had to think back. "'Downhill at Ferry, and seven miles through the darkness; in the sun to Hiuja, and there drink to me.'"

"Sounds easy. Nice and short. We're as good as there already. Do you want a carrot, or not?"

Josh, who was starving, ate two carrots and a wizened apple. He felt so reinvigorated and new and full of fresh courage; he just didn't know why. Everything was delightful: Jericho was being extremely friendly to Lucide, and Lucide was radiant as springtime, so cheerful, giddy almost, as he strolled along behind them. From that morning on Jericho and Lucide suddenly seemed to be the best of friends, to Josh's surprise. Jericho never cursed Lucide any more, and she never said anything catty about him either. Josh didn't quite know what to make of it.

It was a lovely morning. The red and yellow leaves glinted in the fresh sunlight, and the earth looked as if it were strewn with diamonds. There was dappled light and shimmering gold everywhere you looked. Singing, they followed the sunny trail, pushed along by the strong wind at their backs. Josh taught Jericho to sing two-part rounds, and she taught him songs from her time, and occasionally Lucide would accompany them on his violin.

The landscape had changed markedly. When they looked back at Bat Zavinam lying in the distance, they didn't see dead, scorched burial grounds, but green meadows with skinny goats grazing in them. The city itself twinkled in the distance, with smoke curling up from roofs glistening in the sun, and even some proud flags fluttering in the wind.

"Oh," Josh concluded out loud, "then time must have run backwards again! We're in luck! We're now in the time before the Black Death. The plague hasn't been here yet!"

"Of course, that's right," said Jericho. "Time must have run back again last night." She halted, mulling this over, and looked at Lucide. "If the plague hasn't been invented yet, you can't die of it either. Hmm." But as she started walking again she muttered, "But once you're infected, you're infected, whether time happens to be running backwards or not." She seemed to be all tangled up in a very knotty problem. Then she shook her head and gave up. "Well anyway! Or maybe he kept you alive until… Or maybe he himself… Oh, whatever, what difference does it make!"

She took his arm and to his astonishment planted a big wet kiss on his cheek. "Yuck," said Josh, and she laughed, delighted. Then she suddenly turned serious.

"I shouldn't have done it. Joined in with the Beez."

He looked surprised.

"That's what I wanted to tell you." She pinched his arm. "Lovely day, isn't it?"

From time to time they encountered colourful medieval folk on the road. They asked a gaunt peasant leading some horses to pasture if he could tell them the way to Ferry. Siparti hadn't made the instructions too hard to work out, for Beez. "Ferry? Ah yes, they must mean the ferry; you know, the ferry across the river. All you have to do is go down this road here, turn left at the crossroads, going north-east, and when you reach the mountains, you can't miss it." He offered them a sip of beer from his own flask, and they drank thirstily. Their throats were parched. "We'll make a real seventeenth-century boy out of you yet," Jericho said approvingly as Josh wiped his mouth with a blissful sigh.

In exchange for three square coins they were ferried across the narrow river by a ferryman who kept a nervous eye on the little panther. They asked him if he knew of any caves near by, or a tunnel, and, without turning a hair, he gladly gave them directions: first downhill for about an hour, then uphill to the entrance of a cave that was situated about halfway to the Bahad-Pass. And of course they could buy some bread from him. Were they interested in some cheese as well? Goat's milk? Sausage? He had some of that too. Butter perhaps? His ferry hut turned out to be a little trading post. Nearly weeping with hunger and relief, they bought as much as they could carry and sat down to eat, not even a hundred paces from the ferry hut. They ate and they ate and they ate until they were about to burst. Lucide ate too, sitting beside them on the ground, smiling as if he were their uncle, on holiday.

They reached the cave and, before entering the tunnel that led from it, they gathered some twigs and fashioned torches from them. Once they were inside, out of the howling wind, Josh could put on his big black hat again. Zizi climbed eagerly on top of it. For the first half-hour, the wide, smooth-sided tunnel was lit by air shafts. Little pastel birds had built their nests under the cavernous roof, and they flew back and forth, chirping. White mice scurried back into their holes at the travellers' approach, but the small dark brown animals that lay rolled up in furry balls on piles of dead leaves didn't twitch a whisker when they passed. Josh held the little panther firmly by the scruff of the neck as they walked steadily on.

At the end of the tunnel they found rough-hewn stone steps. These led them deep into a silent darkness reeking of wet clay. In the flickering light of their torches the walls danced eerily back and forth. They first started up the steps energetically, then slower, and finally, panting, on automatic pilot. There seemed to be no end to the steep, rough treads.

When Josh was sure they must have climbed the Eiffel Tower at least thirty times over, they felt a current of air. The inky-black shadows faded to grey and light blue, and suddenly they were out in the open air. Jericho uttered a cry. The tunnel came out on a semicircular platform halfway up the mountain. Someone had piled a mound of stones there, and planted a sturdy wooden cross on top, with red and yellow strips of cloth tied to it fluttering in the wind. From this vantage point you could survey the whole westerly world.

"Look, Bat Zavinam!" Josh pointed out.

There lay the city, in the sunlit distance. Beyond the city were the endless orange-brown forests that harboured waterfalls, and pigs, and washerwomen.

"How far we've come," Jericho sighed. She held her slim white hand to her eyes. "Dinak lies on the other side, remember? And beyond that the desert, and Ixilis. And beyond that, more mountains, and then the sea." She peered at the shimmering, misty horizon. "Do you think London is out there somewhere too?"

"Are you homesick?" Josh laughed.

"Who knows?"

"London," said Josh, "is that way." He pointed his thumb over his shoulder, to the next opening in the mountain wall.

"Seven miles through the darkness," Jericho sighed. "I don't think my knees will take it."

They dived into the second tunnel, and found that it climbed steadily upwards, without the benefit of steps, twisting and turning in an endless series of bends. Little bats fluttered off in alarm. Some parts of the tunnel were so wet that there were strings of green moss hanging from the roof, slapping them in the face. In these underground passages it felt as though they were walking on the bottom of the sea, through a rustling green silence. They climbed on steadily, sunk deep in their own thoughts. Josh found himself ahead of the others most of the time, behind the brave little panther, with Zizi perched on his hat. He was surprised to hear Lucide and Jericho having a long conversation behind him as they climbed. At one point he caught a few snatches of their exchange. Jericho's voice sounded unusually gentle and meek: "Yes. Then I suppose I'll just have to. Again."

Lucide's reply was inaudible.

Her reaction was more vehement this time: "All right, but not without him! It's just starting to be fun!"

Again came the deep, indistinct sound of Lucide's voice.

"But why not? Why not that, of all things?"

And a little later: "Oh, fine, fine – but let me think it over, all right? I need some time to think!"

And she ran forward, bumped into Josh on purpose and grabbed his arm: silly girl, in her dark red dress. Her messily shorn hair stuck out wildly in all directions, but her dirty face was beaming.

"Everything all right?" he asked, feeling a bit left out. She nodded, but didn't say anything.

Gradually their torches burned out as the dry passages gave way to wet, mossy and slippery tunnels. They kept hearing the sound of rushing water behind the rock. In some places the water came streaming through the tunnel itself, down the walls, across the uneven floor. For the last hour of their ascent they had to wade, slipping and sliding, through a couple of inches of gushing water. Little by little the tunnel turned into a shallow stream, the water gurgling and cascading back into crevices in the rock.

Suddenly the rock above their heads split open, and they were walking in harsh sunlight. Once the rock walls on either side receded, a grand new landscape unfolded before their eyes. They had climbed very high. The stiff mountain wind pricked their skin and made it tingle, and the fierce sunlight dazzled their eyes. They climbed up the grassy river bank and followed the stream until they reached a waterfall. Jericho stuck her hands into the bubbling cascade and splashed water on to her face and hair.

At the top of the waterfall was a green plateau, criss-crossed by little streams and glistening with ponds. Wet grass and water glittered in the sunlight. And there, on the other side of this bright mountain plateau, they saw a square wooden building.

"Hiuja!" cried Josh. "That must be Hiuja! Let's drink to Siparti!"

"Fine with me," said Jericho. "But which Siparti, Josh?"

* * *

They walked to the mountain lodge, whose door and shutters were open. A couple of donkeys waited around the entrance, with some bundles and cases scattered at their feet. Josh and Jericho politely knocked at the open door, craning their necks to peer inside. An enormously fat man with a gleaming bald head emerged from the dining room.

"What's this? Good God, children! What are you doing here, for heaven's sake!"

He lugged a heavy crate outside, dropped it, and then sat down on top of it, panting heavily. "You weren't thinking of spending the night in Hiuja, were you? I've just come to remove the last bits and bobs, and to lock up. The season is over! Good day!"

But he was a kind man, this mountain custodian of Hiuja, and he invited them to join him in drinking the last of the ale left in the keg, as well as eating the leftover food. Even Lucide drained a mug of ale, which gave Jericho the giggles. The little panther was fed scraps under the table; Zizi likewise, but on top. So they sat for quite a while, putting up their warm, throbbing feet and stretching their stiff legs, happily guzzling down all that the custodian found in his nearly empty cupboards: donkey meat sausage, garlic bread and chunks of salted thistle root, which tasted as bitter as wild artichoke.

"I like to close up the hostel on my own," said the custodian, contentedly sipping from his own mug. "On a lovely clear day like today, I'll come up here by myself to fetch the last things, and then I'll take one last look around at the mountains." He raised his mug. "The mountains are holy, my friends. Here you can hear the breath of God. And sometimes that of the devil too – do you hear it?"

It was very quiet, and in the silence they became aware of a very high-pitched shrieking. *Must be the wind,* they thought to themselves, but a shudder ran up their spines nevertheless.

"Ah yes," continued the custodian, "and then I'll pray for the souls of those who have been crushed by evil, and beg God to preserve the essential goodness of these mountains." He put his mug down and asked, "But what have you come here for? People do often come up here to pray, here in the peace and tranquillity, but it really is getting a little late for that now. November the third! God is already beginning to withdraw. The time of the devil is nigh."

In a few words they explained to him the nature of their expedition. When they mentioned the Tembe, he became very quiet. "It has been many years," the custodian finally said, "since I have heard that name spoken." He got up and stared into the distance.

"They must be *somewhere* around here," Josh reckoned. "Do you by any chance know where they might be?"

"The Tembe," said the custodian, "are nowhere around here. They are not of this world. They are death's wretched hostages."

Josh was silent. Staring at the custodian's wide back, it became painfully clear to him that they'd overlooked something. Beez's *Book of the Cat* had indeed brought them to the mountain lodge, but there was a whole other leg of the journey to go. They were miles removed from the civilized world, and they hadn't the least idea of how to go on from here. They were missing one more piece of the puzzle. The very last piece. Gip's piece.

"This *is* Hiuja, isn't it?" he asked. "Siparti wanted us to drink to his health here! So surely you do know something more about them, about Siparti and the Tembe? Don't you?"

The custodian wouldn't even give any sign that he'd heard him. After several endless minutes he solemnly turned round. He unlatched the door, which was caught by the gale-force wind and crashed wide open. He signalled to them, and they followed him outside in their bare feet. He didn't go far. He climbed to a raised platform and put his hands on their shoulders. "Look to the east. See it?"

They saw a leaden darkness rising up behind the mountains.

It was the same threatening storm that Josh had seen looming in the distance before reaching Bat Zavinam. Now it was that much closer. Awesomely closer.

"See for yourselves. There it is," whispered the custodian. "Hell. It's over there, only on the other side of where the world ends. Can't you hear that diabolic shrieking? Didn't you hear me say that the time of the devil is nigh? The time of Siparti. God preserve the miserable Tembe! Praise heaven that nobody knows how to get there!"

That was all they heard said about the Tembe, there in Hiuja.

They helped the custodian load his donkeys, and he closed the shutters and nailed them firmly shut, trying all the while to persuade them to make the descent with him. Finally he jumped astride the lead donkey.

"I'll never see you again," said the custodian, "and I shall mourn for you all winter long, and pray for your souls. I hope that you will find wisdom and strength, somewhere in this cold, empty void. You *could* still leave your diabolic master Siparti; it's never too late, you know!"

He shook his head pityingly, darted them a last worried look and turned round. They waved and waved until the mule train descended a steep slope and disappeared from view.

Now we are really alone, thought Josh sadly. *The human world has turned its back on us.* He took a timid sidelong glance at Jericho and Lucide, both of whom were standing motionless, buffeted by the mountain wind, as if intently listening for something. *I'm the only normal person left in this world.* He was suddenly convinced that the Tembe had died out ages ago, and that he was doomed to wander all alone over these high lands for the rest of his life.

These disturbing thoughts were in fact but a dim echo of the night before, the night his body still vaguely remembered, but his mind had already erased. At Jericho's touch he gave a sigh, and his strange mood evaporated.

"Come on," he said, and they hoisted their packs on their shoulders and continued their journey. They followed a trail leading up the mountain, pushed on by the howling wind. At times they had to hold on to the rocks so as not to be blown away. Josh put his hat in his backpack again and tucked Zizi inside his collar. They climbed swiftly, higher, further east, higher, higher. When an hour later, out of breath, they found themselves on top of the pass, an endless range of mountain peaks came into view, sharply outlined against the threatening wall of black clouds that now obscured half the sky. There didn't seem to be any path leading down the other side of the pass. Josh realized they hadn't been following a visible trail for a while now.

Troubled, he ducked into a relatively sheltered spot just below the pass.

"What now?" demanded Jericho, squatting down.

"I have no idea."

"Are we lost?"

Irritated, Josh took a spice cake out of his backpack. Breaking it into three, he distributed the pieces among them. "It must be somewhere under that cloud bank, but I haven't the faintest idea where. The entire horizon is the border. I have no idea how we're supposed to work it out!"

"Ah," said Jericho. "The last stage. The Book of Gip. But wasn't there any mention of it, back at that Gippart place of yours? Aren't you supposed to be a Gip yourself?"

"I'm not Gip, I'm Josh Cope. And the problem is, we'd only just started working there. I believe the other Associates had to go through all kinds of training. The only thing I ever got was that *Gippart Associates' Instruction Manual*."

"Well then!" said Jericho, and started unpacking his backpack. "Oh, what a mess, Joshie." It was true, the stuff she was spreading out in the sun was an unappetizing, sticky mishmash. Something in his pack had leaked, and now everything – damp dirty underwear, old crusts of bread, questionnaires, travel papers, bird calls, books, bits of string and picklocks were all stuck together in an unrecognizable tangle of rubbish.

"Can I help it?" Josh spluttered.

"We really ought to do some washing sometime," said Jericho, picking a piece of crumpled wet paper off a crust of bread. Josh began disentangling his metal picklock hooks from a dirty sock and half a sausage. Jericho fished a dog-eared book out of the backpack, and began leafing through it.

"They don't even know the first thing about the Tembe, at Gippart," Josh grumbled, reading along over her shoulder. "Useless bits of advice. 'What to do if you can't fall asleep in *umaya*. Tips one, two and three.' Ha, ha, ha. 'Calculating exchange rates… Accounting practices… Customer relations. Assorted investigative assignments. Time and dream-time theories. Important to pay attention to signs of abnormal time disorders…'"

"Actually, it does say something about the Tembe in here," said Jericho. "Did you ever bother to read this book? Look, 'A Little History', see for yourself!"

Josh took the book from her. "Oh yes, I know. But Jericho, it doesn't help us. Look: '*The year 1000, mercantile beginnings and the birth of our founder… Gippart International established in* AD *1017… Ancient sources … first mention of Gippart … first commercial achievements. The key to our success…*'" He stopped short.

"Wait a minute. 'Gippart: Siparti's heir.'" He raised his eyebrows. "Was that really in there? How did *that* happen?"

"You just haven't done your homework, idiot," said Jericho. "His Excellency has a book and he doesn't even bother to read it. Read it now!"

"But—"

"Read it!"

Jericho peered over his shoulder and read along eagerly. Under the heading there was a rather crude drawing of a cat standing face to face with a large bird. Josh leafed through the book hastily, looking for the key names. Siparti. Temberi.

"Yes!"

They read aloud. "'Siparti, the greatest trader that ever was and ever will be...'"

"Look." Jericho giggled. "'And he took unto him a fifth wife Idadde...' Fifth wife? He had quite a harem, didn't he?"

"'...and gave birth to Gip Siparti and Kat Siparti, on the first day of the Second Millennium,'" Josh read.

They leafed on. And then they found it. Josh read the words, his voice trembling: "'And my father took my hand and my sister's hand and he kissed us. And he pulled me close and he spoke: "My dearest son, apple of my eye, son of Idadde, Gip Siparti: lead your brothers and sisters to the threshold of Temberi. Take the narrow path to the lonely pass, lead them through the empty void to the tower. Choose the dark road, the quiet road, the glittering road. These are my last words, my last request: renounce all desire, and do not touch anything. Renounce your desire and go up to Temberi. Tell him that I love him. Not the wealth, my Gip, not the splendour, but the love." And when he had spoken he let go of my hand, and he sank back, and he died. Thus departed from this life Siparti, of the House of Siparti, Siparti the incomparable, Emperor of Trade. Purveyor of luxury and good fortune. Siparti, my father, his brother's doom and his children's benefactor. And he kept his promise in the end.'"

"Good," said Jericho. "So that's it."

"It isn't all that clear, really. 'Dark road ... quiet road.'" Josh sighed. "Don't you feel sorry for them, though? Why didn't that idiot Siparti go back to his brother himself when he still had the time? Those rotten children of his didn't give a damn."

They first retraced their steps, to find the trail again. Josh had lost it about half an hour before they reached the pass. That was where the path split almost imperceptibly, and if you followed the narrower fork, you ended up on another mountain pass, lower down. It was a desolate spot, all shrieking emptiness. But to their great relief, in the distance, at the far side of a hollow rock-strewn wasteland, they spotted a squat tower. It gleamed yellow in the sun.

It was further than they'd estimated. They didn't reach the imposing tower until late in the afternoon. The stone was crumbling and weathered, but it looked as if it had been built to last an eternity. A small door squeaked opened easily, and they found themselves standing inside the colossal structure. There was a gigantic, empty fireplace built into one wall. The stone floor was bare and empty. But on the first floor there was a big pile of hay. They sank down on it gratefully. It was wonderful to be out of the wind. The tower shook in the storm, but inside it was mercifully quiet. Josh, stretching out in the hay, kicked off his boots.

"You may not be able to get them on again later," Jericho warned.

"We're staying here tonight."

"Oh, good," said Jericho, curling up beside the panther in the soft hay. They dug themselves deeper into the hay, like hedgehogs in their burrow, sheltered and safe.

After a while Josh got up. He walked to the corner where he had flung his backpack and knelt down next to it. He took out his Braxan sword and rested it lovingly across his knees. He caressed it all over, blew on the metal and polished it, rubbing the jewels until they shone in the golden evening sunlight streaming in through a small window.

"Do you remember when we fought the Beez? It didn't do us much good, did it?"

"Well, we did cut a couple of them down to size with those," Jericho laughed. "They really are razor-sharp, those Braxan blades." She leaned back contentedly, wrapping herself up in the warm hay. Then she opened one eye. "What are you doing?"

He had hooked one of his metal prongs behind one of the jewels, and was painstakingly trying to dig it out. "I'm taking those stones out," he grunted. "*Gotcha!* There goes one."

"I can see that. But why?"

"Well," said Josh, keeping at it intently, "you see, I want to keep those precious stones. I don't want to lose them."

"But surely you're not going to lose them?" A little light went on in her brain. "Josh, you aren't going to throw away your sword, are you?"

"Yes I am. That's another one. Ruby, don't you think?" He held it up to catch the sunlight, and little flashes of red light danced all over the floor.

"An unarmed traveller, in this terrible country? You're mad!"

"I don't want to be armed any more. I'm extremely grateful to my sword for having stood me in good stead, but I've had enough. Anyway, I don't know how to fight in the first place, and I don't want to learn, either. And in the second place – look, Jerrie." He raised his sword up high. "See what this is? It's a knife! It's a knife for cutting up people. I'm no Beez. I just find it a horrible thought, to be walking around with a butcher's knife, meant for slaughtering people."

"So you're happy to be slaughtered yourself?"

"Just use your brains, Jericho! Did that sword actually accomplish anything for me? I saved us from the Beez by using my eyes. Well, that's precisely what I'm going to do from now on."

Not answering him, Jericho started unpacking the backpacks, looking for their supper. She grunted approvingly as she took out the bread, the hard-boiled eggs, the goat's cheese and the bottle of sweet ale. "You certainly did an excellent job mastering that skill," she said finally, without a trace of irony. "You aren't an apprentice any more, are you? You've got another scar to show for it."

"What do you mean?"

"Next to your eye, remember? That Beez knife – why, doesn't it hurt now?"

Startled, he touched the deep cut by his left eye. She was

right. Smiling, he went on digging out the precious stones. *Seer, second-class; how about that!*

When he finally succeeded in prising free a glittering rhinestone, he turned to her. "What did *you* learn to be good at anyway, Jerrie? Baz is good at drumming, and Teresa at talking, and I'm good at using my eyes. What about you?"

"Nothing," said Jericho mournfully. "I haven't even got any scars." She gestured dismissively at her unscathed wrists. "I'm just empty air, that's all. A load of nothing."

"That isn't true! You saved all of our lives, don't you remember? On the raft, and then at Braxassallar-Takras, and you dragged me out of Bat Zavinam too!"

"Yes, but I didn't learn to do anything new myself. I haven't changed."

"Don't say that. You used to enjoy hurting and upsetting people, and now you no longer seem to. Isn't that true?"

Jericho gave a short laugh.

"It's true, isn't it?" her brother insisted.

"Oh, you're right, you're right." She hunched over and cradled her head in her arms. "So I've acquired a heart. And now I'm a frightened little mouse. Call that progress?"

He stared at her, bewildered. She muttered something else, and then began to hum. A nasal, monotonous tune. And Lucide, out of sight on the stairs below, was humming a countermelody.

But when Josh had finished taking all the gems out of his sword she was watching him again. "What are you going to do with it now?"

"Hide it somewhere safe. Toss it down a crevice in the rocks or something. I don't want anyone else to find it."

"You have to say goodbye to it," Jericho urged him. "It did save your life, after all, and it was magnificent, and proud, and it was loyal to you, and it wasn't afraid of anything or anyone!"

"Goodbye!" Josh chuckled. But he stopped when he saw that

she actually had tears in her eyes. Slowly he went downstairs to the entrance. Jericho quietly followed him. On the tower's threshold he stood still, a lump in his throat. He stretched out his arm, and the unsheathed sword caught the golden sun's rays for the last time. "Farewell," he said, "farewell, brave heart, heart of steel!" He turned to Jericho, embarrassed. "Teresa would have known what to say a lot better than me."

"You've got to give it a wonderful name. Or you won't be able to remember it. You'll forget what it was really like. It's got to be the perfect name for it. That's very important."

"Lightning-bolt," muttered Josh. "Flash. Heart-slasher?"

"Desastre. Name it Desastre. It was a disaster for your enemies. Their unlucky star."

"But Desastre..." Josh didn't understand. "Wasn't that *your* name?"

"For goodness' sake, I don't *have* a real name," she snapped. "What's my name then? Betty? Desastre? Or what do you think of Jenny, the stupid name you lot gave me at my cremation?"

"Jericho..."

"Oh, yes, someone's idea of a joke! Because they called *you* Joshua. Jericho! Why not, let's name *her* after a pile of rubble! Tumbledown Cope! I don't have any name, but what's the difference anyway? Just call your sword Desastre, and then whenever you think of it, maybe I'll be lucky and you'll think of me too!"

Josh stared at the ground. After a little while he said, "Desastrus, then. It's sort of you, but it's also sort of its own name. All right?"

She nodded, and wiped her nose on her sleeve. Josh softly ran his finger over the little sword's sharp blade, and then he gently tapped it on Jericho's shoulder, her head, and then her shoulder again. "I hereby knight you, Jericho, in the name of the sword Desastrus," he said, "and that will be its last deed. Sir Jericho, sister and hero."

Jericho grinned. She took Desastrus from him and tapped her brother solemnly on the shoulders and head. "Sir Josh," she said, "brother and hero." Then she grabbed his hand. "Desastrus has one more thing to do before it dies." He stood there as she very tenderly carved a little nick underneath his thief mark. "Now you do it to me," she whispered. He cut, very carefully, until the blood began to ooze. She didn't make a murmur. Then she bent forward and licked some of his blood, and he sucked at the cut in her wrist. Finally she rubbed her cut on his. "Now we are blood brothers," she said.

"We already were."

"And I finally have a scar." She swallowed, and sniffed deeply. "Where are you going to hide it?"

Josh looked around. Suddenly he remembered that there had been a deep cleft in one of the rocks they had passed. Gripping the sword tightly, he walked back up the path a hundred metres or so. He wasn't mistaken. There was a deep crevice in the rock.

"Thank you, Desastrus," he whispered, and he dropped it into the crevice. He heard the clash of metal on stone, descending deeper and deeper, and deeper, and then all was quiet.

After supper they went on talking about all kinds of things. Down below, on the stairs, Lucide took his time tuning his violin. Meanwhile they chattered away. About the Braxans, about the comforts of Mur, about those strange knights of Dinak. They fondly remembered the sweetness of morning in the metropolis of Ixilis.

Jericho linked her hands behind her head. "Once you're home again – you know? What's the first thing you think you'll do?"

"Have a bath," Josh said immediately, playing with a handful of precious stones. "A hot bath. With loads of food beside me. What about you?"

Jericho sniffed.

"Oh," said Josh. "Sorry." He clenched his fist, perplexed. The gemstones grated in his hand.

Later, when outside the moon was playing leapfrog with the racing clouds, he dimly heard her get up and creep downstairs. Her voice wasn't much louder than the wind whistling around the tower. Josh pricked up his ears, hovering somewhere in between sleeping and waking, and before nodding off he caught just one full sentence: "But I'd like to make a bargain with you, Lucide. I'm serious…" And a couple of phrases: "In ninety years' time… Is that long enough? Ninety years? Him and me, together…"

The dreams he landed in were bright and sweet, and they were all about himself and Jericho.

The next morning the storm was raging so violently that they could hardly keep upright once they got outside. Zizi had to be tucked deep inside Josh's collar. They had to shout at the top of their voices to be understood, and had to concentrate on where they planted their feet. Every so often, Jericho would suddenly totter forward a few metres, rammed in the back by a gust of wind. The little panther pressed close to Lucide, its ears laid flat to its head. They followed the path that led from the tower up into the mountains, deeper and deeper into the shade cast by the looming cloud cover. After several hours' trek, they ducked into a shallow cave.

"Ouch, my ears!" complained Josh. "This storm is driving me mad! It isn't normal, this horrible wind that just keeps blowing and blowing and getting stronger by the minute!"

"Nothing's normal about this place," said Jericho, combing her fingers through her choppy hair. "But weren't we supposed to find a dark, quiet road?"

"Those directions don't do us a blind bit of good, as usual. Or do you think it means we should be looking for another tunnel?"

He started exploring the cave, but it dead-ended almost immediately. So, anxious and vigilant, they braved the storm again. Slowly they climbed on, toes clenched, fingers clamped around rocky outcrops. Through watering eyes they looked for the entrance to another tunnel.

Jericho was the one who found it. Suddenly, halfway up a zigzagging route, up a slope strewn with fallen rocks. A low entrance, which grazed the top of their heads, led them into a small circular space.

"This was built by humans."

"Maybe it was those Tembe of yours," said Jericho.

They looked around, and thought they could make out some sort of drawing on the rock wall.

"Look!" Jericho pointed. There, faint, barely visible, was the outline of a cat.

"It's a cat with wings," muttered Josh, tracing the lines with his fingers. "Siparti. It's Siparti's cat. *He* made this tunnel."

"Siparti, the cat lover; Temberi the bird lover." Jericho smiled. "A winged cat, Siparti and Temberi together."

A round tunnel with a slight gradient led upwards into the mountain. Cautiously they followed the compass's bright beam. Josh, in the lead, suddenly felt the little panther's warm, friendly fur rubbing against his legs. The animal was trembling oddly and it was making squeaky little sounds. Might there be small animals for it to hunt up here?

They plodded endlessly through the silence of the mountain's interior. They only stopped to eat something, and then walked on in silence through the close, stagnant air. It was a long time before Josh felt his eyes beginning to get used to the dark. Slowly he started being able to see the rocky walls. The further they went, the more acute his vision became. Jericho, behind him, whispered cheerfully, "There's the way out!"

But she was wrong. The light wasn't from the sun.

It was the strangest thing. They found themselves in a circular hall glittering all around with precious stones. The stones flashed not because of any outside reflection; they seemed to be emitting light of their own. Deep, saturated red; the glorious velvety blue of a summer evening; a warm, melancholy tint of gold; and bright, cheerful white. Sparkling ochre and sienna, shimmering rainbows, sudden explosions of dazzling mauve. They had stepped into a wild fireworks display, except without any sound. Josh spun round, elated. He ran his fingers greedily over the glittering gems set into the walls. He polished them, caught their light in his hands, licked them cautiously. "Jericho, can you *see* this? Jericho, this is worth a fortune!" His voice brayed with greed.

He stretched out his hands and tried to see if he could prise the stones loose. He broke one of his nails on one, and started swearing ferociously. His face flushed, he dug out his thieves' tools. The first stone he tackled was a ruby: his favourite jewel.

"Josh," Jericho's voice warned.

"I'll just take a dozen or so. They don't belong to anyone, anyway. Wait, it's coming."

Jericho put a hand on his shoulder, but Josh kept working at it, until the ruby bounced on to the floor with a soft ping. "Oh, what a beauty! Jericho, have you ever seen anything like it? It's so huge, it must be worth a fortune!"

"Josh, leave those things alone! Don't you remember Siparti's words to Gip? That means they're meant for you too! Don't touch anything! 'Renounce your desire.'

He heard her, but couldn't understanding what she was saying. "'Renounce your desire.' Come on, what's *that* supposed to mean?"

"That you shouldn't feel the need to *have* it! It's a warning, Josh! You weren't supposed to touch anything."

Annoyed, he started rubbing the ruby to get off the remaining bits of rock clinging to it. "Anyway, too late now. Do you really think he was talking about *this* place?"

"I'm sure." She walked around the space attentively, her grave face lit by the colourful sparks flying off the jewels.

Yelping, the little panther ran after her. It was twitching its legs nervously. "And I'll tell you another thing. We can't go any further. It's a dead end."

He jumped to his feet. It was true. Apart from the opening through which they had entered, there was no other way out.

"What do we do now? That idiot Siparti! How does he expect us to get to the Tembe this way? It's completely impossible. Damn it, him and those stupid riddles of his!"

Jericho crouched down, her head in her hands. Josh stubbornly continued polishing his ruby. Slowly his anger receded, and he began to think clearly again. They were on the right track. This was the ultimate proof. Maybe he had already ruined everything, but still, the riddle's solution must be within reach. He looked over at the whimpering panther, which kept pawing at the wall, standing on its hind legs. As if it were trying to climb up the wall.

But there wasn't anything up there.

Or was there?

He switched on the compass, and there, among the spiralling lights, its beam shone straight into the air. Up, up – up into emptiness. There was no roof above their heads. There was nothing. The glittering, flashing walls rose to a height of about three or four metres, where they faded into darkness. Beyond that there was nothing.

Jericho had been following his gaze. She jumped to her feet with a cry.

"'Go *up* to Temberi,'" Josh said softly, remembering.

"We have to get up there."

"Oh, by flying, I suppose!"

"That's right." Jericho sounded calm and resigned.

"Ladies first," said Josh, laughing nervously.

Jericho didn't reply, but turned to look at Lucide. Josh was startled to hear her asking him for permission in the meekest voice: "Is that all right with you?"

Lucide, leaning motionless against the wall next to the

entrance, remained silent. Jericho sighed, and peered upwards. "Well, I'd rather not. It's too dangerous. I might just shoot off if I make myself lighter." She turned to Josh, and her eyes were pale, extremely pale. "But that's no help to you. I can't take you with me."

"Can't you teach me? You said you could."

"Yes, but then we'd... Then we'd slip in between, and if Lucide catches us..."

Josh racked his brain to find a solution to this absurd riddle. Might he be able to get somewhere by using his eyes? Make a ladder appear? Ropes? But he didn't have a clear idea of what this place looked like, and he couldn't risk randomly changing anything about this unstable *umaya*, not when they were so near to the Tembe, so near to the end of time.

All of a sudden they heard loud scratching, whimpering and growling. The little panther was trying to climb up the wall. It slipped back down, clawed its way up again, fell down again – until suddenly it gave an ear-piercing howl and, gathering all its strength, started scrabbling up the precious stones, claws extended, striking sparks and flames, until it reached the top of the wall. There, in the shadows, with a sweep of its tail, it disappeared, as if had suddenly been caught up in a whirlwind.

They stared after it open-mouthed.

"So *that's* how it's done," said Josh.

Jericho pursed her lips. "But this really is it! How are we going to get up there?"

"I could give you a leg-up." But that would be nowhere near high enough to reach the edge of the shadow.

"Hell!" cried Jericho furiously. "I can't stand this!" She stamped her feet, hurled her backpack to the ground, then her oilcloth cape, and in the dazzle of that rainbow prison, began hopping up and down furiously in her red dress. And then, as if it was normal and the easiest thing in the world, she leapt straight up in the air, and was sucked noiselessly up and away into the darkness.

Josh whimpered in shock. She'd just abandoned him! Anxiously he looked around for Lucide, but he was still standing in the same place, very placid, very tranquil. Then he smiled at Josh and walked to the centre of the cave. And with an elegant sweep of his arms, he wafted upwards, following Jericho.

To Josh, it felt just like that terrifying moment when everyone's been laughing and jostling up to the highest diving board at the swimming pool, and one by one the others have all jumped in, and you're last in line, and you realize that you simply don't have the nerve. And you are up there, all by yourself on that petrifying board. Or perhaps it was more like skydiving: there they all go, stepping out into the void, and suddenly you realize there's absolutely no way you can do it, and you crawl back inside the empty plane in disgrace.

There was just one way forward, and he couldn't understand. He broke into a sweat. He started hopping up and down hopefully, the way Jericho had. Nothing, not even a breath of wind. The glittering reflections were beginning to really get on his nerves. He sat down on the ground in despair.

Despicable *umaya.* Was it because he'd touched the precious stones, was that why he wasn't allowed to go on? "I am not Gip Siparti!" he bellowed, incensed. "I am Josh Cope!" But the dancing lights took no notice, and went on flitting imperturbably over his body.

He sat for a while with his face buried in his hands, until he felt sharp, familiar little claws in his hair. His parrot, his brave little friend, always loyal. But Zizi had wings, and he didn't. He let her hop on to his finger. "If only I were like you," he muttered. *Yes, a bird-person. Like the Braxans.*

The thought suddenly lit a spark inside him, just a spark of understanding. *The Braxans?* "Possessions weigh you down."

He scratched his head. "Renounce your desire and go up." *The Braxans believe that if you can master your greed, you can fly. Back to Zaam.* He thought he understood it, finally. If *this* wasn't the answer, then he gave up. With great reluctance he took the ruby out of his pocket and wedged it back into the rock wall. It fell out again, but he managed to stick it in place with a gluey piece of chewed bread. He jumped up in the air, hopefully; but nothing happened. He took off his cape and dropped it on the floor, as Jericho had done. He jumped again… Nothing.

With his face set grimly, he let his backpack slip off his shoulder. His magnificent Gippart bag, with its contents: some perfectly good food, his blanket, the book of instructions. And the compass! Pulling the bag towards him, he dug around for the compass and slipped it into his trouser pocket. But he did angrily shove his splendid hat back into the bag, with one last glance of regret. Naked and unprotected he was, without that bag. He took a deep breath, and jumped as high in the air as he could.

No good!

He stamped his foot just like Jericho had, and tears filled his eyes. He took the compass out of his pocket, fingered the smoothness of the wonderful gadget for a moment, and then tossed it into the backpack.

But the next jump was still useless.

"What else? What now?" he cried, at the end of his tether.

He felt in his pockets and found them: the precious stones he had prised out of his Braxan sword. Bursting into tears, he hurled them to the floor. They rolled all over the place, tinkling, and wherever they came to rest started glittering, as if to mock him, scattering lovely, clear rays of light. His stomach churned as he gazed at them through his tears. It had all been for nothing, for nothing! Everything he cared for, lost. He felt deprived, robbed.

Now he had nothing of any value left on his person. Worried about the last attempt, worried that this, his very last chance, would fail too, he paced back and forth aimlessly for a while in the glittering space. Then he took a very deep breath.

He broke into a little run, and startled himself with a roar that came from somewhere deep in his gut: *"Siparti!"*

And then he jumped.

And he was flying! It all happened so incredibly fast that he didn't even know what had hit him. It was as if he had leapt right into the centre of a storm. Spinning like a top, gasping for breath, he was hurtling through an immense, shrieking void. As he flailed around for something to hold on to, his speed just kept increasing.

He didn't fly, he was being catapulted! Faster than sound, faster than light, he tore through the night. Until he suddenly came to a bone-crunching halt. His breath was knocked out of him, and his body shook violently from the shock. Instinctively he latched on to something hard, clinging on for dear life. He lay still.

He had arrived.

Very cautiously he opened his eyes. In a strange half-light he saw square red stones with grass growing between them. The grass was flattened by the howling wind. The same gale that kept him pinned against a wooden door. He mopped the hair out of his eyes. He was lying on the threshold of a very large building – how large exactly, he couldn't tell from here. The raging storm battered the walls. Ahead of him he saw, glowing in the dusk, snow-covered mountain tops stretching endlessly into the distance.

He knew perfectly well where he was. They had accomplished their mission. After fifteen long days in *umaya*, they had finally arrived at the fortress of the Tembe.

PART V
SATURA'S MAW

18
What the Wind Blew In

What's supposed to happen, at the end of a quest? Cheers and accolades, Josh knew; people throw their hats in the air, and you glow with pride as they lift you on to their shoulders. What else? Medals, speeches and a great feast, and then a ballad about your exploits, and finally, as the fireworks go off overhead, a soft, clean, fresh bed. But what happens if you come as a messenger of the villain Siparti, and you present yourself to his irate victim with empty hands? Without the secret that could set him free, and obviously there only for your own ends. Josh couldn't imagine his welcome here would be very warm.

Jericho, who had landed in the bushes next to the door, followed him inside through a little window. They landed in a low-ceilinged white cellar, empty but for Lucide, who was sitting in a corner. There was no sign of the panther. Jericho was in the best of moods. She had flown here within the restrictions of this *umaya*, and she hadn't broken any of Lucide's rules. Now she was all set to go looking for the Tembe, here in this building: "Just tell me what we're going to do."

No, Josh wouldn't. He was crouching down, biting his nails and looking around gloomily. "Jericho, we've got to be extremely careful. I think the Tembe are out for Siparti's blood.

We absolutely mustn't let ourselves fall into their hands."

"What the hell are you so afraid of? You're not Siparti, are you?"

"No, listen to me. I *am* Siparti. No, that doesn't make much sense, I know. But I'm a thief like him, and I just understand what makes him tick, his greed and all that – I've felt the same thing so often in this *umaya*!" He looked at her helplessly. "It's just inside my head all the time, and then I'll say, '*Siparti!*' and then everything seems to get easier. I really do think I've turned into Gip Siparti, or that I'm the original Siparti, the stupid fool. Do you understand now why we absolutely mustn't let ourselves fall into their clutches?"

She listened to him patiently, but then laid a motherly hand on his shoulder. "You're my Josh," she said, very sweetly. "The rest is just rubbish. Dream away – you'd like to be Siparti, wouldn't you! The richest merchant of all time! You're much too slow and good-natured, you." He started to object, but she went on firmly, "If you're afraid of the Tembe, then we'll stay out of their way. Fine with me. Stealth and secrecy. That'll be fun."

Josh sighed. "There must be a way out somewhere around here. Maybe we'll find it without even bumping into the Tembe."

"You mean the exit that you can't get through alive?" Jericho asked, turning sarcastic all of a sudden.

He paid no attention, but lifted his head, listening. "Wait," he hissed. "I can hear something."

They kept quiet, holding their breath. Over the pounding of their hearts, over the storm lashing against the walls, they heard vague, shuffling sounds. From all sides, sighing, vibrating. Jericho grabbed Josh's hand. Suddenly she let her breath out again.

"Look! Birds!"

Now he saw it too: a great host of birds was nesting on the crooked beams of the vaulted ceiling. The birds were sleeping, grooming, cooing, cawing, jostling each other, falling down, fluttering back up and loosing their droppings on the floor. Just as Josh was looking around to see where Zizi was, she came flying up to him. She landed on his shoulder and crept up close to his ear.

"The Tembe! Bird lovers! Of course! It's teeming with birds here," said Josh. "Now we *know* we're in the right place."

There was no door separating the cellar, white with bird droppings, from the hallway. They had to duck under the low opening to get out. "Are the Tembe that short, do you think?"

The dark passage shook and hummed, as if buffeted by a raging sea. Birds were huddled together in holes in the crumbling walls. The place stank of bird droppings.

"If you ask me, nobody ever comes here," whispered Josh.

"Maybe the Tembe died out a long time ago," Jericho ventured cheerfully.

The corridor split into two, and they found themselves in another echoing passage. Their hearts pounding, they stole through the empty, smelly corridors of this haunted shell, recoiling at the sight of jittery birds, always on the lookout for unexpected holes in the floor or walls. The fortress was nothing but a shuddering ruin, constantly battered by a fierce storm, and in the process of being demolished by it, bit by bit. At times they thought they heard voices, drowned out by the wind. Or a very low boom, as if someone had sounded a gong.

"Funny, isn't it?" said Jericho. "All those birds. I've never heard of birds taking over an *inhabited* building."

"You mean this fortress must be uninhabited."

"It must be, mustn't it?"

And it did seem as if she was right. At one point there was a thundering roar, and a wall came crumbling down right in front of them. When they cautiously lifted their heads again, they realized they were now looking outside, over the piles of rubble, at the mountains' weird twilight. As they peered out, a few last stones tumbled into the void with a lonely, clattering sound that went on echoing for quite a while.

"Come on," said Jericho. "Let's go upstairs."

But it wasn't easy to find the way up. They wandered for what seemed like ages through the crumbling passages, which mostly ended abruptly in mid-air. Finally, at the end of a series of cellars teeming with birds, they found a spiral staircase that brought them to a hallway on a higher level. But here they came upon something quite unexpected. They found an oil lamp burning in an alcove. A weak, flickering flame. They stared at it, shocked.

Josh scratched his head. Someone must have been here. He didn't know if he should feel relieved or scared. With his back pressed to the wall, he went on ahead of Jericho, keeping in the shadows. And a little further on he found proof beyond doubt that there were indeed people living here. A flock of white birds flew up, screeching, as they drew near; on the floor lay the bread they had been pecking. Bread that could have been left there only by human hands.

They were irrevocably drawn deeper into the inhabited part of the fortress. It didn't appear to be a very comfortable dwelling; far from it. They kept having to brace themselves as they passed one of the many gaps in the wall. Gusts of wind blasted through these without warning. Here, too, there were crumbling openings in the walls in places where they least expected, as well as in the ceilings and in the floors. Through all these gaps a dim light bored its way inside, blending with the light of the hanging oil lamps swinging in the draught. Huge, menacing shadows quivered up the walls. And then suddenly came clearly audible snatches of voices and a door slamming shut. There was even a warm blast of cooking smells wafting from a corridor they didn't dare turn into.

The closer they got to the inhabited sector of the fortress, the more indecisive Josh became. In a lofty corridor he pulled Jericho to a halt. They slipped back round the corner of the corridor they had come from. Just in the nick of time too. A man came into the passage through a hole in the wall. "And I'm telling you I'll wring his neck if he ever dares to come here!"

Heavy footsteps thumped in their direction, accompanied by the twitter of birds. The clash of metal on stone. "Come along now, birdies! The coast is clear!" From all around now came a rush of flapping wings. It was as if the walls had turned into birds, all of them homing in on one spot. Cawing, squawking, the rattling of beaks and wings. Josh breathlessly clutched Jericho's hand to his chest.

"My God, that brute!" the voice roared down the corridor. "Just look here, blood – a fracture, if you ask me – *mat-ran-zal*! That's Siparti all over – he always brings murder and death! I'm right, aren't I?"

There was a mumbled response.

"What do I care! Isn't he their arch-enemy – yes or no? And so, by association, mine as well, by goodness! And I'm going to crush him to death next time I see him, I'll throw him into a vat of boiling oil, I'll pull his nails out one by one..." Then the man disappeared into one of the side passages again.

Later, in a safe little nook, where they collapsed on the ground next to a dozing heron, Josh said shakily, "You see? We absolutely cannot allow them to get their hands on us!"

It was lucky that Josh had had a chance to perfect his breaking and entering skills in Ixilis and Bat Zavinam. They had to zigzag through the corridors and dive through holes in the wall like lizards whenever they heard footsteps approaching. They crept into a storeroom, where they stole some bread and water. They shrank into the shadows, and held their breath whenever someone came rushing past them. It turned out to be a huge, confusing edifice. In a way it was a little like Gippart, the same warren of twisting and forking corridors. And why shouldn't it be? After all, they were related, the Tembe and Gippart. But this building was a lot more draughty, more vulnerable to the elements, and bird droppings. Not only that, it was a ruin on the verge of total collapse.

They wandered through flocks of birds, and were regularly spattered.

"How long are we going on like this?" asked Jericho. "What are you looking for?"

"The way out," said Josh. "You know."

"What does the way out look like?"

"How should I know? It must be at the border, just where the dark and the light meet."

"So it must be outside!"

"Yes, probably," said Josh, and shuddered, "but in this storm, it's too dangerous out there."

"And so for safety's sake we're limiting our search to where we're certain *not* to find it? That doesn't make much sense to me."

Josh looked over his shoulder at Lucide, who seemed more silent than ever here. He shrugged and trudged on, sighing. They ended up hiding in a broom cupboard, with no idea what time it was, and fell asleep, hungry.

They might have gone on plodding along those passages until the end of time, if it hadn't been for Jericho. Leading the way the next morning, she turned into yet another corridor and suddenly halted. Cupping her hands to her mouth, she started shouting loudly, to Josh's horror: "*Aho-oy! Hello-oh!* Come and catch us if you can! I give up!"

"Jericho!" Josh ducked down into an alcove. A door opened and a little man dressed in dark red rags stuck his head out. He stared at Jericho in astonishment. Josh was going to make a run for it, but Jericho grabbed him by the arm.

"What are you doing?" she hissed. "Stay! I thought you'd stopped being a coward!"

He wrestled himself free and, on his knees, waited for whatever was going to happen. Which wasn't too bad. The man, who was short, with a brown face, dark eyes and short black hair, examined them curiously. He bent over Josh, wiping his hands on one of the many layers of his red, monk-like habit.

"Did you fall down, my boy?"

Josh scrambled to his feet. "No."

He was a couple of inches taller than the kindly man facing him.

"Have you just blown in?" asked the man.

"That's right," said Jericho.

"Aha," said the man, laughing. He went on laughing for a while, chuckling to himself.

God, thought Josh, alarmed, *he's mad. That's another possibility we hadn't thought of. The Tembe are insane.*

"My, my, the things that get blown in, these days," said the man, shaking his head. "Just come with me."

"Where to?" asked Josh.

"To the others. But first I must check the fires. Steam baths. Come, walk with me."

Hesitantly, Josh followed, walking behind Jericho. "Are you a real Tembe?" she asked, without a trace of fear.

"Me?" He stepped inside a chamber where a fire blazed in the hearth. "Shut the door," he called over his shoulder at Lucide. "Of course. Who else would live at the end of time?"

Josh suddenly felt faint. He turned and went back out into the corridor. There he walked straight into the arms of a taller man.

"Gotcha!" he cried, clamping his arms firmly around Josh. "I've got him! Bonode, what have we here?"

"Let me go!" protested Josh, trying to kick himself free. Zizi flapped her wings angrily overhead.

"These just blew in," the little man called back jovially. "Three new 'uns!"

"Let me go!" Josh cried louder, biting through several layers of cloth. Both men wore shapeless layers of musty rags – a kind of rough sackcloth, just what you'd expect poor people living on top of a storm-swept mountain to be wearing.

"Now then," said the tall man, holding Josh at arm's length.

"Vicious, are we? Biting? Kicking? What *is* this?" He grabbed Josh by the chin to peer into his face. "What's your name? Where are you from?"

"Joshua Cope. I'm from London."

"We were with a trading expedition," said Jericho, "and then we got lost and were blown here by the storm."

"Trading expedition?" The two men exchanged a look of surprise. "It's been ages since any traders came to these parts! Where was it then, that you got blown away?"

"Not far after Hiuja."

They didn't believe a word of it. "What would a trading party be doing in these godforsaken, deserted mountains?" The keen-eyed taller man suddenly grabbed Josh by the wrist. "And what have you got there?"

Oh no, thought Josh, *the Gippart wristband!* It was so light he hadn't given it a thought for days.

"J.M. COPE? GIPPART? Look, there's a picture of the Cat!"

Josh tried to wrench his wrist free, but in vain.

"The Cat!"

"Oh, now I see. The Cat! This must be that cursed… Of course! It's another of those…"

"Gippart," chuckled the little man. "Gippart! That made-up name again! Gip Siparti rejecting his family name!"

"And who can blame him!" cried the tall man. "Come on, quick, let's take them to the others straight away! How this will tickle Numo! More Sipartis! He wanted to kill that monster with his bare hands! Come along!"

As he was being dragged off Josh felt worse than he had felt in a long time. Hadn't he learnt anything, stupid idiot that he was? He could have *kicked* himself for forgetting to take off the Gippart wristband. Here, in the lion's den, to wear the name Siparti was asking for trouble. To come waltzing in here as proud as a peacock bearing the name of Siparti, devil of all devils, the very source of all their misfortune – how stupid could you get?

"*Please* let us go," he begged. "We were sent; we really have nothing to do with all of that. We hate Siparti as much as you do, trust me."

But who would believe him? The men grinned as if they were enjoying themselves. "We'll see, we'll see," they muttered.

They climbed several sets of stairs and came to a higher floor of the building, which was rattling from the constant barrage of blows. Little stones kept being shaken loose from the rafters. Turning a corner, they walked straight into a whirl of flapping mayhem. For a brief moment they were caught in a flurry of panicky wings and shrill shrieking. In an instant, the turmoil had flown on, swerving, bumping into the walls: a swarm of birds, white, blue, grey. As the shocked children tried to recover their breath, the men laughed. "Just one of the many hazards of the Tembe citadel! All the birds have moved in here with us. It's too dangerous for them out there! But the only ones you really have to be careful of are the vultures – they're treacherous."

They were dragged along, left, right, ducking to avoid birds zooming through the corridors, tiptoeing cautiously past a vulture sleeping in the middle of the floor, which suddenly raised its head and screamed horribly at them. That vulture was too much for Zizi. With a squawk she detached herself from Josh's shoulder and shot away into the shadows.

The little man ran up a couple of steps and flung open a door. A wave of voices and the sound of clattering plates swept out into the corridor. Josh glanced over the man's shoulder to look inside. He saw a spacious, low-ceilinged hall, with two blazing fireplaces set into opposite walls. Light streamed in through small stained-glass window panes, scattering splashes of colour all over the floor, the furniture and the diners. There were many people, most of them quite short, all dressed in dark red rags, chatting over their meal. One of them, closest to the door, looked up. "Who have you got there now, Bonode?"

"Guests. Three new guests. Where is Awè? Is he in here?"

Awè, whoever he was, apparently wasn't; but Numo, who had sworn to kill the Siparti monster, was – somewhere in the back of the hall in fact – and the news was passed along to him in whispers. A few people stopped talking and craned their necks to see who was at the door. But Bonode and his colleague waved, closed the door again, and continued through the building, escorting the children firmly.

After opening and shutting a series of doors, the smaller man flung open a low door halfway up a spiral staircase leading to the top of a tower. "Ah, *there* he is. Finally."

They peered inside past him. The little room was crammed to the rafters with birds of all feathers, all rather sick and mangy-looking. As soon as the door opened all the sickly birds flew up into the air, and amid the tumult of feathers and wings they saw a little old man who had been hidden among them. He was dressed, like the others, in layers of faded red clothing speckled with bird droppings. In his smooth dark face twinkled two bright, foxy eyes. "Hello, Bonode, Tibid!" He took a step forward, then caught sight of Josh and Jericho. "Who've you got there? What's this?"

"Awè," said the taller man solemnly, "the wind has blown in three more." He looked back at Lucide. "Two, actually, and a very odd third one. Can you feel it?"

The old man stared at Lucide for a moment, then seemed to glow from inside. Lucide stared back at him. They both gazed at each other for a long, silent interval, and it was as if they understood each other, and were mutely communicating something very important, something very ancient. Finally Lucide averted his gaze and withdrew quietly to stand beside the door.

"Awè," the little man now said, "the boy is wearing a wristband of the Cat."

"The Cat!" Awé looked startled.

"So..."

"Siparti? They're from Siparti!" Awè beamed. "Tibid, they're from Siparti too! They were all sent by my brother Sipa! They're all coming here!" He grabbed them by the shoulders and looked searchingly into their faces. "Who are you? You must be grandchildren, great-grandchildren – who sent you?"

"I am Jericho *na* Joshua," said Jericho. "And he is Joshua *na* Jericho. Cope."

"But you were sent by the Cat," said the old man. "Come on, please, don't lie to me, after all this time!"

Something strange was happening to Josh. At first it was as if everything inside him was trying desperately to wriggle away, away from the truth and deep into a web of excuses and lies. And then he looked at the man they called Awè and the panic dissolved, and he was suddenly calm and clear-headed. "It's true," he sighed. "We were sent by Gippart. Gip Siparti."

He stared at the little dark-skinned man in front of him, waiting for him to explode. He had never seen anyone with such a lively, intense face. Who was he? The chief of the Tembe? He didn't look much like a leader, more like an eccentric hermit, curious and merry, enchanted with life. No matter what people might say about the Tembe, this one was not a pathetic victim, bent on revenge.

"Gip? But how can that be? There's a Gip here already!"

"We aren't Gip," said Jericho. "We were sent. Well, *he* was. I've just come along too."

"Oh, I see," said the old man, puzzled. "But what about the others? Do please tell me. Mono? Brax? Are they on their way too?"

Suddenly Josh understood what he was getting at. "Just us, we're the only ones that were sent," he explained. "From Gip."

The old man shook his shoulders, like a bird ruffling its feathers. "But Gip – that's enough, it's fantastic," he said. "I wasn't expecting anyone to come any more, and now suddenly I have all these visitors from Gip! Sipa did think of us after all. Bonode, Tibid, he has kept his promise!" He grasped the children's hands, laughing and peering into their faces. "But wait a moment. You are twins, so who else could you possibly be, but Gip and Kat? Am I right? I see a little bit of Sipa in you," he said to Josh, "there, around the nose. But, in actual fact, he looks more like me, don't you agree, Tibid? Can you see the resemblance?"

"I can." The tall man smiled. "And he's also got a bird with him."

"A bird? What kind of bird?"

"A lovebird – a little parrot," said Josh. "But the vulture scared her; she's flown off."

"A lovebird? I've never heard of those. I hope she will come back soon." The old man cupped Jericho's face in his hand. "But you have a *lot* of Sipa in you. That fierce gaze – I recognize it. You are welcome here, Gip's girl. Are you sure you aren't also Kat's?"

'Bu-but," stammered Josh, who couldn't contain himself any longer, "who are *you*?"

A sharp gleam came into the foxy eyes.

Tibid whispered reprovingly in Josh's ear, "But can't you see that for yourself? Why, that is Awè, the first; Awè, the eldest – he is Temberi, of course."

"Temberi? Are you…?" But it was impossible! He must be a grandson of a grandson, at the very least. Born before 950! And here they were, centuries later.

Temberi closed one eye. "Am I what?"

"Siparti's brother?" Josh stammered.

Temberi chuckled. He shut the other eye. "I am Temberi. The only one, as far as I know." He rubbed the short, grey hair that lay flat across his brown skull. "Temberi *na* Siparti."

Josh stared at him open-mouthed.

"Awè must be about two hundred and fifty years old," Tibid explained.

"There is nothing unusual about us, don't worry," said Temberi. He laughed, baring his sharp yellow teeth. "We live to be so old because we are here at the edge of time. Can't you hear it?" He raised his forefinger, and, indeed, they heard it: the fury of the raging storm pounding mercilessly against the walls and making the tower they were in shake. "Not a very peaceful place, this, but it's a place where you can live to a very ripe old age. We have my little brother to thank for that."

Josh was toying nervously with his sleeve. He had the feeling he should kneel, or make a speech. He felt uncomfortably inept. Temberi. Age-old, legendary Temberi himself! Goodness and wisdom incarnate. Innocence betrayed. But what he saw before him was just a funny, twinkling, modest old man, without any airs.

The strangest thing of all was that the outburst Josh had been expecting never came. When was he going to start spitting fire, cursing Siparti, and ordering them to be thrown in the dungeons?

"But – aren't you angry?" he asked.

Temberi frowned. "Well, you aren't exactly early, I suppose. In fact, you're almost too late. The fortress is about to collapse. But angry…? I used to be angry, once, but now that you have finally, finally come – Gip and Kat, little Gip – dear God, I am so happy! Come, sit down, sit down!"

He waved his hands about and shoved a large eagle-like bird aside to make space for them on the floor. "Tell me all about Sipa, please. Everything, I need to know it all."

"But Siparti," said Josh unhappily, "Siparti isn't alive any more. Didn't you know?"

Temberi froze. The storm held its breath for a moment, and the birds sat petrified on their poles. It lasted a long, breathless spell. Then Temberi slowly buried his face in his hands, sighing deeply. The birds imitated his sigh, shifting on their perches.

"I didn't know," he said softly, "but, naturally, it was to be expected. Sipa." He laid his hands in his lap, and they saw a tear rolling from his closed eyes. "I had hoped that he too would just go on living. I should so much have loved to see him and hear his voice once more. Ah, God, Sipa!"

"He is buried in Ixilis," said Josh, trying to lift the mood.

"Ixilis," Temberi repeated. "Yes, he liked to go there. His eldest son Mono's mother lived there. When did he die?"

"It said 1050 on the tomb."

"He lived to be exactly one hundred." Temberi smiled, blowing his nose on his sleeve. "That's a ripe old age. Was it a handsome tomb?"

"Very handsome," said Josh piously.

"Good. But you are still alive. There are some Sipas left in the world. Are the others still living? Little Kauri? Mono? Brax? And that Beez, he was always a difficult one – what happened to him?"

Josh took some time explaining as best he could what he knew of Sipa's children: how Kauri had gone travelling to distant lands, about Gip's legendary achievements, and about Kat's equally dazzling triumphs of trade. About Brax's philosophy of greed, and, to end with, something about Beez as well.

Temberi shook his head, saddened. He said that Siparti had always worried about his middle son. And then Temberi hesitantly asked if they had a message for him.

Josh blushed. This was the moment he had been dreading. He began to stutter, floundering under Temberi's expectant gaze, which before long started glazing over. "Oh, yes. Teresa had something for you: a bracelet!"

Except that Teresa was gone. And he couldn't exactly remember what Maam Sagal had told them, that riddle about a beginning and an ending and the earth being round. The whole situation was becoming more and more painful. Until Jericho stood up and took Temberi's hand in hers.

"There is a message. Siparti wanted us to tell you that he said he loved you very much. Isn't that right, Josh?"

Relieved, Josh began to nod. The message in the Associates' booklet!

Temberi broke into a strange, crooked little smile, blinking his wide-open, moist eyes, like a young owl. "Thank you," he sighed. "Now that's something the fool never told me himself!" He shook his head. "Not that he needed to. Brothers don't usually tell each other these things, do we? But it's good to hear it, now that night is coming. It is a good message to bring to a brother who was abandoned." He bent his head and they waited shyly for him to go on. After a while he leaned back. "And what else? He promised me something else as well."

It wasn't as if they didn't know that. Oh, the hellish disaster that was time-travelling. Temberi was asking them whether the riddle had been solved. So was that the message he was expecting them to be bringing him?

"No, nothing else," said Josh.

"But you children come from another time. That's what the other one told me, anyway. You were sent by a great-great-great-grandson of Gip's, isn't that right? And you've travelled back in time to the far side of this year, 1200, the place where time has got stuck and no longer can be budged."

"Yes, but we had nothing to do with it. We got caught in a time that kept running backwards. It ran us back until we arrived here. But we didn't make it happen. It happened by itself. We're stuck here too."

Jericho added, "There's supposed to be a way out, though, somewhere around here. Josh was trying to find it when your people caught us."

Temberi stared at the floor. "So then Sipa never mastered the art of time-travelling either. Still – I think we should all discuss this together, including the other two as well. There are still things I don't understand. But I am tired now, and I would like to think about what you have told me – and I want to mourn Siparti. I can't tell you how happy it's made me that you have come, but you have also brought me heartbreak."

Tibid tapped them on the shoulder. "Come along now," he whispered. Quietly they followed the two other men, leaving Temberi alone with his birds.

* * *

Again they made their way through a labyrinth of passages and halls. A little further on, the small man said a curt goodbye and went off in another direction, and they carried on behind Tibid. Passing a courtyard, they heard strange music coming from the opposite side of the open space, where the wind was whipping up the air into little whirling funnels. It sounded like a huge orchestra playing somewhere. They heard loud percussion sounds in various tones and pitches weaving intricate rhythms, and in between they could hear blaring trumpets, wailing horns, high-pitched bells and chimes, humming and squeaking.

"What's *that?*" asked Josh.

Tibid smiled. "Our most important line of defence. As long as the music keeps playing, we can hold out. Without the music, the fortress would crumble in a day. You'll see for yourselves later."

They entered a dusty hall and slowly made their way across it. Suddenly they heard rapid footsteps approaching from the left, from where the music was coming. A Tembe in flowing red robes with black hair ran up behind them. He greeted Tibid with a curt hello as he raced past. Suddenly he slackened his pace and yelled "Hello, Josh!" before dashing off and disappearing into a corridor to their right. A cheerful little black and purple spotted panther darted along behind him, its tail swishing happily from side to side.

Josh's heart stopped. Impossible. It couldn't be. But it was.

It was Baz.

Josh shouted and started running after him. But Tibid grabbed him by the collar and sternly pulled him back. Josh stared at him in bewilderment. "That was Baz! That was—"

Tibid laughed. "But of course it was Baz! Our hero and saviour! Your brilliant friend got here two days before you."

"But—"

Jericho laughed, glancing over her shoulder at Lucide, who

was staring with a frown in the direction in which Baz had disappeared.

"But," said Josh again, with a lump of joy in his throat, "how on earth…?"

"You are at the edge of time here, my boy," said Tibid, "and here strange things happen. It is here that everyone who gets shipwrecked by time eventually washes up, all the truants and early birds."

"But I thought he'd left *umaya*! I had no idea he could get back! How did he do it?" Suddenly he was no longer tired, but happy and excited. "Why did he just run off like that? Where did he go? I've got to speak to him!"

"I think that he was probably on his way to find a stand-in, so that he could take a break from his drumming and come and talk to you. He must have heard that more Siparti children had arrived. But he can't just leave his post! You haven't heard about all that yet, but Baz got here just in time to give us priceless advice on strengthening our defences, just as the fortress was in imminent danger of collapse, and he showed us how to use our drums, and what sort of rhythms to play. I don't know what we'd have done without him! And if he just abandons his post at the drums, the music will weaken, and our position will weaken further, and then we're back in great danger."

"Will he return?"

"Certainly. But keep walking, I'm taking you to your dormitory, which is where he sleeps too. I'll bring you something to eat in there, and then you'll see, he'll come at some point."

As he followed Tibid, it dawned on Josh for the first time that the Tembe had kept mentioning "other" guests – that "more" guests had blown in. Why, Temberi himself had told them they already had one Gip here, and hadn't he said something about "those other ones" who had already told him about certain things – that they came from some other time, for example?

* * *

Their dormitory was on a lower level, a windowless little room with an open hearth, in which Tibid quickly lit a fire. There were six low beds with straw pallets; the sheets were made of the same faded red material they saw everywhere. They lay down, contented. Their little room was cosy. The storm seemed far away. Here all they felt was a gentle rocking, as if they were in a ship's bowels.

They were already half asleep as Tibid went to get them something to eat; but the hearty, appetizing food made them feel quite refreshed and wide awake again.

"What is it?" asked Jericho. "Wheat?"

"Mountain barley," said Tibid, "with our special herbs, and a sauce of bren, odil and mannelé. Like it?"

"Delicious," said Josh, who was wolfing it down much too fast.

"Our kitchen," said Tibid dreamily, "used to be the finest in the world. We do our best, but, well…" He left a jug of some kind of hot drink on the mantel and took his leave.

"Ha, the Tembe!" said Jericho when he had left. She sniggered. "Temberi! So it was *these* people you were so afraid of?"

"Funny, isn't it? They seem so easy-going. And Temberi himself isn't even angry! But did you hear what they said? This whole building could collapse at any minute." He licked his wooden plate clean and went to the door to watch for Baz, then walked over to the fire. He poked at the logs, took a sip from the jug and then turned back again restlessly. And then his heart leapt.

There he was. In the doorway. With a wide grin on his delightful face.

"Baz!" cheered Josh. "Baz, Baz!"

They ran to each other and fell into each other's arms so enthusiastically that they ended up in a heap on the floor. They pinched and patted each other and were so overjoyed they didn't know what to do with themselves. The little panther jumped on top of them and snapped at their hair, yelping. Josh ended up lying heavily on top of his friend. All red in the face, gripping Baz's head between his hands, he asked him, "Where the hell did you go? Where were you, all this time?"

Baz wrestled free and jumped on one of the beds, where he made himself comfortable, grinning. "Hi, Jericho! Did you cut your hair? It looks great."

"Hello, Baz," said Jericho shyly. She remained quietly seated on her bed.

Baz was still the same old Baz, except that he was wearing a strange assortment of red Tembe rags. He was bristling with energy, yet he still had the occasional worried look in his eyes. Fondling the contented panther's furry neck, he started telling them his story.

It was just as Josh had suspected. Baz had heard amazing, irresistible rhythms wafting out of the little chapel. "You know," he said, "it wasn't just the drumming. It was the way the rhythms played off the strings, and off the trumpet..." He waved his hands helplessly. He had just stood there, mesmerized. When the music had finally died away he noticed he was standing in a lovely flower garden, beside a limpid green sea. A boat came ashore, with a veiled woman in it, and she wanted him to go with her. But he refused. There seemed to be some sort of misunderstanding: she kept going on about the untainted virgins she wanted to carry away in her boat, and even though she smelled nice, he thought she was weird. "All that stuff about virgins!" he spluttered. "I mean, *I'm* no girl, am I?"

"Virgins," said Jericho with a crooked little smile, "can be either girls or boys, if they haven't done it yet."

"Done what?" asked Baz. Then he blushed to the very roots of his hair. "Oh..."

"So you see, you're a virgin too."

"Well, I wouldn't have gone with her anyway," retorted Baz crossly. "I walked out of the garden, into a forest – it was all fantastic, Josh! These strange lights, and women in white dresses, and sometimes a white bird in a halo of light. I kept getting the feeling I was supposed to *do* something, and I hadn't any idea what it could be!"

He had encountered a unicorn, and strange, blind old men with long beards, and a knight on a white horse who wanted to challenge him to a duel. But all he was interested in was getting away from there. "It was a very strange *umaya*. An extremely faint rhythm, Josh. It was feeble and eerie."

He finally wound up in a small town where a festival was in full swing. People were drinking, feasting, flirting and dancing, and he'd found a slightly stronger rhythm there, which let him work himself backwards and drum himself to a more stable *umaya*. And after that, towards an even steadier rhythm.

"But – do you mean that you were moving from one *umaya* to the next?"

"No. It was always the same one, actually. This one, except that the beat was quieter and less complicated. It was the same rhythm, only I nearly lost it."

"Were you in heaven?" asked Josh.

Jericho held her breath.

"No, no!" laughed Baz. But then he went quiet. "Or perhaps I was."

They were silent for a while. Then Baz told how, halfway through his attempts to get back to the right rhythm – the one at which he'd left the other Associates – a howling wind had picked him up and carried him off. It was a gale that came out of nowhere, just as he was switching rhythms. He had panicked. The storm blew him from rhythm to rhythm, from one time to the next, and he could barely steer a straight course. "And then I crashed into this building. Wham! The end. Dumped on the front steps of the Tembe's fortress."

"What a coincidence," said Josh.

"Not really. This is the end of time. Everyone travelling through time ends up here eventually. So I knew you would arrive here too!"

Josh stared dumbly into space.

"Don't you remember how you thought it was so strange that the wind just kept getting stronger in this *umaya*? Stronger and stronger. First that stiff west wind in Tsumir, but then in Dinak it was even windier, and as we went on it turned into a full-blown storm, didn't it? Well, that was the storm of reversing time! Do you see? Everything gets sucked this way, that's what that wind was. And here it just disappears."

Josh had to think that over. "So the reason it was so windy all the time was because of time running backwards?"

Baz nodded. "And at the end, it's running back at breakneck speed. But here time gets stuck, because you can't get any further back. There's nothing more."

Josh laughed. "Well anyway, it's great to see you again. You always seem to work it all out!"

"But tell me, now it's your turn. What happened to you two? And where's Teresa?"

And then it was Josh's turn to tell. Baz whistled and swore and said, "Awful," in just the right places. And it was quite a hair-raising tale. A tale with a huge gap in the middle. The gap of Josh's illness and unconsciousness. Baz stole a furtive glance at Jericho, who smiled at him conspiratorially. He gazed thoughtfully from Josh to Jericho, and from Jericho to Josh. And kept his thoughts to himself.

When he'd finished his story, Josh stretched out on his bed. They all listened contentedly to the crackling of the fire in the hearth.

"Now I understand why the little panther was behaving so strangely, and why it made such an effort to scramble up the wall in the jewelled hall," said Jericho. "It must have smelled you, Baz! It was following you!"

"Yes," Baz chuckled, his hands linked behind his head. "That was the best thing of all, when it came bounding into the music chamber. It made a beeline for me, and leapt on top of my drum. I had to stop drumming, which made a whole chunk of the lower fortress slide into the abyss! Everyone screamed!"

"You're very important here, aren't you?" said Josh.

"Yes. Come, come and see for yourselves."

They ran to the orchestra, with the panther and Lucide following on their heels. This time they were enthusiastically greeted by all the Tembe they met, and that felt good. They were deliverers, all of a sudden. They could hear the noise of the music chamber from far off. It wasn't a particularly lovely sound; it was deafening, a cacophony of grating, droning noise. Jericho put her hands over her ears when Baz opened the door and dashed into the chamber. There they saw a peculiar assortment of people behind an even more peculiar collection of instruments. Large singing bowls, gongs, dangling copper pipes, bellows, various string instruments, trumpets, blowers, alpenhorns, triple-horns, bells, xylophones, a glockenspiel and an enormous assortment of drums. The musicians seemed to be jumping around haphazardly from instrument to instrument. They weren't all Tembe. Some of them were much taller, or darker-skinned; others were pale redheads, with goatee beards. The musicians were dressed in different styles, in all the colours of the rainbow. A woman with an olive complexion in a flimsy blue shirt banged away on a large xylophone. She laughed loudly when she saw Baz. "Back so soon? I haven't even started!"

"Keep going," cried Baz, "I've just come to show my friends!"

The woman nodded and went on, working up a sweat.

"What a racket!" yelled Josh.

"Can you hear it?" shouted Baz. "It's the rhythm of the hurricane! We're slowing it down!"

"Crazy beat!" shouted Josh.

"Crazy hurricane!" cried Baz.

They walked past the musicians, who were concentrating on their instruments.

"Some of these people were blown here like us!" shouted Baz.

Josh could see that. Then he caught sight of a sombre figure dressed in red rags sitting, slumped, against the back wall, who was beating very slowly on a little drum. He was taller than the other Tembe, and he had a cloth wrapped around his head that hid his nose, mouth and hair, like a nomad of the desert.

"That one too?"

"Yes," said Baz. "That's the one who blew in here last Thursday. They patched him up a bit with some of their special potions. I haven't talked to him, but I told them to tell him he'd be expected to do his bit today too. According to Tibid, he has perfect pitch. But if you ask me, that one's mad as hell about being stuck here."

"I would be too," said Josh, "if I suddenly found myself blown here by the wind, against my will."

He sauntered over to the back wall, past a little round Tembe man tooting away like mad and an old woman who was banging a cymbal, a serene smile on her face. When he got close to the tall man, Josh faltered, then stopped. The noise here was a little less deafening. He had a sinking feeling as he stood there listening to the slow tapping of those sick grey hands on that little drum. The sound made him unaccountably sad suddenly. He felt Jericho's warm hand slipping into his. Baz was standing on the other side of him. Josh bent forward slightly to get a better look at the man. And when the man suddenly lifted his shrouded face to his, it only confirmed what he had known already. Of course. Who else could it be?

Josh saw that Spratt's eyes had gone even redder. They now looked like bloody wet blobs with pinpricks of black in the centre. He wasn't sure if Spratt could actually see him. But his arch-enemy gave a loud groan, as a sign that he had recognized Josh.

"Well, the whole gang of little psychopaths!" he whispered. "Get lost."

They could barely hear him.

"Are you back, then?" asked Josh. "I thought you'd escaped from *umaya*. That you'd flown away. Just like Garnet."

"Oh, that's what you thought, was it?" Spratt muttered sarcastically. "Do you really think there's any way I can get out of here, as long as your little psychopath-brain goes on believing in this made-up world? *I* can't smash my way out of your hysterical hallucination."

"What's he *talking* about?" asked Baz.

"*I'm* not the one who's been making all this up," said Josh. "Is that really what you think?"

"*Umaya* is rhythm." Baz tried to jog Spratt's memory. "By the way, you should keep drumming."

With one limp, flaking hand Spratt kept the piece of cloth pressed to his nose, but with the other he obediently resumed tapping out his sad rhythm. Josh wasn't an expert, but he did recognize that Spratt's beat was exactly right.

"Rhythm immobilized by the brain activity of a demented child," Spratt breathed. "The most powerful impulses originate in early pubescent brains. That's why Gippart selects kids like you in the first place!"

He wasn't coughing any more. His health really did seem to have improved a lot, now that he was getting medical treatment from the Tembe.

"What on earth do you mean by that, Spratt?" asked Baz.

"That I've finally worked it out. Gippart's shrink was right. Cope here is exactly the type of disturbed Gippart 'Associate', as they're so charmingly called, that can turn an *umaya* into an impregnable prison. It's his fault the rest of us can't get out of here. God, surely you've worked that out for yourselves by now!"

"Josh isn't disturbed," argued Baz.

"Oh, come on," Spratt snapped, "I know the type, I'm telling you. Overworked imagination, broken home, emotional neglect, borderline personality."

Josh had never thought of himself in those terms, and he seethed, offended.

"You are all seriously disturbed," groaned Spratt, tears streaming from his infected eyes. "And that's how this *umaya* – this horrific hallucination – is kept alive. If the lot of you weren't here, the whole illusion would vanish into thin air – if you underwent psychiatric treatment, or if you'd just get lost."

"*I'm* not disturbed either," said Jericho angrily.

Spratt turned his head away. "You don't even exist," he sighed.

"If you want to make me *really* mad, tell me I don't exist, scum!" She was about to thump him, but Baz held her back in the nick of time.

"All you are is the sorry dream-wish of your autistic little brother," said Spratt stubbornly. "And the minute this dream does finally break open, you'll vanish into thin air too."

"Rubbish!" cried Josh, who wasn't sure exactly what "autistic" meant, but was quite sure that he didn't agree.

"You kids must go," panted Spratt almost inaudibly. "Or else nothing will change. You must go. It's either you or me. And I..." He pulled the cloth further over his head and collapsed against the wall, as if he were fainting.

"Let's go," said Baz, and they walked out of the room.

"What a monster," spat Jericho as they walked down the corridor. "It's *him* who doesn't exist, not us!"

Baz laughed. "Don't let it get to you. I think he's the one who's gone mad."

"That's right," said Josh. "He's lying, isn't he? Even if he's such an expert. Baz, he's lying, isn't he?"

"May God help me!" Jericho exploded, leaping at Josh and snapping at his neck. She nipped him hard, then kicked him behind the knees. He stumbled and fell, just missing a couple of huge snowy owls sleeping on the floor. They flew off indignantly.

"You aren't sure, are you?" cried Jericho. "You aren't sure I exist, are you? Well? Well?"

"You do exist, you do exist!" Baz shouted. "We *all* exist, we aren't disturbed, nor is it Josh's fault that *umaya* is stuck shut, and Spratt's the one who's demented!" He shook his head. "I just don't understand how a Senser can come out with such utter rot! Isn't it obvious that there's a distinct rhythm here? And that rhythm isn't Josh's rhythm!"

In the afternoon they explored the fortress in Baz's company. He showed them where it was crumbling – especially on the eastern side, which took the full force of the storm. Next they ducked under low arches leading into rooms that must once have been quite splendid. A Tembe lady told them that all the magnificent drapery had been used for clothes and bedding, and that the tapestries, the magnificent furniture and the glassware had all been sold off a long time ago, when the Tembe still had contact with the outside world. But the murals remained. Josh thought they were wonderful. Most of the colours had faded, but the blue was still dazzlingly bright. There were lovely scenes of gardens high up in the mountains, filled with dancing, happy, colourful animals and humans; there was a picture of a laundress stirring colours in a washtub, and from the lather spilled a bright world of houses, animals and people; and crammed between and around everything, there were pictures of birds, carefully depicted. There was also an unusual painting of two boys standing on either side of a tree. Both were looking up at a snake with an apple in its mouth, which was twisting down around the tree.

"Temberi *na* Siparti," said a woman who had come up behind them unnoticed. She was carrying a load of red washing in her arms. *"Awè na Kide da sirriwillin zeme, din moliwibe am badid."* She laughed. *"Ba zadi i labanne ti Kide, a? Muswodin si kane mer!"* And she scuttled away, laughing her head off.

"You've said it!" said Josh.

Baz raised his eyebrows. "Sometimes I can understand them, and sometimes I can't. I don't know why."

"Wouldn't Siparti speak Tembe?" said a man passing them from the other direction, who had overheard.

"Do you always understand *us*, then?" asked Baz.

"Most of the time. But every Tembe can speak at least three languages, so it isn't all that remarkable."

Josh and Baz exchanged a glance, and shrugged.

Then they went on exploring the fortress: the torrent that coursed right through the middle of it, and the courtyard gardens where wind-resistant vegetables and herbs were grown – the favoured spot of the grumpy goats. The goats were also allowed to wander about in the barn-like lower levels. There they saw a big man carting wheelbarrows of manure to and fro. When he caught sight of them he let go of the wheelbarrow, planted his feet, and pointed his pitchfork at them. "Don't you dare come one step nearer! *Ti!* Siparti scum!"

"Numo," said Baz, but the man brandished his pitchfork angrily at Baz and the little panther. "Go away! Get out of here with that brute, that assassin!"

"Numo!" Baz said again, grabbing the panther by the scruff of its neck. "I'm sorry, I'm sorry, I've apologized to you three times already! But how was it supposed to know those birds belonged to you? It was famished!"

"Oh, my poor birds, magnificent Idè and Irè!" fumed Numo. "I'll – I'll skin him alive! I'm going to boil him in oil! Out of my sight, Sipartis!"

Sensibly, they made themselves scarce, and after running through some more corridors and up and down some more staircases, Jericho burst out laughing. "Josh," she cried. "There's your vengeful Tembe, the one who wanted to drink Siparti's blood! It was the little panther he was talking about! You coward!"

Josh pulled a face. But Baz could very well understand what

had made Josh so convinced the day before that the Tembe hated the Sipartis with a vengeance.

They walked until their legs ached, and then they went to the dining hall with the stained-glass windows and talked to the Tembe who came over to sit with them. But they couldn't really answer all their questions properly. Had they discovered how to time-travel? Could they turn the storm around? How was that old scoundrel Siparti, and the whole Sipa tribe? How were things in the outside world? What kind of birds did they have in the lands they came from? What kind of remedies did they have for parasites? Had they discovered a cure for that stubborn blue-pen disease? And how did they keep their swallows alive in winter in a freezing climate? In the end Baz returned to the music room, and Josh and Jericho couldn't keep their eyes open as a group of Tembe around them got involved in an animated discussion about the wonderful fresh chirping sounds of a nest of robins.

They saw no more of Temberi himself that day, neither at the evening meal (which was out of this world, with at least ten different fragrant herbs that must have gone into it, and which, the woman seated next to them told them, was a stew of old rock owl and young brush sparrow), nor during the convivial after-dinner hour. Numo made a point of walking around them in a wide arc; then he spat on the ground. At the end of the daily story hour, in which one of the Tembe, cheered on by the others, told really tall stories, Josh and Jericho helped with the dishes in a steaming room of fire and water near the interior waterfall. Finally Tibid led them back to their dormitory. When Baz joined them at around eleven o'clock, worn out and with throbbing eardrums, they didn't wake up.

In the middle of the night a gong sounded. Josh slept right through it, but Jericho and Baz ran barefoot through swarms of startled birds down to the lower gate, shivering in the bitter cold, to see who had arrived this time. Hearing a happy commotion of excited voices and laughter, they presumed a new guest must have blown in.

Josh was the only person in the fortress who had remained fast asleep through it all. And yet he was the one who had to be woken up. The new arrival demanded to be shown to the dormitory immediately. She stormed through all the corridors, striding furiously on long, sturdy legs, taking no notice of the Tembe, or of Baz and Jericho, both of whom, delirious with happiness, kept grabbing her arms. When she reached the dormitory she jumped on top of Josh's bed and pulled him up by the collar. "Wake up, you bloody pain in the neck! I've got a bone to pick with you!"

Josh opened his sleepy eyes.

She shook him. "How *dare* you, you little brat! Skipping out on me in the middle of the night like that!"

"Teresa," mumbled Josh.

"That's right, Teresa! Remember me? What the hell got into you, you idiot? Sneaking away as if you were better off without me? And letting me stagger through *umaya* all by myself?"

"Teresa," said Josh, grinning stupidly. He scratched his head. "It's so good to see you here!"

"Oh, you make me so mad," said Teresa. "You idiotic, stupid know-all! What ever were you *thinking*?"

"Didn't you call Kat? Didn't she come and rescue you? Why are you here? You were supposed to phone Kat! That was what I wanted!"

"Oh, my God," Teresa cried despairingly, "I *told* you I didn't want to, didn't I? But if you really want to know, yes, I did phone Kat and I made a bargain with her, and then I went charging after you, to Bat Zavinam, where they told me that you'd succumbed to the plague, then through those blasted caves and tunnels and up all those bone-breaking stairs, and I kept searching for you until I was blue in the face. Creep!"

"I *wanted* you to call Kat," Josh repeated. "Then you, at least, would have been saved."

Teresa let go of him, and sat down on the edge of the bed. Stunned, she stared at the smiling faces surrounding her. "Please forgive me," she said to them quietly, after a moment. "I haven't been very polite. Could I have something to drink, please?"

Tibid, who was standing closest, nodded, and gave orders to fetch food and drink. "Four Sipa children," he said. "This really is an honour. Is this all? Or are there more of you?"

They shook their heads. Exchanged glances, smiling. The Tembe began filing noisily out of the room. When everyone else had left, the children saw that Temberi had stayed behind. He looked at Teresa closely. "Fourth Sipa child," he said, as if he still couldn't believe it. "Whose are you? You are from Mono, am I right?"

"Excuse me," said Teresa, "but who are you?"

Baz said solemnly, "That is Temberi. In the flesh."

Teresa stood up. "Temberi," she repeated, awed. "Temberi himself? Really? Oh!" She bowed reverently. "What an honour to make your acquaintance, sir. You are probably not very happy about our arrival. We are all so terribly, terribly sorry about everything."

Temberi shook his head in his special way. "Oh, Mono, no need to excuse yourself, please. It is such a wonderful treat to be paid a visit by my brother's offspring!"

"But I am not from Mono, sir," said Teresa. "I was sent by Gip Siparti. And also by Kat Siparti, actually. My name is Teresa Okwoma." They shook hands solemnly.

Then Temberi gazed around contentedly, his hands folded behind his back. "Sipa, Sipa." He beamed, but then frowned. "No. You are not just Sipa children, of course. Neither are you only of Gip and Kat. Baz, Josh, Jericho, Teresa, panther and –" He nodded very respectfully in Lucide's direction. "And you aren't here without a reason. Perhaps you will indeed be able to help us to leave this place. Baz has already devised one rescue strategy, and it may yet work." He nodded firmly. "Eat and drink your fill, Teresa, and get some rest, and then we'll see each other again in the morning."

A jug was brought in, and a wooden platter with a helping of the evening's stew, and Temberi bowed to them, which made them blush, and then left them.

They spent a wonderful hour talking into the dead of that night, in the rocking bedroom in the bowels of the Tembe's fortress. They told each other about their blood-curdling adventures; Baz had to tell his whole story all over again for Teresa's benefit, and Josh and Teresa bickered a little more before finally making up.

"You stupid dope," said Teresa fondly. "You still don't get the whole picture, do you? We're supposed to stick together, and we're going to get it done together. You know, Josh, I still think it was mean of you, and stupid, but it was also a brave thing to do."

Josh smiled and made himself comfortable in bed. "I didn't like sneaking off like that either," he said. "But I thought it was your only chance."

"Oh, you idiot." Teresa yawned. "Ah, a bed, a bed!" She burrowed under the covers. "And you, Baz – hero of the Tembe, the great saviour!"

"Well, but I *am*," said Baz.

"That doesn't sound at all like you. Putting on airs now, are you?"

Baz chuckled. "We're *all* the saviours of the Tembe. Look, in the legend it said that Siparti would send his favourite children to share the secret of time with them. Well, that's exactly what we're going to do. We're not just going to get out of here ourselves. We're going to help all of them escape!"

"Bravo," muttered Jericho, half asleep.

But Josh was gazing wide-eyed into the creaking darkness.

19
The Hurricane of the World

Monday November the sixth began with the morning gong calling them to breakfast. Josh was happy. Now that Teresa was here, everything was right again. She had that same old determined look in her eyes. Josh leaned back sleepily, and he ate and drank and let his mind wander. He didn't have to take command any more, and that was blissful. It had been hard, being in charge of an expedition through a nightmare. Even if that party had consisted only of your sister and yourself.

It was a day for ambitious preparations. Everyone was excited, including the Tembe, who kept an eager eye on the Associates. Teresa kept looking around to see if she could spot Temberi. But Temberi, always elusive, was never where you expected him to be, and he seldom took his meals with the others. It was Tibid, instead, who came up to them. "Come with me, will you, please?" He had been sent by Temberi, and he was to take them up to the parapet, where they'd finally be able to see the situation for themselves. They nodded, wiped their mouths and jumped to their feet. But Baz left them to go to the music room, because it was his turn to relieve his crew of drummers.

They followed Tibid down the groaning, howling corridors.

"These walls aren't going to withstand this much longer,

are they?" asked Josh worriedly.

"No," said Tibid. "The place is about to cave in. Oh, there's Mim. Will you please accompany me and our guests up to the parapet, nephew? Awè wills it."

Mim, a stout young man with curly black hair and small piercing eyes, nodded curtly, looking at Josh, Jericho and Teresa with interest. "Siparti's people, are you? Welcome. I've heard about you."

As they walked on, Mim asked softly, "Do they have any idea what they're in for?"

Tibid shook his head, with a warning look at his guests.

"You can tell us," said Teresa.

Tibid frowned. "It's best if you see it for yourselves first. But be prepared. It's staggering. Besides," he added quickly, "I'm not even sure what it is that you'll see. Nobody knows what the Sipa children will see. I know what *we* see, we of Temberi's tribe."

They walked on, tense with anticipation.

"I don't really understand, though," said Mim. "Awè said you were looking for a way out?"

They nodded.

"But why does he think you'll find it at … at… Well, up there on the parapet?"

"The exit is at the edge of time," said Josh. "That's all we know, really."

"Haven't you ever tried to find the way out yourselves?" asked Teresa.

Tibid and Mim exchanged a quick glance. "Actually, we do our best to stay as far away as possible from the border. If that's the exit…"

They were silent. Josh instinctively linked arms with Teresa. This passage led to a staircase, and the stairs rose to a hefty wooden door. Tibid and Mim managed to open it with difficulty. On the other side, in the dark stairwell, the hurricane shrieked even louder. Deafened, they crept up the shuddering stairs, the din of the storm pounding in their ears. At the top of the stairs was a metal door that seemed to be bulging and shivering. It was like standing on the deck of a ship, a creaky ship at the mercy of a raging sea. "Careful!" shouted Tibid. "Hold tight!"

He drew the bolt and opened the door slightly, but it was whipped out of his hands, and they had to grab each other quickly, or they would have been sucked outside. Tibid held them in an iron grip. They couldn't see much at first. There was a heavy darkness, as if night had fallen, a night of hellish noise, a night of brutish might, tied into the most awesome hurricane.

"Hold on tight!" Tibid yelled again, grabbing Josh and Teresa even more tightly. Keeping their backs against the wall, the three of them inched on to the small parapet. Mim followed, with Jericho. They found themselves on the ramparts of a tower, behind a high wall of battlements. Their hair was sucked straight up into the air. It was petrifying. As if they were standing in front of the gaping mouth of a gigantic roaring, sucking vacuum cleaner. A huge funnel-shaped tornado seemed to rise right in front of them. They gasped for breath, desperately trying to see something – a border? An edge?

Then Josh saw it, through the tears streaming from his eyes: the border. A border that looked like nothing he'd ever imagined, even in his wildest dreams. You'd think a border would be something you could simply step over, with an "Adieu, my friend" on one side and "Salaam" on the other. But no. Before their eyes, grotesquely huge, grotesquely violent and noisy, a roaring black wall of cloud in the shape of a menacing head with a ravenous mouth loomed above the mountain tops. The head bulged and billowed around and around that sucking black hole, yet never seemed to grow any larger. It rose halfway up to heaven, and above it the sky was a sulphurous brown. Josh clung to Tibid for dear life as he edged grimly around the parapet, his back to the tower in the middle, holding on to the railing. It was time to face everything now. He wanted to know, he had to see for himself exactly what was happening. He now saw that the black wall wound itself around and around the entire earth, obscuring the lower half of the sky; like a gigantic snake wrapping itself around the world, squeezing the whole world in its terrible grip. And at the same time the snake was sucking the whole world down its gullet with gale-force strength. Through half-closed eyes Josh saw uprooted trees and bushes being drawn up into the billowing head of cloud, and then vanishing into the darkness.

When he had made a circuit of the tower, he had had about as much as he could stand. Tibid understood. He pushed them back to the steps and, using all his might, wrestled the door closed again. They stumbled down the stairs, went back along the passage and down a second flight of stairs, until they reached the relative calm of a room with a fire blazing in the hearth. They sank down beside the hearth, their backs to the heat. Gradually they got their breath back. Jericho combed through her choppy hair in silence.

"What did you see?" asked Mim.

"A huge, raging snake," said Josh.

"Ha," said Teresa. "Yes, that's what it was! A horrible snake curled around the horizon. I saw it too."

"Aha," said Tibid, and he laughed. "So, it fits! Sipa sees a snake. What else?"

"A hideous head," said Josh. "Everything was disappearing inside it. It was swallowing up everything – it's going to swallow you up too, isn't it? When the fortress finally collapses?"

"Yes. That's why we have been constantly making music all these years, and meditating and singing. To ward off the storm and postpone the inevitable. I am glad that you saw a snake."

"Do you see something else, then?" asked Teresa.

"We don't all see the same thing," said Mim. "But we call her Satura."

At that moment the door opened. Temberi entered, in his quiet, unassuming way. He walked up to them softly, carrying a couple of sleeping birds on his head and shoulders.

"Well?" he asked.

"The snake," said Mim.

Temberi smiled. "Sipa. He was fond of snakes, wasn't he? He wasn't afraid of them. That's a good sign. What else?"

"A head," said Josh.

"Snake's head?" asked Temberi insistently.

"No. I'm not sure, yet. Who is Satura?"

"Satura is she who swallows her own children. The end of time. She gives life and takes life. We are on the wrong side of the divide. The side from which she takes."

They were at a loss for words. But it came as no surprise that the end of time might manifest itself that way. An unstoppable tornado girding the whole world, devouring everything in sight.

"Time," sighed Temberi, "is a snake that encircles the world, marking the border between life and death. Satura, the world's snake. But is it a way out?" He looked at them searchingly.

Josh swallowed. He didn't dare look at Teresa. If this was an exit, then it was, quite simply, an exit into the jaws of death. Was that what Max had meant when he'd said they would never get through? The significance of this dawned on him slowly. This way out was impassable. Yes, you could dive into Satura's maw, if you liked. But it would lead you straight to your death. It appeared that finally, after all their hardships and difficulties, they had come to the end of their journey. They had discovered the only way out of *umaya*: a dead end.

"Yes," said Teresa. "This is the exit."

He looked at her, baffled.

"It is," said Teresa, her eyebrows raised. "It is, isn't it, Josh? You did see it too, didn't you?"

"But we can't get through that way!" Josh objected.

"We have to."

"Are you telling me that you want to hurl yourself from the tower into that terrible mouth? Have you gone mad?"

"No," said Teresa, "but you seem to have forgotten everything we've learnt! Didn't you *see* anything up there?"

"The end of time!" cried Josh.

"Right!" Teresa laughed, her mouth wide, her head back.

"Doesn't that remind you of anything? Doesn't it remind you of anything at all?"

"No," said Josh.

Teresa looked at him in despair. Then she resolutely stood up, turning to Temberi. "I should like to give you a message. You see, we were given a message for you." She fumbled in her pocket and took out the snake bracelet Maam Sagal had given her. "Here you are. And I was supposed to tell you this: The earth is round, and the end of time is the beginning of time. Everything is interconnected. And the end of time is also the beginning."

Temberi turned the bracelet round and round. He nodded thoughtfully. Josh looked at him, wide-eyed. He was beginning to understand what Teresa had been trying to show him. *The end of time is also the beginning.* Would Temberi understand the riddle?

Temberi lifted his head. "A new beginning?" he asked hesitantly.

Teresa nodded. "Won't you… Is that all right?"

Temberi stared over her head into space. "But without Sipa – what would be the point?"

"There will always be Sipartis in the world," Teresa replied. "But there aren't very many Temberis. I'm sure you would find a new Siparti, if you started all over again."

"That is an odd answer to a difficult question," said Temberi, rubbing the bracelet. "But I had already lost Siparti anyway. And then you came. So nothing is lost for ever, it seems."

"Not if you're willing to begin again," Teresa insisted.

Temberi nodded, and then nodded again. "Very good. I will go and discuss it with the others. You do have a plan, Sipa child, don't you? Will you make the necessary preparations? We will talk later."

"Wait," said Teresa. "There was something else. Siparti says that he's very sorry, and that he misses you every day, and that he loves you."

Temberi nodded and stared past her, his face glowing and

flickering as if he were being buffeted by dozens of emotions at the same time: joy, sweet sorrow, happiness. Finally he smiled. His whole body seemed to be beaming with joy, right through his rags. Then he turned round without another word. Soundlessly he disappeared through a little door.

"There," said Teresa, both anxious and moved. "So let's get started."

Josh was beginning to get really worried. "Teresa, what are you up to?"

"We're going to find Baz and devise a plan. It isn't going to be easy, but it should work. We'll *make* it work between the three of us! And as far as I'm concerned, Jericho can join us too. Baz will do the drumming, you'll use your eyes and I'll do the talking. It *has* to work. Come on!"

Josh got to his feet, shaken. "You mean – you're going to talk to that hurricane? And you want me to use my eyes to turn it into something else? You're out of your mind; it's never going to work!"

"Josh, we're in *umaya*! You used your eyes on those pigs of Maam Sagal's, and that Beez surgeon, and even on yourself and Jericho at Maam Sagal's. And Baz can slip in and out of this *umaya* with his drumming tricks, and I can change *umaya* around in my own way, with words. Had you forgotten?"

"But this is the whole world! I can't even hear myself *think* in that racket! It's too huge, Teresa!"

"Are you scared?"

"Yes, I'm scared! I'm terribly scared! Can't you remember what it was like up there?"

But Teresa was the chief of their expedition. Chief strategist, and a relentless chief at that. Josh followed her unhappily, in search of Baz.

"OK," said Teresa.

They sat huddled together, four conspirators. Lucide sat on a beam above them, flanked by a couple of sleeping eagles. His long legs dangled just above their heads, but they didn't pay any attention to him. They had important matters to discuss.

"This will be our master stroke." Teresa's eyes gleamed. "If we can do this, we can do anything. And we *can* do it!"

Baz scratched the deeply contented little panther behind the ears. Worriedly he asked, "But how were you thinking of doing it, exactly? We'll be sucked inside before we can change anything!"

"We'll have to find a good position," said Teresa. "Close enough for Satura to hear us. But we mustn't get sucked inside straight away. I'll bet the Tembe will know where to find just the place."

"But what do you mean, you want her to hear us?" Josh asked. He was still convinced she'd gone crazy. "Do you really think you can talk to that thing? It's a hurricane, the hurricane of the world!"

Baz shook his head. "He's got a point, Teresa."

"No, Baz, think! We're in *umaya*, you keep forgetting that. Satura isn't real! She is a nightmare. And nightmares are things you can fiddle around with."

Josh and Baz exchanged a dubious look. But Jericho nodded enthusiastically. "You are all super-talented," she said. "You can do it! And I want to help too!"

Josh sniffed. "*You* don't even want to believe we're in *umaya*!"

"I don't," said Jericho. "But I do see that you want to get to somewhere else, by way of Satura. It's London that's on the other side of that divide, isn't it? Well then!"

"You'll start, Baz," said Teresa. "That's the most crucial part of the plan. You've got to slow her down with your drumming. Do you think you can do it?"

Baz frowned. "I do know her rhythm. We've been drumming to for the last few days. We've already slowed her down a bit. I'm not sure if I'll be able to slow her down even more… But I think I might, if I could get closer to her. And the rest of the orchestra has to keep playing. But…"

"You need someone to back you up, is that what you're saying?" asked Teresa.

"Yes, but I don't think you'll like it."

"Who?"

"Spratt," Baz muttered.

They thought it over, but it didn't take long to reach a decision. "All right," Teresa and Josh agreed.

"But someone will have to keep an eye on him. What do you want him to do?" asked Teresa.

"I want him to accompany me on the drums. He's by far the best at getting the rhythm. Seriously. But he doesn't believe in my method, that's the problem."

"I'll stand behind him," said Jericho, "and if he tries to mess it up, I'll give him a thump. All right?"

Baz nodded, and Teresa went on "So, you'll start, Baz, and when Satura has slowed down a bit, you come and do your thing, Josh. Change her around using your eyes. You have to make sure that she actually sees us, and that she is willing to listen."

"But we're dealing with a hurricane here!" Josh protested.

"Not quite a hurricane, because Baz will already have calmed her down. The way he did with those silly knights, can't you remember? But you must make sure she's really listening."

"I have to change her into a human being, you mean."

"It's up to you. And when she's ready to listen, I'll step in. I'll talk her into letting us through."

"Do you know how to do that?"

"I do. It'll work, I think. And then we'll go. And we'll take the Tembe with us. Well, what do you say? Is everything clear?"

"But Teresa," Josh asked, "where will we end up, then, once we've passed through Satura?"

"At the beginning of time."

"I'm not going where there are any dinosaurs," said Baz hotly.

"No," said Teresa, "I wouldn't want to either. But our only

way out is through Satura, and going that way takes us to the beginning of time. I have no idea what it will be like. We'll have finally broken our way out of this locked-up *umaya*, though, so it must be possible to return home from there."

"But how can you know for sure that Temberi will be able to begin again, over there?" asked Josh after a tense silence.

"Oh, Josh, I've been thinking and thinking and thinking, and this is as far as I can get. As for what happens next, I really haven't got a clue, any more than you have! We'll just have to see what happens."

"But—" Josh objected.

"I can't wait!" said Jericho, grinning.

"But—" Josh tried again.

Teresa raised her hand. "Enough talk. It's time for action. We're going home!" She laughed and slapped Baz a high-five, and then Josh, and then Jericho.

None of them noticed Lucide, smouldering quietly but dangerously up there on his beam. He had overheard every word, every single word.

It was a strange day, that long, interminable Monday. They weren't the only ones on tenterhooks; the whole fortress seemed to be crackling with electric tension. Everywhere they went they'd come across animated little groups deep in discussion. The children were constantly being asked by the Tembe: when was it going to happen? What exactly would they have to do? What could they take with them? What was to be done with the ailing birds? These were matters that the Associates hadn't considered, and they'd look at Teresa, and Teresa would say, cool as a cucumber, "Temberi will explain everything to you later."

Temberi. Only now did they see that this small man really was the heart of the fortress. He seemed to be everywhere, in the most unlikely places; they saw him surrounded by little knots of worried people bombarding him with questions; or among the goats, calming them with his voice; touring the sickbay; and then standing by himself in the deserted dining hall, staring outside through one of the orange stained-glass windows.

It was by chance that they happened to walk in there, but Temberi calmly turned round to face them as if he'd been expecting them. "Everyone has now been informed," he said, as if they had agreed to assemble there and the meeting had started. "We don't need to pack anything, do we?"

"No," said Teresa.

They went and perched on the table by the window. Little patches of orange light flickered across Temberi's smooth, round face. "Well, then there's nothing left to be done," he sighed. "Except to say goodbye. We'll go tomorrow morning."

Teresa nodded. "Is there a place where we can get closer to Satura without being blown away?"

Temberi told them of two parallel tunnels running east. At the end of each tunnel was a large sheltering rock, anchored deep in the ground, and reaching to the height of about a grown man's chest. It was possible to hold out there for a little while, at least.

They discussed other matters – where the Tembe should wait, who should carry the sick birds and sick people, and what to do about Spratt. The reality of it began to hit home. Josh was a bundle of nerves.

"Do please go and speak with Mervin Spratt," Temberi said worriedly. "He isn't doing at all well. The Tembe medicines we have been giving him have worked wonders, but he is in a terrible state mentally."

There was a pause. Temberi sat across from them in the stone window alcove, his eyes turned inwards. He was there, yet he wasn't really there. Finally a light flickered in his eyes, and he chuckled. "And now tell me exactly who *you* are," he said, with genuine interest. "Teresa, Baz, Josh and Jericho. Where have you come from? Are you related to one another, or are you just friends? Why did Gip choose you, in particular, to send to me?"

It felt strange telling him about their own lives. Everything they said sounded so far-fetched. But Temberi really did want to know all about them. He wasn't confining his questions to information about birds, like the other Tembe; he insisted on hearing about *their* lives. Slowly their memories were refreshed, and they were reminded that they were really just very ordinary schoolchildren from London. Jericho eagerly joined in, telling about her own life in the rapidly growing seventeenth-century London, teeming with ships, merchants and newcomers from overseas. Temberi didn't seem to notice that she was talking about an entirely different era. Three hundred and fifty years, more or less, didn't make any difference, viewed from the year 1200. In any case, Temberi also seemed to know exactly what questions *not* to ask. They gabbled on, constantly interrupting each other. In the end they were all burning with the longing to go back. Home!

"But what about you?" asked Teresa, after they'd told their stormy tales. "I'm still not sure why you aren't angry with Siparti. Wasn't Siparti responsible for sending you to your ruin? Wasn't he really out for your blood? And he very nearly succeeded, too!"

Temberi shrugged impatiently. He cajoled a little pygmy owl to come to him and climb on his finger. Josh looked around to see if he could spot Zizi.

"Everyone keeps asking me that," said Temberi tetchily. "Angry! Yes, of course I was angry! Especially once I'd managed to work my way to the end of time, and realized I couldn't get back! I was furious! What a dirty trick, to deceive me that way! That Sipa was always tricking me, wasn't he!" He smiled at the little owl. "It wasn't the first time I had reason to be angry with him, was it!" He glanced at them, adding, with a broad grin on his face, "But to tell you the truth, Siparti always knew how to make me laugh too." He stared off into space, chortling. "That time when we were about your age, and he took me along on a tiger hunt, and he tied two tigers together by the tail, so that they'd get caught around a tree trunk when they chased us – I was petrified!"

"But he's a scoundrel and an underhanded, immoral crook,

to betray you that way, just so that he could get richer," said Josh. "Everyone says so!"

"Ah, yes," Temberi sighed. "People just don't have a sense of humour, do they? I was an idiot, that's all there is to it, to have fallen for his conniving. Who's the guilty one, the one who deceives, or the silly fool who walks right into the trap with his eyes wide open? In the end all I can do is laugh about it."

"But you're in serious trouble now," said Teresa.

"That's right. I do wonder if we'll ever get out of here alive."

"And yet you *still* don't hate him!" Teresa couldn't understand it at all.

"But can't you see? I *love* the old thief, the silly, greedy prankster. Sipa. I miss him terribly, every day. The fool."

He leaned back against the wall and stared at them impassioned. "You know, when people hear the name Siparti, what do they think of?" He pointed at Teresa. "You. How do you picture him?"

"Well," said Teresa. "Like … like…" She smiled apologetically. "Well, actually, like – you know the type, with an evil stare, tall, in a very expensive suit, with a diamond tie-pin and lots of rings on his fingers, and a gold tooth, and one of those pencil-thin moustaches, constantly rubbing his hands together. I'm sorry."

Temberi nodded. "Exactly. That's what they all think. A cold, ruthless merchant, obsessed with money. But that wasn't what he was like at all! Sipa was a short, lithe, energetic little fellow, just like me, with a face like mine, only fiercer and livelier. A bundle of sparkling energy, that's the way you should picture him. He wanted to know everything there was to know, and he wanted to have everything there was to have, and he wanted to make millions and millions. He was so hungry!" Temberi beamed as he recalled his brother, tripping over his words in his eagerness. "Siparti. Ah, my God, Siparti! He loved food, and gold, and treasure. And cats. He loved women too, you know, and the women loved him back. He had six children by five wives, but that wasn't enough for him. He would have liked hundreds of children. Hundreds of children, hundreds of cats, a hundred thousand jewels and gold ingots and outrageous costumes and horses and ships and camels – out of curiosity, out of hunger, out of sheer passion. Oh, I just can't explain it. It wasn't even so much about having, it was about getting, it was about the chase. You know, other great merchants become jaded. They eventually lose interest. Not Sipa. His passions tore him up, his heart was always breaking, and he was constantly on fire. He had no defence against his own passions. That's why I loved him so much. But he could also be terrifying, of course, and utterly ruthless, and he sent others to their ruin without even a second thought. But by the same token, he might very well do the same to himself. Can you understand?"

They tried. Josh muttered, "It's true, actually. I did think he was awfully short. I had imagined him much taller."

"What?"

Josh turned bright red. "Oh, hell," he said. But then he had to come out with it. "I saw his skeleton. In the tomb, in Ixilis."

Temberi stared at him.

Jericho came to his rescue. "You can go inside it. There's a sort of thieves' escape route through the tomb. But Josh put Siparti's bones back in order. He's properly at rest now. With heaps of precious gems scattered among his bones."

Temberi put his hand very slowly to his mouth. A deathly silence fell.

Then Jericho said cheerfully, "But you know, he'd probably have loved it. Being in a thief's grave. With lots of exciting things happening around his bones all the time."

"A thief's grave," Temberi repeated almost inaudibly. "Oh, Sipa!"

Unhappily Josh scratched his head. He steeled himself, waiting for the uncomfortable silence to end. It took a while, but then he felt a hand on his shoulder. Temberi gazed at him warmly.

"But that was a very kind thing that you did. It was a loving thing to do. Thank you, my boy. You did not abandon my brother." He paused, musing, before going on. "And he didn't abandon me, either. We have not lost each other. And now that we are reunited again, we shall see to it that we don't lose ourselves, either." He stood up and scuttled off, the little owl on his finger, and a whole flock of birds fluttered up to swarm after him.

They had never experienced such a nerve-racking day. Josh was too jittery to eat. He couldn't get that terrifying hurricane out of his mind. From time to time he'd stand stock-still, staring endlessly through a gap in the wall at the bellowing pandemonium in the east. Jericho was no help. She stayed close to his side, but he could see she was shaking too, and she kept giving him strange looks, as if she knew something he didn't. Even Lucide was on edge. Every so often his body would flame red, and then his eyes would burn, hard, lacking their usual warmth. He didn't let Josh and Jericho out of his sight for a moment.

Finally Josh decided to go down to the dormitory, and there, surprisingly, he fell into a deep slumber. When he reluctantly awoke, with a hollow stomach, Teresa was sitting on his bed.

"I've talked to Spratt," she said.

"Oh?" He scratched his itchy, unwashed head. "Was he still acting crazy?"

"He's as mad as a hatter. He thinks it's all your fault, doesn't he?"

"Yes. But it isn't, is it?"

"Of course not." She leaned back against the wall, relaxed. They were being rocked to and fro gently, to the slowed-down rhythm of the storm. "You know, he really is completely nuts. He is absolutely convinced that there is just one kind of real time, which we have been insane enough to stray away from. He thinks *umaya* is insanity."

"But *isn't* there just one kind of real time?"

Teresa shook her head. "No, not really. True, there is only one reality. But that reality consists of a mishmash of past memories, of nightmares, and of dreams for the future. And for some people life zooms by very rapidly, while for others time stands still; and some people live in the here and now, others in the past, and yet others in the future." Josh was trying hard to follow what she was saying. "I had a talk with Kat about it on the phone. I now understand the whole thing a bit better."

"But … do you mean to say that our own time isn't real?"

Teresa laughed. "Of course it is. I mean that there isn't just a single kind of time. Our time is made up of all different kinds of time. We all experience time a little bit differently – and we keep weaving in and out of all the different time-strands that mesh together to constitute our time. That's why it's too complicated for Baz to copy the rhythms of our own time on his drum, but he is able to drum the rhythm of the *umayas*. Spratt thinks he's above all that, as if he isn't actually living in time. But he's just stuck with his own deluded idea about time – as if his idea of time is the only valid one. Arrogant fool."

"Did he have any suggestions?"

"No. He despises us, and refused to help. Baz may try talking to him again, in a while. But Spratt's very ill. His face, Josh – it's horrible – I think it's almost disintegrated."

Josh shuddered. "But what kind of plans did you make with Kat?"

"Kat!" Teresa's eyes glowed. "Well, that I'll come and work for her. If, that is, I'm still as thrilled with it once I've had a chance to see it all with my own eyes."

"You're going to work for Kat?"

"Come on, Josh, Kat Siparti! Katz Imagination! That's quite a different kettle of fish from Gippart! Kat knows how to seduce and entrance people using words, images – and she never lies, you know. Not one word is a fabrication! It sounds absolutely terrific."

"But how did she know you're so good with words?"

"Hasn't the penny dropped yet? Kat knows everything about Gippart. She's been spying on them for years. For centuries. And vice versa too, you know. Don't you remember? She's been eavesdropping the whole time, through that mobile."

The blood drained from Josh's face. "But Teresa, if Kat was spying on us using Garnet's phone – that means that Garnet Gippart..."

"Exactly," said Teresa. "You're catching on. Garnet was one of Kat's spies. She worked for Kat."

Josh fell backwards, flabbergasted. "But then it's Kat who's got it in for us!"

Teresa jumped to her feet and started pacing the dormitory. "No, no, no! Absolutely not! Kat is furious with Garnet. That was never the intention! Kat was really shocked when I told her everything. It seems Garnet had her own agenda, and meanwhile she was also in league with the other ones, Tal Sow Fall..."

"And Max?"

Teresa shook her head. "I don't think so. Kat wasn't quite sure. But Garnet Gippart and Tal don't care if there are casualties. All they care about is setting up a profitable trade in time. If some people lose their lives in the process, they're not too bothered."

"On the company's orders," muttered Josh.

"I'm not so sure," said Teresa. "Actually, Josh, I think there's some sort of secret power struggle going on at Gippart. Now that the President has lost his mind. You know – I told you about him, up on the top floor."

She went quiet, and starting kicking the stone rim of the empty hearth with her foot. "But what made him go mad? What was it that's driven Gippart's big chief round the bend? I've been wondering about that ever since I started working there."

"Have you ever seen him?" asked Josh.

"What do you think?" She laughed. "I did decide to go and check on him, once. I'd heard such hair-raising tales about the stuff going on up there in the penthouse. But I had barely reached his floor when this dishevelled lunatic came bursting out of a door and stormed up to me, shouting his head off! I've never made it down so many flights of stairs in so short a time. Luckily, they managed to get him under control again quickly, and no one ever realized that I'd been up there."

"What was he shouting at you?"

"Well," said Teresa. "I didn't understand, at the time. I still don't, to tell you the truth. *'Kat Siparti!'*"

"Kat Siparti?"

"'Kat, Kat, Kat Siparti,' that's what he was shouting. With such loathing and hatred, like a madman – I'm telling you, if he had caught me, he would have beaten the hell out of me."

"But that's his own sister, kind of," said Josh. "I mean, he is the President of Gippart, and Gippart's founder was Kat's brother, Gip Siparti. So what would make the heir to Gippart hate his ancestor's twin sister with such passion, enough to want to murder her?"

"Gip didn't hate his sister. They always fought a lot, but he loved her. And Kat loved him. I found that out from the master storyteller in Ixilis."

Josh nodded.

"It's a strange family," sighed Teresa. "Temberi is the only one of the lot who seems normal to me. Well, are you coming? I want to see if I can draw any more stories about Siparti out of him. It's our last chance to learn about Siparti's curse and the Gippart President's madness."

But Temberi was nowhere to be found. Nor was Zizi. They did bump into Tibid, though. Tibid, who always seemed to pop up at the crucial moment.

"Why don't you all have a bath? A steam bath, that will make you forget your worries. And take Baz with you – he really needs a break. The fourth steam room is free if I'm not mistaken, the one with the red door."

That wasn't such a bad idea. The day stretched before them interminably. Teresa went to fetch Baz, but Jericho tugged at Josh's sleeve. "You said you could draw from memory the way Teresa's storyteller hairstyle used to look, didn't you? Could you draw it for me, please?"

"Why?"

She gave him a sweet smile. "Will you?"

He asked for permission to fetch pencil and paper from the writing chamber, and had just finished his sketch when Teresa and Baz returned to the dormitory. Jericho, looking pleased, took the piece of paper from him and quickly put it into her dress pocket. Then they all went downstairs, to the passage where Josh and Jericho had first bumped into the Tembe. But the steam room wasn't unoccupied. Sitting in a corner of the wide bench, without the omnipresent birds for once, was Temberi.

"Take off your outer clothes, come in, and splash a little more water on the floor, will you?" he said as they entered. With a hiss, a thick fog misted up the little room. "The steam room," puffed Temberi, "was another of Sipa's discoveries! A godsend, because of all the cold draughts."

They installed themselves contentedly on the bench. Jericho whispered something in Teresa's ear, and Teresa sat down next to her with a delighted smile. With the help of a small comb, a handful of ties and Josh's drawing beside her on the bench, Jericho began combing out and rebraiding Teresa's hair. She chewed her lip in concentration, asked for advice in a subdued voice, unravelled her work and then started all over again.

It was so comfortable and warm in there, as if the world had folded itself around them like a mother, and nothing bad could possibly happen any more. They felt languid and happy. Sweating, they sat there, drowsing. Temberi was equally content just to sit next to them in the hot, wet mist. He was the kind of person who made you feel at ease without the need to make conversation.

"Could you tell us more about Siparti, please?" asked Josh

curiously after a little while.

"What do you want to know?"

"Was he good, or was he bad, for a start?"

Temberi smiled. Then he launched into a story about two young boys who lived long ago in a wild, wonderful land in the heart of the world. They could see it all before them: the eldest, dreamy, soft-hearted Temberi; and the keen, quick, impish younger brother – Siparti.

"I was sitting in the highest branches of a huge gnarled apple tree, talking to the magpies, the way I often did. Sipa was strolling below, under the trees. I wasn't paying any attention to him, but then I heard a loud sucking noise beneath me. I had the most awful shock. It was a big, fat, scaly golden snake. Bigger than the boa constrictor we used to hunt. It was slithering down the trunk of the tree, making right for where Sipa had halted. I was so paralysed with fear that I couldn't make a sound. The magpies and I sat there frozen, as if turned to stone. And the serpent just continued its menacing descent, lower and lower. I caught a glimpse of it through the leaves, and saw it had something red in its mouth. And suddenly it dawned on me that Sipa knew perfectly well that the snake was on its way, and that, in fact, he was waiting for it. Then the snake stuck its head out at him, with that red thing in its mouth, and it hissed something. I couldn't understand what it said, but I heard Sipa say, in his inimitable warm, self-assured voice, 'No, no. You're going about it the wrong way.'

"He took the red thing from the snake's mouth, and then I saw that it was an apple. And Sipa said, 'You have to convince me that this is something extremely valuable, something I just *have* to have. So the way you go about offering it should be something like… Wait, I'll show you!'

"And he walked away a few paces, and then turned back, and shaking his head with the warmest concern said, 'Snake, snake, your life really is miserable. All you do is hang around in the trees with your head down, always having to hide from birds of prey and nasty, stupid humans!'

"And the snake replied equally sadly, 'You are right, my boy, you are so right.'

"And then Sipa said, 'But you know, snake, if you eat this fruit, you'll become wiser than all humans and animals put together. This is the fruit of the tree of knowledge, and he who possesses that knowledge can go into the world with his head held high, and will always be able to outwit his enemies.'

"'I'll be darned if it isn't true,' said the snake.

"'It is a precious fruit,' said Sipa. 'It is meant only for the wisest and highest orders of being. Lower creatures would never be able to bear the burden of such knowledge.'

"'But I am very wise,' said the snake. 'I play an important part in the world. Everyone is afraid of me.'

"'That is true,' said Sipa gravely, 'but superior to you are the very wisest beings, they who float on air, and are no longer earthbound or tied to their fears. This fruit is meant for them.'

"'No,' said the snake angrily. 'Give it to me! Come on, boy, enough of this nonsense, it was mine!'

"'If you truly prize this fruit,' said Sipa solemnly, 'then you will pay the necessary price. It's a matter of principle. And this fruit is meant only for creatures of the highest principle.'"

"And he *fell* for it?" asked Josh, incredulous.

"When Sipa does his sales talk," Temberi chuckled, "heavens, you'd even put down good money to buy your own teeth from him. The snake begged him to name his price, and Sipa said, 'An egg.' The snake shot away, seething and swearing, but he wanted to have his apple back at all costs, and Sipa was such a pain, and had talked him into such a corner, that it had given him a splitting headache. He was back in a trice with a blue egg in his mouth. Sipa carefully took the egg from him and with a bow handed him the apple, and the snake couldn't take a bite out of that apple fast enough."

"Uh-oh," murmured Teresa.

"Yes," said Temberi. "The sky immediately went black, I was hurled out of the tree by a gust of wind, the earth shook and then there was a terrific clap of thunder. And Sipa just laughed and laughed! He was rolling on the ground, laughing."

"And the snake?"

"The snake streaked out of there, squealing, but the thunder and lightning followed it, while Sipa and I ran like the devil in the opposite direction. That's all I can tell you."

He laughed at the memory. "Are you beginning to get the picture, what he was like? My brother?"

There was so much steam in there, so much mist, that it gave them the illusion that they could see right into the past, peer into the old stories that had taken place in those two strange brothers' early years. The kind-hearted brother and the ruthless one who had introduced greed and trade into the world; together they had set the course of the world. And everything they now heard was contrary to what they had been led to believe. To his relief, Josh saw that Siparti wasn't just any old ordinary, unscrupulous scoundrel. He was feeling better about having rearranged Siparti's bones back in Ixilis. And he also secretly was proud of the fact that sometimes he could feel Siparti's all-consuming greed coursing through his own veins.

"Awè and Kide, the first and the second. Also known as Temberi and Sipa. Sipa the jester, the thief, the pedlar and the traitor," said Temberi in a sort of sing-song chant, "and I the thinker, the dreamer, the seer and the flier." He went on in a normal voice. "We used to drive our parents mad. You see, we were princes, and we were supposed to succeed our mother, the Empress. But they just didn't know what to do with us. Neither of us had the slightest sense of responsibility! If we were expected to meet our tutor in the morning, in order to study the laws of the land, more than likely Sipa would not yet have returned from his night-time escapade of stealing honey from the forest bees. You'd find me somewhere high on a mountain peak as usual, riding the air currents with the eagles. Thermals, updraughts, you know? I was mad about thermals. And our poor old tutor would become angry and chastise us yet again." He grinned. "In the end they simply decided to tie us physically to our desks, to make us stay in our seats. I became very good at daydreaming. In the end it made no difference to me whether I was sitting at my desk or not; I might as well have been standing high on the mountain top. But that is how Sipa finally learnt maths. He ended up liking it, actually."

Josh could just imagine it: rugged little Sipa with his flashing, wicked eyes, suddenly sitting up when he learnt that you could buy two apples for a penny, and then sell them again for a penny apiece.

Sipa's eyes lit up.

"So, Siparti? How much profit would you make, in that case?" asked his tutor.

"Two pennies. Two pennies!"

"Wrong!" A stick banging on the desk. "You only make *one* penny, because you spent one penny when you bought them!"

Sipa squinted. "But are people really stupid enough to pay that much? To pay twice what it's worth?"

"Never mind, that's not what we're talking about, young man. Let's say that you just bought six apples for three pennies and you sell them for a penny apiece."

"No," said Sipa. "For *two* pennies each. Because I'll polish them until they shine. And I'll claim that they have some very special powers. I'll say they were the very last apples from the royal tree, and that they've got the power to give you a very long life. I could even charge three pennies each!"

"But that's not the point here!" cried the tutor in despair. And meanwhile young Temberi sat there daydreaming, his shoulders spattered with droppings and a bird nesting in his unruly hair.

* * *

Yes, Josh could just picture the scene.

"Were you really able to fly?" asked Baz.

"Very occasionally," Temberi replied. "If the thermals were exceptionally strong, and if the eagles would take me with them into the heights, and if I wore certain clothes. Yes, I do remember flying. But all that was done with once I started trading."

"Greed," said Teresa, "weighs you down."

Temberi smiled. "Greed is mainly behind us, these days. But I've never been able to fly since." He splashed some more water on to the floor. "But now tell *me* something. We never get any news here. Tell me something about little Gip. What kind of goods is he dealing in, these days? Is he still on such bad terms with Kat?"

They told him all that they knew, but gradually Teresa took over, and from her the others learnt something new. They already knew about Gip and Kat spying on each other; as well as Garnet, there were lots of other spies at Gippart, Teresa said, and Katz had its share of double agents as well. But the fact was that Kat had quite another role in this whole business.

"So it was Kat's plan? Not Gip's plan, but Kat's?" asked Baz.

"If what she told me is true," said Teresa, "then Kat contacted Gip a couple of years ago to see if they might join forces on an expedition to the Tembe. She couldn't do it herself, because Kat isn't a traveller. That's Gip's department." She grabbed Jericho's hand. "Ouch! Watch what you're doing! The braid's too tight!"

"Oh, *pardon*," said Jericho in a French accent, and Teresa continued her story.

"Besides, Gip had already started exploring the possibility of time-travel. But Kat had done her own research by digging through the family archives, which Gip had lost, and she had already found out quite a bit about time-travelling for herself."

"But why now?" asked Temberi. "Why now, all of a sudden? What did they care, after all these years? It's been a thousand years, as I understand it. That's right, isn't it?"

They nodded.

"I'm not really sure," said Teresa, "but there's something going on with Kat and Gip. With their descendants, I mean. Gippart's President is crazy. Then Kat said on the phone that it was all becoming unbearable, or something like that. And then she hung up."

Josh nodded. "Tell him about the curse, Teresa."

"Of course. The curse! But what exactly *is* the curse?"

"What sort of curse?" asked Temberi apprehensively.

"We were told there is a curse on Gippart, on Gip's head," Josh told him. "I think that means the curse of Siparti. Maybe that's what made the President of Gippart lose his mind."

"Oh, fiddlesticks!" Temberi exclaimed crossly. He rubbed his hand angrily over his bony chest, wet with perspiration. "Despicable family curses! Why didn't they ask *me*? If I'd wanted to put a curse on my brother, surely that's *my* business and I don't need anyone else's help, for goodness' sake? And now Gip has lost his mind!"

"Not Gip," Josh said, startled. "The President."

"They're one and the same," said Temberi. "Oh, how I wish I'd heard about this sooner! All that business about curses and revenge! It's about time I did something about it! I have to get out of here."

He stood up, a towel wrapped around his waist. They followed him into the cold-water chamber.

"Tomorrow," said Teresa. "Tomorrow we're getting out of here."

But before the next day dawned, something disturbing happened. It was a little before ten thirty. The inhabitants of the fortress always went to bed early. The Associates had followed suit, and in spite of their nerves, or perhaps because of them, feeling totally drained, they were already fast asleep. They talked restlessly in their sleep, disturbed by all the birds that came to sit on their beds and kept trying to nest in their hair. A bald, evil-tempered vulture had quietly settled at the foot of Josh's bed. Which was lucky. Because when the intruder, knife raised, crept stealthily up to his bed, and was about to strike, the vulture viciously lashed out at him, clamping its beak on the murderous arm. There was a loud scream, and the clatter of steel on the ground. The Associates, startled out of their sleep, saw a shadow wrestling with a big bundle of feathers, and then they saw it stumble out into the corridor.

"What was *that*?" Josh stammered.

"Do you need to ask?" said Teresa.

"Spratt!" Baz exclaimed.

They dashed into the corridor, but he had already disappeared. Jericho picked the knife up off the floor.

"Well! So without his gadgets to hand, he now resorts to the use of a knife! Bastard!" Teresa raged, taking the knife from Jericho.

They pushed two unoccupied beds and a heavy blanket chest in front of the door to block it, and went back to bed. But suddenly Teresa sat straight up in bed and feverishly started searching through her clothing and her Gippart backpack. "Oh no!"

"What?"

"My mobile. It's gone!"

"Did you still have it, then? Did you call Max?" said Josh.

"No, I only talked to Kat. She at least was a real help."

"How did you manage to keep your backpack and things, anyway?" wondered Josh. "Weren't you forced to leave everything behind in the great jewelled hall, in order to fly here?"

And Teresa, in spite of her anger, couldn't help breaking into a grin. "Didn't you say yourself that *Gip* had to renounce his desires? Gip, not Kat. I came here as Kat."

In all the excitement of the following day, the incident with Spratt was completely forgotten. Unfortunately.

20
Satura's Maw

In the early hours of the morning Josh felt a hand on his back. Someone crept into his bed and snuggled against him.

"Jerrie?"

"Joshie. Josh *na* Jer."

It was still dark, and he couldn't see her face. Only her eyes gleamed softly in the darkness.

"What's the matter?"

"Nothing. Everyone's still asleep."

"Today's the big day."

"Yes."

She put her arms around him and held him tightly. "Josh, I'm afraid."

"Afraid?" He gave her a comforting hug. Big brother. "Why?"

"Just. Afraid."

They felt their hearts beating in sync. What was about to happen was too huge and too strange to be put into words. And Josh knew, he just *knew* that Jericho's journey would be different from his. He knew this would be their last day together. Or rather *she* knew it, and her knowledge of it was involuntarily passed on to him.

"You'll really have to be careful of Lucide today," she whispered. "Lucide doesn't trust us. He's watching us like a hawk."

He dozed off, and woke up again still safe and snug in her arms. Big sister. As he was nodding off once more, he heard her muttering to him softly in strange, seventeenth-century slang. It sounded warm, foreign, comforting.

The third time he awoke, the room had become lighter, and Jericho and Teresa were sitting around a small fire burning in the hearth, talking.

"Hello, Josh," said Teresa. "Are you ready?"

He sighed and tossed the warm, threadbare blankets aside. There was tea – the sweet, herbal, slightly oily tea of the Tembe. Teresa looked her magnificent self again in her storyteller's hairstyle. The braids weren't all perfectly straight, but Jericho had done her best, and there was even a new red feather sticking up in the right place.

"Didn't it come out well?" asked Jericho proudly.

He nodded. "Where's Baz?"

"Drumming. And giving last instructions."

"When are we going?"

Teresa inclined her head. "In about an hour, I think. Is there anything else we have to discuss?"

Josh couldn't manage another word, his throat was so dry and tight. He couldn't remember ever having felt this nervous in his entire life. Or maybe he had, just the once when he'd been expected to recite a stupid poem in front of the whole school, and he had simply put his foot down and refused to learn it by heart. It had been at the time when Mo and Pete were constantly fighting. He'd known in advance it would be a disaster, and it had indeed been a nightmare, in front of hundreds of spectators. And now, too, he knew that what they were about to try probably would not succeed. But this time there was so much more at stake. Their lives, for a start; and the lives of the Tembe as well; and maybe even more.

Teresa eyed him with concern. "You're looking very pale,

I must say. Come on. You can do it, remember? It's only a nightmare. Remember, you've done it before!"

He nodded, bit his lower lip and clenched his fists, which were dug deep down in his pockets.

The dining hall was strangely quiet. The Tembe ate in silence, then got up and left in search of their pet birds, or to say a last goodbye to the fortress that had been their home for two hundred years.

Just as the children had decided they might as well stop pretending to eat, the door was flung open wide. A solemn procession entered, with Tibid at the head. Temberi was next. Beside him walked an old woman they hadn't seen before, with some lengths of cloth folded over her arms. Behind them came a small group of elderly people in clothes that were less drab than usual. Temberi greeted the Associates quietly, and sat down, subdued, on the edge of the bench.

"We are ready," he said. "Let me introduce my most trusted one, Wiseri, the mother of my children. And these are my eldest daughters and sons: Bezamène, Lim the Singer, Imen, Mersele and Pann. Allow me to introduce the Sipa children: Teresa, Baz, Josh and Jericho."

They exchanged polite greetings. It amazed the Associates to think that all these elderly people could actually be the children of someone even older. Every one of them must have been over two hundred years old.

"I really wanted you to meet one another. It may transpire that we are too old to begin again."

Teresa, alarmed, cried, "Oh, no, surely not! There *has* to be a Temberi in the beginning; Temberi *has* to go back into the world!"

Temberi smiled. "I will do my best. Shall we go?"

They stood up in silence. Then the aged Wiseri came forward, holding out the folded garments. "I should like you to wear these."

Teresa took the clothes from her and inspected them. They were long red tunics embroidered with bird designs. The colours had faded, but traces of blue remained.

"The young folk put on these clothes the day that we celebrate their coming of age," said Wiseri. "We tell them that when they put on these clothes, they'll be able to fly – back to Zaam. And even if that doesn't actually happen, at least the clothes serve to remind us of Zaam. Please wear them today."

They took the tunics from her and slipped them on over their other clothes. They felt soft, light and festive. "Thank you so much," said Teresa, hoisting on her backpack. "Hopefully we will indeed get back home today. I'm sure they'll bring us good luck."

Then they were ready to go.

But Josh hung back.

"Zizi," he said. "I haven't found Zizi yet. I can't go without Zizi."

"Oh, Josh!" cried Teresa.

But Temberi rubbed his chin. "Ah, your bird! Wait." He whispered something to Tibid, and Tibid hurried away. "We've sent everybody out to look for your Zizi, and meanwhile we can make our way to the tunnels."

"But where's Baz? Where is Spratt?" Teresa asked anxiously. She too was on edge now. "Jericho, you follow Baz and Spratt into one tunnel. Josh and I will take the other. We can't all fit behind one rock. You'll keep an eye on Spratt, OK? Don't hit him too hard, or he'll faint. What's keeping them?"

Fortunately they both walked in just then. Baz came in first, looking flushed with a drum under his arm. Spratt came behind him, very unwillingly, his forearm bandaged and his face hidden behind his scarf. But at least he was there. Hard to believe, but he did seem to be coming of his own free will. He was even carrying a drum, a big, bulky drum that barely fitted under his arm. Temberi went up to him and reached out to touch his hand, but Spratt brusquely turned away. Temberi said something, and he muttered something in reply, but they couldn't hear what was said.

"Very well," said Temberi. He looked around wistfully as Baz put on his red tunic. "Well then. To the tunnels it is."

They descended into the bowels of the violently shuddering fortress, down into deep catacombs that Josh and Jericho had never visited before. They walked along a long, dark passage, deserted even by the birds, until they came to two hefty doors.

"This is it," announced Temberi. "The left-hand tunnel is Temberi's tunnel and the right-hand one is Siparti's. They run parallel and come out right beside each other, with no more than the width of a garden between them." He pushed open the doors. They couldn't see anything. A sultry darkness awaited them inside.

"Here goes, then," sighed Teresa. She turned round to face Temberi. "Temberi – Mr Temberi – sir…" She couldn't get the words out. He grabbed her by the hand and pulled her close.

"Whatever happens," he whispered in her ear, "whatever happens, you have already put things right, as right as they can be. You have made up for two hundred – no, a thousand – years of sadness. Nothing you do now can better that."

She rested her forehead on his shoulder and nodded. Then she stood up straight and smiled. She took a very deep breath. "Let's go! Baz! Jericho! We'll see each other on the other side!"

Josh was so stiff with dread that he couldn't say a word. Baz, his hand stroking the panther's back, glanced at him with the anguished look of an animal near death. They understood each other perfectly. The Battle of Satura had begun.

Jericho followed behind, after Baz and Spratt, with Lucide following her like a shadow. She gave a whistle through her fingers, and waved. "See you later!" Breezily, fearlessly, she skipped into the tunnel.

But to Josh, the other tunnel felt more like a tomb. He hung back at the entrance.

"Josh!" hissed Teresa. "Don't make it any harder!"

"Zizi!"

"Oh my God! Isn't everybody out looking for that bird of yours? She'll come after us soon, don't worry!"

"Follow us to the beginning of time? You really think so?" He suddenly started fuming. "You and your stupid plans! I'm not going, I tell you, without Zizi! I got myself into this confounded mess in the first place because I had to find Zizi, and I refuse to go on without her now!"

He spun round and stormed out of the tunnel, right into Temberi's arms. Temberi caught him, kissed his cheek, placed Zizi on top of his head and pushed him back inside. Dazed, Josh followed Teresa down the tunnel. She gave an exasperated sigh. "It's about time!"

Josh slowly started smiling to himself. Everything was starting to fall into place, it seemed. It was great to feel Zizi's warm little body perched on his head, and her claws digging into his hair again. Maybe, just maybe, everything would turn out for the best. Who knew – after all, it was only a nightmare. "It's only a nightmare," he told himself, trying to follow Teresa's echoing footsteps. "It's only a nightmare," he told Zizi. "I'm a seer, second-class! I'm wearing the costume of a Tembe hero! Onwards, Siparti! Siparti *na* Temberi, *go*!"

But spurring yourself on is one thing; when you come face to face with the ultimate terror, your sensible, frightened body will tell you quite another story. When Josh crawled with Teresa towards the mouth of the tunnel, he put Zizi under his tunic. As he emerged into the roaring, sucking darkness, he knew with certainty that he was hopelessly out of his depth. He flattened himself against the sheltering rock, next to Teresa. He could hardly see a thing in the shifting light of the hurricane, which was sucking in a steady stream of dust and rubbish; he barely perceived Baz and Jericho behind the other rock.

Teresa tapped his shoulder, then wriggled cautiously up to the rock and peered over the edge. He did the same, with no idea of what he was supposed to do next; and he looked in the direction in which Teresa was gaping; and saw.

Saw, heard, felt; knew that he was nothing but a helpless pawn, witness to something more terrible and spectacular than anything that had ever existed on earth. High above his head towered that hungry hurricane. He saw what it was. It was inexhaustible, ravenous death: death in all its glory, greater by far than anything that existed on a human scale.

He couldn't think. He sank back, trembling. It was too huge.

Teresa knelt beside him, as shaken as he. She said something, but he couldn't understand her. From the fortress, behind them in the semi-darkness, snatches of music reached his ears. From time to time he thought he could hear a dull beat coming from his left. Were they really still going to try it?

He lay flat against the rock, as if he had crashed into it. He felt Zizi, who was scared stiff too, nestling on his chest under his tunic. He couldn't think, wouldn't look. Then Teresa poked him in the ribs. "Your turn! Josh, it's up to you now!"

Startled, he sat up. It was strange: the noise seemed to have subsided. He hadn't even noticed. There was a little less debris tumbling through the gap between the two rocks. The roaring had lessened too. The hurricane had abated to a dangerous storm, the sort he'd seen on TV, causing uprooted elms and smashed roofs.

He gulped, and turned his face towards the east. Teresa put her hand on his back and gave him a push. Taking Zizi from out of his tunic, he handed her to Teresa. He peered over the edge once more. There it was, the bellowing, looming wall of clouds; and there was the horrible gaping mouth, down which everything disappeared in slow motion; and as he looked, he saw ghastly red eyes forming in that awesome head, eyes that seemed to bore right into his. He thought he would faint. He remembered the look in the Beez surgeon's eyes; and then something even more horrible – the faint memory of a night outside the plague city of Bat Zavinam.

He didn't have any conscious thoughts, but a little later,

shaking, he found himself back in the safe, dark tunnel, beyond reach of the storm. His lower lip was trembling uncontrollably. Wrapping his arms around himself, he hugged and stroked himself, as if he needed there to be two of him, one to be scared and one to console the other. It was no time to be alone.

But he wasn't. There was the sound of shuffling feet at the mouth of his tunnel, a little cry, and then a bright familiar face appeared. Jericho knelt down quietly in front of him with gleaming, keen eyes. By way of greeting, he told her hoarsely, "I can't do it!" And went on repeating the same thing over and over again: "I can't do it!"

She said nothing. Waited in silence.

"It's death," he said finally, a little calmer. "There is no end to it; it's much too huge. It's death, Jericho! I *can't* use my eyes on it, because there is no beginning or end to it!"

It was warm and tranquil, sitting there in the bowels of the earth.

"Well," said Jericho. "I can tell you it isn't death. I'm the expert, aren't I? And believe me, it isn't death."

He couldn't get his arms and legs to stop shaking.

"Besides," she said quietly, "as far as death goes, well, you've faced it before, you know, and you've always managed to get the better of it, each time."

He lifted his head, confused.

"The first time was when you were hurtling through space, about to go over the edge of life, when I finally caught you. Remember?" She laughed. "You could easily have shot right past me, into the darkest night. But it turned out you didn't really feel like going there. So."

He nodded. That had been on Trellis.

"And the second time," Jericho went on, "was the time you died of the plague."

"Huh?" He stared at her, and she returned his gaze calmly.

"Lucide brought you back. I'm not quite sure how far gone

you were. But the plague that gets into your lungs, that's the lethal kind. And yet you allowed yourself to be brought back. So again you refused to go."

He was unable to ask any questions, his head was pounding so much. He started scratching his head, wide-eyed.

"And you probably have head lice too," Jericho added.

"I … *died*?" Josh stammered.

"Well, I'm not absolutely certain. Put it this way – you were able to negotiate with death. You stared death in the eye, and you challenged it to a game of chance – Lucide and you – and you won. Or Lucide won. The Reaper didn't, anyway." She took his trembling hand in hers and began to rub it. "It's a secret. Lucide should never have done that. He's supposed to stay out of it. He's a guardian, you see. But isn't it wonderful? I think that after all the horrors we went through in the land of the Beez, he just felt too sorry for us." She smiled. "Now you know. You must never mention it to anyone, though, but I'm telling you so you'll know this isn't the first time you've stared death closely in the face. And managed to slip through its fingers. So this should be easy for you, because this isn't even really death."

"To look death in the eye," said Josh.

"My mother always said that no pain or sorrow, no matter how great, lasts for ever. Nothing on earth is that eternal or infinite. No tragedy, no nightmare." She sniffed. "For instance, you don't even remember the plague of 1665! For me, it really was the end of the world, and you didn't even know it ever happened!"

"I bought a lesson once," Josh reflected, "that said: 'Stare whatever makes you afraid straight in the eye.' That's what the master said. 'Stare the nightmare straight in the eye.'"

"You see?"

They remained seated a little while longer, until Josh finally gave a deep sigh. "Let's go."

"Avaunt, Siparti!" said Jericho, with a twinkle in her eyes.

* * *

Overhead the pitch-black storm still raged. Teresa was panicking. When Josh poked his head out again she staggered wildly to her feet. Josh put on a brave smile, and grabbed her.

"Hang on!" he yelled. "Hang on to me tight!"

Teresa understood. She handed Zizi to Jericho and threw her arms around Josh. They felt safe and strong. Grimly determined, he stuck his head out above the rock. And there she was, as if she'd been waiting for him. As he looked up at her, she started billowing menacingly again: he had to tilt his head back to see the very top of that giant head. Although her fury did seem to have abated a little. The roar was a bit tamer. His hair was being sucked upwards, but he was confident now that he could withstand her force, and not be swept away.

He searched for the spot in the cloud where he had seen the eyes take shape earlier, and he made two bright spots appear in the same place. Neither too close together nor too far apart. Then he tried to follow the contours of the head. What was she, in fact? A snake? No, the head was round, not flat. A sphinx? No, something wilder, more ancient, primal. After all, Temberi had said she did devour her own children. His heart suddenly began beating faster. He was beginning to detect shapes forming. The darkness rearranged itself, swelled larger again. It seemed to take an almost human shape. He stared at it so hard that he started to sweat: there, a broad nose; over there, a mouth. An enormous gaping mouth; but no teeth inside that maw, no teeth! He pushed them away, made them disappear, and the maw yawned open wider and wider and wider, until the head seemed to tip over backwards, with two little eyes and a nose just visible above that huge, empty mouth. No, back! Come back! Satura tilted her vast, sky-obscuring head back down, and stared at him. She now had glittering eyes and a proper nose, and shapely ears were growing from either side of her head, and she still had her mouth open wide. But the storm had died down. Her breath came, formidable and menacing.

"Oh, wow," Teresa sighed into his neck. She was squeezing him nearly to death.

Jericho giggled, a sharp little sound that sliced through everything.

Josh braced himself and then stepped boldly out from the shelter of the rock. There he stood, very small in his flapping red tunic, opposite Satura. She stared at him, and he stared back at her.

Teresa and Jericho nudged one another. "That brother of yours," Teresa said gleefully. "That little devil is pulling it off!"

"Yes, he's putting on a fine act," Jericho agreed, looking pleased.

Josh gazed up at Satura. He couldn't stop staring at her. It felt as if by staring like that, the rest of him was quietly fading away. He was nothing but a pair of eyes. He was staring straight into the very heart of everything. If he went on staring now, he'd see everything: the way the world really was, the meaning of omnipotence, the nature of life, the nature of mortal fears.

And then he finally understood. Jericho was right. This wasn't without end. Fear made you think it was infinite – fathomless and devastating. But it wasn't too vast; you could stand up to it and meet it halfway. If you kept staring at it long enough, you might end up losing your fear of it altogether, and stand tall, and look it squarely in the face, and stare back at it.

Then he shuddered, and looked away. He'd had enough, suddenly. It was so overwhelming, he could only keep it up for a little while. He edged back to the rock where Teresa and Jericho were waiting, and it wasn't until he was safely sheltered behind the rock again that he ventured another glance at Satura. She was still clearly a face. So it had worked! She was ready to listen. The noise had died down. The ears seemed to be pricked with the desire to listen. Still, an icy shudder ran up his spine. It all hinged on a very precarious balance; just one wrong move and she might change back to what she had been before. He gave Jericho a worried look. But she smiled at him in return, put Zizi on his shoulder and skipped back to the other rock to keep an eye on Spratt again. Josh tapped Teresa on the shoulder. "Your turn now," he said. "But be careful."

Teresa smiled. She tugged at her tunic and stepped boldly out from behind the rock. Satura swivelled her astonished eyes at this new little runt. They all held their breath. Josh went on staring, to maintain Satura's shape; Baz kept up his drumming. And Jericho hovered around Spratt, her hand poised, ready to strike.

It was quiet now, in the dark mountains at the end of time. There Teresa stood, insignificant and frail in comparison with Satura's gaping maw. She threw her head back and shouted as loudly as she could. Her voice sounded clear and bold.

"Satura!" she cried. "Terrible Empress of time, I greet you, and I challenge you!"

To Josh's utter astonishment, there was a reply. First a heavy rumble, as if there was an earthquake somewhere near by. Then words began to take shape and come tumbling out of the enormous mouth.

"Ha! Do you *dare* to challenge me, child with no name? Challenge *me*, the end of time herself?"

"Yes, I challenge you!" said Teresa. "I am challenging you because I am going to defeat you! And if I do emerge victorious, the prize I claim is this: that you will let me and my friends pass through you, unimpeded."

The earth shook. It was a terrifying sound. It was Satura laughing. And she spoke again.

"Pass through me? Silly girl! Oh, go ahead and play your little game, show me how brave you are, and if you win – if you *win*" – the earth shook again – "then you can show me how a time-bound child can manage to travel through the end of time!"

"My game is this," cried Teresa, undaunted. "I will tell you your story, and you have to tell us ours – that of the four of us children. Whichever of us is most accurate in relating three things in the other's history wins!"

"And what if *I* win?"

"Name your prize!"

A gust of wind blew over their heads, as if she had taken a deep breath while thinking it over.

"I, who *always* win – I, who devour everything, whom nothing ever escapes...?"

Teresa laughed. "In that case, what you should ask for is to lose!" she suggested boldly. "That's the one thing you don't yet have, and the one thing you'll never have otherwise. Being a loser."

"Very good," came the startled answer. "To lose! That is an excellent prize. Very well! I agree. But remember, child without a name, that I will insist on having my prize, and woe betide you if you cannot deliver it!"

Teresa spread her arms wide. "Right. I will start. Satura, Satura, this is your story! Long, long ago, before there were people on this earth, before the sun and the earth had appeared in the heavens, you came along, and you settled here in the form of a ring of light, a ring encircling life and time."

"That's quite close," Satura thundered. "Now it's my turn. You, little nameless one, were born out of your mother's womb, as were your little friends, and then, as you slipped out of her belly into time, which is sealed in by me, you gasped for breath in alarm, and wailed out of utter terror of me."

"Nearly correct," cried Teresa, "but not quite! One of the four of us did enter your ring of time, but then just shrugged and laughed, and trod on your tail, and danced on your back, to her parents' shock and dismay!"

That's right, Josh thought, delighted. She was talking about Jericho! Who had turned her back on time the moment she was born! Satura had lost that one. It grew quiet, and the wall of cloud bulged dangerously. Alarmed, Josh trained his gaze on Satura's outline again. He had to keep focused on her.

"One–nil," said Teresa. "Now it's my turn again. Satura, Satura, you breathed light into the darkness where you lay, and children came forth from your starlight, and you found them lovely and multicoloured, and you allowed them to grow in thousands of different shapes and a rainbow of hues."

"That wasn't a very hard one," Satura rumbled. "And you, nameless one, you grew up, as did your friends, drinking your mother's milk, and playing on your mother's soil, and eating the food that the land grew."

"Wrong again," said Teresa. "I did drink my mother's milk, but I played in the dust of my *father's* land, and in the dust of the land of strangers, and I ate food grown in countless foreign soils, but seldom in my mother's."

"Well!" said Satura, swaying gently. "Is this really what the world has come to? Well! Two–nil."

Teresa thought for a while, then spoke. "But then, Satura, then your children grew to adulthood. They grew as big as you and as proud as you, and they no longer obeyed your laws. One of your sons, sweet Temberi, preferred the sky above your holy earth, and another of your sons wanted to have the whole world for himself, with a hunger even greater than yours."

"So," asked Satura severely, "what did I do then?"

"You were about to devour them," said Teresa. "You were going to devour them, the way you devour all your children the moment they grow too powerful!"

"You lie!" thundered Satura. "That is a lie, child! I did *not* swallow them!"

"No!" shouted Teresa at the top of her voice. "Because you *couldn't*! Because they broke away from you!"

"Broke away!" Satura whipped her enormous head and looked around, shaking. Josh, teeth clenched, barely managed to keep her in check.

"Yes, broke away!" Teresa cried out, elated. "And you have to let them go! You *have* to let them go!"

But now Satura grew massive and menacing again, a solid wall of foul weather. "Why should I let them go? Explain that to me, you little cheat!"

"Because," shouted Teresa, "because you aren't the end of time, but the *beginning*!"

A shudder ran through the earth. Teresa was hopping up and down in excitement.

"The beginning?"

"The beginning, and it's wonderful to be the beginning. That should be enough!"

"The beginning *is* the end!" Satura rumbled threateningly.

But Teresa turned back and called out to Jericho. "Throw me your bracelet! Quick!"

Jericho dashed out and tossed the bracelet to her. Teresa held the gold circle high up in the air. It was so dazzlingly bright that Satura must have been able to see it. Josh caught sight of the golden tail that ended next to the snake's head. Not in its mouth, the way it did in Maam Sagal's bracelet – next to it.

"Look," said Teresa, pointing at the gap between the head and the tail. "See? The end is not *in* the beginning. *Out* of the end flows a new, separate beginning – everything doesn't necessarily always stay the same."

Satura was silent, shrinking down even smaller. Then she exhaled, suddenly billowing precipitously to the uppermost reaches of the sky. Josh, frustrated, pounded his fists against the rock shielding him. *Come on, stay small, stay small, remain a distinct shape!*

"And that's supposed to be my story? The beginning only?"

"But Satura, isn't that the best, the most desirable thing to be? Isn't it horrible to devour your children and lay waste to what grew and bloomed so beautifully, in thousands of different shapes and sizes?"

For what seemed like an eternity, the wall of cloud billowed up and then shrank again before their eyes, as if Satura was unable to make up her mind. Then she unleashed a huge rainstorm somewhere up north. She retreated to the east, then changed back into a face. A calm, noble face.

"You spoke truly," Satura blew back softly. "It is horrible."

"Three–nil?" asked Teresa.

"Three–nil," sighed Satura. "I have lost." The earth shook rhythmically. "Which means that I have won! I have won the happiness of losing! And here is your prize, my child."

She opened her mouth. A huge tunnel came into view, leading deep inside. Satura's last words wafted around them. "What about your name, child? Am I right in venturing to say it must be Siparti?"

Teresa grinned. "My most revered great-grandmother," she said. "Who am I to contradict you, if you recognize your children?"

She turned to the others, tossed the bracelet back to Jericho, and raised her arms in the air, in a victory salute.

"Let's go, quickly, come!"

It was unbelievable. She had succeeded in making it happen. Uncertainly, Baz stopped drumming. Spratt, still guarded by Jericho, followed suit. The mouth remained open, immobile. Josh walked out from behind the rock, with Zizi sitting on his shoulder. The wind toyed gently with their hair. No more than a couple of dozen metres from them, the tunnel beckoned. This way to the beginning of time. This way for home.

They were all in a triumphant mood. Elated, overconfident. Even Josh had forgotten his doubts. Just a few more paces, and they'd be out of there for good! Nothing could go wrong now. What could go wrong? They were jubilant, cheering with delight as they ran towards the opening.

But things did go wrong. At first they assumed Satura had recovered her senses and had hurled a thunderbolt at them, just as they were about to escape. Jericho was the only one who immediately understood what was really happening.

It was a sudden boom, a blast of fire that sent them sprawling to the ground. When they dared open their eyes again, they saw their way into the tunnel blocked by a livid column of fire, spurting a shower of sparks and thrashing about, and they heard a terrible voice cry out, "You may not pass! You may not pass!"

At the same time came a shrill cry: "Lucide! *No! Bastard!*"

And like a lesser streak of lightning, Jericho threw herself at the burning column. Josh, open-mouthed, watched her go up in flames. Scrambling to his feet he walked stiffly towards the blaze. "Jerrie," he panted, his hands raised helplessly in the air.

But nobody saw what was happening behind their backs. Nobody saw Spratt, released from Jericho's grip, pick up the phone and point it. Nobody saw his wasted face, and nobody saw the hate in his red eyes. He pressed a few keys, and aimed.

Behind the struggling column of fire, Satura's head suddenly began to shudder and swell. The maw opened wider, and a bellowing roar made the earth shake. Josh looked from the fire to the burgeoning head of cloud and back again, and shook his head in utter despair.

"No," he cried. *"No!"*

The wind picked up. Its force increased with dizzying speed. They heard a great thud, and now once again Satura's head towered above them nightmarishly, her maw gaping wide, devouring everything in sight. To his horror, Josh saw the fiery column being sucked inside.

Then he found himself being dragged in. First he was dashed to the rocky ground; next he was lifted into the air, and he flew into the blackness. Instinctively he shut his eyes tightly. Grimacing, he opened them again, and saw a red light straight ahead of him, bathing him in light, a light he seemed to be following at breakneck speed. "Jerrie," he groaned, "Jerrie, Jerrie," and he forced himself to keep his eyes open. It was as if someone was telling him to "Look! Look!" And he did his best to keep looking.

Josh had heard that just before you die, you see your whole life flash before you. Josh saw quite a bit more than that. He saw thousands of lives, thousands of unfamiliar scenes flash by. Strange little clips: a child falling into the fire and being snatched out again by a man dressed in an animal pelt; a miniature boat made from a leaf and a twig bobbing in a gutter; a stag casting off its antlers; a cat with a gilded tail-tip; elephants caressing the bones of a bleached elephant carcass with their trunks; a rat becoming hopelessly lost inside a pyramid; a child feeding a red spider. As he went hurtling along, the images changed: now it was mainly plants, and it was hard to comprehend what he was seeing. A blackened branch, a strange wooden ball plunging into tropical waters, a grain of sand. He looked and blinked and looked and looked, and then – stripped of all sense of time – he dropped down in the grass.

The sun shone. The grass was moist and fresh. The air sparkled, bright and vivid.

Josh was lying on his side in the grass, staring at the stems before his eyes. If you look at grass from very close up, it looks just like a jungle. A few ants scrabbled in and out among the blades. *Lucky things. Hidden in those green shadows. Safe and sound.*

He felt the sun on his back. It had been a long time since he had felt the warm sun. A springtime sun.

He tried to think. Springtime? But it was November! Very slowly he raised his head. He saw blue skies, with a few wisps of white cloud and the sun winking off the leaves of tall trees. He sniffed the fragrant smell of flowers and grass. His heart still seemed to be beating faster than normal. He put his hand up to his shoulder but felt no little parrot there. He got on his hands and knees, then took a deep breath and sat back, his head tilted up to the sun. He saw that he had landed in a clearing, in a glorious forest of giant trees. Everything seemed to be simmering and quivering with zest for life. Zizi sat on the ground near him, calmly preening herself. He pounced, with a cry of delight, and let her climb on to his finger. She winked at him and went on rubbing her beak on her glinting green feathers.

"Josh? *Finally!*"

A girl's voice behind him. She rushed up to him. "So there

you are! What *happened* back there?" She dropped down next to him in the sunny grass. She seemed to have lost her red feather again.

"Oh, Teresa! Where *is* everybody?"

"I've just started looking for them. Baz must be around here somewhere as well, and Spratt. Have you seen anyone?"

Shaking his head, he got to his feet. Only now did he notice the impenetrable bank of dark cloud behind him. It was so close, it felt as if he could just walk inside it.

"That's where we've just come from," said Teresa. "The mouth of the tunnel is inside that fog. Can't you feel it?"

Indeed, when he got nearer he could feel a powerful stream of air whooshing out in one spot; the fog was seeping out of that hole. As they looked, something came shooting out of that misty vent. It was a length of faded red cloth, which, gracefully billowing, floated on a little way before draping itself over a bush. They turned back and walked through the tall grass, looking behind the bushes and the trees, in hollows and in ditches. The happiness of this place was so infectious that, involuntarily, they began humming to themselves. And they found Baz, who was sitting in a thicket of ferns, rubbing his neck fretfully. His little panther lay next to him, much more at ease.

"Look!" cried Baz indignantly. "My drum is ruined! It was a very special, exceptionally good Tembe instrument, and I don't even know what it's called!"

They patted him on the back and said he needn't get so excited about something as easy to replace as a broken drum. Baz grumbled a bit more, but then his face split into a grin.

"We made it, didn't we? We made it through! It hurt like anything, but that drum helped me bear the pain. We've really made it!"

"Yes," agreed Teresa, "but not quite the way I'd expected!"

"Not quite," said Baz, "but you were terrific. Did you think of all those arguments yourself? I couldn't really understand it, actually, all the things you were saying."

Teresa chuckled. "Really? You couldn't? Well, I'd gone over it beforehand with Kat. She gave me some excellent advice. But what a show we put on, didn't we! You were both great too."

Josh was looking around frantically, not really listening. "She went up in flames," he said wretchedly.

Teresa went over to him. "Jericho?"

"That fire burning. It was Lucide," Josh explained. "He didn't want us to get through."

"Damn him," swore Baz.

"But they were blown in here too," said Teresa. "Surely we can find some sign of them?"

They made a systematic search of the forest. Josh told the others as much as he understood: Lucide had evidently wanted to block the border of time so that no one would get through, as he was charged to do, and then Jericho had gone for his throat – and as for the rest; well, he didn't quite understand what had happened next. Satura had suddenly become enraged again, perhaps stung by the blazing fire on her lips. Who knows.

"So Jericho sacrificed herself for our sake," said Teresa.

"No, she can't have done. I won't have it, Teresa!"

"My dear Josh, if she did give up her life, that means she's gone home again, can't you see? Don't be sad; she didn't really *belong* – ouch!" She grabbed the back of her head. "Ouch!" She glared up at the tree above her head. "All right, have you finished, up there?"

"What's the matter?" asked Josh.

"A pine cone fell on my head. Well, anyway. But do you understand what I – ouch!"

She covered her head with both hands, and just in time too, for now a storm of pine cones rained down on her head. Teresa ran off, swearing, and didn't turn round until she was at a safe distance. "What the *hell* was that! What—"

Josh looked up, and started laughing uncontrollably.

She was straddling a branch high up in the tree, swinging her bare legs, spiky hair sticking out all over the place, pine cones in her hands and a wicked, defiant look in her eyes.

"A heroic act!" she bawled at Teresa. "It was an act of heroism, the thing I did! I saved you all from death! And if anyone has the nerve to say I don't belong here just once more, I'll make this whole tree fall on her head!"

Josh called her name, delirious with joy.

"Yes!" cried Jericho, letting all the pine cones tumble to the ground as she spread her arms wide. "Say it! Say my name! All of you! As loud as you can!"

They stood in a row under the tree, applauding, shouting and cheering, *"Jericho! Jericho! Jericho!"* until their throats were sore.

"That's enough," Jericho said finally, from up above. "So tell me, where are we now? This isn't London, not by a long way!"

They looked at each other uncertainly. "We're at the beginning of time," said Teresa. "Or somewhere like it."

"Don't you recognize it, Josh?" asked Baz. "You do, don't you?"

"I suppose so."

"Of course. Jericho, we're at the dawning of the world."

Teresa looked at Baz in wonder.

"Yes," he cried, "I would know that rhythm anywhere. We're in Max's favourite *umaya*!"

Now all they really had to do was lie down in that fresh, new grass, and dreamily breathe the delicious air of this *umaya* and sweetly drop off to sleep, a sleep that would surely transport them back home. They had broken out of the nightmare of the Royal *umaya* and there was nothing stopping them from returning to Gippart. They'd probably be home in less than a quarter of an hour.

Except for one thing: their party no longer consisted only of dream-travellers. They wouldn't all be able to get home the same way. All three Associates glanced furtively at Jericho, their saviour, who had by now climbed down from her tree. Her face and arms were covered in soot, and the lower part of her red dress was scorched. Her hair stank of fire and smoke. But her face was ecstatic as she looked about her. She walked around. She picked a grass stalk and chewed it. She put her ear to a tree trunk, beaming. They watched her sheepishly.

"Josh," she said finally. "You were right! That other world wasn't the real world at all. *This* is the way it's supposed to be! *This* is life!"

"This is Max's *umaya*, actually," said Josh.

"I recognize it, I do! That's the wonderful thing about real life, isn't it, that happy feeling, as if life never ends?" She rubbed a minty leaf between her fingers, sniffing the strong scent.

"Where is Lucide?" asked Teresa.

"Oh," said Jericho, "he went for a walk. He didn't understand. He was so embarrassed about getting it all wrong again."

"What did he get wrong?"

"Well, he thought you were about to walk out of life! He's completely confused; he doesn't know *which* borders he's supposed to guard any more and which he isn't. When we get back, he'll probably be in trouble; he's made such a mess of everything."

They all stared at her in alarm. Back? Lucide and she? But Jericho didn't take any notice. "But where are those Tembe of yours, I wonder?" she said.

Nobody had thought of that yet. Jericho was right: the Tembe didn't seem to have followed them! Well, of course they hadn't; the arrangement had been that they would wait for a signal, back at the mouth of the two tunnels – a signal that it was safe to pass through Satura's maw. But the signal never came, so they must still be standing there – waiting for a sign that never would come!

"Come on," cried Teresa, and they ran after her, back to the billowing bank of dark mist that marked *umaya*'s border.

"What can we do?" asked Baz. "We can't do anything to lull the storm from here, Teresa!"

"We don't need to," said Teresa. "Baz, it's all or nothing! We *have* to help them!"

"What are you going to do?"

Teresa fumbled in the backpack she had dropped in the grass. "The bird calls," she said. "We'll call them, that's what we'll do." She gave each of them a bird call. "Over there, where the vent is. Do you think we'll be able to get inside a little way? Let's try to get inside, as far in as we can. Come on!"

With their eyes squeezed shut, they fought their way into the bank of mist, the air blowing in their faces. It was like swimming against the tide. They didn't manage to get in very far; but they braced themselves, standing shoulder to shoulder, and all started twisting their bird calls at the same time. The shrill squeaks merged with the whooshing of the draughts, setting off piercing echoes that buzzed around in the strangest distortions, soon filling up the whole space. The sounds reverberated, shrieked and cut through the air; some were so high-pitched, they were nearly inaudible. The noise filled their heads and filled up the mist. Suddenly the flow of air started blowing harder, blasting them out of the mist bank. But they went on with their tweeting and chirping, even as they were driven back, step by step.

And then it started. Baz hastily had to duck to avoid a pigeon hurtling past his head. The bird was blown out of the depths of the mist bank, straight at their heads. It squawked with fright, flapped its wings wildly, and then it was off like a shot, into the world that lay beyond.

And that was just the beginning. Next came a flock of little bluebirds, chirping in alarm. Next was a heron, sailing along upside down; they just caught a glimpse of its expression of surprised indignation. Then came seagulls, starlings, magpies, mountain birds; then the smaller birds of prey; and then the first of the giant vultures.

The four of them were sitting on the grass just outside the bank of mist. They stared open-mouthed at the endless flocks of birds being spewed out. The birds came out cackling and screeching, but recovered rapidly from the shock: first they would do a complete flip in the air, then just hover there a few seconds before flying off, jubilant, pirouetting through the air. An owl hanging upside down from a tree suddenly started hooting a strange melody. Three vultures flew on, low to the ground, armed with a determined expression, as if they knew exactly where they were going and, once they got there, what kind of unpleasant things they would do to other creatures.

Occasionally a stone would pop out, landing on the ground with a dull thud. A blue drinking glass came flying out of the aperture in a wide arc, hit a stone and smashed to pieces. Next, with a loud hum, a whole collection of musical instruments came zooming out.

"I think we're about to see the entire fortress come through that hole," said Baz, scrambling to his feet to get out of the line of fire. "Watch out!"

Alarmed, they followed his example. And it was true, more and more things kept landing in the grass. Chunks of stone, a fork, a stool. But that was about it. Satura did not like to let objects pass through her. Rather than letting them through intact, she preferred to crush, pulverize and digest them.

And as they stared, keeping their eyes peeled for dangerous debris, a large bundle of red rags flapped out and landed at their feet with a thump. "Aah!" he cried.

It was Numo. Of all the Tembe, he had made it out first. "Where is Sig?" he asked, dazed. "She needs her birdseed! I was just feeding her..." He stared at them in confusion. "What are you doing here? Where am I?"

"Where is Temberi?" asked Teresa, but then they heard other voices.

And there they came. Every one of them, one after another. They landed softly and elegantly, or head over heels, swearing, or in groups of three. They arrived, and sat in the grass in a daze, and scratched their heads and looked up at the sky.

And then they began to laugh. It was a wonderful sound. Dozens of chuckling Tembe, sitting in the grass. Hearing their voices, their birds began to return. Dozens of delighted birds landed on their bosom friends' shoulders, and everyone basked in the lovely sunlight of the dawning of the world.

It went on raining down Tembe. The Associates ran to them laughing, to welcome and reassure them. Some were thrown quite a way into the clearing. Others ended up in a tree. From time to time a guest, one of the visitors blown by the wind to the Tembe's fortress, would drop down near them. Halfway through this search-and-rescue operation, Baz and Josh found to their delight that their backpacks had been blown there too. Their Gippart backpacks, that were guaranteed always to find their way back to their rightful owners. It was a very happy day, and it felt wonderful to hoist their packs back over their shoulders and be prepared for anything again. But just as they were busy pulling two of the Tembe out of a ravine, a cry from Jericho alarmed them.

She was standing over a strange heap of something that had just crashed to the ground. A shapeless bundle of red rags and some grey, gooey substance. They all stared at it in disgust. Teresa pointed a trembling finger at the colours.

"Tembe clothes."

"Yuck," said Josh. "Did he just get smashed up? How did that happen?"

Baz picked up a stick and started prodding the grey mound. A piece of cloth slipped off, and suddenly Josh saw what it was. "It's Spratt!" he gasped. "Look, there, those eyes!"

Halfway down an elongated triangle of slack grey flesh glittered two red eyes.

"He's still breathing," said Josh.

It was true: the flabby mound rose and fell very faintly. But otherwise, nothing moved, and the eyes were completely blank.

"What's happened to him?" asked Jericho. She was unmoved by the sight of a decomposing body.

"He was already very weak and spongy before, and he no longer had a proper face." Teresa grimaced. "And getting sucked through the hole must have stretched him out of shape completely. Ugh."

"Won't he be able to just fall asleep, and wake up again at Gippart?" asked Baz.

"He's nearly dead," said Jericho brightly, full of interest.

They looked down on their ravaged enemy.

"Poor thing," said Josh.

"His own stupid fault," Teresa said.

"What should we do?" asked Baz.

Teresa thought for a moment. "At Gippart we learnt that if you're dying, you can't return home. Shall we see if we can get him to wake up?"

They prodded him, called his name. But he gave no sign of life. His breathing grew shallower and shallower.

"It's useless, we can't help him," sighed Teresa. "He's dying. He's nothing but a great blob of jelly."

Baz began clapping his hands rhythmically, humming softly to the beat. After a little while, however, he gave up. "That's no good either. He's not reacting. I think his heart is about to stop altogether."

"Poor thing," Josh said again. Then he frowned. His eyes hardened. He stared intently at the formless lump in front of him.

"Go on," Jericho said softly.

"What are you doing?" asked Baz, but Josh did not reply. He stared, stared with intense concentration. And of course they could see for themselves what he was doing. He was using his eyes; and the shapeless blob was changing. They saw it happen. Under Josh's gaze, the stretched, distorted features grew shorter and more distinct. The blob grew a set of teeth. A bony skull materialized behind the eyes. Angular bones started to appear inside the grey mass.

Suddenly an enormous wing burst forth from its side. They saw sharp talons at the end of the grey membrane. Hastily they all jumped back.

The last remaining scraps of red cloth wafted to the ground, and the outline became sharper. The creature before them shuddered. It stretched and turned its bony neck towards them.

"He still looks exactly the same," said Teresa.

It stood up on claw-like, short legs and flapped its gigantic wings. The Associates scurried backwards, out of reach of its talons.

Then the beast craned its neck, and screamed – a horrible, prehistoric cry. It turned its neck round like a bird's, until it caught sight of Josh. For a moment it stared him straight in the eye. Josh couldn't read its expression. Fury? Gratitude? But the next cry the pterodactyl uttered before flying off was, without question, triumphant. Clumsily it moved forward, flapped mightily with its huge wings and flew off, screeching.

"Farewell, Spratt!" cried Baz.

"Now he can finally lord it over everyone," laughed Teresa. "That's what he wanted, wasn't it? He ought to be grateful to you, Josh!"

"As long as Max doesn't get annoyed," said Josh, "about having such a monster in his *umaya* now."

"On the contrary, it's nice for Spratt," said Teresa. "He can visit his old Gippart friends."

"This is the last time I'm using my eyes to change anything," decided Josh. "It certainly worked this time, didn't it? Once I get home I don't suppose I'll be able to do it again."

"You're amazingly good at it," said Teresa. "Perhaps you will still be able to do it a bit, once you're home. It's always a possibility, isn't it?"

Josh shrugged.

On the forest floor, at the spot where Spratt had been lying, was a mobile phone. When they saw that, it finally dawned on them what might have happened at Satura's maw. Grimly Teresa put the phone in her pocket. Then they walked back to the wall of cloud, making their way through throngs of happy Tembe.

"What's keeping Temberi?" asked Teresa worriedly.

Had he been too old for this, after all? Was it really too late for him to start again?

They needn't have worried. It was a blessed day, and Temberi was the last to emerge from the fog bank, very easily and lightly, as if he were flying. He landed quite a distance from the wall of cloud, and they all raced over to him.

"She looked like my mother," he said, wide-eyed. "Satura. The terrible Empress. Our mother." He rubbed his head, dazed; it took him a while to absorb his surroundings. "Well," he said, with a deep breath. "Is this it? It must be. Good heavens…"

He stood up a little stiffly, rubbing his back. But his face twinkled and shone, as if he was sniffing hundreds of wonderful smells at the same time. "Good heavens!" he said again. "Zaam. A new Zaam, isn't it?"

"Could be," said Teresa, who was dying to know if he was happy with the way her plan had turned out. "What do you think? Is this a new beginning?"

Temberi started to chuckle. "Kat," he said, "dear child of Sipa, Gip, I mean – Teresa! I think you've managed it wonderfully. Whether I like it or not, this is a new beginning. I don't have to begin again, but this begins *me*, whether I want it or not. Perhaps I'll go back to being young again."

Teresa grinned broadly. "So it worked, didn't it?"

He took her hand in his, looking up at the sky. A couple of birds spotted him and, with a cry, landed on his head and shoulders.

"It worked," he said with satisfaction. "We are free."

They sat around for a while with all those amazed, delighted people, going over all that had just happened; but suddenly the Tembe became fidgety. They seemed to have been galvanized with boundless energy. One after another, they came over to Temberi and told him, "Well, I'm off, then. Goodbye!" They gave the Associates a wave, with a "Thank you again!" and then they disappeared into the forest. In the end only Temberi and his trusted ones remained. They too were fidgety and impatient. Their birds swarmed around their heads, as if feeling the call of migration.

"We're off," said Temberi.

"What are you going to do?" asked Teresa.

"Have a look around. I want to see if there are any cats here." He looked at the little panther, which lay stretched out on its back in the grass.

"For Siparti's sake?"

"Ah well, yes," said Temberi. "You never know, do you?"

"Good luck," said Teresa. "Well, see you soon, then."

"I don't think so," said Temberi softly. "I must thank you for everything, now and for ever. Teresa, I have nothing left, nothing with which to express my heartfelt thanks. All I can give you is my blessing. That I still have." He kissed her on the forehead and whispered something in her ear.

Then he hugged Baz, and blessed him too, and he whispered something in his ear. And he approached Jericho, rather warily, the same way. As he was whispering in her ear, she smiled her crooked smile. She nodded briefly, and went quiet.

And then it was Josh's turn. Temberi put his arms around him in a warm, loose hug, a hug he seemed to have invented specially for Josh. And he whispered something in his ear too. Then he kissed him on the forehead and said fondly, "Thank you so much, Joshua, brave boy," and Josh felt as if, for the first time in his life, someone had really seen him, the way he really was, and had found him to be just right the way he was. Not perfect – far from it. Simply the way he was, and *had* to be, and that was good enough; it was just right.

Temberi seemed at a loss for words. Then he grabbed Teresa's hand. "When you get home," he said anxiously, "in your harsh times, will you tell them what Sipa was really like? So that they'll know? Will you tell them how much Temberi loved Siparti?"

Teresa nodded solemnly. "I'll tell them."

Then Temberi gave a deep sigh. He turned round and sniffed the free air, and they heard him starting to hum, deep down in his throat. Tibid and his father Bezamène went and stood by his side. They shook themselves, then wandered off in a cloud of birds, slowly at first, but gradually faster and more determined. Temberi, the shortest, was the most light-footed of them all. He was practically dancing, and the children thought they could hear him laugh. Then he and the others disappeared into the bushes and the tall grasses. There was a gust of wind, and they heard the earth singing all around.

Now that it was all over they didn't know quite what to do next. They were a little hungry and they felt overwhelmed, and tired. Too tired to make decisions. They walked into the open forest, and drank from a stream, next to a couple of gleaming purple deer fearlessly drinking at the same watering hole. Josh started stroking them unthinkingly.

"What do we do now?" asked Baz. "Shouldn't we be off too?"

Teresa shrugged and inclined her head at Jericho, who was trailing a few paces behind. Josh, looking pale, was walking next to Teresa and Baz.

"But we've got to get home," said Baz.

All three turned to look at Jericho. She gazed back at them calmly.

"Jericho," Teresa began.

"Yes, yes," said Jericho crossly, "I know what you're going to tell me. It's always the same story, isn't it? Home, home – and Jericho, who saved your lives over and over again, can't come. Who says I even *want* to go with you in the first place?"

That came as a surprise.

"As far as I'm concerned, you two can go right now, this very minute," she said, "and good luck to you. But I'm not going to let Josh go. He left me once, and I won't allow him to be the one to abandon me again. Of course not!" She walked away from them on bare feet, head held high.

Josh smashed his fist into his palm. In a flash, it suddenly came to him: he knew what he would do. He'd stay with her today. Baz and Teresa would have to return to Gippart without him. And then he would ask her to stay here, at the dawning of the world, where he could always come and visit her. She loved it here, didn't she? He'd visit her every day after school. Simple!

Hastily he explained his plan to Baz and Teresa, oblivious to the unhappy glances they exchanged. They began to object, but Josh wouldn't listen. Jericho had already wandered off into the distance. He started running after her, with Zizi flying close behind.

"Jerrie!" he called. She'd already vanished out of sight, and when he finally caught up with her, he found her leaning calmly against a tree. The breeze caressed her bare arms, and the sun shone on her smudged face.

"This is the most wonderful place I've ever been," she said dreamily.

"Isn't it? Look, if you'll just stay here, I'll stay as well, for today at least, and after that I'll come back to visit you every day after school."

She pretended not to hear him. She tilted her head to the sun with her eyes shut.

"Say something!"

Her eyes still tightly closed, she replied, "Didn't you hear what I just said? I don't want to see you leave me ever again."

"But I'll come back every day, with delicious food and lots of presents."

"What about at night?" she snorted. "When there are lions on the prowl? Where will you be then?"

"I could—" he stammered, but she cut him short.

"Josh, it was exciting, I loved being with you, and I'm glad I came back to you. But I don't want to have to see you leave me again." She opened her eyes and peered around.

"What's keeping him? He said he was just going for a walk!"

"I don't *want* to leave," said Josh, who didn't really understand what she was talking about. "But, since you can't come with me, since I *have* to be at home for at least part of the time..."

But she wasn't listening. She was worrying about something else. Nervously she paced back and forth. "Maybe he got lost! He's been getting so muddled recently!" She was silent a moment, and then added, "Or maybe he's gone to be someone else's guardian. That *would* be funny, wouldn't it?"

Josh had no idea what she was talking about.

He didn't understand until he saw her walk to a clearing in the forest, and halt. She stared into the open space, all her attention focused on what she saw there. Josh heard a sharp intake of breath; then she exhaled slowly.

A figure came striding across the field, a dark, radiant figure glittering in the sun's golden rays. He walked slowly towards her, magnificent and solemn. Lucide was his name. He is the messenger and the guardian. At the most important times in and around your life he will come to you; and he will hold your hand, and he will be your companion on roads about which there are no stories.

As he strode towards Jericho, he smiled his lovely, warm smile. A little like Temberi's smile, but sweeter, more ancient. And undeniable.

At a few paces' remove, he halted. His eyes gazed deeply into Jericho's eyes, and she looked back quietly. Then, with an elegant, commanding gesture, he held out his hand.

The wind ruffled Josh's hair. He stared at that outstretched hand. He forgot to breathe. Nothing moved. The earth was still and expectant.

Then Jericho bared her canines in that funny, crooked smile of hers.

"Right," she said.

And she put her hand in Lucide's.

* * *

Josh stood there and he saw it happen. Slowly his legs buckled under him. Teresa caught him from behind in her strong arms, and held him close. He couldn't stop looking. There they went, wandering off into the distance, Jericho and Lucide, hand in hand, as if they had all the time in the world. He wanted to call her name, but his mouth was dry and his lips were trembling.

And yet she did, she did hear him. For Jericho would always hear when someone tried to say her very own, unhappy name. After all, it was the only thing she possessed.

She hesitated briefly. She looked up at Lucide and said something, let go of his hand and fumbled with her wrist. Then something sailed through the air. It fell in a graceful arc right by Josh's knees. He picked it up. It was Jericho's bracelet.

Trembling, he pressed it to his mouth, and hunched his shoulders in grief. But Teresa pushed his head up again, so that he could go on watching the two figures moving away from him, hand in hand.

"Look at her, Josh! Look at her, because this is the last time you'll see her! You *must* say goodbye to her, Josh. *Look* at her!" And she added urgently, "She did save your life, after all, and she was magnificent, and proud, and she was loyal to you, and she wasn't afraid of anything or anyone!"

After that, everything was simple, as simple as sadness. Silently they wandered around until they found a suitable spot: a mossy clearing surrounded by giant trees, with quite a few birds flying about, blithely twittering and chirping. They arranged their belongings around them: three Gippart backpacks, which they now knew would follow them of their own accord; the little panther at Baz's side; and Zizi on Josh's shoulder. No one said anything. Only Baz whispered something, burying his face in the panther's fur. Then they nodded at each other, and nestled on the warm belly of the forgiving earth. The lovely earth, which understood everything and always made everything right.

21
FINAL RECKONING

When Josh woke up he realized he was weeping. It was a strange way to wake up, and he was a little embarrassed. He wiped his eyes and was surprised to see that he'd been sucking his bracelet. He quickly slipped the wet snake bracelet over his wrist.

He was lying on a hard vinyl floor, with Zizi dozing on top of his head. Baz lay next to him, snoring softly. There was no sign of the panther. Where were they? He sat up and saw that they were sprawled on the floor of the Reception area. He sighed. So they had made it! But it didn't feel quite right. The little room was unusually dark, and there was no receptionist seated at the computer terminal. Stranger still, there wasn't even a computer. The red plastic bucket seats were still there, as was the desk, but all the electronic equipment was gone. He nudged Teresa, who was lying face down on her stomach.

"Wha...?" She quickly came to. "What's going on? Why is it so dark in here?"

Baz couldn't understand it either. They stood up, stretched, picked up their backpacks and warily opened the door.

Gippart's splendid Great Hall was dark and deserted. There were a few removal crates piled up along one wall.

"Has everyone left?"

It was very quiet. Their footsteps rang hollowly in the deserted hall. They turned down a corridor and, peering through the glass, they could see that all the rooms were empty. The abandoned desks still had computers on them, however.

"You'd think there'd been an outbreak of the plague *here*," said Josh, laughing nervously.

They climbed the stairs to the upper floors. They could see traffic down on the streets below, but the enormous trading corporation was completely deserted. Something terrible must have happened.

And then, finally, they heard voices. They were on the sixth floor, where the management's offices were. From an open door, angry voices echoed down the corridor.

"No, if I may, Sow Fall! Now it's our turn to speak! You've had your chance!"

"Just *one* day!" They heard Tal Sow Fall's unmistakable voice. "All we're asking for is a twenty-four-hour grace period! How can you refuse, for a firm that has been in existence for nearly a thousand years?"

His questioner laughed sarcastically. "To tell you the truth, dear colleague, I've been dreaming for years of the day when I would prevent Gippart ever celebrating its millennium." There was a click, as if a metal briefcase was being shut. "But to the press, I will naturally express my most sincere regret over this commercial tragedy."

"Come on, Inspector," came a deeper voice. "What would a day's grace period cost?"

When there was only an indignant hiss in reply, they heard Tal's voice again, threatening: "Our lawyers will destroy you, if it transpires that this allegedly scandalous infringement of your employment regulations turns out to be just an innocent misunderstanding!"

"The general public is extremely sensitive to this type of violation," said the inspector, coming out into the corridor.

"It shouldn't even be necessary to go through the official procedure to close down a firm that has several juvenile murders on its conscience. This, however, has hereby been formally done. Good afternoon, gentlemen."

He marched past the children without paying them the slightest attention, with a small group of men in expensive suits at his heels. They heard a loud crash from inside the room.

Then someone else came out. He started running after the businesslike group, then froze, as if nailed to the ground. His mouth dropped open.

"Moussa," said Teresa delightedly. "Hi!"

"You're back..." he stammered. "My Associates are back!" With one step he was at their side, touching them and punching them on the shoulder, hysterical. "You're back! You're back! How long have you all been here? Why didn't you report to me immediately? You're back, for crying out loud!"

He was shouting so loudly that the others stuck their heads out too. There was Max, pale as a ghost, his clothes rumpled, with several days' growth of beard. Behind him, Tal Sow Fall, impeccably dressed, but with bloodshot eyes. Behind him came Marmeduke Fawcett. They all stood rooted to the spot. No one breathed a word; they all just stared at the Associates.

"The children," sighed Tal finally, with a weak smile. "Well, perfect timing! Moussa, do me a favour and run after the inspector to give him the happy news, will you?" He gave another deep sigh and looked down at them from on high. "I am delighted, young people. I'll just have to take care of a couple of things, and then I would like to see you in the Dispatch Board room, in an hour's time." He turned round and went back into his office, head held high.

Moussa, looking ashen, but suddenly buzzing with energy, laughed, then ran after the team of inspectors. Max, meanwhile, spreading his arms wide, threw himself at them. He drew all three into a single bear hug, making choking sounds. "God," he finally said, rubbing the tears from his eyes with both fists, "I really had given up hope. I still can't believe it. How … how…"

"Oh, you know, through the exit at the end of time, where the Tembe lived," said Teresa. "It wasn't that hard. But what's going on here?"

"The employment inspector," explained Max. "Three missing children – that was it for Gippart."

They giggled in surprise.

"But now everything will turn out all right after all. Most of the offices had already been sealed shut, and we were packing everything into crates. Those inspectors can be merciless! You hadn't even been missing for twenty-four hours when they started banging on our doors. Oh God, how simply wonderful to see you again! You look well – disgustingly filthy, of course, but you are all in good health, I trust?" He couldn't stop talking.

Above their heads a light suddenly came on. Then came the sound of a machine rattling in the distance and telephones started ringing again.

Beaming, Max escorted them to his own room, the shabby office with the group photos and trophies, where, a long time ago, Baz and Josh had changed their clothes for their first *imayada*. Max invited them to sit down on the couch, which they did, squashed up cosily together, legs curled under them, blissfully contented. He offered them drinks, put a plate of chocolates, peanuts and wafer biscuits in front of them, and then he made them peanut butter sandwiches with stale bread, which tasted delicious anyway. They ate and ate. Real, normal food! Finally Max pulled up a chair, and sat down. He gazed at them, sighing.

"I should never have let you go. It's all my fault. *I* set up that bloody Junior Associates' Committee. It was *my* fault that children ever became involved in Gippart's dirty business in the first place! I haven't slept a wink the whole time you were gone!" He rubbed his eyes. "But you're back now, thank God, and I swear, I'm going to personally see to it that no minor ever gets sent back into *umaya*."

"Oh, don't say that," said Teresa, taken aback. "We've only just discovered how to transform things in *umaya*!"

"Are you being serious?" asked Max. "How?"

"It's simple, really. You just turn it into a different story. You just tell the story in a different way."

"Or you do it by drumming," said Baz. "All you have to do is change the rhythm, and the whole world changes."

"Or by using your eyes," added Josh. "You just look at it, and look through it, and you transform things that way. It's all just nightmares anyway – nightmares made of nothing. Fear, that's all it is. Just fear."

Max smiled. "You seem to have all the answers. But adult nightmares are tough, a very tough nut to crack."

"So? *We* aren't adults," said Teresa, shrugging.

"Thank heavens for that," declared Max. Taking a sip from his glass, he gazed at them over the rim. "Well, then tell me. It can't have been worse than the nightmares I had about what you must be going through. And how *did* you manage to get out, in the end?"

And then they told him. Gave him the full story. They started every sentence with "But the *worst* was when…", vying with each other to see who could tell the most harrowing story. Max was suitably appalled. He became more and more distressed, till in the end he was deathly pale. The things they were describing to him in gory detail were infinitely worse than his very worst nightmares.

"But there's still a lot that I don't understand," Teresa said thoughtfully. "Take us, for example. Like…" She looked from Josh to Baz and then at Max, who looked back at her uneasily. "Why were Baz and Josh affected by that gadget of Garnet's, and I wasn't? And how did we manage to come through Satura's maw in the end, without getting hurt?"

"It did hurt!" cried Baz. "I nearly fainted. I had to drum like mad not to lose it!"

Josh said nothing, and remembered the red light that

had protected him during his flight.

"That's something I *can* explain," said Max sheepishly, embarrassed at having to own up. "Teresa, you weren't just chosen for this expedition out of the blue. Do you remember your open-heart surgery?"

"What about it?"

"After your time-experiment accident, they fixed you up again, but then Gippart decided to give your heart a little extra reinforcement as well, so that you'd be super-resistant."

"What?"

Max chewed his nails. "Without your consent, of course. You could sue them."

Teresa brought her hand up to her chest. "Without asking me first? You mean I was a *guinea pig*?" She gulped.

Max refilled their glasses; his hands were shaking. "I quite understand what you must be feeling now, and perhaps you should insist that they reverse the operation and make your heart normal again. I'd never have agreed to it, but by the time I heard about it, it was already too late."

Teresa shook her head, but she was in such a good mood that she'd much rather continue with her story, and have her questions answered, than complain just now. There would be plenty of time for that later. "But Baz and Josh survived too, and *they* didn't have surgery," she asserted. "Tell him about the drumming, Baz!"

But before they had time to explain to Max how they were able to manipulate *umaya*, or tell him about Siparti and Temberi and the whole unpleasant Siparti-clan saga, there was a loud commotion outside the door.

"*There* you are!" Moussa burst into the office, with a whole train of Associates behind him. Grinning from ear to ear, he started slapping Josh and Baz on the back again. Everyone was shouting at them at the same time. "Did you break your way out?" "Can you really travel through time?" The girls, jubilant, flung themselves at Teresa, pressing a bouquet of flowers into her hands. "We're all playing truant!" "I was just about out of my mind with worry, I swear!" "Are you hurt?" "Aren't you famished?" "Moussa called us!"

Sita presented Baz and Josh with a bunch of red and yellow flowers, which promptly got squashed when Moussa enveloped them in another bear hug. "How did you manage to fight your way out of there? Tell us!"

Josh giggled. "We got into some real sword fights, Moussa!"

Moussa's eyes flickered. "Even you, Joshie?"

"But you're much better off changing things around by using your eyes."

"Or by drumming."

"Or by storytelling," Teresa interrupted.

"But how?" asked Moussa. "How do you do that? I want to know!"

"Oh, Moussa," said Amina, laughing. "Can't you give them a break?"

Moussa sat down on the couch, grinning. "Max, do you have anything to drink?" He took off his glasses and rubbed his eyes. "Four nights! Oh my God, I hardly slept a wink for four whole nights!"

"What's next on the agenda?" asked Max, clumsily filling more glasses and making a mess.

"A party," said Moussa, "and official pronouncements. To announce that Gippart is not going out of business, after all. And my farewell speech."

There was a sudden hush; everyone turned to look at him.

"Farewell?"

"I'm leaving," said Moussa.

"Because of...?" asked Max.

"Gippart is crap," said Moussa. "I refuse to go along with it any longer. All that underhanded business with the Associates! I've had enough."

Nobody knew what to say.

"Have you decided on a successor?" asked Max.

Moussa smiled. "Teresa," he said. "If I'm right in assuming she was the one who managed to drag these boys all the way through that *umaya*."

"You're right," said Baz.

Josh nodded too. But Teresa shook her head. "We all did it together," she said. "Josh and Baz are incredible, they really are."

"You're cut out for it, Teresa," said Moussa. "You really love those kids. Will you do it?"

Teresa smiled shyly. "No. Sorry, Moussa. But I'm going to go and work for Kat."

"What?" Now everyone stared open-mouthed at Teresa. *"Katz?"*

"That's right," said Teresa. "Katz is the greatest. Kat offered me the job, and I said yes."

There was another knock at the door, and a woman in Gippart uniform came in and asked the three travellers to accompany her to the boardroom. They waved goodbye and cheerfully went with her. She looked at them curiously, but didn't ask any questions. They walked taking long strides, their Tembe tunics flapping around their legs. Josh had retrieved his crushed black hat from his backpack and put it on, with Zizi sitting on top. He felt like an eccentric hero who didn't have to worry about what anyone thought of him. In other words, a Gippart Associate! Heroic victor of *umaya*!

The woman brought them to the large room where it had all started. The lights were still lit – or lit again. The logo of the crowned cat was as dazzling as ever.

"Siparti," whispered Josh as they walked across the carpet to the big table, and he grinned.

"They're going to have to change the logo," whispered Teresa.

"A bird," Baz suggested.

"No, it should be a winged cat," said Teresa. "Siparti will never become Temberi. But it wouldn't do any harm to combine them."

Several Board members awaited them on the other side of the table. They recognized six of the adults who had been present at the first meeting. Garnet Gippart was missing. Tal stood in the centre, smooth as ever.

"Welcome back," he began. Max came scurrying into the room after them, and joined the ranks on the other side of the table. The Associates sat down on three tall stools arranged in front. "The entire Board is extraordinarily pleased that you have successfully completed your mission. Your assignment was to seek out the Tembe, and from your presence here we can deduce that you did indeed find our kin. May we have your report now?"

Everyone looked expectantly at Josh, who looked up, startled. "Report?" he muttered.

"Joshua M. Cope, expedition leader." Tal read from a form he had taken from an impeccably neat folder. "The expedition leader is charged with delivering the final report."

"I haven't finished it yet," Josh stammered. "We've only just come back..."

"Just the forms will do, in that case," said Tal generously.

Josh pulled his backpack on to his lap and fumbled through it. Jericho had been right, it was a disgusting mess in there, and it hadn't improved. Blushing, he pulled a couple of wet, tattered and nearly illegible forms from out of the jumble. "They're a bit dirty," he said apologetically, dangling them between his thumb and forefinger to show the Board members. "But I can copy them out again, this afternoon sometime..."

There was an icy silence.

"Tal!" cried Max angrily. "These children have braved terrible dangers! Is it really necessary to bother them with formalities now?"

Tal coughed and sniffed. "All in good time, then, we will expect from you legible forms, ready for filing, as well as a full report," he sighed. "Well, anyway. Just a few questions. You found the Tembe. Were you able to gather any information pertaining to Gippart's key project, temporal manipulation and navigation?"

Josh stared at him blankly. But Teresa answered for him. "Time-travel is impossible," she informed him coolly. "The Tembe looked into it, and they found that it can't be done."

The Board members leafed through their files.

"What about Dr Mervin Spratt?" asked a tired-looking man. "Where is he? What are *his* findings?"

Baz smiled, then quickly bent his head.

"Well?" asked Tal. "What about Dr Spratt?"

"He is … dead," said Teresa with a straight face.

"He too reached the conclusion that time-travel is impossible," added Josh.

"That is shocking news," said the tired man.

"You should have reported this to us at once," said Tal. "How did he meet his end?"

The tired man sighed. "He must have been extremely ill. He would have run out of medicine. A Senser in *umaya*, you know what that means…" Overcome with emotion, he began rubbing his eyes. He, Ouahabi, could picture only too well what had happened; he too was a Senser, and Spratt's colleague.

The Associates nodded mournfully, and proceeded to answer all questions meekly and politely. Only Max gazed at them rather sceptically, one eyebrow raised.

"In other words, your expedition was a failure," Tal said finally, snapping his folder shut.

"Not at all!" protested Josh. 'But you haven't been asking us the right questions! We freed the Tembe, and we lifted Siparti's curse! We now know all of Gippart's secrets and we managed to pass through Satura's maw, and we even know how to manipulate *umaya*. It was an amazing success!"

"Naturally, naturally," said Tal condescendingly. "But I'm talking about a failure from a business point of view. I have no doubt that you young people learnt some valuable lessons."

But an elegant woman to their left raised a finger. "Was

there anything in those … secrets of Gippart's that might throw light on the manipulation of time?"

"No," said Josh. "But Siparti's curse—"

"The folklore of our firm is not really of much interest to us at this time," interrupted Tal. "You are able to manipulate *umaya*, you say? Does that mean that you have explored the borders between *umaya* and real time?"

Baz answered this time. "You can't get out," he said. "I am a Senser too. We really tried everything, and you can't get out of time!"

"But," said Ouahabi the Senser in the silence that followed Baz's pronouncement, "what about that bracelet then? Mervin was absolutely convinced that that bracelet came from another time!"

All eyes swivelled to the gold bracelet on Josh's wrist. He stared at it himself, as if he had never seen it before. Baz glanced at it out of the corner of his eye, and then he looked directly at Ouahabi. The two Sensers measured each other up in silence, senior Senser and boy drummer.

"Spratt was very confused," said Baz slowly. Ouahabi was listening carefully to his younger colleague. "He simply got it all wrong. Living beings can't travel in time." He took a deep breath. "Time is inside you, you see? Time is rhythm. You can't get out of it."

"And yet—" Ouahabi began.

But the elegant woman interrupted him sternly. "Enough!" she cried. "Enough of the riddles and the mystery! You experts are even worse than these adolescents, Ouahabi! Oh, that damn bracelet! I wish you Sensers had never found it. It's cost us millions so far! Now we must put an end to it!"

Tal blinked. "Mrs Gippart… Ida—"

"Enough!" she repeated, and everyone looked down. The Board members sighed, and shuffled their papers.

"So, that's it, then!" said the woman firmly. "Gentlemen, ladies, I hereby dissolve the Dispatch Board. That ought to make the employment inspectors happy, if nothing else." She stood up and clicked out of the room on her high heels.

"Wait," said Josh as all the other Board members prepared to leave. "I mean, I had another question. About the money, and things."

Tal turned to the secretary sitting at the end. "Oublassi? You should have had the financial details from Comptesso."

"You mean your salary?" Oublassi asked Josh, with a frown.

"Yes," said Josh, blushing. "I've added it all up. I worked four hundred and thirty-two hours, if I'm not mistaken, because we have been away for eighteen days. That's seventy-two times six hours, and I'm supposed to get five hundred pounds per six-hour shift, so that's thirty-six thousand pounds all together."

Max chuckled. Tal bent over his papers, and the secretary slid out his laptop from beneath the table.

"Hold on," he muttered. "You left – on Saturday October the twenty-first. Correct? Today is Wednesday October the twenty-fifth. How did you arrive at eighteen days?"

"Wednesday October the twenty-fifth?" chorused the children, flabbergasted.

"Yes, of course!" said the secretary.

The Senser Ouahabi began to laugh. "Ah, yes, *umaya*-time! Too bad! Your salary calculations are based on *real* time!"

"But that's not fair!" complained Baz.

"Read your contract," said the secretary. "You've been gone three times twenty-four hours plus nineteen… Mind you, it still comes to a considerable sum. You cannot expect the full hourly wage you might normally command, of course, but I would venture to guess that your pay for this *imayada* will be around, um, three thousand, four hundred pounds, roughly."

Josh smiled weakly.

"As for your friends, I'll have to work out what they can expect," said the secretary agreeably. "But in your case that's probably about it. Give or take a ten per cent margin of error."

"Unfortunately," said Tal, "we have overlooked something

in our calculations. Oublassi, check the liabilities ledger for damages."

"Oh, no," said the secretary. "Are you serious, Tal? Come on, man."

"Indeed I am," said Tal. "Damages are damages. Your final balance, my dear boy, is, alas, in the red. But we won't make an issue of it. Gippart is very grateful to you for your efforts."

"What?" cried Josh.

"Don't you remember your little jaunt to Lamerika, the day of the Traders' Trial?" asked Tal. "Can you remember selling some matches to a group of children in the vicinity of a petrol station?"

Josh and Teresa nodded.

"There was an explosion. Children playing with matches. In Lamerika everything is very costly, exceedingly costly. Gippart was stung for the damages, which were naturally entered in your account as deferred liability. After all, it was your Trial, and your sale. The total came to one million, eight hundred and seven thousand, four hundred pounds."

Josh's jaw dropped.

"Which, offset against your pay – and of course we are obliged to deduct the usual fine of three hundred and fifty from your pay as well – is a sum we are entitled to claim from you, although we won't press the issue for now. Do try to be more careful in future, however, won't you? Anything further?"

Max walked out into the corridor with them.

"Never mind," he said. "You are all heroes, and they know it. They just want to warn you, officially, that you won't get a penny more out of them than they are contractually obligated to pay."

Josh was too angry to say anything.

Baz, walking beside him, was just as furious. "Next they'll think of a way of making us pay for the collapse of Temberi's fortress! Or they'll hold us responsible for the Tsumirans' doctors' bills, Teresa!"

As he spoke, a lift door opened, and their Associate friends spilled out noisily and ran up to them.

"Let's have a party!" cried Sita. "Come along to the Great Hall. Everyone is going!"

Her words were drowned by the sound of a gong. Shouting and cheering, the Associates hoisted the three heroes on to their shoulders, and with much laughing and stumbling they were carried down the stairs and into the Great Hall. Josh had never been carried in victory. He blushed, and, half embarrassed, half proud, he held on for dear life to Zak's hair, on whose tall shoulders he was riding.

In the hall the Traders' Trial stage had been erected again, and the glittering light show beamed over the revellers. The smiling crowd filling the hall broke into thunderous applause as the Associates threaded their way to the podium. Waiting for them on the platform were Tal Sow Fall, Max, Marmeduke Fawcett and a master of ceremonies wearing a shiny gold tuxedo. Standing next to them were some people in such formal suits that they were obviously VIPs.

"Unbelievable!" cried Teresa beside him, full of awe. "All the most important members of the family."

"Is it the President?" asked Josh as Zak lowered him on to the platform.

"No," hissed Teresa, "they're the Vice-presidents."

The next hour was entertaining, but also something of a blur. People were constantly climbing on and off the podium. Max hovered over them like a mother hen. There were speeches that Josh didn't follow, because his mind kept wandering. People came up to them to shake them by the hand, flowers were heaped on them, they were congratulated and applauded, and everyone kept telling them over and over again that they had single-handedly rescued Gippart from bankruptcy. Many other people were thanked as well, people they'd never heard of, but who apparently had worked themselves to the bone trying to get them out of *umaya*. Moussa too was heaped with praise and heartfelt thanks. You could have heard a pin drop as he gave his extremely brief farewell speech. He was presented with a commemorative medal and a special suitcase. One of the Vice-presidents whispered something in his ear, and he nodded doubtfully.

After many more speeches, the microphone was finally thrust under their noses. Teresa tried to tell them something about the Tembe, and to explain how freedom had finally been achieved for Temberi, but no one seemed to be very interested. The master of ceremonies broke in and cut her short, shouting enthusiastically. Now Josh was beginning to feel out of it, strangely indifferent. He smiled faintly at Baz, who was leaning rather listlessly against the barriers too. Josh coaxed Zizi on to his finger. For the first time since their return, he felt a gnawing, hollow ache inside. He missed Jericho fiercely.

And nobody seemed in the least interested in the story of Siparti and Temberi. Finally the speeches were done, and the music began. Trays of coffee, champagne for the adults, soft drinks and cake were offered round. Josh and Baz climbed off the podium. Josh was feeling a bit depressed, and somewhat indignant.

Baz pulled a face. "Grateful, aren't they?" he remarked sarcastically.

Josh laughed bitterly. "So grateful that they're willing to pay us for only four days out of the eighteen we were away!"

Baz suddenly stiffened. "Oh, I forgot, that's right! What day is it today, again?"

"Wednesday October the twenty-fifth," said Max, who had climbed down after them. "Why?"

"My sister," said Baz, beaming. "My sister! The wedding! I was supposed to play the drums at her wedding. What time is it?"

"Around eleven."

"She's getting married at noon! I can still make it! I've got to go, I've got to get out of here! Josh! Teresa!" He started pulling his red tunic off over his head, babbling excitedly. "Twelve o'clock, at the town hall. I'll just make it!"

They squeezed through the merry crowd, which wasn't easy because people kept slapping them on the back and trying to engage them in conversation. Max had abruptly left them and gone off elsewhere. He caught up with them again at the lifts.

"Here, Baz," he called, "for your sister! A little something from Gippart!"

Max threw a package at him: a set of voice-activated visiophones in the form of two sleek wristwatches. With video-game option, and wrapped in a lovely gift box too. Baz blushed and shot a delighted look at his friends; then he darted into a lift, and was gone.

Josh had no time to debate whether to follow Baz's example and sneak off home, leaving all the official nonsense behind. He didn't get the chance. Max tugged his sleeve just as he was once again mobbed by Associates, who were finally ready to hear about his adventures.

"What's the matter?"

Max pulled him into a quiet corridor. "Joshua," he said, "we have just received a summons from upstairs. A personal invitation, for you. From the President."

"What? But isn't he—"

"Mad. Yes. And he wants to see you. It's up to you to decide whether you want to go. Or I could send someone up to tell him you've already left."

Josh thought about it. "But just how crazy is he, exactly? Is he dangerous?"

Max rubbed his stubbly chin. "I suspect that you know more of Gippart's whole family history by now than I do. But I'll tell you what I know of this madness. It may very well mean more to you than it does to me."

Josh sat down on a lighted glass cube.

"As you know, the President is a descendant of the man who founded Gippart in 1017."

"That was Gip Siparti," said Josh, "Siparti's favourite son, and Kat's twin brother."

"Aha," said Max. "So now we know! I did have an inkling that there was some kind of family connection between Katz and Gippart – that must be it. They're descended from the twins, Gip and Kat Siparti. Well, well! But be that as it may, our President himself always maintained that he was tainted with the family curse. But it only got really bad when he reached the age of fifty, fifty-five. He told us it felt as if hundreds of desperate souls had taken up residence, uninvited, inside his head, together with all their horrific memories, their regrets, their nightmares. Retribution for a thousand years of greed, he claimed – he did get a little over-melodramatic about it. That's all we know, really. His condition keeps deteriorating. He hasn't dared leave his penthouse for a long time, and he just paces up and down like a lunatic, arguing with those ghosts of his. He'll sometimes attack people and hurt them. He's been seen by hordes of psychiatrists. One shrink even made a chart showing all the different personalities tormenting him – Brax, Kauri, Mono; there was Beez, for instance…"

"Oh, Beez – I can just imagine," said Josh, shuddering.

"Hundreds of them," said Max. "But there was one name in particular that he kept crying over and over again. *Kat.*"

Josh smiled. "Gip and Kat, Kat and Gip, they were two of a kind, those two," he said. "They were twins, always at each other's throats, but they were inseparable too. Do you understand?"

"If you say so," said Max. "Well, the only other thing I can tell you is that the old man seems to have calmed down a bit these past few days. He told his nurse that the pain in his joints seemed to have vanished overnight, and that his head was beginning to clear. On the other hand, he seems more than ever haunted by his obsession with Kat. Now he wishes to see you. He has asked for you specially."

"For me?"

"Yes, for you," said Max. "I don't know any more than that."

Josh looked down at his hands. The thief's scar he'd acquired in Ixilis was still there. He smiled. *Go, Siparti!*

"I'll go and see him," he said, jumping to his feet.

A nurse was waiting for him. She knocked on a heavy door, pushed it open and called inside, "Here's the boy you had asked to see."

She turned and whispered in Josh's ear, "If he becomes aggressive, just run, or shout for help. At once. I'll wait here."

Josh nodded. The door closed behind him.

"Come closer," came a dark, muffled voice from the shadows.

He shuffled reluctantly closer. He thought he could make out the shape of a person seated in an armchair behind a large desk.

"No, stop there." A click, and the soft yellow light of a desk lamp came on. Someone was sitting behind the lamp. Josh noticed that the light was reflected off the man's glasses.

"Ah. You are the boy?" It was an imperious, croaky voice.

"I am Joshua. Joshua Cope. Josh." He swallowed. "Josh *na* Jericho."

"Josh *na* Jericho?" There was a pause. "How old are you, boy?"

"Twelve."

"Well, well. That's very young."

Josh felt himself being inspected.

"I am glad to see you, Josh," said the hoarse voice. There was another pause. "I wanted to thank you in person. That surely is the least Gip Siparti can do."

Josh balanced shyly on one leg. "I didn't do it by myself."

"Of course not." Now he sounded impatient, as if he found Josh a little slow on the uptake. "But if it hadn't been for you, nothing would have happened. And what you did is literally priceless, Josh. I am a Siparti, and I know what things are worth. You have cleaned up the mess the Sipartis have left lying around for a thousand years. You, and your young friends."

Josh smiled. That was something he'd tell Mo the next time she complained that he never cleaned up after himself. "You're welcome," he said sheepishly.

The old man snorted. "It's my sister who really ought to be thanking you. She has such a way with words. I don't have her smooth tongue. But Gippart will give you a reward!" He said it vehemently, as if it had just come to his attention that nobody had thought of praising or thanking Josh. "Tell them I said so. They'll have to give you a damn fine reward. No one can say that Gip Siparti doesn't pay his debts. Be sure and tell them!"

"Gip Siparti?" said Josh, who had only just realized by what name the man had referred to himself.

The man behind the desk chortled. "Don't worry, my boy. The first Gip Siparti turned to dust many years ago, of course. I am the last of a long line, the thirty-third Gip, if I'm not mistaken." He paused a moment, and then sighed deeply. "And yet you do have a point – that curse means that in a way I am Gip Siparti. I am all of those Gips at once. Gip – that greedy, self-satisfied little rat, and the whole wretched lot of power-hungry, conceited company presidents after him."

"That's Siparti's curse, isn't it? That you become convinced you are all of them?"

"Yes, that's it," the thirty-third Gip replied dully. "Every single Gip, and all those thousands of other selfish Sipartis as well. And then all the rest on top of that. The Beez's victims came to haunt me, and the victims of the slave trade and land-grabbing, which was another sideline for some of us. The sort of thing that eats at your soul, you know. It eats away at your soul, and your bones."

He was whispering so softly that Josh had to strain to hear him.

"And Kat was right when she said that that curse was no joke. She was right about it the first time, a thousand years ago. I thought she was exaggerating. As the favourite son of the richest and most cunning man in the world, you're convinced nothing bad can happen to you. Especially if your own company is one of the greatest trading companies in the world, and if you yourself are a millionaire many times over before the age of twenty-one…"

"So then the Royal *umaya* must be the *umaya* of the Sipartis' nightmares, mustn't it?"

"*Of* the Sipartis and about the Sipartis. Nightmares of greed." He took off his glasses and rubbed his eyes.

"But then why didn't you go and look for Temberi earlier?"

The man sitting in the dim light laughed shortly. "Because we were too busy, because Temberi had long vanished from this earth, because we didn't believe in that whole fairy tale – and because the curse wasn't that bad, at first. And by the time Kat and I realized, a thousand years later, that the curse had become intolerable, it was too late."

"But in the end you did go, after all. I mean, you sent us," said Josh.

"That's right," said the President, as if he himself were surprised by that fact. "When Kat heard we had started exploring the *umayas*, she emailed us her plan."

"So Teresa was right? The idea of sending us to the Tembe was hers?"

"Of course! Who else? The first thing she suggested was to sweep *umaya* clean of nightmares, since those nightmares were driving us mad. Next she decided that, as long as we were in *umaya* anyway, we might as well send a party of envoys to the Tembe. It seemed the only possible way to lift the curse: to travel into *umaya* in order to make good Siparti's promise. It stands to reason, since the real Temberi has been dead for centuries, unlike his counterpart in *umaya*."

"But if you want to stop the nightmares," said Josh, "all you have to do is make up for all the bad things that people do in the real world. The nightmares come from the evil that's in the real world. Not the other way round."

"Hmm," said the President. "Fine. All right, I hear you."

Now Josh caught a glimpse of his face. It was still a strong face, a bit square, he saw, with a full head of grey hair. He thought he recognized the typical Siparti eyebrows, which lent the Siparti face its mocking, defiant expression. But there was no mockery in Gip's voice as he resumed.

"Still, the method isn't the point here, my boy. The point is the result. And this project has certainly succeeded. It is so much quieter in my head, I can't tell you what a relief that is! And the pain in my bones is gone. Again thanks to you!"

"Thanks to me?" asked Josh. "But … surely I had nothing to do with *that*, did I?"

"You did it without knowing you were doing it, my boy. Out of the pure goodness of your heart. When you restored order to my ancestor's desecrated bones – don't you realize what that meant to us? When you laid Siparti's bones to rest, you laid to rest the aching bones and limbs of all of us, our entire cursed dynasty. I knew at once what had happened when I felt the pain in my bones dissolve. That was a darned nice thing to do, my boy, downright kind of you."

"Oh," said Josh, who was having trouble making sense of it all. All this gratitude was making him a bit uncomfortable. He thought of the Beez's poor victims, and all the other deaths the rapacious Sipartis had on their conscience. "Well, I'm truly sorry about the curse – but so many people lost their lives, and there are so many others suffering, all because of the Sipartis and their descendants! I don't know – if, as you claim, you really want to pay off your debts, you ought to pay *those* debts as well!"

To his surprise the President didn't become angry. "That," he replied calmly, "sounds reasonable to me." He thought about it for a moment. "I'll call a meeting. I'll do what you're asking me to do, dear boy. There is nothing I can refuse you."

"Great," said Josh. "But now something else. You sent children out to explore *umaya*, and some of them ended up dead!"

"Yes … it's true. I really am terrible sorry about that. We were definitely careless, and took insufficient precautions to protect you. You, and the other children. That is a complete contravention of business ethics. I heard about it too late. Kat was furious."

"Garnet Gippart was out to kill us," Josh continued stubbornly.

"Garnet has been redeployed. But don't forget that she was convinced you were able to travel in time, that you were the only one who could help Gippart capture a huge new market – world history! It's that younger Gippart generation – their thinking is purely commercial, you must understand. Surely you can see that! They are dedicated heart and soul to the company!"

"You remind me of Brax," said Josh.

"Brax!" Gip laughed. "My noble sister Brax! By God, how is she? Have you talked to her?"

"To the Braxans, not to Brax herself." He grinned. "Those Braxans, they're terrific."

"Brax," Gip repeated. He started muttering softly to himself. "Kauri," Josh heard. "Mono – I should really get in touch with the Mono tribe, if at all possible." Then he turned his face to Josh. "May I ask you something? Temberi, my uncle. How did he look? How did he treat you? Did he curse you? Was he furious?"

"No, on the contrary. He was incredibly nice, and glad to see us."

"Glad?"

"Yes. And, uh … he wanted us to tell everyone here how much he loved Siparti."

It was oddly silent on the other side of the desk.

"Yes, and he was really glad to hear about Gip. And Kat. He wanted to know everything about Gip and Kat, how they were."

"About us? He was glad to hear about me?" The voice sounded shocked.

"Yes." He went on resolutely, "You should have gone to see him a long time ago. He's incredibly nice, and he was upset, actually, that you were living under this curse, and I think it was unbelievably mean of you to ditch him the way you did."

"I agree," said the President, barely audibly. There was a long-drawn-out silence. It was so quiet that Josh wondered if he'd gone too far. But Gip Siparti hadn't become such a successful businessman by being insulted easily. He laughed, suddenly aware of Josh's presence again. "Oh dear, all those stories," he said, putting on his glasses again. "All the endless stories, and you being forced to wander around lost in there. They probably bored you to tears – the follies of a band of thousand-year-old merchants. But would *you* now step in and take over? Please?"

"What do you mean?" Josh suddenly had the unpleasant feeling that the cursed *umaya* was slithering back in his direction, snaking its tentacles around him, getting ready to throttle him in a slow stranglehold.

"I didn't ask you up here just to express my gratitude. There's something I must ask you. The Sipartis are an insatiable lot, my boy, we always want more..."

He paused again. Josh waited patiently. He could hear a cat purring somewhere in the darkness.

"The rift isn't completely healed yet – Gip Siparti is a difficult customer. Gip and his twin sister, Gip *na* Kat. The nightmare is behind us, and I am no longer in its thrall. The madness is gone. I am here, and Kat is there. Far away. But the point is, I miss her." He gave a long sigh. "You know what it is, my boy, to miss someone, to miss the one whose pulse you feel beating through your own veins. Ah, Josh, you know..."

Josh thought of Jericho, and felt an unpleasant emptiness in his stomach. He rubbed his forehead. "But – how do you mean, you miss her? I thought you wanted to kill her, didn't you?"

"Of course! But only to free myself of her – don't you understand? I was fed up with being her mirror image, her shadow – being her! I am *not* Kat, I am Gip, Gip Siparti! It drove me wild, always having to compete, my entire trading empire vying with hers, constantly spying on each other, always afraid she would make more money than I did, that she'd steal my secrets, or take over my business! But that's all over now, my boy. And isn't it absurd, really – the way we fought each other tooth and nail for centuries, for the very reason that we were so terribly close?"

Josh had no idea that he was the first person Gip had ever confided in at such length. Gip was talking to Josh as if to himself. As if he were warning his younger self. His partner twin brother.

The President's voice was suddenly very confident. "Well, what do you think?" he asked. "Does it appeal to you at all, my boy?"

"What do you mean?"

"Well – are you ready to take over? Do you want to become the President, and start negotiating a merger with Katz Imagination? To see the companies pool their resources?"

Josh's mouth fell open. "But I don't know a thing about any of that!"

The old man waved his hand impatiently. "When you're older, of course. What difference does it make, ten or twenty years? You'll have to finish your studies first, all that business and management nonsense at the London School of Economics, whatever. We'll pay for it, of course, and for our own special Gippart training, that's not a problem. You'll become filthy rich too, but that's not the point either. As long as you take care of that merger! Gippart and Katz. Promise me!"

"But," Josh stammered, "what if they don't want a merger? I mean—"

"Oh, by that time that girlfriend of yours will already have been at the helm there for a long time, that Teresa girl, and you have sufficient understanding of the issues; if you give me your word, I'm sure it will happen. Come on, I'm begging you. Josh *na* Jericho, on behalf of our twin sisters, because we miss them so! You and I, Josh, you and I – we're the only ones who can understand."

Josh couldn't take it all in. He, head of Gippart? Become filthy rich? President? It was so unbelievable that he couldn't even take it seriously.

"I don't know. Not that I wouldn't want to help you reconcile..."

Then, out of the blue, his whole history to date with Gippart came back to him, like a punch in the stomach. Suddenly he was reminded of the company's betrayal, the heartless greed, the misery, the nightmares. His breath caught in his throat.

"No," he said vehemently. "I won't do it."

The old man laughed softly. "That's fine, it's fine, my boy. We'll have another chat sometime, a few years from now. I didn't want to either, at first. That's hard to believe, isn't it, coming from a Siparti? But when I was twelve, I refused to have anything to do with the business for at least three months. My forefather, Siparti the great, Siparti the terrible, was irresistible, a force of nature. He was the greatest salesman of all time, a champion manipulator and trickster, but also a terrible tyrant, Josh! Just forget it for now. We'll discuss it again at a later date. But just to be on the safe side, you'd better take some economics courses at school, my lad."

He stopped talking and switched off the desk lamp. Josh turned and walked to the door.

"Goodbye," he said softly in the direction of the dark armchair.

There was no reply.

He walked back to the noisy Great Hall in a daze. The Associates, travelling salespeople and other Gippart employees applauded when they saw him come in, slapped him on the back or cheered enthusiastically. Bemused, he made his way through that comforting show of admiration to a group of Associates sitting on the floor, talking.

Teresa looked up, beaming, surrounded by her girlfriends. "Hi, hero of *umaya*! What did he want?"

Josh just grinned, and Teresa understood. She disengaged herself from her friends and found a quiet corner for them to sit down.

"Was it really the big chief?"

Josh nodded. "Gip Siparti himself, the thirty-third. Roughly."

"But what did he want?"

"He wanted to know if I'd take over running Gippart, later. Arrange for a merger with Katz. When you're boss over there."

"Huh?" said Teresa. *"What?"*

"You heard me. But I won't do it. I've had enough of Gippart."

"Merger," she muttered. "The boss, me, at Katz?"

"That's what he said."

"And you don't want to?"

Josh shook his head.

Teresa stared straight ahead, and giggled. "But that's a great idea!" She smiled broadly. "You and I, arranging for that merger! Can't you just see it now? You and I, two fat-cat presidents, puffing away at cigars, drinking champagne, playing with billions!"

"Not my thing."

"What do you want to do, then?"

"I dunno. See everything. Look around. Go and see the world, see everything..."

"You won't make any money that way."

"I don't care," said Josh stubbornly.

"Or you should make movies. If you've got a good eye, you should become a film-maker."

"Hey," said Josh, his eyes shining suddenly. "Fantastic! Film-maker!"

Teresa looked at him, smiling. She put her hand on his shoulder and said softly, "It was a horrible adventure we had to go through, but I think it might just be starting to be really fun. We've learnt a lot, haven't we?"

"Yes," said Josh dreamily, already thinking about his first film.

The two remaining heroes said goodbye to their friends. It wasn't clear yet whether the Associates' Junior Committee would be retained. In any case, there were to be no more officially sanctioned journeys into *umaya*: the Dispatch Board was disbanded.

Teresa and Josh stood and faced each other a little awkwardly. They kept it short, promising to come and see each other soon. Then Teresa disappeared behind the lift doors, her arms overflowing with flowers. One after another, the Associates took their leave, and Josh saw the hall emptying, and saw his friends turning their backs on Gippart. Funny old indestructible Gippart, rooted where the world of dreams began.

Josh was sitting on the floor in front of the door of one of the Reception areas. Max ambled up to him out of the deserted Great Hall.

"Haven't you gone yet?"

Josh shook his head.

Max knelt down beside him. "What's up?"

"I miss Jericho. I do want to go home, but I'd have been really happy if she could have come too."

"Jericho?" Max whistled softly. "I knew there was something you hadn't told us. Who is Jericho?"

It was good to be able to tell him about it. Max listened attentively. At last, someone willing to listen to the things that were really important.

When he'd finished, Max took his hand in his. "You know, your Jericho… I'm going to tell you something that isn't going to make you very happy."

"Oh," said Josh. "There's nothing to be happy about anyway. She's gone. Gone for good."

"Have you ever considered the fact that she has never actually been in our real world?"

"Of course," said Josh. "That idiot Spratt said the same thing. That I just dreamt her up."

Max gazed at him sympathetically.

"But it isn't true! She's the one who caught me, wasn't she? She's the one who started it, not me!"

"It doesn't matter if you believe us or not. But it may help a bit, to think about it this way – that you loved her so much that you made her come alive by dreaming about her. You dreamt about her so much that she was able to join you in *umaya.* You had given her a face and a story, and so she was no longer lost. And for that same reason she won't ever be lost to you again, not even in your real life."

Josh was shaking. "That only makes everything even worse. Then she never really managed to return."

"Oh, but she did. Because your love for her is real. She really did exist, as a baby, and she really did die before anyone could actually start loving her. But thanks to your love she has become a real, complete, beloved person, with a face and a name."

"No name," said Josh. "Jericho isn't a good name for her."

"Why not? The proud, magnificent city of Jericho! It makes sense too, doesn't it? Your Jericho came tumbling down, just like the city. That is her story. But you already knew that."

"Yes."

"From now on, you will live for both of you. Also, she has truly changed you. You have taken her into your heart. Haven't you?"

Josh nodded and got to his feet in silence.

Max embraced him. "Hurry on home now," he said. "Your parents must be awfully worried. Go, quickly." He studied him a moment at arm's length. "Hero of *umaya.* Thank you, Josh."

Josh walked down the corridor to the lifts. The tantalizing image of his bedroom at home crept into his mind. He was overwhelmed, all of a sudden, with homesickness. Home, home! Just as he was entering the lift, he happened to glance at his wrist. The wrist with Jericho's snake bracelet. His breath caught in his throat. He ran back into the corridor and flung open the glass doors to the Great Hall. "Max!" he shouted. "Max! What about her bracelet then? What about her bracelet?"

But Max was out of earshot, and no one answered him.

22
A Seer in the Kitchen

He sighed deeply as he entered his little bedroom. Something inside him, something that had been very tired and frightened for many days, shook itself, gave a heartfelt sigh, turned around in one spot a few times, and settled down for a comfortable sleep at last. He was home.

His room was the way it always was. Only his duvet had been pulled straight. Outside, in the narrow, rainy street, nothing had changed either. Then he looked at his wrist, and grinned. The mark of the thief, for all to see. And Jericho's scar below it. He stared into the mirror on the wardrobe door. Sure enough, the mark of the seer at the corner of his eye was also still clearly visible. He suddenly saw that he was almost unrecognizably filthy. But the black hat looked splendid on him. He stared at himself in the mirror again, and recognized Jericho's face. Was he imagining it, or did he look less of a dreamer now? Fiercer?

He thought of Max, and then of Temberi:

"You can't ever lose her, because she *is* you. Look hard, my boy. Look inside yourself, at all the fear in you and all the bad in you and all the fierce, dreamy and sweet sides of you, and then you'll see that she is in there too. I like all those different aspects of you, and you must let them all show, won't you?"

Hesitantly he walked to the door, opened it and stood under the door frame. Then he jumped up, hooking his fingers over the top of the door. Groaning, he tried a pull-up. His arms were shaking, but his feet found traction on the smooth door. For the first time, he was doing it! Slowly he worked his way up the door. His elbows were already on the top. But then the door slowly swung to, his hat fell off, and he had to jump down. "There, I can do it!" he said with satisfaction.

Maybe not quite the mighty Siparti, but still, a great improvement! Whistling, he put his hat back on his head, winked at himself in the mirror and strode out of his room.

"Edwin?" Mo called from the kitchen. "Come on, please try that number again! Surely they have to get home *some*time?"

She was doing the dishes. With angry, violent movements.

She heard someone come in, and went on. "And if they still haven't come home, I'll go to that Scouts place myself, and I'll bloody stay there until they give me the address! The irresponsibility of those people..." She turned round and froze, as if turned to stone. Josh grinned at her. Suds from the scouring pad dripped on to the floor. Then she took a deep breath, tossing the scourer over her shoulder into the sink.

"My God!" she said. "Do you have *any* idea..." She went red in the face, and then white, and for a moment he was afraid she'd burst into tears. But she didn't. Instead she folded her arms across her chest, and growled, slowly and dangerously, "Where in heaven's name have you been?"

"Hey," Josh replied lightly, "it doesn't matter where I've been! What matters is where I'm going!"

"What!" said Mo, fuming.

But Josh coaxed Zizi on to his finger, opened the door of the birdcage and let her hop inside. With a screech of delight she scooted over to Dara, who started cooing and fondling Zizi's neck feathers.

Josh laughed and said, "Look, Mum! I brought Zizi home!"

"Did you take her with you?" said Mo. "Josh, I—"

She was interrupted by an angry voice. "What's all this? Mo!"

"It's all right," laughed Mo, her voice suddenly filled with intense joy. "Look who's back!"

"Four days!" roared Edwin. "Do you realize you've been gone for four bloody days, damn it all! Do you have any idea how worried…"

Josh turned to him, shaking. He saw Edwin holding a beer bottle. His unshaven face was red with anger. For an instant, Josh cringed. That bad-tempered, hefty bully, always yelling at him – and then he *saw* him.

He saw him. Saw a very worried, nervous little man, who didn't really know how to cope. Who was always blowing up, only to collapse again like a tired balloon. *Calm down,* willed Josh. *Go on, deflate. Silly show-off.*

And Edwin *did* deflate. It was barely noticeable, but he calmed down just enough for Josh to say in a firm voice, "Edwin, I'd like to have a word with Mo. Alone, please."

"You little snot-nose—" Edwin began, but Josh repeated, "I'd like to speak to my mother alone."

Edwin gave Mo a bewildered look. Mo nodded. And Edwin shambled off, grumbling.

Mo stared at her son, astonished. He was just standing there smiling to himself, unbelievably dirty and self-assured. What she didn't know was that the cheeky look of confidence in his eyes was Jericho's.

Josh sat down, tossed his hat on to the table and looked on as his mother sliced some bread and poured him a glass of milk. Then she went and sat down opposite him, shaking her head.

"What on earth did you get up to? Where you've been?" she asked. "Was it really Wales?"

"It's a little tricky to explain," said Josh with his mouth

full. "Actually, it was like a survival trek." He nodded. "That's what it was, a survival trek. And the things we went through, you'd never believe it!"

He looked at her, beaming, and she stared back at him with a questioning look, frowning, searching, wondering…

And he began telling his story.

CHARACTERS

Joshua (Josh) Michael Cope, 12 years old, son of *Mo* and *Peter Cope*
Bhasvar (Baz) Patel, Josh's best friend, 12 years old
Edwin, boyfriend of Josh's mother Mo
Liz, Edwin's daughter, 18 years old
Mervin Spratt, Liz's boyfriend

Gippart International, founded in 1017
Marmeduke Fawcett, Secretary of Youth Affairs, Dispatch Board
Max Herbert, Talent Scout, Dispatch Board
Garnet Gippart, Tal Sow Fall, Miriane Comptesso and *Oublassi,* Board members, Dispatch Board, Project *Umaya*
Ouahabi, Senser in the employ of the Dispatch Board
Moussa, Chief of Associates, 17 years old
Teresa Okwoma, Gippart Associate, 14 years old
B.L. Gippart, President
Ida Gippart, Vice-president

Siparti's offspring
(Siparti – or Kide – was born 950, in Zaam)
Mono, the beloved, is the eldest son, born in 990; his city is Ixilis
Brax, the noble one, is the eldest daughter, born in 993; the Takras highlands are her territory
Kauri, the missionary, is the middle daughter, born in 995; her territory is the coastline around Tsumir and its oceans
Beez, the lethal one, is the middle son, born in 996; the city of Bat Zavinam has been his since the year 1347
Kat, the youngest daughter, born in Arrar on January the first, 1000
Gip, the youngest son, born in Arrar on January the first, 1000

Temberi's offspring
(Temberi – or Awè – was born in 948, in Zaam)
Bezamène, whose eldest son is Tibid
Lim the Singer, whose eldest son is Mim
Imen
Mersele
Pann

ACKNOWLEDGMENTS

With thanks to: Annemarie Behrens, Jonneke Bekkenkamp, Dmitri van den Bersselaar, Inge Boer, J.T. van Dissel, Farid and Omar Gamei, Maria Grever, Jesse Hoving, David Kempenaar, Frans-Willem Korsten, Shani Mootoo, Bart Nuyens, Gemma Rameckers, Jante Salverda, Patricia Spyer, Daan Veelers and family, Gloria Wekker, and the razor-sharp pens of Querido and Walker Books: Nelleke Berns, Jacques Dohmen, Bärbel Dorweiler, Els van Eeden, Chris Kloet and Dik Zweekhorst. Finally, I thank Bridget Browne, Hester Velmans and Jane Winterbotham.